Avalon

Avalon

Peggy Hoffman

CONTENTS

This effort is dedicated to the brave men and
women of our armed forces. Whether you defend
our freedom on the ground, in the air, or on the
waves, thank you for your service and sacrifice.

www.peggyhoffmanauthor.com

1

Michelle Diaz had lived in Avalon all her life and she knew the town like the back of her hand. She was familiar with every inch of Catalina Avenue – the tour plaza where tourists began their exploration of the town and Catalina Island, the Lobster Trap which actually trapped drinkers rather than crustaceans, the Catalina Dive Shop, Vons Express across the street, the pizza shop next door to the bakery. She knew Coyote Joe's Mexican Cantina, and across from it, the Marlin Club. She knew the Marlin Club better than any other establishment on the entire street.

Never before had there been a wall across the sidewalk in front of the Marlin Club's pale blue exterior. But there was one there today, a big solid white wall that she discovered when she crashed right into it and bounced back, almost falling backward.

"Crap!" she yelled out automatically, stumbling to keep on her feet.

The wall turned around and looked at her, and through her wet eyes morphed into a tall, good-looking man in a white tee shirt and cargo shorts.

"I am so sorry, ma'am!" he exclaimed. "Are you alright?"

Part of her was weirded out by being addressed as "Ma'am" by a man obviously older than she was, part of her was unjustifiably annoyed at him for impersonating a wall and being in her way, and part of her was confused by his apology. Why should he be sorry? She'd been the one who'd plowed into him when his back was turned.

"Not your fault," she muttered and turned to walk around him. Just what she needed right now, another drunk. A quick glance inside the open doorway of the bar showed what was obviously a bunch of his friends, whooping it up. At least her dad wasn't in there with the other drunks. He was at home, walking around bumping into things and crying into his beer. Which was why Michelle was speed-walking away from the house with her head down, her hands stuffed in the pockets of her hoody, and with the hood up so she couldn't see where she was going, sniffling like a baby.

She stepped away from him into the street, to pass by so she could avoid contact with another drunk, and then got the shock of her life when the guy grabbed her arm and jerked her towards him.

Panic snaked through her for a second until she realized he'd just yanked her out of the path of an oncoming golf cart. The man gave a little wave to the driver as the cart passed and called out, "Sorry!" Letting go of her arm, he said, "Maybe you should sit down for a minute, ma'am. You look kind of upset."

"I'm fine." Which was a lie, because she was indeed upset and desperate and a little shaky at having just been saved from being run over. Obviously, he wasn't convinced.

"I'm afraid I can't accept that, ma'am. Why don't you come sit down and let me get you something to drink?" He actually put his hand on her elbow like he was escorting a little old lady across the street.

No way. There was no way she was going into a bar, a bar of all places, with a total stranger. Did he think they had some kind of connection merely because he'd just saved her life? He must be insane as well as drunk.

But he didn't look drunk. He didn't smell of booze nor stumble nor slur his words. He was smiling at her, not leering, but just smiling, like he was concerned about her wellbeing. She wasn't accustomed to people being concerned about her wellbeing. She was familiar with this bar, however, even though she didn't drink. She heard a whoop from her new friend's companions inside, but he didn't move to join them.

She pulled her arm away from him, saying, "I don't know you," and gave him her best Bitchy Death Glare. He had a wide sexy mouth, twinkly hazel eyes, and high cheekbones that would make a supermodel jealous. Of all the drunks to try and pick her up, why did it have to be a super cute one?

"I'm terribly sorry, ma'am, that was rude of me." Apparently, he didn't notice, or chose to ignore, the Bitchy Death Glare, and held out a hand. "Chief Petty Officer Eric Hanson, United States Navy."

Great. He was a sailor. The drunkest of the drunk. Well, second drunkest. Her dad could teach them a thing or two.

"I don't drink." She employed the exact same tone of voice the Queen of England would use to say, "We are not amused."

"Good. Neither do I. But you know what? They serve soft drinks here too, on the house when your buddies are running up a tab."

A sailor who didn't drink? That was like a unicorn, you had to see it to believe it.

"I don't *do* sailors."

At that point, most guys would mutter, "Bitch," and walk away. But this one just kept smiling.

"Well, that's something else we have in common. We're like twins separated at birth." He was still holding out his hand and reluctantly she allowed herself to put out hers and shake it. He looked at her with one eyebrow up, those twinkly, friendly hazel eyes expecting an introduction.

"Michelle," she muttered, looking away.

"Just one name? Like Madonna?" He was still smiling at her with a slight questioning tilt to his eyebrows.

She sighed, trying to sound annoyed. "Diaz."

"Great, Michelle Diaz, now that we've exchanged names, and I've saved your life, that makes us friends. How about that drink? Soft drink," he clarified. His voice had just the barest hint of a southern accent.

Fine. Let him buy her a soda. He'd soon find out how much he didn't want to spend time in her company. She took a deep breath and walked into the bar without speaking to or looking at him or his drunk friends.

It was just a door, after all, it was just a bar, she was just going to drink a Coke, her psyche argued. She'd walked in this door before and survived the experience. In a manner of speaking. Although she had never entered this place in the company of a man before, this one seemed harmless enough, her psyche justified.

It was dim enough after coming in from the late afternoon sun that for a moment she was blinded, and had to push down her hood in order to see where she was going. Her hair caught at the neck of the hoody, so she reached a hand behind the back of her neck, yanked it out and let it hang down her back.

There was only one unoccupied seat at the bar, which was shaped like a boat. That and its underwater seascape décor had probably been what had attracted the group of sailors to party there. Or maybe it was merely because it was the first place they'd encountered after disembarking from the boat. It was steps closer to Crescent Avenue than the Lobster Trap or the Locker Room or Luau Larry's, and a block closer than El Galleon or the Chi Chi Club.

The sailor who had somehow managed to entice her into the place walked up to the guy sitting next to the empty seat and waved his hand at him, saying, "Shoo."

To her surprise, the other guy obeyed without protest; in fact, even smiled at them as he gave up his seat, picked up his beer and strolled over to the pool table.

"How did you get him to do that?" she couldn't help asking.

Her escort shrugged, grinned, and indicated the vacated stool. She had no choice now but to sit there.

"I outrank him," he said. "He's only a PO3."

He looked like he was waiting for her to ask him what a PO3 was, but she refused to give him the satisfaction. As she stared at the wood surface in front of her, the sailor sat down next to her and caught the bartender's eye, requesting, "Two cokes, please."

She knew Gary, the bartender here. He had her number programmed into his phone so he could call her to roll her dad home. He set down the two cold glasses of soda and said, "Hello, Michelle. Let me know if you need anything," and gave a pointed look at her unicorn sailor that clearly said, *I know this young lady and I'm watching you.* She half expected him to point at his eyes and back at the sailor's eyes in that "got my eyes on you" gesture. The petty officer was unfazed, nodded at Gary as if to say, *I hear you*, and picked up his glass to take a sip.

That was when she noticed the tattoo. It covered most of the inside of his right forearm, a large anchor with a rope draped over it.

This was just getting better and better. *Not*. She was sitting in a bar. With a sailor. Who had a tattoo. But who said he didn't drink.

"Friend of yours?" the unicorn sailor asked, nodding towards Gary.

"Acquaintance," she said briefly. She was not going to tell this stranger that her main interaction with Gary was when he'd call to say, *Come get your dad again. He's maxed out his tab and bitching that we won't serve him anymore.*

The sailor's buddies across the room were racking up balls on the pool table. "Hey, Doc," one of them called out. "You wanna shoot?" A second drunk sailor poked First Drunk Sailor in the ribs with an elbow.

"Don't bother him! He's flirr-ting!"

He waved at them dismissively and they shot without him. "Don't mind them. They're ... happy."

"You mean falling down disgusting drunk." Michelle flung the pool players a brief glance of distaste.

"Well, they're not falling down yet, and if they get disgusting, I'll handle it." The sailor glanced at his friends also, but his look was more paternal than unfriendly.

So, he was a doctor. She didn't know much about the Navy, but she had the impression that all its members were jet pilots or SEALs. Or at least claimed to be.

"So, who are you running away from, Michelle Diaz?" he asked. "Trouble at home? You obviously must live here – I can't believe a tourist would be all bundled up in a sweatshirt with a hood over your face like the Unabomber, when it's eighty degrees out."

"What makes you think I'm running away?" Man, what a nosy Rosie this guy was. And what in the world was a Unabomber?

"You've got to be running away – booking down the street like an Olympic speedwalker, running into guys, jumping into traffic, endangering life and limb like that. You're lucky I have quick reflexes or you'd be golf cart roadkill." He grinned at her as if he had a right to get involved in her life. Michelle really wished that grin wasn't just so darn cute.

She sneered. "Aren't you a conceited old superhero."

He still smiled, damn him. "Thanks. I'm partial to Captain America myself. Or maybe Iron Man. Or maybe Wolverine? What do you think?"

"I think you're a dork," she retorted.

He didn't even have the sense to look offended. "Let me guess. Boyfriend trouble?"

Ignore him! She told herself. *Don't let his friendliness and cute smile get to you. He's just another guy, and guys only want one thing.*

She took her own advice and looked steadily into her glass.

"Husband trouble? Come on, you can tell me. We're friends, remember?"

She had never met such an annoying person. Maybe he thought they were friends, but really, he was just someone she needed to shut down. If he knew her better, the last thing he'd want to be was friends. She really didn't know why she bothered talking to him, but then she'd also never met someone who kept smiling through her best Raging Bitch. She should be saying, *go away, leave me alone, I'm not going to talk to you*. She should not be sitting here in a bar full of drunks and she should not be telling him anything about her life or feelings or personal anxieties. And yet, her mouth rebelliously disobeyed her brain.

"No boyfriend, no girlfriend, no husband. Just an alleged father."

Shut up! Her brain said. But weirdly, uncharacteristically, some other, rebellious part of her psyche argued, *talk to him. It won't kill you.*

Sometimes she hated her psyche and wanted to just smack that bitch down.

"Alleged as in, the DNA doesn't match up, or alleged as in, poor parenting skills?" The guy had an expression like he actually wanted to know.

"I'm pretty sure the DNA matches," she found herself muttering.

"OK, well now we're getting somewhere. So why are we mad at Daddy? Was he mean to you? Ground you?"

There was just no getting rid of this guy. Her father had never grounded her. You had to care about someone's behavior in order to ground them.

"Fine, try this on for size if you're so interested." She was practically spitting the words because she really didn't want to say them. Well, that sad, lonely minority of her psyche wanted to talk, and somehow, she was having trouble beating that part of her brain into submission this time. "I just told him I got a new job, a great job, with the biggest boat company on the island."

"That's great. Congratulations. What kind of work do you do for this boat company? Wait, let me guess. You sell them by posing on the bow wearing a bikini?"

She wasn't even going to dignify that with a dirty look. "I fix them. I'm a mechanic."

"I don't believe you."

Of course. They never did. "Yeah, well, you're just another misogynistic ass who thinks you need a penis to turn a screwdriver."

He looked a bit shocked at her crudity. Good. That was the effect she was going for. But the shocked look was only momentary, quickly replaced by a smile.

"Wait, you're misunderstanding me. It's not because you're female. It's your hands. They're too clean. No grease under your fingernails. Every mechanic I know has to scrub their fingernails with a brush for half an hour just to go on a date."

There was no point in giving him her bitchy death glare. It clearly had no effect on him. Maybe she should switch to her bitch-queen-do-not-mess-with-me persona. But it really wasn't much different, or any more effective than Raging Bitch. She had to settle for an annoyed sigh.

"I wear gloves."

His eyes lit up as if she'd handed him a candy bar. "You do? So do I!" He held up both his hands in front of her face like a surgeon waiting to scrub, wiggling ten long fingers. "I've gone through enough latex to stretch from here to the moon. And that's just the gloves." He actually had the nerve to wink at her. "I told you we were twins separated at birth. Your dad must be proud."

That was rich. Proud? Her father, Gregory Diaz, the most apathetic man ever to stumble through life, proud of someone as unimportant as his only offspring? How laughable.

"Oh yeah, he's real proud." She didn't try to restrain the sarcasm dripping from her voice. "You know what he said when I told him?" She didn't wait for the sailor to try to guess. He'd never figure it out. Not even Stephen Hawking could figure out her pathetic life. "He says, pop me another cold one, Mickey."

"Mickey? Your nickname is Mickey?"

"No, it's not!" Her denial was firm and expressed a quite a bit louder than she'd intended.

"Oookay, not Mickey then. Why would he say something like that?" The guy looked like he honestly wanted to know. Yeah, right. When pigs flew. Time to shut this fake friendliness down.

"Because he's a damn drunk, that's why!"

Her outburst was loud enough to silence the entire bar. Gary looked up and started to walk over, but she waved him away. Even the three drunk sailors playing pool stopped and stared at her for a moment before resuming their game.

"I think there were some people in San Diego who didn't hear that," the petty officer chuckled. Actually, she'd probably been heard on the international space station.

Did the man never stop smiling? It was getting downright aggravating. Her hand tightened on the glass.

"Fuck off."

"Not until the third date, sweetheart."

She couldn't even piss him off with bad language. *You're losing your touch, Michelle.* She showed him another, even bitchier Death Glare, to no effect, then turned back to stare at the oh-so-fascinating glass of cola in front of her.

"Don't think you're the first person to ever say that to me. I hear variations of it from guys all the time. Especially when I make them drop trou."

"WHAT?" Did he just say what she thought he said? Finally, she stopped staring at the glass of cola and turned to stare at him. He was still smiling.

"In my line of work, I have to give a lot of injections. Not all of them are in the arm."

"Right, you're a doctor." She turned her gaze back to her glass and tried to load her voice with I Don't Care.

"No, Doc is just a nickname. I'm a corpsman. Kind of the Navy equivalent of a paramedic slash nurse slash physician's assistant."

"If you're in the Navy why aren't you wearing a uniform? Don't you guys wear uniforms?" Why did she ask that? She didn't care. But the I Don't Care facade was getting hard to keep in place in the face of that friendly smile and twinkly hazel eyes.

"We're on leave. We would never embarrass the Navy by going into a bar in uniform." They were shipping out tomorrow and he had wanted to see Catalina Island, but it looked like all he was going to see was the boat dock and this bar.

"Is that part of your uniform?" She tried to sneer as she gestured at the tattoo on his arm.

He turned his arm to give her a better view of his ink. Though she would never ever say so, it was kind of interesting.

"No," he said. "That was the result of a bad decision in Norfolk."

"Then get it removed. I've heard that hurts." She let her tone of voice imply, "duh."

"Oh, I don't regret getting it," the guy said. "Actually, the bad decision was letting my mother see it. She was royally pissed off. You know how moms get. 'If all your buddies jumped off a cliff, would you jump too? If your father was alive he would be so disappointed!' Didn't matter that I was twenty-one years old at the time, a legal adult, and had been in the Navy for almost three years. I may not follow my buddies if they all jumped off a cliff, but when they all got tattoos, well, there you go."

He flexed the arm and she couldn't help but admire the ripple of his muscle. Jeez, a minute ago she'd been telling him to F off, and now here he was telling her stories about his mother scolding him. He really was a unicorn. She half expected to see a shiny white horn start sprouting out of his forehead.

"Were you drunk when you got it?"

"No, I wasn't. I don't drink." He'd said that out on the sidewalk but she still didn't believe him. After all, he was a sailor. He went on, "Moms just can't ever believe their kids grow up, right?"

"I wouldn't know. My mother died when I was ten."

That information finally killed his constant, annoying smile. "Oh, I'm really sorry to hear that, ma'am. I can't even begin to understand what you've gone through, but you have my condolences. That must be really hard for you." Did he really look absolutely sympathetic, or was he just a good actor?

"Yeah, why should you care." It was a statement, not a question, but he answered her anyway.

"Because I'm a human being, with feelings. You've heard of empathy, right?"

She'd heard of it, but she hadn't experienced very much.

It was a mistake for her to look around the bar. At the other end, two girls were doing shots. They gulped down whatever poison was in their little glasses, then waved their arms convulsively as the booze burned inside them. One of them laughed so hard, she almost fell off the bar stool.

There was a couple entwined, swaying nearby, though there was no music playing, or at least none that anyone else could hear. Another couple stood behind the swinging doors that had a life-sized, bare-breasted mermaid and merman painted on them, poking their faces through the oval windows placed where the sea creatures' faces should be, while another girl took photos. The photographer said, "Wait, get one of me!" as she traded places behind the door with her friend.

That painted mermaid, with her painted blond hair floating around her head but not covering her generous naked breasts, had always annoyed Michelle. Why were all mermaids depicted as blondes or redheads? Were there no brunette mermaids?

The three sailors playing pool were laughing uproariously, stumbling as they moved to position their shots, swearing when they either made or missed the shot. One of them, a dark-haired guy with big brown eyes and exotic good looks, picked up his bottle of beer and took a long swig that probably drained half the bottle. He looked towards Michelle over the bottle and when he noticed she was looking, gave her a broad wink. Lifting the bottle in the direction of the bartender, his expression requested another one.

Pop me another cold one, Mickey.

This was cutting too close to the bone. Her throat started to feel tight; it was getting hard to breathe. It was like having an asthma attack, except that she didn't have asthma. Her eyes started to tear, as if she had allergies, except that she didn't have allergies. She hopped down from the bar stool so quickly, she stumbled, as if she'd been drinking, even though she didn't drink. The sailor sitting next to her looked startled at her sudden movement, then put out a hand as if to steady her.

"Hands off, Popeye," she spit out, pulling away from his assistance. "I'm outa here!"

She needed air. Fresh air. Air that didn't smell like beer or resound with the sounds of clinking glasses and bottles. Air that didn't shimmer with the laughter of inebriation, or weigh heavy with the memory of smoke and tears.

Pulling up her hood with determination, she booked out the door, took a left because it was as good a direction as any, as long as it put distance between her and the shooting, dancing, stumbling drinkers in the bar.

She just kept turning left, like a race car driver, quickening her step, back into her blind speed-walking mode. Walking fast, trying not to think or feel or cry, she kept moving, away from the bar, away from that sailor's annoying smile and stupid empathy, just *away*.

Under her feet she felt the earth drop away to a slightly lower elevation, so she lengthened her stride to keep steady and jumped ahead.

There was a loud sound in her ear, vaguely horn-like. At the moment she heard it, she felt both her arms being grabbed from behind and she was jerked backward, to scrape her heels on the pavement and bounce off a wall again, and found herself staring up at a surprisingly familiar pair of twinkly hazel eyes.

"Girl, you are a hazard to navigation!" Chief Petty Officer Hanson declared as her hood fell back away from her face and she realized she had just almost stepped out into Clarissa Avenue, the busiest street in Avalon. The sound she'd heard was the horn of a taxi that had almost run her over as it turned up from Crescent Avenue. Again, the sailor waved at the irritated driver and apologized on her behalf.

"Are you following me?" she demanded, her heart pounding from exertion and shock, and quivering with annoyance.

"Apparently someone needs to," he replied, then reached for her arm, took her wrist in his hand, and put two fingers on the inside of her wrist, as he looked at his wristwatch on his other arm. What a dork, who wore a wristwatch anymore? You just looked at your phone for the time.

"What the hell are you doing?" she demanded, trying to pull her arm from his grasp. But he kept his grip, not surprising considering what was on view under the tight sleeves of his tee shirt. The guy had guns.

"Hush!" he commanded, and she blinked a little. Nobody had ever ordered her around like that, and she found herself so bemused and weirded out by the whole bizarre situation that she actually remained still as she suffered the humiliation of having her pulse taken by a stranger along the side of the road, while people walked by looking at them curiously.

"You gonna check my teeth next? Doc?" she asked after a moment. He probably noticed that her hands were shaking, and she hated that show of vulnerability.

"Shh," he ordered, then finally released her wrist and looked at her. "No, I'm not going to check your teeth, but if I had a blood pressure cuff to hand, I'd check that. You have a pulse like a rabbit on speed. You're having a panic attack, aren't you? You need to sit down and get calm."

Get calm? If he knew anything about her life, he'd know what useless advice that was. Maybe he thought she was going to sit down in another bar with him. Not even if hell froze over.

She breathed deep, trying to quell her rabbity heart rate, so he'd quit treating her like she was a patient, like someone who needed help.

"Do I need to call 911?" he asked, reaching into his pocket as if to pull out his phone.

"I'm fine!" she declared. If she was having a panic attack, it was only because this annoying guy had dragged her into a bar.

No, Michelle, he didn't drag you. You walked in on your own two feet, you stupid idiot. But only because this annoying guy had encouraged it.

No, to be sensible, that wasn't true either. It wasn't as if he'd tried to drag her by her hair. He'd only smiled and offered her a soda. She could have gotten away if she'd wanted to. But had she really wanted to? Or had she subconsciously been grateful for some friendly human interaction?

The quandary confused her and she didn't like being confused. Being confused was in direct contrast to her usual, comfortable Raging Bitch.

"You're pale," he said.

"I'm naturally pale." That was lie number two. Lie number one had been when she'd told him she was fine.

"No, you're not. Your skin is the color of cinnamon with sugar mixed in." He gestured at her face. "Now, you're pale."

Cinnamon and sugar? Was this arrogant jerk coming on to her? Was taking a girl's pulse some new type of pick-up tactic?

"I told you, I'm a corpsman. I'm trained to observe people's physical symptoms."

Of course. He wasn't flirting. He was diagnosing.

He'd need a lot more data than a look at her not naturally pale face and the taking of her rabbit-like pulse in order to diagnose what was wrong with her.

She shouldn't be disappointed that his interest in her was merely medical. She was not going to be disappointed about it.

She was an expert in hiding her disappointment in people.

"I want to make sure you feel OK and get your color back. It would totally suck if you were to have a seizure and drop dead on my watch."

"I am not on your watch!"

"Yes, you are. You became my responsibility when you ran into me back there."

"I'm not your responsibility either, you numbskull." She practically screeched. "I'm nobody's responsibility but my own."

"Really? And how's that working out for you, sweetheart?"

His glib comment made her so angry she felt her head just might explode.

"Go back and play with your friends. I don't need you pawing at me," she told him. But he hadn't really been pawing her. He'd just saved her life for the second time in thirty minutes, and apparently, he was well aware of the fact.

"You know," he said with a return of that cute, sparkly smile, "in the olden days, at this point, you'd be obligated to be my slave for life."

She spotted a break in the Crescent Avenue traffic. "In your dreams, sailor," she retorted, and made her escape across the street.

By swinging left again, she entered the pedestrian section of Crescent Avenue, the main drag of the tourist area of Avalon which followed the curve of the shore of Avalon Bay. Motor vehicles all had to turn up Clarissa Avenue, so she was safe from herself for now, but she left her hood down this time. She didn't want to crash into another wall that might spring up in front of her.

The Green Pleasure Pier was just a block down the street. If she had turned the other way when she ran out of the Marlin Club, she would have come right to it without having risked her life defying the laws of physics, trying to share the same space with a taxi. But she hadn't been thinking straight at that moment. She still wasn't thinking very straight.

The pier got its name honestly, due to its bright green paint job. Michelle hurried down its length, winding her way among people lining up for glass bottom boat tours, tourists taking photos, kids eating ice cream, dive shops selling scuba lessons. People who didn't have drunk, uncaring fathers at home or annoying sailors following them around town.

At the end of the main pier, a ramp led down to a shorter section. She managed the incline without tripping and walked to the end, stopping with her toes at the edge of the wood. There was no railing here, nothing between her and the water. She just stood there, looking out at Avalon Bay and the Pacific Ocean beyond it, trying to be calm.

"Don't do it. He's not worth it!" came a now-familiar voice from behind her. She turned around in disbelief. Was it really? Yes, it was really her life-saving, pulse-taking, annoying new BFF, standing behind her with an expression that combined twinkly friendliness with wariness, one hand slightly outstretched as if to grab her again.

"What the hell are you talking about?"

He shrugged and actually batted his eyelashes at her. "I heard that in a movie once. It seemed appropriate, just in case you were thinking about jumping."

She glanced briefly at the water. "I'm not going to jump," she assured him.

"Then that makes three times I've saved your life today," he insisted.

"This doesn't count." Was she actually debating the point with him? "I had no intention of jumping. And even if I did, I can swim." Just to prove she wasn't suicidal, she sat down on the pier cross-legged, trying to look normal.

To her surprise, the guy sat down next to her, dangling his feet over the edge. "Don't worry," he said with a wink. "I can swim too. And I have rescue skills, so don't you try anything dangerous. I'm almost out of my hero quota for one day."

What a conceited jerk. She just kept staring out over the water, trying to ignore him.

"You want to talk about it?" he asked after a minute, not looking at her at the moment as he also contemplated the ripples off the pier.

Talk about it? Why should she? Nobody would care. But then, nobody had ever offered to hear it before. What did it matter if this stranger found out what a pathetic loser she was? She tried to refuse and insist that he leave her alone to her misery, but then he looked at her and smiled.

She didn't talk about it. The words came out all by themselves, completely on their own power.

"He doesn't care. Nothing makes him care. I could turn into a two-headed purple hippopotamus in front of his eyes, and he wouldn't notice, as long as there's cold beer in the fridge. I could disappear," she waved a hand in the direction of the mainland, "and he wouldn't notice, as long as there's cold beer in the fridge. When I was in high school, I'd hear other girls complain that their parents got on their case if they wore too much makeup, or dated guys the rents didn't approve of, or dressed inappropriately. I always wondered what that felt like. I could make myself up like a whore, date a drummer from a rock band, or wear a bikini to church-"

She stopped talking. If this wasn't the most embarrassing thing she'd ever done to herself, venting to this stranger. She glanced briefly at him, then away. His eyes gleamed with amusement, but thankfully, with neither pity nor derision.

"Did you do those things?" he had the nerve to ask.

"I've been known to layer on the mascara a bit thick," she admitted. "But I've never met a guy in a band, and I've only been inside a church once in my life. Not in a bikini," she added quickly, so that he didn't get any ideas.

"So your dad really does have poor parenting skills," he said. "But you know, being a single parent has got to be rough-"

"It has nothing to do with being a single parent," she interrupted. "He just doesn't care, plain and simple. Not about me at least. All he cares about is his booze. Since I'm not a brown glass bottle, that makes me invisible."

She had had enough. She was tired. Tired of stressing, tired of running, tired of panicking, tired of being followed around being rescued. She wanted, surprisingly, to go home, despite the fact that she'd dashed away from the place as if it were on fire less than an hour ago. But really, she was going to be miserable no matter where she was. It might as well be at home. She stood up.

"Where are you going now?" her sailor asked. *He's not* your *sailor, you idiot,* she told herself.

"I'm going home," she said, but maybe she shouldn't have let him know that. The sailor stood up too.

"I'll walk you home," he said.

What was this, the tenth grade?

She was tempted to try her bitchy death glare again, but what would be the point? Clearly it had no effect on him.

"I don't think so. Go take your shoes for a walk. That way." She pointed at the end of the pier, where taking three steps would have him practicing the swimming skills he'd bragged about.

"Aw, come on. Let me walk you home. It's the least you can do for a guy putting his life on the line to defend your freedom."

She snorted. "Does that line actually work?"

He didn't even bother to look embarrassed at being caught out. He just grinned. "It's one of my best."

"Isn't 'putting my life on the line' a bit much? How dangerous can it be, on a ship on the ocean?" This guy was just too much.

"Actually, very," he replied. "Statistically, the flight deck of an aircraft carrier is the most dangerous work environment in the world. Plus, I've had my boots on the ground. I've spent my fair share of time in full battle rattle."

She had no idea what that meant, but she certainly wasn't going to give him the satisfaction of asking for a definition. "Whatever."

"You don't believe me? Are you insinuating that I lie?" he asked.

"In my experience, most guys do, if it'll get them what they want," she retorted, not caring if her honesty was a bit brutal. Her expression made it obvious what she thought most guys wanted, and would lie to get.

"Well, I'm not most guys. I've never had to lie in order to get," he hesitated, then finished, "a date."

She gave him a frosty look. "Oh, I'm sure you haven't." The sarcasm in her voice was as thick as molasses. It was a barrier to conceal her surprise and unfamiliarity at this casual, bizarre conversation with a virtual stranger.

Fine. Let him walk to her house if he wanted. She had a knee and she knew how to use it. She started to walk up the pier back towards land, and of course, the sailor followed her. She was starting to get used to it. When he came up next to her, he offered his arm like the prom king escorting the prom queen.

As if! Her haughty, disdainful, Queen of England we are not amused look did nothing to diminish that wide, cute grin, but he did at least put his arm down as they walked.

She quickened her step, just to see if he was serious about escorting her. Obviously, he was, as he kept up with her, adroitly avoiding a stroller and bestowing a quick smile on its occupant as they passed. When they reached the end of the pier, she crossed Crescent Avenue in the pedestrian zone. No threat of being run over by a golf cart or motor vehicle in this area, though she did notice her unrequested escort glance around, apparently afraid she might crash into other pedestrians in the absence of mechanical conveyances.

Pay attention to where you're going, Michelle! You don't want to give this annoying superhero the satisfaction of saving your life a third time, for real.

When they started up Sumner Avenue, she felt his hand touch her back, briefly, nudging her aside. She found herself walking on the inside, with the sailor on the outside of the sidewalk, closest to the street.

"Alcoholism is a disease, you know," he said.

She glanced at his face. How could someone smile and look concerned, at the same time? Out of habit, despite her realization of its uselessness, she offered up yet another Bitchy Death Glare.

"Duh. You got an injection with the cure for it in your back pocket? Doc?"

"If I did, I wouldn't be here. I'd be in Stockholm, accepting the Nobel Prize."

They turned up Beacon Street.

"I colored my hair purple once." Again, just like at the edge of the pier, words came out of her mouth without permission. Probably as a result of the fact that she tended to talk to herself, in the absence of other live people to talk to. And yes, admit it, she was still trying to shock him, despite her failure at accomplishing it so far.

Even though she wasn't looking at him, she could sense him turn to stare at her hair for a second.

"Purple! That's absolutely outrageous. But it doesn't look purple to me."

"I did it years ago. And it was temporary. Washed out after five shampoos."

"Wow, that is positively bizarre. I don't think I've ever actually seen purple hair on a living person. What else did you do to push your father's buttons?"

He was a good guesser, she had to give him that. "Got all A's all through high school."

"Impressive! That's sure something to be proud of."

"I guess." She stopped walking for a moment and looked at him while she said the next thing. This was too weird. She had no idea why she was telling him this stuff. It was like she was being controlled by some unseen force that made her talk about her least favorite subject-herself.

She bit her lip and clenched her teeth, but the words still escaped.

"I didn't come home the night of my senior prom." Bitterness dripped from her tone. The sailor's eyes blinked with amusement. "He wasn't even upset. I mean, how would you feel if your kid came home from a date at noon the next day, carrying her shoes?"

"Well, if I had a kid, I guess I'd be pretty upset. But I think I'd be more likely to hunt down the date and tear him a new one."

"Yeah, well, he didn't even know who my date was and he didn't care enough to notice."

The street meandered uphill but the sailor had no trouble keeping up with her. If she were in the mood to notice a man in that way, she'd think he was hot. Good looking and a great body, and those eyes – they could only be described as *sparkly*. But she was definitely not in that sort of mood tonight.

When they passed the Hotel St. Lauren, the sailor stopped for a moment to admire its pink cuteness.

"Is this your house?" he asked. "It's so pink and adorable."

"It's a hotel," she said with a tinge of snot in her voice. Had he not noticed the name painted on the awning above the entrance? She kept walking when he paused, hoping, or perhaps dreading, that he'd lose interest while admiring the building's candy-pink facade and the antique buggy parked in front.

But no, a moment later he was at her side again, as she continued up the hill.

"Can I ask you something personal?" He stopped walking and looked at her with those sparkly eyes. Automatically, she paused also, as if they were actually together, and looked at the sidewalk at her feet, to avoid those friendly eyes.

She'd known this guy all of an hour and she'd already told him more personal stuff than she'd ever spoken of to anyone. What was one more thing? He took her slight shrug as permission to ask her something personal.

"Do you talk to anyone?"

She let her lip curl a little.

"Apparently I talk to sailors who impersonate walls." She refrained from calling him a dork again, but it was implied in her tone and attitude.

He grinned. "A wall, huh? Is that a reference to my manly physique?"

"No, it's a reference to you blocking the sidewalk like a big goof," she replied disdainfully.

"Well, Goof is my middle name. Actually, my middle name is Paul. My mother chose it because Paul McCartney was her favorite member of The Beatles."

"What? I didn't know Paul McCartney was a member of The Beatles." Ancient musical history was not her strong suit.

He looked shocked. "You're kidding, right? How can you not know that? Where did you grow up? In a cave?"

That stung. Just because she lived in a small town on an island didn't mean she was some kind of ignorant bumpkin. "I grew up here in Avalon, remember? Where did you grow up?" She didn't really care. She only asked in the hope it was someplace unsophisticated.

"I grew up in Florida, where we know that Paul McCartney was one of The Beatles."

She shrugged again. "Whatever."

"Back to my original question. Do you talk to someone? Someone professional? A counselor, a shrink, Al-Anon? With all the bars and drinking in this town, there has to be a chapter of Al-Anon here."

She'd considered the idea once or twice and had rejected it as useless. But she certainly was not going to let this guy know that. It was none of his business.

"Like it would matter," she muttered as she continued up the street.

"You should consider it," the sailor suggested. "I've spent an hour or two on a shrink's couch, and I found it to be amazingly helpful."

"Nice for you."

Did he actually think she was going to bare her soul to a stranger just because some random guy thought it would be a good idea?

"And what would I tell this amazingly helpful shrink of yours? That my father is a stupid drunk and that I hate him for it? Would that change anything?" She started up the hill again, not bothering to see if he was still following. He was, of course.

"You don't hate him."

"Oh, I think I do. He's horrible."

"No, you don't hate your father, no matter what he's like. He's still your father, and,"

What a presumptuous ass this guy was! Despite her ongoing knowledge of its ineffectiveness, she still showed him her Bitchy Death Glare, accompanied by hands on hips and the snottiest tone of voice she could dredge up from the pit of her being.

"You don't know me, you don't know my father, you don't know anything about my whole shitty life. So just-"

He interrupted her with a hand raised in protest. "Please, please don't tell me to fuck off again. I don't think my ego can handle it. But actually, I think I do know you, and something about your whole – cosmic existence."

"Yeah, what do you think you know about me?"

He gave her an appraising glance that took in her clothes – the hoody, tee shirt, shorts, even her flip flops, and proceeded to dissect her psyche.

"Your favorite color is pink. You're, stand still, let me stand next to you for a sec, five feet six inches tall. You have a forehead like a rock. My T2 vertebrae still hurts. You're academically brilliant-that stuff you said about all A's was on the level, right? You're not in a relationship, though you wear what appears to be a wedding band, on your right hand. I assume it was your mother's and you wear it to remember her by. So, despite that hard-candy-coated Raging Bitch exterior, you're actually sentimental. You're courageous - you work in a field that, despite this being the twenty-first century, is still male-dominated and that has to be tough. You lost your virginity the night of your senior prom. And you have a chip on your shoulder the size of Texas."

How dare he? How DARE he? She really should tell him to-but the unavoidable fact was, that he was right about everything. Apparently, she wasn't as mysterious as she'd thought she was. And he'd noticed the ring. Well, that wasn't so unusual. It was instinct, when meeting someone of the opposite sex, regardless of the relationship or expectations, or lack thereof, to do a ring check. She had glanced at his hands too; he wore no ring.

Barb-sharp anger formed on her words.

"I do not have a chip on my shoulder the size of Texas!"

"OK, maybe the size of Montana. Or Nebraska. Or maybe I should stop talking now. Brenda always told me my big mouth would get me into trouble."

Michelle couldn't help it. She just simply could not help it. She was, after all, a healthy, red-blooded, heterosexual female. She looked at the mouth he'd mentioned, at that wide smile and sexy lips, and thought, *I just bet that mouth gets you into trouble.*

But if it got him into trouble, it seemed to get him out of trouble too, when accompanied by repentant sheep eyes and an expression that said, *please forgive me for delving too far into your psyche.*

"You know, whatever the size of one's shoulder chip, they are a real pain to carry around all the time." (Apparently, his idea to stop talking didn't last long.) "Sometimes you just have to let go of stuff that isn't your fault and that you can't change. Your father makes his choices and if he can't or won't get help, it's not your burden to bear. You know there's this prayer-I'm not much for religion but I think this one makes sense. 'Grant me the serenity to accept the things I can't change.' There's more to it, you can Google it sometime if you're interested."

This wasn't right. She had called him a misogynistic ass, and he'd smiled. She'd told him to fuck off, and he'd smiled. She'd called him names, given him dirty looks and tried to ignore him. And he'd smiled and given her life advice. What on earth was wrong with him?

She tried to squelch an annoying inner voice that insinuated that perhaps the problem lay not with him, but with her.

They had arrived in front of her house. Due to the curve of the road, and the taller height of her neighbor's houses, the Diaz house had no ocean view, which had made it more affordable when her grandparents had purchased it.

If this was a normal situation, in the company of someone she actually knew, she might have said, "This is my house." But this was not a normal situation. She was with an annoying man she didn't know, and what if he asked to come inside?

So, she said nothing, just stood there, Obviously, he guessed why.

"This is your house? It's cute."

She actually found herself appreciating his compliment. She had painted the exterior herself last month. But her dad hadn't noticed. She'd chosen a buttery yellow, a cheerful color. Cheerful on the outside, but still with a distinct lack of cheerfulness on the inside. No paint color could inspire that.

"OK, you've walked me home. Your obligation is fulfilled. I'm not going to put myself into any more dangerous situations. You can go back and hang out with your drunk friends now." She waved a hand back in the direction they'd come from.

The sailor glanced back momentarily in the same direction. "Yeah, about those guys. Look, Michelle,"

How dare he call her by her name? Oh yeah, right, they were friends. She knew what was going to come next. Some kind of pickup line.

She beat him to the punch.

"Don't tell me. It goes something like this." She put a dramatic hand to her forehead and gave her best Scarlet O'Hara impersonation, laying it on as thick as peanut butter.

"Oh, darling, I'm shipping out tomorrow. I'm being sent to the front, to the danger zone. I may never come back. It's a one-way mission, a suicide assault, flying into the teeth of enemy fire. But I'm willing to die for king and country, for you, babe. Can't we just have this one night of bliss? Do it for your country. Uncle Sam isn't the only one who wants you. Send a guy to the front a happy man!"

He stared at her open-mouthed for a moment, then, damn him, he busted a gut.

"Oh my lord, that is the funniest thing I ever heard!" he exclaimed between gusts of laughter. "That accent! It's priceless! Wait, wait, do that 'send a guy to the front a happy man' part again. That was my favorite."

Whoa. This was new. Someone who thought she was amusing, rather than bitchy. It was rare for her to allow herself to escape into humor. The bitchy death glare and snotty sarcasm were far more effective defenses. But she couldn't help allowing just the tiniest smile to leak out.

Darn, the sailor noticed.

"Well, hello, she can smile! There's hope for the world after all."

Then he looked serious, and glanced at the house. "Your dad, when he's drunk - does he hit you or anything?"

She shook her head.

"No. He's too apathetic to get violent. I screamed at him and he just said, quit your bitching."

She'd screamed at him so loud, it had hurt her throat, "Don't you care about anything?" Then she'd grabbed her hoody, pulled the hood up and ran out the door, slamming it so hard she was surprised the neighbors hadn't called the sheriff's department.

"Why should you care? Oh yeah, right, empathy."

"It does really exist, you know," he insisted.

"If you say so."

"I know so." He was like a dog with a bone about this whole empathy thing.

"I'm sorry," he said, "but I have to get back to that smelly bar and pry three happy guys out and onto the boat to Dana Point. We really are shipping out tomorrow, and if we don't report in at NAS San Diego by oh-nine-hundred, we're all in deep shit. Pardon my language."

"Sucks to draw the short straw, huh?"

"Well, since I don't drink, we don't need to draw straws."

Did he think he was going to impress her by claiming he didn't drink? The guy sure had an ego. But, surprise, surprise, no pickup line, no attempt to get fresh.

"Let me give you my email address," he said. "If you ever want to talk, digitally speaking. I may not always be able to reply right away, but I will as soon as I can." He patted uselessly at his pockets for something to write with. Who wrote anything on paper anymore?

"Can I see your phone?"

He had to be crazy, and she gave him a look that said so. "Don't worry, I'm not going to install any spyware or one of those tracking apps or anything."

This entire evening had consisted of her doing things she'd never thought she'd ever do. What was one more insane thing? Almost against her will, she pulled her phone out of her pocket and handed it to him, but watched carefully as he opened the memo app and typed in his email address, then handed it back to her.

"Take care of yourself, Michelle Diaz. It was nice talking to you. Watch where you're going out there. Look both ways when you cross the street." He grinned boyishly at her frown, then held out his hand again to shake. "Send me an email."

He started to turn away as if to leave but quickly turned to face her again.

"Remember back there," he gestured down the hill towards town, "when I said we were like twins separated at birth?"

She nodded, wondering what he was getting at.

"So, senior prom night?" he inquired with a teasing gleam in his eye.

Oh he would have to bring up that impulsive confession. She nodded reluctantly, embarrassment stirring in her.

One long index finger tapped at the center of his chest. "Senior prom night for me, too."

She gaped at him disbelievingly, which apparently he found to be quite amusing as he grinned and chuckled.

"Twins. Separated at birth," he drawled, then turned and walked back down the street towards town, giving her a little backward wave as his flip flops smacked along the sidewalk.

An odd sound floated back from his direction. Was it, was he, was that – *singing*? No, it couldn't be. More likely someone had stepped on the neighbor's cat.

2

Michelle sat on the loveseat on her back patio, watching the last bit of light fade from the sky. When she'd gotten into the house, her dad was in bed asleep, so there was no need to revisit their unpleasant scene. Not that he would have cared one way or another, she thought bitterly. Dad was blind and deaf to anything that smacked of emotional involvement. Why, she didn't know. It might have made sense to assume it an effect of her mother's death, but she had never once heard him say that he missed her mother or that he'd loved her. In fact, he never talked about her at all. And even before her mother's death, she remembered Dad being a heavy drinker.

She took a sip from the bottle of water she'd grabbed on her way through the kitchen, and couldn't help but think about that sailor she'd met this evening. She felt kind of bad now about how she'd talked to him. She'd said some pretty rude things, and he'd been nothing but nice. The Raging Bitch wasn't how she really was, in her heart of hearts. It was mainly a convenient disguise to shield herself from life's inevitable disappointments. Most people took it seriously, but somehow Chief Petty Officer Eric Hanson had seen right through it. He'd said things to her that, if looked at objectively, actually made a lot of sense.

Grant me the serenity to accept things I can't change. Easy to say. Not so easy to live. She certainly had never been able to change her father's actions or attitude, no matter what outrageous or impressive things she'd ever done. Maybe it wouldn't be the end of the world if she let go of some of the emotional detritus that inspired her unnatural bitchiness.

Or, maybe she was just reading too much into a clever guy's pickup line. But if that was the case, it was unlike any other pickup line she'd ever heard, and she'd heard plenty. He hadn't tried to buy her a drink, other than a Coke, nor had he tried to touch her, other than when he'd yanked her from the path of sudden death, and took her pulse. He hadn't even tried to kiss her when they'd arrived at her front door. He'd only nudged her to the inside of the sidewalk as they walked, and shook her hand like a friend. There had been that comment about her skin being the color of cinnamon and sugar, but it had quickly become apparent that was a medical observation, not flirtation.

He'd been so annoying, following her around, giving her advice, smiling constantly. It wasn't lost on her that while he'd insisted on giving her his email address, he hadn't asked for hers, or for her phone number. The ball was in her court as to any further communication.

With that thought in mind, she decided that maybe she would drop him a brief email. What would it hurt? It wasn't like they were ever going to see each other again. Not that it would matter. He'd obviously only spent time with her to kill a boring hour while his friends partied. Sucks to be the designated sober guy.

No, wait. He'd said, "I don't drink." Not, "I'm not drinking today." Like it was a permanent thing. She found that hard to believe, especially for a sailor, but he'd sounded sincere.

She dropped the empty water bottle into the recycling bin and went inside to her bedroom. From her father's room, she could hear his drunken snoring through the door, sounding like a pissed-off grizzly bear. Hopefully she'd be able to pour some coffee into him before she left for work in the morning. Sitting cross-legged on her bed, she opened her laptop and logged on to her email. Pulling out her phone, she opened the memo app to read what he'd written and typed the address into the "To" space.

It would be polite to start with a greeting, so she typed, "Petty Officer Hanson."

No, that wasn't right. There had been more to it. She tried to remember his introduction, erased what she'd written and entered, "Chief Petty Officer Hanson."

Wasn't that a mouthful of awkwardness. It sounded pretty pretentious for someone with a boyish smile and sparkly eyes. What the heck. He'd said, now that we've exchanged names, that makes us friends. So she deleted the whole verbose rank and just typed, "Eric."

OK, now what? "Thank you for buying me a Coke?" No, that sounded trite and juvenile. And besides, he hadn't actually purchased the sodas. Gary had poured them for free because his buddies were running up a tab. And judging by the way his buddies had stumbled and laughed, the tab had probably ended up to be quite expensive.

"Thanks for saving my life?" (Twice, not three times.) No, he'd get all full of himself. After hovering her fingers over the keyboard for a moment, she finally typed.

From: Michelle Diaz
Subject: Sorry
Date: April 20, 2018
To: Eric Hanson
I apologize for telling you to fuck off. That was rude. You may have said a thing or two that made sense. I'll think about it. But you only saved my life two times. That third thing didn't count.

There were other things she could have included, but absolutely, positively was not going to. Things like, "You have the sparkliest eyes and cutest smile I ever saw. It was adorably sweet of you to walk to my house with me. I'm kind of fascinated by the tattoo." Nope, she wasn't going to include any of that in her email, no way!

She thought it might be nice to end her email with something appropriate to say to a guy in the Navy. Sure, it might be corny, but it wasn't like she was ever going to see him again. It didn't matter if he had a girlfriend, a boyfriend, or a harem. They had no relationship. He probably wouldn't even answer this email. She minimized the email screen, opened another page and went to Google. After looking through a few websites dealing with Navy phrases, including a few that were real eye-openers, she found one that sounded nice, and finished her email with, "Fair wind and following seas, Michelle."

She hit send, then remembered something he'd said that had made her curious. Returning to Google, she looked up 'battle rattle.'

Hmm, maybe he hadn't been exaggerating when he'd claimed to be putting his life on the line to defend her freedom.

It was only later, while brushing her teeth, that it occurred to her to wonder. Who was Brenda?

******

Eric stood at the rail of the Catalina Express boat to Dana Point, watching the lights of Avalon as they pulled away from the dock. Off the port stern, he saw a round white building that seemed to glow in the light of the setting sun. His buddies were settling into seats on the deck nearby, and he'd be willing to bet they'd all be asleep in minutes. He had finally convinced the three of them to stop singing "99 Bottles of Beer on the Wall" by the time they'd boarded. They couldn't seem to remember what number came after 98 anyway. At least the faint, fresh scent of salt air flowed around him. It was nice, but not as salty as the open ocean.

Call him weird, but he loved the smell of salt water.

He reminded himself to insist that everyone hit the head as soon as they docked. It would be another hour's drive from the boat dock in Dana Point down to San Diego, if they didn't hit traffic, and he didn't want to have to stop along the side of the San Diego Freeway just because some guy with a bladder full of beer needed to drain the lizard.

Apparently, the guys weren't all asleep just yet. One of them opened his eyes, grinned at Eric, and asked, "So, Doc, did you score?"

"None of your business, Gonzalez," he retorted.

"Aw come on, Doc," Gonzalez wheedled, "You gotta tell us if you got lucky."

"Shut the *fuck* up."

It was unlike him to give his good friends such a quick STFU. It was also unlike him to not divulge to them all the details of his encounters with pretty girls, even if the details were lurid. But he found himself unwilling to talk about this particular young lady to them. She was too special to be gossiped about, no matter what had or hadn't happened between him.

Fortunately, Gonzalez didn't take offense. He just chuckled and settled in for his nap.

Eric couldn't help but think about her, the girl who'd crashed into his back on the sidewalk. So maybe he had been standing in the path. He'd only wanted to get a breath of fresh air outside the bar. He knew she didn't believe him when he'd said he didn't drink. It was true though, and he had his reasons.

A small smile curved his lip when he thought about how hard she'd tried to be a bitch. He'd had to bite the inside of his cheek to keep from laughing when she'd told him to fuck off, the cutest little F off he'd ever had flung at him.

Despite her fake hostility, he'd been glad to pass some time in the company of someone pretty and interesting. But he also felt kind of bad, leaving her there alone with only her drunk, uncaring father and no mother. While his parents were both deceased, he at least had been an adult when each had died, and had certainly never lacked for their love or attention until then.

But realistically, what could he have done? Stayed there to protect her? Not possible, especially not under the circumstances today, though it was his nature, his inclination, his reason for becoming a corpsman, to always try to help people who he thought needed help.

They'd only just met, she didn't know him; he didn't know her. As much as he always hated to walk away from anyone who needed assistance, it wouldn't have been practical, or even possible, for him to stay in Avalon a minute longer. Not only were they virtual strangers, but if he and his three snoozing buddies didn't report in at NAS San Diego by oh-nine-hundred, they'd all be in deep shit.

It was almost dark now, the receding lights of Avalon sparkling in a large curve across the water. He pulled his phone out of his pocket, thinking he'd call Brenda to say goodbye. There wouldn't be time in the morning. But there was no service out here on the water, and maybe it was for the best. It was three hours later in Florida. Brenda wouldn't mind him calling her that late at night. She was always glad to hear his voice. But if her husband heard the phone ring that late at night, he most definitely would not be glad to hear Eric's voice. In fact, the man would be downright pissed.

The phone went back in his pocket.

Eric had had enough psyche training to realize what that young woman, Michelle Diaz, felt. It was anger. She was angry. It shimmered off her in waves, palpably strong. You could practically see it. She was angry at her mother for dying young, angry at her father for looking for his life's purpose in a bottle rather than with his daughter, angry at the world in general for the crappy hand life had dealt her. He couldn't blame her for the Raging Bitch persona she affected, even though he could tell it was totally fake. He suspected a delicate fragility was hidden behind that tough bitch facade, and marveled at the lonely strength required to protect it.

Why had he followed her when she dashed out of the bar? On the surface, it had appeared that the last thing in the world she wanted was his company. But he had seen past the supposed disdain, the fake dislike. That girl needed help. She needed a friend. So, he chased her down like a stalker, but with the noblest of intentions, and just hoped she didn't take it the wrong way and call the cops.

She was undeniably intriguing, with that long dark brunette hair framing a sweet, pretty face and unusual, startling blue eyes. Those eyes reminded him of the ocean on a clear sunny day. It was an unusual combination. Most of the brunette women he'd known had brown eyes. A lot of blond women he'd known had brown eyes too, but he was sure that didn't always come naturally. Michelle Diaz was more than pretty. She was quite possibly the most beautiful woman he'd ever met, and he'd met plenty of women in his life.

She'd seemed sincere when she'd bragged about getting all A's in high school, and he was a bit envious. He'd gotten decent grades himself, though certainly not all A's, because, well, literature. He had however excelled in physical education and in the physical sciences – biology, anatomy, chemistry.

The lights of Avalon had disappeared under the horizon by now and for a few minutes it was almost like being out on the open ocean, until the lights of the California coast came into view off the bow. As he took a seat next to his snoozing companions, he hoped that girl was going to be alright. Too bad she had to use that tough attitude like a shield. The way his life was, he would probably never see her again, though he wouldn't mind visiting Catalina Island again someday, and next time maybe seeing a bit more than the boat dock, one bar, and vehicles that he needed to drag people away from. He'd purposely not asked Michelle Diaz for her email or phone number, not wanting it to look like he was trying to place a move on her. Which surprised him; usually, for him, meeting a girl as gorgeous as she was, would involve moves being made.

His buddies at that bar must have surely thought he was trying to make time with her when he brought her in and waved his friend away from the barstool so that Michelle could sit next to him. It was true that he outranked the Petty Officer Third Class who had been sitting there by three grades. But the real reason the PO3 had given up his seat so readily was that there was an unspoken agreement among them to make way for any of them who picked up a girl. Seeing them had obviously been what prompted Gonzalez to ask him if he'd "scored" with Michelle Diaz after he'd followed her out of the bar, even though he hadn't, and, surprisingly, hadn't been trying to. He'd been motivated more by concern for her well-being, and good thing he had followed her before she'd stepped out in front of that taxi.

If she chose to email him, he would be happy to correspond with her when his schedule allowed. If not, well, that was just how it would have to go. One thing he'd learned in the Navy was how to leave people behind.

He liked her, or rather, he might like her if he'd had a chance to get to know her. She seemed to be really different from other girls he'd known, with an interesting combination of girly-girl with her pink clothes and wearing her mom's wedding ring, and empowered I am woman hear me roar type girl, working as a boat mechanic of all things.

Tomorrow when his ship left the port of San Diego, its entire crew, with the exception of those actually driving the ship at the time, would man the rails as the huge ship pulled away. It was always an impressive site, six thousand Sailors and Marines lined up along the perimeters of the flight deck, all in starched and fresh-pressed uniforms as they stood at parade rest, feet twelve inches apart, hands clasped behind the back, facing forward, out over the water. They would do it again when they got to Hawaii, to render honor at the USS Arizona Memorial in Pearl Harbor.

What would be the chances that tomorrow he might stand on the side of the ship facing in the direction of Catalina Island?

You're an idiot, Hanson. Their route wouldn't take them within view of the island and even if it did, so what? It wasn't as if a certain blue-eyed brunette was going to be watching for him.

More realistically, he should concentrate on trying to finagle it so that he had Danny Gonzalez standing near him during the manning of the rails. It was challenging enough even for those in the best condition to stand at military bearing for four hours. It could get downright painful. Based on how badly he'd stumbled on the walk from the bar to the boat dock, Danny was going to need some subtle encouragement in order to keep upright and in position. If that boy didn't start making some better decisions about the volume of his off-duty consumption of adult beverages, he'd be in serious danger of pickling his liver. He'd already been decidedly tipsy when Eric had brought Michelle Diaz into the Marlin Club, and had obviously had several more by the time Eric returned from walking her home.

Michelle Diaz. What an interesting woman. What a contrast. That pseudo-bitchiness didn't quite mask the wounded hurt underneath. She'd given him a look that said, *I dare you to be nice to me.* He wondered if she realized how beautiful she was.

The inner conflict had shown plainly on her face as she'd talked to him about her unpleasant home life. It was just too bad there was nothing he could do to help her.

3

∽

From: Eric Hanson
Subject: Hello
Date: April 30, 2018
To: Michelle Diaz
No problem. Like I said, I'm used to it. I find that if I smile at people when they say it, it usually throws them off completely. I'm glad to hear you'll think about it. Just don't go jumping off that pier.

From: Michelle Diaz
Subject: Smiling
Date: May 8, 2018
To: Eric Hanson
Don't your cheeks ever get sore from smiling so much? Mine would. Don't worry, I am not even going to consider jumping off that pier, if only so you can't claim to have saved my life three times.

From: Eric Hanson
Subject: Smiling
Date: August 1, 2018
To: Michelle Diaz
No, those muscles are well trained.

Internet access has been spotty here lately.

From: Michelle Diaz
Subject: Smiling
Date: August 15, 2018
To: Eric Hanson
Where are you?

From: Eric Hanson
Subject: Sorry
Date: August 27, 2018
To: Michelle Diaz

Sorry, I can't tell you. Not that I don't know, but I'm not allowed to. I can say that the view is very wet and it's hotter than the hinges of hell. We recommend that the crew all consume at least a quart of water per hour to stay hydrated, but most of it gets sweated out as fast as it goes in. Trying to keep 5000 pairs of kidneys working properly is a challenge.

However, what you said in your first email turned out to be a self-fulfilling prophecy. We are having fair winds and following seas. But I still can't tell you exactly where.

******

Michelle stood in the doorway of her father's bedroom. There was a worn, stained old comforter on the bed that had probably been there since her mother had been alive. It was, as usual, crooked and one corner dragged on the floor. She looked at it for a moment, then dashed into the room and grabbed it off the bed, pulling and yanking until she dragged it out the door, down the hall, and into the living room. A corner flipped up in the air with the force she used to drag it away, and caught a lamp on the end table, knocking it to the floor.

Ignoring the 'clunk' sound it made, and not bothering to check if the lamp was broken, she continued to drag and jerk the stupid, disgusting blanket into the kitchen, along the tile floor and out the back door. It caught on the hinge as if resisting her rough treatment, and she pulled it off with enough force that the fabric ripped. She yanked the thing across the patio until she stood breathless in front of the trash bin.

The laws of physics state that for every action, there is an equal and opposite reaction. When she jerked open the lid of the bin, its equal and opposite reaction was to slam right back down, coming dangerously close to smashing her hand. It took her three attempts to pull the lid open with the correct amount of force for it to stay up.

She was panting with frustration by now as she gathered up the stained fabric and started stuffing it into the can, pushing it down as the folds caught on the lip of the bin and thwarted her attempt to dispose of it. It smelled like beer. When she finally got most of it inside, with just a small portion hanging over the edge, she slammed the lid down with even more force than with which she'd opened it. Again, it bounced but settled down on top of the stained fabric. For good measure, she kicked the side of the can a couple of times until her bare foot started to complain about the abuse.

There was nothing left she needed to do. She had done all she could, all that was expected of her. Leaving the offensive old blanket in the trash, she limped back into the house. She was alone in the house, but she was used to that. She'd been pretty much alone since her mother had died.

Sitting cross-legged on her bed, she opened her laptop and checked her email. There was nothing left she needed to do.

But something she, for some reason, decided to do anyway. It was stupid maybe, useless almost certainly. But for some weird, unknown reason, she composed a fresh email and typed in the address of that sailor she'd met last spring, that petty officer - what had his friends called him? That Doc. They'd exchanged several emails in the months since she'd crashed into his back on the sidewalk, but she hadn't heard from him since Christmas, two weeks ago, when he'd sent her a brief, vague message wishing her seasons' greetings. No indication of where he was or what he was doing, not that it mattered.

Cure this one then, Doc. The email she sent him was brief, just three words. She wasn't sure why she even bothered typing them.

From: Michelle Diaz
Subject: none
Date: January 2, 2019
To: Eric Hanson
My dad died.

There was no reply, and she wasn't surprised. But, ten days later, she did receive a reply.

From: Eric Hanson
Subject: Condolences
Date: January 13, 2019
To: Michelle Diaz
Dear Michelle,
I'm so sorry to hear about your father. I know that has to be really really hard for you and you have my deepest sympathy. No words can describe how sorry I am for your loss. I wish I could have come over there for the funeral, but I'm TAD OCONUS. Keep your chin up, girl. I know it's difficult. But each day, you will find it getting easier to deal with. It may take a while but you will find yourself in a better place as time passes, and be able to remember things with a calmer feeling than you have today. Just be careful crossing the street, since I'm not there to save you.

He actually inserted a smiley face emoji at that point, the big goof.
Thank goodness for Google, she thought as she typed the letters into the search bar.
TAD – temporary additional duty. OCONUS – outside the continental United States. My, the boy sure got around. What was it they said about sailors? A girl in every port. It was nice of him to send sympathy, sweet even, but she certainly was not his girl in this port, even if he had saved her life twice. That third time still didn't count.

For a moment she allowed herself to daydream. If Chief Petty Officer Eric Hanson hadn't been out of the country, out somewhere OCONUS, saving the world one injection at a time, would he really, truly have come all the way to Avalon just to attend her father's funeral? Her mind couldn't help but envision his sitting next to her in the first pew at Saint Catharine of Alexandria Catholic Church, in his Navy uniform, maybe holding her hand in sympathy. It was only the second time in her life she had ever been inside a church – the first having been her mother's funeral – and she had never before felt so alone, despite the other attendees around her. She didn't consider herself a Catholic, or anything else, but this had been the church where her cousin had arranged her mother's funeral, so it seemed like the right thing to hold a service for her father at the same venue.

Her father's funeral was a short one, because the priest didn't know him, and the only person attending who had anything nice to say about him was one scruffy guy who said that Greg Diaz had been a good drinking buddy.

It would have been nice to have a friend sitting there holding her hand. He'd said they were friends, after all, since they had exchanged names and he had saved her life.

But seriously, when he'd said he would have been there if he could, he'd probably just said it to make her feel better. It was an easy thing to say when there was no opportunity to make good on it. His life was far away from this place, both in miles and in substance. He had signed it over to the United States of America, committing everything he had, up to and including his life. And she thought she was lonely? How could that possibly compare to the loneliness and stress endured by the thousands of brave sailors on board that ship, including Chief Petty Officer Eric Hanson, with its most dangerous work environment in the world?

She shook her head to wave away the stupid, sentimental, immature daydreams. *You're so stupid, Michelle.* One sweet, sympathetic email did not make him your rock, or to use a Naval term, your anchor. Sending a friendly email was easy. A few minutes at a keyboard was all it took. Don't read things into it that aren't there.

4

∽

Bills don't lie. They are the most honest things on the planet. They tell the same scary, inevitable truth every month. And the truth they told Michelle was, that she was broke.

The mortgage on their house – now her house – had been in arrears when her father had died two months ago. He'd worked in hotel maintenance when he was sober, but he'd lost a lot of time due to his brown bottle flu. She'd had to max out her credit card to bring the mortgage current, and there was still the monthly payment. A second credit card was necessary to keep up. She made decent money at her job, but there were still more expenses than income. Utilities, insurance, food, her student loan, payments on the used golf cart she'd bought to drive to work. Though most of her work was done at the dock by the casino, she had a fairly heavy tool bag to bring to work with her, as well as her backpack which she kept supplied with a change of clothes and a couple of towels. Working on boat engines meant frequently getting wet.

There were times when she had to go out to the boat repair company's facility on the other side of town to pick up parts. It was way out past the south side of town, on Pebbly Beach Road, and it took too long to walk out there. Though Avalon's residents always gave each other rides, and even stopped to pick up visitors, she couldn't always depend on that assistance. The golf cart was invaluable.

She needed another source of income. She didn't have the time or inclination to work a second job. Almost all of the part-time jobs in town would be in the tourist industry – in hotels, restaurants, bars, tour companies. She had nothing against the tourists who were Avalon's lifeblood source of income. But she just didn't have the outgoing, happy personality that such work would require.

There was no getting around it. She was going to have to take on a roommate to split the household expenses with.

She really had no experience as a roommate, unless you counted her parents. She barely remembered her mother living at the house. Her only memories were of her being sick, then gone.

Her dad had been virtually useless. He'd contributed financially only when a breakfast of ibuprofen and coffee had fortified him enough to go to work. As for physical or emotional support, there had been none. Living with him had been more like having a kid than a roommate.

For the eighteen months she'd lived on the mainland while attending technical school in Los Angeles, she'd rented a tiny room over a garage in a bad neighborhood. It was highly likely that it hadn't even been a legal rental unit. Her frequent trips back to Avalon to check up on her dad during that time had been another expense that made her credit card groan.

There was no way to avoid it. She called Randy Zimmerman, a realtor in town that she knew, and asked him to place an ad for a roommate and to arrange for getting background checks on any applicants.

******

It was only a few days before Randy called her back.

"I think I have a good candidate for a roommate for you, if you're OK with a male roommate."

A male roommate? She hadn't considered that. But this was the twenty-first century. It wasn't unheard of for men and women to be roommates. And yet, the concept of living under the same roof with another person she didn't know was unfamiliar enough as it was. Would it be too weird if that other person was a guy?

"You have to see his background check," Randy said. "It's impeccable. He even sent a letter of recommendation."

That was surprising. She hadn't asked for that. "He says he knows you."

Michelle wasn't aware of any guy in Avalon who would want to be roommates with her. There were a few she was acquainted with who might want to be roommates just long enough for wham-bam-thank-you-ma'am, but that wasn't what she was looking for.

"OK, so who is this paragon of virtue?"

She managed to sound casual, but inside, she was dying to know.

"Hang on a sec, I have his email here. I thought I did, I must have closed that screen. His name is – oh wait, where is it?" She could hear him tapping at his keyboard over the phone, trying to retrieve the information. "Something Scandinavian."

She was beginning to get a sneaking suspicion.

"Oh, here it is! Eric Hanson. Do you know him?"

Eric Hanson? It couldn't be. She knew an Eric Hanson, sort of, or at least she'd met him. But he was in the Navy. He lived on a ship somewhere. Somewhere outside the United States. Of course, both Eric and Hanson were fairly common names, but she'd only met one person with that particular combination. Why on earth would he be looking for a place to live in Avalon? And more importantly, why would he want to be roommates with her? The way she had treated him, she thought he'd prefer sleeping on a park bench to spending time anywhere in her vicinity.

"Michelle?"

She'd completely forgotten to keep listening to Randy. "He says he can PayPal the deposit and first month's rent as soon as you give the word."

"Yes, I know an Eric Hanson," she said slowly.

"I'll email you his application and info then," Randy said. "Let me know if I should reply to him or not."

"OK, thanks, Randy," she said, and she disconnected her phone.

"I know him," she'd said. But did she really? They'd had an hour's conversation – some of it bordering on the bizarre – almost a year ago, and exchanged a few emails. Did that qualify as knowing him, at least well enough to live with him? Well, not Live With Him. Live under the same roof with him, as a roommate.

What did she know about him? He was from Florida. He was in the Navy. He was a corpsman, which was like a paramedic. Or a nurse. Or a physician's assistant. Or all three. There was a woman named Brenda in his life. Would this Brenda object to him being roommates with another woman?

His middle name was Paul, which had been given in honor of that old English guy who, apparently, had been in the Beatles. He had a cute smile and a charming personality. He didn't drink – that was a big plus. He was perceptive and observant and had given her advice and insights that had changed her life, despite only an hour's conversation and a few emails.

She had, at his suggestion, attended a few Al-Anon meetings since then and found she wasn't alone in her situation, and sharing her experiences about it had lifted a lot of the emotional weight off her shoulders, maybe even dislodging her Texas-sized chip a little. She'd reconnected with a couple of friends from high school and found out to her surprise that they didn't really think she was a raging bitch either. Maybe it wasn't all completely as a result of her brief acquaintance with Chief Petty Officer Eric Hanson. Maybe she had just grown up and stopped hiding behind her hoody, both physically and figuratively, but his advice had helped a lot.

She had derided him for claiming to have put himself into harm's way, until she'd done that Google search for battle rattle. There was no reason to think he hadn't been truthful about it. When he'd been wearing fifty pounds of battle gear and carrying a serious weapon, she'd stake her life it hadn't been while here in the United States. "I'm TAD OCONUS," he'd said in his email after her father's death. She wondered what country outside the United States he'd been in. Nowhere friendly, doubtless.

Michelle had held a gun in her hands once, but it certainly wasn't under the same circumstances.

A few minutes later she was looking at a rental application from Eric Hanson, U.S. Navy, Retired. There was a copy of his driver's license attached. It was definitely her Eric Hanson. Well, not *her* Eric Hanson, but definitely the Eric Hanson she'd met almost a year ago. The same twinkly eyes and cute, wide smile. Who smiled like that in their driver's license photo? Maybe he'd been flirting with the DMV clerk. His address was listed as a post office box in San Diego. Previous occupation-United States Navy. Current occupation-Avalon Fire Department Paramedic.

So, he'd left the Navy. That was surprising. He'd seemed so dedicated. Living and working in a small town like Avalon might seem pretty tame by comparison.

Randy had been right. His background check was impeccable. If she didn't know better, she'd wonder if he was human. Though there was one line she found intriguing. Marital status - divorced. Interesting.

The next line under his marital status answered another question that had been in her mind. His emergency contact was a Brenda Crawford, with an address in Pensacola, Florida. Relationship - sister. She was surprised at the relief she felt. She'd thought that maybe Brenda - who'd said his big mouth would get him into trouble - might have been a girlfriend. But that shouldn't matter. There were only going to be roommates. Maybe.

She opened the last attachment, the not-requested letter of recommendation. After reading it, she called Randy back.

"Yeah, it's the Eric Hanson I know."

"Great," Randy said. "He said he wants to move in on Saturday."

Saturday? Today was Wednesday.

"But doesn't he want to come to look at the place beforehand?" she asked Randy. Her prospective roommate hadn't even seen the inside of the house. Wouldn't he need to consider the facts that it was a small house, with only one bathroom, that there wasn't even a dishwasher in the kitchen?

Not to mention – this Saturday she had other plans.

"No, I can't do that," she told Randy. "I'm going to the mainland this weekend. I won't be home until Sunday."

This weekend was important to her. When she'd been attending technical school in Los Angeles, there had been only one other girl in her class, and she and Michelle had become friends. Ashley was getting married this Saturday, and Michelle wasn't going to miss it, despite the fact that she really shouldn't spend the money on a boat ticket and a hotel. However, she had booked a room at a cheap motel rather than the fancy hotel where the wedding was being held, and had been able to borrow a suitable dress from a friend. The friend loaning her the dress was a little taller than Michelle was, but Michelle was a little bigger in the bust, so it worked out to a decent fit. It wasn't pink, but her friend had assured that blue was a great color on her and that she'd knock them dead and come home with half a dozen guy's phone numbers in her purse. Not that she was looking for that, but it buoyed her ego to think it would be possible.

"No problem," Randy was saying. "I'll just tell him to wait until Monday. If he really needs to be in town by Saturday, he can get a hotel room."

Michelle thought quickly. It was literally the first day of spring. The weather on Catalina Island was superb this time of year - warm, balmy, not too hot. It was the most popular time of the year for tourism, especially on the weekends. Two nights in an Avalon hotel would cost the earth, assuming there was anything available. But she was not going to pass on Ashley's wedding, not even for a potential roommate with an impeccable background check, an impressive letter of recommendation, and who'd saved her life twice in one day.

"I tell you what," she told Randy. "I'll drop off a key at your office on Friday before I leave, if that's OK with you. He can move in on Saturday if he needs to."

"Not a problem," Randy replied. "With a letter of recommendation like that, I'd rent him a room in my house if you didn't want him."

"Sorry, he's all mine," she said a little too quickly.

"Oh, like that, is it?" She could hear the amusement in Randy's voice.

"No, I didn't mean it like that! I meant, I need a roommate to share expenses and I'm glad you were able to find one so quickly. Thanks for your help."

She hung up, wondering if she'd gone insane. Eric Hanson? The annoying sailor who'd followed her around town, pulling her from in front of moving motor vehicles, smiling constantly despite her rudeness, wanted to be her roommate? He'd seemed like a nice guy, with nice feelings. His sympathy had sounded sincere when her father had died. But really, after an hour's acquaintance and a few emails, how well did she know him? Well enough to have him move into her house with her?

Could she trust him? Trust him enough to live under the same roof?

No, of course not. She didn't trust him. She didn't trust anybody, especially not the male of the species. They were, as a rule, generally untrustworthy. None she had ever met had proved themselves trustworthy as far as she was concerned. Trusting a man was one step short of stupid.

Why didn't she trust him? Solely because he was a man? On the surface, it seemed wrong to mistrust a person solely due to their gender. She would be, in fact she had many times been tremendously insulted when she'd been judged solely on her female gender. Wasn't it just as wrong to judge him solely on his maleness?

But her experiences with men in general had skewed her towards distrust, from her dad to her former dates and boyfriends, to casual acquaintances, to strangers who tried to pick her up with lines they thought to be witty and charming, or with offers of drinks she had no intention of accepting.

Was it fair to paint Eric Hanson with the same brush? The closest he'd come to using a pickup line on her had been that silly justification of the fact that he was in the military to let him walk her home. Although he'd smiled at her a lot more than any normal guy might do, he hadn't really acted like a guy trying to make time with a chick. Saving a girl's life, taking her pulse and checking to make sure her skin tone was healthy seemed more like the actions of the "Doc" his friends had called him, rather than the moves of a masher.

Doc. What a weird nickname for someone who wasn't actually a doctor. Was that a Navy thing? She might have to Google that.

But she had trusted him. She'd allowed him to accompany her to her house, to know where she lived. She'd handed him her phone when he'd given her his email address. If that wasn't trusting a guy, what was?

No matter who she might have ended up with as a roommate, she would have to trust the person, male or female. Maybe she just might be able to trust a guy who didn't drink, who'd saved her life, who'd shown concern for her health, who'd tried to diagnose and treat her anxiety, and who, in reality, had been a complete and utter gentleman. She'd never met a complete and utter gentleman before, but she was pretty sure Chief Petty Officer Eric Hanson was one.

She'd given Randy the OK, but maybe she'd been a little too impulsive in agreeing to it. However, that letter of recommendation had convinced her.

If you couldn't trust a letter of recommendation from the captain of the USS Nimitz, who could you trust?

5

∽

Eric had to jiggle the key a little to get the door open, and walked into his new house. A real house. He hadn't lived in a real house since he'd left his parents' home to go to boot camp, a month after graduating from high school. He waved goodbye, and thanks, to the neighbor who'd stopped along Crescent Avenue and offered him a ride, after seeing him walking up from the boat dock with his bags. Apparently, the residents here did that a lot, just stopped their golf carts and picked up pedestrians, both residents and visitors.

There was a somewhat elderly golf cart parked in front of this house, and he knew it had to belong to his new roommate. There were bright pink beads threaded all around the frame around the front window, along the top of the cart's sides, and down the back edge. She must have acquired it after the day he'd walked her home last year, since he hadn't seen a cart there at the time. There was a hammer laying on the passenger's seat, a sight that amused him a little. He wondered if Michelle used it for her work, or as a deterrent.

It was a small, older house, like most of the houses in the neighborhood. They stood jammed close by their neighbors, with no yards to speak of and only narrow pedestrian alleys between one house and the next. Michelle's house – their house – had just a cement step between the street and the front door. Next to the door sat a potted orange tree that seemed to look at him and beg for water.

He glanced around at the quiet, sunny street for a moment before going inside. At the house next door, a chubby orange cat lay catching rays on the front step. The only indication of life shown by the indolent feline was a smooth, lazy swish of a furry tail.

Though simple and just a little shabby, the house was clean and very well cared for. The front door opened directly into the living room, with the basics – couch, chairs, a TV on a stand. A small table next to the door where he dropped the key and his sunglasses.

The couch had an upholstered chair on either side of it, and none of the three pieces matched. The couch was dark brown and solid-looking, while both chairs were blue and yellow, but they didn't match each other. One of the chairs had a checkered design in a deep shade of navy blue and bumblebee yellow, while the other was patterned in flowers of paler hues.

A rickety end table sat between the couch and the flowered chair, and on it sat an old lamp with a significant crack in its base, but with a very new-looking lampshade, as if that part had been recently replaced. The room's eclectic, indifferent décor would have been charming, except that the only decoration on the wall was a cheap, generic print of the Eiffel Tower, and Eric found that to be quite sad. He himself had mostly lived in extremely cramped quarters, but he'd always found room for a family photo or two.

He set his duffle bag down next to the sofa along with the bulging shopping bag he'd brought with him. The roommate advertisement had indicated the place came furnished, but he'd need to supply his own bedding. He slung the strap of his laptop bag down from his shoulder, laying it on the coffee table. The blinds were closed and the room dim, but when he pulled the string on the side to open them up, the room flooded with light and looked much larger. One thing that existed in abundance here on this island was sunshine; it seemed sad and unnecessary to block it out.

There was a kitchen with a small dining table and chairs. Being an older house, the eat-in kitchen was a separate room, not open to the living room. A closet in the kitchen housed a washer and dryer, and a back door led out to a paved patio surrounded by a stucco wall, apparently all the back yard there was. Behind that patio, the house, along with all the other houses on the block, backed up against a steep hill, which while a bit terrifying considering they were in earthquake country, did also provide significant privacy at the rear of the house.

A short hallway at the back of the living room led to two closed doors, presumably the bedrooms. Across the hall was the only bathroom. He went in to use the head, and after washing his hands, couldn't help but open the medicine cabinet door above the sink.

He wasn't snooping, he told himself. He lived here now. He'd paid a deposit and first month's rent. And look, two of the four shelves were cleared off. She had obviously made room for his things.

He couldn't help but look over the items on the other two shelves. Three hairbrushes. He recalled that heavy, shiny mane of dark brown hair Michelle had pulled out of the neck of her hoody that day at the bar, the way it had flowed like a river of chocolate down her back. Every man in the bar, and a couple of women too, had taken notice. She did have gorgeous hair, but did it really require three different hairbrushes to maintain? Having always had military short hair himself, a comb was all he needed.

There were assorted lotions and cosmetics, and he picked up a wand of mascara, marveling at the courage that was Woman, to maneuver an implement like that so close to one's eyeballs. He glanced briefly in the mirror at his own eyelashes. They were long, and light brown like his hair, and the world was just going to have to continue to accept them unadorned.

There was a flat foil packet of tablets. He may have been a bachelor, but he was a medical professional. He knew oral contraceptives when he saw them. A pink razor. That was heartening to see. He'd heard horror stories of women who stole a guy's razor to shave their legs. Nice to know his would be safe. Next to it was a wicked pair of tweezers that looked like something out of a surgical kit. Did she actually use those things on her eyebrows? At the end of the shelf was a pink box, facing backward. He picked it up and turned it around to look at the front.

Oops. He set the box of tampons gently back onto the shelf, as if they were explosive. Served him right for snooping. He'd only been curious to see if it was purple hair dye. It would be a shame to cover that beautiful chocolate-colored hair with anything artificial. What would that hair feel like, he wondered, between his fingers, in his hands, spread out ...?

Whoa, rein that thought in, Hanson! She's your roommate, not your girlfriend, not some pickup. She's trusting you in her home, trusting you to be a gentleman. She deserves your respect. Remember that.

He went back to the living room and unzipped his duffle bag. In the short time he'd been on the island, he'd realized that the uniform of the day seemed to be tee shirt, shorts, and flip flops. He pulled some out of his bag, looking around to make sure his roommate was really not home, then skimmed out of his jeans and boots and changed his clothes.

There was a pile of thick library books on the coffee table. He sat down and leafed through a couple, even tried to read a few pages. Her tastes seemed to run towards dystopian futures, time travel, and sex with vampires. *Eeww*. His favorite book was Gray's Anatomy.

In addition to the library books there was a thick, almost worn-out paperback with a drawing on the cover of a boy with dark hair, round glasses and a weird scar on his forehead. Inside the cover was stamped the logo of a second-hand bookstore in Long Beach. Apparently, his new roommate was a bookworm.

Next to the stack of books there was another book, flat and square, with a ring binding. When he opened it, he realized it was a sketchbook, with half a dozen of its pages covered with sketches drawn in pencil. They were good, downright artistic. He especially liked one that depicted a landscape of, apparently, the town of Avalon from above. The curve of the bay that gave Crescent Avenue its name and the Green Pleasure Pier were recognizable, along with the boats in the harbor – drawn not starkly but in a soft, subtle manner that was artistic but yet left no doubt that they were the boats filling Avalon Harbor. Even the dark smudge of the mainland was hinted at. The other sketches were attractively charming as well – flowers and birds and smaller scenes of the area, a lizard sunning itself on a rock with a drowsy, amphibian smile on its lips, or at least where its lips would be, if lizards actually had lips.

Each drawing had the initials MRD printed in the lower right-hand corner. The name written inside the front cover of the sketchbook confirmed whose initials they were, who this artist was. Michelle Ramona Diaz, his new roommate.

Today he'd be picking up his new Avalon Fire Department Paramedic uniforms. Still wearing a uniform, just a different one now. He still had his Navy uniforms. He'd be using the working ones for the Reserve duty he'd signed up for. And thanks to his honorable discharge, he was still authorized to wear his dress uniform for special occasions.

His best friend had recently informed him that he and his wife were expecting kid number three, and a future christening qualified as a special occasion. Eric had been a bit surprised to hear they were having a third baby; being certain they'd planned on stopping with the two they had. But he of all people knew that babies tended to show up whenever they felt like it, regardless of the plans their parents made. His own birth was proof of that. From what he'd been told, his conception had come as a really big surprise to his parents. His sister Brenda, who'd been fifteen when he was born, had been horrified to discover that her mother and her stepfather had been doing, well, what people did to make babies, and had declared the entire situation and its result - him - to be gross and disgusting. Fortunately, he'd made it up to her later with charming little brotherness.

He'd had other job opportunities to consider, in addition to the one in Avalon. The San Diego Fire Department had recruited him. It had been tempting. San Diego had been his last duty station, and he had a lot of friends there. Even his best buddy Gabriel, with whom Eric had grown up in Florida, lived in San Diego now.

Cedars-Sinai Hospital in Los Angeles had suggested that if he cared to sit for the qualifications - and he knew he could pass them easily - they'd love to have him as a surgical nurse. That had sounded really interesting.

But in the end, he'd chosen the job in Avalon. Although technically that meant he was employed by the Los Angeles County Fire Department, he was contracted to the City of Avalon Fire Department. Perhaps a job on the mainland might have paid more, but that really wasn't his motivation. He'd been fascinated by the unique prospect of living on, literally, a tropical island, almost remote, almost a backwater, yet only 50 miles from Los Angeles and 80 from San Diego.

Avalon was a small town, both in size and population, yet with an influx of thousands of tourists a week. It was an easy day trip to and from the mainland, with boats running between Avalon and ports at Long Beach, San Pedro and Dana Point. Along Crescent Avenue and the Green Pleasure Pier, the main tourist areas, Avalon was bustling, crowded, noisy. But walk a few blocks inland, uphill into the residential area, and the town was peaceful and quiet, a direct contrast to the beachside bustle. He'd noticed that the day he'd met Michelle and walked with her here.

Because 90 percent of Catalina Island was owned by the Catalina Island Conservancy, there was no room for expansion in Avalon. So, the town stayed small and you could walk almost everywhere. He'd left his car stored at his buddy Gabriel's place in San Diego. The waiting list for a permit to bring a car over to the island was so long that expectant parents submitted the names of their unborn children.

Eric would be one of only four paramedics in Avalon, and the variety of cases and patients would be stimulating and interesting.

Larger cities had a separate water rescue squad. Here in Avalon, its four paramedics also fulfilled that function, and were required to be certified rescue divers, which Eric was. They might be called upon for assistance with anything from a panicked diver who got separated from his buddy, to a fatigued diver with decompression sickness.

This diversity and uniqueness had encouraged him to choose the opportunity in Avalon over the other options. The idea of escaping to Catalina held a certain romantic appeal.

He told all of this to Brenda on the phone. While he was close to all four of his siblings, he talked to Brenda the most. She said, uh-huh, yes, that sounds great, and when he finished, she asked, "Did you ever consider coming home to Florida?"

When he hesitated, she pounced.

"This is about a girl, isn't it?"

He would neither confirm nor deny. He wasn't quite ready to admit to his sister that when Avalon had called, he'd had an immediate memory of a certain angry young brunette with eyes like the ocean, who'd plowed into him on the sidewalk when his back was turned. The fact that she of all people had advertised for a roommate, just when he was looking for accommodations, seemed like a sign of some sort.

"Aw, G.D.," Brenda said. That was her nickname for him. The initials stood for Gross and Disgusting. "Just don't go breaking anyone's heart."

"You know me, Bren," he said. "When have I ever broken anyone's heart?"

"I heard half the girls in your high school cried when you went away to the Navy."

"Only half?" he scoffed. "That was on them. I never made anyone any promises."

"What about that girl you were seeing before you went to Iraq? The second time."

"Puh-leeze. That wasn't even close to serious. Absolutely no heartbreak there."

"What about when you got married?"

If he didn't love his sister so much, he would have been annoyed at her for bringing up that particularly unpleasant bit of ancient history.

"You know that was just a great big mistake. Nobody's heart got broken."

"If you'd been a little better at keeping it in your pants, little brother, you wouldn't have had to make that great big mistake." Brenda never hesitated to give it to him straight.

"Such lovely language to hear from a grandmother. And you know it was over seven years ago. I'd think you could cut me a little slack by now."

"But that wouldn't be any fun at all," she said with a chuckle in her voice. "And speaking of being a grandmother, I have to go. We're babysitting the munchkin tonight."

"Give him a kiss for me. And text me a current photo. The one I have is three weeks old."

She ended the call as she always did. "Stay safe, G.D. Love ya."

"Love you too."

He disconnected and went to go find the fire department. He had papers to sign, orientation to attend, and those uniforms to pick up.

6

∽

Michelle could hear the music emanating from her house from almost a block away. She didn't recognize the song - it was country, and her musical tastes ran more towards Lady Gaga. The sheer volume of it made her feet vibrate as she opened the door and set down her weekend bag.

There was a big duffel bag and a bulging shopping bag from Bed Bath and Beyond set next to the couch, a laptop bag on the coffee table, and a pair of worn leather lace-up boots set neatly next to it, the heels lined up precisely. Unlike her flip-flops, which had a couple of pairs scattered around the room. At the moment, she was wearing gym shoes in deference to being on the mainland, but when she took them off, she decided to set them neatly next to the door with the heels lined up. She didn't want her new roommate to think she was a slob. Maybe later she'd pick up the flip-flops. The couch blanket, which she was sure had been scrunched up and half falling on the floor when she left, was now folded neatly in a precise square and laid over the arm. Some dark-colored clothing in a dry cleaner's bag lay over the back of the chair next to the couch.

The blare was coming from the kitchen. She stopped in the kitchen doorway, and there was her new roommate with his back to her at the sink. He was singing along, actually twitching his hips with the music. Nice butt. Not much of a singer, in fact, he was horribly off-key, but he made up for it with enthusiasm.

Michelle might have admired his butt a little longer, but reminded herself that roommates didn't ogle roommates, and besides, the volume of the music was about to make her ears bleed.

"Ahem!" she grunted loudly.

No reaction. His hips continued to twitch along to the thunderous music.

There was no getting around it. She was going to have to touch him.

Tentatively, she stepped closer, reached out and tapped his shoulder, stepping back as he whirled around. He was armed – with a carrot peeler and a stance like something out of the Karate Kid, and screamed, "What the fuck!"

She jumped back, startled, but still wasn't able to contain a giggle, and he relaxed his threatening stance as he realized it was just her.

He was dressed pretty much the same as he had been the day they'd met, in a crisp plain white tee shirt, tight enough to make it obvious he worked out, cargo shorts and a happy looking smile on that wide mouth that unexpectedly made her wonder if he was a good kisser. He said something she couldn't hear over the din.

"What?" she asked, loudly, and he reached over and hit pause on the phone dock next to the sink. After the ear-splitting volume was abruptly ended, the ensuing silence was deafening.

"Hi there, Michelle," he repeated. And, "Welcome home, roomie."

He looked at the carrot peeler in his hand, still being held like a weapon, and set it down on the counter.

"Don't worry," he assured her. "I don't bite. At least, not hard." A slow smile spread over his face and lit his eyes.

"I'm sorry if I startled you," she said. "I hope you aren't auditioning for The Voice or something."

"I thought about it once or twice, but there always seemed to be a scheduling conflict."

"You're kidding, I hope. What scheduling conflict saved them from having to hear that?" His grin was infectious, and she couldn't tell if he was serious or not. If he was insulted by her disdain of his singing ability, he didn't show it.

"Iraq. WestPac. Afghanistan. Operation Inherent Resolve." He mentioned war zones and military maneuvers as lightly as if they were Long Beach or the Rose Bowl Flea Market. "I got a bit carried away with the volume there, I'm sorry. They never let me sing on board ship."

She shook her head. "I can't imagine why not."

"Really! Something about cats being run over by lawnmowers." His grin indicated that he wasn't particularly hurt by his shipmates' complaints either.

"How have you been?" he asked. "It's been a long time – almost a year now. Bet you didn't think then that we'd end up as roommates, huh?"

"Yeah, what are the odds of that?" Impossibly astronomical and absolutely bizarre was what she'd believed the odds to be. Of all the roommates she could have imagined standing in front of her, never had she anticipated a tall, sexy retired sailor with sparkly eyes, a killer smile, and a singing voice that could curdle milk. She sincerely thought she would never see him again after he'd walked away from her front door last year.

"Well, when I saw your ad for a roommate, I thought, it would be nice to live with someone I already knew, rather than a total stranger."

"How could you know it was me? My name and address weren't in the ad." She'd purposely set it up with Randy that way in order to screen background checks before revealing herself. Even in a small, out-of-the-way town like Avalon, it was prudent for a single woman living alone to take all the precautions she could. She'd also wanted to make sure she only considered permanent roommates, not someone just looking for a vacation rental.

He smiled knowingly. "Oh, I could tell it was you as soon as I read the line 'non-drinker preferred.' I thought, yep, that's Michelle Diaz and her cute little yellow house."

"Well, after I read that letter of recommendation you sent, I figured I could take a chance on you," she admitted.

He smiled. "Yeah, I asked my last C.O. to write it for me. But I haven't read it."

"He spoke very highly of you," she assured him. Actually, he'd written in glowing terms about Eric's honor, integrity, and competence.

"I hope you don't mind, but I raided your fridge for vegetables to make a salad. I'll replace them, of course. But I did have to throw away your cucumber. It was, how should I put this? Elderly."

"That's OK," she said. To be perfectly honest, she'd completely forgotten she had a cucumber in the fridge.

"Your timing is perfect," her new roommate said. "this is just about ready." He set the bowl of salad on the table and asked, "Where do you keep your bowls? There's plenty here for both of us. Have you had lunch?"

She had grabbed a hot dog at the snack stand at the boat terminal in San Pedro before boarding the Catalina Express back to Avalon, but it hadn't been nearly as appealing as the fresh salad her new roommate had made. Maybe this guy was a keeper.

She pointed at the cabinet to the right of the sink and he got out two salad bowls while she got forks out of the drawer, and within a minute they were sitting at the kitchen table eating his salad together.

"How's the salad?" he asked. "Is it OK that it has tomatoes in it? My sister hates tomatoes."

"It's good," she assured him, as she swallowed a bite of tomato. In fact, it was more than good. Although it consisted only of assorted chopped-up vegetables, it was the first time in years that someone else had prepared food for her that she hadn't paid for in a restaurant.

It was a good salad, but despite its simplicity, it was a special meal.

It was impossible not to observe her new roommate as he sat across the table from her. His eyes were lively and smiley and crinkled a little at the corners when he smiled, which seemed to be most of the time. A short, military-style haircut kept the sandy brown hair above his ears and collar. It was several shades too dark to be blonde, but much lighter than her own brunette color. His nose was straight and slender, his skin fair but neither freckly nor ruddy like many fair-colored complexions.

He had long fingers and she remembered that were warm and strong, even though she'd only touched them in brief handshakes and felt them on her wrist when he'd taken her pulse the day they'd met. The anchor and rope tattoo showed dark against his pale forearm as he ate.

But the eyes were the most interesting thing about him. A true hazel color, without green or blue highlights, a smooth warm honey shade that lit up when he smiled.

Unlike eating with her father had been, her new roommate smiled at her, drank water instead of beer, asked how her weekend had been, thanked her quite politely for letting him move in while she was away, and cleared away the dishes and rinsed them off when they were done. He'd made a pretty big bowl of salad and put what they didn't finish in the refrigerator, while she stood and picked up the forks, putting them in the sink and turning back to thank him for the meal he'd made.

He stepped towards her and quite suddenly, put his arms around her in a hug.

Whoa, whoa, *whoa*, this was *so* not happening! She started to pull away from him, raised her hand with the intent to slap his face and order him out of her house, until he said, "I'm so, so sorry about your dad."

She hadn't cried a single tear since her father had died. Not even when the harbor patrol had knocked on her door on New Year's Eve to tell her he'd been found in the water with a blood alcohol level of .200 percent. Not even as she arranged the funeral and accepted the condolences of her friends, her coworkers, her cousins from the mainland. She'd stood dry-eyed in the boat as she scattered his ashes. But now, today, inside this friendly, sympathetic hug, all the tears she hadn't ever cried, over her dad, her mom, her whole cosmic existence, burst out of her in a helpless gush.

She didn't just cry. She became Niagara Falls, and the hand she'd raised to slap him with turned into a fist that she hit once on his shoulder in impotent frustration.

He just stood there and let her cry it out on him, and the soft tee shirt under her face was soaked in moments.

When she was finally reduced to gulps and sniffles, she stepped back, wiping her face with her hand, because of course every tissue, napkin or towel in the vicinity had grown legs and walked away. After a moment of her embarrassed sniffling, Eric muttered, "Oh, hell," and, reaching behind his neck, pulled off his shirt and offered her the dry side, saying, "Go ahead, blow your nose."

She was forced to do just that, and wiped her face and eyes on the soft cotton that smelled really good, like soap and warm male skin, then looked up at Eric.

Well, this was officially awkward. Here she stood, in her kitchen, with her new roommate, a man she barely knew, with him standing there half naked while she held his shirt in her hands, a shirt that was now filthy with her tears and snot and mascara. There was even a pink smudge on it from her lip gloss. Yep, definitely awkward. It was more embarrassing than when she'd let loose and vented to him about her dysfunctional family life, thirty minutes after meeting him.

She told herself to turn her back to him or look anywhere else but at the magnificent male specimen before her, but she just couldn't manage it.

However, if one was going to have a half-naked man standing in one's kitchen, it was at least pleasant that it happened to be one that was so easy on the eye. And it wasn't just the handsome face and friendly, sparkly smile.

Those muscles! They weren't bulgy, lumpy, Dwayne the Rock Johnson type muscles (not that there was anything whatsoever wrong with The Rock or his muscles), but Eric's were more streamlined, more natural. There was just a faint shading of light brown hair on his chest, and those cargo shorts he was wearing must have been just a little bit too big on him because they rode low on his hips, showing off his flat stomach and sexy V-cut of the muscles there. The entire package was wrapped up in a whole lot of fair, unblemished skin.

At least her curiosity was answered as to whether he had any other tattoos besides the one on his arm. He didn't, unless there was one on that cute butt, covered by his cargo shorts. Even his feet were cute, and when she looked at them, he wiggled his toes.

She was *so* busted.

"So, do I pass muster?" he asked. "Do I get the Wi-Fi password?"

You're such a dork, Michelle, she thought. Roommates don't drool over roommates. But then, a guy who looked like him was probably accustomed to being ogled and drooled over. He even smelled good. She'd noticed that even through her crying jag on his shoulder. Himself, not just his shirt. Not like cologne or aftershave. Like sunshine and masculinity. There ought to be a law against a man smelling that good naturally.

"I'm sorry," she said, holding up his dirty shirt. Yeah, make it about the shirt. "I got your shirt all gross. I'll wash it."

He reached out and took the tee shirt from her hands. "Not necessary, ma'am. I've been doing my own laundry since I was twelve." He looked at her a moment, his face tilted to one side, then said, "Come here a second, you missed a spot." Puzzled, she took a step towards him, and he took her chin in his hand, turned the fabric of his shirt to find a clean spot, then wiped it under her eyes. Another section of the shirt was now smudged with the last of her mascara. And the package had said it was waterproof! But certainly not Niagara Falls-proof.

Her face flamed hot with embarrassment. If this wasn't completely humiliating, to have this strange, sexy man washing her face as if she was a grimy three-year-old.

And she'd cried on him. She'd been here with him for all of twenty minutes before she'd bawled on his shoulder like a fool. The evidence of it was right here on his formerly clean shirt.

Eric reached over towards the closet where the washer was, dropped the shirt on top, and said, "If you'll point me towards my rack, I could put on a clean one."

"Huh?" she asked, confused enough to escape her tears. Rack of what?

Eric sighed. The terminology he'd been accustomed to using all his adult life was going to be impossible to dissect out of his vocabulary. He spoke slowly, as if to someone with a limited grasp of English.

"Where – do – I – sleep?"

Oh, god, she was such an idiot! It was bad enough that she'd cried on him like a baby and dirtied his clean shirt, but she'd also left for the weekend and left both bedroom doors closed, with no indication of which one was for his use, and he'd apparently been too polite to risk invading her privacy. Duh, duh, double duh! She could have left a note, or sent him an email, or even called him. His phone number was on the rental application. The whole point of leaving him a key was so that he wouldn't have to pay for a hotel room.

"I'm sorry," she said again. "I'm so stupid. I totally forgot to – wait, where did you sleep last night?"

"Well, I wasn't sure of the domestic arrangements, so I slept on your couch." That explained the neatly folded blanket.

"I am such a dummy. I should have let you know which room was for you."

He smiled broadly. "Not a problem, ma'am. Your sofa is real comfy."

"Come on, this way." With an effort, she tore her eyes off his body and all that fair skin and walked out of the kitchen and into the hall. Behind her she heard him step into the living room and grab his bags as she opened the door to what used to be her father's room, but wasn't anymore.

She had donated or disposed of everything but the bed frame and the dresser, only keeping the few photos and things that had been her mother's. She'd even replaced the mattress, despite the hideous expense of having a new one shipped out from the mainland. One of the hotels her father had worked at had been doing some redecorating and she'd been able to buy a couple of small chairs from them, reupholstered them both with a neutral blue fabric, and placed one in each bedroom. She'd scrubbed and cleaned every inch of the space, painted the walls a neutral beige, hung new curtains, rearranged the furniture to make it a totally different space. Not knowing what kind of decor her incoming roommate would prefer, she'd just framed a poster of an aerial view of the island and hung it on the wall.

She stepped aside so Eric could go in. "It's kind of small," she said apologetically.

He set his duffle bag on the bed and glanced around. "All this, just for me?" His smile twinkled at her.

"Well, I'm certainly not going to share it with you," she retorted a little too quickly.

"Oh, darn," he replied with teasing in his voice. "Compared to a three by six rack in a berthing compartment, it's actually rather spacious. It's almost like the goat locker. That is, the Chief's Mess."

"Do you speak English as a second language?" Goat locker? Whatever did goats have to do with the Navy?

He chuckled. "With difficulty, apparently."

She waved a hand towards the bathroom. "There's only the one," she said hesitantly.

"So I noticed, ma'am."

"We'll have to share." His eyebrows twitched and she blushed. "I meant, take turns."

"Not a problem, ma'am. I can SSS in ten minutes."

She was beginning to wonder if the local public library had a Navy to English dictionary in their inventory. At her irritated look, Eric leaned a bit closer and lowered his voice, explaining, "Shit, shower and shave, pardon my language."

She rolled her eyes. When he unzipped his duffel bag, she decided it was time to give the man his privacy and went back to the living room. He came back a minute later, smoothing down a fresh tee shirt. This one was a faded brown color and had a depiction on the chest of a man wearing a cowboy hat and carrying a guitar.

"Is that your alter ego?" she asked.

He peered down his front at the picture. "It's Garth Brooks."

She looked at him blankly. "Is he a musician?" she asked, looking at the guitar the guy on the shirt was holding.

"Don't tell me you've never heard of him?"

"Nope."

Eric rolled his eyes at her. "Girl, your education is sadly lacking."

"Yeah, well, do you know Lady Gaga?" she challenged.

"I've heard of her."

"Name one of her songs."

"Um..."

"Yeah, thought so."

Eric just grinned at her.

"Eric, I should apologize for getting all freaked out on you back there." She nodded towards the kitchen and the embarrassing memory of her little crying jag.

Eric. It was the first time she had called him by his name, to his face. It was a nice name, strong, fresh, efficient.

"No need to apologize," he said. "Your dad died. You're entitled to freak out a little."

"But it's been almost three months, and that's the first time I, you know, freaked out. You must think I'm a horrible person."

Her voice trembled, wobbled just a little. Great, now he was going to think she was some kind of pathetic baby.

So what. She didn't care what he thought, right?

"If I thought you were a horrible person, I wouldn't have answered your roommate ad," he said. "Look, Michelle, grief doesn't run on a timetable. It's not a train. But it is a journey. It doesn't end, but it does change. Everyone grieves at their own pace and it doesn't matter what the relationship was. Losing a parent, even a bad parent, is losing a part of yourself, losing someone who made you exist. It's not abnormal for it to be delayed. Some people cry months later; some people do it when they lock themselves in the head five minutes after getting the news. There's nothing wrong with being human and vulnerable.

"Did you think I didn't cry when my parents died just because I have the Y chromosome? Or because I'm six feet tall or because I served in the military?"

"Six foot one," she corrected him. "I've seen your driver's license, you know. There was a copy attached to the rental application."

He smiled at her, and she found herself smiling back. His words of assurance about her delayed reactions to her father's death had been surprisingly comforting.

You must have been so lonely here after your dad died," he said.

"Not as lonely as you might think. Even when he was here, he wasn't quite – here. He always seemed to have something else – certainly not me – on his mind. Usually, I think, calculating how much credit he had on his bar tab that day. My cousins invited me to come stay with them in Temecula for a while, so I wouldn't have to stay in the house alone right after the funeral. But I told them I had to work and besides, it wouldn't really be that different than when Dad was here, just fewer beer bottles in the trash." She laughed bitterly. "I think my cousin Bruce was relieved that I declined the invitation. He was afraid of me."

Eric looked incredulous. "How could anyone be afraid of you?"

"I beat him up once, when we were kids. I don't think he ever got over it."

"I can so not picture you beating someone up."

"Stick around a while then." Her words were a challenge.

"I think I will," he replied without hesitation.

"Is that all you own?" she asked. "Just that one duffel bag?"

"No, I'm having the rest of my things shipped out here. They should come in a couple of days. In fact, I bought a weight bench, because I've been told there's no public gym in town. Would you mind if I set it up on the patio back there?" He nodded towards the back door.

"Sure, that would be fine." There was plenty of room on the patio for a weight bench. All it held at the moment was a euphemistically named love seat, the trash can and recycling bin. If Eric put his weight bench out there, maybe she could sneak a peek from the kitchen at him working out, maybe amble out to casually offer him a bottle of water or a towel when he sat up all sweaty at the end of his workout.

She had to squelch down that roommate-inappropriate image when he spoke again.

"Also, in the interests of full disclosure, just in case you have a problem with it. I do have a handgun coming with my stuff also. It's kept in a really strong locked case, and the ammo is in a separate really strong locked case. I have all the permits, and it will be registered with the police department. But if you don't want it in your house, just say the word and I'll make other arrangements."

"I don't mind if you have a gun," she replied. "Under one condition."

"What's that?"

"Let me shoot it."

He looked down his nose at her. "Um, I don't think so."

"What," she scoffed. "You think I can't shoot a gun because I'm a girl?"

"I have no issue with you shooting a gun because you're a *woman*. But this isn't the kind of gun for a beginner. I don't think there's a shooting range on the island, but if you want to go to the mainland some time, I can set you up with something smaller and more suitable for a beginner, like a 380. Or maybe – let me see your arm."

"Huh? My arm?"

"Yeah, make a muscle. Like this." He held up his arm and tensed it so that the muscles tightened.

Lord, those muscles. She was beginning to eagerly anticipate the arrival of that weight bench.

She tried to imitate him but she was sure her effort looked pretty pitiful. But he was too polite to say so, as he squeezed her upper arm and looked thoughtful.

"Maybe you can handle a nine-millimeter," he said, as if that were some kind of compliment.

"Hold that thought, stay right here." She turned and strode over towards her bedroom.

He totally ignored the "stay right here" and followed her shamelessly as she went into her room, and froze in the hallway outside her door before scuttling back to the living room like a cockroach. But he was trained to make expeditious observations, and the one quick glance he was able to get showed a lot.

Her bedroom could only be described as Pink. The walls were painted a pale pink. The bedspread and matching curtains were covered with a pattern of flowers, mostly pink, with a few yellow and blue, and delicate green vines. There was a pink area rug on the floor, and hanging on the wall was a print depicting more flowers. It looked vaguely familiar, probably a copy of something famous. On the dresser sat a big white fluffy teddy bear with a pink bow around its neck. It looked like the bedroom of a twelve-year-old princess.

Apparently she hadn't noticed his snooping, and handed him a photograph. Well, not a real photograph; it was printed on regular copy paper rather than on photographic paper, but the image was good quality. It showed Michelle, wearing safety glasses and a serious expression, holding up a paper shooting target depicting a man-shaped sketch.

There were three kill shots. One to the head, one to the heart, one to the groin. Ouch. He looked at the picture, then at her.

"There has to be a story behind this."

She shrugged. "Bad breakup. I thought he was a nice guy, thought he was different. But it turned out, all he wanted to do was get drunk and get down, just like every other guy. God, I am so sick and tired of hearing, just one, baby, it'll loosen you up. Maybe I don't want to loosen up. Maybe it works for me to be tight and bitchy. So he calls me a frigid bitch, and I tell him that's all due to his assholeness, and that was the end of that. The next day was my birthday, and I was in Los Angeles going to tech school, so my friend there offered to take me somewhere fun that wasn't a bar. We ended up at a shooting range, and I imagined this was that guy." She shook the photo a little.

"Well, you sure showed him," Eric said. "He didn't deserve you." She looked at him sharply, but he grinned innocently. "Assholeness? Did you invent that word? It's a great one. I may have to borrow it someday."

"I guess I did invent it. I was inspired."

"And here I thought I was an expert marksman," he said.

"An expert?"

"I was at my last quals. What kind of gun did you use on this guy, metaphorically speaking?"

"I don't know. I just asked for the biggest handgun they had. The guy at the shooting range called it a Dirty Harry gun."

His eyes popped with surprise. "Oh my lord, are you saying the first time you shot a gun, it was a 44 Magnum?"

"Guess so." She shrugged.

"Did it not knock you on your ass? Pardon my language."

"It sure had a kick. My shoulders were sore for a week. And I missed my first shot. But it was a great stress release."

He looked at the photo again. "You call those a miss?" His voice was incredulous.

Michelle pointed at the head shot. "That wasn't where I was aiming." Eric's mouth rounded in astonishment, and he swallowed deeply.

"Ok, you can shoot my handgun someday. Just, please, not at me."

"I didn't know Navy guys carried guns," Michelle said. "I thought you just shot torpedoes and stuff."

He slapped the side of his head as if she'd told him something he'd never thought of before. "You mean we're supposed to *shoot* the torpedoes? Who knew? We just used them as benches in the mess hall. Just kidding!" he added, but with a wink that said, or maybe not.

"But seriously, I spent a lot of time boots on the ground in field hospitals, and there's a lot of bad guys who have no respect for the red cross painted on the roof, or on a truck, or an armband."

She remembered him saying that first day, *I've had my boots on the ground. I've spent my fair share of time in full battle rattle.*

"Does that mean you've been shot?" She'd gotten a pretty good look at, well, a lot of him but hadn't seen anything that looked like a bullet hole.

"No, never shot, fortunately. Shot *at* more than once. And isn't this a depressing conversation to be having on a beautiful Sunday afternoon on a tropical island. If you're not busy, would you take me for a tour around town in your golf cart? So far, I've only seen the boat dock, the Marlin Club, the fire station, and this house. Oh, and the Green Pleasure Pier, where I convinced a certain young lady not to jump into the water."

"You did not!"

"Sure did. You stayed dry, didn't you?"

"I wasn't going to jump."

"Because I talked you out of it."

"Do you want a tour or not?" She glared at him.

"Yes, please, ma'am." He sounded like he was giving in to her side of the discussion, but his twinkly grin made her uncertain.

"Let me just grab some flip-flops." There was one in front of the sofa and she crouched down on the floor to look underneath for its mate. There was a second one there, but not a mate to the first one. One was pink, the other black.

"I'm guessing you're not a very good dancer," Eric said from above her.

Oh, yikes. She'd gotten down on the floor to retrieve the shoes and inadvertently stuck her butt up in the air right in front of him. How stupid. How inappropriate. She scrambled quickly to her feet with the mismatched flip-flops in hand.

"Why do you say that?" she asked. "What has it got to do with my shoes?"

He gestured at them. "You have two left feet."

"Oh, goodness, that is corny. I must have another pair just like these around here somewhere."

They looked around until Eric spied the mate to the pink flip flop in the corner by the television, and she slipped them on her feet, leaving the odd black shoe by the door. She was not going to go crawling around on the floor searching for the other missing one in Eric's presence!

Outside, she hopped into the driver's seat of the golf cart. Before Eric sat in the passenger's seat, he picked up the hammer that was lying there and looked at her questioningly.

"Pick up the back seat," she told him. "You can put it in there."

He lifted the back seat and placed the hammer into the empty space under it. As he sat in the passenger seat, he said, "Oh, by the way, I watered your little tree." He nodded at the potted tree next to the front door.

You didn't have to do that," she said. "But thank you."

"She was really thirsty," Eric said.

"She?" Michelle repeated with amusement. "How do you know she's a girl?"

"Because she's so pretty. She's downright appealing."

She could only look at him in confusion.

Eric rolled his eyes. "It's an orange tree! It's appealing. As in orange peel? Get it?"

"So that was a joke?" she asked.

"Well, I thought it was," Eric replied.

Michelle started up the golf cart, but just before they pulled away from the curb, she stopped and looked at him. "Do you have life insurance?" she asked.

"Um, yeah."

"Who's your beneficiary?"

He looked wary. "My sister Brenda."

"The same one as your emergency contact?"

"Yeah. Why do you ask?" He was starting to look a little scared.

"So I know who to call, just in case."

"Wait, does this have to do with my handgun?"

"No, it has to do with you riding in my golf cart."

The look of panic that crossed his face as he grabbed onto the side was priceless, and she laughed out loud. "Just kidding! I haven't killed anyone yet."

He looked at her for a long moment before saying, "That's the first time I've heard you laugh. It looks good on you. You should do it more often."

Michelle had a feeling that with his big goof around the place, she probably was going to find herself laughing more often. It felt good.

The golf cart seemed somehow smaller than before, with the addition of Eric's muscles and cute butt. She'd never had a passenger riding with her before.

Eric watched the scenery go by with bright interest. Another golf cart passed them going in the opposite direction. Two little kids sat in the back seat, a boy and a girl. Eric gave them a little finger wave as they passed, exactly the way she'd seen the Disney princesses do the one time she'd visited Disneyland.

From Lower Terrace Road, they turned left onto Crescent Avenue, and she could just tell from the expression on Eric's face that he was keeping an eye out for idiots wearing hoodies. When she made the turn up Clarissa Avenue, and the Green Pleasure pier came into view across the pedestrian walkway, Eric pointed at it. "I remember that place," he said with his twinkliest boyish grin.

She took a hand off the steering wheel to point a warning finger at his face. "Don't. Say. It."

He made a zipping motion across his mouth, as a pelican flew over them and set down on the curved decorative wall along the sidewalk. A couple of tourists approached it with bread in their hands.

Pelicans were odd birds. Up close, on land or on a pier, they were homely, bordering on ugly with their long beaks and pouches, bony wings and hopping-style walk. They were so ugly they were cute. But once it took flight, gliding on wide-spread wings over the water, the homely bird became a thing of grace, and of courage when it plunged into the water, diving for prey.

"You can feed the pelicans?" Eric asked with a hopeful look in his eyes.

"Depends," she replied. "Do you like your fingers?"

He picked up his hands and wriggled his long fingers in front of his face. "I'm kind of attached to them."

"Then you don't want to feed the pelicans."

"Aye, aye, ma'am!"

After winding through the streets, passing souvenir stores, gift shops, restaurants, until Metropole Avenue took them back to Crescent and they turned left onto the far side of the pedestrian area, she pointed out hotels and the Tuna Club, where celebrities such as George Patton, Zane Grey and Charlie Chaplin had once gathered. By now they had left the main part of downtown Avalon, and Crescent Avenue became Casino Way. Past the Yacht Club, the round white building Eric had noticed from the boat came into view. Michelle stopped the golf cart in front of it.

"That's the Casino."

Eric's eyes gleamed. "Casino, huh? Great. I like to play a little black-jack every once in a while."

"It's not that kind of casino. There's no gambling there."

His disappointment was obvious, and a bit disbelieving. "How can it be a casino if there's no gambling?"

"Shows what you know. Casino just means little house in Italian. It doesn't necessarily mean a place where there's gambling,"

"Then that makes our place a casino, doesn't it? It's a little house."

Our place. It sounded so intimate, like a couple living together. But no, they were just roommates.

"That casino has a ballroom and movie theatre. There used to be a museum there too, but they moved it to a bigger place over on Metropole Avenue."

"Cool. Let me know if the theatre runs a Star Wars marathon."

They drove around the back of the east side of the casino building, past a gas station and a small dock where Michelle did most of her work on her client's boats. Eric winced at the price on the gas pump.

"I thought gas prices were high in San Diego."

"Welcome to island living."

Behind the casino, the area was paved, and lined with dive bags, scuba gear and Mexican blankets along the perimeter. Michelle stopped the golf cart and pointed out the steps leading into the water. "That's the dive park."

"Do you dive?" Eric asked.

She looked at her new roommate's face. He seemed like the type of person who could take a joke.

A visible shudder ran through her. "I went snorkeling once. But I haven't been in the water since..." She let her voice trail off and pasted an expression of terror on her face.

"Since what?" he asked with bright curiosity. "Did you have a problem?"

"I guess you could call it a problem." She lowered her voice. "I haven't been able to get up the courage to go back in the water, ever since I saw the sea monster."

His eyes went wide with curiosity. "Sea monster? You have a sea monster here? You mean, like the Loch Ness monster or something?"

"Maybe the Loch Ness monster's more scary cousin. It's out *there* somewhere," she waved a hand towards the south, "Between here and San Clemente Island."

Eric was watching her tell her fish tale with an expression of intentness, like listening to a lesson in school. He looked so attentive that she decided to test the limits of his gullibility.

"Lots of divers have seen it, but nobody has ever been able to get a photo. It's a big, barrel-shaped creature with a long neck, like maybe twenty feet. It kind of looks like a plesiosaur. That's a marine dinosaur."

Eric nodded, his eyes never leaving her face. "I know what a plesiosaur is."

"But there's a difference between the Catalina sea monster and a plesiosaur like you might see depicted in a museum. Our monster has hair, like a horse's mane but shaggy, almost like dreadlocks, two feet long and orange. And its eyes are a foot across, and bulgy, and have this dead look in them like it's seen all the death and misery there's ever been in the world. There've been boaters and divers who went out looking for it and never came back, and all that was ever found of their remains was a shred of a life jacket, or a mangled dive mask."

She was really enjoying see his intent, half-believing expression, but after a moment it was replaced by a knowing, joking smile that spread across his face and lit up his eyes.

"You know," he said thoughtfully, nodding as if he accepted her story. "I think I saw that guy, or one of his brothers or sisters, off the coast of Australia a couple of years ago. He was towing a boat with a couple of leprechauns and mermaids riding in it."

She tried to contain the giggle but it escaped her lips. "Well, it is a local legend. But to answer your question, yes I do dive, but it's been a while."

"That's OK," he said. "You know, I'm certified as a rescue diver. I can buddy you." Again, that casual intimacy. *Our place, I'll be your dive buddy.*

He pulled his phone out of his pocket and tapped at it, then turn the screen towards her, saying "See?" and she found herself looking at a digital copy of his NAUI rescue diver certification.

The next thing she knew, they'd be grocery shopping together.

"It's nice to see you joking around," he said. "It sure beats pale and panicking like before."

She had to agree.

"Wait just a sec," he requested. Hopping out of the golf cart, he strode over towards two guys who had just come up from the dive park. One of them was trying to reach the cord on the zipper on the back of his wetsuit, but it swung just out of the reach of his fingers. Eric tapped the guy on the shoulder, retrieved the cord and put it in the diver's hand. Michelle could see them talk for a minute, then Eric pulled his phone out of his pocket and typed something into it, before shaking hands with both divers. Eric Hanson had obviously made another friend in Avalon.

He bounded back to the golf cart, saying, "Thanks for waiting," as he hopped back into the passenger's seat.

"How do you do that?" Michelle asked disbelievingly. "Just make friends with people like that?"

"It's easy. You just put out your hand, like this." He held out his hand as if to shake. "And you say, Hi, how you doing? My name is Eric. You try it."

She held out her hand, as if to shake, tried to make her voice deeper, like his, and repeated, "Hi, how you doing? My name is Eric." She shook her head. "Nope, not gonna work."

He pulled down his sunglasses, just enough to look at her over the top. "Nobody is ever going to believe your name is Eric. Not with boobs like those."

Immediately, he slapped his hand over his mouth. "Oops! Did I actually say that? Out loud?"

"You did." Somehow, she couldn't take offense, not with those repentant sheep eyes he made.

"I sincerely apologize. That was inappropriate." She tried to look outraged but somehow she just couldn't.

"You're just lucky Brenda isn't here."

"Yeah, my ass would be grass, and she'd be the lawnmower. What you should try instead, is," he pitched his voice a little higher, "Hi, how you doing? My name is Michelle."

Now she pulled her sunglasses down a little. "Nobody is going to believe your name is Michelle. Not with muscles like those."

He looked surprised, then grinned as she slapped her hand over her mouth. "Oops! Did I just say that? Out loud?"

"You did." He actually held his arm up and flexed it. Show-off. "I'm glad to know that all those hours in the gym weren't wasted."

"Big goof." She started up the golf cart and made a U-turn back onto Casino Way.

"By the way," Eric said. "Those guys back there? They called total BS on your sea monster story."

"You mythbusted my sea monster story already?" she asked with mock insult. "Do your new friends live here on Catalina?"

Eric shook his head and nodded in the direction of the mainland. "They're from Torrance. They come over here to dive about once a month. We're going to get together to dive the next time they come over to the island, and you're welcome to join us if you'd like. We'll keep an eye out, and I'll bring my dive knives just in case."

"Knives? Plural? How many dive knives do you have?"

He looked thoughtful "Three. I'll let you borrow the biggest one, so you can defend me if we see the monster." He winked at her. It wasn't a flirty wink. It was an *I'm on to you* wink.

As they approached the pedestrian area of Crescent Avenue, before she turned up Metropole Avenue, Eric asked, "Is there a place here where you can park for a little while? I'd like to walk up the pier if you don't mind. It'll be nice to actually see it without having to dodge kids in strollers, chasing you down. I'm sure I'm a blur in the background of a bunch of people's photographs from that day."

She turned her face in his direction long enough to stick her tongue out at him. He just laughed and said, "Be careful, a bird might poop on that. Uh-oh! Here comes a seagull."

There was a spot to park the golf cart in front of the Bluewater Restaurant, and they walked down Crescent Avenue and turned companionably up the pier. It was pleasant, she had to admit, to actually see it and feel the warmth and gentle breeze, rather than dashing along like a maniac, trying to get away from the bar and the annoying sailor who seemed to know her too well. But he wasn't annoying anymore; he was her agreeable, likable roommate. How in the world did that ever come about?

They still dodged kids in strollers, but it was at a leisurely pace this time, without the threat of crashing into any. In fact, Eric tended to smile and nod at people they passed.

At one point, he stopped to pick up a shoe that one of those kids in a stroller had pulled off and dropped, unbeknownst to the parents. After returning it to the mom and dad with a smile, he crouched down to the kid's eye level and told him, "Don't be throwing away your shoes, dude. Your mom and dad paid a lot of money for those." Then he made a quacking noise like Donald Duck, and the kid laughed. Chalk up another new friend for Eric Hanson.

As they continued up the pier, Eric bumped fists with a guy walking the other way, and the two of them said "Hooyah" in unison.

After they passed, Michelle asked him, "Do you know him?"

"No," Eric replied. "But he's Navy."

"How do you know?"

"Spidey sense."

She rolled her eyes at that, and yet, she was surprised at how easy she found it to just hang out with Eric, like a friend. Had she only known him a few hours?

They didn't go down the incline leading down to the smaller end section of the pier, because it was full of people waiting to board a boat for a tour. Instead, they leaned against the rail on the main pier.

"I was trying to take your advice," she admitted after a minute.

He looked at her and smiled. "Which advice? I tend to give a lot of advice. Too much sometimes."

"You said I should sit down and get calm." She gestured out over the water. "Looking at the ocean is the closest I could get to being calm. It's always there. It doesn't change. It doesn't ignore you or let you down. It's just – the ocean. You can look at it, and forget, and get calm."

Continuing to look at the water, she said quietly, "When anxious, uneasy and bad thoughts come, I go to the sea, and the sea drowns them out with its great wide sounds, cleanses me with its noise, and imposes a rhythm upon everything in me that is bewildered and confused."

She glanced at him, wondering if he thought she was a total dork.

Apparently not. He was looking at her as if she'd just discovered the formula for cold fusion.

"Girl, you may be wasting your talents as a mechanic. Maybe you should be a writer. That was … poetic."

"As much as I'd like to, I'm afraid I can't take credit for that, other than for memorizing it. It's a quote from a German poet from the nineteenth century."

"I guess I was right when I said we were twins separated at birth. I did the same thing - when I was ship-board, looking at the ocean when I was stressed out, or at the stars, if it was nighttime. Say that again."

He repeated the poetic words and he listened with concentration, as if committing them to his memory also.

"How can you give too much advice?" she asked, thinking of what he'd said a minute ago.

He looked at her with a grin. "Have you ever had to tell someone they have an STD?"

An STD? Yikes. She shook her head. "No. That's one nice thing about boat engines."

Eric nodded in agreement. "Yeah, well, the first time I had to, I almost wished I'd gone into mechanics instead of medicine."

"I don't believe that," she said quickly. He gave the impression that he was truly dedicated to his work in the medical field.

"You're right. I didn't mean that. Signing up to be a corpsman is kind of like taking a wedding vow – for better or for worse."

"I'll have to take your word for that. You're the one who's divorced."

She was afraid she might have touched on a sore spot, but he didn't seem to mind.

"Well, that's a whole other story for another day.

"So, I start out by telling this guy that maybe he needed to have a conversation with his girlfriend about their, um, histories, and whether they were really in an exclusive relationship. He ended up crying, and I felt like shit, pardon my language. Let's just say that the both of us ended up looking out over the ocean that day, trying to get calm."

"Did it work?"

"It worked for me. But then, I only had to deliver the news. I wasn't the one getting pumped full of penicillin and anticipating an awkward conversation with my significant other."

"What about you?" Eric asked. "Why did you choose to become a boat mechanic? With your brains and good grades, you could have gone to university, and gone into a professional field."

"I am a professional. A professional mechanic."

"Yeah. Poor choice of words on my part," Eric agreed. "I'll rephrase – why did you choose the profession you did?"

"Well, a part of it was due to my dad. It was hard enough to leave him here unsupervised for the eighteen months I went to technical school. I was always terrified he'd forget to turn off the stove, or drop a beer bottle and step on the broken glass. Or not be able to find his way home from the bar when he was really skunked. If I'd gone to a four-year college, it would have been twice the worry. And I couldn't afford to hire someone to keep an eye on him. Even if I could – can you imagine being a babysitter for a grown man?"

Eric looked so sad at hearing her story that she almost wanted to give him a hug of comfort.

"So you're saying you gave up college to take care of your dad? That's one of the saddest, and yet most noble things I've ever heard."

She shrugged. "But it wasn't just that. I'd always been interested in motors and engines and mechanics. I never played with dolls when I was a kid. I preferred Legos. A couple of years after my mom died, when I was lonely and bored and kind of lost, I came across an old broken lawnmower. I was kind of poking around it, and the guy who owned it said I'd be doing him a favor by taking it off his hands because it didn't work. So I took it home and started playing around with it. It took a while, but I got it running, and I took it back to the guy who'd given it to me. He was ecstatic – he thought he'd have to buy a new one, and it costs a fortune to have stuff like that shipped here. He actually insisted on paying me for fixing it. I mean, he paid me money! That blew me away. I'd worked on it for the fun of it. But there I was – thirteen years old and I'd done something worthy of earning money. And that first customer recommended me to someone else who needed their golf cart engine tuned up. Suddenly I wasn't just Michelle Diaz, the daughter of the embarrassing town drunk. I was Michelle Diaz, the girl who could resurrect dead lawnmowers. I've even worked on the mowers at the golf course."

"You were the engine whisperer," Eric noted.

"Yeah, something like that. The summer between my junior and senior year of high school, I got a job as an intern at the marina. It was mostly fetching tools and coffee for the real mechanics, but I managed to get my hands on a few engines, and I liked it even more than bringing dead lawnmowers to life. And I was good at it."

She looked up in the air, smiling in remembrance, and after a moment looked to Eric with a smile that warmed him to the backbone.

"I still remember the first time I fixed an engine on my own. It was just an outboard, but when it roared to life for me, I felt like a million bucks. And there's the extra added bonus – engines don't get drunk and embarrass you by making you drag them home from the bar. They never ask you to pop them another cold one. And they didn't hit on me. Their owners did, a lot, but the boats, they were cool. The only thing I didn't like was how dirty the other guys' hands got. I'm not some kind of prissy princess who needs to get a manicure every week. I leave that to my friend Tracy. But after seeing some of those guys with their dirty hands, I started wearing gloves."

She held out her hands, looking at her clean, unvarnished fingernails. Eric actually took them in his hands and smiled at her.

"That was a good decision on your part. Very pretty."

The brief touch of his hands was warm and comforting.

"So when I graduated from high school, I decided to go to a good technical school to get official training. When I was done, the marina hired me full time, and there I am."

She leaned her arms on the pier's railing next to him as they gazed at the dozens of boats floating in the bay.

"I really was a bitch that day," she admitted.

"Yeah, you were," he concurred.

"You didn't have to agree with me!"

"Hey, I tell it like I see it. It really hurt my feelings when you called me Popeye."

If his feelings had been hurt, his boyish grin certainly didn't show it.

"That's what hurt your feelings? Not when I told you to, you know?" Of all the rude things she'd said to him that day, she wouldn't even put Popeye in the top three. "I'm surprised you wanted to move in with me. I mean, be my roommate."

"I could tell you didn't mean it."

"I'm going to have to work on that then."

"No, don't. I like the real you better. But you know, if you're nice to people, they're usually nice back. Look at me – I was nice to you that day, and now look. I'm living in your house."

He turned and leaned his back against the pier's railing, crossing his ankles and his arms, smiling at her.

"Is this totally weird?" she asked.

"Weird? How can you say that? It's beautiful here. The climate, the ocean, this beautiful island-"

"That's not what I meant. I was referring to us, being roommates. I mean, you're a man." She waved a hand at him, indicating his muscles, his general masculinity.

"Last time I checked." He grinned like a child. "Let's just verify, though." As she stared in horrified amazement, he looped one finger into the waistband of his shorts, pulled the fabric a bit away from his body, and peered down his front. Was he actually looking at ...?

"Yep, still there."

She could barely choke out a strangled, "Wha?" before he looked right and left, as if to verify nobody was eavesdropping on him, cupped a hand around his mouth as if to direct his words directly to her ears alone, like it was a secret, and intoned, "And you know what? You're a woman."

"Yes, you pointed that out back there." She gestured back towards the Casino across the bay where he'd made that crack about her boobs. At least he'd taken his finger out of his waistband and let his shorts settle back against his skin.

"And I apologized for that," he reminded her quickly.

Yes, and his apology had been so sweet and sincere, she had forgiven him immediately.

"And you're a goof." He was, truly.

"Yeah, you keep telling me that," he agreed. "But seriously, it doesn't have to be weird, just because we have different plumbing. We just have to establish some guidelines."

He held up one finger. "I promise not to walk around the house in my underwear." He showed her a teasing grin. "As long as you promise the same."

A second finger unfurled. "I never drink milk directly from the container, and if I finish it, I'll replace it and never put it back empty."

"What about sports?" she asked.

His middle finger came up to join the other two. Now he looked like a boy scout.

"Well, I'm not the kind of guy to sit in front of the TV and scream and yell and get all freaked out about every play. I'm not really into football or basketball or hockey, But I do like to watch the occasional baseball game."

That piqued her interest. "What team?"

"Tampa Bay Rays, of course."

She let her lip curl. "Oh. American League."

He cocked an eyebrow at her unfriendly tone.

"Wait. Let me guess. You're a Dodgers fan."

"Is there something wrong with that?" She hesitated sometimes to admit to guys that she liked baseball. They seemed to take it as an affront to some sort of exclusive boys-only clique, perhaps finding it intimidating that she understood, and enjoyed, ERA's and RBI's, the satisfying crack of a bat against a ball coming in at 90 miles per hour. It was stupid, but she got the impression that some males felt somewhat less manly in the face of a woman who kept better track of standings than they did.

Hopefully her new roommate was made of sterner stuff.

He put down his boy scout hand, put his hands on his hips and gave her a chin nod. "And the most important roommate parameter for us will be, I will be very considerate and respectful when I explain the absolute righteousness of the designated hitter concept to you."

She snorted. "You can try."

"That sounds like a challenge. Look, they designate someone to bat for the pitcher so that the pitcher doesn't get injured at the plate, doesn't have that extra strain on his body, and can focus solely on pitching"

"Ha," she scoffed. "Designated hitter, what a joke. A bunch of whiny prima donnas who aren't athletic enough to be able to pitch and bat. While over in the National League the real athletes can bat and play their field positions with equal skill. Why can't the pitcher bat too, like all the other players? Are they not good enough to hit a ball as well as throw it?"

Eric looked somewhat serious at that. "It's specialization, sweetheart. It's an art. The artist has to be allowed to hone his art. Pitching is the most difficult aspect of baseball, and the AL pitchers are specializing in what they do best. You specialize in boat mechanics. I wouldn't ask you to change the oil in my car."

She snorted. "Oh, puh-leeze. Wimpy divas. And I could change the oil in your car with one hand tied behind my back."

"Really? Now that presents a real interesting mental image. Good thing my car is in San Diego at my friend's house, or I might call you on that. Let's just agree to disagree on the designated hitter concept."

She scented victory. "Giving up, are you?"

"No, just postponing the discussion. Do you always argue with your roommates like this?"

"No. I've never had the opportunity. I've never had a roommate before." Eric opened his mouth but she forestalled him. "My dad doesn't count. He barely spoke to me, let alone argued."

"Seriously, though, it's all about respect," Eric said. "That's how it will work for us to be roommates. It doesn't matter that I'm a man and you're a woman. Well, it matters, of course, in the general scheme of, you know, cosmic existence, but as long as we have respect, it'll work."

"I can do respect," she admitted. "But since I've never had a roommate before, either male or female, the concept is a little weird for me."

He smiled broadly. "Well, I have, pretty much always, and we all managed to survive. I should let you know, I'll be working nights a lot of the time, but I'll try not to be noisy if I'm coming and going while you're asleep."

That was considerate of him. "OK, if you're working nights and sleeping during the day, I'll try not to be noisy too," she agreed.

"Nah, don't worry about it. Just don't yell out 'general quarters' and we'll be cool. Unless you want to get up close and personal with that handgun I told you about."

"You did say I could shoot it."

"Yes, at a proper shooting range. With proper safety precautions, and me standing behind you to pick you up when you get knocked back on your ass. Pardon my language."

"Oh, and one more thing," he warned.

What now? They'd discussed gender anatomy, baseball, milk etiquette and work schedules. What more could there be?

"We'll need to clarify what body parts can and cannot be scratched in the common areas. I promise I'll never scratch my privates outside the privacy of my bedroom, if you'll promise the same."

She put a finger against her cheek, as if considering whether or not to agree.

"Wow, that is really considerate of you," she said.

"That's me, Mr. Considerate."

"It's your middle name, right?"

He nodded happily.

"OK, I think I can manage that," she said.

Eric grinned at her. "I think we'll be really compatible roommates."

"And yet you didn't believe me when I said I wasn't going to jump." She gestured out over the water.

"Well, I just had to cover all possibilities. You know, worst-case scenario."

Some impish impulse in her inspired her to test his reflexes. She put one foot on the bottom rung of the pier's railing, and stepped up.

Immediately, he pushed off his flip flops, grabbed off his sunglasses and dropped them on the pier, and leaped towards her, all within about a nanosecond. She stopped, put her foot back on the pier, and laughed. She laughed so hard she almost cried. After a moment of shocked panic, Eric grinned, retrieved his sunglasses and shook a finger at her.

"Girl, do not do that unless you mean it!" he scolded.

"Maybe I should take your pulse," she suggested.

"No need. It's seventy beats per minute." His demeanor showed absolute confidence in his knowledge.

"How can you know that?" She was sure he had to be making that up.

"I'm in tune with my body," he asserted, as he slid his feet back into his flip flops, and she rolled her eyes at him. He held out his wrist towards her, and for a moment she stared at that anchor tattoo.

"Go ahead. Check it if you don't believe me."

Oops, her bluff had been called. "I don't know how to do that," she admitted.

"Then, you're just going to have to believe me."

"Would you really have jumped in after me?" she asked.

"Of course. It's what I do."

"Then you'd do that for anyone?"

"Yep. If it bleeds, I bandage it. If it jumps, I jump in after it."

"Why did you do it?" she asked, looking down at the water.

"Do what?"

"Chase me here that day? Some people might think that was creepy."

His eyebrows went up. "Are you calling me creepy?"

Actually, she hadn't thought him creepy at all. Annoying, but not creepy. Realistically, the idea of a strange man following her, chasing her down, should have creeped her out, but hadn't.

"No, you weren't creepy," she assured him. "Just kind of weird."

"Aren't they the same thing?"

"No, there's a subtle difference."

Eric's smile softened a bit. "You just looked like you needed a friend."

She was astounded. He was right. She had needed a friend. She'd worked so hard to push people away, to make them dislike her, in order to avoid the supposedly inevitable hurt and disappointment that a real human relationship would inflict. But maybe she'd been wrong. Maybe she should be taking each person on their own merits. Maybe not everyone would hurt or disappoint her. Maybe a friend was just what she needed. She was usually guarded and cautious and private. They were mechanisms she put into place as protection. For the first time, she felt safe opening up to someone.

She felt a smile bloom on her lips. "Yeah, that's what you do, right?" She held out her hand again, but spoke in her normal voice. "Hi, I'm Michelle. How you doing?"

He grinned back and shook her hand. "Hi, I'm Eric. Nice to meet you."

"OK, now that we're friends, can I ask you something personal?"

"Of course, ask me anything you like. My life is an open book."

She started to open her mouth to ask him something personal, but he held up a hand.

"Wait, just a sec. I'm sorry to interrupt you, but there's something I need to do before I forget. Stand here."

He pushed himself away from the pier's railing and put his hand on her elbow, nudging her to stand where he had been, against the railing, and pulled his phone out of his pocket, tapped the camera icon, and held it up.

"Why are you taking my picture?" she asked suspiciously.

"To put in your contact info. All my contacts have photos attached. See?"

He turned the phone towards her and scrolled through a very long list of phone numbers, and as they rolled across the screen, she could see that each one had a photo attached. A lot of the photos were girls. Some were really pretty girls, she could tell even as they scrolled by quickly.

So what. It's not like you're dating and have a right to be jealous.

"Wait, first, what's your phone number?" he asked. "If we're going to be living together, we need to be able to get in touch with each other, right?"

She told him her number and he typed it into the phone, then raised it back to picture-taking height.

"OK, smile. No, wait, that's too bright. Move to your left just a little. No, your other left."

She had moved to the right rather than the left, just to see if he noticed.

"That's good. Now lift your chin a little."

A breeze blew the hair across her face and he actually reached out and pushed it back.

"Let's try this again. Chin up, smile."

"OK, Andrew Liebowitz."

"I thought it was Annie Liebowitz," he replied, as he finally took the photo and made the necessary adjustments to add it to her phone number in his contacts.

"You're right, the photographer's name is Annie, not Andrew. But I couldn't call you Annie. Not with muscles like those."

He laughed. It was a beautiful sound, fresh and forthright without being loud or braying. She was still standing at the rail, but he quickly nudged her aside and stood in the spot again, looking at her expectantly.

"Well, what are you waiting for?"

He expected her to take his photo too apparently. She didn't have photos in her contacts list, and she had a much shorter list in her phone than he had in his, but his number from his rental application was already entered into the list.

She tapped her own camera icon and looked at him through the screen. He smiled automatically, taking off his sunglasses, the wide sexy mouth curving up and his eyes crinkling a little in the bright sunlight, as fair and friendly as a sunbeam.

"Are my socks straight?" he asked, as she took the photo. She looked at his feet, at those cute toes wearing only flip flops.

"You aren't wearing socks," she reminded him.

"Oh, good. My socks were crooked in my high school yearbook photo and I've been paranoid about it ever since."

"Did your feet show in your yearbook photo?"

"No, it was just a head and shoulders photo."

"You're such a goof." She added his cute photo to his number in her contact list.

"So what's this personal question you wanted to ask me?"

"Why don't you drink? You were in the Navy. Isn't being in the Navy and not drinking an oxymoron?"

"Do we really have that kind of reputation?"

"Around here they do."

"Are you saying that other sailors visiting here were rude to you? Hit on you? Treated you with less than complete respect?"

"Not everyone is like you, more's the pity."

"Give me names. I will have words with them."

"That's silly. You're not responsible for the actions of every guy in the Navy. And the guy who said to me, hey baby, want to see my submarine, didn't exactly introduce himself by name first."

"Still, I apologize on their behalf. As for my not drinking-" He laughed a little but it was tinged with an edge of memory. "I don't because I can't. I'm allergic to alcohol."

"I didn't know you could be allergic to it. Is that really a thing?" She'd heard of people being allergic to peanuts, to shellfish, to chocolate, but never to alcohol. If it was for real, why couldn't her father have had that allergy?

"Picture this. I'm sixteen, at my nephew's wedding. I had just gotten my braces off, so I thought I was The Man."

"Wait, you had braces?" she couldn't help interrupting. It was hard to picture this tall, confident man as a teenager with a mouth full of metal.

"I sure did," he replied, baring his very straight teeth at her to show that the braces had done their job. "For three years, my dad would say, 'Open your mouth, kid, let me see our trip to Europe.' Anyway, at Josh's wedding reception, my dad let me have one beer in honor of the special occasion. I didn't really like it, but being sixteen and stupid, I snuck some more anyway. You'd be amazed at how people don't pay attention to their drinks at parties. An hour later, I'm in the ER, puking and with this horrific rash that would really gross you out if you'd seen it. I heard the doctor say that if he didn't know for a fact that smallpox had been eradicated, they'd test me for it. But then I solved the mystery when I let out this huge belch."

"That was a good thing?"

"Yeah, because the doctor smelled the beer on my breath. See, alcohol allergies are kind of rare so they don't usually think to test for it. A lot of people who think they're allergic to alcohol are actually allergic to gluten – that's wheat. It was kind of awkward when they asked how many drinks I'd had, and my dad said, one, and at the same time, I said three. And then my mom got mad at my dad for letting me have that one when I was only sixteen. Normally you'd think it was just a hangover, but because I'd broken out in hives right away, and then started to go into anaphylactic shock, they did a blood test and it came back, allergic to alcohol. Not wheat, actual alcohol. So instead of quarantine, I got an injection of epinephrine, a two-week course of steroids and a lifetime of being the designated driver. I can't even have cold medicine. But after seeing some of my mates get shit-faced, pardon my language, I can't say I miss it much."

"Steroids? So that's how you got the muscles!" The words popped out before she could help herself.

"Not anabolic steroids. Cortical steroids, to treat the rash. Anything I've got here," he squeezed his upper arm, and Michelle didn't miss the small look of pride, "I got the honest way." He shook a finger at her as if she might be considering it. "Cortical steroids, good when used correctly. Anabolic steroids, bad."

"Yes, Sir," she replied and he grinned.

"No need to call me sir, I wasn't a commissioned officer."

"I thought you were a petty officer. Chief and everything."

"I was. But that's not an officer."

"What do you mean? It has the word officer right there. So how can you say it's not an officer?"

"It's not a commissioned offer. A petty officer is still an enlisted person. You don't get a salute and you aren't addressed as Sir or Ma'am. It's like a corporal or sergeant in the Army or Marines."

"That doesn't make sense. Why don't they just use corporal or sergeant like the others?"

"Because John Paul Jones said so. If you must play Navy, you can call me Chief. Or Doc."

How silly of the Navy to address a man as Doc when he wasn't actually a doctor. What was up with that?

Google had served her well before. There was no reason to doubt it wouldn't explain this one. She had, after Googling the meaning of battle rattle, literally typed in the question, "Why is a Navy corpsman called Doc?"

Like before, the answers were an eye-opener. Apparently, corpsmen like Eric didn't only treat fellow Navy personnel. They were also assigned to Marine units and facilities, since the Marine Corps didn't have its own medical unit. They ended up boots on the ground, as he had put it, in places where IEDs were real dangers and the terrorists who planted them were real, close-by threats, rather than the shadowy, mysterious figures talked about on the news. No wonder he'd worn the rhymingly named battle rattle.

She also learned that the nickname was not given out automatically. It was earned. It was given with respect to corpsmen who treated casualties and saved lives in places where many times they were literally the only medical assistance available, and doing it many times while being shot at. No, he wasn't a physician, but apparently he'd had to act as one in situations that would make most people freeze up with trauma.

He'd said it so casually, "I've been shot at more than once," and while he was being shot at, he'd been caring for warriors with gunshot wounds and burns and other injuries she didn't even want to think about it. How absolutely terrifying that had to be.

And yet despite his joking, goofy, singing persona, he'd earned that title, that nickname of Doc. He'd probably seen horrible things and yet he came through it with a cheery outlook and positive attitude, and a continued willingness to help others despite having seen the worst the world had to offer. She couldn't imagine any life experience that would produce a stronger person as its effect.

She had felt a little like a cyber-stalker, Googling information pertaining to him and his life. But she justified it by reasoning, she was trusting him to live in her home, so she had every right to investigate information that might pertain to him.

"How do you prevent something like that?" she asked. "That kind of allergic reaction sounds pretty unpleasant."

"You're right, it is unpleasant. You can't prevent it, really. The only prevention for an allergy of any kind is to avoid the substance you're allergic to. So as long as I don't drink alcohol, I'm fine. And I haven't, not since then. How about you? Do you still get panic attacks?"

She looked away. "A few, when my dad was still alive, and I had to go to the bar and fetch him home."

Eric looked contrite. "I'm sorry about that. If I'd known... Do you blame me?"

The old Michelle would have blamed him six ways to Sunday. But she was smarter and more mature now.

"No, I don't blame you. You had no way of knowing."

She looked back over the ocean, at its blue calmness. Eric was standing next to her, arms resting on the railing in front of them.

"Do you want to talk about it?" he asked. It was like déjà vu. The day they'd met last year, only a few feet from this spot, he'd sensed her despondency and asked her the very same thing. And like that day, she didn't talk about it, just let the words come out all on their own.

"I shouldn't have been surprised when she died. Even though I was just a kid, I should have been able to tell she was sick, and been prepared, you know, so I wouldn't have been thrown for such a loop."

If he was confused by her sudden shift from her anxiety about her father, to her anxiety about her mother, he didn't show it. He just said, "It wouldn't have mattered."

She looked at him sharply. How could he know such a thing? But then – she suddenly remembered one of the first things he'd ever said to her, about his mother being mad at him for getting a tattoo at age twenty-one. He'd quoted her as saying, "If your father was alive." So, he'd lost a parent young also. Maybe he did know what he was talking about. Had that been when he'd locked himself in the head to cry?

"It doesn't matter if you know someone is going to die," Eric said.

"Even when they're terminal, when they do pass away, it's just as bad as if they had dropped dead in perfect health."

She was still a bit doubtful.

"I know this from both my parents, Michelle. For both of them, it was expected, and shouldn't have come as a surprise. But it still hit me just as hard when it did happen. You shouldn't be ashamed of it hitting you that hard too. I'm sorry for your loss."

She tried to be the big brave girl Eric thought she was, but despite her best effort, her lip trembled just a little.

"It was a long time ago," she said, yet she was touched by his sincere sympathy.

"I know," he replied. "I don't think that makes it hurt you any less. But I'm still sorry."

She put a hand on his arm, which surprised her. She wasn't the type to express affection or sympathy in a physical way. "How old were you when your father died?"

He looked briefly at her hand on his arm, smiled faintly, then looked back at the water.

"Eighteen. About a month after I graduated from boot camp. He'd survived the first stroke. It was the second one that did him in. I was still at Great Lakes, just starting corpsman training."

"That's awful. I'm so sorry."

He looked at her and smiled. "Thanks. That means a lot to me."

A brief glance off the pier took in the blue water, the small whispering waves, boats passing by, the faint fishy, salty scent of the ocean. It was only a momentary glance but he still had time to remember the day the Recruit Division Commander had called him into his office and handed him the phone receiver from his desk, saying, "Family emergency, Hanson."

His sister Brenda was crying so hard she couldn't even get the awful words out, but Eric understood with horror what she was trying to say. His brother Philip came on the line after a few seconds and just said, "It's Dad, Eric. You need to come home. Your mom needs you."

He recalled dropping the phone onto the desk but couldn't remember if he asked the RDC for permission to be dismissed. He barely made it into a stall in the head before sinking to the floor, as the hot, stinging tears took over, as uncontrollable as a hurricane, and pain bloomed in his throat and his head.

Irrationally, a hot smack of anger rolled through his gut and assaulted his stomach, so hard he almost had to take advantage of the fact that he was sitting next to a toilet. God *damn* the whole unfairness of it all, the fucking cruelty of the universe obliterating Kenneth Hanson from existence. And yet at the same time, the rational part of his brain tried to raise its hand and remind him, *you shouldn't be surprised. You should have expected this.* Dad had been debilitated by a stroke months ago and the prognosis then hadn't been good. A second, fatal stroke was devastatingly likely at any time.

But that rational thought process was steamrolled into oblivion by the grief and the tears that practically had him howling, until his RDC followed him into the head, bringing with him a chaplain, and, ironically, a corpsman, to pry him out of the stall and help him make arrangements for bereavement leave and a flight home to Florida. Eric sucked up the tears, washed his face, and tried really hard to keep it together as he gratefully accepted the sympathetic pats on the back and multiple mutterings of, "Shit, Hanson, that sucks," from his friends and classmates.

He knew all about the five stages of grief, but experiencing them was another thing altogether. The first four stages – denial, anger, bargaining, depression – rolled over him simultaneously in a crushing wave. The fifth stage, acceptance, was going to take a lot longer.

Only the fact that he'd been in uniform when he arrived at the Pensacola airport to be met by both his sisters had kept him dignified in public, until he got home and saw his mother.

When she glanced at him upon hearing him sing a few words, softly but still off-key, he said, "Hey, you have your German poet. I have Kenny Chesney."

"I almost tried to quit the Navy," he said after another moment.

"You mean, before this?"

"I didn't quit now. I retired. But, after my dad died, my mom was alone, or so I thought. For about half a nanosecond, I considered leaving.

And wouldn't that have brought a shit-storm of hurt down on my head. But just for that moment, as I was about to go back to Great Lakes after the funeral, I thought, I can't go back there and leave my mother to cope with this alone. I actually opened up my mouth to say that, but Mom could read my mind. She took one look at my face and said, 'Eric, your dad was so proud of you.' She looked around to make sure my brothers weren't nearby and said, 'don't you ever tell your brothers, but you were his favorite. He was proud of you when he was alive, and I know he will continue to be proud of you as you progress through this amazing career you're training for.' She said a lot of other nice and encouraging things, but I told her I didn't want to leave her alone at a time like this. I had no idea what kind of places I'd be sent to or how far away I'd be stationed. That had been the main reason I'd chosen the Navy over the other services. I really wanted to serve on board ships. Well, she said a few more embarrassing things about what a wonderful son she thought I was, but she wouldn't be alone. She had my sisters, as well as my brothers, who loved her even though they weren't her sons by blood. Just like my sisters weren't Dad's biological daughters, but they had still loved him like a father. Mom said, 'you go put that uniform back on right now.' She told me I looked incredibly handsome in it."

His cheeks tinged a bit pink with embarrassment as he said that. "But moms are supposed to say stuff like that. She told me, 'you go back and finish your training and make us proud.' Of course, I did go back. I never seriously considered trying to leave."

He glanced down at Michelle's hand, still on his arm. She followed his look and realized her hand was on his tattoo, her thumb unconsciously tracing the rope design.

Whoa. She hadn't intended to get so ... intimate. She took her hand off his arm a bit too quickly, then changed the subject. "Do you like ice cream?" she asked, nodding towards the snack bar nearby. Eric nodded vigorously.

"Who doesn't? I think it's a law." A minute later they were walking back to the golf cart licking ice cream cones like a couple of kids.

7

The next thing she knew, they were grocery shopping together. Eric insisted on stopping at Vons before returning to their casino, saying the cupboards were bare. Michelle tried to keep her items to one side of the cart, so that she could pay for them separately, but he kept dropping things into the cart and messing up her arrangement. There were an awful lot of vegetables in the cart, more than just replacements for the ones he'd chopped up earlier.

A whole gallon of milk?

"Are you going to drink all that?" she asked him.

He grinned. "Of course. I'm all about the healthy."

"What is your cholesterol level?"

"It's excellent, thanks for asking, ma'am."

He stopped in front of the display of laundry products, and gave Michelle a quizzical look. "What do you recommend for removing makeup?" he asked.

She was confused until he tapped at his shoulder, the one she'd cried on earlier. She couldn't help but blush when she remembered smearing her mascara and bodily fluids on his clean white shirt. "Look, I'm really sorry about that," she mumbled, looking away.

He nudged at her with an elbow.

"Don't worry about it! I'm completely machine washable. Cry on me any time you feel the need." The offer was nice, but she hoped she didn't

94

need to take him up on it again. His shoulder had been just a little too warm and comforting.

"I've got some stuff at home that should work on that."

"OK, we're cool then." He pushed the cart past the laundry supplies and into the next aisle, where he tossed a package of paper napkins into the cart. "We need these for the kitchen."

In the cereal aisle, they each reached for a box of cereal, and each gave the other a wrinkled-nose look of disapproval at the other's choice.

Twins separated at birth.

Eric chose a box of something depressingly healthy. Seriously, the picture on the box looked like twigs and bark. He cast a disapproving glance at the box of cereal Michelle chose for herself.

"Are you really going to eat that for breakfast?" he asked. "That's not cereal. It's a box full of sugar and red dye number five." He gestured at the picture on the box. "Those colors don't exist in nature."

Secretly, she admitted to herself that the cereal she'd picked out was more sucrose than anything else, but his disapproval raised her defenses.

"Yes. I'm going to buy it, I'm going to eat it, and I'm going to enjoy it. You have a problem with that?"

"No, ma'am," he replied with a grin. "But if you want to develop the muscle you're going to need to shoot my handgun someday, you're going to need some nice healthy protein. You're not a vegetarian, are you?"

He looked relieved when she shook her head. "Good. Let's head over to the meat department."

She might have been irritated at his judgmental attitude towards her dietary choices, but the prospect of him letting her shoot his handgun someday repressed the irritation.

At the checkout stand he grabbed three candy bars and dropped them in, as she gave him a look. "All about the healthy, you said?"

"It's my reward for eating all my vegetables."

"Do you need to be bribed to eat vegetables?" she asked with amusement, thinking about that salad.

"No, I like veggies. When I was a kid, my parents never had to nag me to eat mine."

"Neither did mine."

"Really?" He looked surprised. "You strike me as more of a rebellious type."

"It was more that nobody cared what I ate." From his look, he'd obviously picked up on her dejection at the memory of silent meals and her father's lack of interest.

"I'll make sure you eat right," Eric said. "Protein, veggies, carbs in moderation. Maybe I'll even talk you into a better cereal choice one of these days."

Some part of her should have been annoyed at his presumptuousness, his bossiness over her life and dietary choices. Another side of her appreciated his concern and helpfulness.

She didn't exactly live on potato chips and soda. She ate normal, healthy food, when she was in the mood to prepare it. Sometimes it seemed unnecessary to cook for one. But Avalon was also full of top-notch restaurants of all types, from sushi to pizza to prime grade steak, all of which she enjoyed. But eating alone in a restaurant was kind of lonely and pathetic. She sometimes could convince her friend Tracy from high school to join her, but occasionally found Tracy's people-watching, or rather, man-watching, to be a bit tedious.

She made a face at him, and he chuckled. "You want a candy bar too? Promise to eat all your veggies?"

When she hesitated, he snagged a chocolate bar. "I bet you want this one. All girls like chocolate."

"That's a sexist thing to say." She frowned at him.

"You're right. I apologize, ma'am."

He reached for the chocolate bar to put it back, until she declared, "touch it and die," and he laughed.

He also insisted on paying for all the groceries, even the cereal he disapproved of, despite her protest, saying it was a "thank you for taking me on as a roommate" present, carried all the bags out to the golf cart, and somehow still managed to open the door for her, leaving her with only the chocolate bar, which she ate before he got his hands on it.

They put away the groceries when they got back to the house, finished off the rest of the salad Eric had made, and then he went to his room, unpacked his duffel bag and made up his bed, all of which took a total of about three minutes. Then he came back to the kitchen, folding up now empty Bed Bath and Beyond bag, where Michelle was sitting at the kitchen table with her laptop, supposedly checking her email, but really more ruminating on how this roommate situation was going to work out, and he asked her for the Wi-Fi password.

She blushed a little when she recalled earlier in the day when he'd first mentioned it. She had a feeling that if she looked at his toes, he'd wiggle them again.

"I'll write it down for you." Every once in a while, the internet service in Avalon would fritz out and you had to reconnect everything. But of course, there were no writing materials at hand. Who wrote anything on paper anymore?

"Let me see your phone," she requested, and he lifted his eyebrows at her.

"Don't worry, I'm not going to install any spyware or tracking apps on it."

With a chuckle, he pulled his phone out of his pocket and handed it to her. "Go ahead," he said. "Install a tracking app. I won't mind."

She shook her head at his silliness, found the memo app and typed in the password, then handed the phone back to him.

He looked at it, looked back at her quizzically, looked at the display again, turned the phone sideways until the screen rotated, turned it upside down, then back before turning his gaze back to Michelle.

"What the heck does that mean?"

She looked over his shoulder to make sure she'd entered it right. "I had to put a number on it for the network to accept it," she explained.

"OK, but what does the rest of it mean? Or is it just random letters?"

"No, it has meaning." Was he blind? She took the phone back and pointed at the letters.

WWHermioneDo?2

"What Would Hermione Do?" Why did she have to explain it? Wasn't it obvious?

Apparently not. "What's a Hermione?"

She rolled her eyes at him. "Not a What. A Who. Hermione. You know, from Harry Potter."

He looked blank.

"Oh my god, are you saying you never read Harry Potter? Or even saw the movies? Where did you grow up? In a cave?"

"I've heard of it," he said slowly. She shook her head.

"Boy, your education is sadly lacking."

He snorted and grabbed the phone away from her. "Give me that. I've got people to Skype."

And apparently that was what he spent the rest of the evening doing. She could hear him talking and laughing from his room. She snuck a glance into his open door on her way to the bathroom, and saw him sitting cross-legged on the bed with his laptop, apparently enjoying his Skyping quite a lot. She wasn't purposely eavesdropping, but she still heard him say, "How much snow is in your front yard? I'm wearing shorts and flip-flops here."

Whoever he was Skyping with must have lived far away.

Later, as she sat on the couch in the living room, supposedly reading a book but really more pondering the dynamics of living with a roommate, and specifically with this particular roommate, she heard him go into the bathroom, close the door, and start the shower. After a moment, the singing started. At least, she thought it might be singing. She was pretty sure the neighbor's cat hadn't gotten into her bathroom to start howling.

The more one tells oneself not to think about something, the more one ends up thinking about that very thing. And Michelle failed miserably in not thinking about the fact that there was a wet, naked, attractive man in her bathroom.

When the shower, and the howling/singing stopped, she buried her nose in her book and firmly did not look in the direction of the hallway. He'd promised not to walk around the house in his underwear, but he'd said nothing about the possibility of walking around wet and naked with a towel around his waist, and she didn't dare turn around to look. She kept her gaze firmly on the page of her book, whose print suddenly seemed to make no sense to her. But she did hear him call out, "Good night, Roomie!" just before his bedroom door closed with a click. Then she felt it safe to go into her own room to sleep, after laying there for quite a while, amazed and bemused at this whole bizarre situation.

8

~

When her alarm went off in the morning, she thought she hadn't actually woken up. She had to be dreaming. She smelled coffee. How could she smell coffee when she hadn't gotten up yet?

The memory floated in with the sweet and bitter combination that gave coffee its unique aroma. She sniffed the air as she picked up her phone and canceled the alarm.

Roommate. She had a roommate now. A roommate who apparently knew his way around a coffee maker. How could she have forgotten, considering the amount of time she'd spent standing in the bathroom last night, looking at his toothbrush?

The toothbrush holder could accommodate up to four brushes. It had come with the house and was screwed to the wall. Since her father's death, Michelle's toothbrush had sat there alone. Now, comfortably in the next slot, rested Eric's bright purple toothbrush. It seemed so incongruous a color for a grown man, a military veteran, to have chosen. She was beginning to realize that he wasn't your typical guy.

Maybe this whole situation was going to work out. She hopped out of bed and opened her door to investigate, then stopped herself. *Male roommate, Michelle!* She closed the door and rummaged in her closet until she pulled out the long, fluffy pink bathrobe she rarely wore. Would it be weird for her to appear in the kitchen in the presence of her new, cute, male roommate wearing a bathrobe over the skimpy shorts and old tee shirt she'd slept in? The long fleece robe had a high neck and long sleeves, and fell past her knees. It was extremely non-sexy, and covered her more than any clothes she owned.

It would be fine, she reasoned. Now she could seek out that delicious smelling coffee.

He must have just finished consuming a bowl of that depressingly healthy cereal when she walked into the kitchen, because he had the bowl to his lips, drinking the leftover milk. "Good morning, roomie," he said with a smile, as he set the bowl back on the table.

How could anyone be that chipper first thing in the morning?

He had a milk mustache.

"How do you take your coffee?" He already had two mugs sitting on the counter and he stood up quickly and filled them both.

The old Michelle would have answered such a question with a snotty, "Duh," but she was going to be a nicer person now. So, she smiled back and said, "Black, please."

He handed her a cup of warm, steaming, fragrant coffee, and suddenly, unexpectedly, her throat got tight and she felt her eyes water a little as she sat down at the table.

Why was she getting all emotional? The man had made a pot of coffee, poured some into a mug, and handed it to her. No big deal. It wasn't as if he'd handed her the world on a string, or his heart on a silver platter. It was a simple cup of coffee, in a simple mug. And it was quite possibly the sweetest thing she had ever experienced.

Yes, big deal. It was an uncomplicated, ordinary thing and yet, it touched her as if he'd given her a solution to all her life's problems. Not even her last boyfriend, who had been so long ago she barely remembered his face, had ever bothered to make her coffee. In fact, nobody had ever made her coffee before. Eric, her new roommate, had, however. It was a simple, ordinary, everyday thing to do, and yet it somehow tugged at her emotions way more than she would have imagined.

You've turned into an idiotic sap all of a sudden, she thought. *Getting all misty-eyed over something as mundane as a cup of coffee.*

Her roommate was looking at her with puzzlement.

"Michelle? Are you OK?" he asked. "Are you going to cry on me again? Let me know so I can go grab a clean shirt."

She waved away his offer of fresh laundry for her to cry on. She was not going to do that again, she hoped.

"I'm OK," she muttered.

She put the cup to her lips, letting the warmth of it loosen her throat tightness and melt her weird moment of emotion, then looked at Eric standing in front of her, and giggled a little.

Should she tell him? The milk on his lip was really, truly cute, but it would be downright mean to let him walk around in ignorance. She set down her coffee, picked up a napkin from the package he had purchased yesterday and handed it to him.

"Um, Eric?" She tapped at her upper lip as she handed him the napkin. "You might want to wipe your face."

He blushed a little but still smiled as he took the napkin and erased the milk.

"First day at my new job, wish me luck." He was dressed for work in a crisp dark uniform with a patch on the shoulder reading "Avalon Fire Department Paramedic" and his name on a pin above the right breast pocket.

"Don't you look handsome," she teased. Wow, that was another new one for her. She didn't usually tease people. But it was impossible to be grouchy in the face of that twinkly smile.

The twinkly smile got even bigger, "Why, thank you. The uniform's not bad either, huh?"

He set down his coffee and actually twirled around so she could check out the whole package. What a goof. But that butt was just as cute as it had been yesterday in his cargo shorts. Not that she should be checking out her roommate's butt, she reminded herself.

When he finished his little pirouette, he said, "And look!" He held out his right arm towards her so that she was staring at his tattoo again.

"It looks the same as it did yesterday," she said. Of course, it did. There wasn't a tattoo parlor in Avalon and even if there was, he hadn't left the house since they had returned from their drive around town. "You weren't thinking of getting it removed, were you?"

"Of course not. I've heard that hurts." He grinned at her as they both remembered her rudeness to him that day at the Marlin Club.

"Notice, it's not covered up. I was afraid that in civilian life I'd have to wear a sleeve over it. Most public service jobs don't allow employees to have visible tattoos. But apparently they're more progressive here, because my boss said it wasn't a problem."

She saw a small expression cross his face, not a frown, but just a little less smiley. "Something wrong?" she asked.

"Not wrong, just weird. Being a civilian. I've never really been a civilian before. It's going to take some getting used to. Do you know what my boss told me the other day when I picked up my uniforms?" From the look on his face, his boss must have told him something pretty horrific. "He said I had to call him by his name!"

"Well, what else would you call your boss?"

"Sir. Or Ma'am, for female officers."

"Don't officers have names?"

"Nope, they have ranks."

"You can't have never been a civilian. Were you born on a ship? Or did you enlist right out of the maternity hospital?" Hadn't he said he'd grown up in Florida?

Though she'd never been the type of person to tease people, she was finding it rather fun to tease this guy. He was just so downright smiley.

"No, I wasn't born on a ship. My parents found me under a rock." At her *Come On* expression, he added, "Well, that's what my sisters told me, and they were pretty convincing for a while. And I couldn't enlist as a kid. They made me wait until I was eighteen and had graduated from high school. But I was at boot camp at Great Lakes a month after graduation. I had really planned on making a thirty-year career of it. I'd planned on going for Senior Chief or even Master Chief."

"If you liked it so much, why did you leave?"

Was that too personal a question? No, he had said yesterday, ask me anything, my life is an open book.

He sat down at the table with her and took a sip of his coffee. "Well, I loved the Navy and my job, and I was incredibly proud to serve my country. I re-enlisted three times and got deployed to a field hospital in Iraq two times and Afghanistan once. But after that tour, I was starting to get burned out. I felt like the possibility existed that I might not always be giving my best, and that wouldn't be fair either to the Navy, to my patients, or to me. So, a couple months after I got back to San Diego after that last deployment, I made the decision to request terminal leave.

"I'll be honest with you, I admit I did get a little choked up when I drove away from the base after signing out for the last time." He looked up into the air as if seeing something in his mind's eye. "In fact, I had to pull over and stop for a few minutes to have me a little cry before I could suck it up to see well enough to keep driving over to my friend's house." He looked at Michelle with a sweet smile. "Now that's a secret, sweetheart. I haven't told anyone else that, not even my sister. So do me a favor and don't rat me out, OK?"

Michelle was touched. This was a totally new situation for her. She and Eric had been roommates for less than twenty-four hours, and he was already telling her a personal secret that nobody else knew about. Not even the sister that he seemed to be very close to.

Or was he joking? His seemingly permanently happy disposition made it hard to tell.

"Do you want more coffee?" he asked, standing up and reaching towards the coffee pot.

She took a second sip of the coffee. It was good. In fact, it was delicious. More delicious than any pot of coffee she'd ever made, and she'd made plenty of pots over the years, trying to keep her dad sober, or to get him sober.

"This is amazing." She raised her cup in salute. "What did you do to it?"

Eric smiled, then pursed his lips and shook his head. "I'd tell you, but then I'd have to kill you."

"Seriously? Over a coffee recipe?"

His twinkly grin came back. "It's an ancient Chinese secret, passed down in my family for generations."

"Yeah, Hanson is such a Chinese name."

"Oh, OK, it's an ancient Danish secret. Twist my arm and I'll tell you." He held out his arm towards her as if he actually expected her to physically twist it. Before she could decide if he was serious or not, he snatched the arm back.

"Alright, I give, I give! It's cinnamon. I mix a teaspoon of cinnamon in the grounds of each pot. And don't bother saying, you can buy cinnamon flavored coffee premade. It has to be actual fresh cinnamon, added separately."

So that explained the two jars of ground cinnamon he'd bought yesterday on their grocery shopping trip.

"Uh, oh, you've told me the secret. Does that mean you have to kill me now?"

"Nah." He reached out and actually chucked her under the chin like she was a five-year-old. "You're too cute to kill."

She wasn't sure if she should be complimented or insulted at the way he called her "cute". Eric stood up and flashed her a brilliant smile. "It's a beautiful day. I'm starting an awesome new job. I got compliments on my coffee, a pretty girl called me handsome, and I'm living on a tropical island. I'm stoked."

"How many cups of coffee have you had?" This was just way too perky for a normal person to be in the morning.

"Just the one."

"So, this is normal?" She waved a hand at his smile.

"Yep. Better get used to it. I'm off," he declared. But before he actually walked out the back door, he turned and leaned down, so that his face was right in front of her.

"Is my face clean?" he asked with laughter in his eyes.

She was so stunned by having those laughing hazel eyes six inches from hers that she could only nod.

"Thanks! This is going to be great, having a girl for a roommate. Another guy would have let me walk out the door with milk on my face.

Have a nice day." He gave her a quick wave as he bounced happily out the door, heading up the street towards the fire station with a quick, loping stride.

Before he got away, she poked her head out the door and called out, "Thanks for making coffee!"

He flipped a backward hand wave and replied, "My privilege to serve, ma'am."

Michelle had to get ready to go to her job too, but she sat and finished her coffee first. It would be a shame to waste coffee that tasted so good. She wondered if she should feel honored that he'd revealed his ancient Danish secret, or would he tell it to anybody who expressed interest?

She also wondered if he'd mind if she tried a little of his bark and twig cereal, just for the sake of comparison.

9

Eric Hanson was without a doubt the most polite roommate a girl could ever have. He not only put the toilet seat down, he put the lid down too. He cleaned up after himself, never hogged the bathroom, and always apologized when he uttered a four-letter colorful metaphor. He actually texted Michelle from the grocery store and asked if she needed anything. She'd never heard so much, please, thank you, yes ma'am in her entire life. She wasn't sure if it was his nature or his military training, but she liked it.

He expressed sincere and copious gratitude and many thanks that she had rearranged things in the medicine cabinet, the tiny linen closet, the kitchen cabinets and the refrigerator to accommodate his possessions and groceries. It really had been unnecessary for him to thank her. He was paying to live in this house, of course there should be space for him. He didn't need to thank her for making room for his stuff. But he thanked her anyway.

He smiled and joked and asked her how her day had been. And he actually seemed interested when she told him how her day had been.

One day he brought her two home-made chocolate chip cookies, from a batch that his boss had brought in, baked by his wife. He said he'd managed to grab her a couple before the rest of the crew scarfed them all down.

That went way above and beyond the duty of a roommate.

She also found out that having a tall roommate was convenient when it came to swiping down the occasional spider from the ceiling.

"It's not that I'm afraid of them or anything," she assured him. "It's just that since you're taller, I don't have to stand on a chair."

Eric just smiled as he deposited the paper towel containing the deceased arachnid into the trash can. "Not a problem, ma'am. It's my privilege to serve."

A jar that she couldn't get open, no matter how much twisting, tapping or swearing she used, he opened with one quick twist. Although he had moaned and groaned dramatically and pretended to fail, and had handed the jar, with its already loosened lid, back to her saying, "I can't get it. You try."

There were adjustments to be made as new roommates, especially roommates of opposite genders. Without actually discussing it, they both remembered to put on their long, concealing bathrobes when traveling between bedrooms and bathroom. They had clarified, on the first day, which body parts could and could not be scratched in the common areas. They agreed to take turns cleaning the bathroom. Eric never shirked or complained when it was his turn, in fact he did a better job than she did. And he actually sang as he cleaned. Off-key of course, but he sang nonetheless.

"How can you sing when you're scrubbing the toilet?" she couldn't help asking.

"Well, I look at it like this. You can scrub the head and sing, or you can scrub the head and be miserable. Either way, you're still scrubbing the head."

She realized she had adjustments of her own to make, one morning when she was in the bathroom drying her hair. Since her hair was long, it took a while. Over the hum of the dryer, she heard a pounding on the door and Eric's voice from the other side yelling desperately, "Michelle! Hate to bother you, but there's a guy out here needs to pee like a racehorse! And I don't think the neighbors would appreciate it if I go out and do it in the street!"

Oops. She turned off the dryer and set it down, opening the door to see Eric hopping up and down in the hall like a demented kangaroo. There was no opportunity for her to ogle as he pushed past her and slammed the bathroom door in her face. A moment later she heard a loud, relief-filled howl of "Gaaah!"

After that, she took her hair dryer into her bedroom and plugged it in next to her bed. That way, she could sit down while drying her hair, and didn't need to inconvenience a roommate when he needed to pee like a racehorse.

One day she went to work and left a load of laundry in the washing machine. When she got home, it had been dried and folded neatly. When she next saw Eric and thanked him, he just said, "Not a problem. I needed to wash my skivvies."

She was just glad her laundry that day had consisted of sheets and towels, and not her underwear.

When he went out to the patio to use his weight bench, Michelle went into the living room and unrolled her yoga mat. With him back there lifting and sweating, he wouldn't be able to see her yoga routine. Some of those poses were kind of – exposing. She especially didn't want him to see her doing Downward Dog. She made a point of finishing up before he was done so she could be in the kitchen drinking water and sneaking glances at him from the back door.

When she realized he had stopped, she quickly pretended to be washing a glass at the sink as he came in wiping his face and reaching into the fridge for a bottle of water.

"If you want, I can help start you with some weights," he said. "Develop your biceps a little." He held up his arm and turned his fist back and forth.

Her mouth went a little dry at the sight of that well-developed bicep.

"That way you can beat me up if I get out of line."

She wondered what, specifically, he meant by "getting out of line", or if he was just being his usual joking self.

"OK," she agreed. "That sounds like fun. I could show you some yoga poses too if you want. It's great for relaxing and reducing stress and PMS."

Oops. TMI.

Eric was polite enough to ignore her accidental mention of PMS, which she appreciated. Most guys got seriously freaked out at the mention of something so feminine. But he did look a little dubious at the idea of doing yoga with her.

"I don't know about that. When you do that one where you stick your butt up in the air," *Damn, he had seen her doing Downward Dog.* "I'm afraid I'd fall on my face and break my nose again."

"You've done yoga before? And you broke your nose?" She tried not to laugh, and looked at his straight, slender nose. It had no bump or crookedness that might indicate having been broken. "You don't look like you've broken it."

"Here, feel it." He actually took her hand in his. His long fingers were warm and strong. He held her index finger and pressed it against the top of his nose. The bump was tiny, too small to be visible.

"I didn't break it doing yoga, or any other kind of exercise. My first day on a ship, the first hour in fact. I was so excited to be there. Then, I tripped over a knee knocker and fell flat on my face. Boy, did I feel like a dork! Bled like a stuck pig too. Not that I've ever actually seen a stuck pig, but I've heard they bleed a lot. I was the first patient in my own sick bay. How sad is that? You know how they set a broken nose?" She was already giggling at his expression of wounded pride. He held up his hands with the bottoms of his palms squeezed together. "Imagine your nose in here," and he twisted the hands with a hard jerk that made her own nose hurt just to imagine it.

"Did you set it yourself?"

"No, another corpsman did it. Laughed his ass off the whole time. Called me Knee Knockers for the whole cruise. That's six months in civilian time. He still sends me a Christmas card every year, addressed to Knee Knockers Hanson. And, I got blood all over my brand-new uniform." Somehow, he made it sound like dirtying his uniform was as painful as the broken nose.

"Guess that was hell on laundry day," she said with a giggle.

"Yeah, but since then I've learned a dozen ways to clean blood off things."

Despite the ominousness of that statement, she couldn't help but laugh at his dismay over the event. He looked pouty. She'd never realized how cute it was to see a grown man pout.

"You're laughing at me. That's not nice."

"I'm sorry if I'm damaging your tender male ego," But her continued giggles didn't back that statement up.

"Hey, I was wounded! I was deformed! Have some sympathy."

"You are not deformed." It was impossible to tell the nose had ever been broken just by looking at it. The tiny bump on the cartilage could only be felt under her finger and wasn't visible on the outside. "Did you get a medal?"

"Yeah, the Biggest Dork on Board Award."

"Is that an official Navy award?"

"No, they made it up just for me."

"I like your nose," she said, then immediately found herself blushing at her impetuous statement.

He turned towards her and grinned, his only indication that her observation had surprised him being that his eyebrows nearly touched his hairline. He briefly touched the proboscis in question.

"Thank you," he replied politely. "It's my father's. As long as we're exchanging compliments, I like your," he looked at her for a moment, as if undecided as to which feature to mention, "hair."

He was so much more of a social person than she was. He liked to talk and he seemed to have friends everywhere. She'd be willing to bet he had a thousand friends on social media. He liked country music and Star Wars and X Men and all those geeky movies, and seemed to make a new friend every day. He'd experienced a lot in the Navy, maybe more than he actually talked about, and he'd been everywhere. She'd barely been outside the state of California, and compared to him she felt like an unsophisticated country bumpkin.

There was something about him, a serenity running under his skin, flowing through his soul. Not placidity – that insinuated sluggishness, and Eric was the antithesis of sluggish. His boundless, bubbly energy was a thing of wonder. But some sort of peacefulness, of calm, thrummed beneath his skin, only occasionally interrupted by a brief spark of worry that once in a while escaped in a swift, quickly suppressed glance. Amazing it was, for someone who'd seen death and been shot at. If she'd had those experiences, she'd be a hot, quivering mess, even more than she already was.

A few weeks after they became roommates, Michelle asked Eric how his new job was going. He was cooking dinner for them both. She'd told him it wasn't necessary for him to feed her, but he'd merely said that it was no more effort than cooking for one. His culinary specialty seemed to be cremating cow flesh on the grill.

"Job's great!" he said enthusiastically. "We've had four heart attacks, all of whom survived, three divers with the bends who had to go to the decompression chamber, one dislocated shoulder, three anaphylactic shocks, one of which I had to intubate. You'd think people with peanut allergies would be more careful. Three broken wrists, two of them on the same person. If I ruled the world, skateboards would be illegal. Eight, count 'em, eight sunstrokes. When will people learn the three rules of sun protection – hat, sunblock, hydration. One fainter who was probably pregnant. The boyfriend proposed right there in the ambulance, it was so romantic. I've lost count of the bee stings. Be careful up on Bird Park Road, I think there's a big beehive in the bushes there. One kid who put a fish hook through his cheek. That one was the worst. Lord, I hate seeing kids get hurt. I almost had to treat his mom too; I thought she was going to have a stroke." He paused a moment. "And a bunch of other stuff you probably don't want to hear about."

"You mean bar fights, right?" She knew he was probably referring to calls to treat the victims of alcohol-inspired altercations. She'd witnessed more than one herself when escorting her dad out of various watering holes. It was one time when her dad's lack of interest in the world around him had worked to his advantage. He at least didn't bother getting involved in any brawls.

Eric nodded. "Yeah. They call us in to determine if the participants are healthy enough to go to jail."

"And one kitten rescued from a tree," he added.

"You're joking about that last one, right?"

"Nope, it really happened, but it was on my own time on my way home from work. The poor kid was sitting there crying. I couldn't just walk by, could I?" He put a finger to his lips. "Just don't tell the firefighters; they think they have a monopoly on cat rescues."

She smiled and said, "Don't worry, your secret is safe with me."

Eric grinned back. "You know, one of the odd things about this island is that there's a casino with no gambling and a bird park with no birds."

"There used to be a bird zoo up there," she told him. "You can still see the cages. But all the birds were sold to the Los Angeles Zoo in the 1960s."

"And a casino just means little house, not a gambling den," he said, showing that he'd paid attention to what she'd told him the day he'd moved in.

10

Michelle stood in the bathroom doorway looking at the shower curtain. It had fish on it. Bright orange and blue and red tropical fish. It was a colorful and cheerful addition to the otherwise plain bathroom.

It wasn't the shower curtain that had been hanging there this morning.

Eric came out of his room, dressed for work. He was on the night shift this week. She gave him a stern look and hooked a thumb in the direction of the fish-printed curtain.

"What happened to my shower curtain?"

"You mean, our shower curtain? I replaced it. The other one was nasty."

"Where's the one that I had?"

"In the trash, where it belongs. There's not a lot of options to choose from in the shops here, but I think this one looks nice. It's cheerful. And look, it has matching hooks, shaped like fish. I think that one is winking at you."

His nonchalance about just marching in as if he owned the place and changing things annoyed her. She knew deep down that it wasn't a big deal but she couldn't help getting snotty over the situation.

"Who do you think you are just throwing out my shower curtain and putting up this gaudy aquarium? You had no right to do that. You just threw mine away without even asking me? Where do you get off doing something like that?"

"What's wrong with it?"

She had no good answer to that question, because really, there was nothing wrong with it. It was an adorable shower curtain, and the old one had been in need of replacing. So what was the problem?

You started this stupid fight, she thought. *Now what do you say?*

"It clashes with our toothbrushes!"

He glanced at his toothbrush, resting in all its purple glory next to her pink one, the two brushes sitting companionly side by side, calmly observing the whole stupid argument. Eric probably had no idea how difficult it had been for her to find a pink toothbrush that was intended for use by an adult and didn't have Disney princesses on it. She knew her whole complaint sounded stupid and juvenile, but she couldn't help herself.

"Seriously? That's your problem? You don't like the shower curtain because it doesn't match the toothbrushes?"

No that wasn't really the problem. She wasn't quite sure what the problem was, she just knew that there was a problem.

Eric turned in the direction of his bedroom. "Where are you going?" she asked sharply. She'd never have pegged him as the type of person to walk away from an argument.

"I'm going to get my laptop to look for a shower curtain identical to the one you had, if you want it back so badly. I refuse to dig that POS out of the trash. Maybe Amazon will have a plain white boring shower curtain with a ripped corner and mold along the edge. They have everything."

"Are you calling me boring?" Of course she zoomed in on the most negative word he'd said.

"No, you're not boring. But that shower curtain, in addition to being torn and dirty, was bor-ring with a capital B. Seriously, I almost fall asleep every time I shower."

"So if you're asleep in the shower, then it must be a tortured cat howling in there."

"Now that's mean," he said, and yet, just like before, he still smiled through her Raging Bitch. But even his sweet happy grin didn't pacify her.

"That was my shower curtain in my bathroom and you should have consulted me before just changing it."

His grin diminished a little but didn't disappear entirely. "Look, Michelle, I realize it's your house and I'm just the tenant here. But I didn't think you'd mind if I replaced something that needed it."

Technically, that was exactly how it was, her house with him as her renter, but when stated out loud like that, made her sound petty and mean, uptight and bitchy. That was her, Michelle the Bitch. What had happened to her being a nicer person? What had happened to the respect she had told Eric she could do? She was regressing back to the Raging Bitch she used to be, and she didn't like that.

The realization of it made her angry. Angry at herself for being unable to function in a normal human relationship. Being angry made her lash out.

"Fine, keep it," she snapped.

"I thought you wanted the old one back."

"No, that one is fine. Keep it."

"Are you sure?" He tilted his head questionably.

"I said it's fine! It's fine!"

"Why is it fine now if it wasn't fine a minute ago?"

"Because it just is, that's why."

"So it's fine?"

"Yes it's fine! Are you deaf? Leave the fish curtain there."

"So the fish curtain is fine?"

Was he purposely yanking her chain? She was seriously getting sick of hearing and saying the word *fine* over and over.

"Yes, it's fine. It's wonderful. It's perfect. It's the most gorgeous shower curtain in the world. Everyone in California should run right out and get the same one."

Just like in the past, he still smiled despite her snotty sarcasm.

"OK, if you're sure it's fine."

She flashed him a look that made him dance back out of striking distance.

"I'm leaving for work now. Have a nice evening. Enjoy that *fine* shower curtain."

She stomped in the direction of her room, yelling at him, "You're a jerk!" as he chuckled on his way out the door, but she returned to the bathroom as soon as he left.

It wasn't actually about the shower curtain. She wasn't really that petty. The shower curtain he'd put up was actually really cute and fun. Much like Eric himself. And he'd been right, the old one had been in need of replacing.

The problem was about her inability to function in an actual human relationship.

You're such a nitwit, she thought. *Just when you think you have this roommate/friendship/respect thing figured out, you go all psycho over something as unimportant as a piece of plastic.*

He probably thought she was bat-shit crazy. She'd thought for a minute that he was being a jerk about the issue. But no, she had misjudged him. Again. She had misjudged him the day they'd met when she had assumed him to be just another drunk sailor trying to pick her up. That hadn't been the case then, and it wasn't the case now. She was the one who'd been a jerk, and as usual, he was too polite to call her out on it. She felt like a five-year-old trapped in an adult's body.

Maybe she didn't deserve him. Maybe she wasn't good roommate material. Maybe she was still a Raging Bitch.

She should apologize. But when she got up in the morning, he was still at work. When she got home from her job, his bedroom door was closed, which meant he was already in bed asleep, and she was not about to go into his room and wake him up. That would be rude, and besides, he probably slept naked. He really didn't seem like the pajama type.

How did Eric manage that weird changing schedule he had?

It was Saturday before she saw him again. She made a point of getting up early so as not to miss him.

"I'm sorry," she said as soon as he walked in the door. Surprisingly, he was dressed in civilian clothes and carrying his uniform in a plastic bag.

He tilted his head and smiled. Of course. He always smiled. The man did not know how to frown.

"Is this about my fine shower curtain?" he asked.

"Our fine shower curtain."

"No need to apologize. But if you want to talk about it, can we do it in the kitchen? I need to get this into the washer ASAP." He lifted the plastic bag a little. "I've been bled on, puked on, and sneezed on in the last twelve hours. Good thing I had a change of clothes at work or I'd be walking home in my skivvies."

"Eeww," she said as she followed him into the kitchen and watched him put his soiled clothes in to wash. "Not about you walking home in your skivvies," she qualified. That sight would have been a gift to the women of Avalon, though she wouldn't say that to him. "The eeww is about you getting bled, puked and sneezed on. I hope not all from the same person."

"Well the puking and sneezing were. But everyone is fine."

"Look, Eric," she said, "I'm really sorry I went off on you about the shower curtain. It was so stupid. I mean, the shower curtain isn't stupid. It's nice. But I was stupid. And mean, and bitchy. I'm such an idiot!"

"Sweetheart," he started to say, which she knew from previous experience meant that he was about to make a joke or say something funny. But she was on a roll and didn't give him a chance.

"I acted like a jerk and I'm a bad roommate who can't even discuss stuff without turning into a psycho, but sometimes I just can't help myself and it's so stupid and moronic, and the shower curtain really is fine and I mean that, I'm not being sarcastic. I'm such a moron, an idiot, a complete and utter nincompoop! I shouldn't have gotten all snotty and bitchy over something as trivial as a shower curtain. It's actually nice, and it was nice of you to get it. The other one was old and torn. But did I appreciate your help? No! I go off like some sort of bat-shit crazy lunatic and you probably think I'm insane. And you'd be right. I don't deserve to have a roommate, much less a great one like you. I can't believe you actually want to live here with me. If I were you, I'd run away screaming. But I couldn't help being a snot and maybe I'm just not good roommate material, and I suck at relationships, especially with men, and-"

She was working herself up into a mini panic attack, complete with tingling skin on her face, a cold sweat and pounding heart, not even looking at Eric anymore. She ceased her rant only when she felt two hands grab her upper arms and twitch a little, almost shaking her to get her attention and shut her up.

"Michelle! Take a breath." Eric instructed. "In through the nose, out through the mouth."

She gasped a little, jerking her eyes towards him, trying to breathe. *In through the nose, out through the mouth.* It took a little panting, but she managed to calm herself into something resembling normalcy, and she stuck her hands behind her back so that he couldn't try to check her pulse again.

"It's OK," he insisted. "Don't work yourself up into a fit. Seriously, you're not nearly as neurotic as you seem to think you are and for the record, you are good roommate material. And by the way, I think 'bat-shit crazy lunatic' is a bit redundant, but I don't think you're either." He let go of her arms and she had to catch herself, having in those few seconds become dependent on him to keep her on her feet.

"Is nincompoop a real word?" he asked. "Or is that one of your creations, like assholeness?"

"I didn't make that up. It's in the dictionary."

Having him ask that silly question helped her break out of and defeat her moronic ranting and raving. If Eric sincerely didn't believe she was a redundant bat-shit crazy lunatic, she'd have to take his word for it. He hadn't steered her wrong yet.

Why was he so damn nice? Why was he being helpful and sweet, rather than unpleasant like her? Even his disagreement about her assessment of herself was offered helpfully.

She looked at his face, and inspiration hit her. "Wait a sec," she said, and pulled her phone out of her pocket.

He looked surprised. "Hey, we haven't finished our fight yet, and you're playing on your phone? Someone needs to get their priorities straight."

She held up a finger in a 'wait a minute' gesture. "This is important." She swiped and typed as he goggled at her.

"More important than our fine shower curtain fight? I was just getting into it. More important than you asphyxiating over your anxiety?"

She finished her task, hit the final button, and slipped the phone back into her pocket. "Yes," she said simply. A moment later, Eric's phone chirped, and she nodded at his pocket. "You have an email."

"I know, I heard it. I'll read it later."

"I think you should read it now. It's from me."

His eyes went wide. "Seriously? You had to send me an email when I'm standing right in front of you? You can't just say what you have to say in actual vocal words?"

"Seriously. This has to be conveyed by email."

With a put-upon sigh and a muttered, "this is stupid," he pulled out his phone and swiped it, then stared disbelievingly at the screen.

"Read it," she insisted.

From: Michelle Diaz
Subject: Shower curtain
Date: May 18, 2019
To: Eric Hanson
Dear Eric,
I apologize for calling you a jerk. That was rude. You may have said a thing or two that made sense. I'll think about it.
Sincerely, Michelle

He burst out laughing. The shower curtain controversy was over.

"Come here," he invited, giving her a brief hug and pat on the back. "Obviously I'm not the only big goof in this house."

"Well, I'd rather be a big goof than a redundant bat-shit crazy lunatic," she said. "I'm sorry about the fight. I really do like the fine fish shower curtain, and it was nice of you to put it up."

He released her and went on, "I have a theory about why me replacing the shower curtain bothered you so much."

"A theory?" she repeated, still a bit stunned at that brief hug, the small back pat that seemed like the answer to all life's trials and tribulations.

Slow down, Michelle. Get a grip. It was just a hug, from a man whose nature was to be physically affectionate.

"Yes. I think I know why it was an issue for you," Eric said. "And it's not that you're any of those unpleasant names you called yourself, because those aren't true."

"Please explain it to me, then. I'm dying to know." She didn't mean that sarcastically. She sincerely wanted to hear his theory. Maybe it would help explain, and help her defeat, some of the faults in her psyche.

Eric leaned against the washing machine behind him. "I think it's about control." At her disbelieving look, he said, "Hear me out. I'm guessing, from what you told me about how things were with you and your father, that you probably felt like you had no control over your life. Of course, you could control what you did, the training you took, your job and so on. But you couldn't control how your father chose to live his life. You couldn't control the destructive path he took, and you couldn't control the circumstances that led to his death. So you find it, let's just say, upsetting, when things are taken out of your control."

He was well aware of the feeling of inadequacy that had been pounded into her since childhood. No wonder she had control issues. Another reason for him to think she was bat-shit crazy.

"So you're saying I have control issues? That sounds so neurotic. Like a crazy person."

He held up a finger. "Do not say the word bat-shit, please."

"If you insist."

"I insist, sweetheart. There's nothing wrong with trying to be in control of your life. Just as long as you don't-"

"Go bat-shit crazy?"

'More like, as long as you don't eviscerate your roommate over a shower curtain."

"Eviscerate? Doesn't that involve bleeding?"

He held up his arms in front of him as if looking for signs of laceration.

"I'm a quick healer." Then he yawned.

"Am I boring you?" she asked.

"No, sweetheart, you never bore me. But I've been up for over twenty-four hours and it's catching up with me. Time for me to hit the rack."

He reached out and put a hand on her shoulder. "Don't be sorry for being yourself."

"What if myself is b-"

He gave her a censorious look.

"If you're going to keep calling yourself crazy, I just might have to take away our very fine fish shower curtain."

"You better not. I adore that thing. In fact, I'm really hung up on it."

"Actually, I think it's the curtain that's hung up."

He walked over and looked at the washer, which still had twenty minutes to go in its cycle, then rubbed a hand over his face, yawning again.

"You poor thing," she apologized. "You're exhausted and here I am blathering. You should go – what's that term you used?"

"Hit the rack. I just have to wait until the washer finishes so I can put this stuff in the dryer."

"I'll do it," she offered.

His look of gratitude was heart-warming. "Great! Thanks. Do you want to come tuck me in?"

Tuck him in? No. Yes. That was a question with absolutely no right answer.

He grinned apologetically. "Sorry. I'm so tired I'm talking nonsense. Good night."

"Good night," she managed to mutter. "Even though it's eight a.m."

"Smarty pants," he called over his shoulder as he walked towards his room.

"I'm sorry about the fight," Michelle called after him.

He closed his door gently, and then leaned against it briefly.

"Oh, sweetheart," he muttered to himself. "You still think this is a fight."

11

Slicing bagels is the most common type of kitchen accident and a leading cause of trips to the emergency room. But Michelle didn't need an emergency room. She had her very own personal paramedic, sitting in the living room with his laptop, Skyping with a buddy.

For a moment she stared at the red, dripping slice running down the length of her left index finger, then called out, "Eric?"

"Yo," came floating back from the living room.

"Remember when you said, if it bleeds, you'd bandage it?"

There was an immediate loud *thunk* sound – had he dropped his laptop on the floor?

It was amazing how quickly he was at her side, even considering the small size of the house. In a nanosecond, he was holding her bleeding finger over the sink. Sparkly, joking Eric was set aside, and medical professional Eric took over.

"What did you cut it on?"

She nodded at the bread knife on the floor.

"Do you feel faint? Come over and sit down."

He was trying to nudge her towards a chair at the table, at the same time opening a cupboard door to pull out a first aid kit.

"I don't feel faint." She resisted his nudge toward the kitchen chair. "I'm sorry to bother you. I think I have a box of Band-Aids in the bathroom under the sink, but I don't want to drip any blood on the floor."

"Band-Aids are for amateurs," he said. "And don't worry, I know a dozen ways to clean blood off stuff. Have you had a tetanus vaccine?"

"Yes. I had my booster six months ago."

That surprised him. Most civilians didn't bother.

Obediently, she sat down as Eric set the first aid kit on the table next to her.

"When did we get a first aid kit?" she asked.

"I brought it with me when I moved in. I can't believe you didn't have one," he said a bit disapprovingly.

Despite her sore, bleeding finger, this was kind of fun, seeing Eric in his serious work mode.

He pulled out an antiseptic swab and cleaned the cut, then dropped the used wipe on the table and inspected her finger. His look of solemn competence was downright captivating. "This is a nice shallow cut. Easy-peasy. You don't even need stitches."

"If I needed stitches, would you be able to do them for me?"

"I can, and I have. But you don't need them. It's too long for a bandage, though. I'll need to gauze it." He next pulled out a white stick that kind of looked like a crayon.

"Are you going to draw a picture?"

"It's anhydrous aluminum sulfate. It acts as a vasoconstrictor."

"You know, Eric, I'm not a paramedic. Or a nurse. Or a doctor. I'm just an ignorant mechanic."

He gave her a brief apologetic smile. "Translation – it's a styptic pencil. It inhibits bleeding. Same thing guys use when they cut themselves shaving. This might sting a little."

It did sting a little and she couldn't help just the tiniest intake of breath as Eric rubbed the styptic pencil along the cut until the bleeding stopped.

"Sorry," he said briefly as he put the pencil down and pulled out a roll of gauze in a plastic wrapper, which he opened up and wrapped the gauze around her finger, then picked up a roll of adhesive tape to secure it. His treatment was quick but not rushed, efficient, skillful.

A tiny drop of blood had fallen on the floor. Not to worry; he knew a dozen ways to clean up blood from stuff. Sand soaked it up pretty good. It was only a tiny drop, but it was also a man-sized pool of it as, unbidden and unexpected, the compartment door he usually managed to keep tightly shut managed to slide open just a little, just enough, just too much. He closed his eyes, only for a moment, but it was enough to conjure up the dusty field hospital in the desert. All the sutures in the world hadn't been sufficient that day, not from him, not from the surgeon across the gurney, and certainly not for the unlucky bastard on the gurney whose truck had run over an IED.

It was the sounds that assaulted his brain the most: the screams, the rumble of trucks just outside, the barked orders and his clipped responses of, "Aye, Sir," muffled behind the surgical masks they'd hurriedly slipped on, hooking the elastic over their ears. The squishy sound of rubber tourniquets, the rattle of an IV stand. The screams. And the horrifying silence when it all went to shit.

He somehow managed to squeeze it all back into its compartment and slide the compartment door shut in the endless fraction of a second, before Michelle noticed, and finished bandaging the easy-peasy little sliced finger that didn't even need stitches. He'd wrapped on little more gauze than such a minor cut required, but she seemed satisfied with the job.

He had never, ever in his career had a problem with the sight of blood. No issue with the sight of it or the smell of it or the sound it could make when gushing. He'd never even flinched at the taste of it when it sprayed in his face. But there was a reason that medics at any level were advised not to treat family members, or friends, or even roommates. It made them vulnerable, vulnerable to losing focus, vulnerable to the unexpected opening of usually closed and locked compartment doors.

His voice remained the cool, calm professional tone that he always succeeded in maintaining. "There you go, all pretty." He tore off the adhesive tape securing the gauze and returned the roll to the first aid kit. "Just don't get it wet for a few days."

"Dang. I was just about to wash my hair," she said, looking at the wrapped-up finger and wiggling it a little.

"That could be a problem," Eric replied. "Well let's see. What are your options?"

After a moment of consideration, he got out a yellow dishwashing glove from the drawer and gave it to her. "You can wear this and put one of your hair fru-frus around the wrist to hold it tight, and you should be OK."

"Hair fru-fru?" she asked with amusement. Eric grinned.

"Yeah, that elastic thing you put on your hair. It should hold the glove tight enough to keep water out. Or better yet, a work glove. We both wear them, you know." He grinned and wiggled his fingers in front of her face, reminiscent of the day they'd met when he'd declared the two of them to be twins separated at birth. "Why do you wear those things anyway?"

"Work gloves? To keep my hands clean. So people don't believe me when I tell them I'm a mechanic."

Eric chuckled. "Actually, I meant why do you wear those hair fru-frus?"

"Duh. To hold my hair back, silly."

"I know that. I mean, why the ponytail? You have such pretty hair. Why hide it?"

Whoa, that sounded kind of flirty. But now that he was done bandaging her finger, he had his usual silly, teasing grin showing. He wasn't flirting with her. It was just Eric, being Eric.

"It gets hot. Or it gets in the way. Have you ever had long hair?" she asked him.

He gave her one of his incredulous, down the nose looks.

"Sweetheart, I decided to enlist in the service when I was fifteen. What do you think?"

"Well, take my word for it then. Long hair can be a pain sometimes. Every once in a while, I'm tempted to cut it off." Her hair was laying loose over her neck at the moment and she reached up – with her unbandaged hand – and grabbed the length of it, looking around as if for a pair of scissors.

"No, don't do that!" He actually sounded a little panicky at the notion for a moment. "That would be a crime against humanity."

What a goof he was.

"Easy for you to say. You don't have to brush it or wash it or dry it."

"Well, I could."

Wait, had he just offered to wash her hair? Had she heard right?

"Huh?" Her response sounded really stupid but it was about all she could manage at the moment.

"I'll wash it for you. You won't have to worry about getting the gauze wet, and it will help me understand your life challenges, caring for it."

"Why would you want to do that?"

"Let's just say I'm curious about other people's lives, and I like to help my friends. What do you say? Let me wash your hair for you."

She looked at him. "Why do I have the feeling your next sentence is going to be, it's the least you can do for a guy putting his life on the line to defend your freedom?"

He grinned childishly. "Well that worked last time, didn't it? You let me walk you home, and now we're roommates. Win-win."

What could it hurt? It was nice of him to offer to help her out. "Sure, knock yourself out," she agreed, trying to sound casual. It was just a friend helping out a friend. It wasn't like a lover running his hands through her hair or anything. Still, she couldn't help wondering, just for a moment, in a manner totally inappropriate for roommates, if the kitchen table would bear the weight of both of them.

It took him only a minute to go to the bathroom and come back with her shampoo, conditioner, two towels, and the wide-tooth comb. She looked at the stuff in his hands.

"Wow, for someone with no experience with long hair, you sure figured out all the required equipment."

"Sure beats an M16 or a flak vest. Here, lean over the sink. Is that uncomfortable? Does it hurt your back?"

"No, it's fine."

She felt a bit awkward, having her roommate washing her hair. But he'd seemed so childishly eager to help her out. That was a big part of his persona – he helped people. Of course, that made sense, given his profession.

He was always helping her, and she found she really liked it, whether it was swiping away spiders, drying the dishes when she washed them, or texting her from the grocery store to ask if she needed anything. The last time, she had hesitated when she read the text. Yes, she needed something, but wasn't sure if she should ask him to get it. She'd texted back, "Yes, but I don't think you'll feel comfortable buying it."

His quick return text showed what good intuition he had. "Don't worry, I'm a big boy. I know what tampons are. Same brand as usual?"

She'd almost dropped her phone when she read that, but then realized, they had been sharing a medicine cabinet for a couple of months now. There were no secrets there. And yes, he'd come home with the tampons, her usual brand, and hadn't even let her pay him back for their cost. Unlike most other guys, he had refrained from making crude jokes about her mood when the time came to use them.

He turned on the water and they waited for it to warm up, then he held his hand under the stream. "Feel this. Is the temperature OK? Too warm, too cold?" He actually picked up her right hand for her to check the water temperature, probably to make sure she didn't accidentally put the bandaged one in the water.

"Maybe just a little warmer."

He adjusted the faucet and when she told him the water temperature was perfect, he let her lean into the sink and gathered up her hair to put it in.

This was nice. It felt good to have someone else do this simple task for her. She enjoyed the feeling of his fingers against her scalp as he applied the shampoo and kneaded it through her hair, as he said, "You have a lot of hair, gonna need a little more shampoo."

She closed her eyes, not only to prevent any shampoo or water from getting into them, but also to relish the sensuous feel of his hands on her scalp as he rubbed her head and separated her hair to make sure the shampoo was distributed evenly.

She shouldn't be enjoying this so much. She shouldn't be getting turned on by the mere feeling of him squishing shampoo suds through her hair and the sensation of him rubbing her scalp.

But she couldn't avoid it.

"Have you washed girl's hair very often?" she couldn't help asking, considering how good he was at it.

"Not often, but I've done it before," was his casual reply.

She just couldn't keep herself from conjuring up a mental image of Eric and some past – or present – girlfriend in the shower together, washing each other's hair. Washing each other's – everything. But as his roommate, she just got the kitchen sink.

Jeez, Michelle, quit letting your imagination run away with you!

"I was sixteen," he started to say. "My sister Diane had broken her wrist after her son convinced her to try out his skateboard."

She shouldn't have felt relieved, but she did.

"Was this before or after the wedding reception where you ended up in the ER?"

"Before. Good thing too. Nobody would get near me for weeks after that incident. For a while, I looked like I had a cross between smallpox and the bubonic plague."

"I thought your sister's name was Brenda."

"This was my other sister. I have two. And two brothers. Diane's husband was out of town on business and her kids weren't old enough to do it, so she came over to our house to ask our mom to help her. But mom was at the store so rather than waiting for her to get home, I offered to do it. But Diane didn't have as much hair as you do. Only about this long," she felt his hand briefly touch her shoulder. "And not all chocolatey brown like yours. Diane's hair is pretty much like mine, not quite blond, not quite brunette. She calls it dirty blond." He'd rinsed out the shampoo and reached for the bottle of conditioner.

Chocolatey? Had he just compared her hair to chocolate? She wasn't quite sure how to take that.

"I wasn't serious about cutting my hair," she admitted as he worked the conditioner down the length of her hair.

"I'm really glad to hear that," he replied instantly.

"It has to do with my mother."

Eric paused his hairdressing service for a moment, as if uncertain how to respond.

"She was sick and weak for a long time before she died. In fact I don't really remember her doing much of anything. But she did brush my hair. I'd sit on the floor in front of the couch, and she'd brush it, and pet it, and tell me how pretty it was. It's pretty much my only memory of her. That's why I've always kept it long."

Every time she put a brush to her hair, she'd close her eyes and think about her mother, doing this simple task, their only mother-daughter bonding experience. She tried to remember what her mother looked like, what kind of person she was, but with every passing month, every year, the memories faded a little and she feared that eventually she wouldn't be able to remember her at all, as if she'd never existed. It scared her to consider that possibility. Only a pathetic loser could forget their own mother.

She had photos. Not many though, and she kept them in her top dresser drawer rather than in a frame on a shelf or hung on the wall. Looking at photos to remember one's mother was somehow, in her mind, cheating. If she couldn't remember with her brain, her psyche, her own cognition, what kind of daughter did that make her? What kind of person? Not a good one.

She'd never talked to anyone about her mother brushing her hair before, not to her cousins from Temecula, not to her friend from high school. It had always been awkward, downright impossible, to talk about personal or emotional things to other people, even to the sociologist at Al-Anon. It might reveal how false her tough, bitchy persona really was. But with Eric, it was different. He knew how fake the Raging Bitch facade was, and he was her friend in spite of it. She could tell him anything, and he never made her feel like a pathetic loser.

Well, maybe there were a few things she couldn't tell him. Like what a cute butt he had, and the weird, inappropriate things about him that she couldn't help her imagination from conjuring up, and how much she enjoyed hearing his silly, loud singing around the house, despite how bad he was at it.

"You're all rinsed out now." He turned off the water.

"Hold still a sec," he instructed, as he picked up her wet hair, piled it on top of her head, and grabbed a towel with the other hand. Wrapping it around her head like a turban, he said, "OK, stand up now."

He set the second towel he'd brought over her shoulders, and she reached up to adjust it around her neck, but he nudged her fingers aside and arranged it himself.

"I've got this," he said, then took the first towel from her head and tossed it across his shoulder.

"You look like an Italian waiter," she said with a smile.

"Ciao, Bella," he replied. "That is the extent of my Italian."

"Don't forget about casino," she reminded him

She reached for the wide-tooth comb. If she didn't comb out her hair before it dried, it would end up as a long brown rat's nest. But of course, Eric never did anything by halves. He took the comb away from her, and pointed at the chair she'd sat in when he'd bandaged her finger.

"Turn around," he instructed. When she sat down, he pulled up the other chair behind her, turned it backward and straddled it, gathering up her hair and smoothing it down her back. He picked up the comb and drew it gently through the strands, discreetly following each stroke with his other hand. Just to make sure it didn't get tangled, of course.

"Tell me if it's too rough," he said. "I don't want to pull your hair."

"It's perfect," she replied, a little too quickly, a little too enthusiastically.

He'd always wanted to get his hands into her hair and he was enjoying the sensation of smoothing its length under the comb and his palms.

Having him comb it out like that, so gently, so careful not to pull or yank on any tangles, made heat curl down her spine just as much as the way his fingers felt smoothing the shampoo and conditioner through it.

This was so not like having her mother brush her hair. Eric's hands along her hair were sinfully sensual, but he obviously had no idea what his touch did to her.

"What if I forget her?" The words snuck out from between reluctant lips, and she couldn't help but wince at the shame that spiraled through her at the possibility. "What if I forget what she looks like? What if I forget she existed?" She knew she didn't have to remind Eric that the "her" she was referring to was her mother.

"You won't forget her," Eric assured her. "If you'd been younger, like three or four, when she died, then maybe you wouldn't be able to remember. It's called childhood amnesia. But at ten, that's old enough to retain memories. I doubt you'd actually forget. Do you have photos of her?"

"Yes." Her voice was small and she worked hard to prevent it from wobbling. Why was she getting like this over something as mundane as washing her hair? She hadn't been so sentimental back in her Raging Bitch days. But since she'd met Eric, somehow the Raging Bitch facade now seemed unnecessary.

"Are they out somewhere? Displayed in a frame? I haven't seen them anywhere around the house. Or do you keep them hidden away in a drawer.?"

"In a drawer." He really did have Spidey sense.

"I think it would help if you put one in a frame and set it someplace where you'll see it. It's not like you'd need it to remember her. It's more that it would be like having her near you, so to speak. Everyone seems to have their photos on their phones or computers, and that's great and all, but there's still something to be said for old-fashioned printed photographs too. Do you look like your mother?"

"No, I look like my dad. Except for being female of course."

"Well, then your dad must have been a good-looking man."

"Are you flirting with me?" She wasn't hoping for it, she wasn't, she wasn't. But still. It was a good thing her back was to him so he couldn't see her face.

God, she was so pathetic. Bitchy one minute, whiney the next. Why would someone as cool as Eric ever flirt with someone as pathetic as her?

He didn't answer right away, being busy combing. "Of course not. It would be highly inappropriate to flirt with my roommate."

She wasn't disappointed at his response, she wasn't, she wasn't.

She turned around quickly, and he stopped combing, lifted his hands away from her as he stared at her in surprise. In one swift movement, she took the comb from his hand, set it on the table, stood up and slid her arms around his neck, and kissed him with a passion and longing she had never experienced before.

What was weird was that he didn't respond. He didn't embrace her, didn't kiss her back, didn't melt into her closeness as she'd thought he might. Neither did he reject her.

"Ouch." A slight tightness tugged at her scalp.

"Oops, I'm sorry!" Eric said. "I missed that tangle there. I'll be more careful."

She blinked, and realized she was still sitting in the chair with her back to Eric and he was still combing her hair out.

Freya, she had just fantasized about making out with her roommate. What a complete and utter dork she was. It was a good thing she had her back to him so he couldn't see the blush of embarrassment on her face.

"Stop twitching," Eric scolded lightly. "I don't want to accidentally pull it again."

When he was done serving as her hairdresser, he put the towels on top of the washer for the next load, then turned back to her with a smile.

"Well, that was fun. Your hair is really beautiful."

Whoa. She hadn't expected that. Her stomach kind of fell out beneath her.

He'd said he wasn't flirting with her.

"Is it OK for me to say that?" he asked. "I don't want to make you feel uncomfortable. It's just an observation."

She turned and looked at him, feeling confident in his silly, friendly smile.

"Well," she said with an exaggerated pause. "As long as we're exchanging observations-" She looked him over, trying to be casual and roommate-like, trying not to drool. What to mention? There was so much to consider.

"Your muscles are-" Gorgeous, sexy, what? "Handsome."

How utterly lame. How woefully inadequate. What an understatement.

What would he say to that?

He was smiling and his eyes were twinkling. "Thanks, sweetheart. Tell me more. I'm a glutton for praise."

This was the kind of teasing she could get into.

"OK, if you insist," she said obligingly. Eric returned to the chair he'd sat in while combing her hair and looked at her expectantly, grinning like a kid. So she obliged him. It was easy to compliment him.

"Your eyes are sparkly. Your nose is pretty." Eric nodded solemnly.

"Yes, I believe we've already established that."

"Your cheekbones make me jealous. Hold up your hands."

He obligingly showed her all ten fingers.

"Your hands look strong. And warm."

Oops, maybe that last compliment went a bit over the line. But Eric just grinned goofily and said, "Well that really boosts my confidence for today."

"Thanks, Eric. For this," she held up the bandaged finger, "and for washing my hair, and for – listening. It's nice of you to put up with me."

"Well, that's what friends are for. You know I don't think I told you how sorry I am about your mother. Not only that she died, but that she missed out on being your mom and having you for a daughter."

"You did tell me, that first day we met when I told you she was dead. You were so sympathetic even though you didn't even know me."

Just his simple, empathetic offering of "You have my sympathy" had meant a lot to her, though she hadn't appreciated it at the time.

Suddenly she remembered what he'd been doing just before she'd cut her finger.

"What about your friend? Weren't you Skyping with someone? I totally barged into your conversation with my clumsiness."

Eric smiled a little guiltily. "Oh yeah, him. He probably hung up. It's pretty late in Iceland. I'll text him tomorrow and explain there was an emergency."

She giggled a little. "Do you think your friend will believe that washing your roommate's hair was an emergency?"

"Well, since it was precipitated by you bleeding, yes that would qualify as an emergency."

She held up her finger and its white gauze wrapping. "If this little cut qualifies as an emergency, what would actual serious bloodshed be considered?"

"A bigger emergency, but let's hope we never have to find out. Speaking of being interrupted, what were you doing when you cut yourself?"

What had she been doing? For a moment, she couldn't remember. It took concentrating on something besides the feel of his hands in her hair, and his words of reassurance regarding her memories of her mother.

"A bagel," she finally said. "I was cutting a bagel. The package said they were pre-sliced, but that was a lie. Another myth told to us by advertisers, along with waterproof mascara."

Eric grinned, obviously remembering the day she'd stained his shirt with her supposedly waterproof mascara. He looked back towards the sink and saw the forgotten bagel sitting on the counter. Picking up the knife, he put it in the sink, and said, "I don't think you're going to want to eat this one now. It's getting dried out and there's blood on it. I'll grab you another one."

"No, don't. I'm not hungry anymore. I think I'll just go dry my hair now. In my room, you know, just in case you need to pee like a racehorse."

"You're never going to let me live that one down, are you?" He was twinkling again.

"Are you kidding? I could hear you howling through the door. The people on the next block probably thought I was torturing a coyote in here."

"Ha-ha, very funny. Thanks, though, for making other arrangements to accommodate me."

"Well, that's what friends are for." She stood up and took a step away, towards her bedroom and hairdryer.

"Do you need help with that?" Eric asked.

Oh, no, she was not going to go there. "I've got it, thanks," she replied, trying to keep it light and casual.

"Thank you," he said unexpectedly.

"What? I'm the one who got my hair washed and combed. I should be thanking you."

"Yes, and you're welcome for that. But I meant, thank you for telling me about your mom. I know it must be hard for you to talk about her, and I don't blame you for that. Thank you for trusting me to tell me about her. I wouldn't mind hearing more when you feel like talking about it. I've been curious, when she died, why didn't your relatives step in to take care of you rather than just leaving you here with your dad? Didn't you say you had cousins on the mainland?"

"Yes, a cousin of my mother's. My dad didn't really have any family. They did have me stay with them in Temecula for the summer that year, and I hated it. Not that I'm bashing Temecula itself. It's a nice place and a pretty area, but it's so far from the ocean. It took two hours to drive to the beach, and that was when there's no traffic. But there's always traffic over there. So I hardly got to see the ocean at all, and that was when I needed to see it the most."

Eric could relate to that. He and some of his buddies had occasionally visited the casinos in the Temecula area when on leave, and the traffic on the I-15 freeway was the stuff of nightmares.

"My mom's cousin, Joyce, she was nice and sympathetic and all, but she had a job and a family too and couldn't spend all her time babysitting me. And when I kicked her kid in the leg for calling my dad a drunk, well that was the end of that vacation. They brought me home and it was a good thing too. Someone needed to keep an eye on my dad, make sure he went to work and ate and stuff like that. Joyce came out here on weekends for a while to help, but she didn't get along with my dad, and it was expensive and time-consuming. So after a while, she came less and less and then stopped coming altogether. I don't think she ever forgave me for kicking her precious little Brucie baby."

"So I'm guessing you're very not close to your cousins?"

"Not really. They come over here maybe once a year, and we met up a couple of times when I was going to technical school on the mainland, but that's about it."

After she'd gone to her room, and he heard her turn on the hairdryer, Eric quickly grabbed a paper towel and a bottle of spray cleaner from under the sink, and obliterated that tiny, huge drop of blood that had fallen on the floor from Michelle's finger and been forgotten during the convenient, delicious distraction of washing her hair. The crumpled, bloodstained paper towel was hurled into the trash can with enough force to hopefully ensure continued closure of compartment doors.

Michelle wanted to remember her mother, and that was good. Remembering deceased loved ones was admirable, a celebration of their lives and the love their survivors felt.

But there were other, unpleasant things that a person would rather forget.

He'd seen blood in much larger quantities, in much more traumatic circumstances, and not once had it ever bothered him. He'd kept his cool, always, even when everyone around him was going to pieces. Sometimes literally going to pieces.

But this wasn't just any blood. That tiny little red dot on the floor was Michelle's blood, and the fact that it was her blood transformed that tiny dot into a huge key, a key large enough to unlock his compartment doors, doors he strived to keep closed.

A dab of bleach, a wet paper towel, and the little, huge drop of blood disappeared. But the memories remained, even with the compartment doors closed and locked.

Just for good measure, he fished the paper wad out of the can and flung it back in with a hearty, but silent, *Take that, memories!*

12

TEN YEARS EARLIER, IRAQ

It was a day of firsts for Petty Officer First Class Eric Hanson.

Eric had grown up in Florida, so he thought he understood hot weather. But the heat of Florida was nothing compared to the moisture-sucking furnace blast of the desert. Some of the guys tried to justify it by saying, but it's a dry heat. It was true that Florida's humidity could be oppressive, but it also was nothing compared to the absolute dryness that soon left both his skin and his innards feeling like the hide of a crocodile.

And the dust! There was no escaping the dust. There was dust in his mouth when he woke up, dust between his toes when he hit the rack. Eric struggled to keep the surgical wards and instruments dust free. There was dust in the water, even somehow, he tasted dust when he consumed sealed MRE's. He was surprised that every living creature in the country didn't have intestines completely blocked by their ingestion of dust.

But he never complained about the heat, the arid air, or the dust, and neither did any of his comrades. Eric had a small plaque stored in his locker, a gift from his mother, that was kept in a zippered plastic bag to try and protect it from the dust. It read, "Home is where the Navy sends me." For the next year, home would be here, in the dust and searing heat. He could only dream about the kiss of salt air, the smell of jet fuel that wafted around the avionics techs, the thump of the catapults that vibrated even down to sickbay as jets launched on the flight deck. That was in the past, and might yet be in the future, but today, he sucked it up in the desert, even as the desert in its turn sucked him dry.

Once a week, if medical staff were available, they held a free clinic for civilians outside the base, about a mile away from the gate to prevent groups of people from gathering close to the facility. This week the clinic had almost been canceled because the base hospital was busy enough that there were no physicians and only one corpsman available to work the clinic, and today that one corpsman was Petty Officer First Class Eric Hanson.

Perhaps some people might not consider it the best possible use of the American taxpayer's money to fund three armed-to-the-teeth Marines, one armored truck, one Navy Corpsman turned temporary Marine, and an officer who was both the CO and the translator, spending half a day administering first aid to Iraqi civilians, but in Eric's mind, it was totally worth it. It offered a brief glimpse of why they were all there – the Navy, the Marines, Army, Air Force and National Guard reservists, of why they were all sweating in this dusty desert – to try and bring this country back from what it had been under Saddam's dictatorship.

"Let's wrap it up, Hanson," Lieutenant Nazari ordered. "Time to get back on the bus to kindergarten."

Eric had to smile at the analogy. Their bus was a heavily armored combat vehicle and their kindergarten was a Marine facility. Before leaving the old school building they'd used to hold the clinic, he'd have to put his battle rattle back on. It was just too heavy and confining to wear while treating patients, and it made some of the civilians nervous and uneasy about talking to him. Of course, he couldn't talk much to the people he saw there. Eric's knowledge of Arabic pretty much consisted of "Hello" and "Goodbye'. But Lt. Nazari, who was of Iraqi descent, was an excellent translator and today at least, with Eric being the only medical person working, he didn't have to wait his turn for her assistance.

"Just one more patient before we head out, Ma'am?" he requested.

"Jeez, Hanson," Nazari replied. "You sound just like my five-year-old nephew when he wants five more minutes and another story before bedtime."

"I have a five-year-old nephew too, Ma'am," he told her. Well actually, the kid was his great-nephew but they didn't need to quibble about details at the moment. "And when I'm home on leave, and he asks for another bedtime story, I always oblige him. Mr. Popper's Penguins is our favorite."

The lieutenant gave in. "Fine, Doc, you had me at penguins. We can take one more."

They looked up to see who was next, who would be their last patient of the day. There were two of them, a young couple, husband and wife, standing with arms around each other's shoulders. Eric glanced at the lieutenant when he heard her quick intake of breath, and she said, "I am neither a physician nor a corpsman, but even I can diagnose this one."

She was right. It was painfully obvious what the couple was here for. The wife, like most Iraqi women, wore a hijab, the headscarf covering her hair, ears, neck and shoulders, and the traditional loose, long-sleeved blouse and ankle-length skirt common in the country. That skirt looked like she had a pumpkin concealed under it. A pumpkin that had been cultivated in close proximity to a nuclear power plant. But what was even more nerve-wracking than the extremely advanced stage of pregnancy was the fact that her bare feet were stained with the blood that dripped from under her skirt.

Lt. Nazari looked at the Marine who had escorted the couple into the clinic. "Did you pat them down?" she asked.

The Marine nodded, his eyes wide as he leaned forward and said in a low voice, nodding towards the expectant mom and her nuclear pumpkin of a belly.

"That thing is alive!"

"That's the plan, Corporal," Eric told him.

As soon as they made eye contact with the husband, he started talking. Talking fast, desperately, gesturing at his wife's belly, looking panicky. Lieutenant Nazari held up one hand to stop him for a moment, and glanced at Eric.

"You know, Hanson, Arabic is not my first language. I was born in Boston, not Baghdad. But I'm pretty sure what he's saying is that the local midwife who was supposed to deliver this baby is unavailable and things don't seem to be progressing the way they should."

Eric's mouth went a bit dry, and not just because of the dry heat. He looked at Lt. Nazari with concern.

"Ma'am, you realize I'm not a doctor. I'm just the Doc."

Most civilians at this point would be saying "Huh?", but the lieutenant understood what Eric was saying.

"You just got a temporary promotion, Doc," she said. "I certainly am not going to deliver this baby, and Corporal Rasmussen there looks like he's about to puke."

Rasmussen did look a bit green about the gills as he stared at the nuclear pumpkin, which chose that moment to visibly roll and heave in an alien-like ripple.

At the same moment, the woman's knees buckled and she sagged towards the floor with a loud moan. Eric leaped to his feet and went to her other side with an additional supportive arm.

"In here," he instructed, and led the couple into the former headmaster's office that was now their exam room. Their treatment table had once accommodated children's schoolwork, but it was as clean as Eric could get it. He flipped a clean paper cover over it, then he and the husband helped the soon-to-be mom, who was white-faced and groaning, onto the surface.

Eric introduced himself to the couple. After all, he was about to get up close and personal with his lady in a way that only her husband had before, and the least they could do was exchange names. He pointed to his name badge, then held out his hand to the father.

"Hanson," he said, and the man understood, shook Eric's hand, then touched his own chest, saying, "Fadhil."

Eric wasn't sure if that was the man's first name or surname, but he nodded and said, "Sir."

Fadhil indicated his wife and said, "Rayah."

Rayah didn't acknowledge the introduction. She screamed and arched her head back in pain. The time for pleasantries was over.

He started to position the patient's feet on the makeshift delivery able, but the husband suddenly stepped in front of him with an outstretched arm between them, and announced loudly, "*La*," which Eric immediately realized was the Arabic word for "No."

Fadhil turned to Lieutenant Nazari and spoke quickly, almost angrily, as she argued back with whatever he was telling her. After a minute she held up a hand to stop his complaints, or at least pause them, and turned to Eric.

"He's saying he won't allow another man, especially an infidel – sorry, Doc, his words, not mine – touch his wife. He brought her here because he'd heard there was a female medic. I think he means me." She paused and gulped, looking at Eric with scared eyes. "I think they expect me to deliver this baby."

If the situation hadn't been so deadly serious, Eric would have laughed at the notion of Lieutenant Nazari delivering a baby, or accomplishing any medical procedures.

In order to be successful in the military, it was important for a person to know their strengths and shortcomings. One used his or her strengths to their best advantages, and depended on one's comrades to do the same. Commanding Marines and translating were Lieutenant Nazari's strengths, not medicine. She had the good sense to leave those tasks to Eric and the other corpsmen.

Eric looked at the husband and prospective father, feeling both sympathy for the man's beliefs and wishes, and irritation at them at the same time. He looked at the husband, who had both distress and fear filling his face.

"Mr. Fadhil," he said. "I respect your wishes and your faith, I truly do."

He paused to let Lt. Nazari translate. Some medics spoke to the translator, saying, tell him this, ask him that. But Eric felt that was demeaning. Just because there was a language barrier didn't mean you didn't speak directly to someone's face.

"But you may have been given some incorrect information. I am the person with medical training. The lieutenant here does not have that training. She can translate our words but she cannot do medical tasks.

That is my job. My only desire is to help your wife and your child. I do not see her as a woman, only as a patient. If you wish for them to live, please allow me to help them."

He watched the man's face as Lieutenant Nazari translated and could see conflicting feelings bloom there. As soon as the lieutenant finished, he added.

"She," he nodded towards Nazari, "Can assist me and she will be right here with us."

He saw her blanch a little and give him a, *do I really need to help* look, to which he responded with an encouraging nod. "I promise you'll survive, ma'am."

At this point, Rayah made her opinion on the subject known with a sound that combined the pain of labor and exasperation towards the man who had caused her pregnancy, and even while the contraction pain still lingered on her face, she reached over and grabbed her husband arm, talking to him quickly and angrily and apparently faster than Nazari could keep up with as her eyes narrowed with concentration as she listened.

The lieutenant gave Eric an amused glance. "One of the things I like about this language is the poetry of their insults. Apparently, the lady believes her husband is being more stupid than a goat that's had its head stepped on by an elephant for refusing the help of someone trained to provide it. I haven't seen any elephants here since we've been here, have you, Doc?"

"No, ma'am, I haven't," Eric agreed, but he continued to observe the heated marital discussion going on.

"I believe," the lieutenant added, "she is now telling him that he will never, ever touch her again in this lifetime or the next."

"I believe all women in labor are of that opinion towards the fathers of their children at this point," Eric told her.

"But there may be a slight chance of future marital bliss if he has the sense to accept our help even if you are a man and an infidel." The lieutenant glanced at Eric's face with apology. "Her words, Doc, not mine."

"Not a problem, ma'am," Eric said, watching the father's face closely. Relief filled his being when Fadhil's expression seemed to indicate that he was appearing to finally relent, and the man spoke a few sharp words to them.

"This is a literal translation of the gentleman's words, Doc. 'Very well, the infidel may perform the task of the midwife. As long as you, a lady of the true faith, assists and supervises.'" She leaned a little closer and whispered to Eric, "I think I'll wait until later to tell him I'm a Catholic."

"Good idea, ma'am," Eric replied as he turned away from them just long enough to squirt some hand sanitizer on his hands, rub it in and pull on a pair of gloves. He gestured to Lieutenant Nazari to do the same, to give the impression that she would actually be participating.

There wasn't time for a full scrub. There also wasn't going to be time for a saline solution IV or a fetal heart monitor or to coach the mom on breathing techniques, nor for the freakin' obstetrical surgeon he wished he could conjure up at his side.

What he wouldn't give to have a genie appear and give him three wishes at this point. Wish number one would have been for an operating theater in a first-class hospital. Wish number two would have been for the obstetrical surgeon he'd thought of a moment ago. Wish number three would have been for the opportunity to wipe the sweat off his face.

There was also certainly neither the time nor supplies, for an epidural. Eric said to the father, who now looked more terrified than anything, "Please stand behind your wife and support her shoulders. A little higher. Yes, just like that. Ma'am, please move your feet inwards and bend your knees. Here, let me help you."

He grabbed a sheet, draped it over the patient from the waist down, and motioned to the lieutenant to push up her skirt so he could assess the situation.

"You're going to have to stand next to me, ma'am, for appearance's sake. Please try not to faint."

"I'm a United States Marine, Doc," she replied sharply, as she positioned herself next to him. "We do not faint."

Mrs. Rayah was panting now, between contractions. Eric looked at her face, contorted with pain. "Is this your first baby?" he asked.

The lieutenant spoke, and the mom shook her head, though the husband answered the question. Lt. Nazari looked sad when she translated his response.

"It's their second, but the first one was stillborn."

Great. That just put a whole lot more tension in the room.

As he suspected, the birth was imminent, but it wasn't a baby's head he saw crowning.

It was a foot.

"Not good!" he muttered to himself, then looked up at the lieutenant with a tiny head shake that requested, "Don't translate that."

The lieutenant was a United States Marine, and as such, she did not faint, but she still went a bit pale. Eric sucked in a whole lot of, *you can do this, Doc,* even though he was painfully aware that this young woman should have had a Cesarean an hour ago. However, it did no good whatsoever to dwell on could have, should have, would have.

He saw one tiny foot, but where was the other? Bent up backward? Next to its mate? He hated to cause the young lady further pain, but he had to figure that out if there was going to be a happy outcome to this event. He looked at Rayah's face.

"Ma'am," he said. "Ma'am!" A little louder, so that even though she may not have understood his actual word, she understood he was talking to her. "I need you to try not to push for a minute while I try to help your baby."

When Lt. Nazari translated, the mom nodded, and her face strained with her effort to ride out the contraction without giving in to the basic, age-old maternal need to push. He didn't bother asking how far apart the contractions were now because he could tell just from looking at her that there was no space whatsoever between her contractions at this point; they were just rolling one after the other.

He slid his fingers along the leg attached to the protruding foot and thankfully, found that the other leg was barely bent at the knee, and just a small nudge encouraged it to pop out next to the first one. Using his fingers to only support the limbs, not to pull, he instructed next, "Now you can push, ma'am." He hesitated, but had to say it. "Bear down as if you were trying to have a bowel movement."

Glancing up at Lt. Nazari, he could see her expression was asking, "Do I really need to say that?" He nodded at her, and she muttered, "Good thing I graduated top of my class in language school," before repeating Eric's words in Arabic. Both parents went a bit pop-eyed as they heard the translation, but Rayah didn't hesitate to push as he'd requested, accompanied by groans of pain that bored into Eric's brain and made him glad this was something he was never going to have to go through himself. He doubted he'd have the strength for it.

Gently, supporting the baby, assisting and guiding, but not pulling or yanking as one might be tempted to do in order to hurry things along, the upper legs slid out with the next contraction. He could see from the position of those little legs that the child would present face down, and he was grateful not to have to deal with the added complication of a face forward delivery. He just prayed the umbilical cord wasn't tangled around the neck or body.

The legs were out now, and the buttocks. "Push!" he ordered like an admiral, and Lt. Nazari's translation added one more word to Eric's tiny Arabic vocabulary.

"*Iidfae!*" he said the next time.

"Very good, Doc," Nazari commented, but he didn't bother to acknowledge her compliment. Rayah no longer needed instructions to push. Her whole body had been transformed into one pushing, moaning muscle, her only focus being performing the act of birth. Her hands were clenched into fists at her sides, her shoulders and head trembled with her effort, and her hijab was stained damp at the edges with perspiration.

The father was now silently terrified as he supported his wife's shoulders, and he dripped perspiration as well. Eric was sweating too, and not only because it was a hundred and ten degrees. If he'd had a third hand, he would have wiped his face, but since that wished-for third hand didn't obligingly sprout out of his body by mere wishful thinking, he dealt with the sweat, swallowing the saltiness of it running into his mouth.

When the shoulders appeared, he placed his gloved hand underneath, feeling for the head and pushing the vaginal wall away from the face with two fingers. The head quite suddenly popped out and thank you Mother

Nature, the cord was not tangled nor prolapsed. Quickly he turned the baby face up, maneuvering his right arm under the tiny body for support as he swept his fingers inside the mouth to clean it out. The child gasped, then cried, just like a live newborn was supposed to do. His color was good, and tiny clenched fists waved as if to express his outrage at this undignified situation he found himself in.

"It's a boy," Eric announced, his voice calm but his psyche reeling with relief and pride and terror and a bunch of other emotions he didn't have time to consider at the moment.

Both parents beamed with pride, and the mom cried, as Eric laid the breathing, squalling baby on the mom's belly, grabbed a towel and did a quick wipe of the face and torso before clamping off the umbilical cord. The clamps were intended to secure bleeding arteries rather than an umbilical cord, but he wasn't about to get picky at the moment.

By this time, neither of the new parents noticed that Lieutenant Nazari had stepped aside from the makeshift delivery table to give Eric room to maneuver. Their only focus now was on their new living, breathing baby.

The new mom was reaching for her baby, touching his head, obviously yearning to have him in her arms. Eric snapped a pair of surgical scissors out of their sterile pack and offered them to the new father, who looked shocked. "Dad, would you like to cut the cord?" When Lt. Nazari translated that, the dad looked painfully startled. "It's your right," Eric said. "But if you choose not to, please just say so."

To his credit, Fadhil grasped the scissors and placed them between the two clamps under Eric's guidance. Eric could tell from the expression on the man's face that the cord was tougher to cut than he'd thought it would be. Once it was severed, he handed the scissors back to Eric, who put them back on the table as the dad stepped back to admire his new son, wailing on the mom's belly like a goose under torture.

In a normal situation, this baby would have been delivered by a doctor, with a nurse assisting. But this hadn't been a normal situation. Not only had Eric been "temporarily promoted" to the doctor's role, but he was also forced by necessity to be the nurse too. He picked up the little boy and cleaned him more thoroughly, but quickly, wiping away the birth fluids, checking the mouth again for obstruction, and taking advantage of his brief private moment with the brand-new human he had brought into the world.

"Hi there, little guy," he said softly. "Aren't you a handsome boy. Welcome to the world."

He couldn't help but wonder, what would it feel like to have a little kid of his own like this? A baby he had helped create. Would he, or she, have a cap of dark hair like this little man? Probably not. Most likely, any child he might father would be fair-skinned and blond, like him. It was only when he'd hit puberty that his hair had darkened to its current light brown. He'd been a complete tow-head as a child. Of course, it would also depend on what the mom looked like. But since there was nobody even remotely resembling a baby-mama in his universe at the moment, the point was completely moot. He'd have to live vicariously through other people's babies.

He had been casually seeing a girl before this deployment. It had really been more of a friends-with-benefits situation. The benefits had included hot, moany sex in her bed, against the wall, and on her living room floor. However, the benefits apparently hadn't included seeing a guy off to a year-long military deployment.

When his sister took him to the airport, she'd refused to just drop him off at the curb. Brenda had insisted on parking in the garage and walking with him all the way to the security checkpoint. Once they'd said goodbye and he'd passed through security, he looked back to see she was still standing where she'd left him, but with her back turned, and he suspected she was crying.

And while he'd been boarding that plane and remembering his sister crying over his departure, he suspected that his erstwhile friend with benefits had most likely driven up to the main gate of NAS Pensacola, rolled down her car window, and called out, "Next!"

In his current role as both doctor and nurse, he had another task to complete. He wrapped the little guy up in a fresh towel and placed him in his mother's arms, saying, "Congratulations. Your son is beautiful." Then he went back to take care of the afterbirth. He placed his hand on the mom's abdomen and said, "Sorry, ma'am, I need one more push."

He pressed down on the belly with his right hand as she gasped and pushed again, then he shifted down to catch the afterbirth as it popped out, looking like a bloody, gelatinous bag. He checked quickly to make sure it was complete, and heard Lt. Nazari say, "Eeeww", as the new dad simultaneously said what was obviously the Arabic word for, "Eeeww."

After disposing of the afterbirth in the medical waste bucket, he turned to the new parents. "I'm sorry, but I can't stay with you any longer." The Marines at the door had been itching to leave when the couple had arrived, and itchy Marines were not the people you wanted to keep waiting. Now that the delivery was accomplished and everyone appeared to be alive and healthy, even the terrified new father, Eric knew they would have to be on their way back to the base within minutes.

He pulled off his gloves and stepped up to take another glance at the baby he'd just delivered, then offered his hand in congratulations to the new father. But rather than shaking his hand, the new dad grasped Eric's arms, leaned forward, and kissed him on the lips.

Yowza, that was not what he'd expected! Before he could panic, the man stepped back and shook Eric's hand, speaking fast in what were obviously words of thanks.

Lt. Nazari was smirking. "That's what they do here, Hanson. It's their culture. He wasn't asking you for a date."

"Thank you for the clarification, Ma'am. That was officially weird." He wasn't sure he'd ever get over the feeling of another man's beard on his lips. He had to restrain himself from saying, "Eeeww."

Lt. Nazari was having a laugh at Eric's expense. "You know, Hanson, my grandparents were born here and I can't get used to it either. At least I know he's not going to kiss me. And you know what – I think I'll keep the fact that I'm not actually Muslim to myself."

After a moment's hesitation, the new father settled for a nod and word of thanks to the lieutenant, with no touching.

As the new parents started counting their son's fingers and toes, the lieutenant said to Eric, "You know, Doc, I don't have kids myself but I'm still pretty sure they're supposed to come out head first."

"So I've been told, Ma'am," Eric replied, breathing heavily with the rush, the giddy sensation of having successfully brought a child into the world, and one that chose to not present itself in the usual way.

"Wait a sec," Lieutenant Nazari gasped. "Are saying this was your first delivery?"

Eric grinned. "Yes, Ma'am."

The lieutenant's mouth gaped. "You've got to be shittin' me!"

"No, ma'am," Eric replied. "I would never do that. I'm pretty sure that's a court-martial offense."

Nazari was shaking her head in amazement. "I have to say, Hanson, you have a pair of steel ones."

"Thank you, Ma'am, but I just did what had to be done."

"Don't be so humble," Nazari argued. "How did you know what to do? I wasn't aware they taught obstetrics in corpsman training."

"Only the basics, Ma'am. But you know what? My favorite things in the world to read are letters from home, but my second favorite thing to read is medical textbooks."

She paused for a moment, her face lighting up in memory. "Now I get it. When we were talking to the father, you said you had training. You didn't say you had experience. Way to split hairs, Hanson. You read medical textbooks for fun? Are you-"

"Still not shittin' you, Lieutenant."

He was packing up their gear as they spoke, and as the lieutenant picked up one of their carry bags, she said, "Ordinarily, Hanson, I'd say that was weird, but now I'm glad you're that kind of weird. I'm sure they are too." She gestured at the couple behind them, bonding with their new son.

"Thank you, Ma'am," he said again. "I'll take that as a compliment." He turned to say goodbye to Fadhil and Rayah, but stayed out of kissing range, saying, "Congratulations, again," and the man said something to them that made Lieutenant Nazari nod with relief.

"The two grandmothers are both waiting outside to help them

home," she said, and Eric was relieved that the new little family would have some support, and some female assistance for the new mom.

As he donned the fifty pounds of battle rattle that he'd taken off and set aside during the clinic, he felt himself transforming, from Doc to Marine, like a snake shedding its skin, or in this case, putting it on, in the form of a flak vest and a helmet. Within minutes, gear was stowed and the two grandmothers waiting outside were ushered into the building to reunite with their children and new grandchild.

"Go red," Lt. Nazari ordered, as the combat vehicle turned towards the base. Five weapons had their safeties switched off and were pointed outward, and five heads remained on swivels as they drove the short distance back to base.

Twenty minutes ago, Eric had had latex gloves on his hands, bringing a new life into the world. Now he was seated in the back of a Humvee with Lieutenant Nazari and three other Marines, with a safety-off M16 in his hands that could belch out over 700 bullets per minute.

He'd much rather be wearing the latex gloves.

As they entered the compound and the heavily guarded gate clanged shut behind them, he turned to the lieutenant. "May I have a few minutes before reporting back to sickbay, Ma'am?"

"Of course, Doc," she replied. "I think you've earned a little breather, under the circumstances."

"Actually, I wanted to go visit Fuentes for a few minutes."

Nazari's face darkened with a touch of sadness. "Fuentes."

She sighed, saying just one short word, but it was replete with feeling. "Shit."

"You took the words right out of my mouth," Eric replied, and the lieutenant nodded. "Go ahead, Doc. You can tell Fuentes he's leaving for home tomorrow."

"I'll do that, Ma'am." As soon as they were out of the truck, Eric took off his helmet, stowed his rifle, and turned to go visit a wounded Marine.

He was grateful to run into one of the female corpsmen (and yes, females in the job were still called corpsmen), on his way to the other side of the hospital, and was doubly grateful it was Melanie Andreadis, who was a good friend.

"Andie, you got a minute?"

"Sure. What's up, Doc?" Andreadis made a rabbit chewing mouth.

Eric rolled his eyes. "Oh, that is so clever! I never heard that before." Andreadis grinned, as Eric undid the shoulder fastenings of his flak vest and pulled it off. Under it, his fatigues were soaked with sweat. It was, after all, a hundred and ten degrees.

"Where have you been?" she asked him. "It's been crazy here all day. We just got a little breather but I don't think it'll last long."

Eric hooked a thumb toward the gate. "Civilian first aid clinic," he said. "It was crazy there too. Last case was a delivery."

"Delivery?" Andie repeated. "As in, a baby?" Eric nodded.

"Who delivered the kid? Not Lieutenant Nazari?"

Eric spread out his hands in a "you're looking at him" gesture.

"Doc! I thought you were an obstetrical virgin."

"Well, my cherry's been popped."

"Good for you!" Andie's dark eyes glowed with vicarious happiness. "Weren't you scared?"

"Scared?" Eric echoed. "I was fuckin' terrified. It was a breach birth too, kid came out feet first. It was a boy, cutest little thing ever. The mom and dad-"

Andie interrupted him. "Doc, I'd love to hear all about it but I can't sit and chat right now. But before I go back on duty, can I tell you something personal?"

"Jeez, Andie, haven't you told me more than enough personal stuff already?"

"Look, I know you like to run your mouth, Doc, but you know when to keep it shut too, right?"

"I can be the Sphinx if I have to."

He and Andie hung out together enough that Eric knew rumors were floating that they were shacked up. They weren't, but he managed to keep his big mouth shut about it. For her sake, for her protection, he let the rumors float.

"You know," she said, "you're the only guy here who almost makes me wish I pitched for the other team."

Eric looked around, terrified they'd be overheard. "I'm really, really flattered, but you need to keep that kind of shit under your cover. Don't ask, don't tell, remember?"

Andreadis sighed. "Yeah, I know. But that's not the real thing I wanted to tell you."

"You mean there's more?"

"Don't get your knickers in a twist, Hanson. I'm not going to tell you when I have my period or anything."

"For which I am truly grateful."

"My enlistment is going to be up in a few months, and when I get back to the States, I'm not re-enlisting."

"Andie, no!" he responded with shock, taking her arm and nudging her towards the wall to avoid a gurney being pushed towards the OR at double-time.

"You can't be serious. You're the best, we need you."

"It's not like I want to leave. But I can't keep living this double life. I want to come out of the closet. I want to live with my girlfriend without having to tell a bunch of lies."

"Your girlfriend isn't here, is she?" Eric looked around in panic.

"No, she's a civilian. When I get out I'm moving to San Francisco to be with her."

"You're leaving me?" He made a silly pretend lovesick face at her. "You're gonna dump the only guy who makes you want to pitch for Team Hetero?"

"I said almost, Hanson. Don't get all full of yourself."

"How can I not? Lt. Nazari just told me I have a pair of steel ones."

"Well, call me when they're solid diamond," Andie said with a smile, "and then maybe we'll talk. But I'll keep in touch. And who knows, someday if they ever wise up and repeal Don't Ask, Don't Tell, and my girlfriend and I can get married, maybe I'll re-enlist."

"I hope so, Andreadis. You're an asset to the Navy. I'm going to miss you. Don't forget to say goodbye before you leave."

"Where you off to?" Andie asked.

"Fuentes," he said simply, nodding in the direction of the recovery ward and shifting the heavy flak vest in his arms.

Andreadis lost her smile. "Poor guy," she said softly, then looked at Eric. "You want me to take care of that for you so you don't have to carry it around the hospital?"

He handed her the vest with a sigh of relief. "Thanks, Andie, I appreciate it," he said as she turned in the direction Eric had come from.

"Got your six, Doc," she called over her shoulder.

In the recovery area, he found Marine Private Javier Fuentes, one of four Marines who yesterday had been in a Humvee that ran over an IED a hundred yards outside the gate and had been torn open like a tuna can. Fuentes had survived; he'd even kept all his limbs. But the shrapnel flung about by a Humvee exploding around him had shattered both his legs and done extensive nerve damage, and it was going to be a long time before he walked again, if ever. The driver of the truck had come back DOA, or more accurately, DIP – Dead in Pieces. The other two had both bled out on operating tables, one of them while Eric had been assisting the surgeon trying vainly to keep him alive.

He was surprised to see Fuentes sitting up in bed, considering the level of narcotics in his system, but the Marine was sitting there with a thundercloud for a face. Eric pulled up a chair next to the bed and gave his comrade a friendly shoulder nudge.

"How's it hanging, Jarhead?" he asked, with a joviality he didn't really feel.

"Fucking crappy," was the morose reply. "But thanks for asking, Doc."

Eric tried to keep a neutrally pleasant expression on his face. It was one of the most difficult skills he had ever mastered. Inserting IV's and breathing tubes was easier.

"You're going home at least, Javi."

Although Fuentes was going home, his journey would not be direct. His trip home to Albuquerque would be interrupted with a stop in Bavaria, Germany. But he wouldn't be there to admire the Black Forest or to hoist a Pilsner. He'd be admitted to Landstuhl Regional Medical Center for surgery on his legs in hopes of repairing some of the nerve damage so that maybe, someday, he'd walk again.

"Not the way I wanted to," Fuentes replied. He glared at his legs as if his anger could make them work again. "I just got married before I shipped out. She's pregnant."

"That's great," Eric replied. "Congratulations. You'll be there to see your kid born. A lot better than meeting your new kid via Skype like some of the other guys."

Fuentes swept a hand towards his mangled limbs. "She's not going to want me back like this. I'm a freak."

"Come on now, that's not true. You're not a freak. You're a wounded vet. You should be getting a Purple Heart."

"I'd rather have the use of my legs back. And my guys." Fuentes closed his eyes for a moment, and Eric knew he was mourning his three deceased comrades. "Patel was going to teach me how to play chess. He loved that stupid game and he nagged me every day to learn it, and I kept putting him off. Finally I said OK, you can teach me how to play your stupid chess game if it'll shut you up. He's not going to ever play chess again and the last thing I ever said to him was to shut up. He'll never nag me to learn to play it because he's-" Javi flapped a hand, obviously not wanting to enunciate the word "dead" out loud. "Patel," he repeated in a despairing voice. "And Kowalski and Robertson. They'll never learn to play chess either. Fuck."

The one profane word held volumes of grief and despair in its four letters.

Eric put a hand on Javi Fuentes's shoulder. "Don't forget them," he advised. "Grieve for them. But think about your wife too. And that baby you guys have coming."

"We just found out it's a girl."

"Congratulations, dude. I'm jealous. Make sure you send me a photo when she's born." Eric was sincere in his jealousy. Another someone else's baby for him to admire.

"What if she wants to play sports?" Javi asked with despair in his voice.

"How am I going to be able to keep up with her? I won't be able to run or jump. What about when she grows up and gets married? How am I going to walk her down the aisle?"

"You're going to be able to do all those things," Eric assured his friend, hoping like hell that he was right. "There have been great improvements in treatments for nerve damage. You'll be playing ball and walking that kid down the aisle before you know it."

Fuentes didn't look convinced. "You know the last thing my wife said to me before I left?" he asked.

Based on his experience, Eric would hazard to guess that it would be "I love you." That had been the last thing his sister had said to him when she'd dropped him off at the airport, right after, "Stay safe, G.D." He'd been touched that she had enunciated all three words, rather than the casual "Love Ya" they usually flung around.

Apparently, that hadn't been Fuentes's experience, because the guy started to cry.

"She said, you better come home just the way you left, or I'm going to kill you. She's going to fucking kill me."

Seeing a Marine cry had to be the most heartbreaking thing in the universe. Eric hitched his chair up closer to the bed and put an arm around Fuentes's shoulders.

"It's OK," he said, though he knew in his heart that it was not really OK. Fuentes broke down completely and the next thing Eric knew, the guy was collapsed against Eric's shoulder, sobbing. Eric was just glad that in this position, Fuentes couldn't see his face, because by now, Eric was crying too. He made an effort to keep it quiet, though. After all, he was the one who was supposed to be comforting Fuentes. It was part of his unofficial training. Don't cry in front of the patients. Silently, the hot tears streamed down his cheeks and into his mouth, even more copiously than the sweat had just an hour ago during the delivery.

He cried in relief for the new life he had just brought into the world. Cried over the plight of a good friend who couldn't live her life the way she should have been able to. Cried for a twenty-one-year-old Marine who wasn't going home the same man he'd been when he'd left. Cried for three families who had just answered a knock on their door, to find two somber officers standing on their front porch. Cried over the three flag-draped coffins that were leaving on the same plane with Fuentes. And most of all, he cried over the thought of one of those coffins, which contained a comrade who, despite every bit of training, skill and experience he had, had died under Eric's hands.

It was a day of firsts for Petty Officer First Class Eric Hanson.

13

～

Michelle and her friend Tracy sat on the edge of the dock by the Casino, next to the boat Michelle was working on. Both girls were on their lunch break, but while Michelle usually just stopped long enough to actually eat, then went back to her work, Tracy's lunch breaks started an hour earlier than they were supposed to and lasted an hour longer. The two of them dangled their feet over the water as they ate their sandwiches.

Tracy was a friend from high school that Michelle had reconnected with recently, someone who had actually been a help to her in their school days. They were polar opposite personalities, which actually made them better friends than would someone who was just like her.

Tracy liked to flirt and have fun and paint her nails and dye her hair as the whim struck her. She took very little seriously, flitted from one fashion fad to another and spent as little time as possible at her supposed job of managing her father's gift shops. On the surface, it would seem that a person like her, the opposite of Michelle's reserve and anxiety, wouldn't be the person she'd keep in contact with. But somehow, their differences made them stronger friends than similarities might have. Tracy had a sister and parents who, despite her flightiness, noticed her, praised her accomplishments and punished her transgressions, just like normal families were supposed to do. Her family sympathized with Michelle's lack of parenting and the two girls had spent much of their adolescence hanging out

158

at Tracy's house when Michelle just couldn't stand being at home any longer.

It had been Tracy and her older sister who had helped Michelle take care of things when she got her period for the first time, Tracy who'd giggled and demanded details when Michelle told her about the first time a boy had kissed her, and later, expressed jealousy when she'd found out about Michelle's prom night adventure. Michelle had helped Tracy with her homework and coached her on test preparations that had enabled her friend to pass more than one class that she might have otherwise failed. As much as Tracy's flirtatiousness and frivolity were Michelle's polar opposites, still she'd been a good and loyal friend and Michelle was grateful that she'd stuck around when she'd gone through her Raging Bitch phase. Tracy had even loaned Michelle the dress she had worn to the wedding she'd attended the weekend her new roommate had moved in.

They went to the mainland for the day once in a while, to shop for things they couldn't get on the island. Michelle would spend her very small discretionary budget at the secondhand bookstore, while Tracy made a beeline for the beauty supply store, questing for new colors of hair dye.

Tracy had come down to the dock to tell Michelle about her favorite local gossip, which was the Avalon dating scene.

"Is it really worth it, to go out with a guy who's visiting here?" Tracy mused. "I mean, once they go back to L.A. or Oxnard or wherever, won't they just conveniently forget about our little island adventure and hook up with some girl at UCLA?"

"I think it would depend on the guy," Michelle replied. She didn't really have any useful input on the subject, considering that she hadn't gone out with anyone, either a tourist or a local, for a very long time. Well, she hung out with Eric a lot, but that wasn't a date.

As they sat at the end of the small dock, drinking the cokes that Tracy had brought, the owner of the boat Michelle was working on popped up out of the hold, startling them. Just a minute ago he'd been sitting in the captain's chair, observing the insides of his eyelids.

"I am in so much trouble!" he called out when seeing the two girls.

"I was supposed to meet my wife for lunch at the Descanso Beach Club twenty minutes ago!"

Tracy grinned at him. "Uh oh, maybe someone's sleeping on the couch tonight."

The tardy husband didn't respond, and rushed up the slope of the dock, then slipped on a previously unnoticed puddle of water and went down with a yelp of pain and a swear word that could be heard in Long Beach.

When Michelle hurried over to where he lay, the man was laying on his back, cradling his left arm and moaning out colorful metaphors that would make even Eric and all his Navy friends blush. She crouched next to him and advised, "Don't move, we'll get you help." She turned to Tracy, who had stood up and was staring at them. "Call 911!" Michelle requested.

As Tracy pulled out her phone, she asked, "Is he bleeding? I hope not, I can't handle the sight of blood."

"No, he's not bleeding, just call!" Michelle repeated. Sometimes Tracy was a bit selfish. Her squeamishness at the sight of blood was certainly secondary to the poor man's obviously painful injury. Michelle would have made the call herself, but her phone was in her tool bag on the boat she'd been working on.

There are eight fully trained full-time paramedics on Catalina Island. Four of them live and work in Avalon, and the other four are on the other side of the island in Two Harbors. That dynamic meant that the odds of any particular paramedic responding to their 911 call were four to one. Today the odds were in their favor. Eric and his partner, Tony Campos, pulled up in the ambulance and hurried towards them with a gurney and their medical bags. The injured man lay between the two girls and the land end of the dock, so they were more or less trapped there for the time being.

Eric's bubbly smile was of course set aside as he knelt next to the patient, snapping on a pair of blue gloves at the same time. He glanced briefly at Michelle and Tracy, giving Michelle a brief nod of recognition, saying, "Hey," then, "Did you ladies call this in?"

"I did," Tracy said, stepping forward, as if her obeying Michelle's instruction had been a feat deserving of a medal.

"Thank you, ma'am," he said gravely, then turned to his patient.

Tracy turned to Michelle and mouthed silently but dramatically, "Ma'am?"

"Don't take it personally, he says that to everyone," Michelle replied. Tracy's eyebrows twitched up, then she turned to watch Eric. Actually, she more than watched. She stared.

"Good afternoon, Sir. My name is Eric Hanson. I'm a paramedic with the Avalon Fire Department," he said to the man. "We'll be taking care of you, don't you worry. May I ask your name?"

"Bob," the man replied. "Bob Morales."

"Can you tell me how this happened, Mr. Morales? Are you injured anywhere else? Did you hit your head when you fell? How old are you, Sir? Are you on any medications? Do you have any allergies?"

As the man answered Eric's questions, his partner Tony, kneeling on the other side of him, repeated the information into the microphone on his shoulder.

Michelle had met Tony Campos once or twice. He and Eric worked as a team most of the time, from what Eric had told her, and they'd apparently become friends as well and spent some of their time off whacking at balls on the golf course.

"Can you sit up?" Eric put an arm around the patient's shoulder and assisted him into a sitting position, while he hissed with pain and swore again.

"Sorry," Bob said, glancing at Eric's face.

"Not a problem, Sir," Eric replied gravely. "I understand you're in pain, go ahead and swear if you like. I have heard it all, I assure you."

Michelle smiled to herself, thinking that Mr. Morales should at least be grateful that Eric didn't need to make him drop trou. She watched the treatment as avidly as Tracy, not only because there was really nothing else they could do at the moment, but also because watching Eric at work was quite possibly the most fascinating thing she had ever seen. His serious, professional demeanor as he listened to the man's breathing with the stethoscope that had been draped around his neck, checked his blood pressure, took his pulse, was in direct contrast with his joking, goofy exuberance when he was off duty. It was almost like seeing an actor performing his role, though she realized that neither of these two personas was an act, not his serious professional treatment at this moment, nor when he sang and laughed at other times. They were just two sides of one remarkable person.

She smiled with remembrance when he took the patient's pulse, remembering warm fingers on her own wrist on the day she and Eric had met, when she'd been in full panic attack mode with a pulse like a rabbit on speed. At least Mr. Morales was too smart to try to run out into traffic.

The assessment completed, the two men assisted their patient onto the gurney, which had one end raised so that he could sit up. Eric gently prodded the man's left arm above the elbow, closing his eyes for just a moment as if imagining in his mind's eye the extent of the damage under his hands. When Morales yelped with pain at the touch, Eric said, "I'm sorry, I realize that hurts, Sir. We just need to determine what's going on here."

Tony was talking into his phone now, saying, "white male, age forty-five, possible closed fracture of the left humerus."

Despite his pain, Morales still quipped, "I don't find this humorous at all," and Eric nodded.

"I understand completely, Sir. Nothing humorous about breaking your humerus."

Tracy turned away and made a gagging noise when Eric inserted an IV needle into the vein on the top of Mr. Morales's hand, even though the man said, "That didn't hurt at all," with surprise in his voice. Tony hung the bag of fluid on a hook sticking up at the top of the gurney, and nodded at Eric, as Eric pressed tape over the needle to secure it to the patient's hand.

"We're going to give you something for the pain," Eric said, as he inserted a syringe and pumped medication into a port on the IV tube. "This is morphine. Be warned, it may make you nauseous later."

The two men fastened the safety straps over Mr. Morales's legs and waist, and Eric pulled a long paddle-like item out of his medical bag, which he placed against the man's injured arm.

"I'm going to splint this now," he told him. "This is going to hurt, I have to tell you, but we need to stabilize the arm while we transport you to the hospital for further treatment. They will probably advise you to see an orthopedic doctor on the mainland." Eric held the splint against Mr. Morales's arm and wound a long cloth bandage around the arm and splint, and from the look on the patient's face, Michelle could tell he was holding back further swear words.

"Is there anyone we can call for you?" Tony asked, and Mr. Morales's expression changed from painful suffering, to remembered dismay.

"Yes, my wife. I was already late to meet her, hopefully this will be enough to get me out of the dog house for being late. But my phone is over on the boat." He nodded towards his boat parked on the other side of the dock, where Michelle and Tracy stood.

Eric looked at her and for the first time since he'd arrived, smiled, but just a small smile. "Michelle," he said, "would you mind terribly getting the gentleman's phone from his boat so he can contact his wife?"

Michelle noticed Tracy looking at her sharply at hearing Eric addressing her by name, showing that they obviously knew each other. Mr. Morales added, "It's on the passenger's seat. Thanks so much, dear."

She found the phone where he'd said it was and when she walked up and handed it to him, Eric and his partner were releasing the locks on the gurney and starting to push it up the slight incline towards the ambulance.

"Thanks, see you at home," Eric said quickly, then looked at Tracy and added, "Thank you for your assistance, Ma'am."

As soon as Eric wheeled the patient towards the ambulance, Tracy grabbed Michelle's arm. "My gawd, you sly little vixen, why didn't you tell me you were shacked up with a hot stud?"

"Shhh! I'm not shacked up with him," Michelle said quickly.

"You don't fool me, I have eyes and ears. He looked right at you and said, see you at home."

"We're just roommates. Remember, I told you I have a roommate now." Michelle had, however, not mentioned to her friend that her roommate was, as Tracy phrased it, a hot stud.

"Roommates with benefits?" Tracy was watching avidly as Eric hopped into the back of the ambulance with the patient, closing the door behind him as Tony got into the driver's seat. "I wouldn't kick him out for eating crackers in bed!" she declared.

"It's not like that. We're just roommates. He has his room and I have mine."

"Wait just a gosh darn second. You mean to tell me you live under the same roof with, with, *him*, and you're not jumping his bones? What are you, insane? Wait, paramedics are part of the fire department, aren't they?" That was obvious; the ambulance pulling away clearly had City of Avalon Fire Department printed on it in big blue letters. "Is he on one of those fireman calendars? Please tell me he's Mr. July or something."

"I don't think so," Michelle replied, though secretly she thought, *I wish*!

Tracy sighed. "Well, he ought to be. That man is positively lickable. I can't believe you actually live with him and you aren't doing the nasty together."

"Tracy, that's gross," Michelle replied, while another secret thought crossed her mind. *Never could one put the words nasty and Eric in the same sentence. With Eric, it would not be nasty. It would be phenomenal.*

14

Eric's schedule tended to change regularly, sometimes being on duty during the day, sometimes at night, sometimes over the weekend, and occasionally being called away on an emergency. As Michelle found out one Saturday night as she sat up in bed way too late, engrossed in a good book. She heard Eric walk by her door in the hall, heard him say, "Be there in five," apparently on his phone, and a moment later, the front door opened and closed.

She'd stayed up way later than she'd intended to, finishing that book, so she was bleary and yawning in the morning as she shuffled into the kitchen to make coffee.

Again, she heard the front door open and a moment later Eric bounced into the kitchen with all the energy of a chihuahua on a sugar high. He smiled broadly when he saw her sitting at the table like a zombie.

"Great, you're up! Let's go for a hike. I want to see the buffalo."

She was barely awake enough to do more than stare at him stupidly. He wanted to see buffalo? To native Avalonians, the feral buffalo roaming the island's interior were so much a part of their surroundings that they hardly seemed unusual. After a dozen bison were left behind from a movie shoot in the 1920s, their descendants still roamed the mountains of Catalina Island, sometimes even venturing into the gardens of homes on the outskirts of town.

"Didn't you work all night?" she asked. "Aren't you exhausted?" How dare he be so perky?

"Nah, I'm not tired. I delivered a baby this morning, and now I'm pumped. You know, that whole circle of life thing."

"If you start singing The Lion King, I will slap you silly."

"Really? That could be interesting." He opened his mouth, but shut it when she lifted a warning finger in the air.

"Wait, how could you deliver a baby here? We don't have any maternity facilities here in Avalon. Everyone has to go to the mainland a couple of weeks before their due date. I was born at Kaiser Permanente in Temecula myself."

"I understand that's how it's usually done," he said. "But this kid decided to be born four weeks early, while mom and dad were having a last, pre-baby vacation. Then the mom decided not to bother with early labor, just went straight to pushing. At that point, you take what you can get, and what they got was me."

"Weren't you terrified?"

"Nah, this one was easy. The hard part was keeping an eye on the dad at the same time. He looked like a fainter. They're going to name it Catharine after the island. Good thing it was a girl."

"Wait, were the parents visitors? They don't live here?"

Eric nodded. "I think they live in Pasadena."

"Where was this kid born?"

"Room 212 in the Portofino Hotel."

"Wow, that must have ruined their vacation."

"No way." Eric looked incredulous. "You can't say 'ruined' and 'had a baby' together! It may not have happened exactly when and where and how they planned, but they got a beautiful healthy baby out of it."

She was a bit amused at his enthusiasm for the event. "So, the baby you delivered was beautiful?"

"Of course. All babies are beautiful. Especially mine."

She couldn't help making a choking noise. His babies? Was he saying, he had kids? She knew he'd been married and divorced, but nothing had been said about progeny. Where were they? Why did he never go see them?

She never would have pegged him as the neglectful father type. He seemed the type of person who would be an attentive parent, involved in his kids' lives. She remembered how he'd smiled and quacked like Donald Duck at that toddler on the pier when he'd retrieved the kid's shoe. It was so charmingly paternal, it had made her ovaries tremble.

"Your kids?" she managed to squeak out.

"Yeah," he said with a grin. "The ones I've delivered. I've got three catches. One in Iraq, the one today, and one in an elevator in the base hospital in San Diego. Another lady who couldn't wait for her regular doctor."

Oh. That's what he'd meant by "his". He made it sound like a baseball statistic.

Although he had referred to the babies he had delivered as 'his kids', she could totally imagine Eric as an actual father. She could just picture him playing catch, holding a kid by the hand and walking him to school, kissing boo-boos, oohing and ahhing over a kid's good report card. All the things her friend's fathers had done. All the things she'd want the future father of her children to do.

Where did *that* roommate-inappropriate thought come from?

He waved a hand at her. "That robe is really cute, I mean seriously, it's adorable, but not for hiking. Go get dressed. I want to see those buffalo. It will only take me a minute to change." He was already unbuttoning his shirt. "Unless you've got something better to do?" The expression on his face hinted that he'd be devastated if she had something better to do.

Not possible. How could she have anything better to do on a Sunday than hang out with Eric, despite her bleary sluggishness, next to his perky adrenaline high. He sealed the deal by promising, "I'll buy you breakfast."

By the time she'd brushed her teeth and hair, splashed some water on her face to wake up, and got dressed, he was already waiting on the step outside the front door. His crisp paramedic uniform had been exchanged for tee shirt, shorts and boots. He had a cap tucked under his arm and a tube of sunblock in his hand, as he rubbed some on the back of his neck.

He handed the sunblock tube to her as she stepped out the door. Her hair covered the back of her neck but he gestured at her front, so she squirted a little out and applied it to her throat and at the top of her tee shirt. She noticed that he watched as she applied it. Probably to make sure she didn't miss a spot.

She handed him back the tube and he almost tucked it into his pocket. "Wait a second!" he said in an accusatory voice, as if she'd tried to pull some sort of fast one on him. "Hold still a second."

He uncapped the sunblock tube and squirted a dab of the cream onto his finger, leaning towards her.

She looked at those sparkly eyes and her breath caught a little. He dabbed the sunblock onto the tip of her nose.

She stood there like a dimwit with the cool blob of cream on her nose and after a second, Eric said, "OK, this is the part where you rub it in."

Blushing and embarrassed at how his smile and eyes tended to mesmerize her, she rubbed the sunblock into the skin of her nose while he grinned, squeezed out another dab and rubbed it onto his own nose.

She'd never realized how sexy it was to see a man protecting his nose from the sun's UV rays.

"Where's your hat?" he asked, as he put the sunblock tube in his pocket, and put his cap on his head. Of course, the cap had a ship embroidered on it and the lettering, "USS Nimitz, CVN 68."

"I don't need a hat."

"Yes, you do. Three rules of sun protection. Sunblock, hat, hydration."

She rolled her eyes. "I'm fine, Doc. You're off duty now, remember?"

"Doc is never completely off duty," he insisted. When she tried to step away from the door, he just pointed back at it, ordering, "Hat. Now."

Obviously, Mr. Bossypants wasn't going to budge. He had a really implacable, immovable look in his eyes that made her wonder if he'd really only been a chief petty officer in the Navy, or if he'd actually been an admiral. He was being presumptive again. She worked outdoors most of the time. She knew about the potential harm of too much exposure to the sun's UV rays. She did use sunblock, but hats got in the way of her work.

Annoyed, she turned back to the door, muttering as she opened it, "For someone who wasn't an admiral, you're awfully good at giving orders."

"I heard that," he said, then just laughed when she stuck her hand behind her back and showed him her middle finger.

Despite her irritation at his bossiness, she kind of liked the fact that he cared enough about her health to insist on it, rather than just letting her take her chances in the sun.

Eric nodded approvingly when she came out with her floppy pink sun hat firmly in place.

"I like it when you're obedient."

"Bite me," she snarled in reply.

"If you insist."

She couldn't stay irritated him when he got goofy like that, she realized as they finally set off on their hike. The walk up Avalon Canyon Road was a pretty easy uphill incline, but once they got close to the Wrigley Botanical Garden, the trail branched off into a serious climb. Michelle explained to Eric about how the Wrigley family, of chewing gum fame, had once owned the island and had used it for spring training for the Chicago Cubs baseball team, except during the years of World War II when the military had taken over the island for training. In 1952, the Cubs had moved their spring training to Arizona, and twenty years later, the island had been transferred to the Catalina Island Conservancy. The Cub's practice field had in fact, been located where the fire station, Baywatch Avalon lifeguard headquarters, and Avalon City Hall now sat. When the Cubs had trained there, the Wrigley family home had sat perched on a hill with a view of the baseball field. William Wrigley, and later his son Phillip, would watch their practices with binoculars, and players who failed to perform at their best would be called to visit the Wrigley home to be scolded for their deficiencies.

Eric nodded. "I'd sure rather be here in February than in Chicago."

"I've never been to Chicago," Michelle said. There were lots of places she'd never been to.

"It's not a bad place, but you don't want to go there in February. It's fucking *cold*, pardon my language. I'm talking frozen toes, hurts to breathe, chip a nipple cold. It was even worse for a southern boy like me, growing up in Florida. I was used to going to the beach in February. And someone with long hair, like you, didn't dare go outside with it wet. It could freeze into an icicle and literally break off."

Reflexively she ran a protective hand over her hair. "Some people complain that they don't like the lack of seasons here in California, but after hearing that about February in Chicago, I think I can manage without them."

Eric nodded. "We have seasons in Florida, though not the same as in the Midwest. Hurricane and Monsoon. I knew a guy in boot camp who was from Minneapolis – he said you could experience all four seasons in one day there. He's stationed in Iceland now. Says he feels right at home." He looked at the expression on her face and added, "Let me guess. You've never seen snow?"

"Not close enough to touch it." When she had been in Los Angeles, on those rare clear days when the Santa Ana winds blew the smog away, she'd caught occasional glimpses of snow on the peaks of the San Gabriel Mountains north of the city. From the way Eric had described it, that faraway glimpse was close enough.

"But did you use sunblock on the beach in Florida in February?" she asked.

"Of course. By the gallon."

"I bet you wore a Speedo." The thought of it made her gulp a little.

He looked a bit surprised at her teasing, but smiled and said, "Nah, I'm more of a board shorts type of guy."

The trail was steep and uneven and rocky, twisting back and forth up the slopes, surrounded by prickly pear cactus, fragrant white sage and the long, thin petals of the aptly named Liveforever flower. Below them, Echo Lake glittered in the sunshine, but by midsummer, it would be a dry bowl between two hills. The chaparral habitat of the island was sparser than its mainland counterparts, giving the Catalina ironwood, mahogany and oak trees there the look of a dwarf forest.

Michelle had grown up hiking these hills. No wonder she had calf muscles like an athlete, a fact that wasn't lost on Eric as he followed her up the hill, to the next hill, ascending higher into the mountainous interior of the island.

She stopped suddenly and turned to look at him with a direct, serious gaze that he found a bit disconcerting, and also rather sexy.

"When you were in the Navy, did you have safety drills?" she asked.

"Of course, all the time."

"Well, this is your Catalina Island safety drill." She looked so serious and intense that Eric was tempted to stand at attention as she spoke, perhaps salute when she was done.

"If we see any bison, it will probably be at a distance. But if we encounter any up close, move aside and let them pass. And watch out for signs of agitation, like raising their tail, pawing the ground, swinging their head, stuff like that. Look for an escape route or a place to hide, like behind a rock or tree. If it charges at you, do not run. You'll piss it off, and you'll lose. Try throwing something off to the side to break its concentration on you, and if that doesn't work, get on the ground, make yourself as small as possible, protect your head, and pray."

Pray? He didn't pray, borderline pagan that he was. Although technically on his service record, it said Lutheran, that was really only for the comfort of his family in case anything had ever happened to him. As for actual beliefs, he was uncertain. Mother Nature, the Force, Norse mythology, any, all, or none of them. The only religious item he owned was a copy of the Koran, which he had received as a gift. He had never read it, because he didn't read Arabic, but kept it for sentimental reasons.

"Who should I pray to?" he asked.

"Whatever goddess you think likes you best."

"How about Freya?" He watched Michelle's face, to see if she knew who he was talking about.

Of course, she did know who he was talking about. "The Norse goddess of love and war? She'll do. I'm partial to Venus myself."

"Venus?" He had to think. "Isn't she the goddess of beauty?"

"Among other things."

He looked at her. "Yeah, I think that's just right."

They hiked up high enough that they could look down and see the town of Avalon below them, curving around the bay, the harbor filled with dozens of white boats. It was a clear enough day that they could actually see the Palos Verdes Peninsula on the mainland, a dark smudge twenty-two miles to the east. Though it was clear today, tomorrow there could be fog, sometimes wispy and translucent, sometimes so thick it was like being inside a wet wool sweater, obscuring any possibility of a view. No two hikes were alike here.

A small animal darted into their path, stopped and looked at them for a moment with bright dark eyes, then skittered off into the bushes.

"Why was that cat wearing a radio collar?" Eric asked, looking in the direction it had gone.

"That wasn't a cat. It's a Catalina Island fox. They're native to the island. You won't find them anyplace else in the world. They're collared because they were almost wiped out by an epidemic of distemper years ago, and now the Conservancy tracks their numbers."

She looked around and gave a small wave, to indicate the hills around them. "There are a lot of species of animals and plants here that are endemic to Catalina Island and not found anywhere else in the world."

"Endemic?" he repeated with an amused glance.

"It means native," she explained.

"I know what it means. I've just never heard anyone use it in real conversation before. You'd make a great tour guide, you know, as much as you know about this place."

"Well I have lived here all my life. But no, I would not make a great tour guide. In fact, I'd be a horrible tour guide. If you don't believe me, go down to the tour plaza on Catalina Avenue and sign up for a sightseeing tour. It's right next to the miniature golf course. Listen to the real tour guides. They're bubbly and nice and outgoing. I couldn't do that. They don't hire bitches to be tour guides."

"You're not a bitch," he said quickly.

Why wasn't she surprised to hear him say that? She was getting used to the way he argued with her whenever she was brutally honest about herself. She was about to argue back when she saw his hand reaching towards a clump of Saint Catharine's Lace.

"Don't pick that!" she warned quickly.

He snatched his hand away as if the flower were actually a poisonous snake.

"I wouldn't even think about it," he claimed. Instead he pulled out his phone and took a photo instead.

As they passed by an island oak tree, another endemic species on the island, with its branches contorted in an asymmetrical but artistic fashion, a sharp twig end scratched across the top of Michelle's hand.

"Ouch," she said briefly, rubbing at it.

"Let me see that," Eric instructed immediately.

"It's nothing," she assured him.

He insisted on inspecting her hand, and she let him, but stressed, "It's just a little scratch."

"I'll be the judge of that," he countered. "Do I tell you when some weird noise in a boat engine is just a little noise?"

She rolled her eyes but patiently let him look at her hand and just enjoyed the feel of his warm fingers holding hers, until Doc was satisfied that the scratch hadn't broken the skin and did not require further medical attention, other than his instruction to keep an eye on it and to let him know right away if it started to bother her.

"Yes, Sir!" she responded with a heavy eye roll, as he gave her a stink eye.

"Yes, Doc," she corrected herself. "What's that other title?"

"Chief," he replied with a look that said, you knew that.

"Like an Indian?" she teased.

"Like an E-7."

Eventually, they did find their buffalo, at a safe distance, a line of dark brown humps trudging up a distant slope. Eric turned his cap backward, pulled out his phone again, and unabashedly took photos like a tourist.

Before heading back down the hiking path, Michelle turned to the side and took a few steps towards the cliff.

"Where are you going?" Eric asked with a hint of panic in his voice. "You know I have rescue skills, but I can't fly."

"Really? And here I thought you could do anything." She sat down on the flat rock at the edge of the drop-off and looked up at him.

Please don't think I'm a total dork.

His smiling eyes invited confidences, and held a complete lack of judgment.

"This is my rock," she said.

"Your rock?" He peered at the flat ledge with interest. "Really? Hmm, I don't see your name on it."

"Well it might as well have my name on it. I spent a lot of my adolescence sitting on this rock, looking at the ocean or reading."

"Oh, that makes sense then." Eric gestured at it dramatically. "From now on this spot is named Michelle's Rock. Next time we come up here, I'll bring a can of spray paint and label it. May I?" He indicated the space next to her and she slid to the side so he could sit next to her.

"You can't spray paint my name on this rock," she said regretfully. "That's vandalism."

"Yeah, I suppose it would be. How about a discreet label?"

"Even that wouldn't be allowed. This rock doesn't actually belong to me. It belongs to the Catalina Island Conservancy. I just borrow it."

There had been sufficient space on the rock's flat surface for one skinny teenager, but it seemed to shrink significantly when occupied by an adult woman and man. A man with guns. Eric actually scooched in a little to maneuver his butt onto the rock's surface, and they sat there with knees, hips and shoulders touching, gazing out over Avalon Bay below them.

To some people, the concept of spending a Sunday morning sitting on a rock on the side of a mountain might not be their idea of fun, but Michelle couldn't think of anything else she'd rather be doing at this moment. Sure, her butt was getting sore due to being squished to one side of the rock by her larger roommate, but their knees, hips and shoulders were touching, and every time she shifted a little as the two of them occupied a rock built for one, they touched some more. She could get used to this.

It was peaceful, serene, the air hot but with a slight breeze that kept them from sweltering. Eric took off his cap and she could see that his head was sweating a bit under it, and she removed her sun hat too, lifting her hair up with both hands to let the breeze cool her neck.

"This does seem like a good place to sit and read. What a beautiful view. As long as the buffalo don't follow you here," Eric said.

She looked at him and couldn't help smiling. She liked sharing her special spot with him. He seemed to appreciate how much it meant to her. She decided to ask him a question, but she knew he'd probably find it a thorny one.

"Who's your favorite author? Who would you read if you were up here alone?"

Oh, jeez, he was supposed to have a favorite author? Was that a condition of being roommates? It hadn't been on the rental application. The only author he could think of off the top of his head was Shakespeare, and he certainly had never read any of his works. An old girlfriend had once dragged him to see a film version of Macbeth but he hadn't understood a word of it. Although the battle scene had been pretty cool.

"I don't really have a favorite. I don't read much fiction."

"What do you read then?" she asked. "Playboy?"

He chuckled. "Only for the articles."

"Comic books?"

"Only when my nephews ask me to look at theirs. I don't collect them or anything."

She'd called him a dork once, and this conversation was kind of proving it. But how could she think dork when looking at a face that made Brad Pitt look homely, attached to a body like Adonis?

Oh, jeez, Michelle, did you just mentally compare your roommate to Adonis? Maybe you've been reading too many fantasy novels.

"Why do you read so much?" Eric asked.

Bradonis. That was what she should call him, at least to herself. Certainly not out loud. Brad plus Adonis equaled Bradonis. But he looked sincere in his question, so she gave him a sincere answer.

"Well, I read because I enjoy it. And also, because it takes me away to another time and place for a while. I can get immersed in another world, another planet if you will. It's like a break or a vacation from reality, worrying about someone else's fictional problems and issues, instead of my own, for a while."

Her eyes looking out at the ocean were dark with memories.

"It's somewhere I can escape to, far away from this real-world bull-shit."

He gave her a look and she grinned and added, "Pardon my language. For a while, I can be a different person. For a while I can be this fantasy person, this – I don't know – not me."

"I know we haven't known each other very long, but I don't see anything wrong with you, as the type of person you are, other than that baseball thing."

She gave him a wrinkled nose and an eye roll that conveyed what she thought of his baseball thing.

"Sorry," she said. "I'm being silly."

"No, I don't find that silly," Eric insisted. "It's fascinating, and kind of sad. But in any event, being silly once in a while might be just the thing for you. I think I can relate. I listen to music a lot for the same reason. It can be a pleasant escape. You might say, it's my book. My escape from the stresses of reality. That, and stars too."

"Stars? You mean, like," she furrowed her brow trying to remember. "Garth Brooks?"

"Actually, I meant stars in the sky rather than celebrities. When I was at sea, if I got a chance to get up on deck at night, I'd go up to the vulture's row and watch the sky. You would not believe the stars you can see out on the open ocean. If you stand still long enough, you can even sometimes see a satellite moving across the sky. I loved to stand out there at night when I could and watch the stars and try to pick out constellations, while at the same time listening to the jets launching and landing down on the flight deck. Over in San Diego, and even more so in Los Angeles, you can hardly see any stars because of the urban light pollution. It's better here on Catalina, but still not like being at sea."

His passion for stargazing was obvious by the way he lifted his face to the sky and closed his eyes for a moment, as if recalling the multitude of celestial bodies seen from the sea.

He shifted a bit next to her, causing their hips and knees to brush together. "Didn't your butt get numb after a while, sitting on a hard rock like this for so long? Based on the thickness of the books I've seen you hauling home from the library, I'm guessing your reading sessions up here were pretty lengthy. There's a sharp piece poking me right in the gluteus maximus."

"Sometimes it did get uncomfortable. But a lot of the time, even with getting a numb butt or getting poked in the -?"

Eric stood up and offered her his hand to help Michelle stand up too.

"Gluteus maximus," he repeated, and slapped his rear with his other hand. "The largest muscle in the human body."

"If you say so. Sometimes I preferred to having it be numb or sore to going-" she gestured towards the town below them. "Home."

Home. Where she had been ignored and unappreciated, unless she was willing to pop another cold one. But now, home was a whole lot more pleasant, in the company of this laughing, sweet goofball, her friendly, considerate roommate, who always said please and thank you and didn't seem to take her for granted.

She started to head back towards the hiking trail, but Eric said, "Wait a sec."

"Are you hoping to spot more buffalo?"

"That would be nice, but at the moment, I'd like you to sit on your rock again for a minute."

"OK," she agreed, but wondered why he wanted her to do so. To her amazement, as soon as she sat back down, Eric pulled his phone out of his pocket again, turned it towards her and said, "Say cheese."

"Why are you taking my photo? You already have the one you took at the pier on your contact list."

"Well if we can't label the rock as yours, we should at least have a photo to commemorate it." He looked at his screen and shook his head. "You weren't smiling. Let's do this again."

Maybe his middle name really was Goof. Obligingly, she smiled as he took another picture.

"Much better!" he said enthusiastically. "I'll text it to you."

When she stood up, she said, "Let me see your phone."

"I said I would text you the photo. See, I'm doing it right now."

"Yes, and thank you. But I left my phone at home. I set it down when you made me go back for my hat and forgot to pick it up." She gave him a look that indicated it was his fault she was phoneless at the moment. "Don't worry. I'm not going to install a tracking app or anything."

He looked a bit puzzled but smiled and handed over his phone, and she indicated the rock she'd just been photographed sitting on. "Your turn. It's only fair."

He grinned but didn't sit down. "Let's do a selfie instead. Come on."

He stood on the rock and reached for her hand. "Don't worry, I won't let you fall off."

The next thing she knew, she was sitting on the rock again, squished against her goofy roommate who put one arm around her shoulder and leaned against her as he held up his phone in front of them. She could see the two of them on the screen, with the ocean behind them. This time she didn't need Eric's request to smile as he took their photo. She didn't only smile in order to end up with a pleasant photograph to commemorate their hike. She smiled because he'd put his arm around her shoulder and leaned against her, and she really liked how that felt. She liked it way more than she should have.

Just before they turned away from her rock, Eric took a last look and said, "I recognize this view."

"You've been up here before?"

That surprised her. She'd thought this was his first exploration of the island's hiking trails.

"No," he admitted. "I recognize it from your sketches."

Her sketches? Had he been snooping in her sketchbook?

"I admit it," he said, as if reading her thoughts. "I looked at your sketchbook. It was lying right there on the table the day I moved in. I'm sorry, I know it was snooping, but I couldn't help it. And your drawings are really good. You should be proud of them and show them off."

His words of praise for her sketches ameliorated her first tendency, to be annoyed at his snooping. Her sketching was another escape, the concentration required to reproduce the scenery of Catalina Island helping to aid in a temporary escape from life's anxieties.

"In fact," he went on, "I'd like to buy one of them."

Buy one of her sketches? That was crazy. She wasn't a professional artist, just a hobbyist with a sketch pad and some old colored pencils.

"Which one?" she couldn't help asking.

Eric swept a hand towards the view of Avalon below them. "That one. The view from up here. I love that drawing. How much?"

"No. I won't sell it to you." Her roommate's disappointment was obvious. "But I will give it to you if you really want it. Call it a thank you for being my roommate present."

Eric's look of disappointment was replaced with a happy grin. "Really? Thanks bunches! Someday when you're a famous artist, I'll be able to say I have an original Michelle Diaz sketch."

She rolled her eyes again. "It's just a little sketch. Not exactly a Van Gogh or anything."

"Oh, it's better than a Van Gogh," Eric insisted as they started back down the trail.

By the time they hiked back down to town, it was late enough that the promised breakfast became lunch instead. They ate at the Sand Trap, across the street from the edge of the golf course. On the other side of the green they could see the fire station. Eric looked towards it, through the screen that protected the restaurant's patio from misguided golf balls, and put a finger on his mouth.

"Don't let them know I'm here. They'll draft me, and I'm supposed to be off duty the rest of the day."

"How can they make you come back to work after you went in last night, and delivered a baby to boot?"

"Because they need someone to wash the ambulance, and I really don't want to have to do it."

"Can't anyone else wash it?"

"Not like me. That ambulance," he gestured towards the fire station doors, "has never been so clean and spotless as since I got here. But I have better things to do on my day off." He smiled at her. If that smile of his wasn't so sweet, it would have been sinful.

"Like hunting buffalo?"

"Yeah, that too."

"You're not at all modest, are you?"

"Why should I be?" That might have sounded arrogant, if it hadn't been accompanied by a twinkly, boyish grin. "Besides," he added, "those guys have no appreciation for good music."

Michelle was surprised, and a bit disconcerted, at the small pang of jealousy she felt when she saw the flirty smile he gave the waitress when she took their order and asked him how he'd like his cheeseburger cooked. "Well done, please, ma'am. Thank you."

He can flirt with whoever he chooses to. He's not your boyfriend or anything. "You're so polite," she commented.

She was glad to see that his flirty smile was not only for the benefit of waitresses. "I like to think that my mama raised a gentleman."

When their food came, he looked askance at her plate. "I can't believe you're eating them!" He gestured at her buffalo tacos.

"What's the problem? You're not exactly a vegetarian." She indicated his well-done cheeseburger.

"Yeah, but I didn't just take pictures of this cow on the hoof an hour ago."

She let him stew about that for a minute before admitting, "This doesn't come from the local bison. It comes from an Indian reservation in North Dakota. There are no meat processing facilities here. When the herd here gets too big, they put them on birth control."

Eric almost spit out his food as he laughed. "Are you kidding me? Birth control? I'd hate to have to be the unlucky bastard who gets the assignment to put condoms on those boys!" He shuddered.

"It's oral, you goof. They put it in food."

Just then the waitress came back to ask how their food was, and out came that flirty smile again. "It's delicious, thank you for asking, ma'am."

"I'm jealous," Michelle said after the waitress walked away with a smile on her own face.

"You should be. This is a great burger."

"No, I meant what you said before. That your mama raised you."

He kept smiling, but it was tinged with regret. She'd never met anyone with such an expressive face before. "I'm sorry, Michelle. I didn't mean to bring up bad memories for you. Me and my big mouth."

"It's OK, don't worry about it. I guess I'm just envious of people who have normal families."

"Well, I'm not sure I'd call us normal. With my family, sometimes it was like having three sets of parents. And no, I did not join the Navy to get away from them. I love them all to pieces, but they still drove me crazy sometimes." He took another bite of his burger and a sip of his glass of milk. What was he, six years old? "Since I was the youngest, they tended to treat me like some kind of walking, talking toy to play with. Can you imagine being thirteen, and having your sisters trying to pick out your clothes, and your brothers trying to tell you about the birds and the bees?"

"No, I can't imagine it. When I was thirteen, I was stealing money out of my dad's wallet to buy tampons and my first bra." She took a bite of her taco, looking at him over the food as he chewed and swallowed his own lunch. "Even though I don't have siblings, I can imagine having your brothers telling you about the birds and the bees must have been pretty embarrassing. Even more embarrassing than ninth-grade biology class."

"Yeah, that was the second most embarrassing conversation I ever had with them."

"Second? What could be worse?"

He rolled his eyes at her. "Well, I would have to say, several years after that. The night before I left for boot camp, my mom had a little going away party at our house. Just the immediate family, so there were like twenty people there."

"Wow, you have a big family."

"We could start our own village, sweetheart. She even had a cake decorated with a Navy design on it." Eric tapped at the tattoo on his forearm and looked at her with mischief in his eyes.

"Is that where you got the idea from?"

He nodded. "Anyway, my two brothers took me out into the back yard to have a little going away talk, as they put it. Oliver said that they didn't think our dad would feel comfortable discussing this kind of thing with me so they were going to take care of it."

"This kind of thing?" she asked with amusement, trying to imagine what kind of important discussion an older brother might need to have with a young man about to fly the nest to the military.

"Yeah, it took a lot of hemming and hawing and euphemisms, but they finally managed to start talking about stuff like safe sex and protection and responsibility and all that stuff you don't want to have to talk about with your brothers. You're an adult now, Eric," he mimicked. "You have to understand that you need to be responsible and that there are consequences to your actions. I just wished I could curl up and disappear. I was dying for them to stop talking about it. I kept muttering, I'm eighteen, guys."

"Wait, was this before or after you went to your senior prom?"

He chuckled. "Oh, it was after. But you know, there are some things even a bigmouth like me doesn't confess to his siblings."

And yet, he'd confessed it to her. *Senior prom night for me too.*

"Finally, I just had to put us all out of our misery. I yelled out, I know what safe sex is! I know what STDs are, I know what condoms are and I know how to use them! It was a good thing we were out in the yard where nobody else could hear us."

"Weren't you afraid someone in the house would hear you through a window?"

"Sweetheart, it was Florida in July. Every house in the state is sealed up tight with the AC going. They both stared at me for a minute in absolute shock, then Phillip said, well all righty then. Our work is done here. And we all went back in the house and nobody ever mentioned the subject again, thank goodness."

She smiled at his story, but still felt jealous that he had such a large, caring family, at the casual manner in which he'd said that "just the immediate family" consisted of twenty people. What she wouldn't give to have had normal parents, siblings, people to share her life with. A bit of sadness weighed in her chest and she looked at the floor next to their table.

"You know, I do have a big mouth," Eric said. "But I've got big ears too."

She looked at his ears. They weren't big. They were perfect. He saw the direction of her gaze and chuckled. "I meant, I'm a good listener."

There was just something about his smile, his voice, his attitude, that made her willing, even eager, to say things she'd never felt comfortable saying to anyone else. She never felt stupid talking to him. It had been like that since the day she'd crashed into him outside the Marlin Club, which was probably why – never mind that.

"When my mother died," she said, hesitantly, wondering why she was taking this risk, "my cousin from Temecula came here, had me put on a black dress and took me to a church service I didn't understand. They didn't even tell me she was dead. They just said she was gone, like she went to the mainland for the day. When she didn't come back, I thought maybe she ran away, because of my dad's drinking, and I was mad that she didn't take me with her. It took a long time for me to figure out that by gone, they meant dead. I kept asking my dad how she died, but he couldn't be bothered to tell me. All he would say was, her heart stopped. I mean, duh. Doesn't everybody's heart stop when they die? It made no sense to me, but it was all I could get out of him." She looked away and put on her tough face. "He refused to talk about her at all, probably because it interfered with his drinking to actually have a conversation with his stupid kid. I had to wait and send for a copy of the death certificate when I turned eighteen."

"What was it, if you don't mind me asking?" Eric's smile exuded sympathy.

"Pneumonia. Who dies from pneumonia, at age thirty-two, in the twenty-first century? It's like dying from a cold. Sometimes I think she didn't bother getting treatment for it or trying to fight it because she didn't care enough about us, about me, to want to live. What did she have to live for anyway? A drunk for a husband and a stupid kid."

She hadn't noticed until she stopped talking, that at some point, Eric had rested his hand over hers on the table. He obviously meant it only as a gesture of sympathy, but those warm long fingers felt just a little too affectionate. She had a feeling that his fingers, in fact all of his skin, would be warm to the touch, even in Chicago in February.

She took her hand away on the pretext she needed it to finish her lunch. "I'm sorry, I didn't mean to burden you with my stupid personal shit." She remembered Eric's manners and added, "Pardon my language."

"It's not stupid and you're not burdening me. Let me tell you something, sweetheart. It's not unheard of for a younger person to die from pneumonia. Unusual, yes, but not impossible, especially if the person has other health issues. I'm so sorry you had to experience that. What a horrible thing for a kid to have to go through. When my mother died, I was twenty-five, not ten. I was still devastated, of course, but I never once thought she wanted to leave us. No mother would ever want to leave her children. I'm sure yours didn't either. It must have been terrible for you to have to go through that at such a young age." He leaned forward, his fingers laced before him on the tabletop.

"You said you didn't understand the funeral service," he said. "Then you thought she'd run away and left you, until you realized on your own that she was dead. I'm hearing confusion, anger and grief, all in one unhappy ten-year-old kid. That's a lot of powerful emotions to deal with all by yourself at such a young age. That would drive a weaker person crazy. And sweetheart, you are not crazy. Quit trying to tell me you are, because I'm not buying it."

"I suppose you're going to tell me I should talk to a shrink about it."

"It wouldn't hurt. You did say you'd think about it."

"When did I say that?"

"In the very first email you ever sent me. I've saved it in my archives. You said, and I quote, you may have said a few things that made sense. I'll think about it."

"You remember my exact words from an email I sent you over a year ago? That is a seriously good memory."

"Sweetheart, I remember everything you've ever said to me, digitally and in person."

She found herself smiling in spite of her memories of anxiety. "I did go to a few Al-Anon meetings after you suggested it."

He nodded approvingly. "That's a good start. There's no shame in asking for help."

What he hadn't mentioned to Michelle was that not only had he saved every email she'd sent him, he'd printed them out and reread them when he'd been on his last deployment, pulling them out of his locker to read in the rare quiet times between working and sleeping, like a bedtime story. The worn printouts had gone with him when he'd been sent TAD to A-stan, tucked into his sea bag, to be read again by flashlight in his dusty rack. They weren't the only emails he'd preserved and reread like that; he had others as well, emails and letters from his siblings and other family members, from his best friend Gabriel. They were all a tie to the faraway world of Home, of normalcy, to the reason he was where he was and doing what he was doing.

But he read the ones Michelle had sent him the most.

Maybe it was weird, to read and reread printouts of emails from a girl who had appeared, when they'd first met, not to even like him very much. That was odd; he thought he'd been rather charming. The emails they had exchanged in the months since she'd crashed into his back had been fun and diverting, but basically superficial. Although she had in her first email apologized for telling him to F off. He smiled every time he read that, and thought, *apology accepted, Michelle Diaz.*

"I'm surprised that, considering how things were with your dad, that you didn't bug out of here and move to the mainland after high school," he went on. "I'm glad you didn't, of course. But if I'd been in your situation, I think I would have considered it. I can think of several people I've known who enlisted in the service mainly to get away from a bad situation at home."

"I did consider it, once or twice." Or twenty or thirty or fifty times. "But I couldn't have left my dad here alone. He was like a baby. He couldn't take care of himself. When I finished technical school, I suggested we both move to the mainland. There might have been better job opportunities for me there. But he didn't want to leave his drinking buddies or the bars where they let him run up a tab. Plus, I actually like living here. It's beautiful and unique and there's no traffic like in L.A. And you can always see the ocean."

And yet, no amount of care or supervision had prevented her dad from getting drunk, falling off a boat, and drowning. Even after that, she could have sold the house and bolted for the mainland. And then what? Finding a job probably wouldn't have been difficult, but living there would be. She'd pay a fortune for a tiny apartment in a bad neighborhood, far from a view of the ocean.

She would have to buy a car and dispose of her golf cart. She'd have to navigate the southern California freeways, after growing up in a town that didn't have a single traffic light and where the maximum speed limit was twenty-five miles per hour.

That concept terrified her. She preferred to stay in Avalon. Despite how much her life sucked, she still felt safer on Catalina Island than she could ever imagine alone on mainland southern California.

And now of course, she was glad she had chosen to stay on the island. If she'd left, she wouldn't be living with Eric. Not Living With Him, she reminded herself. They were just roommates.

"I like living here too," he said. "I'm glad you decided to stay, or I might be fighting traffic in Los Angeles or San Diego instead of hiking around seeing bison in my back yard and walking to work."

"Oh, I'm sure you would have found someplace to live here even if it hadn't been with me. I mean, at my house. As a roommate."

"Maybe," he said. "But it wouldn't have been nearly as much fun."

She decided not to pursue what he might mean by that and instead turned her attention to finishing her lunch.

When they got back to the house after their hike and lunch, Eric said he had to go get some shut-eye because he was still assigned to the night shift. Before he disappeared into the sanctuary of his bedroom, Michelle got out her sketchbook and carefully detached the sketch she'd promised to give him, the one depicting the view of Avalon as seen from up on the mountain.

On receiving it, Eric's grin came out in a full-bloomed smile.

"Thanks. I will treasure this always. What other artistic mediums do you use? Watercolors? Oil paint? Sculpture?"

She opened her mouth to inform him that no, she only did pencil sketching, but he rolled right over her.

"Do you draw nudes? I totally volunteer to be your model."

She didn't know if she should laugh, or gulp for air.

"I just draw. Pencils, not paint. Not people, and certainly not..."

"Nudes," he supplied helpfully. "Aw come on. I've always wanted to be a nude model."

He struck what he probably thought was an artistic pose, with one hand on his hip, the other in the air in a dramatic gesture, his chest puffed out – and a smile beaming in her direction that could have melted chocolate at twenty paces.

"I'm ready for my close-up."

She chose to laugh. It was safer.

15

Eric was arriving home off the night shift as she was leaving for work, like ships passing in the night, when he asked, "You got a minute?"

"Sure, what's up?"

"I need to tell you something."

Oh no, this was it. The moment she had been dreading. He had a date. He had a girlfriend. He wanted to bring her here. She was going to spend the night here with him, at their casino. They'd be having sex in the room right next to Michelle's. The walls in this house were thin. She could hear the water run every time he showered, and presumably, he could hear her showers too, when they were home at the same time. Michelle would have to listen to them making love in the next room. Would they be loud? Or quiet and smooth? The head of her bed was against the wall separating their two bedrooms. Maybe she should move it over to the other wall, and get noise-canceling headphones. Maybe she should sleep on the couch.

There would be an awkward encounter in the hall in the morning. Eric would introduce her, because he was so polite. "This is my pathetic roommate," he'd say, "who hasn't had a date in a year." He'd caress the blonde's cheek. He was such a touchy-feely type person, and Michelle was sure he'd have a preference for blondes. He'd say, "This is my girlfriend." Or, "This is my lover." Or, "This is my woman."

They'd have to takes turns in the bathroom. Would Eric and his woman shower together? Expect Michelle to eat breakfast with them in her kitchen, with her having to sit there while they cuddled, laughed and whispered together? Would she have to watch as they slithered back to the bedroom?

Maybe she should call her friend Tracy and ask if she could come over and sleep on her couch.

"I'll be leaving Friday," Eric said. "I'll be gone for two weeks."

Two weeks? Maybe his girlfriend lived on the mainland. He was taking two weeks' vacation to be with her. Did she live in Los Angeles? In San Diego? Somewhere in between? Would he stay at her home, or would they spend the two weeks shacked up in a hotel? After two weeks, he'd come home a half-dead, dried-out husk. But he'd probably have a really big smile on his face, even happier than his usual smile.

Get a hold of yourself, Michelle, you're obsessing over something you have no idea about, and which is none of your business anyway.

A hand waved in front of her face, and she blinked at Eric's fingers. "Hello?" he inquired. "Earth to Michelle."

"Sorry." She tried to keep from blushing at her imaginings.

"I thought I lost you for a minute there," he went on with a grin. "I'll be doing reserve duty."

That didn't sound very romantic. Or very sexual. Even though it was none of her business, she still asked, "What's that?"

"The Navy Reserve. I signed up for it when I retired. Two weeks a year, they get me back. Gotta go defend our freedom. Do you think you can handle two weeks without me?" His grin flashed, teasing her.

The old Michelle would have said something snotty about having managed without him before, and being able to manage now without him for two weeks. The new Michelle, not so much. She was embarrassed to admit how relieved she was to find out that his two-week absence would be spent working, rather than copulating.

"You'll be at sea?" Yikes, her voice sounded so childish and pathetic. *Get a grip, Michelle, it's just your roommate going out of town, not your soul mate abandoning you.* She wondered if his ship would pass by Catalina Island, and at what point along its twenty-one-mile length she might be able to go stand and watch it leave. Most of the island's coastline was inaccessible by road. She might have to rent a boat.

"Well, I'll be on a ship-can't tell you which one-but we won't be leaving port. I'll be helping prep the sickbay for deployment and giving vaccinations to the crew." He looked darn happy at the prospect, which she really couldn't understand.

"Vaccinations? You mean, more dropping trou?"

"Yep, I'm afraid so. But at least I won't be on the pointy end of the needle this time."

"Why? I mean, why do some shots have to be in the rear end rather than the arm? It seems so downright humiliating."

He proceeded to give her a long explanation about doses and muscles, with a bunch of incomprehensible words like intramuscular and subdermal thrown in for good measure. She didn't understand a word of it, but he seemed to know what he was talking about.

"OK, well, thanks for letting me know." She couldn't quite keep the wistful tone out of her voice.

You can't go away, her inner self wailed. *I can't figure out the cinnamon to coffee ratio.*

When she got home from work on Friday, he was gone. She could tell the moment she walked in the door that he was Away. It actually felt different around the place, a different kind of quiet than when he was at work or hanging out with friends or anything else he did here on the island. She'd never realized how unpleasantly quiet her house was until Eric Hanson had shown up with his music and his twinkly sparkle.

Reluctantly, she immediately found she missed hearing his off-key singing, his conversation, his jokes and teasing. She missed his smiley presence. She even missed hearing him swear. It was so sweet when he apologized for his language. He was good company, a good listener, full of helpful insights, and the fact that he was drop-dead gorgeous didn't hurt either.

It was going to be a long two weeks.

Of course, he had left for a six-month deployment the day after they had met, but that didn't count. At the time, she had assumed him to be merely a casual acquaintance. Or, more accurately, an annoying nuisance. They had exchanged a few emails during that time, but they had been casual and superficial. She had truly never expected to see him again. And yet here he was living in her house, and now he was gone, even though it was for only two weeks. She was dreadfully lonely in a way she had never been before. Amazing how that happened.

She did get a text from him. It was a photo, a selfie he'd taken on the boat to the mainland, with the words, "Miss me yet? See you in a couple of weeks."

She almost texted back, "Yes, I miss you," but didn't. He was just a big silly tease who liked to joke. She shouldn't get all clingy, as if they were anything more than roommates. So, she just texted, "Stay safe," and tried to prepare herself for the long, boring two-week duration.

She shouldn't be missing him like this. She'd been fine all on her own before he'd arrived, thank you very much. She had, after all, only taken on a roommate for financial reasons.

And yet, despite all that relational reasoning, she missed him. She may have gotten along before he'd moved in with her, but it had been dull and lonely. She just hadn't realized quite how lonely until he left, just when she'd been getting used to having him around. Was this what it was like for military families – and roommates – when their Sailors or soldiers or Marines were deployed? She was miserable having him gone for two weeks. He had told her that deployments for active duty service members were six months or longer. The first time he'd gone to Iraq it had been for a year. How did people manage that? It had to be even worse for closer relationships – spouses, children, parents.

Was she allowed, as a mere roommate, to be proud of him? To be proud of what he did and of the difference it made?

She liked to think so. They were friends, after all, if not family. She could be, and was, proud of him. And maybe that was, in part at least, what made it possible for people to send their loved ones, and friends and roommates, off on those deployments.

How did they manage to get coffee made right or remove ceiling spiders? How did they dispel the quiet and gloom that threatened to seep back into their homes after the smiley, joking, off-key singer was gone?

Jeez, Michelle, snap out of it. You're spending way too much time in your own head.

******

Eric came home from defending our freedom looking like he'd been in a bar fight. Michelle's eyes goggled at the sight of his big purple shiner.

"Oh my god, are we at war?" she gasped.

He set his sea bag down next to the sofa and said, "Of course, we're still fighting the war on terror. But this was friendly fire."

"You mean one of OUR guys did that to you? I hope they threw him in Navy jail."

"The brig? No, it's cool. In fact, I had to do a lot of fast talking to keep the guy out of the brig."

One of the things she had learned about Eric since she'd known him, was that he was good at fast talking.

"Well they should have. That looks awful. Why didn't you call me when you got off the boat? I would have come down and picked you up in the golf cart so you wouldn't have to walk all that way."

"I didn't want to bother you."

"It wouldn't have been any bother, Eric. You look exhausted. Sit down, I'll get out an ice pack."

"It's OK, I'll be fine," he said. The bruise was mature enough that an ice pack really wouldn't improve it any, but she wasn't having it. She put a hand on his shoulder and pushed him down, so he sat. "But I have to go to work tomorrow and I need to do my laundry," he protested weakly.

"Jeez, take a load off, you big goof.," she scolded him. "You're always taking care of other people, let someone take care of you for a change. Your laundry will be here later. Do you have a clean uniform to wear to-morrow? I mean a fire department uniform, not that cammie thing." She waved a hand at the green camouflage patterned uniform he was wearing.

"I know I should have changed into civilian clothes before I left to travel home," Eric said. "But I was running late and barely made my boat. But I think I have one clean work uniform in the closet."

"I can see why. So, you have clothes for tomorrow, do you have clean, uh, skivvies?"

Did he blush as he nodded at her mentioning his skivvies? If that wasn't just the cutest thing ever.

"Then it's settled. You sit, I'll get that ice pack."

OK, so maybe an ice pack would help. He was absolutely beat, his eye did hurt, and he found he liked the idea of her taking care of him. She went into the kitchen and as he heard her opening the freezer, he unlaced his boots and pulled them off, setting them neatly next to his sea bag. His feet thanked him for the release. Michelle returned with a blue ice pack carried in a dish towel.

She sat down next to him and touched it to his face. "Is that too cold?"

"No, it's great." In fact, it was wonderful.

"So how did you get this? Should I ask how the other guy looks?"

"Well, we had a guy pass out on deck," he started.

"What, did he not follow your orders to wear a hat, apply sunblock and stay hydrated?"

"Guess not. You know how they say, the bigger they come, the harder they fall? Well this guy fell pretty hard. We got him down to sickbay and then he came to. Have you ever fainted?" She shook her head. "Some people wake up from a faint feeling disoriented and freaked out. When he came to, he thought I was trying to hold him down. Actually, I was just trying to get an IV into him. Before he figured out what was going on, he popped me one."

"What a creep." The ice pack was starting to warm up and she took it off his face and wiped the moisture it left with the dish towel. He didn't want to admit how sweet it was to feel her hands on him. She was sitting right next to him and he could smell her hair, a faintly flowery scent from the shampoo he knew was in their shower.

She probably didn't even realize that her leg was touching his as she sat next to him. He could feel the warmth of her skin, even through the fabric of his uniform trousers.

They really weren't supposed to travel in uniform unless it was an emergency. He should have changed into civilian clothes before leaving the base. It was only partially true that he'd been running late to make his boat. If he'd taken the boat he'd originally planned on, he would have had plenty of time to change. But when he realized that if he hauled ass to make an earlier boat, he'd get home early enough to be sure Michelle would be still awake when he got there. It was possible she might have been already in bed if he'd taken his originally scheduled boat. So he'd given the Uber driver an extra fifty dollars, cash, off the books, to inspire the guy to ignore the speed limit on Pacific Coast Highway and get him to the boat dock in Dana Point in time to make the earlier boat.

It had surprised him how much he'd missed their little casino in Avalon, the cute little yellow house next to the hill. He had especially missed his roommate. He'd missed trying to tease a smile or a laugh out of her. Her laugh was infectious, even more so due to its rareness. He'd missed the way she rolled her eyes when he sang out loud. He'd even missed how she ignored him totally when she was engrossed in one of her thick library books.

She subconsciously tried, and failed, to let on what she was experiencing emotionally on those printed pages. Obviously, she was completely unaware of the emotions she revealed as her eyes devoured the words in front of her.

He'd seen her eyes widen in surprised when something unexpected happened in the story, seen her eyes dance around in a smile when the plot held happiness, or frown when something bad was happening to her beloved fantasy characters. He'd seen her get misty when tragedy unfolded on the page. And once in a while, he'd seen her breath catch and her eyes go dark and wide with a look of absolute lust, and he knew she was reading a sex scene. He sincerely hoped she wasn't aware of his arousal when he caught that look in her eye.

But she was completely oblivious to those revealing expressions crossing her face, or the fact that Eric had observed them.

He discreetly shifted his leg a little away from hers, putting a little roommate-appropriate space between them.

"The guy felt really bad about it after," he said. "Wanted to buy me a drink. He was pretty disappointed when all I would take was ginger ale."

He leaned his head back on the sofa and closed his eyes. "Sometimes I just get tired of explaining about it."

"You are going to get so many sympathy points at work this week," she told him, and he raised his head and opened his eyes to look at her. She winced in sympathy at the sight of his injured eye.

"Yeah, that was the first thought that crossed my mind as I was sitting there on the floor wondering if I'd been blinded. Sympathy points."

"Can you see? How many fingers am I holding up?"

He covered the unbruised eye with his hand and squinted with the bruised one. "Eleven?"

"You goof, I didn't even put my hand up."

He stuck his tongue out at her like a little kid. She was glad to see that being wounded in the line of duty hadn't damaged his silly sense of humor.

"Are you hungry?" she asked. "I made pasta salad and there's plenty left." She'd taken a page from his book and when she cooked, made enough for two.

"You don't have to..." She gave him a look that would make an admiral obey and finished, "I'd love some, thank you, ma'am."

"Don't go anywhere. I'll just be a sec." He had no intention of going anywhere at the moment. He just wanted to sit here and enjoy the feeling of her touching him, even if it had been just a small brush of a dish towel in her hand, wiping a drop of moisture from his face.

The ice pack Michelle had applied sure felt a lot better than the one his fellow corpsman had tossed at him on the ship with a brusque, "Ten minutes on, ten minutes off, Doc."

The guy had empathized the "Doc" with a smirk, vastly amused at the sight of Eric being the patient, rather than the caregiver.

She took the ice pack and towel with her back to the kitchen and returned with a heaping plate of pasta, sat there watching him eat it.

"This is really good," he said between bites. "I hadn't realized how hungry I was."

"And yet you almost tried to refuse it."

"I didn't want to put you to any extra effort for me."

"It's not an extra effort to help a friend." She wanted to blurt out, *I'd do just about anything for you.*

When he was done, she took the dish back to the kitchen saying, "I'm just going to rinse this off real quick."

It only took her a minute to scrape the crumbs into the trash, rinse off the plate and put it in the sink for future washing, and come back to the living room. But in that minute, he'd laid down on the couch and was already asleep, just like that.

She sat in the chair across from him and watched him sleep. What was it about seeing a man asleep that made them look so young and vulnerable? Maybe because he'd finally relaxed. He made a small sigh and she wondered what he would do if she ran her hands through his hair, which though still military short, looked very soft. Would he wake up all disoriented and freaked out, and pop her one? She didn't think she'd mind. But he looked so exhausted and the bruised eye was nasty. It would be pretty mean to wake him up just to send him to go to sleep again in his room, so she kept her hands off and unfolded the couch blanket folded over the armrest, laying it over his cami-clad form. At least his boots were already off. The sweet, boyish relaxation of his sudden slumber gave him a precious charm that made her want to pet him like a puppy.

On a whim, she did actually run her hand briefly over his hair and it was really soft, and as fine as a baby's, but he didn't wake up.

"Thank you for defending our freedom," she whispered, and left him to sleep on the couch.

Eric was home. Everything was going to be OK now.

When she got up in the morning, he was already up, had made coffee, and was putting his laundry into the washer. The Navy uniform was gone and he had on his usual tee shirt and cargo shorts. Of course, the couch blanket she'd covered him with was folded into a precise square. Sometimes his tidiness put her to shame.

"I had the weirdest dream last night, before I woke up on the couch," he said with a silly grin. "I dreamt someone was brushing my hair."

"Oh really?" she said noncommittally, trying to sound detached and innocent. "You sure fell asleep fast."

"Yeah, you learn to do that in the service. You never know what kind of timetable you may have, and you have to train yourself to sleep when and where you can. But after I had the hair-brushing dream, I got up and went to bed."

She was glad he didn't ask how he'd gotten covered up with the couch blanket. He had to know she'd done it. "How does your eye feel?"

"Not bad. Your ice pack helped a lot."

"So how was your two weeks back in the Navy? Other than getting punched in the eye, I mean."

Even with one eye bruised and purple, he still managed to sparkle. "It was great, thanks for asking. I was thrilled to be back in uniform, and back in the Navy routine. Nobody tried to correct me when I addressed my superiors as Sir." He looked especially happy about that part. "I was busy, really busy. It was intense, hardly a moment's rest. And yes, I had to make guys drop trou."

"Didn't you get some time off to recuperate after the guy punched you?" she asked.

"About half an hour. Most of which I spent explaining to the shore patrol that it was an accident, not assault.

"And yet, at the same time I realized that I made the right decision to retire and become a civilian. There comes a time when you just know something is right, and I know it was right for me to leave the Navy, and to take this job here in Avalon." He paused. "And it was the right thing for me to live here, on this island, in this house, with you."

She stared at him, at that sweet friendly smile. He felt the right thing for his life was to live here with her? That was – interesting. And, she had to admit, a little bit arousing.

"The whole time I was there, I kept thinking it would be nice to get home." He looked around the kitchen, and she followed his gaze, pleasantly astounded that he considered her little house to be "home"

He grinned at her. "How did you manage without me while I was gone? Did you miss me? Any stray spiders around that you couldn't reach?"

"Of course I missed you." She managed to refrain from blurting out, *it was horrible. It was lonely.* She held her tongue from saying just how much she'd missed him, how he'd become such a part of her life in the few months they'd been roommates that the two weeks with him gone had felt like a prison sentence. And she absolutely positively was not going to let him know how long she had sat there last night and watched him sleep on the couch.

"There was one spider, but he ran away when I told him you'd be back."

Eric stood up to his full height and stretched his arms above his head so that his fingers almost touched the ceiling. "Just goes to show you, size does matter," he joked, as Michelle tried to roll up her tongue back into her mouth.

"I forgot to give you your present last night," he said.

A present? Michelle was, admittedly, unfamiliar with roommate protocol, but she was still fairly certain that having one's roommate go away for two weeks was not necessarily a gift-giving occasion.

"You didn't have to bring me a present."

"I know. I wanted to. It's just a little thing, but I hope you like it."

His smile was almost childish as he handed her a small bag. She opened it and pulled out a package of a dozen colored pencils – fresh, new, sharp.

She looked at him with shining eyes. "Thank you, Eric. That was really sweet of you."

"It's nothing," he said, though it was far from nothing to her. She didn't want to admit to him that her existing pencils had been a set the high school art teacher had been about to throw away.

The gift was small enough and inexpensive enough not to cross the line into inappropriateness, yet the thoughtfulness of it gave her a warm, fuzzy feeling.

The washer had started its rhythmic wet swish, swish and he headed down the hall towards his room. "Gotta go change for work and go get my sympathy points."

16

✻

She was awoken by the slam of the front door at one a.m., and a very loud "Shhh!" that sounded like Eric. Pulling on her bathrobe, she went out into the living room to see Eric and his friend Danny Gonzalez, the guy who had sent her a tipsy wink over the top of his beer bottle that first day she'd met Eric, standing in the doorway, looking guilty. Eric was supporting Gonzalez under the shoulder, and Danny's head was wobbling like a bobblehead doll. It had been a week since Eric's return from reserve duty and the black eye had almost faded away.

Without warning, a horrific flashback assaulted Michelle's brain. A memory of being awakened by an angry knocking on her door at midnight, to find her neighbor from down the street supporting her inebriated father just like Eric was supporting Gonzalez, but with disapproval and disgust radiating from Mr. Johnston's face like a nuclear meltdown.

"He was passed out on my front porch again," Mr. Johnston growled. "He's so drunk, he couldn't tell which house was his. He tried to open my front door and rattled it a couple of times when it didn't open. Scared my wife out of her mind." Her neighbor's brows came together in a scowl as he pushed her dad towards her, and Dad stumbled before she caught his arm and steadied him.

"I'm sorry, Mr. Johnston," she said quickly. "It won't happen again." At least she hoped it wouldn't happen again, but she had no way of ensuring that it didn't. Gary must have been too busy to call her to fetch her dad home. It wasn't the first time Dad had bothered the Johnstons

199

like this, nor were they the only neighbors to have had him pass out on their doorstep. She tried to smile at her neighbor, tried to act like this was a one-time occurrence, but they both knew that was a sham. Every single one of her neighbors knew what her dad was like, and there was nothing she could do to change it.

"It better not happen again, Michelle," Mr. Johnston growled. She wondered if he had a normal speaking voice. All she'd ever heard from him was a growl. "The next time I'll have to call the sheriff's department. He can't be doing this all the time. You need to get him into a program of some kind."

"Yes, we'll work on that," she promised, though knowing it was a lie, and Mr. Johnston probably was perfectly aware of it. She'd been trying to get her dad into a program of some kind for years, with no success whatsoever.

"Thank you for helping him. I'm sorry he frightened your wife. Please tell her I apologize." She shook her dad's arm a little. "Dad, you should thank Mr. Johnston for helping you."

But Dad didn't thank their neighbor for dragging his sorry drunk carcass home. He just slid his arm from Michelle's grasp and ambled away from the door, bumping into the sofa and clutching on to it for support, mumbling things that she couldn't understand, as usual. It sounded something like, "I want a robin," as if he expected birds to be chirping in the middle of the night.

Mr. Johnston turned to go, knowing from experience that he wasn't going to get a thank you from Greg Diaz, because the man probably wasn't even aware of his assistance. All he was going to get was excuses from the guy's pathetic loser of a daughter.

"Good night, Mr. Johnston," Michelle called out to his back. "I'm sorry, really I am. Dad just hasn't been feeling well lately and I'm sure he didn't mean to be a bother and-" She was aware that she was babbling, just making excuses and pathetic justifications, because she was completely incapable of preventing her dad from being a huge embarrassment.

"No more!" her neighbor warned as he stomped away and Michelle closed and locked the door behind him.

"Dad!" she scolded. "You shouldn't have done that. You should call me if you need help. You've got a phone in your pocket." Of course, half the time her dad's phone was dead because he forgot to charge it when he'd been drinking.

Dad didn't respond to her reprimand, as usual. He just stumbled towards his room, ignoring her, as usual.

"Good night, Dad," she called out, and he mumbled something that may or may not have been a response before disappearing into his room and presumably, falling onto the bed in his clothes, as usual.

Michelle had squeezed her eyes to stem the tears that threatened to leak out. Mr. Johnston had not for a minute bought her pathetic apology and Dad hadn't cared a bit that he'd inconvenienced their neighbor and embarrassed his daughter. Why couldn't she change him? Why couldn't she succeed in getting him to try and fight his addiction? Why did everything she attempted to do end in failure and embarrassment?

Because she was a pathetic loser, that was why.

The memory caused Raging Bitch to raise her ugly head.

"Are you two drunk?" she now demanded irately, as anger seared through her. "Because if you are, you can both just turn around and scram out of here."

This was absolutely unbelievable. After what Eric had told her about his allergy, she couldn't believe he would be so careless with his health.

He flashed her a look she had never seen on his face before – anger.

"Do you really think I'm that stupid?" Immediately, Eric's expression changed from anger to contrition. "I'm sorry, Michelle, I really am. I'm not drunk, but this guy is plastered. And they left him! Took the last boat and left him behind. I'm really sorry to have to bring this into your home. But I couldn't just leave him there."

Seeing him there, helping his friend, looking sorry and apologetic, mollified her anger like water poured over a flame, and pushed Raging Bitch into oblivion. *This isn't your dad*, she reminded herself. *And it's not your irritated neighbor threatening to call the sheriffs. It's your room-*

mate, your friend, taking care of his companion who'd been abandoned by his other supposed friends.

That was Eric. He took care of people. He fixed things.

"It's your home too, Eric. Don't worry about it." The words surprised her even as she said them, but she meant them, she realized. It was astonishing to find herself taking this whole situation so well.

Gonzalez seemed to notice where he was for the first time. He winked at her. "Hey doll face, I remember you. You're Doc's squeeze."

Eric got that unaccustomed angry look again, and said just one word, but it was like the voice of God.

"Mouth!"

Gonzalez subsided and looked at the floor, mumbling, "Apologies, ma'am. Nothing but respect."

Michelle's eyes widened in surprise. "You've trained him well."

"Yeah, but those other guys are going to need some remedial education. I'm sorry, but I need to keep him here tonight, until I can get him on a boat in the morning."

"Well then, bring him in."

"I'm sorry we woke you. I told him to be quiet."

"If you say sorry one more time, I will slap you."

Eric glared at Gonzalez. "Look, now you're getting me in trouble with my roommate."

Gonzalez ignored that, and whined childishly, "Doc, I gotta whiz!"

Eric steered him toward the bathroom, warning, "You better aim real good, or you're cleaning it up with a toothbrush!"

While Gonzalez was in the bathroom, hopefully aiming real good, Eric put a hand to his forehead, as if he had a headache.

"I don't deserve this. Come shoot some pool, they said. It'll be fun, they said. Gotta go, Doc, they said. Last boat out leaves in ten minutes. Where's Gonzalez, I ask. Oh, he's at the Green Pleasure Pier, feeding the fish."

"He was feeding the fish?" She'd known people to do a lot of strange stuff while under the influence, but having someone feed fish was a first.

Eric put two fingers in his mouth in the internationally recognized symbol for puking.

"Eeeww. Do you want me to make some coffee?"

"It's sweet of you to offer, but no, thanks. I don't think he's ready for coffee yet; he'll just puke it back up. You go back to sleep, babe, I got this. I'm sorry we bothered you."

Babe? Did he just call her *babe?* She forgot to reprimand him for repeating "sorry" again.

Gonzalez came crashing out of the bathroom, declaring, "I aimed real good, Doc!" Then he looked at Michelle as if seeing her for the first time, smiled a drunk smile, and said, "Hey, girl, where you been all my life?"

Eric rolled his eyes. "Come on, Fish Food, you need to sleep it off."

Michelle expected Eric to deposit Gonzalez on the couch, but he opened the door to his bedroom and shoved his friend inside.

"You're giving him your bed?" she asked with disbelief. "What a friend."

"Well, I'm afraid if I put him on the couch, he'll roll off and hurt himself."

"Where you gonna sleep, Doc?" Gonzalez asked, then looked at Michelle and winked again. "Ooh, you lucky dog, you." He stood with his feet spread apart, apparently to give himself stability. His dark eyes were bleary. Those eyes might have been attractive, big and brown and framed with eyelashes that ought to be illegal for a man to have, but their drunken fuzziness canceled out the effect.

"Again, mouth!" Eric scolded.

By this time, Gonzalez's apology was so mumbled as to be unintelligible, though she did catch the word *respect*. Eric stepped into the room and literally pushed Gonzalez to the bed. Danny collapsed face down, not moving.

From the doorway, Michelle peered in and asked, "Is he alive?" Gonzalez belched.

"Yep," Eric affirmed. "But in the morning, he'll wish he wasn't. Here I thought my couch days were over. I promise, I'll have him out of here first thing in the morning." He closed the bedroom door and walked into the living room, calling, "Good night," over his shoulder.

Michelle went back to her room as she heard Eric muttering rude things to himself about his friends who had left their man behind.

But before she closed the door, she wondered for one brief, insane moment, how Eric would react if she were to walk into the living room, take his hand before he settled onto the couch, and invite him to her room, as Danny Gonzalez certainly seemed to think was happening. What would he say if she twined her fingers into his and invited him to take liberties? Would he agree? Would he walk into her room with her, close the door behind him, and turn those sparkly eyes to her in a very non-roommate-like manner?

Or more likely, would he laugh? Would he chuck her under the chin like a five-year-old and say, *you're cute, thanks but no thanks*? She knew he liked her, but as a friend. She knew he respected her, as a roommate. She liked and respected him too, even if he was the sexiest thing in shoe leather. But he also had a lot of honor, and she should respect that as well.

Roommates don't drool over roommates, she reminded herself. Nor do they get naked together just because the house was short a bedroom for one night. She closed her door quietly and got into bed alone.

She woke up in the morning when she heard a moaned, "God, my head!' from the hallway, then the crash of the bathroom door. *Please be aiming real good!* She dressed quickly and was ready for her turn in the bathroom as soon as Gonzalez was done. Good boy, drunk as he was, it still looked like his aim had been sufficient.

When she came out, Eric was folding the couch blanket neatly, both men still wearing the clothes they'd arrived in last night. Or rather, earlier this morning. Gonzalez sat on a chair, holding his head in his hands and muttering, "Don't yell so loud," even though Eric hadn't spoken.

It reminded her of her dad and how many times she'd had to encourage him to sober up and go to work. Except that her dad had never looked quite as regretful as Danny Gonzalez did this morning.

Then Eric's phone rang, and he had plenty to say, as Michelle stood back and eavesdropped shamelessly.

"There's the man of the hour." He swiped the phone open. "Good morning, shithead. You're a disgrace to the Navy. Yeah, I have him, no thanks to you. Why do I sound so mad? Because you left him behind, dirtbag! We don't leave our man behind. I don't care where he was puking. I'm aware we're not the Marines. We still don't leave a man behind. You're just lucky my roommate is a sweet, understanding person. Yes, my roommate is a female. No, I am not -Jeez, get your mind out of the damn gutter! Of course, I want - we are not having this conversation! Shut up and listen. This is what you're going to do. Get your ass up to Dana Point to pick him up. He is in no condition to make it down to base on his own. No, you cannot use my car. Use Uber if you have to. I know it'll cost you your left nut. I don't care. I will text you his ETA when he's on a boat. You just better hope they let him trade his boat ticket without him having to buy a new one. No, I will not introduce you to my roommate. You are undeserving. Now get your ass in gear and wait for my text." He poked viciously at the disconnect icon without even saying goodbye.

"Wow, you sure told him."

Eric jumped, startled. He hadn't noticed her standing there listening in to his side of the conversation. "I'm sorry," he said, then at her look, amended, "I'm getting him out of here right now, I promise."

"No coffee?"

At the sound of the word coffee, Danny turned a pair of beseeching dark eyes towards Eric with a look like a puppy begging daddy for a treat. But Eric was shaking his head, the big meanie.

"You know what I told you last time, Gonzalez. No caffeine when you're hung over. It'll dehydrate you and make your headache worse."

Danny grimaced. "Ah, jeez, Doc! You're no fun."

"Yeah, remind me of that the next time you dislocate your shoulder."

"You know, I have never seen you angry before," she told him.

"Yeah, I know," he replied. "Usually I'm just a great big old cuddly teddy bear."

Michelle wondered if Eric would drop dead from shock if she asked him to show her just how cuddly he was.

"Do you want me to take you two to the dock in the golf cart?" she offered.

"Thanks, but no. I don't want to make you late for work. The walk will do him good." He pulled Gonzalez to his feet. "Come on, Fish Food. Time to go." Gonzalez groaned. The poor guy looked like death on a cracker.

"Do you have something to say to Michelle for letting your drunk ass stay in her home?"

"Thank you, sweet understanding roommate," Gonzalez said, then at Eric's glare, defended, "Hey, you said it first. I'm just agreeing with you."

"You did say it first," Michelle confirmed. "Yes, I was listening, pardon your language." Eric grinned and made sheep eyes. "What is it you want?" she asked. He looked confused. "You told your friend, of course I want - something. What was it?"

"I want to tell you, you're the best roommate ever." He really looked like he had just made that up.

"Well, thanks. You're a pretty good roommate too."

"Even though I bring home drunk buddies to crash here?"

"Yes, even though you help your friends when they can't take care of themselves."

There went the sheep eyes again.

Michelle stepped up and gave Gonzalez a kiss on the cheek. "Stay safe, sailor," she said, then stepped back quickly as the guy's miasma of beer, vomit and body odor hit her. She looked at Eric.

"You could have let him take a shower. He stinks." She waved a hand in front of her nose. "Seriously. He reeks."

"I've smelled him worse. That's what you get for kissing him."

"I doubt that. I don't think such a thing is possible."

"It's possible," Eric said agreeably.

Gonzalez, who apparently was indifferent to his odor, said in a loud stage whisper, "Doc! She kissed me! My head doesn't hurt anymore! It's a miracle!"

Eric was pouting and turned his cheek towards Michelle. "Hey, what about me? I'm the one who did all the work."

"You big goof." She gave him a fraternal peck on the cheek too, then stepped back just as quickly as she had from Gonzalez.

"What, do I smell too?" He didn't smell, but she'd enjoyed that little kiss way more than she should have.

"No, but you need a shave." That was a lame excuse if there ever was one. Eric's cheek was just mildly bristly. Danny was seriously scruffy.

"As soon as I get back," he promised. "It'll be as smooth as a baby's butt." He rubbed a hand over his cheek. "You can be my quality control." Her stomach did a little flip-flop at the prospect of caressing that cheek when it was as smooth as a baby's butt. She knew he was only teasing, but still...

"I'm also going to have to change my sheets, after letting this stinky guy sleep in my bed."

"You may have to burn them," she observed.

Eric opened the front door, but Michelle stopped them and pointed at Danny's feet.

"Was he barefoot when he got here? They may not let him on the boat like that."

"He had sandals on. They fell off when he laid down."

"You mean when he crash landed."

"Yeah, that. Go on, Fish Food, go get your shoes."

Danny screwed up his face as if trying to recall Pi to a hundred places, then after a minute announced, "Sandals!"

"Yes, sandals," Eric repeated patiently. "Go get them. In the bedroom."

Danny leaned his arm against the door frame and let out a sigh. You'd think Eric had asked him to scale Mount Everest without oxygen.

"Oh for goodness sake!" Eric flashed his friend an annoyed look and walked quickly back to his room, returning with a pair of huarache sandals, which he dropped at Danny's feet.

"It would be easier to get a kid out the door on the first day of school. Do you think you can manage to put them on or do I have to do that for you too, little boy?"

"Just as long as I don't have to bend over," Danny whined, shuffling his toes into the shoes.

As the two men stepped out the door, Gonzalez put his hand in front of his face, wincing at the cruel, bright sunshine. "Gah! Bright light, bright light!"

"What happened to your sunglasses?" Eric asked, then looked at Michelle and said, "You can start calling me Mrs. Gonzalez now. I feel like his mother. We need a list. Shoes, shirt, sunglasses – you got your man parts, Gonzalez?"

Danny grabbed at his crotch. "Yeah, they're attached. You wanna see them?"

"No!" Eric and Michelle yelled in unison.

Gonzalez muttered, "My mother would kick your ass. After she kicked mine," then patted at himself as if thinking his sunglasses might be attached to the front of his smelly green tee shirt. He stopped, looked thoughtful, then his face filled with dismay. "Shit, Doc, I think they fell in the water off that pier." He looked like he just might cry. "They were Ray-Bans."

"Well, you are out of luck. You're a good friend, Gonzalez, and I'll do a lot for a friend, but I draw the line at fishing your sunglasses out of the water. Especially water you puked in." He glanced at Michelle and held up his thumb and index finger about an inch apart. "He came this close to spiffing his biscuits into some guy's boat."

They both made "Eeww" faces, then Eric put a hand on Danny's arm.

"When you get back to base and sober up," he instructed. "You call your mother. Even if she threatens to kick your ass. You call her and tell her you love her."

Danny looked at Eric's face with bleary-eyed curiosity. "Why?"

"Because you can." His hand on Danny's arm squeezed firmly. "You never know when you may lose the opportunity to talk to your mother, Danny."

She picked up on the way Eric called his friend Danny, rather than by his surname, and recalled that Eric had said his mother had died years ago.

"Take my advice," Eric said sternly. "Call her. But when you sober up."

He looked at Michelle. "From the look of him at this moment, that could be weeks from now."

Eric put on his own sunglasses, and cruelly left Gonzalez to wince and squint and put his hand over his eyes as they walked down the street. Actually, only Eric walked. Danny stumbled, partly due to the amount of alcohol still in his system, and partly due to his being blinded by the bright morning sun, and mourning the loss of his sunglasses, now sitting at the bottom of Avalon Bay.

After a few steps, Michelle heard Danny saying in a childlike, sing-song voice, "She called you a goof, she called you a goof."

"Shut up, Fish Food," Eric ordered, as Michelle closed the door behind them, her lips tingling at the remembrance of kissing Eric's cheek, and went to take a shower. A cold shower.

******

The next morning, they were sitting in the kitchen drinking Eric's delicious coffee, and Michelle was thinking about how downright domestic the two of them had become, when his phone made a little beep. He picked it up, swiped it open, and chuckled.

"What is it?" she asked

"Danny Gonzalez just sent me some money, to repay me for the boat ticket I had to buy him yesterday. They wouldn't let him use the one from the boat he missed. And he included a note." Eric scrolled down the screen to read the note. "Thanks for letting me crash at your place, Doc."

Eric paused, as if there was more that he wasn't reading, then looked at her with a strange expression on his face.

"Is there more?" she asked.

"Um, yeah," was the enigmatic reply. He looked reluctant to share the remainder, which was uncharacteristic for gregarious, talkative, my-life-is-an-open-book Eric.

"Well now that you've piqued my curiosity, you have to tell me the rest. Don't worry, I've heard swear words before. Mostly from you. Or is it Navy secrets?"

"It's not profane, nor classified," Eric said hesitantly. "Look, you know Danny was really, really drunk, and I think he took some stuff way out of context." Michelle nodded. "I'm going to have to have a little talk with that boy about his drinking."

"What happened to, accept the things you can't change, and people making their own decisions in life?" she asked.

"That's all true, and I'm not taking any of it back, but I still think Danny would benefit from a little advice about those decisions he's making. The fish swimming off the pier really don't need that kind of fish food." He made a face that clearly said. "Eeww!" at the thought of it.

Michelle rotated her hand at him in a, *come on, tell me the rest*, gesture. "What was the rest of his note?"

"Ok, well, now, don't go all Chewbacca on me." Eric tilted his head back and made a throaty "*hhrraaeerr*" growl – apparently the Chewbacca attitude he was warning her away from. "The rest of his note says, 'Kiss Michelle for me'."

Unbidden, her face started to feel a little warm, and despite his silly growling noise, Eric looked like he was blushing a little too. He stood up, appearing relieved it was time for him to leave for work. Michelle looked into her coffee cup, then up at Eric.

"Well it would be rude not to do what your friend asks you to," she said, trying to sound teasing.

Eric grinned, leaned down and quickly kissed her cheek. "That's from Danny," he said. "Have a nice day." Then he was out the door.

Michelle put a hand to her cheek after he'd left, savoring the brief warm touch, yet aware that it was meant strictly in a friendly way. Danny might have sent the affection as a remnant of his drunkenness, but the actual kiss had come from Eric's lips, and she was a bit scared to admit how much she'd liked it.

The various female components of her body were panting at her, *he's hot. Can we have him?* At the same time, her mind was screaming, *oh dear god, what are you thinking?*

Well now you know you made the right call, not giving in to that brief moment of insanity the other night, she told herself. *You practically invited the man to kiss you, and he did – but exactly the way he'd kiss his sister. He's your nice, sweet, friendly, adorable, respectful* roommate *for goodness sake.*

Too bad she had the major hots for him.

17

SEVEN YEARS EARLIER, AVALON

Considering the island's status as a tourist destination, the beach in Avalon was actually rather small, jammed along the side of Crescent Avenue along the pedestrian zone, next to the Green Pleasure Pier. On a clear day like today, you could see all the way across to the mainland, though even then it was just a dark smudge across the water.

Yesterday had been an amazing day, and she had hopes for today too. Michelle's dad had actually come home from work sober. And he smiled. He was actually a nice-looking man when he was sober and smiling. Michelle had inherited his dark brunette hair and bright blue eyes. Her mother had had blue eyes also, but from the few photos Michelle had seen, her mom's eyes had been pale and faded, and she'd been a blond.

Dad didn't complain about what she made for dinner, though he still didn't help any in the kitchen.

"I got my report card today," she told him. She pulled it out of her backpack and gave it to him. "Straight A's again. Can you sign it, Dad?"

He glanced at it briefly. She'd hoped for some words of praise, acknowledgment for all her hard work. But she'd hoped in vain. He just signed it where she indicated and handed it back to her. At least she hadn't had to forge his signature this time.

After finishing dinner, she went to her room to study for finals, but kept her door open to listen for any sounds of clinking bottles. She'd set a goal on her first day of high school, to come home with the best grades possible. Now, at the end of her junior year, she still had her A average, but she wasn't quite sure why she bothered to keep it up. Even on sober days, he wasn't interested.

The Avalon beach may have been small, but it was warm and sunny that Saturday, and Michelle was sitting on a beach towel in a new pink swimsuit she'd bought with money she'd earned herself, fixing her neighbor's golf cart engine. The boy Justin, from her class at school, sitting next to her – dare she call him her boyfriend? – seemed happy in her company, though his eyes seemed to wander more towards her bosom than to her face.

"I hate that stupid reading class," Justin said with vehemence. He sat behind her in American Literature.

"I like it." American Lit was her favorite class. It allowed her to read on the school's time.

"The only good thing about it is getting to look at your ass," was Justin's reply.

That was a little crude, but she was sure he meant it in a nice way.

"Hey, look what I got." Justin unzipped his backpack and pulled out a plastic bag. It was obvious that what he had was a bottle. Michelle started to get nervous.

"That's not booze?" she asked with trepidation, looking around nervously at the other beach-goers. But they were mostly tourists and unlikely to be concerned with the antics of a couple of local teenagers.

"Of course, it is, baby girl." He pulled the bag's edge away enough to read the label. "Chivas Regal. Sounds fancy, doesn't it?"

"Where did you get that?" She tried to squelch the unbidden squeaky tone her voice had taken.

"At home. The old man won't notice I took it. It was way in the back of the cabinet." Justin peeled off the gold foil over the top of the bottle and unscrewed the cap. He held the grocery bag around the bottle as he sniffed at the opening. "Wow, that's intense! You want to try it?"

"No." She shook her head. "It's booze. I don't drink booze. And neither should you. You're supposed to be twenty-one. Your dad will kill you if he finds out you took that." She leaned away from the offered bottle as if it were a snake.

"Don't be such a prude," Justin said with disapproval. "Try a little. It'll loosen you up." He took a swig himself, and coughed harshly as the whisky went down. "You could use a little loosening up. You're way too uptight." He offered the bottle again, and the smell wafting from it turned her stomach.

"Maybe later you can come over to my house. My parents went to the mainland for the day." He nodded towards the boat dock where the Catalina Express was pulling away. "We'll have the place to ourselves." He wiggled his eyebrows and grinned suggestively.

"I don't think so." She scooted a bit away from him and his smelly bottle. "I don't want any of your smelly booze."

"Ah, jeez, Michelle, don't be such a baby. It's not just any booze. It's," he looked at the label again. "The finest single blend Scotch whisky."

"I don't care if it's the nectar of the gods. I'm not drinking it." Michelle's breath was starting to get a little short. She hoped she wasn't developing asthma or something.

"God, you are such a prude." Justin frowned in disapproval. "Come on, have some fun."

"You don't need that crap to have fun. It's disgusting."

"Fine. I'll drink it then. You can watch." He'd already sipped enough that his eyes were starting to get bleary. He took another slug, then capped the bottle, but left the foil seal laying on the sand.

"Come on, let's go to my house and finish this off." He got that suggestive glint in his eyes again.

If he hadn't started drinking, she might have been tempted. This wasn't how she'd anticipated this day going. She had thought of Justin as fascinating and handsome at school, and had felt flattered when he'd asked her out. But he was getting less and less interesting by the moment.

"I'm not hanging out with someone who drinks." She started gathering up her things as Justin grabbed at her arm.

"Jesus Christ, Michelle, are you really that much of a frigid bitch? I thought you'd be some fun."

She slapped his hand away and stood up, clutching her towel and the clothes she'd worn over her swimsuit. "Get your hands off me, you jerk. Stay away from me and keep that shit away from me or I'll tell your parents."

She shoved her feet into her flip-flops and practically ran to the sidewalk, where she started speed-walking away. Behind her, Justin called out, "Bitch!" as she felt her eyes start to tear. But she sniffled the tears back, refusing to let passers-by see her cry.

Two things she was sure of. Justin was definitely not her boyfriend. And on Monday, she was going to ask her American Literature teacher if she could sit in a different seat in class, one where Justin didn't have a view of her ass.

As soon as she got home, she changed into hiking clothes, grabbed her backpack, and headed uphill. Solo hiking was discouraged on Catalina Island, due to the combined dangers of steep rocky terrain, abrupt drop-offs, snakes and buffalo. But today she didn't care. Michelle was familiar enough with the island's hiking trails to avoid the dangers, and kept a sharp eye out for hazards. Somehow the threat of snakes and bison in the hills seemed like a lesser danger compared to what she'd left back on the beach.

She found a flat rock with a view of the ocean, a good place to sit and rest. Of course, one could see the ocean from the beach, the Green Pleasure Pier, or pretty much anywhere in Avalon. But today she needed space, lots of space, between her and the beach, and Justin and his stupid bottle of Chivas Regal and his suggestive eyebrow wiggles.

Her backpack contained three essential items. One, a bottle of water. She took a healthy gulp, thirsty from her climb. Two, a thick library book. It wasn't the book they were reading in her American Literature class. She had finished that book, though she'd bet money that Justin hadn't even opened it. He was too busy looking at her ass. This book was replete with vampires and magic, and a refreshing lack of reality.

Important item number three was her pink hoody. Sure, it was way too warm for a sweatshirt, but she didn't wear it for protection from the elements. She pulled up the hood enough that she could see only the ocean, and the words in her book.

Everything else was blocked out, unable to hurt her. The hoody worked every time, if only for a little while.

The day had started out so happily. Dad had been sober and was at work. She had high hopes he'd come home sober again and not go out to the bar this evening. When Justin had invited her to the beach, she'd been happier than she'd been in as long as she could remember. But that happiness was ruined the moment he'd pulled that bottle out of his backpack. Justin knew about her father – didn't everyone? Did he think it was, like father, like daughter? No way, she vowed. There was no way on earth she would ever be interested in a guy who drank, especially an underage drinker who stole his liquor from his parents. Maybe she was a prude, a stick in the mud, a bitch. If that was what it took to be everything her father wasn't, that was what she would have to be.

Right. No pressure there.

18

Eric was pounding on her door and calling out her name, interrupting the pleasant dream she'd been having. She'd been dreaming she was laying on the bow of a boat, a yacht actually, wearing a bikini. There was a man reclining next to her in the dream, his features indistinct other than a general impression of fair skin and muscles. The boat bobbed and swayed gently in the sunshine.

But her roommate was obliterating the dream with his pounding and yelling. What was his problem? She was in bed, not in the bathroom. If he needed to pee like a racehorse, there was no impediment.

"Michelle! Wake up! We're having an earthquake!"

An earthquake? They weren't having an earthquake. Or if they were, it was a small one, too minor to wake her up. Maybe that's why the boat in the dream bobbed a little.

"It's fine," she called out, trying to fall asleep again and perhaps return to her pleasant dream. This was way too early o'clock to be alert.

"Michelle, don't play around," Eric called through the door in his maybe-he's really-an-admiral voice, the one he'd used when he'd forced her to wear a sun hat. "You should get up and come out here where it's safer."

"Oh all right!" She might as well get up. He obviously wasn't going to let her get back to sleep. She shrugged into her bathrobe and shuffled towards the door, but just before she touched the handle, Eric added, "Put something on your feet."

Obediently, she slipped her feet into her flip-flops. She shouldn't have needed to be reminded. She was one of that rare breed, the native-born Californian. She should have known to keep footwear handy in case of earthquakes. She was well aware of earthquake protocol. Little ones that didn't wake you up, no worries. If it was The Big One, then you could worry.

Even with his too-sensitive earthquake concern, Eric was still so polite and considerate. He had actually gotten dressed, because he'd promised not to walk around the house in his underwear. He'd thrown on shorts, a tee shirt, and of course, his flip-flops. But his shirt was inside out and backward. The little white tag was right in front of her face.

"Took you long enough," he said with irritation. He'd turned on the hallway light and it took a moment for her eyes to adjust to its brightness.

"Well that's what you get for waking me up from a perfectly good sleep," she grumbled.

"Not a morning person then, are we?"

"Is it morning?"

"Technically. Barely. Call it, zero dark thirty. Come on, let's get out of here."

"And go where? Look, Eric, if there was an earthquake, it was a little one, and it's over."

"A little one!" he echoed. "The earth's tectonic plates are moving, and that hill back there makes me nervous." He gestured towards the back wall, which faced towards the hill behind the house. "What about aftershocks?"

"I'll survive," she said curtly. "I'm going back to bed. If you want to stand in the door frame, knock yourself out." She waved a hand towards the front door before turning back towards her room, her bed, and hopefully, her dream of a bobbing boat and that fair-skinned, muscular man.

Déjà vu. They were reenacting the day they'd met, starting with him grabbing her arm to pull her away from the perceived danger of her room and the hillside behind it, just as he had when she'd almost stepped out in front of a golf cart, as he pulled her into the hallway. He actually looked concerned. Concerned for her?

"Haven't you lived in California for a couple of years already?" she asked. "Don't tell me this is your first earthquake?"

"No, but since I was deployed half the time, I managed to miss most of them."

"Where do you suggest we go?" Tiredness put a touch of snottiness into her voice.

"I don't know. Outside maybe?"

"You're joking, right?" She looked at his face. He wasn't joking.

"Oh for goodness sake!" She detached her arm from his hand and marched into the living room, crossed to the door, and opened it to the dark of early morning. Very early morning. All she saw and heard were dark and quiet.

"Look!" She pointed. "Nobody is outside panicking. If there was a quake, it was too small to bother anyone. All the neighbors are in bed asleep, and that's where I'm going back to. The people in the bars probably didn't even notice their drinks slosh. If you want to stand in the doorway all night, be my guest. This tremor won't even make the local news report."

Eric followed her, looked out the door, observed the lack of panic, and closed the door.

"OK, let's compromise. We can hang out in the living room for a while, just in case there's an aftershock."

"Are you serious?"

"Yes, I'm serious." He sat down and patted the seat next to him. "You know me, I'm all about safety."

She sat down next to him and yawned. "I thought you were all about the healthy."

"The two go hand in hand. I just want to be sure you're safe."

"Aren't you sweet." She'd meant to say that sarcastically, to convey annoyance at him having rousted her from a sound sleep and a pleasant dream as if they were under attack from enemy torpedoes. But in reality, it was sweet of him to be concerned about her safety, and she found it was actually rather sweet to sit next to him here on the sofa, in the dark of technically, barely morning. Maybe if she sat real still, he'd fall asleep and she could sneak back to bed. He'd fallen asleep pretty fast the day he'd come home from reserve duty, right here on this couch. Hopefully he was tired enough to nod off that soon tonight.

"If there are any aftershocks, we probably won't even feel it." She yawned again, to encourage Eric to do the same, but instead he pulled his phone out of his pocket.

"What size do you think it was?"

"Machine wash cold, tumble dry low."

"What are you talking about? Did the earthquake rattle your brain?" He was obviously a bit annoyed at her nonchalant attitude.

She gestured at his shirt front. "Did you get dressed in the dark?"

"Well, yes." He peered down his front, realizing his wardrobe malfunction. With a muttered, "Oh, jeez," he pulled off the shirt, turned it right side in, and pulled it back over his head, so quickly she barely had time to ogle.

"Is this better?"

Tired as she was, she still giggled at him. "Oh, yes. That is way better."

Worn correctly, the tee shirt showed a silhouette of a bucking bronco and displayed the words, "Save a Horse, Ride a Cowboy."

"My sister gave me this shirt, a couple Christmases ago. Apparently, I'm hard to buy for."

"Maybe they should pitch in and get you some common sense about not panicking about a teeny tremor and saving it for The Big One," she teased.

"Well since they live in Florida, they have no concept of earthquakes."

"Don't you have hurricanes down there?"

"Yes," he affirmed. "Totally different concept. With hurricanes, you get a couple days' notice and can make advance preparations."

She wanted to close her eyes, but the light of Eric's phone suddenly shone. "What are you doing?"

"Looking up this earthquake. Here it is, the Southern California Earthquake Center at CalTech. Three point four on the Richter scale. Centered one hundred miles off the coast of Santa Barbara."

"Three point four? That's not an earthquake. That's barely a tremor. I can't believe you even felt it."

"I can't believe you didn't. Let's just wait a little longer, just in case. Please. That hill behind the house makes me nervous."

"Are you scared to be alone?" Tiredness was making her cranky. "Turn that off."

Obligingly, he set his phone on the coffee table and after a moment the screen went dark. Michelle sat real still, instigating her plan of a moment ago to hope that Eric would fall asleep so she could sneak back to her bed. It was rather surreal and eerie, sitting here in the dimness, lit only by the light from the hallway behind them. Just a few minutes, then she was going to sneak back to her room and, hopefully, to that pleasant dream.

She rubbed her eyes, yawned, and rested her head against the back of the sofa. Just a few minutes.

******

A song dimly slid into her brain, nudging her consciousness. It wasn't Eric singing. The music was recorded, and in tune.

Oh jeez, I've joined the Navy. They were playing the Navy theme song somewhere nearby. Eric was going to be so mad at her for joining the Navy when he'd left it.

But her enlistment was brief. Her pillow shifted a bit under her face and the naval music stopped.

Groggily, she came half awake. She wasn't in the Navy, she realized, but she was in the company of a former sailor. In fact, she was practically on top of him. She'd never had the opportunity to sneak back to her bed.

She wasn't just leaning on him, she was half laying on him, and Eric, in turn, was almost laying down beneath her. Her feet were tucked up next to her on the sofa, only completing the laying concept, his arm was firmly around her shoulders, as if to protect her from further tremors, and her face was pressed against the shoulder of that silly cowboy tee shirt, her arm draped casually, intimately, across his midsection. She was cozy, comfortable, warm and safe feeling. Nothing was going to hurt her, not even an earthquake. She was not lost; she was not lonely.

He was warm and solid, his steady heartbeat soothing beneath her face, and she was snug and half asleep. Still not fully conscious, she murmured, "Mmm, you're cuddly."

She came to full consciousness when she heard Eric reply, "Thank you. That's a lovely thing to hear first thing in the morning."

Oh, crap. Had she actually said that? Out loud? Unbelievably, somehow, she had the couch blanket over her. It was a light enough blanket that it wasn't suffocating in the heat, but warm enough to keep a person comfortable when the cool island breezes chilled the air at night. Had Eric covered her with the blanket after she fell asleep, the way she had done for him when he returned from reserve duty?

The cotton under her face was damp. She'd drooled on him. Literally this time. *Freya*, how embarrassing. Maybe he wouldn't notice.

Unlikely. He noticed everything. He'd noticed her accidentally muttering about his cuddliness. He certainly must have noticed she was practically laying on top of him, because otherwise how could the blanket be covering her?

Despite how delicious that felt, she sat up, trying to discreetly wipe at the small wet spot on his shoulder.

He even smelled good, like cotton and plain soap. At this time of day, a guy should smell like B.O. and morning breath. But no, Eric smelled like heaven.

Eric sat up also, and she sensed him setting his phone back on the coffee table. It was still dark out.

"What time is it?" It was eerie, sleeping here on the couch with her roommate. Eerie, and way too comfortable.

"Five a.m." His voice was soft next to her and she felt him shift, sitting up. "I'm sorry I woke you. I tried to sit still after you fell asleep but I had to turn off my alarm."

So the Navy music was his phone alarm. Figured. You can take the boy out of the Navy, but you can't take the Navy out of the boy.

"You mean you sat up awake all this time? And why is your alarm set for five in the morning?"

"No, I drifted off to sleep after you did." He squinted down at his shoulder, where a moment ago her face had rested.

"Hey, now I have your DNA. I can have you cloned."

Darn. He had noticed the drool.

"Please don't. I think one of me is more than enough bitchiness for the world."

"I'm on shift at six," he explained. "That's why my alarm was on."

"Well I don't have to be at work until nine, and my phone is in my room, so if you don't mind, I'm going back to bed. I'm pretty sure the earth's tectonic plates aren't going to shift anymore tonight."

She stood up, quickly, shoving aside the blanket that had covered her. Their half laying down position had been definitely a bit too intimate for platonic roommates and she was scared to admit how good it felt.

Eric came to his feet also. Of course, he had to get ready for work. She didn't, not yet.

"Good night." She stepped towards her room. "Or, good early morning."

His hand was on her elbow in his helping a little old lady across the street gesture, and it stayed there until she was in front of her door. He was probably nervous that the walls might come tumbling down on them.

Walking her home. Déjà vu all over again.

Now it was a bit awkward. Was he going to come into her room and tuck her in? The concept of it was both thrilling and totally scary. To cover up her ambivalent mindset, she gave him one of her sisterly cheek kisses.

"Thanks for being my hero."

His hand lingered on her elbow another moment. "Girl, don't do that unless you mean it," he said, just as he had the day he'd moved in when she'd pretended to be preparing to jump off the pier. Except that he said it a lot softer.

"Go save the world, goof." She stepped through the door and closed it behind her. As she got back into her bed for a couple more hours of sleep, she suddenly recalled the dream she'd been having at the moment Eric had woken her up. That indistinct man next to her on that boat had not been a vague generic male. It had been Eric.

19

When Eric was off duty, he frequently walked into town to meet up with friends and old Navy buddies who came over from San Diego. It was on one of these evenings that he stopped with one foot on the threshold, turned and looked at Michelle curled up on the couch with her nose in a very large book, and walked backward until he stood in front of her. It took her ten seconds to notice him standing there.

She lowered the book just enough to look at him over the top. "Huh?"

"I said, I'm going to meet a couple guys to play some pool. Would you like to join us?"

She glanced at the page of her book. "Um…"

"Seriously? You would seriously rather spend a beautiful spring evening with fictional vampires than with real live human beings?"

"I like real live human beings." Actually, she kind of liked the real live human being standing in front of her at the moment.

"Well then, put on your flip-flops and let's bounce." She didn't protest when he took the book out of her hands, but she did wince when he closed it and set it on the coffee table without marking her place. He took her hand and pulled her up from the couch, and there was an awkward moment when they found themselves almost nose to nose. Then he stepped back and let her retrieve her flip-flops from under the couch. "Don't worry," he said as they walked out the door. "If anyone tries to bite your neck, I've got your six."

*****

She hesitated at the door of the Marlin Club, consumed by memories.

Gary calling her at all hours, to summon her here to drag her dad out. Her dad's objections, cajoling, her tears when she pulled his arm and forced him to leave. The stares of the other patrons – some sympathetic, some irate, some condemning. A few other drunks calling out, "Aw, let him stay, spoilsport!" Memories of having to scrounge up odd jobs to pay his tab.

And a more recent memory, of walking willingly into this bar with Eric a year ago, and then dashing out a few minutes later with a pulse like a rabbit on speed.

Beside her, Eric had his 'escorting a little old lady across the street' hand on her elbow. "Got your six, remember?" He smiled encouragingly.

She looked at the open door of the bar. It was just a door, not the gateway to hell. She was just going to be hanging out with a friend, not going through some old trauma. Her friend Eric was smiling at her. He had her six, remember? He held out his arm like some kind of escort, just like he'd done the day they'd met when he insisted on walking her home from the Green Pleasure Pier. That time, she had ignored the offered arm. Today, she giggled and smacked it lightly. "You are such a goof," she told him as they went in.

It was fine, for a while. They played some pool – she was pretty bad at it, since the only places to play pool in Avalon were in bars, so she had no experience with the game. The jukebox had been well fed and the song genres rotated loudly between rock, country and hip-hop. Somebody was apparently a fan of the oldies. When the melodic guitar intro of La Bamba started, Danny Gonzalez, Eric's buddy whom he had brought home that night when his other friends had left him behind, set down his bottle of beer, grabbed Michelle's waist and spun her around in an attempt to tango.

"*Muchacha! Bailamos!*" he crowed.

"What are you saying?" she demanded in a voice gone a bit squeaky.

Eric, who had grown up in a part of the country with a large Cuban population, glanced up from the pool table and said, "He's asking you to dance."

She pulled herself away from Gonzalez as her breath grew short. "Get your hands off me!"

Danny obeyed her shriek, and looked contrite. "Hey, I'm sorry, I didn't mean..."

But he was talking to himself. She was already out the door.

At least this time she didn't dash out into traffic. She stood next to the door and leaned against the wall, breathing deep, getting calm. In through the nose, out through the mouth. She wasn't surprised when Eric came out and stood next to her, but she crossed her arms over her chest. He leaned against the wall also, and mimicked her posture, arms crossed over his own chest.

"You're not taking my pulse," she told him, looking into the street without really seeing it.

He turned towards her and grinned. "I don't think I need to. Look, Gonzalez didn't mean anything. Don't be mad at him."

"I'm not. It's not him, it's me."

"I'm surprised you didn't understand him. Don't you speak Spanish?"

She felt a bit annoyed, and pushed herself away from the wall she'd been leaning on to give him a dirty look. From inside the bar, La Bamba faded away and Uptown Funk started playing.

"You think that just because I have a Spanish name, that I automatically speak Spanish? Isn't that a bit presumptive? Do you speak," she waved a hand at him, at his fair skin and Scandinavian features, "Danish?"

"No, I don't speak Danish. I've never been to Denmark." Wow, that was a first. Someplace he hadn't been to.

"Well, I've never been to Mexico. Or Spain, or South America."

"OK, fair enough. I apologize for assuming. Ma'am." He smiled apologetically, but she wasn't actually mad at him. Or at Danny Gonzalez.

"Look, I'm sorry," he said. "I didn't realize this place would be such a bad experience for you. Do you want me to take you home?"

No, she didn't want that. It would be unfair of her to take him away from this evening that he'd planned on hanging out with his buddies, just because of his crazy roommate. She remembered the first day they'd met, right here, and how she'd rudely told him to go back and play with his friends. That wasn't who she was anymore, or who she should be.

"No, you don't have to do that. I'm sorry if I'm ruining your evening. If I need to go home, I can go by myself."

"You are not going home by yourself. I brought you here, and I'll leave with you."

Despite her anxiety and near panic attack, she was still amused at him. "How very old-fashioned of you. Let me tell you a secret. The fifties are over."

"I'm not ditching a friend when I invited you to hang out with us. Remember,"

She finished his sentence. "Your mama raised a gentleman."

He smiled and said, "Well, yeah, she did."

"You shouldn't have to be stuck out here with a roommate who's insane."

"You are not insane."

"I think I am." Danny Gonzalez surely must think she was insane. She'd treated him as if he were some kind of pervert, which she knew he wasn't.

Eric was shaking his head. "No, you're not. You're just a girl with, well, with issues. But there's nothing wrong with that. Everyone has issues."

It was nice of him to try and make her feel better like that. But she didn't quite agree with him. "Not everyone has issues."

He nodded. "Yes, everyone."

"Then what are your issues?" Being too nice, too helpful, too sparkly?

"Sweetheart, you're not ready to hear about my issues." But his smile disproved that. Someone with an upbeat attitude like his, did not have issues.

She defensively kept her arms crossed over her chest and looked across the sidewalk.

"It's OK," Eric said, patting her arm.

"No, it's not OK," she snapped. "You can't possibly understand."

"Well, I could if you told me." He tapped the side of his head. "Big ears, remember?"

She so regretted the childish way she'd just snapped at him. If he was going to stick around while she obsessed over her issues, she at least should give him the courtesy of an explanation, such as it was.

"See that bench there?" She nodded at the green and white seat across from where they were standing. "It's been painted a couple of times over the past few years, but it's been there forever."

"Do you want to go sit there?" he asked. Obviously he thought she'd mentioned the bench because she might be tired. But no. She would never ever sit on that particular bench again. She'd sit on the concrete first. She'd sit in the street in the path of an oncoming golf cart before she'd ever sit on that particular bench.

As much as she never wanted to sit on it again, she couldn't help staring at it.

"There was a big fire here on the island when I was twelve," she started, trying to keep her voice level as she spoke. Like she had experienced the day she'd met Eric, words that she'd never enunciated aloud before came out into the warm light of the tropical sunset. "It burned ten percent of the island's area, and reached the outskirts of town. People were being evacuated to the mainland. The Los Angeles County Fire Department was out here with helicopters, trying to drop flame retardant, and the Coast Guard came to help with the evacuations. The Marines brought volunteer firefighters over from the mainland in their helicopters."

Eric nodded in appreciation. "Hooyah for the Marines," he said with a small, grim smile.

"I kept waiting for my dad to come home and get me. It got dark and he still didn't come. I went out into the street in front of the house and I could see the smoke and a red glare in the sky from the flames. Ash was actually falling from the sky. Finally, I walked into town. I peeked into the doors of the bars and found him sitting in there," she gestured towards the inside of the Marlin Club, "drinking with his buddies. They wouldn't let me go into the bar to get him, of course, since I was only twelve. After a while I had to ask some guy walking by to go in and get him." She took a deep breath, willing her voice not to wobble. "Dad came out looking all irritated that I was bothering him. I told him we had to go now, they were evacuating people. All the tourists had already left and they were putting residents on the boats to Long Beach."

She gathered in oxygen for steadiness, in through the nose, out through the mouth. "You know what he said?"

Eric just shook his head, as if he was afraid to guess.

"Did he say, thank you for coming to get me, let's go? Did he put his arms around me and say, don't worry honey, Daddy will take care of you? Did he say, we'll go visit Cousin Joyce in Temecula and she can tell you about your mother? No, he did not. He just said, I ain't going nowhere, and he went back into the bar, and I heard him call out, Pop me another cold one."

"What did you do?" Eric asked, in a tight voice, as if he was trying to keep some kind of emotion bottled up inside. Michelle for her part was trying to channel anger, in order to keep away tears.

"I sat on that bench, crying like a stupid baby. A couple of people passing by stopped and asked if I was OK. I couldn't tell them that I was scared to death that our house might burn down, that the fire might make its way into town and burn the whole place down, including the stupid people who didn't leave in time. I sucked it up and told them I was fine, my dad was on his way to pick me up, he'd be here any minute now.

"I kept watching people walking down to the boat docks, and I wanted to just jump up and run down there and jump onto the first boat and get away. It was getting pretty chaotic by then. I'm sure a kid could slip into a group and pretend to be with some other family.

"But I could see into the door of the bar and I could see my dad sitting there drinking his beer. What if I left and the place burned down? He wouldn't be able to escape, not in his condition. What if he tried to walk home? He'd be going towards the fire, not away from it. What if he did try to get on a boat and I wasn't there to help him walk straight? They probably wouldn't let him on the boat if he looked too drunk.

"So I just sat there on that bench, like an idiot. A pathetic loser who had no control over her life. I must have sat there for two hours, and I closed my eyes, both to hold back the tears, and also so I wouldn't have to see all the normal people, being normal, you know, leaving town when there was a huge fire on the horizon.

"I must have fallen asleep for a few minutes, because I woke up feeling chilly. I opened my eyes, and there was fog rolling in, rolling up from the water towards the hills. The wind had changed direction and was blowing that wet marine layer into the fire, and just like that, it wasn't pushing towards town anymore. About half an hour later, Dad came out of the bar, because they closed the place and made him leave. His daughter couldn't make him walk out that door, but locking the beer fridge and turning off the lights did the trick. He stumbled out and stood there for a minute, like he'd forgotten which way to go, and I came over and said, let's go home, Dad.

"He didn't say anything, not so much as a thank you for sitting on a bench for two hours to make sure he didn't burn to death. He just let me take him home and when we got there, he just went straight to bed like it was any other evening, and I went and cried myself to sleep, like it was any other evening.

"They stopped evacuating people in the morning. It took five days until the fire was put out completely, but the danger to town was over and the people who'd evacuated came back, and in a few days, everyone went back to school and work and tourists started to come back. Later they figured out the fire had been started by accident by a careless contractor working with a torch."

Eric just stood next to her, listening to her talk. She was, in this particular instance, glad. If he had touched her, even just a tiny pat on the arm, never mind a full-on hug, she would have instantly, completely fallen apart into as many pieces as the wine glass under a groom's heel at a Jewish wedding.

"I'm so sorry, sweetheart," he said. "You deserved so much better than that. I wish I'd been there."

"No, you don't. It was terrifying."

"That's why I wish I'd been there. There is no way I would have let a twelve-year-old kid sit there like that, unsupervised and terrified. I would have had you over my shoulder in a fireman's carry in a heartbeat and not put you down until you were on a boat. And then I would have gone back and done the same for your idiot dad."

"But he refused to leave."

"Do you think I'd let that stop me?" He held up his arm and flexed his muscle, and she was well aware he wasn't doing it to just show off. "I didn't start working out just yesterday, you know. I've moved a few unco-operative adults from point A to point B in my time."

She realized that he was most like referring to people who couldn't cooperate because they were unconscious and wounded. She also felt a slight thrill at the concept of his flinging her over his shoulder and carry-ing her away.

"He should have come with me just because it was the sane thing to do and because I'd begged him to. But he didn't. Because of course who would listen to a stupid loser of a kid anyway."

Eric looked at her with complete and utter disbelief in his warm hazel eyes. "You can't possibly feel like any of this was your fault, like it was any kind of personal deficiency on your part that your dad was the way it was. Lord, you are the furthest thing from a stupid loser in the universe. You can't blame yourself for any of this. Your dad-"

She waved a dismissive hand at him. "Yeah, I know, he had a disease, and that's what made him dislike me."

She continued to stare at that traumatizing green and white bench, not because she wanted to see it, but because if she looked at Eric, she'd end up on his shoulder again, and people would really get the wrong idea about them.

Eric could see that Michelle was bravely trying to restrain herself from crying at the memory of that night. He was amazed at her strength in keeping the tears at bay. How absolutely terrifying that had to be, for a twelve-year-old kid, to have to sit there alone, wondering of her house was going to burn down, if her town was going to burn down. How coura-geous of her to stay there to take care of, and wait for, her uncaring father, rather than bolting for safety and leaving the undeserving drunk to his own devices.

When he'd been twelve, his most traumatic experience had been being told he was going to need braces on his teeth. A far cry from being traumatized over the possibility of a fiery death or sudden homelessness.

How incredibly unbelievable that an undeserving man like that should have been blessed with such an amazing daughter, and yet had not appreciated the treasure he had. And at the same time, people who probably would have made excellent parents and who would have loved and cherished their children, were childless.

Sometimes the universe was just fucking unfair.

He wished he'd known this stuff the day he'd met her, the day he'd walked her home from the Green Pleasure Pier. He would have walked into her house without an invitation and tried to shake some sense into the guy.

And after shaking the man, he would have sat him down and said, "Mr. Diaz. Sir."

Yes, he would have given the man the respect of a "Sir" even though he didn't deserve it.

"Don't you know you have an amazing, strong, smart, loyal daughter here?" he would have said. "Do you not appreciate all she's done for you, even though you don't deserve her? Could you not put down that damn bottle for a minute, open your eyes, and be a father for a change? You're being given an amazing opportunity," his imaginary conversation with Gregory Diaz continued, "one that not everyone is privileged to have, and you're blowing it with your selfishness. And to top it off, you're making your daughter feel like it's somehow her fault, like there's something wrong with her, when nothing could be further from the truth. Don't you realize you're ruining her childhood? No, more than ruining it. You're stealing it, and no kid deserves that."

On second thought, maybe it was for the best that he hadn't been aware of all the painful details of Michelle's dad's idiocy and poor to nonexistent parenting skills. He would most likely have ended up being arrested for assault, and wouldn't that have been a black mark on his otherwise unblemished service record.

But from what Michelle had told him about the man's apathy, all the scolding, respect or shaking Eric might have used probably would have had about as much effect as a fly trying to bore through a mountain. How was it possible that a man so absolutely clueless could have had a part in creating an awesome young woman like Michelle?

He found her lack of family to be disturbing. Though he had lived a bachelor life, away from most of his relatives, the distances were only in miles, not in sentiment. He could always count on them to be there for him, and he for them, even if it was mostly via Skype or text or email.

And when he did have the chance to get home to Florida, he reveled in the chaos of a big family, the kids running around, the scanning about at the appropriate age group of female relatives and in-laws, asking, "Who's pregnant now?" and looking to see who blushed. His niece Joanna called him the hormone whisperer, because he had more than once diagnosed a pregnancy just by looking at a face, sometimes before the mom-to-be even knew it yet.

He was flattered that his assorted relatives came to him for advice when he visited, and he flat-out adored playing with the kids. He was always up for a game of tag or soccer, or a visit to the golf course or batting cages. He minded the little ones so their parents could have date nights, even changed dirty diapers while giving the offending little pooper an expressive sermon on why he or she was the absolutely stinkiest kid he'd ever met. But once the child was all cleaned up and sweet-smelling, it was all cuddles, kisses and peek-a-boos. The little ones especially enjoyed his piggy-back rides and he needed little to no encouragement to roar like a dragon while doing it.

How incredibly sad that Michelle hadn't been able to experience that. He considered occasionally asking her if she'd like to take a few days off and fly to Florida with him for a visit. Might she find the noisy, rowdy bunch of them intimidating, or exhilarating? Brenda most likely would adopt Michelle. His sister was usually critical of the women he'd dated, and had flat-out detested his ex-wife. But Michelle was neither his date nor his wife. She was a friend with little real family other than a cousin in Temecula that she apparently wasn't close to, and that was why Brenda would adopt her.

"Look," he went on, verbally now rather than in his mind, "I would never, ever, wish someone dead. But your dad, well, he's gone now, and whatever your relationship with him was, however dysfunctional it was, you don't have to go through that anymore. I'm not saying you should just forget everything that's ever made you unhappy, but you can compartmentalize it."

He glanced at the amused expression she showed him, glad to see her relaxing a little after the tight anxiety she'd been experiencing this evening.

"Yes, I know a few five-syllable words," he informed her. "I know the last thing you want to do right now is to go back into the lion den, but I think someone in there wants to apologize to you. If you'll be OK out here for a minute, I'll go get Gonzalez and have him come out here."

She shook her head. "No."

"You need me to stay with you?" He pulled his phone out of his pocket. "No problem, I'll call him and get him out here."

"Don't call the guy on the phone when he's six feet away, you goof. I meant, no, I don't need to stay out here and neither do you. I can go back in there and talk to Danny myself. I'm supposed to be an adult and I should be able to act like one."

"Nobody is doubting that you're an adult. And nobody thinks you're insane, either. In fact, I think you're one of the bravest, strongest people I've ever met."

He thought she was brave and strong? And here she'd thought he was a smart man.

"Wow, I really have you fooled."

"No," he argued. "You're only fooling yourself if you don't think you are a strong person. Look at how well you did in high school. How did you get those good grades? Yeah, because you're really smart, but it takes more than just brains. You have to work at it and dedicate yourself to it and be strong, or it won't happen, no matter how smart you are."

She looked away for a moment. "I just wanted my dad to notice me. But it didn't work. I guess I wasn't so smart after all."

For a moment he looked like he was going to argue that point, but instead said, "And remember, this is our place."

"Our place?"

"Yeah, the place where we met."

She looked towards the street. "I wonder if that's the same golf cart that you saved me from?"

"Let's not find out," he replied quickly. "Sweetheart, I know you have bad memories associated with this place, and I don't blame you for getting upset about them by coming here. I'm really sorry that my bringing you here brought them back. But good things have happened to you here too, right? I hope the fact that we met right here can kind of cancel out the bad shit. Pardon my language."

"I can manage it, going back into the lion's den. As long as you've got my six." Jeez, she was even starting to talk like him now. She turned back towards that door. *You can do this Michelle. Nobody is going to hurt you or force you to do anything you don't want to.* Especially not Eric.

"Hey," he said, "I thought you said you got all A's in high school." She read his mind, knew what he was referring to.

"I didn't take Spanish. I took French."

"Ooh, sexy," he intoned in his silliest voice. "Say something to me in French."

"*Où sont les toilettes.*"

"What does that mean?"

"It means, where is the bathroom."

He hooked a thumb towards the door. "In there."

"Then let's do this." She glanced at the door to the bar. "Put on your big girl panties, Michelle." She'd meant to say that under her breath but realized her mistake when she saw the look on Eric's face. "Oops! Did I just say that, out loud?"

He was laughing and staring at the same time. "Is that actually a thing? Is that why you wanted to know where the bathroom is? So you can put on your big girl panties? What do big girl panties look like? Can I watch?"

His boyish grin made her realize he was teasing her big time, so that she'd laugh and let go of her *issues*.

She started to step towards the door, but Eric put a hand on her arm.

"You have every right to be happy, you know," he said. "It's in the Declaration of Independence."

"What does the Declaration of Independence have to do with my cosmic existence?"

"Hey, Miss Straight A's. Didn't you study it in American History?"

"Yes. And the Constitution. We had to write out the entire preamble, word for word, by memory, in order to graduate."

"Remember the part about life, liberty and the pursuit of happiness? Yeah, I know it may sound facetious, but it's true. And not just because it's in the Declaration of Independence. You have every right, as a person, to pursue happiness, to find what makes you happy, and to strive for that. It's a whole lot more fun than living with sorrow and regret."

"Do you pursue happiness?"

"All the time. It's my favorite thing to do.. Come on, let's try it."

He put his hand on her elbow. She was actually starting to like his "escorting a little old lady across the street" gesture. She walked in that door like a big girl, compartmentalizing the bad memories, looking around for Danny Gonzalez, expecting him to be at the pool table or sitting at the bar.

Instead, he was sitting on a turquoise-colored bench along the wall by the pool table, by himself, looking morose. He held his beer bottle loosely but wasn't drinking it, and set it down as soon as he saw Michelle return, standing up quickly, his hangdog expression radiating apologies.

"I'm very sorry, ma'am," he said politely, a far cry from the tipsy dancing guy he'd been a few minutes ago. "I didn't realize-" She saw him glance towards Eric and realized, *he thinks we're a couple and that he was infringing onto Eric's relationship.* Why did everyone assume that because the two of them hung out together sometimes, that they were romantically involved? She had to take a few steps to be standing in front of Danny, because he apparently was afraid to approach her again.

"No need to apologize," she told him. "It wasn't you. You didn't offend me or anything like that. It's me, it's just my issues, nothing you did. I mean it. I'm sorry if I was rude to you."

"Thank you, ma'am," he said politely. Apparently, Danny Gonzalez was a graduate of the Eric Hanson School of Manners. She surprised herself by giving the poor guy a fraternal kiss on the cheek, to show she wasn't mad at him.

Eric, leaning against the pool table, said, "You do that again, and he's going to get down on his knees and propose to you."

Danny was both grinning and looking embarrassed. She turned to look at Eric. "Are you jealous?" she asked.

"Insanely," he teased, tapping at his cheek with one finger.

She glanced back at Danny, saying "Is he not the world's biggest goof?" before giving Eric his requested cheek kiss. Those two were like competing siblings. Give one a piece of candy and the other one had to have one too.

But she totally missed the very non-teasing expression that crossed Eric's face when her back was turned. His smile faded just for a moment and he muttered under his breath, "Yeah, I am the world's biggest goof."

They did end up having an enjoyable evening once she compartmentalized away her bad memories. Maybe Eric was right. Maybe she wasn't insane after all.

20

After that, Eric invited her to hang out with him and his buddies on a regular basis when they came over from San Diego. It wasn't like a date or anything, just a couple of roommates hanging out, grabbing a bite to eat, playing the occasional game of pool. She learned to get over her reluctance to socialize in a bar, especially since Eric, bless his little non-drinking heart, always deflected the guys who tried to buy her drinks. He had a way of looking at his Navy friends with a glare that made them behave like children, though it was always followed up with a friendly grin and exploding fist bump.

One day while walking down Metropole Avenue to meet up with some of those friends, they ran into Eric's boss.

"Hey there, Hanson, how are you?"

"I'm fine, Sir. Nice to see you."

"Now, Hanson, we talked about this. It's not Sir. It's Dennis."

"Yes, Sir. I mean, Dennis."

Dennis, looking amused at Eric's inability to call him by his name, looked at Michelle with a smile, and Eric introduced her.

"This is my roommate, Michelle Diaz."

"Michelle? Little Michelle Diaz? Is that you?"

"Yeah, Mr. Brandt, it's me."

"Do you two know each other?" Eric asked.

Michelle nodded. "Mr. Brandt taught first aid classes at my middle school. He flunked me and I had to take the class over."

Eric looked shocked. "You flunked a middle school first aid class? How is that possible?"

Michelle snorted. "Hey, we're not all Mr. Blood and Guts whose Navy buddies still call him Doc."

Dennis Brandt was looking between the two of them. So, his newest paramedic was "roommates" with little Michelle Diaz? Was that what they were calling it these days? He almost hadn't recognized her, and not just because she was grown up now and no longer a middle school student. It was also because she was smiling and teasing Hanson. He remembered her from when she was thirteen, and she'd been the grouchiest kid he'd ever met. Not that he could blame her. Everyone in Avalon had known that her father was the town drunk, and with no mother either, he hadn't been surprised that she wasn't exactly a little ray of sunshine. But she sure looked like one now.

Hanson was still looking a bit shocked that anyone could not pass something that to him was as basic as breathing.

"Michelle," Dennis said. "I think you could just call me Dennis too. Mr. Brandt is my father. Maybe it will remind Hanson here to do the same. And maybe you should tell your ... roommate ... why I had to make you take the class a second time."

He wasn't going to make her confess it, was he? Yep, he was. Both men were looking at her expectantly, and she felt herself blush.

"Fine! I wasn't paying attention to the class because I had a copy of Harry Potter under my desk and was reading it instead."

Eric hooted with laughter. "I knew it! I have to practically pry those vampire books out of her hands to get her out the door. You're such a little rebel."

She could laugh about it now. She had to admit it, she'd been a real snot back then. But now, she couldn't help but smile, despite having to reveal her childhood misbehavior. She also had to correct Eric's lack of literary education. "Harry Potter isn't a vampire. He's a wizard."

"And what kind of mythological creature was in that book I had to pry away from you today?" he countered.

"That one was vampires," she admitted. "And werewolves."

"Well," Dennis said, "I'll let you two get on with your evening. Take care, Michelle. Hanson, I'll see you tomorrow."

"Yes, Sir. Have a nice evening."

"Hanson!"

"Sorry, Sir. Dennis."

Dennis Brandt shook his head with amusement as he watched Eric and Michelle walk away. He admired Eric Hanson quite a bit. Hanson was the most experienced and knowledgeable paramedic Dennis had ever known, and he was grateful to have him on his team. The man should have gone to medical school instead of to the Navy.

There were only two issues Dennis had with Eric. One was Hanson's inability to call him by his name rather than Sir. It came so naturally to Eric that he didn't even realize he was doing it. The other issue was Hanson's singing. In between emergency calls, the staff had plenty to do around the fire station, and unless they were participating in some form of training, Hanson had the most annoying tendency to break out into song. The last time it had been something about mamas not letting their babies grow up to be cowboys. It wouldn't be so bad if he could actually sing, but he had no shame whatsoever at being totally off-key. When he had been requested to cease that racket – a request that was made loudly and included swear words – he simply switched to a different song, and the entire station had been treated to an even more off-key rendition of Thank God I'm a Country Boy.

But he sure seemed to have been a positive influence on little Michelle, who Dennis had always felt kind of sorry for, given her unpleasant home life. Nice that she seemed so much happier now with Hanson.

Roommates?

He watched as Hanson put his hand briefly on Michelle's back, nudging her aside so that he could walk on the side closest to the street. Hanson leaned down and said something to her that made her stop, laugh and punch his arm lightly. He heard the words, "You big goof!" float back on the breeze.

They might call it just roommates, but Dennis Brandt knew foreplay when he saw it.

21

The day that Eric walked into the house and found Michelle laid out on the kitchen floor, he almost panicked. A twitch of her legs revealed, to his relief, that she wasn't laying there dead. She had her head under the sink, and Eric leaned against the counter and took advantage of the opportunity to admire her legs without getting caught.

"Watcha doing?" he asked in a boyish voice.

"I'm getting a pedicure, what does it look like I'm doing?"

Was it weird of him to feel that when she got that slightly bitchy tinge to her voice, that it kind of turned him on?

"Pass me the pipe wrench." She must have regretted her irritated response, because she added, "Please."

There was a mean-looking red tool on the floor near her hand, and he nudged it within her reach.

She owned a pipe wrench. His adorable little roommate owned, and wielded, an actual pipe wrench.

Eric didn't own a pipe wrench. The years of living in base housing, cramped shipboard berthing compartments, and field hospital barracks shared with twenty other guys, hadn't allowed him the luxury of accumulating bulky possessions like tools. The closest thing he owned to a tool was a Swiss army knife. It was doubtful that anyone would consider dive knives or the cleaning kit for his handgun to be tools. He wasn't even a hundred percent positive that the mean red tool actually was a pipe wrench. Now show him a sphygmomanometer, a tourniquet, or a hypodermic syringe, and he was your guy.

Michelle attacked the innards under the sink with the mean red pipe wrench and a noisy gusto. Eric was willing to bet she was taking out her frustrations just as much as fixing her sink. A minute later she slid out with a U-shaped piece of pipe in her hands.

He quickly averted his gaze from staring at her legs. She sat up and peered into the pipe, then looked up at him with narrowed eyes.

"Have you been letting grease go down the sink?"

He flattened an innocent hand against his chest. "Who, me? Never!"

"Hmmph," she replied disbelievingly as she picked up a screwdriver-that at least he was familiar with, though he still didn't own one – and poked it into the pipe, digging around into whatever contraband was blocking it. With a second skeptical "Humph," she handed the pipe segment up to him.

What was he supposed to do with the thing? Take its pulse? Fortunately, she instructed, "Hold this a sec."

"My privilege to serve, ma'am," he told her, and the look she flashed him obviously said she knew he was just trying to charm his way out of possible culpability for the blocked pipe.

She stood up and took the pipe back, upending it and shaking it over the counter next to the sink. A few bits of dirt fell out. After significantly more shaking, pounding, digging into it with the screwdriver, and a few muttered swear words, out popped the offending blockage.

Eric held his breath for a moment until they recognized the item that fell from the pipe – a thick black hair band exactly like the one currently holding Michelle's hair back in a ponytail.

"Ha!" he said. "And you tried to blame me."

She looked sadly at the gunky hair band before throwing it away. "I wasn't blaming you. I just asked. I guess this one is on me."

"And don't you forget it, sweetheart."

"I'm sure you won't let me."

"Not for a minute. Where did you learn to do that?"

"Fix a clogged pipe? I taught myself, from watching videos on YouTube. It's not like I ever had anyone else around here to fix things."

Eric didn't fail to notice the look of sadness that crossed her face. She'd had to do all the repairs here herself, with no help from her father.

"You have me now," he said.

"I have you?" she repeated, looking at him wide-eyed, appearing a bit stunned.

Yes, she had him. She just didn't know how much.

He nodded. "I could help you with stuff like this. I'm more than just a pretty face, you know."

That made her smile. "Yeah, you're a human being with feelings."

Feelings for you, he thought but didn't say.

"I may not own any tools myself," he did say. "But I'd be totally willing to help you with stuff that needs fixing around here. I think I can do more than reach spiders and hand you tools. You did say it was my home too, right? We're living here together. You don't have to do everything by yourself anymore."

Her smile was like sunshine. Lord, her eyes were blue. A strand of hair had escaped her ponytail and her pink tee shirt had a few smudges on it. How could someone disheveled and dirty look so beautiful?

He wondered how badly she'd slap him if he were to slide that hair band off her ponytail, and throw it in the trash with the one that had fallen down the sink.

"I'd like that," she said. Was she getting a little misty-eyed at his offer of domestic help? "I'm going to take this outside and rinse it out. You grab that bucket and move it out of the way."

He followed her glance to the pail, half full of water, that sat under the disconnected pipe.

"No problem," he replied, as he picked up the pail and moved it away from the sink, and Michelle turned to go out the back door.

"You talk to me all bossy-like," he told her, "and I'll do anything you say." He lowered his voice, and emphasized, softer, "*Anything*."

Lord, why had he said that?

Because he meant it. Because he couldn't help it. Because he had a big mouth that got him into trouble.

What he wouldn't give to have her turn around, smile, and repeat, "Anything?"

But she just hesitated for a moment, turned her head a bit as if she might turn around but didn't, and went outside to clean the pipe.

He had the water pail moved away from the sink when she returned, and to avert the trouble that his big mouth was getting him into, he grinned and sat down next to her on the floor in front of the open under-sink cabinet, took the pipe segment from her hand and peered into it.

"Clean as a whistle. You could be a plumber on the side if you wanted. A lady of many talents. Let's put this back together so we have a working sink tonight."

She was staring at him a bit as she sat down next to him in front of the sink, probably wondering how to react to his previous comment. Maybe she'd think he was just teasing. He had to hope so.

Like twins separated at birth, they simultaneously scooched their heads under the sink. He grinned at her nose two inches from his as he handed her the cleaned-out U pipe.

"Do you need that mean red wrench?" he asked, feeling around on the floor with his hand for it.

"Maybe not," she said, as she stopped staring at him and inserted the pipe segment back between the two exposed open ends. "I should be able to just tighten the collar manually. Someday I'd like to repipe this with PVC. It's a lot easier to work with than steel. Hold this in place for me."

He kept his big, inappropriate mouth shut and did as she requested, thoroughly enjoying the tight quarters under the sink as Michelle slid a collar over each end of the formerly clogged pipe and tightened them with her hands.

"That should do it," she said.

"Darn," Eric replied. "I was hoping to see you wield that pipe wrench again."

"Will it make you happy if I do?" she asked.

"Absolutely. It will make my day."

"OK, well just to keep domestic harmony."

"Hooyah." He slid back from the sink, located the pipe wrench again and gave it to her, and she obliged his teasing request by pretending to use it on the pipes.

"Happy now, you big goof?" she asked.

"Yes, ma'am," he replied, and stood up, offering his hand to help Michelle up too.

She even smelled good, and he quietly, discreetly inhaled in that brief moment of physical closeness. Not perfumey, though he didn't usually mind the scent of perfume. But some girls overdid it. His roommate, however, smelled faintly strawberry-like, sweet and feminine.

They tested the sink by pouring the water from the drain pail back down the sink, and everything flowed freely with no leaks or clogs, so she put away the wrench under the sink.

"Thanks for your help," she told him, though they both knew that his help had been mainly ceremonial, rather than practical.

But he had never before had so much fun doing a simple household task as he had watching his roommate wield that pipe wrench.

22

She walked in the house the next day, dropped her keys and phone on the table by the door, and flopped onto the couch, leaning her head back against the back. Eric had been in the kitchen and hearing her, came in, took one look at her face, and asked. "What's wrong?"

"My feet are killing me. Seriously, they are dying. I think I've killed them."

He looked down at her feet, encased in stiff leather lace-up boots. "Those things are hideous. What happened to your pink flip-flops?"

"A decked-over boat with a rat hole."

"And you complain about me using Navy terms you don't understand."

"Yeah, I never used Google so much as since I met you. And that thing you said yesterday? That was crude. Took me seven websites to find out what it meant."

Eric grinned down at her. "Well, I do have certain a rep to maintain. So what's a decked-over rat hole?"

"The boat is decked over, meaning the only access to the engine is through a small opening called a rat hole. It's one time when being a girl in this job is actually an advantage. Some of the big manly men can't physically fit in there. So I get to be the rat climbing down the rat hole. There are lots of hot parts and tools getting dropped. Can't wear flip flops there, so I've had to wear my back-up boots all day." She indicated the leather hideousness on her feet. "My boss gave these to me after his kid outgrew them."

"A rat hole? If anyone there dares to call you a rat, we're going to have a problem. I can't imagine anyone in the world who is less rat-like than you. Maybe it would help if I rubbed your feet."

That sounded like something a bit intimate to get from one's platonic roommate but the prospect of relieving her foot pain won out.

"Knock yourself out." She leaned down to unlace her boot but Eric put out his hand.

"I'll do that. This is a full-service foot rub."

He shifted the coffee table over and sat on the floor cross-legged in front of her. Picking up her right foot, he unlaced the boot and pulled it off, with a bit of resistance. "I think it's time to pass these things down to someone else. They're at least a size too small for you." He dropped the offending piece of footwear on the floor. "Here's another part of your problem. Where're your socks? You should wear socks under shoes like this."

She shuddered. "Oh, no, not socks."

"I only suggested socks, not a torture device."

"Socks are a torture device. The only thing worse is pantyhose."

"I'll take your word for that one. But you should still wear socks. You're gonna get blisters. I always wear socks under my boots. You don't see me with sore feet."

She looked at him with annoyance but of course he just grinned and unlaced the other shoe. It felt so good to get those boots-and she agreed, they were both hideous and too small - off her feet that her sigh of relief was audible. He picked up her foot and rubbed his thumbs over the top, pressing the toes almost to the point of pulling. It was one of the most blissful things she had ever felt. She seriously hoped her feet didn't smell.

"Bend your ankle," he requested. "Toes pointed up." When she did so, he grasped her foot with both hands but now with his thumbs against the sole, and pressed both thumbs firmly, intensely into the center of the sole.

"Oh, god, that hurts," she groaned. "Do that again."

"Ah, so the lady likes a little pain," he chuckled as he released her foot and did the same to the other. The sensations that shot up her feet and out the toes were almost orgasmic and her groan pretty much sounded that way too.

"If you ever get tired of the paramedic thing, you could have a wonderful career as a masseuse ahead of you." She seriously thought those long, strong fingers of his were the best thing her feet had ever felt.

"I'll take that under advisement." He held her heel in one hand and massaged with the other. "I once spent an entire week's leave rubbing my niece Amanda's feet." He held his arms out in front of himself for a moment, rounded as if to indicate a large belly. "She was, like, twelve months pregnant and her feet were swollen up like balloons. Her husband, who according to her, was a total failure at foot rubs, said that she hadn't been able to get real shoes on her feet since about ten minutes after conception. Those were his words, mind you, not mine. It's a good thing they live in Florida where she could live in flip-flops."

"It's like an orgasm for my feet." As soon as the words left Michelle's mouth, she clapped her hand over it. "Oops! Did I just say that? Out loud?"

"You did." Could his grin get any huger?

To cover up her embarrassment, she quipped, "Do you always give your roommates foot rubs?"

"Well, seeing that my previous roommates have always been other guys, no. I never even rubbed my ex-wife's feet. Maybe that's why she dumped me."

She had always, since day one, been intensely curious about that line on his background check. Marital status, divorced. Despite his openness about himself, his declaration that his life was an open book, she'd hesitated to ask him about that segment. But he had opened the door. She tried to sound casual.

"So, you were married?"

"For a little while." He didn't cease his awesome attention to her aching feet. Which felt much better now but she wasn't going to tell him that in case he was inclined to stop. "Didn't last long."

"That's sad. What happened?"

He made that little "no big deal" expression he had and said, "She thought she was pregnant, so we got married. It turned out she wasn't, it was a false alarm. Then, I got deployed. She got lonely, and I got an email saying she wanted out."

Shocked surprise swept over her. How could someone be married to a great guy like him and not be willing to wait for him? And to dump him with an email? That was cruel. And why should she care about that so deeply?

"That's horrible, what a bitch!" Her exclamation was just a little more intense than she'd intended. "You must have been heartbroken."

Actually, he'd been surprised at how not heartbroken he'd been. "It really wasn't traumatic at all. She sent me papers, I signed them, and sent them back with some money and asked her to put my stuff into a storage locker until I got back, and that was it. My wedding ring ended up at the bottom of the Persian Gulf."

"Still, that's downright cruel, to send you divorce papers while you were out there defending our freedom." She actually couldn't think of anything more reprehensible. How could a woman be married to a guy like Eric, the sweetest person she'd ever known, and be unwilling to wait for him? It wasn't as if he'd gone off to a six-month party. He'd been on a military deployment, putting his life on the line to defend the freedom of his wife, his family, and every other American citizen.

"How did you meet her? Why did you break up?"

She hoped he didn't regret telling Michelle to ask him anything she wanted to.

"I met her in a bar. My buddies had been drinking and I was hanging out to make sure they got back to base on time."

"That sounds exactly the same as when you and I met."

Eric nodded a bit ruefully. "Except that she didn't tell me to fuck off or try to run away from me as if I carried the Black Death." He hesitated a moment. "You want the honest truth?"

She nodded, her eyes wide.

She both wanted, and didn't want, the absolute truth. But she had asked, insisted he tell her.

Don't ask the question if you're not prepared to hear the answer.

"I'll be totally honest with you, Michelle. It was a pick-up, plain and simple. It wasn't love at first sight. It wasn't love at all. We were hot for each other, that one night at least. I had just been transferred to San Diego and hadn't gotten, um, hadn't had a date in a while. I put my buddies in a cab, let the cab driver run my credit card in advance and told him to give himself a big tip, and went home with Karen. I skedaddled back to the base first thing in the morning, and it seemed like it was just going to be a one-night stand, but then she called me and dropped the PG bomb. I probably never would have seen her again otherwise. You see, the condom had broken at, well, the critical moment. It happens sometimes. I didn't even remember giving her my phone number, but I must have.

"I never heard such absolute regret in a person's voice as when I heard her on the phone saying, I'm pregnant. I thought, even under our circumstances, how could anyone regret the possibility of creating a new life? She made it sound like it was a death sentence, and it was all my fault.

"As for me, I turned a blind eye to her unpleasantness, even though I could sense it went bone deep. I didn't ask her to marry me. I just told her it was going to be a done deal, for the sake of the kid we thought we had conceived. A kid that turned out never to have existed.

"But when she called, all I heard was the word pregnant. She had taken a home pregnancy test, but it's not uncommon to get a false positive result. I was so stupid. The correct response in a situation like that should have been something like, are you a hundred percent positive? Did you take a second test? See your doctor? Nope, my immediate response was, meet me at the county clerk's office. We'll see if they take walk-ins. Twenty-four hours later, we were married. Lasted a whole six months, at least on paper. Longer than Britney Spears and Jason Alexander, but not as long as Jennifer Lopez and Cris Judd."

She restrained a giggle at the silly pop culture reference, because they were after all, talking about his divorce. "I didn't think you'd follow celebrity marriages."

"I don't. My friend Gabriel Googled it."

"I don't think it was stupid," she said. "It was incredibly honorable, and kind of romantic." Eric made a small snorting noise on hearing the word *romantic*. "Still, it was pretty mean of the former Mrs. Hanson to serve you with papers while you were at sea, putting your life on the line to defend her freedom. She could at least have waited until you got back."

"Well, to start with, she was never Mrs. Hanson. She kept her own name. Which was probably a wise move on her part. I've heard from a friend of a friend that she's already been married and divorced again since then. It saves her a lot of paperwork to just stay Karen Butler."

Even more the fool, Michelle mused. She thought that Michelle Ramona Hanson had a really nice ring to it.

One would expect such an account to come out sounding bitter and accusatory. But Eric managed to actually sound sympathetic towards the former not Mrs. Hanson.

Out of nowhere, the thought pierced Michell's brain with the swiftness of a bullet.

If I were your woman, your wife, I wouldn't let you go for anything. Not for deployment, not for war. I'd wait for you and be the first person on the dock waiting for your ship to return, and wouldn't even consider-

Yikes, where did that totally inappropriate train of thought come from? *Down girl*, she told herself. The guy is your *roommate*, remember? And yet, if his marriage had worked out, he wouldn't be living here in Avalon with her.

He smiled and shrugged. "At least my ex had the decency to divorce me. I've had more than one shipmate cry on my shoulder after finding out they'd been cheated on."

Unexpectedly, jealousy crept through her. She tried to squelch it. *Don't be silly. His sympathetic shoulder is not your personal property.*

"I'll bet the female sailors on your ship were very comforted."

He gave her an appraising look. "Actually, it's not only females that get cheated on or who need a shoulder to cry on sometimes."

"You had male shipmates cry on your shoulder too?"

"Yes, I have. And whether it's a male or a female, it was never anything sexual or inappropriate. People, just guys in general, need comfort sometimes, and empathy and the knowledge that they have a friend who cares. Crying it out usually helps a guy get through it.

"Now keep in mind, sweetheart," he went on, "when I say guys, I mean that in a gender-neutral way. I don't just mean men. It's a generic term I use to include both male and female shipmates. It's a lot less awkward than 'persons'. After all, I don't want you to think I'm a misogynistic ass who needs a you-know-what to turn a screwdriver."

Dang. Sometimes she wished Eric didn't have such a good memory. He actually remembered all the nasty stuff she's said to him that first day, though he wasn't holding it against her. She was embarrassed that she'd called him that, but at the same time she was touched that he seemed to remember pretty much everything she'd ever said to him. Though he smiled, she could see in his eyes that he really truly did not want her to think of him as a misogynistic ass who needed a ...

"You can say the actual word, you know," she told him.

"Yeah, no. I think I'll stick with you-know-what, thank you very much."

At that, she did giggle.

"Deployments are tough," Eric continued. "On both the sailor, and their spouses and families back home. It can be totally overwhelming for them both, especially the first time. Relationships don't always survive, even strong ones. There are support groups for military spouses, but Karen wasn't interested in joining. It's lonely, both for the sailor and for their significant other. I mean, you're there with your colleagues and shipmates and buddies, guys that you would literally die for, but you still get lonely for the people you've left on shore, and they get lonely too when you're separated for six months or more. The pressure and anxiety are fierce. I know there stresses in any relationship, but it's much tougher for a military spouse. You can exchange emails, and try to call if you have phone cards, but there's always a delay or a lag that makes it difficult. When I was in A-stan, it was next to impossible to get a connection for email, not to mention finding the time. It's hard sometimes for people to keep the perspective, and not unusual for spouses or significant others to feel abandoned. I wasn't the first person to be served with papers while away from home, and I'm sure I won't be the last."

Eric frequently held the hands of patients being treated or traveling to surgery. It wasn't romantic; it wasn't sexual. People, of either gender, who were in pain or scared shitless, or both, needed the reassurance of a comrade who cared. It was neither romantic nor sexual. It was human.

He'd received requests on more than one occasion from a patient to tell (insert loved one's name here) that they loved them. He always saw that the appropriate C.O. or chaplain relayed the request to the patient's spouse, child, mother, whoever. You never knew when it would be the last words the guy uttered.

"Did she cheat on you?" She regretted the words as soon as she asked her impulsive question, afraid it might hurt Eric if he had to relive the unpleasantness. Though he looked a bit surprised at her asking it, he didn't seem upset.

"Not that I know of. But then, I never saw or spoke to her since then. I, on the other hand, was a completely perfect and honorable gentleman right up until the bitter end." He smiled his sparkly, teasing grin at her. "But once things were final, all bets were off."

Oh, *Freya*, he was probably talking about dating again after his divorce was final. She did not want to go there. Fortunately, he'd left open a different direction of conversation.

"Wait, there's something wrong with your math here."

He rolled his eyes. "I know. I was exaggerating when I said my niece Amanda was twelve months pregnant. I know that human gestation is forty weeks."

"That wasn't the math I was referring to," she said. "You talk about your nieces and nephews as if they were your age or older. You said you were at your nephew's wedding when you were sixteen and got sick. I know I don't have much of a family, but I'm still pretty sure that nieces and nephews should be younger than you. Are you sure you meant your niece and not your cousin?"

He chuckled. "In most families, that would be the case. But my family, well, we're not exactly typical. All of my cousins are actually old enough to be my parents. You see, when my parents got married, it was a second marriage for both of them, and they both had kids from their first marriages. My dad was already a grandfather. Mom and Dad didn't plan on having kids together, so when they found out I was on the way, it was a really big surprise to the whole family. When I was born, my mother was forty-two and my father was sixty. I have two half brothers and two half sisters, all a lot older than me. My sister Brenda is the closest to me in age, and she was a sophomore in high school when I was born. She thought the entire concept of people my parent's age having a baby was gross and disgusting, at least at first. I figured out that my family dynamic was not quite the norm when I was in the second grade, and realized I was the only kid in the class whose dad was retired. And that, boys and girls, is why Eric's nieces and nephews are his contemporaries. My great-nephew little Kenny is twenty-three."

"My, that's different. Is he called Little Kenny because he's short?"

"No, he's like six foot six. Went to college on a basketball scholarship. But he's named after my dad, his grandfather. Since they were both named Kenneth, he was called Little Kenny from birth, and everyone still called him that even when he grew taller than Dad and everyone else."

"So do your nieces and nephews call you "uncle" even though they're older than you?"

"They make a point of it. They think it's hysterical."

He sat back and released her feet, and she immediately missed his touch. It was tempting to claim that her feet still hurt and need more treatment, but he'd probably see right through that weak excuse. She could only thank him for the massage.

23

SEVEN YEARS EARLIER, THE PERSIAN GULF

Though he wouldn't have volunteered the information to his commanding officers – because Home was where the Navy sent him – Eric was thrilled to be back on the blue side and reassigned to his old ship. Along with the shipboard orders, he'd also just received his passing score on the Chief's exam and would be pinned on this cruise, so he was doubly happy as he greeted old buddies he'd served with previously, met new ones, and settled into the sickbay. Recalling previous experiences, he was very observant of the knee knockers and stepped over them carefully.

The guys who knew him were quick to notice the new wedding band on his left hand. Some of them offered congratulations, others offered condolences, and several exclaimed, "Doc! Didn't even know you were engaged."

"I wasn't."

"So, it was a shotgun marriage?"

"Something like that."

"So, does that mean you're going to be a daddy?"

For a few weeks, he'd thought so but, nope.

"Not anytime soon," he said and changed the subject.

Six weeks later, he got the email. There wasn't even a greeting. No, Dear Eric. No, how are you? No, I hope you're safe out there. She got right to the point.

"I want a divorce. This whole thing was a mistake. I'm attaching the papers. I'm glad I can send them electronically. Who knows how long it would take for them to get to your stupid ship in the mail. Just print out the last page and sign it and send it back."

That was it. No, love. No, I'm sorry. No, have a nice life. Whatever. He wasn't upset. He wasn't even surprised. She was right, the whole thing had been a big mistake. It did, however, sting that she'd referred to the Nimitz as "your stupid ship". Maybe he'd been a little too happy when he'd gotten the orders for deployment.

He read the papers over before printing the signature page. She'd listed two things as grounds for dissolution of the marriage.

Irreconcilable Differences. That was pretty accurate. They had nothing but differences, and each and every one of them was exquisitely irreconcilable. Nothing whatsoever in common. Their only agreement had been to jump each other's bones the day they'd met. She hadn't even wanted to get married and had done so only at his insistence. He wondered occasionally, or actually constantly, what he'd ever seen in her. All there had been was a momentary spark of lust, quickly extinguished.

The second justification irritated him. Abandonment. She'd thrown that at him when he'd left and it had done no good whatsoever to try to explain the reality and obligation of the military to her. He was half tempted to refuse to sign the papers, to contest the divorce over that self-absorbed misconception. Not because he wanted to stay married to her, but because of her selfish, mistaken belief that he had somehow engineered his deployment as an excuse for him to leave her.

He could try to explain the reality of it all to her until he was blue in the face, but it would be a waste of breath.

He printed out the signature page of the divorce papers, and his hand hesitated only a moment over the signature line before he signed it with the same neat, precise signature he'd used six months earlier on the marriage license. Without regret, he put it in an envelope to mail out when they docked in Bahrain.

There were a few minutes left before he had to report to duty, so he walked back to the fantail at the stern of the ship, just below the flight deck. Jets were landing practically on top of his head, and foam earplugs and sunglasses weren't going to cut it here. Though he wasn't a member of the flight crew, he put on a cranial like theirs that combined heavy-duty ear protection, safety helmet and eye goggles, to protect him against the volume of the Nimitz's flight operations.

It wasn't just the 140 decibels produced by a Super Hornet screaming in for a landing one deck above him that threatened to cause deafness. It was also the booming, vibrating thump made when the jet's tailhook trapped the arresting wire and went from 150 miles per hour to a dead stop in two seconds. The pilots always aimed for the third of the four wires, the safest and most effective target, and consistently trapping on the third wire was recommended for ambitious pilots who wanted to move up through the ranks.

It was mid-afternoon, and too early for the stars he liked to watch. Though the sun was intense, it was still slightly less hellish here than the body and soul-sucking heat of the desert.

He looked at his left hand for a minute, then pulled off the ring. It slid off easily. Perhaps that was a sign of some sort, an easy ending to his big mistake of a marriage. He hadn't been wearing it long enough for it to even leave a dent in his skin.

Up on the flight deck, the flight crew was raising the blast deflector behind another jet preparing to launch. A shooter in a yellow shirt knelt, pointed, and the F-18 roared off the deck and rocketed over the water, leaving a spray of steam to dissipate off the deck with the jet blast.

Eric had played baseball back in high school. Coach had said he had a pretty good arm. Coach had, in fact, suggested he sign up for the Ray's open tryouts, an opportunity Eric had politely declined.

But apparently, he still had the arm. Accompanied by the roar of the jet launching off the flight deck just over his head, he used his best, out-field to home plate, picking off the runner from third, throw as he sent the ring sailing out over the water. It flipped once, glinted in the sun, then descended down to fall into the Persian Gulf. From this height, he couldn't have heard it when it hit the brine, even if there hadn't been 140 decibels of jet blast going on one deck above him.

He had only two regrets. One was the waste of the money he'd spent to buy the wedding rings. He had no idea what Karen was going to do with hers. She could melt it down for tooth fillings for all he cared.

The second, stronger regret was a fleeting sadness that he wasn't going to be a daddy after all. For a brief time, it had seemed like a possibility, and he'd been honestly disappointed when it turned out not to be the case.

Duty called, and he closed that unpleasant chapter of his life and made his way down to the sickbay, singing the latest Brad Paisley song as he walked, despite his buddies putting their hands over their ears and howling like wolves when he passed by.

What made the whole situation even more bizarre was that he won the First Kiss raffle, a charity fundraiser done during deployment at sea. The crew members purchased raffle tickets in hopes of winning the right to be the first person allowed to disembark and greet their significant other when they returned home and docked at the end of the deployment. Since Eric now knew that at best, he might be greeted by one of his siblings, he gave the First Kiss card he'd won to a friend who'd gotten engaged just before they'd left on deployment. That particular friend had been one of the guys to congratulate him back on day one when Eric had been wearing a wedding ring, and he glanced at Eric's now bare hand, winced in sympathy, and accepted the gift with thanks, and tactfully asked no questions.

24

〜

One day, on his day off, Eric decided to walk down to the marina, maybe see if Michelle could break away and grab some lunch. It was, as usual, a beautiful bright day without so much as a hint of a cloud in the sky. The most boring job in the world had to be a weatherman in southern California, he reflected as he walked down Casino Way towards the small dock next to the dive park, where she'd told him most of her customer's boats came for repair, recalling the last time he'd been here, to respond to the broken arm incident, when Michelle and her friend had been there.

Michelle was standing on the small dock, but apparently not working at the moment. She stood almost nose to nose with a blond, long-haired surfer dude type guy, and they were having quite an argument. As Eric approached, he saw Michelle's eyes blaze like blue lightning, and he hoped she never got that mad at him.

Or maybe he did.

He heard the guy yell, "Cunt!" as he turned away from her and stalked up the dock. He didn't get far, because Eric blocked his path with hands on hips.

"Apologize," he said, nodding towards Michelle.

"Get lost!" The surfer dude was about Eric's height, but didn't bother to look him in the eye as he tried to side-step him.

"I said, apologize, douchebag!" The guy tried to dodge around him but Eric continued to block his path. Surfer Dude sneered.

"You gonna make me?"

"I sure am, if you're too dense to figure it out for yourself."

"Yeah, you and what army?"

A broad, but nevertheless grim, smile on Eric's face confused Mr. Douchebag.

"Army?" he said tightly. "I don't need no stinking army. I've got the Navy. In fact, I know a couple guys from the SEALs." The guy at least had the sense to look a bit scared by now but still offered no apology.

"I'm waiting," Eric reminded him.

"Who are you, her boyfriend?" The douchebag looked Eric up and down as if assessing the possibility of taking him on.

Ha, sucker. You'd lose.

"You don't want to be with her, she's a total-"

He didn't get to repeat his insult because Eric grabbed him by the shirt and literally shook him. The guy's streaky blond hair fluttered wildly, and his eyes got big and scared.

"Don't – you – dare." The douchebag opened his mouth, but made no sound, as Eric, with his jaw muscles tightened with anger, pulled back his right hand and made a fist, showing a grim smile. He confused the guy again by asking, "You like Clint Eastwood movies?"

"Huh?" Sweat broke out on the douchebag's forehead.

Eric cocked his fist, aimed it in the direction of his adversary's chin. "OK, I changed my mind. Say it. I dare you. Go ahead, make my day."

The douchebag wriggled a little, trying to extricate himself from Eric's other hand which still held onto the folds of his shirt, and dredged up enough of a spine to demand, "Let go of me, you creep."

But he still offering no apology.

"It's Chief, to you, douchebag!" Eric retorted, still with his grim, confusing smile. "You know what? You're not worth bruising my knuckles on. You just better watch how you talk to people." Instead of punching the guy, Eric gave him a shove and released his hold on his shirt at the same time. Douchebag Surfer Dude Guy stumbled backward and fell off the dock into the water, coming up sputtering, his shaggy hair now plastered to his face. Eric gave him a brief glance to make sure he wasn't drowning, then looked towards Michelle to see that she'd be grateful that he'd had her six. But all he saw was the back of her as she disappeared into the hold of the boat parked on the other side of the dock.

Obviously, she wasn't interested in having lunch with him today. Disappointed, he turned and headed back towards home.

******

When Michelle got home from work, Eric was asleep on the couch. That geeky sci-fi movie on Netflix had apparently not been as interesting as he'd expected. She looked down at that sweet, innocent, adorable sleeping face - and kicked the couch so hard that he sat bolt upright, as if she'd jabbed him with a needle.

He smiled, with a complete and utter lack of just-woke-up confusion. "Hi there, how was your day?"

"Just what the hell were you doing out there today!"

He played it all innocent and totally ignored the "the hell" portion. "Well, let's see, what was I doing today? I did some lifting." He nodded towards the patio where his weight bench sat. "I stopped at the store and bought some shaving cream and some shampoo. That kind you like was on sale. Oh, and I took a walk down by the marina."

"Yeah, let's talk about that part." Her voice appeared calm but the blue eyes blazed fire.

"It's really pretty down there. All those boats, just bobbing in the water. And they run so well, there must be a really competent mechanic working on them."

"Don't try to butter me up. Who do you think you are, roughing up Justin like that?"

So, the douchebag's name was Justin. Even his name sounded like a surfer dude. Eric gave up all pretense of not knowing what she was talking about.

"He deserved it, and more!" he insisted. "He insulted you. He called you a..." He couldn't even say the word to her.

"I know, I heard him. He's been calling me that since high school."

Justin had upgraded his insults since that disastrous beach date, when she'd refused to have anything further to do with him.

"You went to high school with that douchebag?" Eric asked.

"Yes. This is a small town, Eric. I see people from school all the time."

"Wait, was he your prom date?" Damn, he could not help the tiny note of jealousy that crept into his voice.

"My prom date? Absolutely not. I wouldn't have gone to the prom with him if he'd been the last living, breathing boy in town."

"But you obviously have a history with him."

Why was he harping on her romantic past like a jealous boyfriend? He certainly had plenty of history behind him and she didn't give him any grief about it.

"I wouldn't call it a history. We went out once. It didn't go well. And quit trying to change the subject. You had no right to rough him up like that. I mean, seriously? Go ahead, make my day? Could you possibly get any dorkier?"

"I don't think dorkier is a legal word. I think you made that up, like assholeness."

She flared at him. Lord, she was gorgeous.

"Who cares! I can't believe you threatened to sic the SEALs on him. Don't you think they have better things to do than come over here and help you channel your inner Neanderthal? I've heard about testosterone poisoning, but I never realized it was a real thing until today."

"I'm not a Neanderthal, he was the Neanderthal! I'm surprised he didn't try to drag you away by your hair. He was way out of line saying that to you. He's lucky I didn't make his teeth bite his own ass, from the inside out. And why are you mad at me about it? You should be thanking me, not yelling at me. Oh, and I did not threaten to sic the SEALs on him. I just mentioned that I know a few. Which I do. He can infer from that what he will."

She'd been standing over him but now she sat down on the chair across from the couch.

"It wasn't your fight. It was mine. Look, Eric, I know he was insulting. But it's hard enough to be a woman doing this job, without having my roommate jumping in and beating up every guy I have a conflict with. Do you know how many of the boat owners I deal with think I'm the company secretary when I show up with my tool bag? Do you know how many times I've had to listen to guys tell me I should go type something and let the man take care of the repair? It makes me want to bash their knees with a wrench, but of course I can't. I can only bite my tongue and do my job twice as good as a man, for half the respect. And if some guy gives me shit, I have to give it back just as bad, because if I cry or back down or let someone else-" she gave Eric a pointed look- "fight my battles for me, it destroys all the credibility I've built up and just makes me look like a little girl pretending she can do a man's job. It might help if I were taller, looked more imposing, but unfortunately five foot six is all I've got to work with."

She paused and looked at his face. He tried to look contrite, sorry that he'd potentially made things more difficult for her, but she was just so darn adorable, sitting there scolding him. Five foot six of adorableness. Seriously, how could she not have expected him to smack down that douchebag?

"And don't give me those sheep eyes," she reprimanded.

"What sheep eyes? I don't have sheep eyes," he said, as he showed her his sheep eyes. "Are you saying I should just stand there and let some jerkface throw inappropriate insults at my - friend, and do nothing? That's not how I operate. Friends don't let Neanderthals disrespect their friends." Boy, wasn't that a mouthful! "I'd better not hear him, or anyone, talk to you like that again, or I won't show the considerable amount of restraint I did today."

"You call that restraint? Your little chest-beating exhibition embarrassed me. I felt like I ought to get out a measuring stick. None of the guys would look me in the eye after that. When I left work, my boss called me "Ms. Diaz." He's known me since I was six and he never called me anything but Michelle before."

Yes, merely demanding an apology had required quite a lot of restraint. His first impulse had been to give the guy an immediate fist in the solar plexus, one that took advantage of every weight he'd ever lifted in every gym he'd ever been in.

"Good, well maybe they've learned a little respect. Seriously, I was just trying to help you. Isn't that what friends are supposed to be for?"

"So, are you my defender now?" she demanded.

"If necessary, yes. Is there something wrong with that?"

He could see annoyance flare in her eyes.

"So, let me ask you this," she said. "If I were your male friend, and someone said something rude to me, would you still get in their face about it?"

That made him pause, but just for a moment, trying to imagine Michelle as a male. Nope, not buying it, not with that feminine figure and gorgeous face and silky hair. He almost blurted out his former inappropriate comment of, *not with boobs like those*, because yes, he was a dirty-minded dog with a big mouth that got him into trouble. She had forgiven him the first time he'd said that, sweetheart that she was, but he couldn't risk making the same mistake again.

He managed to suppress his big mouth for once, and settled for, "Yes. I would still stick up for another guy if he was being given undeserved guff. But maybe not with quite as much Clint Eastwood-ness."

She just couldn't be mad at him anymore. Those sheep eyes got her every time. "You're just incorrigible, you know that?"

He breathed a sigh of relief at escaping the dog house. "Incorrigible is my middle name."

"No, your middle name is Paul, remember? Your mother named you after a bug."

"Not a bug, a Beatle. Tell you what, I'll make you a deal. If you ever hear anyone insulting me, you have my permission to knock their block off, OK? I'll just stand there and cheer you on."

That conjured up an interesting mental image, of her beating up on some guy who may have stupidly said something insulting to him, and him standing off to the side yelling, "Hooyah! You go, girl!"

"Fine, that works," she said. "But just not the guys you make drop trou for injections. I don't want to see that."

"It's no picnic for me either, sweetheart. And Mr. Justin Douchebag better learn to behave if he knows what's good for him."

"Actually, he climbed out of the water after you left and apologized to my feet."

"Your feet? Does he have a foot fetish as well as a bad case of misogyny?" Maybe he was going to have to hunt this guy down and educate him further.

"Not that I know of. I told you they wouldn't look me in the eye."

"So, I fixed the problem after all! I was right. And you got mad at me." He pretend pouted. "It's a good thing you're cute when you're mad." Actually, she'd been more than cute. She was amazingly beautiful when she was mad, with her hair flying wildly and her eyes wide and hot.

A face that could launch a thousand ships. It was a euphemism for off-the-charts beautiful. The phrase was a reference to Helen of Troy. Eric wasn't particularly interested in Greek classics, in fact he had zero interest in the subject, but the reference to ships had interested him enough to look it up.

He was a dog, a hound, a degenerate. He wanted her, in a way that went beyond lust or even sex, in a way that scared the hell out of him.

She was wearing shiny pink lip gloss, the same color she'd smeared on his shirt the day he'd moved in. Was it strawberry flavored? How much trouble would he be in if he tried to find out?

"You weren't right, just intimidating," she told him. "And close your mouth, intimidating is not your middle name."

"Hey, I think that Eric Paul Goof Incorrigible Intimidating Hanson has a great ring to it, don't you? You want me to come down there after work tomorrow and talk to your boss, tell him it's OK to call you by your first name?"

"No, do not do that, you big goof. They already think you're my boyfriend. When I tried to tell them you were my roommate, everyone just kept saying, yeah right, sure."

"Maybe I don't want to be just your roommate anymore." He hadn't meant to blurt that out, but he couldn't help it. His big mouth got him into trouble every time.

Not only was he a big-mouth, he was a selfish insensitive jerk too, because his impetuous declaration made Michelle look really upset at what he'd said.

"You mean, you want to move out?" Her voice wavered just a little, but he could see her repressing it, as her defensive shields went up, and her eyebrows drew together in concern, "You signed a lease, you know. If you don't want to – what's that term – re-enlist when it expires, that's your decision, but you're stuck with me for now."

She'd totally misunderstood him, and maybe that was for the best.

"No, I certainly don't want to move out!" he reassured her. "I meant," he thought fast, because he couldn't say what he really wanted to, that he'd like to be more than roommates, maybe he would like to be her boyfriend, as in, sharing the same bedroom as well as the same house. No, he could not tell her that. That would freak her out totally.

"I meant," Jeez, now he was repeating himself in his anxiety to put Michelle at ease. "I hope we can be friends *and* roommates. Friends stick up for friends, you know, when douchebags give them trouble. What were you two fighting about anyway, if you don't mind me asking? Or is it private?"

Slowly, reluctantly, he could see those defensive shields come down slightly, as she made a little twisted mouth of irritation. Lord help him, he wanted to kiss that unhappy expression right off her lips, right along with that cute pink lip gloss she wore. He wondered if she used it just to turn him on. If she did, it was working.

"His father owns a charter fishing boat, and for some reason, he thought that gave him the right to tell me how to do my job. He didn't take it well when I told him he didn't know what he was talking about."

"Lord help him," Eric said with a shudder, and was rewarded with a small expression of agreement from Michelle. Not quite a smile, but at least she wasn't glaring daggers at him anymore.

"OK, I'm sorry if I embarrassed you by being intimidating," he said.

That, finally, made her smile. Hooyah. "Why can I not stay mad at you?

"Because I'm adorable?" he theorized.

"Yes, you are. And humble. I'm sorry that I yelled at you when you were just trying to be, uh, helpful."

He held out his hand. "Friends?"

She took the hand he offered. "Friends." His hand was warm, and the long fingers held on to the handshake just a little longer than just friends usually did.

When he let go, he said, "I think I do understand a bit of what you've experienced. I saw it in the Navy, times when female sailors, both enlisted and officers, didn't receive the respect they deserved. I saw how some guys – and in this case, I mean male guys – didn't believe that female sailors could be as smart, as strong, as capable or as in-command as men. It was wrong, and stupid, and I hated that it happened. Not from me, of course. I never hesitated to give the salute or follow an order from a female officer, or to take a female corpsman seriously."

"Wait, wouldn't a female be called a corpswoman?"

"Nope, they're still called corpsmen, regardless of gender. You know, there are women in every aspect of the Navy, up to an including admiral rank. But female corpsmen are still called a corpsman. Not to be discriminatory, it's just that corpswoman or corpsperson is just too difficult to say.

"That, and the lowest enlisted rank is called a Seaman regardless of the gender of the person wearing the uniform. It's the same over in the Air Force, where they all start out as Airmen, even the girls. That was one thing that bothered my niece Pamela when she enlisted."

"You let a member of your family enlist in a service branch that wasn't the Navy?"

"Well, I tried to talk her into being a Seaman rather than an Airman. But when you're a great big grown-up eighteen, the last person you'd probably take career advice from would be a dorky fifteen-year-old uncle with braces."

"You were an uncle by age fifteen?" She still couldn't quite wrap her head around his weird family dynamic.

"Sweetheart, I was an uncle before I was born."

"And when you observed that discrimination, did you threaten to punch the offenders, or sic the SEALs on them, or throw them in the water?"

"No, that was strictly for your benefit, sweetheart. Though I was tempted, a time or two. I had words with a couple of misguided crewmates on the subject, more than once, but managed to not throw anyone overboard. The Navy really frowns on that kind of thing.

"I'm really not the kind of guy who picks fights. In fact I've only hit someone on purpose once in my life, and I was a kid then. But hearing that guy call you that name ... Nobody has a right to call a woman, or anyone, something like that."

When she went to bed that night, laying there thinking about Eric, as she usually did, she couldn't help but actually be grateful to him for giving Justin Douchebag (she was going to think of the guy by that name forever now, even though his surname was actually Moore) a load of grief over the way he'd talked to her. She'd been truthful and honest when she'd told Eric about her difficulties in being taken seriously as a mechanic, and yet, still. It had been rather gratifying to see him sticking up for her, like her personal knight in shining armor. She would of course never, ever let him know that, but she smiled to herself as she turned off the bedside lamp and slid down on her pillow, remembering him shaking Justin and demanding an apology for his crude insults. Nobody had ever championed her like that before and surprisingly, she found she kind of liked it.

Now if that wasn't the most unliberated thing she'd ever felt. But it wasn't just that someone had stuck up for her, but that it was Eric who'd stepped up and helped her. She couldn't think of anyone else she knew who would have done something like that. It was wonderful, downright incredible, to have a friend like that, despite the incorrect assumptions that his gallantry had given to Justin, and to her boss, about her relationship with her roommate.

She suddenly realized that she trusted Eric, more than she'd ever trusted anyone before in her life. She trusted him with her emotions, with her anxieties. She'd trust him physically, if it ever came to that.

She'd trust him with her life. He would never, ever let anything hurt her, emotionally or otherwise.

How had she gotten so lucky to have him in her life?

I am so lucky to have you as a friend, she thought, just before she fell asleep.

25

After several days of having to work late to finish a job, Michelle was glad to get home a little early the following day. As a thank you for her extra work, her boss had given her a couple passes for the miniature golf course, and if Eric was free, she thought she'd ask him if he'd like to play some pretend golf. She knew he occasionally played golf with his work partner; the real golf course being conveniently just across the street from the fire station. The mini golf course in town next to the tour plaza should be a breeze.

Just as she pulled up in front of the house, he walked out the front door carrying a garment bag over his shoulder. For a moment, she thought he'd been replaced by an evil twin, because he looked so somber and non-sparkly, and didn't even say hello as he started down the street.

"Where are you off to?" she asked brightly.

He called over his shoulder, "Mainland. Be back tomorrow."

OK, so maybe he was in a hurry to make his boat, but it was so unlike him to be so curt and just leave without a word. It reminded her of how she used to be. If he'd been a girl she would have suspected PMS. But she could be the bigger person.

"Would you like me to take you down to the dock in the golf cart?" She had to speak a little louder as he kept walking.

"No!" he yelped with the same firmness with which he might decline poison.

"Fine, be a grouch!" she yelled at his back. He stopped, stood in his tracks for a moment but didn't turn around, then just kept on walking away, the black garment bag twitching a little as he disappeared around the corner.

He'd never been in a bad mood before, since the day she'd met him. He'd never complained, never frowned, never spoken sharply in any way. The closest he'd ever come to grouchiness had been the day he'd demanded access to the bathroom when he'd needed to pee like a racehorse. But that had obviously been driven by desperate physical need, not a bad mood.

Even his occasional bossiness had only been in the intent of being helpful. His insistence on her wearing a sun hat, that she move away from the hill behind the house in case of an earthquake, had only been in order to protect her, not due to grouchiness. What was different about today?

******

When he arrived home the next evening, Michelle was curled up on the couch with a book. He gave her a brief "Hey" without even looking at her, and went into his room, closing the door. After twenty minutes or so, she heard him come out and go into the bathroom, then heard the shower running. For the first time since he'd moved in, she heard no shower singing.

It was an anomaly. She had actually gotten used to hearing his off-key singing in the shower.

When he came out of the bathroom, he walked into the living room and sat down across from her, wearing his bathrobe. She ignored him. After a few minutes of awkward silence, he said, "I'm sorry I snapped at you yesterday."

She put down the book and looked at him, but he wouldn't meet her eyes. This was totally weird, not like him at all. Where was his twinkly smile? She wanted to accept his apology, but she also wanted him to look her in the eye. So she didn't respond, and after a minute he finally looked at her.

Sad. *Freya*, he looked so sad. Was this really her goofy, smiley roommate, or a pod person?

"OK, apology accepted," she said. "What's up with you anyway?"

She had to restrain herself from standing up and going over to him, sitting there looking so uncharacteristically morose. It was crazy, but she wanted to sit on his lap, feel the terry cloth of that bathrobe he was wearing on her legs, put her arms around his neck, and draw his head to her shoulder. She wanted to ask him, "What's bothering you? Tell me. Let me make it all better."

But she didn't. He was her roommate and her friend, but sitting on a guy's lap went way beyond the roommate/friend parameter.

"Nothing," he said, which she didn't believe for a minute.

"I'm not buying that. Are you alright?"

"I'm fine. I'm wonderful, haven't you heard? I'm abso-fucking-lutely peachy-keen."

"You can't lie for shit, Hanson."

She purposely spoke crudely, purposely did not add their usual "pardon my language", just to get a rise out of him. Not so much as the tiniest smile crossed his face, not even at hearing her swear, when it usually got a laugh out of him. She was even more certain now that something was wrong. He got up and started to walk back to his room, but stopped, and without turning around, said, "I went to a funeral."

Well that explained a lot. Now she felt bad, having called him a grouch when he'd most likely been upset and grieving. She put down her book, stood up and stepped towards him. "I'm sorry, Eric. I didn't know," she said to his back. "Was it a friend of yours?"

"Yeah, a guy I served with in Afghanistan." He still stood there with his back to her but she could see his shoulders slump a little.

Freya, this was awful. "So that garment bag you had?"

"My dress whites."

"I'm so sorry, Eric," she said again. She actually felt her throat get tight, even though she hadn't known the deceased. Eric hadn't mentioned his name or anything about him. He'd only referred to him as "a guy I served with." And yet, the sadness she felt on his behalf was heartbreaking. It might as well have been a close family member or his best friend. Because Eric, her friend, grieved, she felt an intense sorrow also. That must be the empathy thing Eric had talked about.

Empathy sucked. Empathy hurt.

She stepped close, wanting to give him a hug of sympathy, but he must have had eyes in the back of his head. He held up his hand in a "stop" gesture, still not turning around.

"Don't," he said, then went back to his room, closed the door, and didn't come back out.

She stared at his door for a minute, with a mixture of sympathy and annoyance. This was so not like the Eric she thought she'd come to know the past few months. When she had experienced her delayed grief, the day he'd moved in, he'd given her a friendly, sympathetic hug and let her cry on him. She'd only wanted to give him the same sympathy, and he'd rebuffed her as if she had leprosy. Weren't they supposed to be friends?

It was several days before Eric came back to his usual, familiar twinkly self, and while Michelle really wanted to talk to him about his unfriendliness that day, she decided, in this case, not to pester him about it.

26

TEN YEARS EARLIER, AVALON

"Dad, let's eat dinner," Michelle entreated, calling her father from where he sat on the couch, not watching the baseball game on the television in front of him, and drinking a beer. It wasn't his first of the day. It wasn't even his third.

After offering the food a second time, he finally asked, "What is it?"

"I made spaghetti, Dad. And garlic bread."

"Again?"

She was hurt at his disdain for her limited culinary repertoire. She wasn't even in high school yet. How could he expect restaurant options?

Finally he shuffled into the kitchen and sat down as she put the dishes of pasta, sauce and bread on the table. He drained the last of his beer and set down the empty bottle on the table so hard it fell over, and his plate rattled.

"Pop me another cold one, Mickey," he requested as he put food on his plate.

"We're out of beer, Dad," Michelle lied. "How about some lemonade?"

Her dad just got up and opened the fridge, grabbing out another bottle and popping off the cap, which fell on the floor. He didn't bother to pick it up. Somehow, there was always more beer in the fridge. A brief dirty look for her lie was flung in her direction as he ate.

As she ate her own meal, feeling a little sick inside, she said, "Tomorrow is open house night at school, Dad. Are you going to come?" She both wanted, and feared, that he would attend. She hated being the only kid without any parents showing up, but unless he was sober, she didn't want to risk suffering the embarrassment of him stumbling around smelling like a brewery.

"Dunno. Maybe," was all the response she got.

As she cleared the table and put the leftovers in the fridge, pushing aside some beer bottles to make room, her dad shuffled back to the couch, clutching another beer, and not watching the baseball game on the television in front of him. Michelle washed and dried the dishes. She knew better than to ask for help. When she was done, she took out the trash, which clinked with empty beer bottles, and swept the kitchen floor, including several discarded bottle caps.

She snuck quietly into her room, hoping her dad wouldn't notice her creeping past behind the couch and demand that she pop him another cold one, Mickey. She hated that nickname. Her name was Michelle. Mickey was a mouse.

After she finished her homework, she picked up the pamphlet the counselor at school had given her. Al-Anon. A support group for the families of alcoholics. There was a meeting in a few days. But it was being held in the parish hall of Saint Catharine of Alexandria Catholic Church, the same church where her mother's funeral had taken place, and she had no desire to ever set foot in that building again.

What did they do at these Al-Anon meetings? Talk about their drunk fathers who didn't care about anything? What would that accomplish? Would telling other people, strangers, about her horrible home life make her dad stop drinking? Not bloody likely. If it would, she'd talk about it until she was blue in the face. But no amount of talking, to anyone about anything, was going to change anything at the Diaz house. Her mother would still be dead, her father would still be a drunk, and she'd still be a pathetic loser.

When she went back into the living room, her dad had gone to bed to sleep it off. She gathered up the empty bottles he'd left behind, and wiped up the wet rings they had left on the coffee table. After depositing them onto the trash, she turned off the lights he'd left on, and made sure the doors were locked.

While brushing her teeth, she looked at her reflection in the mirror. *You look sad, Michelle.* She heard that a lot. She supposed she did. There was little to be happy about. Maybe occasionally, when her dad was sober and acted like a real parent. But those were rare occasions.

She was sick of looking, and feeling, sad. It was pathetic. It was weak. It was vulnerable. Her reflection stared back at her, daring her to change.

OK. She wasn't going to be, or look, sad anymore. Instead, she'd be mad. Angry. Strong. Bitchy. Anything but sad and vulnerable. In a few months she would start high school. So far, she had gotten fairly decent grades, when she paid attention. Starting with high school, she would get even better grades, she vowed. She'd pay attention, stop sneaking her fantasy books into class, and get the best grades possible. That wouldn't be sad. That would be strong. That would make her father pay attention.

The next evening, when it was time to go to her school's open house evening, Dad was passed out drunk on the couch, so she went without him. When she got home, she threw the Al-Anon brochure into the trash.

Briefly, she wondered if maybe she did something drastically different with her hair, if he would notice it.

27

There is no home mail delivery in Avalon, so all its residents utilize post office boxes. With the small size of the town, walking to the post office to pick up one's mail was little inconvenience.

Michelle had willingly conceded custody of the post office box key to Eric within a week of him moving in. They received very little in the way of actual paper mail. All of their bills came by email. Both Michelle's and Eric's paychecks were direct deposited, and the notifications when that happened came by email also.

Taking that into consideration, they only checked the post office box about once a week. The vast amount of what they found there was advertising.

But every once in a while, Eric pulled out an envelope that made him grin. The advantage of coming from a large family was that every so often, some of his great-nieces and nephews would send him an envelope filled with he thought of as Great Works of Art.

In reality, they were crayon drawings and homemade greeting cards, but to him, they were just as precious as any Picasso or Van Gogh.

Although there had been one drawing in the last batch that he and Michelle were still discussing. They still couldn't decide if the drawing depicted a Navy ship, a commercial vessel, or an alien spacecraft, and they didn't want to hurt the feelings of his great-nephew Andy by asking him what it was.

Today was his lucky day. With a quiet, "Hooyah," he pulled out an envelope with his niece Amanda's return address, whose crinkly thickness indicated the presence of more childish works of art. He just hoped that Andy might have labeled his later drawings.

"Hi there, Mr. Paramedic."

The voice came from behind him. He turned around to see a slightly familiar woman standing there, quickly raising her eyes to smile at him.

Had she been looking at his ass? He couldn't quite place her, though he was certain he must have met her somewhere. "Good morning, Ma'am," he said politely. She noticed his puzzled expression and held out a hand.

"Tracy," she reminded him. "Tracy Cook."

Oh, right, Tracy. Michelle's friend, the one who had been with her at the dock the day he'd responded to the fractured humerus. He hadn't recognized her at first because her hair was a rather unnatural shade of red today. The day he'd treated Mr. Morales's arm, she'd been a blonde.

"Eric Hanson," he said, shaking her hand. He had to, of course. His mama had raised a gentleman. She was smiling at him in a manner he recognized as flirtatious. *Yikes. Please, no.*

"You're Michelle's roommate, right?" She put a slight emphasis on the word roommate.

"Yes, ma'am. How have you been?" he asked, for politeness sake.

"I've been great," she said. "Even better, now." She actually looked him up and down. She was checking him out, her eyes lingering long enough on his muscles to make sure he knew she appreciated what she saw, and when she finally met his eyes, he saw a definite spark of interest and appreciation in hers.

Now, he had seen women check him out before. Not to brag, but it happened. He'd been accustomed to that up and down, head to toe and everything in between look, one that usually lingered on his biceps. In the past, he'd appreciated the looking. He'd worked hard to develop, and maintain, those muscles, and female appreciation had admittedly been in part a motivating factor.

Michelle had done that – checked him out – that first day in her kitchen, after crying on his shoulder and wiping her face on his shirt. Despite their brand-new just roommate status, and his respect for her, he'd gotten a warm fuzzy feeling when she'd unconsciously looked him up and down. She probably hadn't intended to do so, but then he had stripped off his shirt right in front of her.

He hadn't done it to be suggestive or pushy or even flirtatious, but merely as a necessary action to provide her with something to wipe her face with. He had all sorts of respect and platonic liking for her, and yet, he'd really enjoyed it when she looked at him and let her gaze slide down all the way to his feet. She probably didn't even realize she was doing it, until he'd wiggled his toes at her. Her look of dismay when she looked away had been the most amusing thing he'd seen in ages.

He'd managed to be a lot more subtle when he looked at her.

In his hound-dog past, he'd checked out right back with no subtlety whatsoever, completely willing to smile and flirt. He used to unashamedly return that up and down glance, a look that usually lingered on the bosom.

But somehow, he had lost his desire for that kind of thing since living in Avalon, since being roommates with Michelle. What he really wanted to do right now was to get home and share his treasure trove of artwork with her. But of course, it would be rude to just run off when Michelle's friend was standing there trying to talk to him.

"I was hoping to run into you," Tracy went on. "I wanted to tell you, it was really amazing what you did that day, helping that guy who fell. You didn't even get grossed out or anything."

"That's my job, ma'am. Not getting grossed out is one of the first requirements." She seemed to have totally forgotten the fact that there had been two of them there attending to that patient. He hadn't done everything by himself.

He refrained from mentioning that Mr. Morales's broken arm had been a fairly routine case to treat. Stabilize the patient, take his vital signs, and transport him to the hospital for x-rays. There'd been no bleeding, no bullet wounds, no burns, no severed limbs. No screaming.

Tracy smiled warmly. Maybe she was attractive, but that bright dyed red hair was bizarre. It was smooth and sleek, but of a color completely nonexistent in nature. He didn't mind chemically assisted hair color in general. But was it too much to ask for it to be at least close to a natural color? Maybe Tracy had influenced Michelle to experiment with her youthful rebellious purple hair.

She had a shiny gold ring pierced through her nose on the outside of her right nostril. *Eeww.* How did she clean that thing if she sneezed? There were two earrings in the lobe of each ear, and when she flipped her hair back flirtatiously, he could see another stud pierced into the top of her right ear, through the scapha.

Yikes, how many holes had the girl pierced into herself?

"I was wondering if you'd like to get some coffee. Or a drink?"

A drink? If it wasn't bizarre enough to have this friend of Michelle's practically asking him out, even if he did drink, it was eleven-thirty in the morning. However, the bars in Avalon were already serving. He did not want to have to explain to Tracy the reasons why he most certainly did not want to have a drink with her. Not only due to his allergy, but because he suddenly didn't want her to think he was interested in her flirting.

Wishing for a moment that his mama had not raised quite so much of a gentleman, he replied, reluctantly, "Coffee sounds nice, ma'am, thanks for offering."

There was a coffee shop just steps away from the post office, still inside the indoor shopping area attached to the Atwater Hotel. He closed up the post office box and followed Tracy as she led him to the counter.

The coffee she ordered had, seemingly, twelve ingredients and eight instructions. The barista seemed distinctly disappointed when Eric just ordered a plain black coffee. No fru-frus, no swirls, no half double shots of flavoring. Wouldn't a half double shot be, just a shot? Why did they take this complicated coffee setup so seriously?

He politely paid for both their beverages and they sat down at a small round table. How fortunate that they were in a smaller, more out of the way part of town, rather than in one of the busy places along Crescent Avenue. Less chance of people who knew him, or Michelle, seeing them sitting here together and possibly getting the wrong idea.

"How long have you lived in Avalon?" she asked him. "I don't think I've seen you around town. I'm sure I would have remembered you."

"Just a couple months," he replied uneasily. "I moved here to take a job with the fire department."

She flipped her unnaturally red hair over her shoulder in a movement obviously intended to be flirtatious. She wore a skimpy, low-cut tank top in a garish leopard print, shorts that were barely decent, and sandals with inch-thick soles. The straps of her tank top were thin enough to clearly reveal the bright red straps of her bra. Her fingernails were painted a ghastly shade of green. It clashed with the red hair.

She put a casual hand on his shoulder. It didn't give him the warm delightful feeling he got when Michelle touched him. And Tracy wore way too much perfume.

"I'm thinking about getting my belly button pierced," she said. "What do you think?" She actually picked up the hem of her shirt a bit to expose her navel.

Navel and nose piercings, and all those earrings? How many holes did the girl plan on putting into her body? A tattoo was one thing, but piercings were a turn-off. Michelle didn't even have pierced ears. He'd noticed that the day he'd washed her hair. Her natural, non-artificial hair.

Tracy pulled a tube of lip gloss out of her pocket, applied it, and winked at him. He could see her staring at his tattoo. Oh Lord, her hand was moving along the table, creeping towards his. Was it his imagination, or did she scoot her chair a little closer to him?

It wasn't his imagination. She leaned in a little and said, in a low voice, "You know what? I think you're hot."

He had to suppress a cowardly urge to bolt and run.

"How did you and Michelle meet?" he asked quickly.

"We went to school together," Tracy replied. "She always pretended to be a snot, but she wasn't really."

"She told me she used to help you study in high school," Eric said, trying to discreetly put distance between his chair and Tracy's. "I bet that was really helpful. And she said you helped her out a lot when she had issues at home. You know she had a really tough childhood, with her mom dying and her dad's drinking. I'm sure it meant a lot to her to have a friend to spend time with."

"So now she has you to hang out with?" Tracy gave him a look that he read easily. She was fishing to see if he and Michelle were a couple, or if he was fair game.

"We're very compatible roommates. It helps that she likes ice cream as much as I do. I was really lucky to be able to move into her house just when she needed a roommate. It's amazing how she basically raised herself and yet turned out to be strong and successful despite her unpleasant home life."

Tracy was seriously flirting with him, leaning forward so that he could see down the front of her shirt, which he avoided looking at, flipping that impossibly red hair, giving him a definite come-hither smile. He recognized it – he'd been on the receiving end of that kind of flirtation before, and in the past, had returned it enthusiastically. But he just wasn't interested now.

Michelle didn't flirt. She told it like it was, without artifice. If he saw down the front of her shirt, it was completely by accident. He tried not to look then too, but in that case, it was due to respect rather than disinterest.

"So you and Michelle spent a lot of time together in high school?" he asked, trying to discreetly scoot his chair away from Tracy as he took a sip of his coffee.

Tracy looked a bit irritated at the way he kept steering the conversation back to Michelle, but answered, "Yes, we did, I helped her color her hair one time."

"Was that when she went purple?"

"She told you about that? Usually she doesn't tell people stuff like that."

Really? Michelle had told him about coloring her hair purple, and even more personal stuff, the day they'd met.

"It took two boxes of dye to cover all her hair," Tracy replied. "I thought it looked cool, but she wasn't interested in keeping it up when it washed out."

"Well yeah, why should she, when her natural color is so beautiful."

There went his big mouth again.

"You know she really only did it to see if her father would notice," Tracy said. "But he didn't."

"That must have really upset her."

Tracy nodded. "Yeah her dad was a real piece of work. He didn't even bother to come down to the school when she ended up in the principal's office."

"Why was she in the principal's office?" His sweet little Michelle, being sent to the principal's office?

"Maybe you should ask her," Tracy said with a bit of a frown when he declined to request more gossip from her.

"I think I will. It couldn't have been due to her grades. I know she got straight A's."

"So tell me about you," Tracy suggested, emphasizing the word "you".

He briefly spoke about retiring from the Navy and coming to Avalon to work as a paramedic.

"The Navy?" Tracy asked with interest. "Oh, those white uniforms are sexy."

"I mostly wore khaki. Or camouflage. Or Marine green."

"I saw Top Gun. Were you a pilot?"

"No, I was a corpsman."

"But now you're a fireman?"

"A paramedic," he corrected.

"You know what would sell great in the gift shops here? One of those calendars with firemen on it. And paramedics. You know, posing shirtless, holding their firehoses."

She put a slight emphasis on the word "firehose".

Oh, lord.

"Do you think you'd be interested in doing something like that?"

He knew she'd be insulted if he refused outright, even though something like that would be the absolutely last thing he'd ever want to do.

Where was a medical emergency when he needed one?

When Eric had told Michelle, and by extension her douchebag ex-boyfriend, that he knew a few guys from the SEAL teams, he hadn't been exaggerating. It was impossible to be stationed in San Diego without running into them, or seeing the trainees going through BUD/S. As a member of the medical team, Eric had met more than one in the clinic.

Eric liked treating the guys on the SEAL teams. They were stand-up guys who didn't whine and curse about a little thing like getting a dozen stitches in their scalp. While Eric had been suturing that particular scalp, its owner had only complained about having to have his hair shaved off in the process. Since the SEALs frequently were inserted into places where they had to blend in with the local population, they were usually exempt from standard military grooming regulations.

In order to have something to talk about while Eric stitched the guy's now-shaved scalp, his patient had told him about learning a tactic called Escape and Evade as part of his SEAL Qualification Training. E and E was a tactic that they used to remove themselves from difficult situations.

Eric suddenly wished he could have sat in on that class, so that he would have an Escape and Evade tactic at hand at this moment.

"Um, well, I'd have to think about it," he said vaguely. *For about two seconds, before declining.*

Lord help him, he was a changed man now. Here was an available young woman, attractive despite her unorthodox style choices, hitting on him, and all he could think about was his roommate and how soon he could get away and get home to her.

At that moment, salvation walked towards him in the form of Johnny Del Risco, the manager of the Portofino Hotel, where Eric had delivered a baby.

Thank the universe for small mercies. He caught Del Risco's eye and smiled in recognition, giving the guy a, come on over here gesture.

Johnny hesitated, looking at Tracy sitting there with him. Eric could see in his eyes that he was reluctant to interrupt what he wrongly thought to be a date. Lord, what he wouldn't give at this moment to have ESP so that he could telepathically communicate to the guy, this is *not* a date.

"Hey, Johnny, how are you, man?" he said jovially as Del Risco approached with a wary look in his eyes. "Sit down, take a load off." He pushed a chair towards the other man, as Tracy's expression morphed from flirtatious to irritated at Eric's inviting an interloper to their not-a-date.

Johnny sat down and Eric, being a gentleman, performed the introductions.

"This is Tracy Cook, she's a friend of my roommate. Tracy, this is Johnny Del Risco, he's the manager of the Portofino Hotel."

Johnny shook Tracy's hand, smiled at her and said, "It's really nice to meet you." In fact, he held her gaze for kind of a long time, in just-met-a-person time. Apparently, the guy was into unnaturally colored hair and nose rings.

Suddenly, Tracy's look of irritation disappeared, to be replaced with the same come-hither smile she'd subjected Eric to. *Oh, Lord*. She looked Johnny Del Risco up and down, just like she'd done to Eric, and her gaze lingered on his dark eyes, magnified behind wired rimmed glasses. The other man's hair was long enough to be held back into a ponytail, and the combined effect with the eyeglasses gave him a scholarly, college professor look. Eric would just bet from the look that now crossed Tracy's face, that she was imagining taking those glasses off Johnny's face and undoing that ponytail.

Salvation indeed.

"Cook?" Johnny was asking. "Are you part of the Cook family that owns the gift shops here in town?"

Tracy nodded. "Yeah, that's my dad. He has a shop in the Metropole Marketplace and another one on Sumner Avenue. I'm his assistant manager."

Eric took a sip of his coffee to hide his smile. From what Michelle had told him, Tracy's title of Assistant Manager of her father's shops was mostly honorary. She spent more time coloring her hair and flirting with guys than actually working.

"I'm so glad to have met you," Johnny said enthusiastically. "We're thinking of putting a gift shop inside the hotel, and I was thinking it would be so much easier to have it set up by someone who already has the experience, rather than doing it ourselves from scratch. Do you think your father would be interested in exploring an idea like that?" He looked so earnest behind those glasses that Eric almost laughed out loud.

"I'm sure he would," Tracy replied, just as enthusiastically. "I think that's a great idea. I could totally help you with that. We could work on it together. I have some great ideas on how to arrange it. Where in the hotel were you thinking of locating it? Maybe I could come over and scope the place out, help you choose a spot."

Johnny Del Risco was looking like he'd just been handed the winning Super Lotto ticket, and just like that, Eric became invisible, as Tracy and Johnny started brainstorming about the idea of her family placing a shop in the hotel, accompanied by a whole lot of flirting.

One thing Eric had never been before, was a third wheel. Though he obviously had just become one, he didn't mind a bit. He wasn't accustomed to being brushed aside by a woman, and if this had been Before Michelle, he wouldn't have liked it. Today, he was delighted to have this woman's attention diverted elsewhere. It gave him an excuse to roll on out of there. He was doubly lucky when his phone chose that moment to chirp with a text message and he quickly pulled it out to check. Which was something he totally did in any circumstance, since it might possibly be a text from work announcing some kind of emergency. Although most emergencies requiring the assistance of off-duty personnel would be communicated by the voice pager clipped to his belt, it wasn't unheard of for a phone call or text to be used.

It wasn't an emergency; it was a text from his buddy Gabriel saying that his kid had lost a baby tooth, including a photo of said kid pulling his lips back to reveal the empty space in his teeth, but Eric didn't reveal that. He just said, "Oh, sorry, gotta go," and held up the phone as if it had called him away.

"Another tourist go into labor?" Johnny asked.

"Um, no," was Eric's vague reply.

Johnny turned back to Tracy, saying, "Do you know that this guy," he nodded towards Eric, "delivered a baby at the hotel last month? In fact, I've gotten a couple of requests from guests requesting that specific room.

Apparently, some people who are trying to get pregnant think it's good baby luck or something."

Tracy blinked at Eric for a second as if she'd forgotten he was still there. "Oh that's nice," she said, then turned her attention back to Johnny. She actually reached over and ran her hand down the length of Del Risco's ponytail. "I'm thinking of getting my belly button pierced," she told him.

That was Eric's cue to escape. He stood up, still holding his phone up. "Sorry to bail on you guys, but duty calls." The two lovebirds sitting there didn't need to know that his immediate "duty" was replying to his friend's text message.

"See ya later," Johnny replied vaguely, though he continued to focus on Tracy. Tracy was looking into Johnny's eyes, and he was looking back, as Eric stood up and picked up his coffee cup and the envelope from his niece, preparing to escape.

He was three steps away when he heard Tracy's voice call his name.

Dang! He thought he was going to be successful at slithering away from her attention. His heart sinking, he politely turned back to look back at her, pulling up a friendly smile.

"Ma'am?"

"Do me a favor?" Tracy asked. A favor? He was afraid to ask, but felt obligated to nod agreeably.

"Give Michelle a message for me," Tracy said with a knowing smile. "Tell her she's a really lucky girl."

Then she turned back to Johnny. He was gazing into her eyes.

The man was toast.

******

As soon as Michelle got home from work, Eric felt obligated to confess about his non-date with Tracy. "I saw your friend Tracy in town this morning," he said. "We had coffee."

He felt, weirdly, like he'd somehow cheated on Michelle by sitting down and socializing with another woman. There was really no reason why he had to tell her about seeing Tracy. He could have coffee or whatever with whomever he chose. *Stupid.* It wasn't like they were a couple, other than friends and roommates. Why then did he feel bad about the incident? Why did he feel like he had to confess it and be forgiven? He hadn't done anything wrong. He hadn't even initiated the encounter. And yet, he felt as if he'd cheated on Michelle.

How pathetic was that, to feel like he'd cheated on a woman who wasn't even his girlfriend.

Admit it, Hanson. You care about this girl and you don't want her to think you're interested in someone else.

Lord, he was so screwed.

Michelle's eyebrows came together a little, almost looking – what? Upset? "You had a date with Tracy?"

Tracy? *Tracy?* Her supposed best friend, had flirted with Eric, *her* Eric? She knew Tracy. If it had the Y chromosome, she flirted.

She was going to scratch the bitch's eyes out.

Whoa, girl. Down, Michelle. He wasn't *her* Eric. He was only her roommate. He could have coffee with, have dates with, have a flaming hot affair if he chose, with anyone he chose to have it with.

But that didn't mean she had to like it.

She'd known Tracy since middle school. Tracy was a self-confident, talkative, happy person whose greatest concerns were what color hair dye to choose next, and whether she had a date every weekend. She was outgoing and vivacious and not at all above allowing a potential date to get an eyeful of her cleavage, just to see that drooly expression overwhelming a guy's face. She'd been flirting her way from man to man ever since Michelle could remember.

She was everything that Michelle wasn't.

And yet, despite their disparate personalities and their different home lives, somehow they had remained friends. Michelle had spent a significant amount of time at Tracy's house in her high school years. Though Tracy frequently had disagreed with her parents, still the family had been way closer to normal than Michelle's living situation.

"No, not a date." Eric insisted. "We just had coffee. At Old Ben's by the post office. It was her idea." He plastered on his silliest, most teasing grin. "Are you jealous?"

"Insanely," she assured him. Of course, it was their little joke, a reversal of their joking exchange the night at the Marlin Club when she'd kissed Danny Gonzalez's cheek. But Eric had been jealous that evening, even though that kiss had been nothing but fraternal, though he'd hidden it from Michelle with his joking.

"I introduced her to Johnny Del Risco. Do you know him?" Michelle shook her head. "He's the manager of the Portofino Hotel. He was working the night I delivered the baby there. We've kept in touch. I think they hit it off."

Michelle smiled then. Yes! She believed him that he didn't have any interest in Tracy.

"She also said she thinks you're lucky." He held his breath a little when he relayed that message, wondering if Michelle would come to the same conclusion about his feelings for her that Tracy apparently had. After all, he had spent pretty much the entire time he'd sat with Tracy talking about Michelle, until Johnny Del Risco showed up and saved him. He was going to have to stop by the hotel tomorrow and thank the guy, maybe bring him a basket of muffins, or at least a latte.

"I am lucky," Michelle said. "I have you for a roommate."

"Aren't you sweet," he teased, though he actually meant it. "I've got a couple of steaks in the fridge I can make for dinner." He went out to the back patio to fire up the grill. This was totally how he'd rather spend his time, cooking dinner with his roommate, rather than squirming at an awkward non-date with her friend.

28

"One of these days you're going to have to let me pay for the ice cream," Michelle said.

They were sitting on a bench on Crescent Avenue, enjoying cones from Scoops Homemade Ice Cream shop. Behind them was Avalon's small beach and the backs of the buildings along the Green Pleasure Pier.

"Maybe," Eric replied vaguely as he finished off the rest of his cone and cast a covetous eye at Michelle's.

"You encouraged me to get two scoops because you knew I wouldn't be able to finish it, didn't you?"

He nodded guiltily.

"You were right," she said as she handed him the remains of her treat, and wondered how he managed to keep that slender waist, cute butt and general all-around fit body, considering how much and how often he enjoyed ice cream. Maybe it was rude to stare, but she was mesmerized by his mouth and the way his tongue licked away the little drip of ice cream that threatened to fall off the bottom of the cone.

"Thanks, sweetheart," he said, accepting her leftovers and making quick work of it. She started to get up but he put a restraining hand on her arm.

"Can I ask you something?" He actually looked a bit less sparkly than usual, so she took that to mean he had a serious concern to ask her about. Had she left her laundry in the washer again, or forgotten her turn to clean the bathroom?

"Did you ever wonder why your father was the way he was? Why he was so apathetic about life?"

The bright sunshine they'd just been enjoying went behind a cloud.

Of course, she'd wondered. She wondered about that every waking moment of her life. If it were anyone other than Eric asking her about it, she would have said, mind your own business. But she knew him by now. He didn't ask out of morbid curiosity or to create gossip. He truly wanted to know and if possible, make things better. She sat back down on the bench next to him.

"He was a drunk, Eric. You know that. Like you said, it was a disease, and one that he refused to get treatment for."

"Yes, I realize that. But did you ever investigate his life, his situation, to try and find out what his problems were, more than just his alcoholism?"

She stared at the people walking by along Crescent Avenue without really seeing any of them. "I tried asking him, hundreds of times, what his problem was, why he didn't care about anything. All I ever got were non-committal grunts and half answers and an occasional mention of something stupid like birds. He didn't want to talk to me about whatever went on in his life. There were so many things I wanted to know. How he felt about my mother. Did he love her? Or did he resent the fact that he had to marry her?"

"Had to?" Eric asked.

She nodded. "Remember I told you that I sent for a copy of my mother's death certificate when I turned eighteen? Well as long as I was retrieving public records, I got copies of their marriage certificate and my birth certificate too. They were only married five months when I was born, so obviously my mother was pregnant already. I think they call that a shotgun marriage. They probably didn't even want me, but felt obligated to get married because I was a bun in their oven."

"Don't automatically think you were unwanted, just because of that," Eric tried to assure her. "Not all unexpected babies are unwanted. From what I've been told, it was a huge surprise to my parents when they found out they were expecting me, and the rest of the family was really shocked too, but that didn't mean they didn't want me or didn't love me, despite the unplanned nature of my existence."

"So did your parents get married because they were expecting you?"

"No, they were married almost five years before I was conceived. They didn't think they would have kids together so they were all pretty shocked when it happened. There had to be another reason for your dad's outlook on life. Maybe it had to do with your mom's death. Wouldn't you want to know?"

"How? I couldn't read his mind, and he wouldn't say. If there even was a reason other than his alcoholism. The only thing he ever said was occasionally mentioning birds, and that's nothing."

"Maybe you should ask around, talk to some of his friends."

Her mouth twisted. "You mean drinking buddies."

"Yeah them, maybe they knew something. Maybe Gary at the Marlin Club knows some of them. Didn't you say your dad spent a lot of time there?"

Eric had that eager, I want to help, look on his face, but Michelle wasn't going for it.

"No, I don't want to open that can of worms. I'm afraid I might not like what I find out."

"But wouldn't knowing the truth be better than wondering for the rest of your life?" he asked.

"It would depend on what that truth was. What if the truth was, my Dad just didn't care about me or want me and just thought I was a pathetic burden to him, unless I was willing to pop him another cold one. What if the truth was my mother didn't care enough about her family, about me, to fight for her life."

"Sweetheart, I seriously doubt it would be like that," Eric insisted. "It's true, whatever they were thinking or feeling, it may have been unpleasant, but I can't believe any sane person would not want you or care about you. I'm sure your mother loved you even before you were born."

"How could she love me before I was even born?"

"Trust me on this one," he assured her. "I come from a big family. When you find out you're going to become a parent, you love that kid from the moment you find out it exists, even if it's still an embryo." He looked away for a moment. "Or so I've been told."

"They didn't want me," she insisted. "I was an accident."

"Please don't call yourself that. It hurts me to hear it."

"Why should it hurt you?" For a smart man, sometimes he didn't make sense.

"Because you're my friend and it hurts to hear you put yourself down unnecessarily. I hate it when you call yourself stuff like pathetic and loser and bat-shit crazy, because those are just not true. None of what your parents did or didn't do are your fault. You survived a bad situation and came out of it as a strong, brave, amazing person, and you should be proud of that, rather than running yourself down."

"I just wish I could have your optimistic attitude about all that."

He leaned over and rubbed his hand briskly up and down her arm.

"What was that for?" she asked in amazement.

"That was me rubbing off some of my optimistic attitude onto you."

She smiled. "You are such a goof."

"Hey, it worked. You're smiling. Michelle, seriously, let's ask around town and see if we can find some people who knew your dad socially, and see if they know things that maybe you don't. If I were in your situation, I'd be dying of curiosity."

"No, I told you that's a can of worms I'd rather not open."

"But why?" He seemed completely disbelieving that she didn't leap at the chance to open that can of worms.

"Maybe I'm scared to hear the answers."

A couple of days later she was chopping some vegetables to make a salad to go with dinner. Eric had promised to cook his famous well-done steak tonight, but he was an hour late getting home. It didn't concern her. She was well aware that injuries and accidents didn't always follow his work schedule, and there were always reports to complete after each call. He'd told her, if it's not documented, it didn't happen.

When he did get home, and grilled their steaks, and was drying the dishes as she washed them, he said, totally out of the blue, "I found a guy that knew your dad. Gary at the Marlin Club pointed him out when I asked if he knew of any of your dad's friends."

She went very still, poised with a plate in her hand that she'd just washed and rinsed and was about to hand to him for drying. Had he not listened to her the other day? Had the ice cream he'd eaten numbed his brain, affected his memory?

"Eric, I asked you not to do that, didn't I?" She had a slight difficulty getting the words out.

"Well, not in so many exact words."

"Don't get picky. You knew I didn't want to pursue it."

"How can you not want to know the truth of the situation? Even if it's unpleasant, knowing is better than ignorance."

"No, it's not. You don't understand." Sadness started to drag on her heart. "You grew up in a real family that cared about each other. You have no idea what it was like for me. You can't possibly understand. What I do know is bad enough and I don't want to go down that particular rabbit hole. I told you that, and yet you went behind my back and looked up some drunk that knew my father so that I can have salt poured into my wounds. I thought we were friends. Friends don't cut friends off at the knee like that."

"I wasn't trying to hurt you," he defended himself. "I was trying to help you."

"You're not helping."

She handed him the plate she was still holding in her hand, and he set it down without drying it, looking both irritated at her lack of appreciation for his supposed "help" and relieved that she didn't break the plate over his head.

When he'd annoyed her by replacing the shower curtain without consulting her, she'd practically grown fangs as she yelled at him, called him names and stomped away. But this upset her a lot more. She didn't yell, she didn't stomp and she didn't insult. She turned and quietly walked away, saying, "I'm going to go take a walk," leaving him in the kitchen among the half-washed dishes and the leftovers and the glasses of iced tea they hadn't finished yet.

"Can I come with?" he asked from behind her.

"No," she replied briefly, as she slipped on her flip-flops and walked out the front door.

For some reason however, she found herself unable to fume at what he'd done. She was upset, but not at Eric. She felt no inclination to cry or throw things or be angry at him. She just walked down to the pier and stood looking at the ocean, breathing in calmness.

It wasn't actually accurate that she didn't want to know about her father's life and why he was the way he was. She really did want to know. As Eric had guessed, she was dying of curiosity. It was more that she was a complete and utter coward about the possibility of hearing things she might not like.

You are such a wimp, Michelle. All these months since she and Eric had been roommates, he'd been telling her that she was, in his opinion, strong and brave and impressive. She wanted to believe him, but she had just proven him to be completely wrong about all those upstanding traits he'd attributed to her. And yet, she knew he was a smart, observant and perceptive person. She was not wrong in believing those things about him.

An arm appeared in her peripheral vision, leaning on the pier's railing next to her. That arm bore a familiar tattoo, depicting a fouled anchor. She'd been concentrating so hard on the color of the water in front of her, on the patterns of the waves and the slight, mobile scents of salt and seaweed, that she hadn't even heard him approach and stand at the railing just a foot to her left.

"Are you following me?" she asked, though with much less irritation than she'd had when she'd asked him the same question the day they'd met.

"Absolutely not. I heard you say no when I asked if I could come with you on your walk. I decided I needed to come down here and look at the water all on my own. It's strictly a coincidence that you're here too."

He didn't look at her and she didn't look at him. There was no need to at the moment; they could just enjoy each other's companionship and watch the ocean at the same time.

Like Michelle, Eric had grown up within sight of the ocean. The sea could be as comforting as a mother's embrace when she was in the mood – calm, smooth, loving. The sea could also be as tempestuous and exciting as a lover when it foamed and roared with waves that bit with excitement. And like a lover, the sea could be a fickle bitch whose mood changed in a heartbeat.

The sea could also be a best friend, a confidant who invited a person to talk, to share, at least internally if not aloud. She would listen to whatever you had to say without judgment. You could tell the ocean the good stuff, the bad stuff, the embarrassing stuff, and she calmly kept your secrets just like a best friend should.

Of course the ocean could also be a monster, a threat to be defeated, or at least survived, when she raged and roared and pounded. While Eric, and every other sailor with an ounce of brains, held a healthy respect, even fear, when the sea raged and threatened, he'd never hated it. Some of the storms he had seen at sea had scared the hell out of him, but when they were over, he and the sea forgave each other – her, for scaring him, and him, for being afraid of her. He knew that his watery lover would, always, eventually morph back into the calm friend, the affectionate mother.

He surmised that Michelle's lack of a stable family life had been a motivating factor for her own desire to appreciate the ocean and its consistent existence, its dependable, always there to listen state of being. Eric had plenty of friends he could talk to, hang out with, depend on to have his six. He had a family who loved him and whom he loved and appreciated. He'd had his share of love affairs, ranging from one-night stands to almost real committed relationships. And along with those human interactions, he had the Ocean – his mother, his friend, his lover, his child. Her salty scent was always there, whatever her mood or persona. She never left him and never disappointed him, and he realized that she, Ocean, Sea, Watery Deep, whatever she was named, held Michelle in the same consistent, listening, non-judgmental embrace.

Michelle could be like the ocean – beautiful, changeable yet constant, inviting emotional confidences. He'd found himself telling her things he'd never even told his best friend or his closest family members. Which rather surprised him, as a natural-born big-mouth, concealing anything from his friends and relatives, was something extremely rare for him. He'd never hesitated to talk to them, big-mouth that he was, and yet, Michelle was the only person he'd told about the day he'd officially left the Navy, about how he'd pulled over, parked his car, and cried over the end of that phase of his life. It was rare for him not to share everything – the good, the bad, the ugly, with Gabriel or Brenda or his other friends and relatives, or his shrink, but somehow, that little event had stuck in his psyche until he'd revealed it to Michelle. She'd looked at him with those ocean-blue eyes, curious and friendly, and he'd been glad to tell her, just like he told his mother-friend-lover, the Ocean.

He suddenly wished that Michelle had been there with him that day. Sure it was an absolutely insane thing to wish for. He hadn't even known her phone number yet, hadn't yet responded to her roommate ad. But he couldn't help wishing that he had been able to contact her that day.

And say what?

"Hey there, remember me? Sidewalk Guy? I know you haven't seen me in almost a year, and we have no relationship other than a couple emails, but would you mind terribly hopping on a boat right now this minute and then getting an Uber down to NAS San Diego so that I can cry on your shoulder?"

Brenda always told him his big mouth would get him into trouble. It was a good thing he hadn't yet known Michelle's phone number that day.

"When anxious, uneasy and bad thoughts come," he said softly.

"I go to the sea, and the sea drowns them out with its great wide sounds," she replied.

"Cleanses me with its noise."

"And imposes a rhythm upon everything in me that is bewildered and confused," she finished the quote.

"I'm sorry," he said.

That was it. Just, I'm sorry. Not a long diatribe of justifications for his actions or reasons why she should forgive him. For someone usually as talkative as him, it was quite surprising.

Just, I'm sorry. And that was all she needed.

"You don't need to be sorry," she told him, and was rewarded by a look of confusion. He also became his familiar, talkative self again.

"I should have accepted what you told me and not gone behind your back when you said to drop it. I'm sorry I disrespected our friendship like that. I won't pursue it if that's what you want."

"But you said you thought I should try to find out."

"It doesn't matter what I think. It's your decision and right to pursue or not to pursue the situation and that's all that matters. I'm sorry I ignored that. That's all there is to it. I'm sorry."

"OK, three sorries is the charm. But, you were right. Knowing the truth, if there is more truth to know that is, would be preferable to living in ignorance."

"So you're not mad at me?"

"No, I'm not mad at you. I wasn't ever mad at you. In fact, I'm glad you instigated this because I was too chicken to do it myself."

He opened his mouth but she beat him to the punch. "Yeah, yeah, I'm brave and strong. Well, I'm going to put my money where my mouth is."

She turned and leaned against the rail as Eric looked out over the water. "I'm just glad you're OK with this," he said.

"I'm more than OK with it. I'm grateful." To show him how grateful she was, she leaned over and kissed his cheek, just like they frequently did in moments of happiness. He looked really surprised when she did that, but recovered quickly.

"So you forgive me?" he asked. "Are we good now? Or do I need to send you flowers?"

She was taken aback. Send her flowers? Was that actually a thing? She thought that only happened in movies.

"Do people actually send flowers in real life?"

"Of course. There are lots of reasons why people send flowers. Congratulations, sympathy, apology, thanks for last night, all sorts of things."

"Have you sent thanks for last night flowers? You said I could ask you anything."

He grinned and blushed at the same time. "Once or twice."

"We're good. Save your money. I forgive you. So, who is this friend of my dad's that you dug up and when are we going to talk to him?"

The next day at work, her phone chirped with a text message. She had her hands full of greasy parts at the moment so it was half an hour before she could read it. The text was from Eric. A picture of a large, colorful, gaudy display of flowers whose assorted blossoms and hues verged on the tacky, accompanied by the message, "Virtual apology flowers don't die."

She texted back, "You big goof" and made a point of saving the image.

******

Sunday morning, they walked out the door and Eric asked, "Do you know where Pete's Café is?"

"Yes, it's right across the street from the library."

"The guy we're meeting is named Brian Gallagher," Eric said. "Does that name ring a bell?"

"No, but my father didn't exactly introduce me to his buddies or have them over for tea. You know, you don't have to come with to see this guy. I'm sure there are more interesting things you could be doing on your day off."

"No. I am not going to make you face this alone. I opened this can of worms and I'm going to be there to see it through."

"You know, that's really a silly phrase," she said. "Have there ever really been worms in cans?"

"Yes. The military just dignifies them by calling them MRE's."

He hesitated a moment as they turned down Sumner Avenue.

"Unless you'd rather not have me there? I'd understand if you wanted to talk to this guy in private."

This time she was the one to put an escorting hand on his elbow.

"I really would rather have you there, if you don't mind, just in case I need someone to pick up the pieces."

"It would be my privilege, ma'am," he assured her with a grin.

Pete's Café was a combination bar, restaurant and open-air café, with a large banner advertising happy hour next to its name sign, and they took a table in the patio, close to the street and away from the bar. She sat in the red plastic chair, feeling nervous, while Eric went to the counter and returned with three cups of coffee, which he set on the table and gave her a determined look.

"I don't care what this guy may want, I'm not buying him a drink."

They waited for what seemed like hours, but was really only ten or fifteen minutes, and Michelle had just about decided that this supposed old friend of her dad's wasn't going to show, when a scruffy, somewhat shabby man of indeterminate age, with mousy longish hair and dull eyes, walked in, saw Eric, and walked over to their table.

Michelle recognized him, though she hadn't known his name. It was the guy who'd come to her dad's funeral and said that Greg Diaz was a good drinking buddy.

"Mr. Gallagher," Eric said politely, standing up and shaking his hand. "Have a seat. I got you some coffee."

Brian Gallagher sat, with a glance towards the bar that clearly indicated he'd prefer something stronger than coffee, but realizing he wasn't going to get it at the moment.

"You know Michelle Diaz?" Eric asked, giving her a small arm pat.

Gallagher nodded, saying briefly, "Hey there."

Now that she thought about it, she recalled seeing this man with her dad at bars around town when she'd gone to escort, aka drag, him home. She'd never spoken to him nor asked his name, and Dad hadn't volunteered it. It wasn't as if he'd expected them all to be friends or anything.

The two of them, Eric and Brian Gallagher, were looking at her as if waiting for her to get the conversation rolling, but she suddenly felt tongue-tied.

On the one side, she wanted to bombard the guy with questions. How long did you know my dad? Did he confide in you about his life or feelings or motivations? If so, why to you and not to me? Are you going to get help for your addiction too, or just roll on down the alcoholic road like he did?

On the other hand, she wanted to get up and run away and hide her head in the sand like an ostrich, without risking finding out the truth.

Eric, being the perceptive man he was, saw her conflicting feelings and took over the interview for her.

"You knew Michelle's father, Greg Diaz?"

"Yeah," Brian said. "We hung out."

Hung out. More like got drunk together four or five times a week.

"Do you think you could tell us, that is, tell Michelle, if her father ever talked about his personal life with you? He was rather reticent with her."

Reticent. What a classy word. It would be more accurate to say uncaring, unresponsive sot, but of course Eric was too polite to get that real with dear old Dad's drinking buddy.

Brian hesitated, but Michelle suddenly had had enough of tiptoeing around these particular tulips.

"Look, Mr. Gallagher. I know my dad spent a lot of time drinking with you and I want to know what he may have told you about himself, about why he treated me like crap and why he didn't care about anything in the world other than his next bottle of beer. If you know anything about his feelings, if he had any, I'd really appreciate hearing about it. Especially since he's dead now and we'll never get anything out of him, not that I ever could when he was alive."

The man looked between Eric and Michelle and sighed.

"OK, well if you want to know so bad. Yeah, he did talk to me about his life when he was really, really wasted. Sometimes he'd look down the neck of his bottle and just start saying stuff."

Just start saying stuff. Michelle did that sometimes, just started saying things that she usually kept inside. Did that mean she had something in common with her father, a shared personally trait? *Please, Freya, no.*

But when she did that, it was usually due to Eric's encouraging smile, rather than the influence found in a bottle.

"And sometimes I could understand what he was saying," Gallagher said. "Not all the time, but enough to realize that he was a real head case. It really messed him up when Robin left him."

"My mother's name wasn't Robin. It was Rachel. He must have been so wasted he couldn't even pronounce her name correctly. And she didn't leave him, more's the pity."

"I know your mother's name was Rachel." Brian Gallagher took a sip of the coffee Eric had provided. "But before Greg met her, he was madly in love with a girl named Robin. Robin Osorio. She lived here on the island for about six months as an intern for the Catalina Island Conservancy, counting foxes or something. He wanted to marry her, asked her to stay here on the island with him. She said no, it was more important for her to get her master's degree or whatever she was working on at USC. He begged her, and she said that they were just having a summer fling, it was no big deal. But it was a big deal to him. He never got over it. He'd go to the mainland every month or so to try and see her until she got a restraining order against him. He gave up on that then, and started seeing Rachel, you know, to try and get Robin out of his mind. He married Rachel when she got pregnant, but it wasn't the same. She wasn't Robin. Eventually, he started to accept that he was never going to have Robin, but it didn't stop him from drinking more and more, way too much and way too often."

For an obvious drunk like Brian Gallagher to say her dad drank too much, it had to be really bad. And she positively could not imagine her apathetic father being so passionate about someone that it took a restraining order to dissuade him.

"Then when Rachel died, he lost it. Just snapped. He didn't care about anything after that."

"Yeah obviously, he didn't care about me, that was for sure." She could feel Raging Bitch stirring inside her, and tried to squelch her down, like Bruce Banner trying to suppress the Hulk. "I used to think sometimes that maybe he wasn't really my father. Robin and Rachel are pretty similar names. Do you think he started dating my mother because of that similarity, so maybe he could pretend that she was really Robin?"

"I don't know about that," Brian Gallagher said quickly. But his expression seemed to indicate it was a possibility. "He was definitely your father. No doubt. You look just like he would have if he were female. Same hair, same eyes, same nose, chin. The only difference, other than gender, was that you have a spark in your eye and he didn't.

"I think he just got tired of caring, and having what he cared about disappear. You know his parents died when he was about twenty, and he was an only child."

That kind of explained the lack of family on the Diaz side.

"They went to the mainland for the weekend and were killed in a car crash. Didn't you know that?" Brain Gallagher looked at her speculatively.

"No, I didn't know my grandparents died in a car crash." She'd never even thought about having grandparents, on either side of her family. Grandparents were another thing only other people had. No wonder her father had been reluctant to go to the mainland.

Quite suddenly, and practically without thinking, she found herself reaching out her hand. She was floundering, adrift, lost at sea. She needed an anchor. When she put out her hand, she found her anchor. It was Eric's hand. Maybe it was inappropriate, but at the moment she needed something solid to grasp, and she looked at his face.

The man could read her mind. "I never knew any of my grandparents either."

Brian Gallagher was nodding, his mouth twisted in an expression that could have meant sadness, sympathy, or more likely, thirst. "The whole Robin fiasco happened about a year later, and then later, your mom, Rachel, died. I think he was afraid to care about you or anything else after that, like maybe if he did care, you'd disappear too."

She thought about all the times she'd considered, and rejected, the idea of running away from the island, of disappearing from her father's view and life. What might have happened to him if she had?

Brian Gallagher was still talking. Michelle had already heard more than she'd wanted to about her father's past, but apparently, once the drinking buddy got rolling, he couldn't stop.

"He did see her, that is Robin, one last time. It was years after they'd split up, years after Rachel died, but he went to the mainland for a couple of days and he managed to get her to talk to him. She was married by then, happily, had a couple kids. Greg told her he still loved her and if she'd leave her husband and be with him, he'd never touch another drop of booze again. Greg said she just laughed at him and said even if she believed that, she was happy with her life and her family and didn't want anything to do with him."

"A couple of days?" That wasn't like her dad. "The only time he ever went to the mainland after my mother died was when I finished technical school." She looked at Eric. "He actually came over to see me get my certificate, but instead of us coming back to Avalon together, he disappeared for three days and when he got home, he was so drunk he passed out on a neighbor's front porch." She felt her throat get tight. "That was why he disappeared. He went to see her. The woman he loved. He offered to give up drinking for her, a woman who didn't want him, but wouldn't consider it for his own wife or daughter, who might have loved him if he'd cared about them like a husband and father should, rather than treating us like burdens he was stuck with."

The brutal knowledge rocked her psyche for a loop.

She looked back to Brian the drinking buddy. The man appeared uneasy at having told her all these things about her father. Too bad. Now that she'd gotten him talking, she needed more information.

"Did he ever talk about my mother? Did he care about her at all, or was she just an obligation because she'd gotten pregnant?"

"He might have cared but it was such a burden. She was always sick and unhappy and he couldn't handle it. I think her unhappiness made him miserable, and being miserable made him drink."

"Of course, who wouldn't be miserable," she said bitterly. "If all you had was a drunk for a husband and a stupid kid you didn't want. I don't remember either one of them ever smiling, not once."

"He said she had CAH," Brian said. "But I don't know what that meant. He wasn't always clear."

"Yeah," Michelle replied bitterly. "People tend to mumble and slur their words when they're drunk. I couldn't understand half of what he said."

Eric perked up at hearing Brian Gallagher's words. Of course. He was interested in the medical aspect.

"CAH?" he asked. "Are you sure that's what he said? Could he have meant CHF?"

Brian Gallagher just shrugged, indicating a lack of comprehension.

"What's CHF?" Michelle asked.

"Congestive heart failure. No wonder she died so easily from pneumonia, if she had congestive heart failure." He looked at Michelle with raised eyebrows.

"She coughed a lot," was all she could add.

"Did she smoke?" Eric asked her. "Was she overweight, have diabetes, or take a lot of medications?"

Michelle had no memories of cigarettes or prescription bottles at their house.

"No, I never saw her smoke. She wasn't overweight, in fact she was very thin. I don't know about the other stuff. I don't know, Eric. I don't know!"

She noticed Mr. Gallagher jump a little at her loudly expressed frustration and tried to tone it down.

"She's dead. You can't diagnose her symptoms now."

"I know," Eric conceded. "But if she did have congestive heart failure, it might explain why she died so easily from pneumonia at such a young age. Plus the strain that giving birth with a condition like that puts on a woman's body..." He trailed off when he noticed the effect his big mouth had on her.

She felt herself go pale and cold. If Eric tried to take her pulse now, he probably wouldn't have been able to find it.

"Are you saying my mother may have died because of me? Because she gave birth to me?" Her already fragile psyche started to crumble like dust.

She'd forgotten she was still holding onto Eric's hand, and he squeezed it now, but she pulled hers away.

"I'm sorry, sweetheart," he said quickly. "I didn't mean it to sound like that. It's just a guess, and like you said, we can't know for sure.

When she'd yanked her hand away from him, he got an expression on his face like a puppy expecting to be punished for peeing on the rug, and she felt bad about that.

Brian was sending furtive glances towards the bar on the other side of the patio from where they sat. The coffee Eric had bought them was obviously not what he really wanted, and his telling Michelle about her dad was apparently a bit more sobriety than he was interested in. It didn't matter that it was noon on a Sunday. Drinkers gotta drink.

She tried to keep the look of disgust off her face, reminding herself, *it's a disease*. One however that this guy was as uninterested in treating as her father had been.

"Do you have children, Mr. Gallagher?" she found herself asking.

"Two," he answered, looking away from her, away from the café. "They live on the mainland now, with their mother. I don't see them much."

"Do you ever wonder why?" she asked harshly. "Do you think maybe it has to do with how much time you spent sitting in a bar with my dad, when you could have been spending time with them?"

Brian Gallagher didn't answer.

It wasn't exactly a panic attack, but she had to get out of here. Maybe it was rude to get up and leave Eric and Brian the Drinking Buddy sitting there, but she wasn't burdened with Eric's good manners. Her red plastic chair tipped over when she stood up. She was tempted to dash out of the place like a coward, like she used to do, but actually surprised herself by first managing to say, "You should get yourself into a program of some kind, Mr. Gallagher, before you fall off a boat and drown too."

It surprised her how calmly she spoke, as if his revelations hadn't just torn a great big rip into her already wobbly persona. It was all like an out-of-body experience, like a bad dream. She felt like she was looking at this scene from a distance, seeing her pale, strained face and miserable eyes, feeling somehow smaller than she really was.

If you wanted to split hairs, she didn't precisely dash out of Pete's Café, but she did a pretty good imitation of it, leaving the red plastic chair laying on its side on the patio, vaguely hearing Eric thanking Brian Gallagher for his time, and stopped outside, standing there with fists and teeth clenched, leaning against a palm tree across the sidewalk.

This was the second time she'd managed to not blunder out into the street in the throes of a panic attack. Eric would be proud of her.

As if conjured up by that thought, her roommate came out, looked at her face and asked, "Do we have any more of that laundry stain remover at home?"

Was he kidding? Her life was falling apart, and he was asking about laundry supplies? What had happened to his famous empathy? But then she saw him tap his shoulder, inviting her to cry on him. She barely had time to gulp before she found herself smearing her mascara on his tee shirt again.

"I've got to quit doing this," she said after a minute, as she grasped the fabric of his shirt in her fingers.

"No, you don't," he replied, patting her back a little in sympathy. "If you need to cry, then go ahead and cry. Sometimes it can actually be helpful, you know, sort of symbolically washing away the things that upset you."

"Easy for you to say," she muttered again his cotton-clad shoulder. "You're not the one humiliating yourself in public."

"Sweetheart, if I had to hear the things you just did, I'd be flooding the place and you'd be the one with a wet shoulder."

As much as he had mentioned himself crying on more than one conversation, she still believed he was just saying that to make her feel better.

"It's not fair of me to use you like this, like my personal sponge."

"I don't mind being your personal sponge. I like it. I've never been someone's personal sponge before."

"What about those shipmates who cried on your shoulder?"

He hesitated. "That was different."

'You know," she said, still with her face against his shirt, because the damn tears were still leaking out, "I never cried so much until I met you."

"So, you're saying I make you cry?"

"No. You let me cry. I've also never laughed so much as I have since I met you. I've never looked forward to each new day so much. I've never lived so much. And I've never been calm so much, as I have since you showed up here."

"It's my privilege to serve, ma'am."

She forced herself to remove her wet face from her roommate's shoulder, and found herself trying to wipe her face with her hands again. Just like last time, she had nothing at hand to clean up with. She saw Eric look-ing at her. One hand started to grasp the bottom hem of his shirt, and she quickly warned him, "Do not take your shirt off!"

As much as she appreciated the use of his clothes to wipe her eyes, they weren't in the kitchen this time. They were on the sidewalk with dozens of customers sitting on the patio of the cafe already staring at her pub-lic display of sniffling idiocy. She was upset enough as it was. It would be even more upsetting to have to start beating women away with a stick at the sight of Eric shirtless in public.

"Wait here a sec." Eric turned and dashed back into the cafe, coming out a moment later offering her a cloth napkin. It wasn't as warm and soft as his shirt, and it didn't have the scent of his skin on it, but it at least let her dry her face. She just hoped she didn't look too blotchy.

"Did you steal this?" she asked.

"No, the hostess gave it to me when I told her it was a medical emer-gency."

"And she believed that?"

"Yes. She knows I'm a paramedic."

"Is she a particular friend of yours?" Yes, jealousy over that possibility crept through her despite her knowing it was unjustified.

"No, I treated her boyfriend when he burned his arm."

Michelle turned away a bit, both to shield Eric from the unpleasant sight of her wiping her nose, and to breathe down the anxiety that Brian Gallagher's revelations had given rise to. It was important to keep breath-ing. Without air, she would just keel over, right in front of him, and wouldn't that be embarrassing. A small headache bloomed and throbbed behind her eyes, threatening to expand.

"He confided all this stuff to some drinking buddy, but not to his own blood. I hate him. If he was alive, I'd tell him to his face."

Eric didn't argue with her this time, didn't try to convince her that she really didn't hate her father, that he was still her father, blah blah blah.

He just stood there, listening to her rant and giving 'mind your own business' glares to the passers-by who stared at her standing there crying and ranting by a palm tree on Sumner Avenue.

She swiped savagely at her cheeks with the napkin that Eric had thoughtfully provided, and her voice caught in her throat.

"God, I am so-"

She couldn't finish her sentence because Eric quite suddenly slapped his hand over her mouth, literally pressed his palm against her lips, shushing her as if her uttering another word would bring the zombie apocalypse down on them.

She stared at him over his hand, torn between the desire to bite his fingers, or to lick the inside of his palm.

"Choose your next words very carefully," he said. "I do not want to hear the word pathetic. I do not want to hear the word loser. I especially do not want to hear bat-shit crazy or any variation thereof. Got it?"

To be perfectly honest, she had actually planned to use a couple of those words he didn't want to hear. But he'd been too nice to her today, and every other day, for her to irritate him. He honestly believed that she was not a pathetic bat-shit crazy loser, and he was a pretty good judge of character.

He removed his hand from her mouth and looked wary.

"Hungry," she said. Relief flooded Eric's face.

"Good. Me too. Let's go get some lunch. Not here." He glanced back at the café they'd just left, where Brian Gallagher was now sitting at the bar. "I'm sure it's a nice place and I'm sure their food is delicious, but I think I'd rather eat someplace else today."

She looked at his shoulder, where she'd cried on him. He was wearing that brown shirt again, the one with Garth Brooks on it. The mascara smears weren't quite as obvious as they'd been previously on his white shirt, but still visible.

"Do you want to go home and change first?" she asked.

Though she wouldn't exactly call him a clean freak, she had come to know that he disliked dirtiness.

"Nah. I'll be fine."

"I'm sorry." She shook her head. "I'm always getting you dirty and creating more laundry for you."

At the look he gave her, she hastened to add, "Yeah, I know. You're machine washable."

She took a final wipe at her face with the purloined napkin from Pete's, then turned to Eric.

"Am I streaky?"

"Just a little. I think most of it is on my shirt." Again, he took the napkin from her hand and wiped away the last of her mascara from under her eyes. She really needed to look for a more tear-resistant brand.

Or maybe not. Somehow she was reluctant to give up having Eric hold her chin in his hand and wipe her face.

They took a shortcut through the tour plaza over to Catalina Avenue and went into Original Jack's Country Kitchen, where Eric told her, "Yes, you may have waffles for lunch. If ever a situation called for comfort food, this is it. We can even have ice cream for dessert."

When she refrained from teasing him about managing to work ice cream into any food-related event, he gave her a stern look.

"Talk to me, sweetheart."

Of course, she obeyed him. She couldn't resist him when he looked at her like that. Just like on the day she'd come home when he'd moved in, he wrapped her in a hug of sympathy, giving her a brief pat on the back and a fraternal kiss on the forehead as he stepped back.

Now she was going to talk to him about things she'd never talked about to anyone else. Again. The man had some kind of emotional psychic force that drew out her innermost demons like a high-powered magnet moving iron filings.

"Tell me about your mom."

"Sometimes I thought she didn't like me. I know my dad didn't."

"You can't possibly be more wrong," Eric said quickly. "I know, I didn't know her or your family, but still, she was your mother; you were her daughter. Children are a gift, a treasure. Anyone lucky enough to be a parent adores their kids. You should hear my friend Gabriel go on about his. You'd think those munchkins were made of solid gold."

He stopped with an apologetic smile. "Sorry. I got a bit carried away there."

She wondered how a man like Eric, who thought children were a gift and a treasure rather than a burdensome obligation, who obviously wanted his own children badly, enough to marry a woman he didn't love, was yet a divorced, childless bachelor.

"Why would my dad tell all this stuff to a casual acquaintance, a drinking buddy, and not to me, his own kid? Isn't this the kind of thing you share with your family before other random barflies?"

A realization hit her suddenly, stinging like a mosquito bite. "Oh my god. Robin. The woman he loved was named Robin. I used to hear him mutter about a robin every so often. I thought he was talking about birds. But he must have meant the name Robin, not the bird. I remember asking him what he was talking about but he would never tell me."

"May I offer a theory?" Eric suggested. "Maybe he couldn't tell you about this other woman or how he was overwhelmed by what he'd lost in his life, because he couldn't face having his child be disappointed in him. Maybe he avoided a normal father-daughter relationship with you, not because there was anything wrong with you, but because he was too psychologically weak to face you. Maybe he cared about your mother, and about you, but was afraid that if he showed it, he'd lose you too."

"Well," Michelle said with bitterness, "he miscalculated that decision by a whole lot, because his child was majorly disappointed in him. I would have had a whole lot more sympathy for my father if I'd known about all the stuff he shared with that other drunk. I might have actually loved him, despite his drinking, if I'd believed it was his problems that made him the way he was, rather than having me feel like his ignoring me was a failure on my part. I kept thinking if I tried harder, talked to him more, that we might have come closer to a real relationship. But the way he was always made me so mad, because he made no effort at all."

She shoved her hair back away from her face with a hand that shook just a little, and when it disobediently fell right back, dug in her pocket for an elastic band to secure it behind her neck. But her crumbling emotions translated into uncoordinated fingers and she somehow couldn't get her stubborn mane contained.

Eric looked at her struggle and asked, "Do you need help with that?"

He actually started to get up from his chair as if to step over to her side of the table and do the job for her.

"No, I've got it." She could tell the words came out a bit petulant and ungracious, but she really needed to avoid having him get his hands in her hair again. It had been just too exquisitely dangerous the last time, the day he'd washed it for her after bandaging her finger. With some twisting, she managed to get most of it looped inside the hair band, so she could at least eat her lunch without getting her hair in it.

Fortunately for her willpower, Eric accepted her refusal of his help with his usual calm aplomb, and simply said, "I know it's upsetting, sweetheart, and it's heartbreaking that it worked out like that. It's just a theory of course. But one thing I do know is that you have nothing to be ashamed of, and everything to be proud of, in how you survived the whole dysfunctional situation."

If only she could believe that. She wanted to not care, to compartmentalize the sad, dysfunctional relationship with her father into the ancient history, doesn't matter anymore box.

She'd always thought she could take care of herself, handle any situation in her life without needing support from anyone, doing her crying in private. It had been an attitude born of necessity, because she had always been literally forced to face it all on her own. Until now. Eric, her friend and roommate, was totally willing to help her handle this potentially emotionally terrifying situation. What she had done to deserve a friend like that, she had no idea.

But she was not stupid. She was not going to throw away the opportunity of his support.

"You don't have to be brave all by yourself," he told her. "It's OK to fall apart once in a while."

"Brave?" she replied incredulously. "I'm not brave. I'm a sniveling coward who falls apart all the time. The evidence is right there on your shoulder." She gestured at the mascara streaks on his shirt.

"No, a coward wouldn't have even talked to that guy."

"I should be able to compartmentalize it by now," she muttered, stabbing a fork into her lunch in frustration. "Like you said, he's gone now and I should be able to let it go. I thought I was finished being hurt by him. But somehow he's reaching out from beyond the grave to unravel my heart like a fucking ball of yarn."

At Eric's look, she quickly added, "Pardon my language. Somehow I just can't wrap my head around him being passionate about anything or anyone."

"You've got to admit," Eric said, "It's kind of romantic, to pine for someone like that all your life."

"Romantic except for the part where he marries a woman he didn't love and virtually ignores their child."

"Yeah, there is that," he conceded.

"Why do I still let still bother me?"

"Because you're a human being, with feelings."

"Like you?"

He grinned. "Yeah. We're twins separated at birth." He gestured towards her plate, still under attack. "I think you've killed it. It should be safe to eat by now."

She stopped stabbing at her plate of waffles, swimming with syrup. The moment Eric had mentioned comfort food, she'd started craving it.

She looked up at Eric's smile. Of course, his plate contained an all about the healthy tuna salad sandwich, and hers was filled with a Belgian waffle covered with liquid sugar known as syrup.

"You are a bad influence on me, Eric Hanson," she said with a sigh.

"That's what all the girls say," he replied with a grin.

"I meant, by talking me into this huge plate of sugar. I'm going to have to starve for a week to make up for it."

However even that prospect didn't stop her from eating them.

"God, what an idiot," she said, after she swallowed.

"You're not an idiot," he insisted. Somehow she knew he'd say that.

"I was referring to my dad."

"It's OK to be angry with him," he said. "But don't hate him."

"I don't. I realize that now."

"I remember you saying that once."

She sighed and looked away for a moment, then back at Eric.

"I pity him."

"Him who?" Eric asked. "Your dad? Or Mr. Gallagher?"

"Both of them. I used to think I hated my father, but you were right. I don't hate him. I pity him for being weak and incapable. It must have been horrible to live your life wanting someone you could never have. But that still doesn't excuse how he treated me. I pity his drinking buddy too."

"Whereas you are just the opposite," he told her. "You may resemble your dad physically, but emotionally and psychologically you are the opposite of weak and incapable. And you're right about the way he treated you. That was inexcusable. None of his issues were your fault. It makes you the bigger person to be able to look past that."

Despite the horrid revelations of today and her emotional reaction, she was able to smile at him.

Gregory Diaz hadn't been a good dad. He hadn't even qualified as a bad dad. As a parent, he'd been positively crappy. But he'd still been her dad. Eric was right about that. And he had stayed. He could have run off after her mother's death, continued to pursue his Robin. But he'd stayed with her on the island, at least until she was an adult and he made his failed attempt to reconnect with his former lover. She couldn't bear to think what would have happened if the mysterious Robin Osorio had taken him back.

"I wonder if my mother knew that my father was in love with someone else," she said as a sudden realization hit home. Maybe that's why ..." she trailed off as Eric looked at her quizzically.

"Was there something about your mom that made you think she might be aware of your dad's feelings?"

Michelle shrugged, uncertain. "All I remember about my mother is that she was always sad. I never saw her smile, not once. She didn't care about my dad or me or anything. Here she lived on a beautiful tropical island with perfect weather and gorgeous scenery, but she never did anything but sit around looking unhappy."

"Maybe she was pining for a lost love too." Eric sighed romantically.

"Please don't suggest I try to find out," she said quickly. "I really couldn't handle hearing more of that kind of thing."

"But don't you have cousins on the mainland?" He nodded in that direction. "They'd probably know about your mom's life before she and your dad were married."

"Probably. And I know I should ask. But I can't. I just can't. I'm not brave enough for that, no matter what you think."

"Well I still think you're brave, but I won't try to push more family revelations on you if you're not ready for them yet."

"You know, that's what I love about you, Eric," she said. "You always know what to say to make me feel normal. You see past the crap and bring out the best in me."

He inhaled a bit as if she'd startled him, but quickly smiled back. "Well, that's what friends are for, right? Besides, you're not normal. You're amazing."

When they walked back to the house after lunch – and Michelle had indeed indulged in a bit too much of the comfort foods of waffles and ice cream – she found herself dragging in exhaustion, and not just physically. Her emotions were exhausted beyond belief.

"Why am I so tired? It's not like I've been doing anything strenuous today." She yawned, sat on the couch and kicked off her flip-flops.

"You don't have to run a marathon to be tired," Eric said. "Emotional exertion can tire a person out even more than physical exercise." He looked at her face. "You do look tired. Why don't you lay down and take a nap?"

"That would be so lazy," she replied sleepily. "I have stuff to do." But her stomach was full and her emotions were shredded and she just wanted to close her eyes for a minute before she tackled the stuff she was supposed to do.

The next thing she knew, her feet had been picked up and set on the couch, and Eric was actually covering her up with the couch blanket, just as he had done the night of the alleged earthquake when they'd slept here on the couch together.

On one level, she hated the way she somehow morphed into an old-fashioned dependent female under Eric's comfort and sympathy, and yet on another level, the safe feeling of protection he provided with his empathy liberated her from her anxiety and anger.

"It seems so decadent," she said, though that didn't stop her from laying down.

"Sweetheart, if you think that taking a nap on a Sunday afternoon is decadent, you really need to get out more."

Exhaustion was consuming her, covering her with its weight just as much as the blanket that her roommate was now pulling up over her. He leaned down and gave her a fraternal kiss on the forehead.

"Have a nice nap." He stood up and made a sound that seemed like a sigh, but she wasn't sure.

For one brief, insane moment, she was tempted to invite him to squeeze onto the couch and take a nap with her, because he was, as they both knew, cuddly. But that would be extremely inappropriate to suggest to one's roommate, even if he had been a huge emotional support for her today. She just managed to mutter, "Thanks, Eric."

She should have qualified, specified what she was thanking him for – gratitude at his putting her in touch with her dad's drinking buddy, because it was, as he claimed, better to know the truth even if it did hurt, appreciation for the physical and emotional support he'd provided that made it possible for her to get past the hurt and devastation of her new-found knowledge of her father's circumstances, and even thanks for the simple, friendly gesture of pulling a blanket over her as the physical and emotional fatigue of the day overlook her and she closed her eyes. It was really no different than the day she'd covered him up when he'd fallen asleep on the couch, right?

Just before Eric stood up and stepped away, he replied, "Anything for you, sweetheart."

As she slid into blissful, healing sleep, she heard a small sound from the direction of the hallway. Maybe Eric had bumped into the wall.

What she didn't know was that the small bump was the sound of him kicking himself.

<h1 style="text-align:center">29</h1>

"Are you doing anything this weekend?" Eric asked over coffee on Tuesday morning.

Was he asking her out on a date? No, he just wanted to hang out, like they frequently did.

"I don't have any plans," she said.

"I have the whole weekend off, barring an emergency." Eric was sparkling with anticipation. "The whole entire weekend, just like a regular person. There's an air show in San Diego. I thought maybe you'd like to go see it. Lots of jets, helicopters, tanks, even the Stealth Bomber is going to be on display. And the Blue Angels are performing!" He looked positively ecstatic. "I love the smell of jet fuel in the morning!"

She wrinkled her nose. "The smell of jet fuel? Now that's weird."

He rolled his eyes at her. "That's a paraphrase of a line from a movie. Apocalypse Now. Don't tell me you've never heard of it."

She shook her head.

"Your education is sadly lacking, padawan," he said with a disbelieving head shake of his own.

"What did you call me?"

"Girl, you really need to see Star Wars."

"Maybe we can watch it on Netflix," she suggested. Eric had signed up for a subscription, at his expense, shortly after moving in, and had breezily given her the login and password information, so that she could access it on her laptop if she chose.

But Eric shook his head at that suggestion. "Oh, no way. Not Star Wars. For that, we'll wait until you can see it in a theatre. Star Wars should be experienced for the first time on the big screen."

He winked at her. "First times should be special, don't you think?"

"Special? If you say so."

She was very aware that by now they were most likely no longer discussing one's first viewing of a popular science fiction film.

Without quite looking at him, she said, "Some first times can be awkward, embarrassing and – unfulfilling."

Eric chuckled. "Well, should the opportunity arise, I will make certain that this first time is wonderful and exhilarating."

And just like that, they were back to talking about Star Wars.

"Is that Apocalypse Now one of your Star Wars movies?"

"No, it's not. It's, well never mind. We can stay at my buddy's house, if you don't mind sharing a room."

Her heart raced. Was he actually suggesting that they sleep in the same room? And at someone else's house, the home of his friend?

"With his daughter. I have dibs on the living room couch. It's practically my second home. We can go over on Friday afternoon, go to the airshow on Saturday, and come home on Sunday. My buddy will even come to pick us up here."

"Your friend has a boat?"

Eric's eyes gleamed. "Even better. He has a bird."

*****

The Catalina Island heliport was just down the street from the office of Michelle's employer on Pebbly Beach Road, south of town. When they pulled in and parked the golf cart, Eric's friend, and his bird, were already there waiting for them.

Eric may have called it a bird, but to Michelle, the helicopter looked more like a huge metallic dragonfly. The pilot leaned against it and as they approached, Eric dropped their weekend bags and the two men grabbed each other with bro-hugs, fist bumps and back-slapping. Except for the fact that Eric's friend was black, she would have thought them to have been long-lost brothers.

When they were done trying to bruise each other, Eric introduced Michelle to Gabriel Jones.

Gabriel didn't so much shake her hand, as he enveloped it, as he intoned, "Well, well, what have we here?"

Eric made a slight snort, reached out and plucked Michelle's wrist out of his friend's grasp, saying, "All right, all right, you old smoothie," in a voice just a shade deeper than his natural speech.

Their words sounded so rehearsed that Michelle looked at Eric questioningly. "He thinks he's Lando Calrissian," Eric explained.

"And welcome to my Millennium Falcon," Gabriel invited, indicating the bird, which actually had the words "Jones Helicopter Charters" printed on the door. As Eric retrieved their bags, Gabriel opened the door and invited her in.

There were four seats, two in front, two in back. To Michelle's eyes, the panel of gauges, controls and buttons seemed like enough to pilot the space shuttle. Not that she'd actually ever seen a space shuttle, but she could imagine.

Gabriel walked around to the other side of the helicopter, opened the other door, and got in. Sitting in the pilot's seat, he held out one hand, smiling and inviting.

"Would you like to sit in front with me? You can help me fly."

She looked at all those space shuttle-like gauges. Help him fly it? The guy had to be crazy. She stood there, paralyzed, unable to even answer him.

Eric had brought over both their weekend bags and come up beside her. Looking at her face, he said, "I think we'll sit in the back, if it's OK with you, Jonesie."

He set their bags on the front seat that Michelle had refused to occupy, then edged around her to climb into the back seat, and held out his hand, also inviting her in.

"I tried that already, dude," Gabriel said.

"Come on Michelle," Eric entreated. "We can't take off until you get in."

She hated to be an annoyance to Eric and his friend, but her feet were molded to the ground. She saw the two men exchange glances, and Eric slid across the seat towards her with both hands outstretched.

The day she'd received Eric's email after her father's death, she had warned herself not to let herself think of him as her anchor to sanity. However, her psyche had ignored that warning since he'd moved into her house. Those warm hands held out to her confirmed it.

He leaned out towards her, grasped both her hands, gave a tug, and before she knew what she was doing, he had her sitting in the seat next to him.

"See, that wasn't so hard." His voice was teasing but she didn't look at him. She was too busy looking at the ground and wondering if she wasn't making a really big mistake.

Eric had to reach across her to pull the door shut. The click it made as it latched was ominous.

The helicopter's engine hummed to life, then roared, and she quickly shifted her gaze from the ground to the front seat. Gabriel was flipping switches and looking at gauges in a manner that appeared to be completely random. The engine noise roared in her ears, and the blades above them started to whirr around, slowly at first, but soon faster, with a loud swishing sound. She felt Eric nudge her arm. He and Gabriel had both put bulky-looking headsets over their ears.

He probably expected her to follow his glance over her shoulder, but she was too paralyzed to do it. He sighed, reached across her and pulled her headset off its hook and placed it over her ears with a smile that looked a bit puzzled.

The engine roar was decreased to a hum with the headset on, and Gabriel's voice spoke in her ear.

"Everyone buckled up back there?"

Eric was buckling a seatbelt across his hips and she hastily grabbed for hers, but one end slipped down next to her seat and she couldn't retrieve it with her suddenly sweaty hands. He saw her struggling and reached across her again with an annoyed grunt to retrieve the buckle and fasten the belt for her.

"Do I have to do everything for you?" he asked in his teasing voice.

"Yes," she whispered, but her voice was so impaired that the sound didn't actually make it out of her mouth, as she stared at terra firma out the window.

"We're go for launch," Eric's voice came through the headset.

Gabriel nodded and flipped a few more random switches, seemingly just for show. Michelle looked down at the ground beneath them. Was this assemblage of vibrating parts actually supposed to take off and fly? Apparently so.

Come on, Michelle, you work with engines every day. You know how they function. This is just another engine.

But the engines in the boats she worked with every day didn't rise up from the ground, leaving nothing but nothingness between their passengers and a violent, bone-fracturing death.

With just a little jerk they started to ascend and the ground moved away. However, her stomach hadn't quite gotten the message about their ascension and lagged behind the rest of her. She gulped and involuntarily let out a deep, "Oh, shit!"

Really, she shouldn't be terrified. People flew in helicopters, airplanes, even hot-air balloons every day, and lived to tell about it. She had no qualms about Gabriel's piloting skills. Eric wouldn't trust their lives with an amateur. But still – there was maybe six inches of metal between her feet and air. The bird's doors were mostly window, and every time they turned or dipped, she found herself looking through a mere inch of plexiglass and the nothingness between her and her death.

Eric reached into the pocket next to his seat and she felt something paper flip into her lap. "Look at the horizon!" he advised sharply. "Barf bag if you need it."

She followed his instruction and moved her gaze from the ground beneath her to the horizon, staring at Mount Orizaba at the top of the island. Her stomach was still lagging quite a bit behind the rest of her, and she couldn't help repeating *shitshitshit* until Eric grabbed her hand and squeezed.

"It's OK," he said in his soothing voice that made people believe they were going to live. "You're going to be fine, I'm not going to let anything happen to you." She nodded, still staring at the horizon but not letting him have his hand back. It was warm and reassuring. In fact, she meshed her fingers between his and held on so that he couldn't take it back.

Admit it, Michelle. That notion she had tried to convince herself of, not to depend on Eric as her anchor, had just flown out the window of Gabriel's helicopter and splashed into the cool blue waters of the Pacific Ocean below them. Without intending it to be so, Eric had most definitely become her anchor to safety.

As the helicopter started to turn towards the mainland, it tilted a little bit, but neither Gabriel nor Eric gave any indication of distress. As the bird straightened, for a moment she lost her view of the horizon. "Shit!" she said again, until she found the horizon of the mainland in her point of reference.

"OK, maybe we can find a new swear word now, just for variety," Eric suggested.

She laughed a bit but that distracted her from the horizon. "Fuck?"

He nodded approvingly. "That's my girl."

Despite his approving nod, she was dismayed that she was once again proving Eric wrong when he said she was brave and strong. At this moment she was the exact opposite of brave and strong. The only thing that kept her from shaking, kept her lunch stationary in her stomach, was the fact that he had a grip on her hand.

She squeezed onto that warm strong hand for the remainder of the flight so he wouldn't forget to remind her that it was going to be OK. The water was below them now. The sea was her friend, her calm, her strength. The sea, and Eric. She squeezed his hand tighter and took the risk of looking down at the ocean beneath them. Nothing bad was going to happen to her, because she was with Eric, and she was looking at the ocean.

It was her ocean. Eric's ocean. The same calm, ever-present waves she usually craved. It was her link to sanity, that and the presence of the man sitting next to her.

"I won't let anything happen to you." Eric had said that a few minutes ago, and she believed him. The ocean beneath them said it too, communicated it to her with blue calmness and soothing, swishing presence, and she believed that as well.

The flight took about forty-five minutes and she spent the entire time looking straight ahead at the horizon, and squeezing Eric's hand. When they landed with just a little bump, she finally released his hand and he flexed it a bit. "Wow," he said. "I didn't realize you were so strong. Have you been using my weight bench without me there to spot you?"

Gabriel turned around to look at them, as his random switch flipping powered down the helicopter and the blades above them slowed their rotation. "Your girl looks a little shaky, dude," he said.

"Are you OK now?" Eric asked. She made no effort to get up. "Deep breaths," he advised. "In through the nose, out through the mouth. Do you need this?" He was opening the barf bag he'd put in her lap and handed it to her. She felt warm fingers touching the back of her neck. Eric had actually reached behind her neck, gathered her hair up and held it behind her head, just in case she decided to barf.

"No, just give me a sec. I'm OK now." She breathed as he had instructed until she felt her heart rate return to something close to normalcy.

"You're sure?" Eric looked like he didn't quite believe her.

"Yeah I think my stomach has caught up."

"I'm so proud of you. You swear just like a sailor." That made her giggle a little hysterically.

"You've never flown in a helicopter before?" he asked.

"I've never flown in anything before." Like most Avalonians, she carried insurance to cover the cost of a medical transport to the mainland via helicopter if needed, but fortunately, she had never had to use it.

"You're kidding! You live on an island, and you've never flown?"

She felt a little defensive, like a country bumpkin, so her reply held just a hint of bitchiness. "I take the boat. I can't afford to fly."

He grinned. "Well, now that I've taken your aviation virginity, how did you like it?"

Gabriel grunted, the sound coming through their headsets. "Dude, you know I can hear everything you say." He tapped his headset and Michelle blushed.

"At least this bird has doors, and nobody on the floor bleeding," he said.

Wrong thing to say, bigmouth! Michelle went pale, and even Gabriel gave him a quick glance of disapproval.

"Can I take this off now?" she asked, her voice shaking as she reached for the headset.

"Yes, but you'd better let me help you." Eric took off his own headset and hung it on a hook next to his seat, then took off Michelle's and reached to hang it up as well. As he leaned across her towards the hook next to her seat, she found their faces very close together, found herself staring into his eyes. Embarrassed, she averted her gaze, and found herself looking at his mouth instead. He smiled. He had the sexiest smile she'd ever seen. She'd always thought that, from the moment she'd met him, but it was getting harder and harder to resist. Instinctively, she licked her lips.

I wonder if he's a good kisser. She'd asked herself that the day he'd moved into her house, and she wondered it again now.

Maybe she should kiss him and find out. Just so she wouldn't have to wonder anymore. Yeah, just for the sake of knowledge.

The charged moment was broken when Gabriel opened the door. Apparently, while she'd been staring at Eric's mouth, his friend had gotten out, and walked around to their side of the bird to wait for them.

"Oh," Gabriel said guiltily as he observed them. "Do you two need a private moment?"

Eric twitched away from her and Michelle felt her face flame with embarrassment. She said, "Um, no, we're good," and looked away from Eric's too-kissable mouth to turn to Gabriel, who was looking past her at Eric with a huge grin on his face.

"Is it going to be as difficult getting her out as it was to get her in?"

Gabriel asked teasingly. He offered his hand again, and this time she accepted his assistance in disembarking. Eric quickly hung up the headset he'd been holding and hopped out behind her, closing the door. Obviously, he thought she was an incapable dunce. For a little while, that was exactly what she had been.

Gabriel pulled a set of car keys out of his pocket and flipped them at Eric, who caught them overhanded. "I'll meet you at the car, gotta call my better half." He pulled out his phone, and as Eric led her towards the parking lot, Michelle heard Gabriel saying, "Hi honey, we just landed. Eric's great. Yeah, he brought her."

In the parking lot, Eric clicked the remote in his hand and a trunk popped open.

"This is your car?" she asked, glancing over the modest white Honda sedan. "Or is it Gabriel's?"

"It's mine," he replied. "What did you expect? A beat-up old pickup truck with a gun rack mounted on the back?"

Given his love for country music, that was exactly what she had expected.

The Honda was kept in storage at Gabriel's house while Eric, as Gabriel put it, lazed around on a tropical island. Eric just tossed a friendly, "Kiss my ass" over his shoulder at his friend as they pulled out of the heliport parking lot.

Both men had insisted that Michelle sit in front with Eric as they drove, and frankly, she was jealous as he merged smoothly onto the freeway and maneuvered into the carpool lane.

She did have a driver's license, and she'd been lucky to get it. The DMV only came to Avalon twice a year, and appointments booked up months in advance. If you missed it, you had to go the mainland and wait at the DMV office there for who knew how long to take the test. Michelle was happy she'd been able to secure one of the precious semi-annual appointments. After all, if she was studying how to repair engines, she really should be authorized to drive them. But she had never owned a car, just her golf cart.

To be honest, the prospect of driving on the southern California freeways intimidated her. When she'd been going to technical school in Los Angeles, she'd relied on rides from classmates, what passed for public transportation, and Uber. But Eric was smoothly confident on the drive to Gabriel's house in the suburbs, and if there were any crazy girls in hoodies lurking in the area, they stayed out of his way,

They pulled up to a small, cute bungalow. Eric parked his car in the driveway next to Gabriel's vehicle, which actually was a pickup truck, but a late model, in nice condition, black in color, without so much as a hint of a gun rack. As soon as the three of them walked in the door, they were greeted by a pretty, fair-skinned blonde lady with a noticeable baby bump who hugged both men quickly as Gabriel introduced Michelle to his wife Susan.

As soon as introductions, hugs and handshakes were concluded, Eric leaned down and put his ear against Susan's six-month bump.

"Hey, little dude!" he said to the occupant. "How's it going in there? Talk to Uncle Eric!" A moment later, he twitched away and said, "Hey, he kicked me!"

Smiling affectionately, Susan pushed Eric away. "You put your head on a kid's foot, he's going to kick you. I keep telling you that, but do you listen?" She shook a finger in front of Eric's nose. "Why is it that you men seem to think a pregnant belly is public property? You try pushing something the size of a cantaloupe out of an opening the size of an egg, and then we'll talk."

Despite the chastening, Eric was grinning. "Have you decided on a name for the little dude?" he asked.

"David," Gabriel said quickly.

"No," Susan said immediately. It was apparent that this conversation had happened before.

"But I like the name David," Gabriel declared, almost whining.

"Yeah, it's a great name," Eric added.

Susan looked back between the two men, putting her hands on her hips. "And when he gets to middle school, where will he put his books?"

Michelle was a bit confused by the question and what it might have to do with Gabriel's choice of a name for his new child, and Susan's objection to it.

Eric and Gabriel looked at each other, grinned like little boys, and announced in unison, "Davy Jones's locker!"

Susan and Michelle both rolled their eyes as the two men laughed. "Cameron," Susan announced. "We're going to name him Cameron." She patted her bump as her husband shrugged.

"Well, we tried," Eric said. "Where are the other two?"

Susan glanced behind her. "Call them," she offered.

Eric grinned, sucked in his cheeks, put two fingers in his mouth and emitted a whistle guaranteed to have every dog in the neighborhood howling in pain.

There was an almost immediate loud door slam and a moment later two brown, curly-haired children pounded into the living room, shrieking, "Uncle Eric! Uncle Eric!" as they launched themselves at Eric's midsection with a force that nearly knocked him over. There was much hugging, high fiving and exclamations of, "what is your mother feeding you, you've grown a foot," until Gabriel cleared his throat loudly.

"Ahem! Dad here! What am I, chopped liver?" The two transferred their affection to their father and he introduced them to Michelle. "This is Natalie, she's eleven, and Tyler, he's nine." He ruffled their hair affectionately.

Tyler looked at Michelle with great curiosity. "Are you Uncle Eric's girlfriend?" he asked.

Michelle just said, "Um," not daring to look at Eric, even though he sounded like he was choking.

Goodness, Tyler was a cute little guy, with skin a smooth brown color halfway in between Gabriel's rich coffee-colored complexion and Susan's milky fairness. Curly dark hair bounced in all directions and he had the most adorable gap-toothed, all I want for Christmas is my two front teeth smile. On Natalie the same coloring and features, softened into pre-adolescent femininity, and minus the missing baby teeth, hinted at a stunning beauty when she grew up. That girl was going to break hearts.

Tyler continued, "Natalie wants to be Uncle Eric's girlfriend, and the last time he came here, she put ketchup on her arm to make it look like bleeding, so he would fix it."

Natalie's face flushed angrily and she punched her brother sharply in the arm. "Shut up, nitwit!" she yelled.

"Stop it, both of you!" Susan ordered, and both children subsided immediately, saying, "Yes, ma'am" in unison.

Michelle glanced briefly at Eric, who had his mouth pressed into a tight, straight line. "Did Uncle Eric teach them that?"

"No, I did," Susan said. "Go outside and blow the stink off you, while I show our guest where she'll be sleeping."

Eric, who was not a guest, but who was family in every way but blood, and who already knew where he was sleeping, dropped his bag on the couch and gave Michelle a brief wink, saying, "Mine," as he and Gabriel followed the kids through the kitchen towards the back door.

Just before they left the room, Tyler tugged on Eric's arm. "Uncle Eric, can I pull your finger again?" he begged.

Eric glanced at Susan. "No, dude, not this time. Your mom will put me in a time out again."

As soon as they got into the kitchen, Gabriel punched Eric's arm.

"You dog! Why didn't you tell me you had a girlfriend?"

"Ouch," Eric replied. "We're not dating. We're just roommates."

"Of course you are. And I'm Denzel Washington," Gabriel replied sardonically.

"I thought you were Lando Calrissian."

"Him too. Are you seriously telling me you live with that pretty lady, and you're just?"

"Roommates. Yes."

"And you're not, you know?" Two black eyebrows rose in disbelief.

"Nope. We're just friends."

"I have one question. Why?"

"Because I was looking for a place to live in Avalon, and she was looking for a roommate. She's a really nice girl, and I like her a lot, but we're not sleeping together."

"OK, I have another question," Gabriel said. "Why not? That pretty lady is into you, dude. I saw you two holding hands back there."

Eric shrugged. "She was scared. I didn't know she'd never flown before."

"Since when did Eric The Hound Hanson become such a saint?"

"Believe me, I have not become a saint." Not with the thoughts he'd been having.

"I saw how you two were looking at each other there, dude. It's more than just hormones with her, I think."

"Hormones? Seriously, dude, we're not sixteen anymore."

Gabriel chuckled. "You're right about that. You'll never guess where I found a gray hair the other day."

Eric put his hands over his ears in a dramatic gesture and yelled, "Lalalalala! I do not want to hear about that, please!" Then he took his hands away and asked, "What do you mean, how we look at each other?" though he had a feeling he already knew.

"Like you hadn't eaten in about a year, and she was a steak. So, you like her a lot. Does that mean you like her, or you *like her* like her?"

Eric rolled his eyes. "Man, that is way too deep for me. Yes, I like her. Yes, I acknowledge that she is a smart, special, beautiful person. And she's my roommate and my friend, and that's as far as it goes." Actually, Eric was glad to be able to tell someone about his feelings for Michelle. He'd made a lot of friends in Avalon since moving to the island, but none that he could talk about this to. Gabriel was different though. They had been best buddies since the eighth grade, and with him, Eric could give free rein to his big mouth.

"Look, yes, Jonesie, I like her in all the ways you can like a person. I like her as a friend. She's a lot of fun to spend time with. I like her as a roommate. We're very compatible roommates, believe it or not, except that she doesn't appreciate the designated hitter concept. But we're working on that, and nobody's perfect. And yes, I'm attracted to her as a woman. I mean, how could any guy not be? Lord, she is gorgeous. And I don't just mean on the outside. She is so strong, as a person, it just blows me away. She had a pretty unpleasant childhood and it amazes me every day how strong and self-sufficient she is in spite of it. I'll admit it, a part of me wants to protect her, even though I know she's perfectly capable of taking care of herself. You should have heard her tear me a new one this one time when I tried to fight her battles for her, as she put it. It was so sexy I just about died. But we're not dating, and at night we each sleep in our own separate rooms. With the doors shut. Like roommates do."

"And you wish it was more than that." Gabriel's words were not a question, and Eric's lack of immediate answer, actually was an answer. Gabriel put a hand on the kitchen door to prevent Eric from opening it to follow the kids into the back yard just yet. He looked at his friend's face and chuckled again.

"Are you trying to tell me that you're suddenly ... shy?"

"Of course not!"

Eric had listened to Gabriel go on and on the day after his first date with Susan, and had later stood up as best man at their wedding. He had, however, declined to ask out the maid of honor, who was Susan's sister. Somehow the concept of dating one's best friend's sister-in-law seemed a little incestuous. Eric was the only person that Gabriel allowed to call him "Jonesie" and he used the nickname now.

"Yeah, Jonesie, I *like her*, like her, in all the ways a guy can like a woman."

"Then why aren't you two dating?"

"She's my roommate. I should respect that, don't you think? She's trusting me in her home, and I can't break that trust by hitting on her."

"Well, I think you should tell her how you feel and let her decide how to take it. How do you know she doesn't *like you*, like you the same way?"

"I doubt it. I know she likes me and trusts me as a friend, but not as anything more."

Gabriel stopped chuckling, and got serious. "So, have you dated anyone else since you moved out there?"

"No."

"Is she dating anyone?"

"I don't think so."

"Then what is stopping you?"

"Like I said, she's my friend and roommate. I respect that."

Gabriel gave him a look of sympathy. "Dude, I saw how you were when you got back from Afghanistan. You were totally burned out. Susan saw it too. That tour was brutal for you, and that's saying a lot considering you went to Iraq twice."

Afghanistan had not been in his original orders. He'd been happily busy in the Nimitz's sickbay, on the deployment that had departed the day after he'd met Michelle on the sidewalk, when Master Chief poked his head in the door and told him to report to the captain's office.

Eric had been both nervous and intensely curious as he washed up, checked his uniform to make sure he was squared away, and made his way to the captain's office. It was unheard of for an enlisted sailor, even a Chief, to be summoned there on his own. Even if he'd committed a serious disciplinary infraction – which he hadn't – it would have been handled by the Master Chief. If the captain needed medical attention, there were six physicians on board to tend to his needs. Even a death in his family would have been relayed to him by Master Chief.

When the captain told him to stand at ease, Eric glanced at the papers on the desk and was able to read upside down enough to see that it was his service record. He quickly moved his gaze to straight ahead when the captain looked up at him. "I see you've been on the green side in Iraq twice."

"Yes, Sir."

"How was it?"

Eric hesitated but Captain said, "Permission to speak freely, Doc."

"Dusty, Sir. With a complete and utter lack of Super Hornets."

Captain chuckled. "That bad, huh? You still have your Marine uniform?" When Navy corpsmen were assigned to Marine units, they wore the same uniform as the jarheads.

"Yes, Sir."

"Good. You'll need to get it pressed. We have to send you TAD to A-stan. Commander Lindstrom recommended you."

"I thought Commander Lindstrom liked me," Eric retorted, before he could rein in his big mouth.

"He does. He says a lot of good things about you, Hanson. Says you're top-notch. In fact, and I quote," the captain glanced down at the file on his desk, "Hanson is the best IDC we've got. That's why he had to choose you for this. We've lost three corpsmen in Helmand Province this week. One killed, one sent to Landstuhl with a burst appendix, one whose wife in the States just died. They need someone to fill in until more permanent transfers can be put in place. Someone who can train one person to do the work of three. Are you up for that, Chief Hanson?"

"Yes, Sir." What else could he say? *Home is where the Navy sends me.*

"You'll be leaving with the COD. You'll probably have to be there a couple of months while it gets sorted out. But, don't forget, Doc, you're a Nimitz man. We'll get you back here if we can."

"Thank you, Sir."

Captain actually stood up and shook Eric's hand. "I owe you one, Hanson. Good luck. When we get home, I'll buy you a beer."

"I'd be honored, Sir, but I'm afraid I'll have to decline the beer. I can't drink. Makes me sick." He started to put his hand on his stomach to make a retching gesture, as he usually did when telling people about his allergy, but stopped himself in time.

Jeez, Hanson, you idiot, you don't make puking motions in front of the Captain!

"Is that so?" Captain looked vastly amused. "I know a couple of guys who could benefit from a condition like that. I don't suppose it's contagious?"

"No, Sir. It's an allergy."

"Well if you ever need some non-alcoholic assistance in the future, let me know. In fact," the captain opened his desk drawer, pulled out a card, and wrote on the back of it before handing it to Eric. "That's my personal email address. I mean it, Hanson, I owe you one. I'm sure you'll do the Nimitz proud out there. Let me know if I can return the favor."

Six hours later, he was a passenger on a Grumman C2 Greyhound that had delivered cargo to the ship, and kitted out in a uniform that almost, but not quite, made him appear to be a Marine. Though he wore a Marine Corps combat utility uniform, the patch above his left breast pocket read U.S. Navy. The caduceus badge on his shoulder and his Fleet Marine Force pin identified him as a combat corpsman.

As he watched the flight deck receding below him, he thought, *this would be a whole lot more fun in a Super Hornet.*

"I never did get back to the Nimitz," he said to Gabriel. "By the time I got things straightened out in A-Stan, she was already back to port so they just flew me straight back to the base here."

"Yeah, I know," Gabriel said. "Must have sucked to be in a place like that for Christmas."

"It did. But there were a lot of other guys there spending Christmas away from their families, and a lot of families who were always going to be having an empty chair at Christmas dinner, so, you just embrace the suck."

He'd spent that Christmas day, what little time he'd had to himself, rereading his email printouts from Michelle and wondering what she was doing. The tactile sensation of reading those printed emails somehow insinuated a more real connection to the sender than just reading them on a screen. The only email she'd sent him that he hadn't been able to print was the very short one she'd sent when her father died. Eric was still in Afghanistan when he received it. He had tried to contact her via Skype but couldn't get a connection from there. He'd been lucky to finally get an email through days later.

At least he'd done the Nimitz, and his Captain, proud. The Captain had said that he owed Eric a favor in return, and had given Eric his personal email address with which to claim it.

Eric had called in that favor when he'd separated from the Navy and accepted the job in Avalon, by asking Captain for a letter of recommendation to be given to Michelle Diaz so that she would accept his rental application.

"I know it was a big part of why you decided to retire from the Navy," Gabriel was saying. "And when you were here with us, before you moved over to the island? You never called any of the girls that Susan tried to set you up with. Don't think we didn't notice. The only female you'd even talk to was your shrink, and that does not count as a date. But for a while there, I thought you were dating your shrink, because you seemed to spend so much time with her. You weren't dating her, were you?"

As his best and oldest friend, Gabriel felt he had the right to push Eric's buttons.

Eric looked at his best and oldest friend with shock.

"You have got to be kidding." He lifted his hand to start counting off reasons.

"One, she's married. Two, she's an officer. Three, she's my physician. All of which combine to equate to a huge lack of chemistry. I may be a hound, but I am still a firm believer in things like morals, ethics and the UCMJ, which before you ask, is what brings a shit-storm of hurt down on the heads of enlisted people and officers who are stupid enough to fraternize."

"Unlike the ginormous amount of chemistry I see between you and that pretty lady," Gabriel said. "No, it's more than just chemistry. It's pyrotechnics. You two could start a forest fire just looking at each other."

"Was I that obvious?"

"To me you were." Then, surprisingly, Gabriel changed the subject for a moment.

"Are you still having those dreams?" he asked.

"Once in a while. Say, you didn't tell the kids about that, when I stayed here last time, did you?"

"No, I just told them that Uncle Eric needed a hug. That's about the only thing I never have to tell them twice."

Eric looked in the direction that Gabriel's kids had gone. "Yeah, Uncle Eric always needs hugs. Dreams or not."

"And how about roommate Eric?" Gabriel gave his friend a little nudge with his elbow. "I bet he needs hugs too. From that pretty lady with the long dark hair. Did you notice those blue eyes of hers?"

"Um, yeah, kind of hard not to. Those eyes can look right through me to my backbone. They're like the ocean when it's calm, and like blue fire when I piss her off. Either way, I can't help fantasizing about them."

"Call me a romantic," Gabriel said, "but I think that smart, special, beautiful person you've got right there under your nose might just be the one to help you keep your head screwed on right. No offense to your shrink, I'm sure she's a big help, but still, being in love can cure a whole lot of what ails you. I learned that when Susan and I first got together."

"Michelle and I do hang out together a lot, but dating? I doubt it. She doesn't want me, not like that. She thinks I'm a big goof."

"Ah, so she's already got a pet name for you, that's a good sign." Gabriel nodded his approval. "What's your nickname for her?"

"I call her sweetheart a lot."

"Dude, you call everyone sweetheart. You call my mother sweetheart."

"Well, your mother is a sweetheart. Do you remember the look on that guy's face that time she introduced you and me as 'her boys'? The guy kept looking at her, and you, and me, and I could practically see the wheels going around in his head as he tried to figure out the DNA. How's your mom doing, by the way?"

"She's great, and quit trying to change the subject, dude. What do you call her, as a nickname? You know, in private. And by 'her', I mean that pretty lady you live with, not my mother."

"Gorgeous. But not to her face." Eric looked around, to verify nobody else was within earshot. "Venus." He'd associated the name with Michelle since the day on the mountain when they had discussed their personal goddesses.

"Well, now we're getting somewhere! There may be hope for you two yet." Gabriel got serious again. "You know, dude, I think I'm a pretty good judge of what couples should be together and which ones shouldn't. I mean, look at me. I have Susan and she's having my babies. We're a match made in heaven. You and that ex – she whose name shall not be mentioned – you two were not right for each other. I can't believe you married her. I knew it wouldn't last. I bet if you say her name three times fast, an evil spirit will pop up and bite your ass."

"So you told me, and told me, and told me. I get it." Eric rolled his eyes at Gabriel's joke about his ex, but didn't dispute the concept.

"But you and that pretty lady – seriously. I think she's the One. And yeah, I know I just met her a couple of hours ago. But I got this feeling, like you say, Spidey sense. I knew it when I saw you two holding hands in the copter. If she hadn't been wearing her seat belt, she would have crawled into your lap when we took off. When we landed, I thought maybe I should have backed off and given you two your privacy."

Eric sighed. "Jonesie, you are such a romantic! I could only be so lucky." Oops, big mouth time again. "Speaking of your and Susan's babies..."

"I know what you're going to ask. No, we didn't really plan on number three, it was a complete surprise. But a great surprise!"

"Yeah, surprise babies are the best. Look how great I turned out." Eric thumped his chest.

Now it was Gabriel's turn to roll his eyes. "Yeah, you turned out real great. Except for being blind." Gabriel started to sing, and despite the childish voice he employed, he, unlike Eric, could carry a tune. "Eric and Michelle, sitting in a tree, K-I-S-S-I-N-G!"

"You've got to be kidding me."

"Hey dude, you did that when Susan and I started dating. Only louder. And off-key."

"Well, yeah, but that was different. You guys were dating."

"And what are you two doing together," his friend challenged, "living under the same roof, on that romantic tropical island, if you're not dating? Tell me about this platonic, roommates, not sleeping together thing, because dude, I'm having trouble wrapping my head around it. You mean, you've never even kissed her?"

Eric's face went dreamy, so much so that Gabriel blinked in surprise. "Yes. On the cheek. Every chance I get."

"And that's all?" Gabriel's voice was completely skeptical.

"Well, there was that one night."

Gabriel's eyes lit up. "I knew it!"

"Not like that!" Eric assured him. "We slept together one night, on the couch, but it was just that. Sleep."

Gabriel looked completely disbelieving.

Eric told him about the earthquake – which Gabriel hadn't felt either, snorting a bit derisively upon hearing it was a mere three point four. He told his friend about waking Michelle up, her lack of concern about the alleged temblor, their sitting on the couch in case of aftershocks, and the sweet, comfortable feeling of her laying her head on his shoulder and sleeping there with him, even though she obviously hadn't intended to end up like that.

"So yeah, we've slept together, but only literally. Not in the naked sense."

Gabriel chuckled. "Well, I can tell, dude. She's yours if you want her. You do want her, right?"

"Lord, yes. I've never wanted anything more. Figures, doesn't it? The one person I shouldn't pursue."

"Dude, you are so wrong. You're just lucky I'm a happily married man."

Eric's face darkened. "Don't you even think that, Jonesie!"

"Oh, don't be so sensitive, dude. You know I'm just kidding. Talk to her. I bet you'll hear she feels the same."

"I do talk to her. All the time. We talk like magpies. But she doesn't want me, not *that* way."

"How do you know?" Gabriel demanded.

From outside the door, Tyler's voice called, "Dad! Uncle Eric! Come on!"

"The bosses are calling," Gabriel said, as he opened the door and the two men went out.

But he had one more thing to tell Eric before the kids heard them.

"Dude, I am so picking out names for your kids."

"Do not mention anything like that to Michelle. She'll slap me silly."

"And you'd love every minute of it."

******

Susan led Michelle back to the hallway and into the third bedroom, which had bunk beds. "Welcome to our guest room," she said, indicating the bottom bunk. "I'm sorry, it's kind of small. I'd love to get a bigger place, especially with this one on the way," she patted her tummy. "But house prices in San Diego are insane."

"It beats a three by six rack in a berthing compartment."

"I can see Eric's been telling you his Navy stories."

What drew Michelle's eyes, more than the bottom bunk she was going to sleep on, were the room's walls. Every bit of available space was covered by posters of military aircraft, mostly Navy fighter jets. Susan noticed her staring and smiled.

"Yeah, we have our very own future jet pilot here. Eleven years old and she's already begging for flying lessons. Gabriel and Eric are already filling out her application to Annapolis. I'm surprised Eric didn't tell Gabriel he was dating someone. When those two get together, they gossip like high school kids."

"We're not dating," Michelle said, continuing to look at the airplane posters. "We're just roommates."

Susan looked skeptical.

"Gabriel called me after you guys landed. He said you two were holding hands on the flight over. And that they thought you might be sick, and Eric was holding your hair back. A guy doesn't do that for a girl unless he cares about her."

"Eric does. He's like that. You know him. He takes care of people. I was scared when we took off. I mean, I was seriously terrified. Eric was just taking care of a friend."

"Yeah, that's our Eric."

They looked out the window to see the kids – all four of them – were kicking around a soccer ball in the back yard. Eric must have scored a goal, because he started to run around in a circle with his hands in the air, then flopped down on his back on the ground as Tyler and Natalie piled on top of him.

A moment later, he was no longer on his back. He was on his side, curled up in a fetal ball, rocking back and forth, because Tyler had accidentally sat on his man parts.

"Ouch," both women said, and Michelle wondered if she ought to run out and do something for Eric. But realistically, what could she do? Offer ice? From what she understood about this kind of thing, a guy just had to ride it out.

Susan clucked sympathetically. "I hope he's just being melodramatic. Eric is crazy about kids, and I know he wants to have his own someday."

"We're just roommates," Michelle repeated. But she simply could not prevent herself from conjuring up a mental image of a cute kid with sparkly hazel eyes, nice manners, who gave good advice and couldn't carry a tune in a bucket.

Apparently, Eric had recovered, because he sat up and hugged Tyler, who had been sitting next to him, crying in remorse.

"What a guy," Susan said.

"You know Eric really well?" Michelle tried not to sound jealous.

Susan nodded. "I've known him almost as long as I've known Gabriel. Those two went to high school together. Eric helped Gabriel get his first job as a helicopter pilot, before he started his own company, because the owner of the company he started out flying for was a-"

"Let me guess. An old Navy buddy?"

"You got it. That's our Eric. He helps people."

"Were you and Eric ever ... uh," Michelle tried to sound casual and not at all jealous.

"A couple?" Susan chuckled. "Oh gosh no. Once I met Gabriel, I never had eyes for anyone else. We love Eric like a brother, and the kids adore him, but, he's all yours."

"No, he's not."

"Well, I think he could be. I saw how he looked at you."

"We're so different. He's so sweet and nice, and I'm not."

Susan laughed a little, and held out one arm towards Michelle, giving a small tap with a finger indicating her very white skin.

"Look at me, and look at Gabriel. I think I know a thing or two about people from different backgrounds making it work, having a successful relationship. If you care about him, you can make it work."

Michelle wanted to repeat, we're just roommates. Or maybe she didn't.

"Of course, I care about him," she said. "He's a great roommate, and a really great friend. He's helped me get over a bunch of emotional stuff I spent way too much time obsessing over. He's a lot of fun to be around."

Oh, shut up, Michelle, she told herself. *You're going on like you have a big old crush on him, when you just gave Susan the 'we're just roommates' line.*

"At least you wouldn't have to worry about your parents objecting to him," Susan said.

"I don't have any parents. They're both dead."

"Really? So are Eric's."

"Yeah, we're twins separated at birth. Your parents objected to your marrying Gabriel?"

"A little. But they weren't, aren't, prejudiced. Not at all. They had no problem with my marrying him because he's black. They were only concerned about us potentially having problems from people who were. But I can't imagine any parents objecting to their daughter being with a sweetie like Eric."

"You sound like a matchmaker."

She smiled. "Maybe just a romantic."

She hoped Susan wouldn't be upset if she changed the subject. "Are you going to the air show too?"

"Not this year." She patted her belly again. "Gabriel and the kids are on their own this time. One whiff of jet fuel and someone will have to hold my hair back."

"Eric apparently likes the smell of it in the morning."

Susan smiled. "You know that's a paraphrase of a line from a movie?"

"Yeah, but it's not a Star Wars movie."

"Eric is a sweetie, but he's kind of a geek too," Susan said, and Michelle had to agree, but with more emphasis on the sweetie part and less on the geek part. "How did you two happen to become roommates?" Susan added just a slight emphasis on the word roommates, as if she didn't quite believe that was all they were, listening with amusement when Michelle recounted the day she'd met Eric on the sidewalk just before he left for deployment, though she left out how rude she'd been to him, and how he'd answered her roommate ad after leaving the Navy.

"So you two live together, but you don't *live* together?" Susan clarified.

"Yeah, I guess that's how it is." It wasn't lost on Michelle that Susan had somehow managed to steer the conversation back to her and Eric's relationship, or lack thereof. However, as the wife of Eric's oldest friend, Michelle really couldn't blame Susan for her curiosity.

"When Eric told us he was bringing a friend with him this weekend, I was sure he meant a girlfriend," Susan said.

"Well, we're friends, and I'm a girl. But not his *girlfriend*."

Susan put a sympathetic hand on Michelle's arm. "You could be if you wanted to," she insisted. "You know there's something that Eric and I have in common. He and Gabriel call it Spidey sense, nerds that they are. Sometimes we can just sense something, without being told."

"Yeah, Eric has it. He can tell if someone is in the Navy even if they're a total stranger wearing civilian clothes." She recalled that passing fist bump and perceptive "Hooyah" she'd witnessed the day they'd walked down the pier when he'd first moved in.

"My Spidey sense is knowing what couples should be couples, and which shouldn't. I knew that Gabriel and I were destined to be together on our first date. You know, don't you, that Eric was married once?"

Michelle nodded. "He told me about it."

"I only met her once, but I could tell just by looking at the two of them that they shouldn't be together. Of course the fact that Eric didn't even tell us he'd gotten married until after the fact was a huge red flag too. Gabriel was pissed at not being able to be Eric's best man. I was actually glad when he told us they got a divorce, because I knew they'd both be miserable if they stuck together."

"But still," Michelle insisted, "It was so totally cruel of the woman to file for divorce when he was deployed and out there putting his life on the line to defend our freedom. She could at least have had the decency to do it in person, and look him in the eye. How mean can a person get?"

Susan smiled at her. She was really very pretty, with a beautiful smile that exuded amusement at Michelle's passionate disgust for the way Eric's ex had acted. "Yes, I agree. But the point I'm getting at is that I could tell those two were wrong for each other, and on the other hand, I have this gut feeling that you and Eric would be, well, compatible. I know you may be different types of people, but still, you seem right together. I think he likes you."

"We are compatible, and he does like me, and I like him, but as friends and roommates, not romantically."

"Why not?" Susan replied quickly. "You're attracted to him, aren't you?"

Michelle was tempted, very tempted, to blurt out everything she felt about Eric to Susan, even though they'd only just met. Part of her wanted to admit, *yes I like him, I'm attracted to him as a man, as more than just a friend, and sometimes I just want to kiss him to pieces*. But she held her tongue. She wasn't accustomed to divulging her innermost feelings to other people, other than to Eric, and as much as she liked Susan and Gabriel, she couldn't make herself say those things to her.

It was difficult for her to make friends. She couldn't just walk up to people and introduce herself, the way Eric did. Though Eric had been her friend from the very first, from the moment he'd turned around on the sidewalk and introduced himself, though she'd been too stupid to realize it at first. Knowing Eric, living with his positive friendliness, had allowed her to risk lowering her tough defensive facade.

Susan was smiling at her. She obviously wanted to be friends, if only because she and Gabriel loved Eric like a brother, and any friend of Eric's was a friend of theirs. She gave Michelle's arm a friendly pat.

"Of course I think he's attractive," Michelle admitted. "He's adorable and he's the best friend I've ever had. But we aren't dating and we don't sleep together."

Susan chuckled. "I have to admit, I am having a hard time wrapping my head around this, we live together but we don't sleep together thing. You know, I told Gabriel I loved him the first time we slept together. It was our third date. And he replied, '*I know*', the big dork."

At Michelle's blank expression, Susan explained, "It's a Star Wars thing. Although usually Gabriel quotes Lando and leaves the Han Solo parts to Eric."

"Eric and I haven't, um, we don't, that is we aren't, you know..." she trailed off in embarrassment.

Fortunately, further discussion of her and Eric's non-romance was cut off by the sounds of Eric, Gabriel and the kids clamoring in from the back yard and Tyler's strident call of, "Mom! When's dinner? I'm starving!"

"Me too!" came a response from the rest of them in unison, and Susan laughed. "Come on," she invited. "We better feed the troops before there's a mutiny."

"Can I help?" Michelle asked, getting up and following Susan out the door and to the kitchen.

"Absolutely," her new friend replied. "Eric is in charge of vegetables, though."

30

When they drove from Gabriel's house to the airfield in the morning, the two men sat in the front and Michelle sat in the back with the kids, who waved enthusiastic goodbyes to their mother as they pulled out of the driveway.

"Don't forget sunblock!" Susan called out to her husband as they backed out into the street.

In the parking lot, Gabriel had his kids stand with their arms outstretched as he sprayed them both down with aerosol sunblock, SPF 50, and squirted some into the palms of their hands so that they could apply it to their faces.

"Just because our skin is dark, doesn't mean it won't burn," he told her, and Eric nodded.

"This is my weekend off," he said. "I don't want to have to treat anyone for sunstroke."

Eric obviously preferred the cream version of sunblock, and after rubbing some on his arms and the back of his neck, handed the tube to Michelle as he put on his Nimitz cap. When she returned the tube to him after applying hers, he looked at her sharply.

"You didn't bring a hat, did you?" he accused, and she nodded guiltily.

"Uh, oh," Tyler interjected somberly. "You're in trouble. Make it a double." However, rather than scold her, Eric just sighed melodramatically as they joined the crowd headed towards the gate.

Gabriel and the kids turned in the other direction after they all went through security, Natalie insisting, "Come on, Dad, we need to go see the planes!"

Gabriel grinned at Eric and Michelle. "We'll meet you at the car later," he suggested. "We need to see the planes like, right now! Because if we wait ten minutes, they might all fly away before she can worship them." He followed his daughter's tugging him in the direction of the airplanes on display. "And no, we are not bringing any of them home with us." His last statement was directed at his daughter.

Eric took Michelle's hand as they wandered in the other direction. It startled her a little. After all, they weren't in a helicopter flying above the ocean at the moment. They were walking past vendor's booths selling tee shirts, handmade jewelry, and assorted snacks. He glanced at her with a quick smile, saying, "It's pretty crowded. Don't want to lose you."

On the surface, it might appear that spending a day walking around looking at military planes, helicopters, tanks and other ordnance might not have been most girl's idea of fun. But, to her surprise, Michelle found it was in a tie for the most fun she'd ever had, right along with sitting on a rock on the side of a mountain on the island with him.

Yes, it was hot. Yes, it was crowded. But she was walking around with Eric and he was holding her hand. Sure, he was doing it because it was crowded and they didn't want to get separated. But she liked to pretend he was doing it because he wanted to, and she didn't hesitate to hold his hand right back.

They took pictures of each other and selfies standing in front of a lot of those aircraft and tanks, perused the vendor's booths, and wandered the field eating churros, after which they gulped down bottles of water to wash away the dryness of the cinnamon.

Eric's eyes lit up when they approached the recruiting tents for the various military branches. Although the Army, Air Force, Marines, National Guard and even the Coast Guard were all represented, he headed straight for the Navy's tent.

"Do you mind?" he asked her. "I just want to stop in and say hello to my buddy."

"Is the recruiter in there a friend of yours?" she asked, though having a feeling whoever was working there would be soon if he wasn't already. Eric seemed to know everyone. He'd stopped to chat with half a dozen friends and acquaintances they'd encountered that morning.

"He will be soon," Eric replied.

She hoped Eric wouldn't mind if she didn't join him to talk to whoever was working that recruiting tent. It wasn't that she was reluctant to meet the person, but the copious amounts of water they'd been drinking to keep hydrated in the heat were catching up to her.

"I'm going to look for the facilities while you talk to your friend," she told him. "I'll meet you back here in a few minutes, OK?"

Eric pointed past the row of recruiting tents. "The heads are down that way."

"We civilians call them porta-potties," she teased, as she disengaged her hand from his and walked towards them. She heard him say, "Hooyah," as he stepped inside the Navy tent to talk to the person who was, or soon would be, another of his many friends.

When she returned, he was just emerging from the tent and she saw him stand there looking at the recruiting poster on an easel next to the entrance, his face in profile to her, a slightly wistful expression on his face.

She couldn't help it. She was inspired to raise her phone to sneak a photo. It was the perfect combination of lighting, composition and an attractive subject. It was only fair, after all. He'd insisted on taking her photo on more than one occasion, even before today.

At that moment he must have noticed her approaching because he turned towards the camera just in time, his eyes squinting against the light, his beautiful mouth curled up in an affectionate smile just as she took the photo.

"Do you miss the Navy?" she asked, thinking about that wistful look she'd briefly spied on his face when he looked at the large poster depicting an aircraft carrier with jets launching off the deck.

"Yeah, a little, sometimes," he admitted. "But I have a pretty awesome civilian life too. Living in a place like Catalina Island, with you – doesn't get any better than that."

She started to feel a little flustered at the way he said, living with you, until she remembered. Best roommate ever.

"Here, I got you a present." He had a cap in his hand that he picked up and showed to her. It was dark blue of course and had the word NAVY in two-inch-tall gold letters embroidered on the front.

He'd gotten a cap for her? She was touched. That was so sweet. She reached to take it but he insisted on putting it on her head himself, and threaded her ponytail through the back opening. "That should keep the sun off your face."

Of course. It was his weekend off, and he didn't want to have to treat anyone for sunstroke.

He took her hand again as they walked towards the Stealth Bomber parked across the field. It was crowded after all, and they didn't want to get separated. But despite that decidedly unromantic reason for holding hands, Michelle still thought, *I could get used to this.*

By the time they'd finished examining all the military paraphernalia on display, checked out all the vendors, had lunch, and talked to the acquaintances that Eric tended to cross paths with, it was almost time for the Blue Angels performance, so they headed to the grassy field and found a spot to sit down. By coincidence, Gabriel and the kids were sitting a few feet away. Natalie was practically bouncing with excitement as they waited for the show to begin.

Eric had, of course, found ice cream and they ate it as they sat in the warm grass waiting for the exhibition to begin. He was like a heat-seeking missile for the stuff. Or more accurately, a cold-seeking missile.

When the six bright blue planes, with the dramatic yellow US Navy printed on each wing, roared into view, the entire audience gasped with delight. Michelle was entranced by the plane's maneuvers, the loops, rolls, and formation flying. She held her breath as two planes hurtled towards each other in what appeared to be a collision course, with each plane turning sideways just before passing each other to roar away behind the nearest mountain before returning for the next maneuver. It was absolutely astounding to see the back-to-back, belly-to-belly, and wingtip-to-wingtip formations the planes executed, even with one jet flying inverted above its partner, the clear canopies of the planes looking as if they were glued together. It was thrilling, and they made it look easy, though Eric informed her they were doing it at speeds approaching seven hundred miles per hour. How did they not crash into each other, as they passed seemingly within inches? At times it looked like the wings of one plane were almost touching the wings of the other.

A few of the other people in the audience around them called out, "I feel the need! The need for speed!" Eric laughed appreciatively hearing the enthusiastic comments.

Michelle had never seen anything so amazing in her entire life.

With all the various maneuvers and formations, it wasn't surprising that few if any of the spectators noticed that one of the jets did not return to the sky in front of them after the inverted flying display. A moment later, that jet came roaring up from behind them, completely unexpected, with a noise like hell on earth above the astonished spectators. It couldn't have been more than 100 feet off the deck.

The instantaneous jolt from pleasure and enjoyment, to abject terror, fear and panic affects people differently. Some screamed, some covered their heads, some launched themselves at their companions for protection.

Michelle did all three, and Eric immediately found himself with a screaming, twitching ball of fear in his lap, trying to burrow her way to safety in his chest. He liked it.

When she realized that instantaneous death was not raining down on her head, she opened her eyes to realize that she'd knocked Eric flat on his back, with her on top of him, and he was laughing his head off. It was a good thing they had finished their ice cream already, or it would have been smeared into Eric's stomach.

All around them, kids were crying and being comforted by their parents. Some adults were crying too, being comforted by their kids.

As the blue and yellow planes flew off with a final wing-waggle, the spectators started to compose themselves and catch their breath after the unexpected climax to the performance. Flustered at her panic, Michelle sat up and retrieved her cap, which had flown off her head when she'd launched herself at her roommate for safety.

"Sorry," she muttered, embarrassment heating her face. "Did I hurt you?"

Eric shook his head, still laughing. "I'm fine. Don't worry, you didn't do a Tyler."

That was a distinct relief, recalling how Tyler's enthusiasm yesterday afternoon had caused Eric significant discomfort for a little while. That was certainly the last thing she'd want to do to him!

When they made their way to Eric's car later, Gabriel and the kids were there waiting, the two children chattering excitedly about the day and especially the Blue Angels. She could see from the gestures Natalie was making that she was recreating the aerial performance. Despite her father's serious pronouncement that morning, it appeared that Natalie was actually bringing some planes home with her, as she clutched a rolled-up poster in her hands. Where, Michelle wondered, was she going to display it? Her bedroom walls were already covered completely, and Michelle was certain the girl wasn't about to remove any of the existing posters. The new one might have to go on the ceiling.

Gabriel gave them a pointed look, seeing Eric and Michelle walking toward them holding hands, but Eric just grinned and exchanged high fives with the kids, asking, "Did you guys have fun?"

The smiles on their faces were a definite answer of *Yes*.

The next day, Sunday, they spent the morning with Gabriel, Susan and the kids. They didn't do anything exciting, but it was still the second-best day Michelle had ever experienced, after the air show yesterday, a type of day she had been completely unfamiliar with until now.

It was a family day.

It started with breakfast. Eric was in charge of bacon. Gabriel was in charge of pancakes. Susan and Michelle were, apparently, in charge of sitting at the table, supervising and drinking orange juice. Natalie and Tyler were in charge of cleaning up afterward, and squabbled over whose turn it was to take out the garbage, and if they really had to clean their rooms.

"I'll help you clean your room," Michelle offered to Natalie. "After all, I've been your roommate this weekend. I should help tidy up."

"Hey!" Eric protested with a pout. "I'm your roommate too, and you never offer to help me clean my room."

"Is your room a mess?" she asked him.

"No," he replied. "I'm pretty squared away. But I'd throw some stuff on the floor if you'll help me clean it up."

At that point, Gabriel made a "Hmph!" sound and pulled Eric to the other side of the kitchen with a tug on his arm. "Smooth move, dude," he said, low enough to evade the kids' hearing. "Is that how you charm a woman into your bedroom? By offering to throw things on the floor?"

Eric just shrugged and gave Michelle one of his teasing winks.

Susan was smiling as if she'd just figured out the answer to the Schrodinger's cat paradox, as Michelle shook her head and rolled her eyes. "Don't take him seriously," she told them. "You know he's just teasing."

He was teasing, wasn't he?

"Yes," Susan said, but with a tone that clearly indicated she really meant to say no. "He's just teasing."

Tyler came crashing in from his trash run declaring, "Garbage is tossed!" and his mom immediately questioned, "In the can? All of it? Nothing dropped on the driveway like last time?"

Tyler nodded vigorously in confirmation, his curly hair bouncing.

"Come on," Michelle suggested to the kids, feeling a bit disconcerted at Eric's teasing about messing up his room in order for her to come in and help tidy it. She hadn't been inside that room since she'd fixed it up before he'd moved in. "I'll help you both with your rooms. It will go faster that way."

Natalie and Tyler led the way to their rooms willingly, looking happy at the prospect of help.

Behind her, Michelle heard Gabriel stage-whisper. "Dude, you need a better line than that if you think you're going to get that pretty lady into your bedroom," followed by an "Oof!" as if he'd been jabbed in the ribs with an elbow.

Eric and Gabriel were just teasing, weren't they?

"Thank you for sharing your room with me this weekend," Michelle said to Natalie as they picked up laundry and made up the beds. "I hope I didn't put you out of your bed." She had enjoyed sleeping there the past two nights, listening to Natalie's soft breathing above her, and wondering if Eric was comfortable out on the living room sofa. He must have been, he had after all referred to it as his second home.

"No," Natalie replied. "I always sleep on the top anyway." Michelle noticed the way Natalie's gaze lingered on the airplane posters, and wondered if the girl chose the top bunk because it put her just that much closer to the wild blue yonder. Her guess was confirmed when Natalie added, "I'm going to fly one of those someday."

"I'm sure you will." Michelle couldn't doubt it, noting the intense look she saw in the girl's dark eyes. "Which one is your favorite?"

It was obviously a difficult choice to make, as Natalie's eyes roamed over the various posters on her wall for long moments, before finally pointing to one depicting a Super Hornet that was pinned next to the window.

"That one. Uncle Eric got it for me."

"That was really nice of him," Michelle replied. It was apparent to her that Eric and the Jones family were as close or closer than most blood-related people. Again, she felt a twinge of jealousy at their closeness, their casual affection, wishing she'd had a family like this. Natalie was only a year older than Michelle had been when her mother had died.

Natalie leaned towards Michelle a little and said, in a lower voice, "And he told me if I get good grades, he'll put some money in a bank account for me to save up for flying lessons when I'm sixteen. Mom and Dad said they're really expensive. Daddy can teach me how to fly a helicopter, but," the girl's eyes returned to the Super Hornet poster, "I want jets."

Michelle suddenly found herself giving the girl a quick hug and repeating her thanks for the sharing of her bedroom, feeling quite impressed at the girl's dedication to a dream at such a young age, and also feeling affection towards Eric with his enabling of that dream.

"I promised your brother I'd help him too," she said, blinking back a tiny bit of moisture that had entered her eyes, "and I bet his room needs more work than yours."

"Yeah, that kid is a slob," Natalie affirmed, as Michelle went next door to help Tyler and Natalie headed in the opposite direction to join her parents and Uncle Eric.

After helping the boy with his cleanup, which wasn't quite as bad as Natalie had led Michelle to believe, they all spent the rest of the morning just sitting in the yard, enjoying the sunshine and chatting. Michelle looked at Eric's face, trying to decipher his expression as he watched the kids sitting in the grass, goofing around. He turned and looked at Susan's rounded tummy, covered in a blue cotton maternity shirt, with her hand resting on top of the mound.

Eric had a very expressive face, she already knew, and it didn't take long to realize what he was feeling.

He was jealous. The man wanted babies.

We're just roommates, she had told Susan.

Eric looked at Gabriel. "Dude, you got a piece of rope?" he asked.

"What for?" Gabriel asked with suspicion in his voice.

"I want to tie one of Michelle's hands behind her back."

"Dude! Not in front of the children," Gabriel admonished.

"Oh jeez, get your mind out of the gutter." Eric turned from his outraged friend to Michelle.

"Michelle, sweetheart, remember you said you'd change the oil in my car with one hand tied behind your back?"

"I said I could. Not that I actually would."

She laughed at the disappointment on Eric's face.

"OK, Mr. Pouty-face. I'll check the oil, at least, if it'll make you happy. But with two hands." She sent an admonishing finger-shake in her roommate's direction.

That at least seemed to pacify Eric and he settled into a lawn chair to watch, as Michelle stood up and looked at Tyler and Natalie. "Do you want me to show you how to check the oil?" she asked, nodding towards Gabriel's truck and Eric's car in the driveway.

"Sure!" Tyler replied cheerfully, and both children followed her as she walked over and opened the hood of Eric's car.

Behind them, Gabriel grumbled, "I tried to show them how to do that and they weren't interested. What's up with that?"

He looked over at Eric, but Eric didn't respond.

"Dude?" Gabriel enquired.

Eric didn't answer.

"Dude!"

Gabriel practically yelled the word in Eric's ear, and Eric jumped. "Huh?"

"What planet are you on, dude?" Gabriel asked, and Susan chuckled.

"He goes a little deaf at the sight of his roommate bending over the hood of his car," she observed.

"Shh!" Eric yelped, and he blushed at being caught staring at Michelle's rear end, bent over the fender of his car as she reached for the dipstick.

"He also gets a little snippy at the sight of his roommate bent over the hood of his car," Gabriel added.

"Shh," Eric repeated, giving his friend a castigating look. "I don't want her to hear you and your wild stories."

Michelle closed the hood of Eric's car, apparently satisfied that his oil level was sufficient, and moved over to Gabriel's truck. It was a taller vehicle, and she had to lean a bit further to reach the dipstick. Natalie followed her instructions on removing the dipstick and checking her father's oil level. The fabric of Michelle's shorts stretched over her derriere and rode up to reveal a sliver of cinnamon-and-sugar skin previously unseen. Gabriel looked at Eric quickly when he heard his friend make a tiny sound almost like a sigh of longing.

"Maybe you should go over there and tell her how you feel," Gabriel suggested. When Eric offered no response, due to his new, temporary deafness, his friend added, "Or, maybe I should go over there, since you've suddenly become so shy, like you ain't never been before, and I could tell her how you feel."

Eric turned a glare towards his friend. "You just keep your ass in that lawn chair, dude!" he ordered.

"Don't you go bossing me around," Gabriel retorted. "I ain't one of your boot camp trainees, messing up your sickbay."

"Boys!" Susan interjected. "Stop your squabbling this instant. You two are as bad as Tyler and Natalie."

"But he started it," Eric insisted as he pointed a finger at Gabriel.

The two men looked at each other and grinned. Gabriel made a motion as if to get up, but desisted at Eric's plea of, "Seriously. Dude." With a glance at Susan, he added, "You don't want to upset the pregnant lady."

"Yes," Susan agreed. "Don't upset the pregnant lady. You," she pointed a finger at her husband. "Stop teasing poor Eric. He will say what he needs to say when he's ready to say it."

Eric stuck his tongue out at Gabriel, a gesture that while childish, was fairly common coming from Eric, as Michelle and Natalie closed the hood of Gabriel's truck and came back to report.

"You're both good. You don't need to change your oil for a while yet."

"Thanks, sweetheart," Eric said with a grin, then looked at the kids. "I hope you guys were paying attention there. You need to tell your dad and me when it's time to get the oil changed."

"OK, but it's not time yet," Tyler piped up helpfully, looking at Michelle for confirmation. She nodded her agreement.

Eric gestured at Michelle. "If she says so. She's the engine expert in the family."

In the family? Had he just referred to her as being "in the family"? The concept gave her a warm, fuzzy feeling she hadn't experienced before.

*****

After lunch, Susan decided she needed a nap, and Gabriel decided he needed to supervise it. Eric made eyes at Michelle and at the kids, and the next thing she knew, the four of them were in his car, heading to the mall.

Michelle had always been under the impression that most men hated shopping and would do just about anything to avoid going to the mall.

However, she had realized, even as far back as that first day she'd met Eric, that he was not most guys.

First, he headed to a children's clothing store, where he found baby outfits with little ships embroidered on them. He bought several, in assorted sizes, as Natalie and Tyler rolled their eyes.

"Hey, kids grow fast," he assured them.

The next stop was the video game store, where Eric let each of the kids pick out a game, although Tyler did have to go with his second choice when Uncle Eric rejected one that was rated M for Mature.

Michelle watched this shopping expedition with a smile, amused at seeing Eric spoiling his friend's kids.

They ended up at a table in the food court with a tray full of ice cream sundaes. As Natalie and Tyler slurped whipped cream and chocolate, Eric pulled the smallest of the ship-embroidered baby outfits out of the shopping bag.

"I remember when you two were this size." He held up the tiny outfit as both kids looked disbelieving.

"Susan and Gabriel got rid of all their baby stuff when Tyler outgrew it, so they have to start from scratch for this one. That's probably why they got pregnant."

"Because they got rid of their baby stuff?" Michelle asked, as Eric put the outfit back in the bag and scooped up a spoonful of his own ice cream.

"Yep, works every time," he assured her. "I have a couple of nieces and nephews that I'm sure were conceived as a result of their parents giving away their baby clothes, thinking they were done with babies."

"Uncle Eric," Tyler asked. "What does conceived mean?"

"Well," Eric said hesitantly, as Michelle stifled a giggle. "Have your mom and dad told you about how babies come?"

Tyler nodded. "The mommy gets a fat tummy, then they go to the hospital and they take the baby out of her tummy, then the mommy and daddy bring it home. But how does the baby get in there? Is that what conceived is?"

Natalie was looking embarrassed – Michelle would guess that she had more of an idea what the word conceived meant – as Eric told Tyler, "Well dude, it's kind of like that, but I really think you need to talk to your dad about the rest of it."

Michelle leaned close to Eric and whispered at him, "Clever way to slither out of that one."

Eric grinned and whispered back, "Hey, I love the kid, but I seriously think it's not my place to tell him about the birds and the bees."

Tyler's curiosity about conception was forgotten when Natalie piped up, "Mom and Dad should have kept Tyler's old baby clothes then. We don't need another stupid baby."

Uh, oh, Michelle thought.

Eric glowered at Natalie's unkind words regarding her upcoming new brother.

"Don't you go calling your little brother stupid," he scolded.

"Yeah," Michelle chimed in. "He's going to be beautiful."

All three of them stared at her, as she reached out and gave Eric's arm a brief pat.

"Uncle Eric says that all babies are beautiful."

For a moment, Eric looked at where Michelle had patted his arm, then he grinned.

"She's right, you know," he assured them.

Natalie looked at him. "Uncle Eric, how come you don't have any babies?"

Oh, this is going to be interesting. Michelle hid a smile behind her napkin.

Tyler piped up before Eric could respond.

"I know! Daddy said that Uncle Eric doesn't have his own babies because he was married to the Navy. But how can you be married to a Navy? I thought you had to be married to another person."

Michelle sat back and listened to Tyler going on.

"But you're not in the Navy anymore, right?" He looked at Eric for confirmation.

"Yes, that's right," Eric said, looking like he had more to say, but Tyler was still talking. Apparently, Eric wasn't the only one with a big mouth.

"When you came here before, you told us that you're a simian now."

"A civilian," Eric corrected. "A simian is a monkey."

"So does that mean you're not married to the Navy anymore? Did you get a divorce?"

"Not from the Navy," Eric replied. Michelle wondered if Natalie and Tyler knew about Eric's real divorce, or had they been too young. "It was a friendly separation. I decided that it was the right time for me to start being a civilian. Not a simian."

He curved one arm over his head and pretended to scratch at his armpit with the other, making a very realistic monkey screech.

"Uncle Eric!" Natalie hissed, looking around, obviously checking to make sure nobody she knew was there in the food court to witness her silly "uncle's" antics. "Don't do that in public!"

"Yes, ma'am," Eric replied sweetly, and desisted his simian imitation.

"I have an idea," Natalie said. "If you're not married to the Navy anymore, then you can get your own babies." She turned to look at her brother. "When Mom has this baby, Uncle Eric and Aunt Michelle can adopt it."

Aunt Michelle? These two children were calling her *Aunt Michelle*? She could understand them addressing Eric as "uncle" due to his close and long-standing friendship with their parents. But Michelle had only met this family less than forty-eight hours ago. Did they consider her an honorary aunt because she'd come here with Eric? Had they picked up on their parent's mistaken belief that she and Eric were a couple? Either way, it warmed her heart to hear it. She'd never been called "aunt" before.

But even more astounding was Natalie's casual suggestion that her new baby brother be given away – and to her and Eric! She was certain that Eric itched to be a daddy, but still, Natalie's plan of action was ab-solutely outrageous, and from the expression on the girl's face, she knew it, as she looked from Michelle to Eric with a determined demeanor, dar-ing them to accept her outlandish plan.

Tyler opened his mouth to say something about his sister's bizarre sug-gestion, but Eric hushed him with a finger raised in front of his face. He pushed aside his ice cream sundae to reach across the table and took Natalie's hands in his in that adorable uncle manner that Michelle immediately found to be one of the most charming things she'd ever seen.

"Now, sweetheart," he said. "You don't really want to give away your little brother."

Natalie's mutinous expression suggested that yes, she did want to do just that.

"To start with, your mom and dad might have something to say about that idea. This is their baby, and they love it. And you're going to love him too."

"Do I have to?"

"Of course, you do. But you won't need to do anything in order to love him. As soon as you see him, it will just happen."

Natalie looked disbelieving. Tyler took advantage of Eric's taking a breath to pipe up, "You can't give away our baby! Not even to Uncle Eric. He's going to share my bedroom, and I get to be a," he scrunched his face, trying to remember. "A role model, that's it!"

He looked at Eric. "Uncle Eric, what's a role model?"

Eric chuckled and looked relieved at the subject shifting away from his lack of babies. He let go of Natalie's hands and turned to Tyler.

"A role model is someone you look up to. Someone you admire, and you want to be like. Like your dad."

"And you too, Uncle Eric."

"OK," Eric agreed. "But mostly your dad. And if you're going to be a role model for your new little brother, that means you need to be a good kid and do good stuff, so your little brother learns how to be a good kid too. But that should be easy for you. You're already a good kid."

Tyler beamed, but Natalie still looked unhappy.

"But Uncle Eric," she complained. "This new baby is going to ruin everything. Our family was perfect the way it was. Two boys and two girls. Now there's going to be three boys and it's all going to be ruined. It's stupid."

"So if the new baby was going to be a girl, you wouldn't mind so much?" Eric challenged.

"Maybe," Natalie muttered.

Eric pretended to look hurt. "Hey, there's nothing wrong with boys! Some of us are kind of cute." He put a hand on Tyler's head and scratched the boy's head with his fingers. "Like this guy."

Impulsively, Michelle reached up and put her hand on top of Eric's head and made the same motion he'd done on Tyler. "And this guy," she said, allowing her fingers to run through his soft hair. It was OK, as long as it was done in jest, right?

Eric's face split wide in an ecstatically happy smile. Then he made a beckoning gesture at Natalie and took her hands again.

"Can I tell you guys a story?" Both kids looked eager and leaned towards Eric. Apparently, they were accustomed to, and enjoyed, Eric's stories. Michelle could relate to the concept. She enjoyed hearing Eric tell stories too. But sometimes she liked hearing him talk just to watch his mouth.

"When I was a little baby," he began, and Tyler interrupted.

"You were a baby?" He sounded disbelieving.

Eric smiled at the boy. "Well, yes, dude. Everyone starts out as a baby."

"Even Mom and Dad?"

"Yes, even your mom and dad. When I was a baby, my big sister didn't want me in the family. You guys remember Auntie Brenda from Florida?"

Both kids nodded.

"Well, Brenda didn't like me at first. She thought I was gross and disgusting."

They giggled.

"But you know what? After a while, she started to like me. I was the cutest baby in the world."

By now they were laughing, and even Michelle found herself giggling.

Eric glanced at her with his special grin.

"Well, I was!" he defended. "I've seen photos."

"Cute and humble," she said. "A winning combination."

Eric actually puffed up with pride, the big goof, as he looked back at Natalie and Tyler.

"Once she got to know me, she started to like me. And now, she loves me more than anyone else in the world. Well, that is after her husband.

And her children. And her grandkid. But she loves me a lot, even though she thought I was a really bad idea at first.

"And when your new little brother comes, I bet you're going to love him, and you won't want to give him away, even to us."

Eric the family man. This was a new side to him, one she hadn't seen before.

Of course, this wasn't his family and these weren't his kids. But the way he interacted with them was so darn perfect. Michelle could recognize it even though she had no experience with children.

His scolding of Natalie at her trying to give away her parent's baby. It wasn't harsh or imposing, so she wouldn't feel punished, and yet serious enough to convey the unsuitability of her proposal. Not too hard on her, not too gentle. Just right.

His gentle deflection of Tyler's questions about human procreation. Not too harsh so as to make him feel bad. Not too flippant.

Just right.

Eric glanced at Michelle and gave her a smile that could melt the sun. And then he did something that made Michelle's heart kick up a notch, right there in the food court with a spoonful of ice cream halfway between the dish and her mouth.

He made a kiss mouth.

The ice cream oozed off her spoon and landed in her lap with a cold wet plop, as Eric said, "We can get our own babies."

Had she heard right? Had Eric just said "we" and "babies" in the same sentence? She was used to his joking, but this was a new level of outrageousness.

"Aunt Michelle, you spilled your ice cream!" Tyler scolded, and Eric handed her a napkin.

Unlike Tyler, Michelle knew perfectly well exactly how babies were conceived. She may not have had parental guidance or older siblings to educate her, but she had spent a lot of time at her friend Tracy's house, and Tracy had an older sister who was only too happy to educate them. The clinical details had been filled in during ninth-grade biology class. And then there had been that awkward, but educational experience the night of her senior prom.

Yes, she knew exactly how a couple got their own babies. The potential mom and dad had to ...

Oh, Freya!

Eric smiled at her. She recognized that particular smile. That was teasing. He was just trying to get her goat with his silly faces and talk about "we" and "babies"

We can get our own babies.

He had to be joking about that. Joking was his modus operandi.

She was both relieved and, frankly, a little disappointed.

Eric was nodding towards a store on the other side of the food court. "Do we need to get you a new pair of jeans?"

"No, I'll be OK," she said, blushing as she wiped at the ice cream stain on her thigh.

He looked at the kids, asking, "Are you guys done?"

He started to place the empty sundae bowls on the tray and gave Tyler a look.

"No, you cannot have another one. You won't eat your dinner and then I'll be in the dog house with your mom again."

Tyler started to laugh, but Natalie poked him in the ribs while giving Eric a scolding look.

"Don't laugh at him! He'll start making dog noises."

Eric picked up the tray and said, "Woof," as he turned towards the trash can to toss their detritus and placed the tray in its spot.

"Come on, guys," he instructed. "We have one more stop to make before I take you home, and your dad takes us home." He handed the video game bag to Tyler to carry and picked up the baby clothes bag.

Michelle followed the three of them as they headed towards the exit, still a bit stunned at the casual use of words like "aunt," "we," and "babies" in their conversation.

As they buckled their seat belts in Eric's car, Tyler leaned forward from behind him and said, "Uncle Eric, can I ask you a question?"

"Sure dude, what is it?"

"Can I get a tattoo like yours?"

Eric put the car back into park and turned around to give Tyler a stern look.

"Absolutely not."

"Why not? You have one."

"Ok, dude, listen. There are some very strict rules to follow here regarding getting a tattoo. First off, you have to be a grown-up. At least twenty-one years old."

"Wait a minute," Natalie interjected. "Mom told me that we would be old enough to vote when get to be eighteen. Isn't that being a grown-up?"

Michelle had to give Eric credit for quick thinking.

"There's a special level of maturity you need to have in order to get a tattoo. Twenty-one or older. That's the rule. No exceptions." He looked sternly at both kids, and also directed a slightly grave glance at Michelle. He was obviously warning her not to inform the kids that legally, they would be adults at eighteen and would technically be allowed to have body art done at that age without parental permission.

"Were you twenty-one when you got your tattoo?" Natalie asked.

"Yes, I was," Eric replied, then leaned towards Michelle and whispered. "Barely. I got it on my twenty-first birthday. Most of the guys would go to a bar on their twenty-first birthday, to order their first legal drink. But I couldn't do that of course."

When he'd gotten his tattoo, his buddies had moaned and groaned when he insisted on checking out several establishments before choosing one that looked the most hygienic. He'd also requested a double application of disinfectant rubbing alcohol, until one of his friends had complained, "It's a tattoo, Hanson, not brain surgery!"

It was a good thing that his allergy only reacted to alcohol ingested orally and not through skin contact.

He turned back to the kids.

"Also," he told them. "You need to understand that if you do ever get one, a long long time from now, you have to realize that whatever you get is permanent and you're going to have it on you for the rest of your life."

"You mean you can't ever take it off?" Tyler asked.

"Well, you can, but it hurts. Even more than it hurts getting it put on." He winked at Michelle, obviously recalling her reminding him of that the day they'd met.

"Does it hurt a lot when they put it on?" Tyler was looking a bit uncertain now about the idea of getting a tattoo.

"You bet, dude. You know how it feels when you get a shot at the doctor's office?" Both kids nodded solemnly. "Well, imagine getting thousands and thousands of shots at the same time, for about two hours."

They both looked a bit scared, and Eric gave Michelle a look of satisfaction. "And!" He paused for emphasis. "There's another thing, even more important than being a grown-up, or how much it might hurt. You absolutely, positively must have your mom's permission before getting a tattoo. Got that?"

"Did your mom say it was OK when you got your tattoo?" Tyler asked.

Natalie gave him a little poke. "Uncle Eric's mom is in heaven," she reminded her brother.

"Yes, she is," Eric affirmed. "But she was still alive when I got this." He pointed at the anchor design. "And no, I didn't ask her before I did it. And she was really really mad at me."

"Did you get grounded?"

"No, but she yelled at me a lot."

Michelle stifled a laugh at the mental image Eric's words conjured up. An image of a mature military man, in uniform, looking at his feet and protesting, "But, Mom!" while being dressed down by his mother. Michelle wondered if Mrs. Hanson had scolded Eric in the presence of his buddies.

"And if your mom gets mad at you, I'll get mad at you too," Eric continued. "You don't want that, do you?"

Both young people shook their heads.

Eric nodded, satisfied that he had done his part in squelching further ambitions of body art on Tyler's part, and put the car into reverse to leave the mall for their last errand.

*****

Their last stop was, surprisingly, at Barnes and Noble. That was weird. She knew Eric wasn't much of a reader.

However, he seemed to have an agenda as he escorted Tyler to the children's department. "You look around in here, dude," he instructed. "Stay in this section and don't go anywhere else. We'll be back in ten minutes."

He put his hand on Michelle's arm in that now-familiar escorting a little old lady across the street manner he had, and a minute later they were standing in front of a section labeled Fantasy and Science Fiction.

Eric started pulling books off the shelf and turning the covers towards Michelle. "Have you read this one? Look, this one has a dragon on the cover. That looks cool. Are there sexy vampires in this one? Wait, it's Book Three of a series – where's number one and two? You can't read book three until you finish the first two."

Every time she replied that she hadn't yet read the book he was looking at, he set it aside, until he had a stack in his arms whose total cost had to exceed a hundred dollars. No, more like three hundred. The books were mostly hardbacks.

"Are you going to read all those?" she asked.

"Nope," he replied with a grin. "I'm getting them for you to read. You can give me a summary afterward if you want to."

She looked at the heavy stack and drooled a little. She'd been lusting for the book with the purple fire-breathing dragon on the cover, but it wasn't available at the local library yet.

"You can't do that, Eric." It caused her physical pain to refuse his generosity, but it just wasn't right for him to spend money on her like that.

"Sure, I can. Just watch me."

"No. It's not right. That's a lot of books. A lot of money. I couldn't ask you to buy all those for me."

"Well, you didn't ask. I volunteered."

"No. It's too much." Even as she said the words, she couldn't help but let her eyes linger on the purple fire-breathing dragon. The creature seemed to be enticing her, murmuring, *Take me home. I belong to you.*

This was outrageous. It would be completely inappropriate to let her roommate buy her a stack of books that Eric could barely see over the top of, and whose purchase price would feed a family for two weeks.

Since she'd known Eric, she'd realized he was sweet, helpful and generous, but still. For him to even consider spending money like that on a gift for her, and it wasn't even Christmas. If it were any other guy, she'd be wondering, in her best Raging Bitch attitude, what exactly he expected from her in order to express her gratitude.

No, if it were any other guy, she'd *know* what he'd expect.

But she knew Eric pretty well by now. If he said he wanted to buy these books for the pleasure of seeing her enjoyment, she believed him.

But the money. Surely he had better things to spend his hard-earned money on than a pile of books for her.

"No. I can't let you buy me those. It's not right. It's not appropriate. And don't give me that, let me do it because I've put my life on the line to defend your freedom line. Just, no."

It made her really sad to have to say that. The stack of books was calling out to her, whispering, *we're yours. Feel us. Smell us. Open us up and love us.*

She tried to keep her book lust from showing on her face, but she had a feeling she was failing.

Over the top of the book stack, Eric was making that scrunched up, pretend pouty face that she found so irresistible. He sighed melodramatically.

"Fine. You leave me no choice. I'll just have to buy them for myself if you won't let me buy them for you."

"Yeah, right. You're going to read all those?"

"No, I'm going to stack them on the coffee table as decorations. The purple fire-breathing dragon goes on top. And if you're really nice to me, I might let you borrow them."

While Michelle had no problem with the concept of books as decorations, still to use them exclusively as decorations, without also reading them, was a travesty akin to buying a chocolate bar and just looking at it, rather than eating it. She threw up her hands in defeat.

"Fine. You can buy them for me. I shouldn't let you do it, but against my better judgment, I'm going to anyway."

His sparkly smile had talked her into it. She just couldn't resist that smile, and she had a feeling he was well aware of the fact.

"Thank you, ma'am," he said, as if somehow she was doing him a favor.

"Why on earth would you want to do this, you big goof?"

"It will make me happy," he insisted.

"How in the world will buying all those books that you'll never read yourself, make you happy?"

"Well, I'll enjoy seeing the pleasure you'll get from reading them."

"That's silly," she replied. "How can watching someone else read give you pleasure?"

"Are you kidding? The expression on your face when you're into one of those vampire books is a real trip. Sometimes you look really intense, almost orgasmic."

Orgasmic? She looked orgasmic when she was reading? And Eric had watched her when she was reading? She had assumed he'd been watching a baseball game on TV or Skyping with some of his many friends and relatives.

He took her stunned silence at his observation as agreement and started to walk away with the stack of books, saying, "Let's go see what Tyler picked out."

At the children's department, they found Tyler sitting on the floor, absorbed in a book with Darth Vader on the cover.

"Don't you have that one already?" Eric asked.

"No, this is a different one."

"Do you want to get it?"

Tyler nodded vigorously, a wide smile splitting his face as he scrambled to his feet with the book in hand.

Michelle looked around, suddenly panicked. "We lost Natalie!"

Neither Eric nor Tyler seemed concerned.

"Don't worry, sweetheart. I know where she is. Grab your book, dude," he instructed Tyler. "Aunt Michelle has me loaded up."

"I could at least carry some of them." She reached for the stack, but Eric neatly sidestepped her.

"Nope. I got this. Come on."

He led her and Tyler, who clutched his Star Wars book, out of the children's department. A minute later they were in the Military History section, where Natalie also sat on the floor, absorbed in her book.

As they looked down, it was obvious the book she was perusing was an encyclopedia of military aircraft, and she was so engrossed in it, she didn't even notice Eric, Michelle and Tyler standing there, until Eric nudged her with his foot and she glanced up, startled.

"Come on, kiddo," Eric said. "Grab your book."

Natalie scrambled to her feet also, clutching the book like a lifeline.

"And that one," Eric pointed a toe at the second book that had been lying next to Natalie, and she hastily grabbed it up.

Eric nodded his head in a *Come On* gesture and the girl smiled broadly, her apparent unhappiness about the new baby forgotten in the rush of acquiring new books.

That's something we have in common, Michelle thought, even though the subject matter of their books differed. At that age, Michelle had been more into Harry Potter and other fantasy fiction than Phantom fighters and Super Hornets, but the book lust was the same regardless of the preferred genre.

Natalie hugged Eric, and exclaimed, "Thanks, Uncle Eric. You're the best."

Actually, she mostly hugged the stack of books in Eric's arms. Tyler, not to be one-upped, gave Eric a book-wall hug too and echoed, "Yeah, you're the best."

Eric smiled at both kids, then grinned at Michelle over the top of the stack.

"See? I'm the best." He shifted the pile in his arms a little, and Michelle could positively read the *hint-hint* in his eyes. She had no choice. She gave him a hug too, but it was awkward and a bit uncomfortable, with book corners poking her chest and belly.

"OK, you're the best. The best goof."

"That works for now. You can thank me properly later," he teased, as he turned towards the cashier.

"Come on guys. Let's check out before your mom and dad think I've kidnapped you."

"Wait!" Michelle exclaimed, before they got a step away. She had spotted something on the top shelf of the section where Natalie had been sitting with her airplane books. Eric quirked his eyebrows at her.

"Did you think of another book you needed? Guess it takes a lot to satisfy that vampire addiction of yours."

"Not for me. For you."

"That's OK, I'm good."

"No. it's not fair. You've been shopping for everyone else. You have to get something for yourself too."

"Don't worry about it."

"Nope nope nope. You are getting a book for yourself." She stepped directly in front of him and he had to stop quickly to avoid a collision. The stack of books in his arms wobbled a bit and he had to shift his weight to keep from dropping any.

"Over here." She turned back to the Military History section, where she perused the top shelf, looking for the book she'd noticed earlier.

"You heard the lady," Eric said with a chuckle in his voice as he waited patiently for her to choose a volume from the shelf. He stood next to her and added, a little lower, "I like it when you get bossy."

"Yeah, it's a change from the norm, isn't it? Usually you're the bossy one." Eric declined to deny it. "Let me see, where is it?" She ran her fingers along book spines.

"You're looking for something specific?" Eric asked.

"Yep. Aha! Here we go. Get this one."

She held up the book for Eric to see the cover, then plopped it on top of his stack. He pretended to stagger under the added weight.

"I've seen the movie." He twitched his chin in the direction of the book she'd picked out for him. In a lower voice he added, for Michelle's hearing only, "I cried at the ending."

"Seriously?" she asked, her heart melting at the thought of his sentimentality.

Eric nodded. "Every service person and vet in the place couldn't help but cry at that. Plus, you know me. I'm just a great big old crybaby."

"The book is always better than the movie," she informed him. "A lot more detail. I'll expect a summary from you when you finish it, and I'll get you a box of tissues when you read it."

"Can I cry on your shoulder?" The grin he showed her was a little crooked.

"Sure you can," she assured him. Why not? His shoulder had been her source of solace on more than one occasion. It would only be fair of her to offer the same. That's what friends were for, right?

But she couldn't be sure if he was serious or being his usual teasing self.

It took four shopping bags to accommodate their book purchases.

Three bags might have held the stash, but Eric leaned on the counter, smiled at the cashier, called her "Ma'am" and requested sweetly if she wouldn't mind terribly letting the kids each have their own bag for their books, emphasizing his faint southern accent as he did so.

Of course, seeing that smile, the cashier, despite appearing old enough to be Eric's grandmother, was more than happy to accommodate his request. She probably would have tossed in a dozen more books on her tab if he'd asked.

Michelle winced in pain when the total price for their purchase was revealed and glanced at Eric's face. He didn't have a stroke or even start to bleed from the ears. He just calmly inserted his credit card into the chip reader and signed the screen with the stylus, just as if dropping several hundred dollars on books was a normal, everyday event, as casually as if it were loose change found under the couch cushion.

The kids each carried their own bags, but Michelle was not at all surprised that Eric wouldn't let her carry either of the other two bags. He had to set one down on the pavement when they got to his car so that he could dig the clicker out of his pocket to pop the trunk and unlock the doors.

Tyler and Natalie dropped their bags into the trunk and let themselves into the back seat. As they buckled their seat belts, Michelle put a hand on Eric's arm as soon as he put the two heavy bags in and closed the trunk.

"Thank you, Eric," she said with sincerity. "And I don't just mean for buying me the books. Although that was pretty awesome, and I'm grateful. But," she hesitated, unfamiliar with this type of gratitude. "Thank you for being my friend, and my roommate, and for helping me to get out of that black hole of bitchiness I used to live in."

"Black hole of bitchiness?" he repeated with amusement. "You have such a way with words. It was my pleasure, ma'am." He held out his arms. "Remember what I said about thanking me properly later?"

It just seemed natural to step into his embrace and hug him, but this time without a stack of poky books between them.

Damn. He was just so utterly huggable. It was downright dangerous, the way he hugged her back and briefly let his cheek rest against her hair.

"You're cuddly too," he said, then stepped back and grinned at her.

He would have to remember, and mention, her half-asleep observation from the night of the alleged earthquake. But Eric wasn't half asleep and mumbling. He was very much awake and alert and standing right in front of her in the parking lot of Barnes and Noble, with Tyler and Natalie watching them through the rear window of his car.

Eric winked at her. Of course. He was just being his goofy self. He quickly stepped up and opened the door for her, then scurried around to the driver's door.

As Eric was buckling his seat belt, Tyler piped up.

"Uncle Eric?"

"What is it, dude?"

"Are you and Aunt Michelle going to get married?"

For a moment, silence reigned. Michelle could only look at her knees, unable to meet eyes with Eric, or Natalie, or especially with Tyler.

Fortunately, both Michelle and Eric were spared having to answer Tyler's question, as a grunt from the boy confirmed Natalie's elbow being jabbed into his arm again.

"You can't ask people things like that, nitwit! You have to wait until they tell you."

"Don't call your brother a nitwit," Eric scolded. "And quit poking him."

His discipline had conveniently allowed him to sidestep Tyler's awkward question. For the moment.

"But I want to know!" Tyler insisted, and looked at his sister. "They're going home in a little while. If they get married, I want to be a ring bearer. It was a lot of fun when I did it for Aunt Cecilia."

Michelle finally hazarded a glance in Eric's direction. He was grinning and raising his eyebrows in a way that said, *don't take the kid too seriously.*

"Cecilia is Gabriel's sister," Eric explained. "Tyler was the ring bearer at her wedding. He was really cute too."

They pulled out of the parking lot and turned towards Gabriel and Susan's house.

"Look guys," Eric said over his shoulder. "If anyone has anything important to tell you, they'll tell you, OK?"

His reassuring, but utterly vague response seemed to satisfy both youngsters and they desisted from further awkward questions or suggestions for the rest of the ride home.

31

∽

Susan's eyes goggled when they piled their shopping bags on the kitchen table.

"Did you leave anything on the shelves for anyone else to buy?"

"A little," Eric affirmed. "But I did clear The Children's Place out of all its baby outfits with ships on them." He handed her the bag. "Now little Cameron will be the best-dressed baby in town, at least for the first nine months."

Tyler and Natalie were unpacking their shopping bags and competing for their mom's attention as they both said, "Look what Uncle Eric got me!"

Susan looked at the baby clothes, the video games, the books. "You shouldn't have, Eric," she said, and her eyes misted. "You're such a silly goose." She wiped her eyes and glanced at Michelle apologetically. "Sorry, pregnancy hormones."

Eric was tapping at his chest proudly, smirking at Michelle.

"See? Not only am I the best, I'm a silly goose too." He made it sound as if being called a silly goose was something to be proud of, then looked back at Susan, mooning over the baby clothes. "Michelle prefers the term Goof."

"That's a good one," Susan agreed. "But I think I'll stick with Silly Goose and let you keep Goof all to yourself." She squeezed Michelle's arm briefly and gave her a knowing smile.

Michelle had no idea what to think of that.

373

"You spoil them too much," Susan chastised Eric, but she said it with a smile.

"Hey, that's what uncles are for. I mean, look at those little faces. How can I not spoil them?"

The kids scampered to Tyler's room to start playing their new video games, Natalie's poking and name-calling of her brother apparently forgotten.

"What's all this?" Susan asked, peeking into the large, heavy bookstore bags.

"Those are Michelle's," Eric informed her. Susan's eyes widened at the sheer number of books. She looked at Michelle, who shrugged a little.

"Look what Uncle Eric got me," she repeated.

"Uncle?" Susan questioned. "Oh, I don't think so."

"She likes to read," Eric added, a bit unnecessarily. Then he switched his gaze from Susan to Michelle. His smile was warm. "I hope you read the one with the purple fire-breathing dragon on the cover first. I want to hear all about that one."

"Anything for you, sweetheart," she replied, caught up in his joking.

Oops! Did she just say that, out loud? Eric's big mouth syndrome was positively contagious.

Susan was smiling knowingly.

"They're not all hers," Eric said. "I got a book too."

A very skeptical look crossed Susan's face.

"Yeah, right. You, reading a book? I doubt that."

"I'm serious!" Eric declared, rummaging through the bags until he came up with the copy of *American Sniper* that Michelle had picked out for him. "I can't wait to read it."

"Didn't you see the movie?" Susan asked.

"Yeah, but there's always more detail in the book." He looked at Michelle and made a small serious mouth, and she caught just the tiniest shake of his head.

Don't say anything about what I told you about crying at that movie, his expression said.

Wow, that was – touching. Another personal secret he was trusting her with. This may be the twenty-first century, but despite that, the man didn't want his sentimentality to become public knowledge, not even to his best friends. And yet he trusted her, Michelle, with the information.

That was almost relationship-like.

Just then Gabriel breezed into the kitchen, pulling a tee shirt over his head. Michelle laughed when she saw the words printed on it.

"My best friend joined the Navy and all I got was this shirt."

"I can't believe that still fits you," Eric said with a grin.

Gabriel winked at Michelle and said, "Dude gave this to me for my birthday right after he enlisted. Back in the Dark Ages."

"Your family is really into giving each other silly shirts," Michelle observed, thinking about Eric's bucking bronco, ride a cowboy shirt.

"He's still upset he couldn't talk me into enlisting with him," Gabriel said. "Although I came close to it, just to get him to shut up."

"You could have seen the world," Eric told his friend.

"I don't need to sail around on a ship to see the world," Gabriel replied. "I can see it right here."

He put a possessive arm around his wife and unborn child, laying a hand on Susan's tummy.

Eric grinned at Gabriel's teasing, but also glanced at his friend's baby bump under its dad's affectionate hand.

Again, Michelle noticed the tiny flicker of jealousy that momentarily interrupted Eric's smile as he observed his friend caress his wife's lush mound of fertility. Not jealousy over Susan herself – Michelle completely believed Susan's assertion that she and Eric were like brother and sister. But since she'd known Eric she'd come to recognize a lot of his facial expressions, and she was certain that what she had just witnessed was a tiny spot of envy that his best friend had a family and Eric didn't.

But he shook the revealing expression off quickly and turned to Susan. "Speaking of your world," he said. "You might want to have a little talk with Natalie. I hate to rat the kid out, but she suggested giving the little dude up for adoption in order to maintain the gender ratio in the family."

"Who did she try to adopt him out to this time?" Surprisingly, neither

Gabriel nor Susan seemed terribly concerned at their daughter's effort to get rid of her future little brother.

Eric grinned, and to Michelle's complete and utter astonishment, he put his arm around her shoulders and drew her close, so that she was standing right next to him.

It was everything she could do to restrain herself from burying her nose in the soft cotton freshness of his shirt.

"Us," he said. Just as if there was an 'us.' "I'm really flattered at the offer, of course," he continued, as Michelle stood there in stunned silence. "And I'm sure Michelle is too, but of course I had to decline the honor."

"I'll talk to her," Susan said. "But I wouldn't worry too much about it. Last week she was negotiating a trade with the Nakamura family across the street, because they're expecting a girl. When Mrs. Nakamura told me about it, we decided to call her bluff and told Natalie that we were thinking of making the deal. She got all upset and said that I couldn't trade away our family's baby. Her feelings about it tend to shift with her mood. The joys of living with a pre-adolescent girl. Between that and me," she rubbed her tummy again, "I'm surprised Gabriel hasn't run screaming for the hills."

"Never," her husband assured her, then gave a nod to Eric. "We'd better head out, dude. I like to get the bird all tucked into bed before dark."

Although it only took five minutes to gather up their weekend bags and shopping bags, it took an additional fifteen to conclude hugs, kisses, offers to come visit again and other assorted goodbyes between Eric, Michelle, Susan and the kids. She was utterly touched at them all treating her with such familial affection, as if she were a member of the family.

Eric leaned down and kissed Susan's tummy, saying, "See you later, little dude. Call me when you're ready to come out and play."

32

Gabriel sat in the front seat with Eric on the way back to the heliport, so that the two men could continue their apparently ongoing debate as to who would win in a fight, The Hulk or Thor. By the time they arrived, the consensus was Thor. Michelle sat in the back looking at her phone and swiping through the photos she'd taken this weekend. Her favorite was the one that she'd taken of Eric waiting for her outside the Navy recruiting tent, with that sweet, wistful smile on his face.

She tapped the Settings button and with a few pokes at the menu, made it her wallpaper photo.

When they arrived back at the heliport, Gabriel didn't bother inviting either Eric or Michelle to sit in the front and help him fly the bird. He just opened the door and smiled knowingly as they settled into the two rear seats.

This time, she was not scared. What a baby she had been the first time! How often does one have the opportunity to fly over a beautiful place like the California coast, in the company of such good friends? She should be grateful, and enjoy the experience, rather than twitching and swearing like some kind of coward.

This time, she buckled her own seat belt, found her headset hanging on the hook, and put it on all by herself, like a big girl. She didn't go into a panic when Gabriel teased that the weight of their shopping bags full of books might prohibit the bird from taking off, she didn't need to stare

377

at the ground or at the horizon, and she didn't swear like a sailor, despite Eric's approval of it.

As the bird lifted off and they became airborne, she reached over and took Eric's hand, just like he had done at the air show. Automatically, he twined his long fingers with hers and looked at her quickly, with a slightly puzzled smile.

"Are you OK, sweetheart?"

"Yeah, I'm OK. This is going to be fun."

A brief sound came to her through the headset – Gabriel's voice, just a brief peep, a little voice of "hmmm."

She made Eric hold her hand the rest of the flight back to Catalina, and he obliged her for the entire time as she looked out the window and actually enjoyed the scenery this time. Her stomach remained right where it should be, but her heart, well that was another situation entirely. Her heart seemed to be skipping around like a kid chasing butterflies, as Eric smiled at her and glanced down at their clasped hands. She wasn't sure if he was deceived into thinking she still needed his professional reassurance, but she took the chance.

She was positive Gabriel wasn't deceived, as he glanced back and caught her eye momentarily as they took off, and winked at her.

When they landed, Gabriel hugged Eric, whispered something in his ear, then they bumped fists enthusiastically in farewell. As Eric picked up their overnight bags and walked towards the golf cart, Gabriel enveloped Michelle in a big, brotherly hug, kissed her cheek and whispered in her ear too. "You take good care of my dude now, pretty lady."

Take care of him? What did he mean by that? She kissed his cheek in return, thanking him for everything, but not really responding to his instruction to "take care" of Eric. He and Susan were such hopeless romantics.

She held her new Navy cap firmly in her hand as they waved and watched him take off, and the draft from the rotating blades washed over them. She'd be devastated if the cap got loose and blew away from her, and placed it firmly back on her head once the helicopter was airborne. Eric watched her and grinned, saying, "Looks good on you."

She dug the golf cart key out of her pocket - and handed it to Eric. He reached out automatically, but hesitated before actually taking it, placing a disbelieving hand on his chest.

"You're letting me drive your golf cart? Are you sure? Is this real, or am I dreaming?"

"Oh, stop it, goof," she said. "If you can handle the freeway in San Diego without killing anyone, you can handle a golf cart in Avalon."

He grinned. "I am truly honored, ma'am," he said, finally accepting the keys. Just before he sat in the driver's seat, he looked at her quizzically. "You're sure, now?"

She sat firmly in the passenger seat. "I'm sure. Do you need me to take down the pink beads? Are they too girly for you to be seen driving my cart?"

"No, don't take them down. I love those beads. I just never thought I'd actually be deemed worthy of driving this thing. It's like having Thor hand me his hammer. I shall make every effort to do you proud and not run into anyone."

"You have good reflexes, remember? If any idiotic girls in hoodies step out in front of you, I'm sure you'll be able to stop in time."

He finally sat down in the driver's seat, looked around wonderingly, then smiled at her. "I never thought you were idiotic."

"Then you would be wrong. Sometimes I think I've been the world's biggest idiot. I mean, look at how I acted last year, running around like a crazy person, like that would fix things. I'm really lucky that you were the one I crashed into, and that you saved me from my idiocy."

Eric started up the golf cart before looking back to her with one of his special smiles.

"Yes," she said. "I am thanking you for saving my life, both literally and emotionally."

"You're welcome," he replied. "It was entirely my pleasure. But you know, I think you're being too hard on yourself again. You are an amazing person. A lot of kids who didn't have good parental supervision would have ended up drinking, doing drugs, being promiscuous. Not getting straight A's and having a valid, skilled career. A lot of kids would have booked on down the road when they reached adulthood, rather than staying and taking care of their incapable parent. I knew several people who joined the service mainly to get away from an unpleasant situation at home. But you didn't do any of those things, you didn't bail on your dad. Although you would have been an asset to the Navy or any other service branch if you had enlisted."

Freya, this man was just too nice for words. She tried to lighten the mood with a joke.

"I could never have gone into the military. They would make me cut off my hair."

He grinned. "Yeah, well there is that."

As they pulled out of the parking lot and onto Pebbly Beach Road, she said, "You're just a great big old softie, aren't you?"

"Uh oh, my cover is blown."

"I saw you slipping money to those kids. And after buying them all that stuff too."

He managed to grin and shrug at the same time, giving her a quick guilty glance before returning his eyes to the road.

"Hey, kids have got to have ice cream, right?"

"Or maybe save up for flying lessons."

"You noticed the posters, did you?"

"Impossible not to. I felt like I was sleeping on the deck of an aircraft carrier."

Eric shook his head. "Sweetheart, I have been on the deck of an aircraft carrier. Trust me, nobody has ever slept there."

"Maybe she'll fly for the Blue Angels someday," Michelle suggested.

Eric smiled broadly. "Wouldn't that make me the proudest godfather ever!"

"You're Natalie's godfather? I thought you weren't much for religion."

"I'm not. But me and Gabriel, well, we've been tight since we were kids, and we always promised each other we'd be godfather to each other's firstborn." He paused for a moment, and she thought she saw a momentary flicker of sadness cross his face. "Gabriel's still waiting."

"You know that girl has a great big old crush on you," she told him.

"All the eleven-year-old girls have crushes on me. I'm a real catch."

She looked at his profile and thought, *some grown-up girls have crushes on you too.*

"So, did you have a good time? Other than the helicopter ride? I wish I'd known you'd never flown before. I could have prepared you."

"Prepared me? What am I, a gourmet meal?"

"Are you getting bitchy on me? I like it."

She looked out from her side of the cart, at the boulders along the side of the road. "I didn't want you to think I was some kind of country bumpkin."

"I would never think that," Eric assured her.

"Actually, I had a wonderful time," she assured him. "Even the helicopter flight, once I got used to it. Those planes at the air show were awesome. And the Blue Angels were amazing. In fact, I'm thinking of taking some training and changing my focus from boat engines to planes." She gestured towards the mountain where the Airport in the Sky served small planes. "Besides, the restaurant up there serves killer buffalo tacos."

He showed her a brief "I told you so" smile as they rounded a curve in the road.

"You knew that was going to happen, didn't you?" she asked, thinking about the jet roaring over their head at the conclusion to the air show.

Eric laughed outright. "Did I tell you that I grew up ten miles from their home base? We used to sit on the beach and watch them practice. You should have seen your face! I thought I was going to die on the spot."

Actually, he'd been thrilled at the way she'd flung herself into his lap when the jet roared over their heads.

"Tyler was really eager to pull your finger."

"The kid is obsessed with flatulence."

"Did you really...?"

"Fart on command? Let's just say it was a good thing I'd had beans with my lunch that day. But don't you worry, it's not something I do on a regular basis."

"That's a relief," she said with a smile. "But Susan didn't really put you in a time out, did she?"

"Sure did. Nose in the corner. Longest five minutes of my life."

"You're not serious."

"Absolutely," he assured her. "Gotta set a good example for the kids."

Michelle decided not to point out that if he'd really wanted to set a good example for Tyler, he wouldn't have gone along with the whole "Pull my finger" thing in the first place. She had to smile at the hysterical mental image she conjured up of Eric standing with his nose in the corner, hands behind his back, stifling giggles and sneaking glances back at the kids when Susan wasn't looking.

"I hope Tyler and Natalie didn't make you uncomfortable with their talk about babies. You know kids at that age have not yet learned to filter what they say. They just blurt things out without thinking sometimes."

"I wonder where they learned that from?" she asked, giving him a teasing look, and he grinned back.

"Did you ever want to be a pilot?" she asked, wanting to steer the conversation away from babies, both real and theoretical.

"No way. I'm more into blood and guts than G forces."

"How can you do that? Be a first responder? Having to be the first one to deal with blood and guts and injuries and stuff?"

He smiled, and even though he was watching the road, she could still see his eyes gleam with passion.

"Well, it started that day when I was in the ER and found out about my alcohol allergy. When they were doing stuff like inserting the IV and taking a blood sample, my parents kept telling me I didn't have to look. But even though I was sick and rashy and scared, I was still fascinated by the whole procedure, and I couldn't not watch. That was when I decided I was going to do something in the medical field. I'd actually considered nursing school, but I'd already decided I wanted to enlist in the Navy too. So, corpsman training was the perfect option. Even though my recruiter warned me I'd probably spend some time assigned to the green side, with the Marines, at a Marine facility, and I was. That's how I ended up in Iraq, and A-stan. It was kind of ironic, having my medical kit in one hand there and an M16 in the other.

"It's not just blood and guts. It's some real person's blood and guts, someone who's in pain, and scared, maybe afraid they might die. Having the ability, the knowledge, to help someone feel better, to heal, to live – well, it's the most awesome feeling you can ever imagine. Well, maybe not, you know, sex awesome, but still, pretty darn awesome." He glanced at her with a brief gleaming smile as they rounded the curve of Abalone Point, with the cliff face on their left and the water on their right.

"Is that TMI?" he asked, seeing that she'd twitched a little at his use of the phrase 'sex awesome'. "It may not be glamorous to pull bleeding people from cars, but it makes you feel like a million bucks, seriously, there is no more amazing feeling in this world than saving someone's life or delivering a baby. It may sound corny, but I love to feel like I'm making a positive contribution to society."

She was fascinated by his obvious passion for what he did.

"And, of course, it's pretty cool that we're just about the only guys in town who get to drive over twenty-five miles per hour when we light up the ambulance.

"I'm sorry you were scared flying over there. I never considered that it might be your first experience flying."

"That's OK," she assured him. "It was a bit terrifying at first, but I knew you wouldn't let anything happen to me."

He grinned. "You know, Gabriel had something to do with it too. It was his skills keeping our asses out of the water."

"Yeah, Gabriel is a sweetheart. I can see why he's your friend." Then she asked, "Tell me, what's the most scared you've ever been? The first time you flew?"

She thought about that information she'd Googled months ago about the experiences of Navy corpsmen, but Eric appeared to gloss right over that.

He put a finger to the side of his head as if thinking deep thoughts. "Well, let's see. The first time I saw a great white shark while diving." (The FIRST time? Did that mean there'd been a second time?) "No, wait, right before I did my first parachute jump." (Again, with the 'first time'.) To her, that definitely qualified as extremely scary.

"Do you mean to tell me that as a Navy corpsman you had to dive with sharks and jump out of airplanes?" she asked incredulously.

"Nah, I did those for fun." He waved his hand in an erasing motion. "No, no that's not it. The scariest moment of my life was the first time I had to give injections to a squad of Marines."

"Oh, come on, that can't be scarier than jumping out of an airplane."

"Are you kidding? They were Force Recon. That's the Marines' equivalent of the SEALs. They eat insects like me for breakfast and spit out the bones like an owl. I swear the first one growled at me like Beast from the X Men."

"But you obviously survived."

"Yeah, I manned up and a whole squad of Marines got inoculated against anthrax."

He remembered the day, age nineteen and about five minutes out of A school, when he'd been assigned to administer routine pre-deployment inoculations to the six biggest, most badass Marines he'd ever laid eyes on. He'd figuratively, if not literally, shook in his boots at the prospect of jabbing a needle into testosterone-overdosed real live human beings, rather than the oranges and mannequins he'd trained on. Guys who outweighed him by forty pounds, and Eric was no lightweight. And it was all muscle, not a gram of fat. With a hypodermic in one gloved hand and an antiseptic swab in the other, he'd somehow managed to produce the cool, calm, *yes I am a medical professional* voice required as he requested, "If you could please roll up your sleeve, Sir."

After a moment of a *you puny insect* glare, the Marine, rather than rolling up his sleeve, had stood up and removed his blouse, under which he wore a sleeveless tee shirt, Marine green of course, to reveal a bicep that looked to be almost as big around as Eric's thigh. Eric had been eternally grateful that the placement of the injection hadn't disturbed the barbed wire tattoo encircling that massive bicep. The tattoo artist had probably had to go out and buy more ink just to complete it.

After finishing with the group, the first Marine, who to this day Eric still thought of as Lieutenant Growls Like Beast, had come over, given him a friendly slap on the arm, and said, "You did good, Squid."

He'd kept that experience as a tool to be used later, when needing to give injections or insert IVs into guys who were bleeding, puking, convulsing, crying for their mamas, or combinations thereof. It was only later that he'd found out that the senior corpsmen always recruited the biggest, most intimidating Marines or SEALs they could find in line for inoculations to "indoctrinate" the rookies, and that they'd been pre-briefed to breathe fire and look scary. Later, when Eric became the senior, he'd reached out to former Lieutenant, now Colonel Growls Like Beast for help in recruiting suitable first patients for the newest crop of rookie corpsmen.

"Can I ask you something personal?" he inquired.

"Sure you can."

"Why don't you date?"

That was the last thing she had expected him to ask.

"A smart, charming, beautiful girl like you, I should think guys would be lining up for the chance to spend time with you."

She turned her head away from him so he wouldn't see that she was literally biting her tongue. She'd been asked out several times the past year. Her old high school date Justin had even suggested they "give it another go", as he'd put it, not long after his unpleasant encounter with Eric on the dock. The owners of the boats she worked on flirted with her on a regular basis. She'd even been asked out by another woman, a tourist from Long Beach, and hadn't that been awkward.

She had declined them all.

And why? Because none of them were Eric. It was pathetic, really, how she yearned for a man who only thought of her as a friend. She didn't date because Eric hadn't asked her. They went out all the time, including this weekend together on the mainland. It had been the most fun she'd ever had, but it wasn't a date. None of them were dates. They were just hanging out as friends, as buddies, despite the incorrect assumptions made by Gabriel, Susan, Danny Gonzalez and Tracy.

She hated to deceive Eric about why she hadn't dated. But she'd hate even more to admit the truth to him and have him decline her.

So she told him a little white lie. Well, no, it wasn't a lie. Just an alternative answer.

"I really have you fooled," she told him. He glanced at her with a question in his eyes. "Charming? Guys lining up to date me? Hardly. I have a reputation in this town, and it's not a nice one."

He went a bit white about the lips as he slowly asked. "A reputation?"

"Not that kind of reputation. More of a rep as a bitch. And a brawler."

"A brawler? As in fisticuffs?" The look of concern was replaced with amusement.

"Yeah, I got into a lot of fights in middle school and high school. Some of my former classmates still avoid me because of it."

Eric looked disbelieving. "I'm really having trouble wrapping my head around you, Miss Straight A, getting into fights."

"Well, I got good grades, but I never got a good conduct award."

"I did," he told her. "A couple in fact. They're fun. You actually got into fistfights with other girls in school? I wish I could have seen that."

"And boys too. Mostly boys."

Eric scowled. "You mean boys you knew in school hit you? Do they still live in Avalon? I think I need to take some names and kick some ass. What about that guy from the boat dock? I knew I should have punched his lights out instead of just tossing him in the water."

"Oh I always threw the first punch. Since most of the guys I had to fight were bigger than me, I used the element of surprise to my advantage."

"You had to fight? You were obligated?" She could see the curiosity in his eyes.

"Yes." She looked out at the weekend tourists lining up at the boat dock as they drove by. "Sometimes, well a lot of times, kids at school would say things I didn't want to hear. Things about my dad and him being a drunk and how he'd been found more than once passed out in public, and what a loser he was. And by extension, that made me a loser too.

I know it was all true, but still, that didn't mean they could say it, right? Just because my dad really was a drunk, didn't give them the right to say it. So I'd tell them to shut up and take it back, and usually whoever it was would look down their nose at me, like I was dirt under their feet, and say stuff like, make me. So, I'd make them, or at least I tried. I thought if I got in there first, with a punch in the belly, or the nose if the guy wasn't too tall, or a knee in the crotch-" She saw Eric wince in imagined pain at that. "That it would make them apologize and take it back. But it never did. All it got me was trips to the principal's office and a couple of suspensions. I never heard one apology. I got into a couple of fights with girls too for the same reason. I was an equal opportunity brawling bitch."

Eric slowed down for a moment behind a slow-moving taxi – what passed for a traffic jam in Avalon – and glanced at her with sympathy in his eyes.

"I'm sorry you had to experience that, sweetheart. Kids can be really cruel sometimes. What about Justin Douchebag? Did you ever beat him up? I'm sure he deserved it."

Eric's obsession with her relationship with Justin was starting to get funny. But what she found absolutely amazing was that his simple expression of sympathy, just that one sentence, *I'm sorry you had to experience that,* comforted her more than any other sympathetic expression ever could.

"No. Justin was a jerk but he never said anything about my dad. He just tried to get me to drink with him the one time we went out, which is why there was never a second date. But one time when I got into a fight with a girl in my math class, he stood there watching and yelling, 'Girl fight! Girl fight! Pull her hair!' I was real close to just shoving that girl aside and giving Justin a punch instead, but then the principal showed up and broke it up, marched me into the office and called my dad. Who, of course, couldn't be bothered to come over to the school and take me home when I got suspended again. After leaving him two voice mails, the principal finally said, 'Just go, and don't let this happen again' like he usually did. I finally realized that I wasn't accomplishing anything like that so

I quit the fighting before I got arrested, and just tried to ignore those stupid kids."

"What about your friend Tracy? Did she ever say anything to you? She seems like a good friend, kind of the yin to your yang."

"Oh, Tracy never said anything about Dad. In fact, that last time I was in the principal's office, she cut her last class of the day and waited for me outside the school when I left and we went over to her house. In fact, it was her idea that I just ignore the jerks instead of trying to fight them. So we spent the rest of the afternoon doing our nails and hair. She had some new boxes of hair coloring she'd gotten the last time she'd gone shopping on the mainland. Her idea of fixing a bad situation is a new hair color."

"I noticed that," Eric replied. "What is her natural color?"

"I have no idea. I've never seen it, and I've known her since ninth grade." She couldn't help but run a hand down her own hair, and Eric noticed the gesture, and gave her a slightly scolding look.

"Is that when you dyed your hair purple?"

His disapproval made her smile, and let go a little of the bad memories of her adolescent altercations.

"Well, yeah. But after it faded out, I never bothered to do it again. That didn't change anything either."

"You were just trying to push your dad's buttons with the hair color, right?"

Sometimes her roommate was just a bit too perceptive.

"I just wanted him to notice me." She was glad, now that she'd asked Eric to drive, so that she could look away and squeeze her eyes for a moment. She looked back at Eric when she felt him pat her hand, and she couldn't help turning her palm up and curling her fingers around his. He squeezed briefly before putting both hands back on the wheel. But that little hand squeeze spoke volumes. It said, I care, I'm here, I'm your friend, you're not alone.

How had she ever managed to muddle through her whole cosmic existence before he'd come into her life?

"It was his loss," he said softly.

"I bet your parents came to every parent/teacher conference and every school event," she said. "My dad didn't. He couldn't even be bothered to come to the school when I was in the principal's office for fighting. The only time he set foot in the place was for the graduation ceremony."

"I did end up in the principal's office for getting into a fight once, in middle school," Eric said.

"I don't believe that. You, fighting? I'm not buying it."

"I did, really," he assured her. "I was in the seventh grade, so I was thirteen. My niece Joanna was in the eighth grade in the same school."

"Your niece was a year older than you?"

"Yeah, I told you I was an uncle before I was born, Well, Joanna was having some trouble with some guys in her class who were following her around school giving her a hard time about her, um, figure. See, she had, shall we say, developed her femininity a bit more than most other girls her age."

"Are you trying to say, without actually saying it, that she had big boobs?"

Eric nodded. "Yes, exactly. I was trying not to say it. They didn't do anything for me of course, because she was my niece, and because I was barely thirteen and at that age, I still thought girls had cooties. But the crude things those other guys were saying to her really pissed me off, so one day between classes when I saw her run into the girl's bathroom crying, I went right up to the guy who'd been harassing her and told him to quit it and leave her alone. I told him to pick on someone his own size, and he made a crude hand gesture about size. So I called him dick breath."

"Wait," she had to interrupt. "You were thirteen and you called your adversary dick breath? Let me guess, you threatened to sic the SEALs on him?"

"I'll tell you a little secret, sweetheart. The boy's middle school locker room is an educational institution all in itself. Unfortunately, even though we lived near Pensacola, I didn't know any SEALs at that age. The guy just laughed at me, especially when I told him I was Joanna's uncle, and made another unrepeatable remark about her. I was kind of scared, because he was bigger than me. I hadn't hit my adult growth spurt yet, and he looked like he had. But still, he refused to apologize to Joanna, so

I hauled off and punched him in the gut. He was pretty surprised, but he hit me back, and the next thing we knew, we were on the floor bloodying each other's noses. Even though I had anger on my side, still this guy was a football player or something and I was starting to feel like I was going to get the snot beat out of me, when a couple of teachers broke it up and hauled us both to the office and called our parents."

She wondered if either of Eric's parents had come down to the school to retrieve him and perhaps even punish him for fighting. His next words confirmed it, and she was jealous.

"The whole drive home from school, my mom and dad kept telling me that violence was never an answer and that even if the other guy had been rude and malicious, it wasn't the right thing to do to start a fight and that it wouldn't solve anything, and they hoped they'd never have to come to pick me up for that reason again. Of course, I blamed the whole thing on the other guy for what he'd said about my niece but that didn't seem to be a justification, at least not to my parents. When we got home they sent me to my room, and I was afraid I was going to get grounded. But about a half hour later, my brother Phillip walks in. He's Joanna's dad. He sits down and pretty much gives me the same speech I'd gotten from Mom and Dad, but then he got up and closed the bedroom door. I really started to get nervous, thinking maybe he was going to spank me or something."

"Did you get spanked a lot?" she asked.

Eric looked shocked at the notion.

"No, never. Instead, he gave me a high five, a big hug and said, don't tell your parents I said this, but, good on you, kid! You are The Man and what you did took real guts. Then he told me to go out to the back yard because Joanna wanted to talk to me too. When I went out there she gave me a hug too, and said I was her hero and if we weren't related, she'd want to marry me. Then she kissed me. It was the first time I ever kissed a girl."

Michelle was laughing by now. "Do you mean to say that you had your first kiss - and it was a relative?"

He looked defensive. "Hey, it was just a little kiss. No tongue or anything. And even if she hadn't been family, I would have been nervous about kissing a girl at that age. I had braces, remember, and I was paranoid about hurting someone with them. I had to get the metal kind, not those invisible plastic braces. But I was glad that she, and Phillip, didn't think I was some kind of bully for starting the fight. But of course, my parents were right, fighting never solves anything."

"You got that right," Michelle muttered.

"Oh, and when Phillip and Joanna left to go home, he had me walk out to the car with him, and offered to take me to the gym and show me how to lift weights. He said maybe if I got into better shape and wasn't such a scrawny thing, which I was at the time, I wouldn't have to fight because the bullies wouldn't want to take a chance on someone who looked like they might win. So we started going to the gym together three times a week, every week, until the day I left for boot camp, and well, the rest is history."

Michelle smiled at him. *And thank you, Eric's brother Phillip for starting you on the path to developing that sexy body,* was the thought that came unbidden to her mind.

"If you got straight A's in high school, weren't you the class valedictorian?" Eric asked.

"No. There was another kid with the same GPA who never got into fights, so he was the valedictorian. Good thing too. He had to give a speech at the ceremony." She shuddered. "I could never do that."

"Can I tell you something personal, without you going all Chewbacca on me?" she asked.

"Of course you can, sweetheart. You can tell me anything you want. I'm all ears."

"You're the best friend I ever had."

His smile held the warmth of a kid who'd just unwrapped the hottest new toy on Christmas morning. "Thanks. That really warms my heart to hear you say that. Same goes for me, by the way."

He couldn't be serious. "Are you saying, you think I'm your best friend? What about Gabriel?"

Eric winked at her. "Don't tell him but yeah, he's fallen to number two."

Happiness sparkled inside her, like a caffeine buzz.

They had turned up Clarissa Avenue, but instead of continuing up the hill towards Tremont Street, he turned back towards Crescent Avenue.

"Let's stop for dinner, OK?" he asked. "I'm starving."

"Sure, on one condition."

"Conditions? You're giving me conditions on whether or not we eat dinner?"

"Yes. You have to let me pay this time."

"You don't have to do that."

"Yes I do. You paid for everything this whole weekend. And it must have cost Gabriel a lot in fuel to fly us there and back."

"I'll tell you a secret – he can deduct it as a business expense."

"You paid for everything at the air show."

"Admission was free you know."

"Yeah but you bought me lunch, got me that cool hat, and even bought me a churro."

"I love those things," Eric said with a grin, "even if they are just a big stick of empty calories. I'm going to have to do some extra crunches when we get home after having two of them."

"You mean two and a half," she reminded him.

"Hey, I wasn't about to let a perfectly good churro go to waste just because you couldn't finish yours. And I'll tell you another secret – the guy at the Navy recruiting tent gave me the hat when I told him I'd served on the Nimitz."

"And you bought pizza for all of us last night, and even made a separate stop to get that salad for Susan."

"Pizza always gives her heartburn when she's pregnant. Most expecting women have trouble handling anything spicy."

"You seem to know a lot about pregnancy. Did they teach you about it in corpsman training?"

"Not really. But with a family as big as mine, there's always someone expecting. Every time I get back to Florida for a visit, I'm always surrounded by ladies with morning sickness, swollen feet and BWS."

"BWS? Is that a medical term?"

"Yeah, it stands for Beached Whale Syndrome. A common complaint among women in their third trimester."

Michelle chuckled. "Between all that, and those books, which I should not have let you pay for, it's only fair that I pay for dinner. In fact, I insist."

Eric grinned and responded, "Yes, Ma'am."

They parked the golf cart on Metropole Avenue, stashed their bags under the back seat, and walked across to Antonio's Pizzeria. They were able to get a table outside on the patio right away. Being Sunday evening, most of the weekend tourists were heading down to the dock to board their boats back to the mainland.

Eric's eyes lit up as they sat down.

"Hey, they're having karaoke here tonight!"

She pointed a finger at his nose.

"No. Just no."

He pouted but turned his eyes away from the small stage inside the restaurant and looked at the menu. Once the waiter had taken their order, he looked at her with a smile.

"Can I tell you something, without you going all Chewbacca on me?"

She nodded. She wanted to call him sweetheart, the way he always did when he talked to her, but the word didn't slide easily off her lips the way it did for Eric. She tried not to take it too seriously when he used it, realizing that it was just his friendly nature to use that term to most people he talked to, not just to her.

"I think you really need to talk to a shrink," he said. "Not that I think you're crazy or anything! But I think it would help you deal with some of your issues from your past. My shrink works for the V.A., but I'm sure she can recommend a civilian for you."

"I don't need a shrink. I have you." Seriously, she couldn't talk about her issues with a stranger, no matter how professional. But she had no hesitation in talking about them to Eric.

Sometimes she was afraid she talked too much to Eric, because she hadn't had anyone to talk to before. But he never seemed to mind. And he didn't press or nag her at her rejection of his suggestion to talk to a professional. He actually laid an affectionate hand briefly on her cheek.

"That's what I love about you, sweetheart. You always see the best in me."

She smiled at him, but then his fingers twitched towards the bill when the waiter laid it on the table, and she snatched it away, reminding him of her intention to pay this time. And like a gentleman, he smiled and said thank you.

******

Eric was yawning when they walked into the house, though he did follow her into the kitchen as she put her to-go box from the restaurant into the refrigerator. Her eyes had apparently been bigger than her stomach.

"Are you working tomorrow?" she asked him.

"Yep. I'm on shift at 6:00 a.m."

"Yikes, that is inhuman. Do you want to take this for lunch?" She indicated the restaurant box just before she closed the fridge door.

"Wow. You let me drive your golf cart, you're giving me your leftover lasagna, and you held hands with me. Does this mean we're going steady?"

She laughed at him. "Yes, goof, we're going steady."

She laughed on the outside, but on the inside, she seriously thought, *If only.*

Eric grinned and went into the bathroom to brush his teeth while she locked the doors and turned off the lights. When he came out of the bathroom, she was waiting her turn.

"Thanks for coming with me this weekend," he said.

He put his hand on her arm.

Oh *Freya*, was he going to kiss her?

He leaned in a little, into her personal space. She could smell his warm skin, with a faint fragrance of coconut scented sunblock. "It was a lot of fun."

OMG, he was going to kiss her. Her mouth went dry and her heart kicked up a notch.

"In fact, you being there made it really special."

Her pulse started to skitter like a rabbit on speed.

He kissed her.

On the cheek. Barely touching her skin. Exactly the way he'd done before. Just like he would kiss his sister.

"Good night," he said. "I'll try to be quiet in the morning when I leave for work." And then his bedroom door closed behind him and she had to lean again the wall for a moment to regain her equilibrium.

Sometimes she wished that Eric Hanson wasn't so much of a gentleman.

******

Michelle lay sleepless on her bed, thinking about her roommate on the other side of the wall. Was he sleeping? Or was he lying awake too? Did he think about her?

Of course, he did. He'd think about her on the first of the month when the rent was due. He'd think about her when the utility bills came and he paid his half. He'd think about her when she was in the bathroom and he needed to pee like a racehorse. He'd think about her when her laundry was in the washer and he needed to wash his skivvies.

But then, he also thought about her at the grocery store when he texted her for requests. He'd thought about her when he left for reserve duty and sent her a picture so she'd remember him. He thought about her when he made her coffee in the morning, and cooked her a steak on his day off, and included her in the group when he hung out with his friends. He'd thought about her when he bought her a huge, expensive stack of books that she shouldn't have let him buy.

But, did he think about her when he lay awake in his bed?

Her first instinct, her gut reaction when he had first moved into her house, had been to think he didn't understand, that he couldn't possibly understand how she felt, her personal anxiety about her whole cosmic existence. He'd led an entirely different type of life than she had, with a different family dynamic and life experience. He'd grown up in a happy, loving and supportive family. How could he possibly understand her, whose experiences had been just the opposite?

And yet, he did understand her and how she felt. Somehow, he got it, even though he hadn't lived it himself. His sympathy and empathy at her lack of parenting were genuine and he never made her feel like a pathetic loser.

He had a childlike appreciation for ice cream, and she encouraged it, just so she could watch his mouth and tongue when he licked it. Once they'd been sitting on a bench along Crescent Avenue with chocolate cones, like a pair of tourists, and she had accidentally bumped his arm so that he ended up with ice cream on his nose. His perfect, straight, slender nose that she knew had the tiniest bump on the cartilage from being broken years ago.

Michelle had felt jealousy towards the napkin he used to wipe it off, because she had a sudden, lustful urge to stand up, straddle his lap and lick that dollop of ice cream right off the tip of that perfect nose, and see if she could feel the tiny bump on the cartilage with her tongue.

Sometimes she found herself arguing with him, not because she actually disagreed, but more to have an excuse to watch his mouth when he talked.

Eric Hanson, she thought, *you are a unique and special human being. Why hadn't some girl snapped you up long ago?*

33

When Eric got home from work the next evening, Michelle was in the bathroom. He sat in the kitchen drinking a glass of water and thinking about what to have for dinner, and trying not to dwell on the image of his roommate naked in the shower on the other side of the wall.

When the shower sound stopped he decided that he needed to get something from his room – what he couldn't tell you – so that he was in the hall when she emerged, wrapped in that fluffy pink robe, toweling her hair and smelling so sweetly delicious he had to restrain himself from pressing his nose to the soft skin of her neck.

"Hey," he said with mock casualness. "What do you want to eat tonight?"

She stepped away from him, towards her bedroom door, still rubbing the towel down her hair. Eric was suddenly, insanely jealous of that towel and wondered if maybe she would let him comb out her hair for her again. *Please please pretty please.*

"I won't be home for dinner," she said. "I'm going out."

"Out?" he repeated stupidly, as if he didn't understand the word.

"I have a date."

"A date?" Jeez, he was turning into a damn parrot.

"Yes, a date," she replied. "You know, where two people go out and do something together. You mentioned it the other day."

Somewhere in the center of the earth, a fiery pit received the stomach that had suddenly dropped out of Eric's midsection.

She had a date? He'd mentioned it? Oh, yeah, he'd asked her why she didn't date and she'd claimed it was due to her alleged bad reputation. But, no, *no*, he hadn't brought the subject up to encourage her to date some other guy. He'd hoped she would have replied with something like, "I don't date because you haven't asked me yet, you big goof!" He'd been feeling out the possibility of her perhaps dating him, not someone else.

You really screwed that one up, Hanson.

Too late now. He covered up his devastation with feigned casual interest. Just roommate curiosity.

"Who do you have a date with?" *Please, not Justin Douchebag.*

"A guy," she replied vaguely.

That only narrowed it down to half the world's population. OK, may to a quarter of the world's population, if you eliminated the guys who were too young, too old, married or in comas.

"Anyone I know?" *Anyone I can have kidnapped and relocated to the opposite side of the world?*

"I don't think so." She stepped away from him. "I have to go get ready now."

She went into her room and closed the door. A moment later, he heard the hum of her hair dryer start.

She was still in there when there was a knock at the front door. Eric waited a moment but when Michelle didn't emerge, he reluctantly went to the door and opened it, drawing himself up to his full height to try and look intimidating to the guy who was arriving to take his Michelle out on a date.

"Yes?" he barked in his most stern Chief Petty Officer voice, the voice that had in the past inspired young corpsmen in his sickbay to snap to and be quick about it. The young man standing there stepped back in surprise, glancing at the Mexican tiles next to the door indicating the house number, obviously wondering if he'd knocked on the wrong door.

He was tall and slender, with black hair, a little on the long side, flopping over his forehead in a manner that some girls might consider cute. Asian eyes, with a wary look in them upon seeing Eric answer his knock.

Casually expensive jeans, a red polo shirt with a small alligator logo. So the guy could afford to spend fifty dollars on a polo shirt.

The man's features were sharp and handsome, the black hair and eyes elegant. Was this the kind of man Michelle preferred, as opposed to Eric's fair Scandinavian looks? Her former boyfriend Justin had been fair and blond too, though even Eric could see that the streaks in the douchebag's hair had not been applied by the California sun but rather with a bottle of peroxide. Michelle obviously didn't like him at all, but apparently that had been due more to his treatment of her than his outward appearance.

No, his Michelle would never be so shallow as to choose, or reject, a man due to the mere coincidence of genetics.

Eric could afford fifty-dollar polos too, but felt no need to flaunt the fact. Besides, Michelle found his tee shirts to be amusing, or sometimes, comforting.

"Um, I'm here to meet Michelle Diaz," the guy asked hesitantly. "Does she live here?"

Eric was strongly tempted to say, "Nope, never heard of her," and slam the door in the guy's face.

But, no. His mama had raised a gentleman. He stepped back from the door.

"Come on in," he offered. "She's getting ready, I think."

With a moment's hesitation, the date accepted Eric's invitation to enter, but looking wary and curious, obviously wondering who Eric was. Eric offered a hand.

"Hi, I'm Eric." He didn't offer his last name, or the nature of his relationship with Michelle, or anything else. Let the guy guess why he was in her house, why another man had opened the door when he came calling for his date. Outwardly Eric presented his usual polite friendliness, but inside he wanted to push the guy out the door and kick him down the street.

"Christopher Wong," the other man replied, returning Eric's handshake.

"Have a seat," he invited. "I'll tell Michelle you're here." *I wish I could tell her this guy took one look at me and ran away screaming.*

Christopher sat down on the sofa and Eric wanted to insist, *"No, not there, that's where I sat when Michelle laid her head on my shoulder and fell asleep and cuddled me."* But instead he walked back to her door, tapped lightly and called, "Michelle," - he was not going to say the words *your date* - "Christopher is here."

If this wasn't the most not fun evening he'd ever had. He'd rather have a root canal done, without Novocain, than send his Michelle off on a date with another guy.

Michelle opened the door so quickly after his knock that he had to wonder if she'd been standing there waiting for it. She stared at him for a moment, then looked away.

She was wearing jeans too, unusual for here on the island, and a short-sleeved shirt with little flowers printed on it, with her shiny, beautiful dark hair streaming down her back, still a bit damp at the ends. Gym shoes were on her feet, but of course without socks. He wondered if she owned any.

After a moment he realized he was blocking her from moving out of the room, and stepped aside to let her pass.

Christopher Wong stood up, looking relieved to see her. "You look nice," he said.

Of course she looks nice, Eric thought. *She always looks nice. She especially looks nice when her head is on my shoulder, or when she's holding my hand.*

"Thanks," Michelle replied. "Shall we go?" Was it his imagination, or did she seem to be in a hurry to get out the door and away from Eric's view? Didn't she realize how he hated to see her with this guy, or with any other living, breathing, unattached male? It wasn't even a reverse of the time he'd had coffee with Tracy Cook, because he'd done that out of obligation, while she was walking out the door with Christopher Wong completely willingly.

He couldn't help but follow them towards the front door. As Michelle opened it, Eric offered his hand to Christopher again.

"Nice to meet you," he said, then gave the other man's hand a squeeze that was brief but nonetheless strong enough to make him wince.

Christopher stared at Eric's face, while Eric lowered his voice to a barely audible growl, low enough that Michelle didn't hear.

"Hurt her, and you will regret it," he promised, then offered his friendliest smile and released Christopher's hand quickly, before Michelle caught him threatening her date. As the two of them stepped out the door, she just gave Eric a little wave and said a brief, casual, "See ya," as they walked away down the street. Christopher Wong didn't even bother to walk on the side closest to the street like a gentleman should, just in case a runaway golf cart or taxi might threaten.

However, Eric did hear him ask Michelle, "Who is that guy? Your brother? He doesn't look anything like you."

Eric couldn't hear what Michelle's answer was, and watched them forlornly for a moment before closing the door.

It wasn't conceited of Eric to acknowledge that he was a brave, strong, competent man. He'd had to be, in the career he'd chosen, and knowing that about himself had been what had encouraged him into the military. He'd seen his first patient die at age twenty. Yes, he had called his mother afterward and cried for ten minutes straight, unable at first to vocalize the reason for his crying, while she kept saying "Eric, talk to me. What's wrong? What is it? Did they kick you out of the Navy?" Then he'd spent the next twenty minutes apologizing to her for it, while she, being his mom, had said it was a perfectly acceptable thing for a twenty-year-old to do in that situation. He'd seen and treated horrific, grievous wounds, seen good men die from those wounds more than once. He'd had to tell patients they had an STD or were unexpectedly pregnant. He'd experienced a mistake of a marriage and been divorced. He'd been shot at.

And tonight, seeing Michelle walk out that door with another man, was right up there with a similar unpleasantness factor.

His Michelle was going out on a date. But not with him. How exactly had that happened? Of course, she had every right to do so. There was nothing in the rental lease he'd signed to prohibit it. She was a free, unattached, attractive woman, and maybe Eric had inspired her to this devastating action by asking her about her lack of dates since they'd met. But that didn't mean he had to like it. He had no right whatsoever to feel jealous, but he did. He couldn't help it.

He flopped down on the couch, suddenly with a complete lack of appetite, though he'd been starving before Michelle's announcement that she was going out, and he tried not to think about what the two of them might be doing this evening.

The things he and Michelle had jokingly said the other evening when coming home from their weekend in San Diego crept through his brain.

I thought we were going steady.

******

The lights were still on when she got home. Not surprising, it was barely ten p.m. As she approached the house she sighed with relief that this whole unpleasant evening was finally over.

It wasn't any fault of the man who'd asked her out. He visited Catalina Island regularly with a sailing club and had asked her out several times before she had accepted today. He was a very nice person: pleasant, friendly, attractive. The evening had been enjoyable, and he hadn't come on to her or been in the least bit pushy. Under different circumstances, she might even have agreed to see him again.

But he wasn't Eric.

They had eaten dinner at Steve's Steakhouse, located, like most of Avalon's upscale restaurants, on Crescent Avenue. Though the establishment was famous for its Omaha corn-fed choice steak, she had ordered fish. Having a steak, even though she was aware that Steve's steaks were divine, would have been too much of a reminder of Eric's cooking, the way he could grill a filet completely well-done without burning it on the outside. Steve's could assuredly do the same, but she'd prefer it coming from Eric's hands.

She had teased Eric once that if he ever desired a career change, in addition to finding success as a masseuse, he could easily secure work as a chef.

"Excuse me? Miss?"

She flushed a bit, embarrassed that the waiter had to speak to her twice to get her attention, while she'd been reminiscing about Eric's cooking. Her date looked just a bit embarrassed. She hoped he hadn't been trying to talk to her too while she'd been daydreaming.

"Um, sorry, what did you say?" she muttered.

"Would you like your mahi-mahi blackened, or seared?"

She requested seared.

After dinner, Christopher had suggested they stop in at Coyote Joe's for a drink, and had been gracious when she declined and told him she didn't drink. Then he uttered the words she'd been dreading to hear all evening.

"Can I see you again?"

His shiny black hair flopped engagingly over his forehead. In a different circumstance, a different girl might have found that to be adorably cute, might have been tempted to brush those bangs away from his eyes. But Michelle's fingers tingled with the desire to smooth over a head of light brown hair, cut military short, hair that she knew was as soft and fine as that of a two-year-old. It wasn't due to its color or texture or length that she yearned for it. It was due to the hope that its owner would smile slowly in response and run his hands through her hair in return.

What a silly daydream.

Christopher Wong was a really nice guy, charming, attractive, smart, successful. He was a chemical engineer with a degree from USC. He was perfectly willing to spend seventy-five dollars on a boat ticket to come back to Avalon if she cared to go out with him again.

But he wasn't Eric.

"Christopher," she said, as they moved to the edge of the sidewalk to let other pedestrians get by. "You're a really nice guy, but,"

"You don't need to say anymore," Christopher replied quickly. "I wasn't born yesterday. I know what it means when a girl starts telling you, you're a really nice guy, but. There's someone else."

She blushed and looked away.

"It's that guy, isn't it? Your," he made air quotes. "Roommate. What is he, like, a football player?"

"No, he's paramedic," she replied.

Despite his disappointment at Michelle declining a second date with him, Christopher apparently found that interesting. "Really? I have a cousin who's a paramedic. Did your roommate," again, the air quotes, "go to USC?"

"No, he was trained in the military. He was in the Navy. He worked in base hospitals and served on ships, and was boots on the ground in Iraq and A-stan before he retired and moved here to work as a paramedic."

Michelle said it unconsciously, but it wasn't lost on her date that she'd obviously picked up some of Eric's military jargon.

"That's impressive," Christopher replied, looking a bit dispirited.

Michelle tried to smile at him. "Look, Christopher, I'm sorry. I mean it, you are a really nice guy and I had a great time tonight, and I'm sure most girls would love to spend time with you."

"Just not you," he added.

"I hope you don't feel I only went out with you to try and make Eric jealous." From the look on Christopher's face, he had probably thought just that. Michelle hoped she hadn't talked about her roommate too much at dinner. "OK, well to be perfectly honest, maybe I did, a little, but also, I wanted to see if I could manage to have a social life on my own, one that maybe,"

"Didn't include him?" Christopher suggested. "So you mean, you and that muscly guy really are just roommates? Does he know you have a thing for him?"

Christopher Wong was apparently as perceptive about her true feelings towards Eric as Susan Jones had been.

"He works out," she said, replying only to Christopher's accurate description of Eric as muscly, and ignoring his observation about her having a *thing* for him. "He has a weight bench on the patio at home. And he uses it a lot."

And Michelle always tried to sneak a peek at him when he was doing it.

"Can I walk home with you?" Christopher asked. "Or will your Navy SEAL boyfriend beat me to a pulp if I show up there again? He looked pretty intimidating when I came to pick you up. For a second there I thought he wasn't going to let me in."

"He's not my boyfriend and he wasn't a SEAL." She couldn't help but smile a bit as she remembered the time Eric had put her former high school date Justin in his place for insulting her. "But he does know a few."

That didn't seem to hearten Christopher any.

"Thank you for understanding." She shook his hand, a sure kiss of death ending for an actual date. "Stay safe."

He had told her at dinner that he worked for an oil refinery in El Segundo, a type of place she knew to be potentially hazardous, though she knew it wasn't the number one most dangerous workplace in the world. That honor went to the deck of an aircraft carrier.

****

When she walked in the door to see Eric sitting the couch, he immediately stood up and asked, "Where's your date?"

"Last I saw, down on Crescent Avenue," she told him.

"He didn't walk you home? That's not gentlemanly." Somehow that information seemed to make Eric look both upset, and relieved.

"He offered," she told him. "I declined. He didn't insist." Not like Eric had the day they'd met. He'd walked her home despite her objection, and it had changed her life.

"Are you waiting up for me?" she asked. Wasn't that fraternal.

He was, but he wasn't going to admit it to her. He'd been dreading the possibility of hearing them walk up to the door but not come inside right away, and wondering if he was going to have to flash the porch light a couple of times as a hint that it was time to stop necking and call it a night, as the mothers of his high school dates had done, back in the day.

"Of course not. I was watching the game." He indicated the television, where the convenient baseball game was in the bottom of the ninth inning.

She glanced at the screen, and her eyes rounded. "Are you actually watching the Dodgers?" she asked incredulously. "Have you finally wised up and given up on that designated hitter concept?"

"No, I'll never give up on that. But the Rays aren't playing tonight, and it doesn't hurt to check out the dark side once in a while. These guys actually think their pitcher should, or can, bat." He grinned at her. "How was your date? What did you guys do?"

She toed off her gym shoes and left them by the door, then turned back to Eric.

"It was nice. We did the zipline at Descanso Canyon, then had dinner."

He could just imagine Michelle flying over the trees on the zipline tour, her cheeks bright with excitement, her hair streaming behind her.

"He seems like a nice guy," Eric admitted. "Does he live here in Avalon?"

OK, yeah his big mouth was running away with him, but he needed to know if he was going to have to run into the guy around town like Justin the douchebag, that is, Justin Moore. Eric had crossed paths with him once or twice since their meeting at the casino dock, and Justin had quickly, wisely, turned and walked the other way.

"No, he lives on the mainland. In Redondo Beach." She waved a hand in the direction of the mainland.

Good. He wasn't going to have to cross paths with the guy around town, but Redondo Beach was still not far enough away for his liking. It was only a twenty-minute drive from there to San Pedro, to one of three boat terminals that could bring a guy to Avalon on the Catalina Express in only an hour. Way too close.

Why couldn't he live someplace further, someplace more inconvenient for visiting Avalon and Michelle, like Outer Mongolia maybe? The guy was Asian after all. That might make it impossible for Christopher Wong to make plans for a second date with Michelle.

You're being unfair, Hanson. He couldn't blame the guy for liking Michelle. If nothing else, he had good taste in women. And at least Christopher Wong had been smart enough to officially ask her out. And she had every right to date whoever she chose to.

She's not your personal property. But he sure wished she could be.

He had to ask the big question, and hope he didn't sound too much like he was interrogating her like some sort of neurotic big brother.

"Are you going to see him again?"

"No, I don't think so," she replied, but what she really wanted to say was that she had only gone out with Christopher to try and get lustful thoughts of Eric out of her head, and that when she realized she was thinking more about him than the man in whose company she was spending the evening, had mercifully decided to end the date early, and didn't plan to see him again. It would be unfair to Christopher, who was a really nice guy, to string him along like that.

She had even waited purposely in her room, so that Eric would have to answer the door when Christopher arrived to pick her up, just on the off chance that Eric would send Christopher away and tell him that she would be going out with Eric instead.

She wanted to say to Eric, I was hoping you'd order me to not go out with him, in that bossy Navy chief tone of voice. She tried to say, I'd rather spend time with you than with anyone else. But fear kept the words silent in her throat.

Instead, she did give in to one unavoidable impulse. She walked right up to Eric, put her arms around his neck, and hugged him.

She felt his arms go around and tighten against her waist. Of course, he was a generally hands-on, touchy-feely type of person. If someone hugged him, he was bound to hug them back.

Tell him. Tell him now. You've always been able to talk to him. You've told him things you've never told anyone else in your life.

But what if he doesn't feel the same? What if he felt it would make him uncomfortable to be roommates with a girl who admitted to wanting to take their relationship to a different level? Would he move out then, and deprive her of even the opportunity to have him around just in their current platonic relationship? Or would he stay and live with the uncomfortable, awkward situation of unrequited feelings?

At the moment, she couldn't do or say anything more, not without revealing that scared, vulnerable little creature rolling around in her psyche like a bumblebee trapped in a jar. And here she had almost started believing Eric's assertion that she was strong and brave. *Wrong.* She was a sniveling coward.

So instead, she permitted herself merely one inhaled breath of the cottony softness of his shirt, then, before she made a complete mess of everything, reached up, kissed his cheek just like they did all the time, said, "Goodnight, Eric," and like the coward she was, left him standing there stunned as she walked on suddenly weakened legs to the bathroom to prepare for another night of sleeping alone.

34

～

She woke up long before her alarm went off, feeling that the universe around her was somehow different. Not bad, not scary. Just different. She picked up her phone, canceled the alarm, and lay back, listening.

It was raining. Real, actual rain. California had been under a drought for so long, she had forgotten what rain sounded like. And for it to rain in the summer was even more unusual. The constant drumming, pattering sound of it above her was almost hypnotic.

She got up and sprinted across the hall to the bathroom, noticing that Eric's bedroom door was open, the room dark. He must have already left for work. So, she decided to leave the big fluffy bathrobe on its hook and went into the kitchen in just the soft, ancient tee shirt and shorts she'd slept in.

The door to the patio was open. She was sure she'd closed and locked it last night, but there it stood open with the sound and simple fresh scent of the rain flowing in. She went over and peeked out the door.

Eric was standing out on the patio in the rain; shirtless, shoeless, wearing only a pair of shorts. His arms were bent at the elbows, palms upturned as the raindrops bounced off his hands. His head was bent back, face upturned to the rain. Did he actually stick his tongue out to catch raindrops in his mouth?

She huddled in the doorway. "What are you doing out there?" she called out.

"I'm communing with Mother Nature," he replied, without looking towards her.

This was silly, a grown man standing out in the rain when they had a perfectly good shower in the house. "You're going to catch pneumonia out there."

He glanced at her briefly before turning his face back to the rain. "Pneumonia is caused by bacteria. You can't catch it from the rain. Come out here and feel this. It's glorious. When was the last time you felt real rain? This is almost like Florida."

His simple, elemental pleasure in something like the feel of rain was contagious. Hesitantly, she stepped out onto the patio, picking her way carefully on the wet tiles, until she stood in front of him. She started to say, "I don't think this is a good idea," but he shushed her.

"Don't think. Just feel."

He was right, it did feel glorious. Cool, but not cold. The rain was steady and intensely heavy, but there was no wind, so it showered straight down on them, and soon her hair was soaked and streaming down her back. Eric was still standing in his Mother Earth worship pose and after a moment, she felt compelled to imitate him, turning up her palms and her face to feel the raindrops bounce off and slide down over her. Yes, definitely glorious, though she did refrain from trying to catch raindrops on her tongue.

She felt a shift, a movement and opened her eyes. Eric's face was no longer upturned to the rain. Instead, he was looking at her. She was suddenly aware that the thin, faded tee shirt she'd worn to sleep in was soaked, molded to her skin, and transparent, her nipples clearly visible through the thin fabric.

He was smiling but it wasn't his usual sparkly smile. It was downright hot, smoldering, burning down her defenses. She was surprised the rain falling on his face didn't turn to steam. He lifted his right hand and she stared at it, mesmerized as he curved his hand around the back of her neck. Her gaze was drawn back to his face as he silently drew her towards him, and she could no more resist than could a magnet resist moving towards true north. Her arms, completely of their own volition and with no instructions whatsoever from the rest of her, went around his neck.

His lips on hers were warm despite the chill of the rain, soft and yet at the same time hard and demanding. Instinctively her mouth opened to him, and his tongue pressed swiftly past her teeth to caress hers with a sensuality that made her bones tingle. This was the kiss she had been waiting for, longing for, despite how corny it sounded, her whole life. She felt his kiss all the way down to her toes.

Don't think. Just feel.

It was insane, to be standing here in the rain, making out with her roommate.

It was glorious, to be standing here in the rain, kissing a man she craved like oxygen. All that mattered at this moment was his mouth, his hands, the feel of him. God his mouth was sweet. His kiss was hungry and eager, but he didn't try to swallow her whole like the last boy she had kissed, a really long time ago.

And that was just the difference. The few other boys that she had dated, had kissed, were just that. Boys. Eric was a man.

She had fantasized so many times about kissing him, and it had been hot and steamy in those fantasies, but her fantasies were nothing compared to the reality of this moment.

She stopped thinking, and she just felt. Felt the warmth and pressure of his lips on hers, felt her arms clinging to his neck because if she let go, she just might collapse. Felt his hands on her, one cradling the back of her head, the other curved around her waist. Felt her breasts pressed against his chest, her tee shirt so wet that they might as well have been naked. Felt the hollow bubble in her stomach and the tingling in her femininity.

His tongue was in her mouth like it belonged there. Yes, *yes* it was supposed to be there.

The gray sky and rain surrounded and isolated them, and the surrounding world faded away. Just them two, kissing in the rain. Nothing else existed. Her cosmic existence filled with a pleasure that spread quickly through her flesh and bones.

When they finally parted, he pressed his forehead against hers. She couldn't let go of his neck, not yet. Forehead to forehead, they couldn't see each other, but she was more aware of him than she'd ever been of any living being.

"Do you know how long I've wanted to kiss you?" he murmured. "I mean, really kiss you. Not just on the cheek."

"How long?" she whispered.

"Since that day."

"You're going to have to be a little more specific."

"That day you flipped me off." She smiled against his mouth.

"That day you cried on my shoulder." She twitched a little in his arms.

His voice lowered to the barest whisper. "That day you told me to fuck off."

She jumped and stepped back, staring at his face. "But wait, that was …"

That burning hot smile filling his face promised ecstasy. It promised heaven.

"Yeah, it was," he said, and he kissed her again. This kiss was proprietary, possessive, and intoxicated her way more than alcohol ever could. It felt like a reward for having waited for it so long

If it had been hot the first time, it was positively solar now. She couldn't help but melt into him, like crayons left out in the summer sun.

Don't think. Just feel.

His arms around her waist slipped down, sliding over her wet, thin tee shirt, until they rested on her butt cheeks. She had to steal breath from him, because she had absolutely none of her own left. Instead, all she had was a swift stab of pure, unadulterated lust racing like fire through her veins.

He pulled her closer, scooped her in, pressed her against him at a molecular level, and *whoa*, the man was sporting wood. And he'd been standing out in the rain long enough that it couldn't just be a guy's usual morning happy-happy. She clung to his neck, cooperating fully in the embrace, straining to get closer, pressing herself against him until they were like two halves of a whole.

She gave herself permission, the right, to touch him, to kiss him.

Dimly, she was aware that they were standing on the patio with the rain pouring down on them, but she didn't care. All that mattered was that his lips and hands were on her, and their bodies were pressed close together. He kissed her until she felt she would faint if he didn't stop, but in spite of that, she didn't want him to stop, delighting in the feel of his muscles – all his muscles – against and around her. At the moment nothing else existed for her other than the man in her arms. She wasn't thinking about how dangerous this was, what it might be leading to. She was just feeling and OMG, it felt good.

But unfortunately thinking did have to be done. They had to come up for air eventually, though Eric was breathing heavily when his lips left hers. Michelle felt breathless as well, and hot and feverish in spite of the cool rain soaking through her shirt, with heat racing like danger through her veins.

Eric pressed her head against his shoulder and spoke with despair in his voice.

"I have to go to work."

"Me too."

"I don't want to."

"Me either."

He stepped back, just enough so they could see each other's faces. There were raindrops on his eyelashes, and when he blinked, they fell on his cheeks. He cupped a hand along her cheek.

What he should do was at war with what he wanted to do, and damn it, what he should do won.

"You should go dry your hair," he whispered, glancing towards the house.

"I don't want to." She repeated what he had said, twining her arms around his neck again, feeling bereft when he grasped her wrists and untwined her. She tried to press her hands against his chest but he was able to hold her hands away from skin to skin contact. Damn those gorgeous muscles of his, preventing her from touching him, from convincing him to kiss her some more.

She'd never seen such a look of regret on a human face before in her life. "I hate to say this. I hate to do this." He took a step back, away from her. Was he rejecting her? Or just doing What Was Right? "But we both need to go inside and get ready to go to our jobs. It's the right thing to do." He bit his lip and sighed heavily. "Lord! I shouldn't have-"

"Yes, you should have," she breathed, hating the fact that he seemed to be regretting having kissed her, and unable to dredge up a normal voice. "I'm not sorry."

"Me neither," he replied quickly. "But, crap, damn it all! We have jobs, and obligations to give them our priority." He put his hand on her rear again and oh, *Freya*! her knees weakened. But he wasn't pulling her against him this time, he was nudging her towards the door to the kitchen, towards her hair dryer, towards her obligation to her job.

"You're so honorable." She couldn't keep the regretful sigh out of her voice.

"Yeah," he replied. "But right now I wish I wasn't."

An impulsive urge to quit her job without notice slammed through her, but she had to admit that Eric was right about their obligations. As much as she hated to do it, she agreed to his nudge and wiped the rain from her face as she stepped away from him, her lips still tingling with the sensation of his kiss, a sensation that even the rain couldn't wash away.

Her heart pounded and she actually felt dizzy. Had she just kissed, made out with, sucked face with her roommate?

She glanced back at him before going in the door, but only for a moment, because if she chanced more than just a quick glance at his wet, glistening semi-nudity, she'd never make it any further.

35

Eric arrived home from work sweaty and irritated. The emergency calls in Avalon tended, in some weird Murphy's Law kind of way, to run in cycles. One week it was heart attacks. The next week it was slip and fall injuries. This week, tourists had been dropping from sunstroke left and right, and he was seriously considering starting up a petition to be submitted to the Catalina Island Tourist Bureau, to assign volunteers to stand at the boat docks, handing out bottles of water and tubes of sunblock to visitors as they disembarked, along with printed instructions on their use, in several languages. It was a good thing he was an expert at painless IV insertion, because he'd been doing it a lot the past few days in order to administer fluids.

But both the sweatiness and irritation dissipated when he got in the shower and mentally let go of the stresses of work, washed away by soap and fantasy, and allowed himself to think about Michelle.

Trying to keep his mind out of the gutter when he talked to her, when they hung out together, was a feat worthy of sainthood. And one thing he had never been, was a saint.

She'd probably laugh her head off if she knew that not only had he not had sex since before the day he'd met her on the sidewalk outside the Marlin Club, but he hadn't so much as had a date. Not for lack of opportunity, but for lack of interest in any woman other than an angry blue-eyed brunette with eyes like the ocean, in a pink hoody. Sometimes he fantasized about her being in bed with him wearing only that silly hoody, though he hadn't seen it on her again since that first day.

He loved the way the bathroom smelled after she'd been in the shower, all moist strawberry scented shampoo and sweet femininity. They shared that fragrant shower, but never at the same time, other than in his fantasies. He always went into the bathroom after she showered, just to breathe in that scent of her shampoo and soap. Then he'd flush the toilet, to give the illusion of a real reason for hanging out in the head. She probably thought he had a bladder the size of a pea.

She was so damn sweet. She thought she was a bitch, but despite her intelligence, she was totally wrong in that assessment. Unconsciously sweet was now his absolutely favorite attribute.

Lord, he'd been dying to kiss her, to touch her, to make love to her, for so long. He couldn't remember not yearning for it. It was the only thing in their relationship that he hadn't been open and frank about to her. All those times they'd kissed cheeks like siblings, he'd had to stop himself from pulling her close and showing her what a real kiss was all about. Especially the day he'd gotten the reimbursement from Danny Gonzalez for the boat ticket and Danny, who obviously had a crush on Michelle, had requested in his message, kiss her for me.

Nope, his first thought had been. *I won't kiss her for you, Gonzalez. I only want to kiss her for me.* And when Michelle had insisted that he actually follow the instruction, he'd thought for a brief, insane moment that she was actually inviting him to kiss her, in a non-fraternal way. But why would she do that? She was his roommate, not his lover, as much as he wished otherwise. It had been difficult, but he'd managed to restrain himself to one of their platonic little cheek kisses, then high-tailed it out the door before he lost control and kissed her for real. For himself, not for Danny.

Gonzalez had assumed that Eric and Michelle were sleeping together when Eric had let Danny have his bed to sleep off his drunk. And yes, so sue him, Eric had been tempted, that night, as he prepared to sleep on the couch, to turn around, go to her door and say, *"Hey, you know, I really don't want to sleep on the couch and Danny's snoring in my room, and maybe I could sleep but actually not sleep in here with you like Danny as-sumes we are anyway, and let's do the wild thing as if we were lovers and not just platonic roommates."*

Yeah, and how would Michelle have reacted to that insane speech? Probably with something like, *"Look, Eric, you big goof, you're a great friend and roommate and I like you and all but no, I don't think so and I really don't think of you that way and well, nope,"* which was really just a more polite way to say, *"Back off and hit the couch, dude."*

Or, would she have invited him in?

Yeah, that was about as likely as her getting down on her knees and of-fering him a blow job.

Christ, why had he allowed that particular fantasy image to creep out of the swamp of his dirty mind? Now he was going to think about that every time he saw her knees. Which was pretty much every day, since in this climate, they both wore shorts every day. The only time her knees were covered was when she had on that big fluffy pink bathrobe in the morning, because she liked to have her coffee before getting dressed and of course now when he saw her in that, he was going to wonder what if anything she had on underneath it and how secure was that sash around the waist.

She even got to wear shorts to work, while his work uniform had him in long pants and boots. Not that he had any illusions that she might want him on his knees before her. Of course, that put another erotic image into his fertile, dirty imagination, one that involved him on his own knees, grabbing those perfect round butt cheeks with his hands and pulling her into his face ...

Christ. Now he needed to turn his shower into a very cold one. Or bet-ter yet, maybe he should just put some ice into a plastic sandwich bag and shove it down his pants.

Of course, a man getting down on his knees had another meaning, but one he was sure Michelle wouldn't want from him. As much as he wanted a family, he knew he wasn't good husband material. Too many old girlfriends in his past, too many former lovers, too many pickups, and a hasty, pre-doomed marriage that had lasted a whole six months, on paper at least.

He'd never gotten down on his knees, never proposed. When Karen What's-your-last-name-oh-it's-Butler-thanks had called him and dropped the maybe pregnant line, he'd immediately looked up the address of the marriage license office and arranged to meet her there the next day. They'd both come straight from work, so he'd worn his service khaki uniform and Karen had worn a beige pantsuit, not even remotely resembling a wedding dress. No church, no reception, no honeymoon. He hadn't even told his family or Gabriel until it was a done deal.

Definitely not good husband material.

But that didn't stop him from wanting her.

He couldn't stop looking at the curve of her cheek and the way it flowed into the perfect curve of her chin, or the way her eyes got even bluer and flared when she showed emotion, be it happiness, sadness, or anger. She seemed fragile sometimes, hidden behind that tough bitch façade, almost like a little girl. But no. A little girl didn't look like her. And yet she was amazingly strong at the same time. He wanted both to protect her, and to be protected by her. It was a tantalizing contrast.

She did something to him, and he wasn't sure what. Wasn't sure what it was, or why, or how. He just knew it was Something. And it made him want to put down roots in a way he'd never felt a need for before.

So many nights he'd lain sleepless in his bed, thinking about her, fantasizing about her, when usually he fell asleep quickly and soundly as soon as he hit the rack. When he did fall asleep, she completely invaded his dreams. More than once he'd woken up reaching for her, certain that his impossibly detailed erotic dream had been real. Though he'd been disappointed when the dream turned out to be just that, an unreal dream rather than reality, it was still a hell of a lot better than his other dreams.

He would have asked her to be his date, his girlfriend, his lover, until she'd played the Best Friend card. It wasn't that he disliked the concept of being the best friend she'd ever had. He was flattered and had meant it when he'd returned the feeling. No, he was more than flattered. He was honored. But being a best friend precluded anything more romantic, more intimate. If he kissed her, other than one of their fraternal cheek kisses, she'd either laugh or slap him.

She was his best friend. He was her damn best friend. It was wonderful and satisfying to be best friends.

It totally sucked to have the hots for your best friend.

He knew he shouldn't look at her breasts. She was his roommate, after all, and he should respect her. He did respect her.

But despite that honorable respect, he was still a healthy, red-blooded heterosexual man, and she had the most beautiful breasts he had ever seen.

Well, not literally seen, of course. But in this tropical climate, with everyone wearing tee shirts and skimpy tank tops, the size of them and their perfect round shape were easily discernable. Not small, not huge, somewhere in between. The perfect size for his hands, at least in his fantasy.

He'd spent so much time and effort trying not to kiss her. It was like trying to pass a particularly difficult test.

Don't kiss her today, and tomorrow you can pat her arm in a completely platonic manner. Anything to be able to touch her in any way. Resist the urge to make out with her like a horny teenager, and your reward will be a fraternal kiss on the cheek. Pretend to be completely freaked out by a teeny tiny tremor that didn't even qualify for the title earthquake, and maybe she'll trustingly put her head on your shoulder, fall asleep there, and drool on you.

He was eternally grateful for those small wonders, and could only hope for more.

It was the contrasts in her nature that attracted him the most. The innocent girl afraid to be hurt, sheltering inside her pink hoody and her fantasy novels. The reasonable adult, confident in her technical skills. The tough pseudo-bitch who got a little bossy once in a while. Lord love a duck, but it thrilled him when she bossed him around. Then there was the sexy love goddess who peeked out once in a while. That aspect of Michelle really turned him on, though he tried to hide that effect with jokes and teasing.

There was the really smart professional woman who could diagnose and repair a boat engine like no one else and keep her hands clean doing it, and the giggly girl, not often revealed, who teased and laughed and even made the occasional joke. And yet, there was a sharp edge to her psyche that kind of broke his heart a little bit to contemplate the despair that had honed it to that edge. She was tough, even when she was falling apart inside.

She was so amazing – that fascinating blend of hard and soft, strong and fragile. Of sweetness and insecurity, and of something that made him want to fix all her problems for her, from the stray spider on the ceiling, to the crushing anxiety of her unpleasant childhood.

She wasn't his ex-wife and she wasn't that friends with benefits he'd been with years ago. She wasn't any of the women he'd dated or slept with or picked up, knowing and taking advantage of the fact that his smile and charm had made it easy. She was his Michelle, his Venus.

He wondered sometimes, with the impressive high school grades she'd gotten, why she had chosen a technical career rather than attending a university and getting a bachelor's degree. It would have been easy, he was certain.

And then there was the girl who, startled by the roar of a Blue Angels F/A-18 Hornet over her head, had turned to him for protection and comfort. Despite the fact that she'd knocked him flat on his back, onto a rock that poked him painfully in the vicinity of his third lumbar vertebrae, he'd still loved the fact that her first instinct had been to turn to him, rather than to cower in place and cover her head like most of the other unsuspecting onlookers.

Yes, that was definitely the side of her he liked the best. The Michelle who wanted him, Eric, to be her safety.

It wasn't just her beauty, although there was that. He'd been with beautiful women before, including his ex-wife. It wasn't just that she was smart, or fragile, or sweet or strong or bitchy or funny. It was the sum of them all.

He hadn't been exaggerating when he'd compared her skin to cinnamon with sugar mixed in that first day. It made her bright blue eyes stand out even more. When she looked at him with those ocean-blue eyes, he wanted nothing more than to take care of her and protect her from all of life's adversities. That long, chocolate brown hair seemed to beg for his hands to caress it.

Her figure could inspire poets. It certainly inspired him. Those perfect breasts, not too big, not too small. That equally perfect gluteus maximus that his hands longed to caress even more than he wanted to caress her hair.

The way she unconsciously broke into a smile when she saw him made it nearly impossible for him to keep his hands to himself. There were times when he wanted to pretend he thought he had a fever, just so she would put her hand on his forehead to check. And if she did, then he probably would contract a fever.

He hadn't followed through with his attraction to her, his burning desire for her, a desire that he couldn't remember starting because it seemed like it had always been the case.

Why not? Because she was his roommate. Because he respected her. Because his mama had raised a gentleman.

Until that day in the unexpected rain. It was as if the rain had washed away his resolve and hesitation. He still respected her, but he'd finally dumped the gentlemanliness and kissed her like he'd been wanting to since the moment he'd first seen her, and, *God!* She'd kissed him back in the most non-fraternal way imaginable. And was it his imagination, or had she pressed herself closer against him when she'd felt – because how could she not have felt – the tree-trunk style boner that her closeness had inspired? If that wasn't an "I want you too" signal, he didn't know what was. It wasn't the first time he'd been aroused by having her near him - hell, it wasn't even the hundredth – but it was the first time he hadn't hidden it from her.

Lord help him, there was no way she could have missed it. She had felt so right, there in his embrace, like peace, like home. And *Lord*, the feeling of her breasts against his chest as she'd clung to him – he didn't need to drink alcohol to get intoxicated. Maybe it was a good thing they'd had to cease their epic kissing and go to work that morning, otherwise he was sure things would have gone much further.

He'd come *that close* to picking her up and carrying her to his bed like some old-fashioned movie hero, but then his damn, stupid honor and respect and idiotic gentlemanliness had surfaced. It was the most difficult thing he'd ever had to in his entire life, to send her into the house to get ready for work. He'd waited until he'd heard the hum of her hair dryer behind her door before going in to dry off himself and change into his uniform. It was the first time in his entire adult life that he hadn't followed through on his attraction to or lust for a woman, but then he'd never felt about any other woman the way he did about Michelle.

Thinking about her curvaceous perfection tempted him to take care of himself right there in the shower, but he was tired of that. He wanted the real thing, and he wanted it with Michelle.

He was going to use his big mouth to tell her he wanted to make love to her, and see if it got him into trouble, or into heaven.

36

Michelle drove home much slower than usual, thinking hard. It had been three days since her little make-out session with Eric in the rain, and since then the universe had conspired to keep them apart, other than a few brief text messages. That afternoon, he'd been called away on an emergency, to accompany a heart attack victim on a life flight to a hospital on the mainland. By the time he got home the next day, she was already at work. Then, he'd had to pull a double shift when one of his colleagues had come down sick. With only four paramedics in Avalon, there wasn't much in the way of backup. She had no idea if he'd be at the house when she got home.

And during those past three days and nights, she'd suffered from serious insomnia. When she did sleep, she was ashamed to admit that she dreamed about Eric, her slumber filled with stunning, erotic dreams. Sometimes the details were vividly lustful, dreams of hot naked flesh against hot naked flesh, and the light of sparkly eyes. Other mornings she recalled no details, but still the dreams were lurking just around the corner of her memory, and she woke up in a sweat that had nothing to do with the weather.

Her stomach still flipped a little when she thought about how he'd kissed her. Ever since that moment, she kept touching her lips, remembering the taste of his mouth. Kissing him had been like drowning, but in a good way.

There was no doubt in her mind as to the direction in which Eric was interested in going. That erection she'd felt against her stomach had said it all.

Sex. That was the direction in which he was interested in going. A man didn't kiss a woman like that, get aroused like that, without intending it to lead to sex.

Be honest with yourself, Michelle. Isn't that what you want too? Hasn't it been what you've wanted almost since you first laid eyes on him?

What if she did sleep with him? What would he think of her? He'd said he'd wanted to kiss her, but if they did have sex, might he not think her unsophisticated and unskilled?

She wasn't exactly inexperienced. She'd slept with a couple of guys during the time she'd lived on the mainland, attending technical school. Mainly out of curiosity, to see if it was any better than her experience with that fumbling boy with whom she'd lost her virginity on the night of her senior prom. They had been better, somewhat, but she still hadn't been terribly impressed.

And what of Eric? She knew, without asking, that he'd had a lot more experience than she had. With his self-confidence and good looks, packaged in a Navy uniform, he probably could have charmed any woman he wanted into bed. He'd been around the world, literally, and had probably been with all sorts of girls. He'd been married, if briefly. Wouldn't a small-town girl like herself suffer by comparison?

And there was another consideration. She liked Eric. She liked him a lot. Not just in the, lust for his body, get naked and do the wild thing sense. She genuinely liked him as a person. He was the exact opposite of herself, and that was what made her like him so much. His outgoing demeanor, his joy of life, his honest belief that the world didn't totally suck, were contagious. She knew that her happiness, her own outlook on life, had improved immeasurably since she and Eric had become roommates, and friends. She could be herself in his company. She didn't have to hide behind the fake Raging Bitch persona she used to wear. He was her best friend.

If she slept with him, would that change? She may not have had scores of lovers; she may not have had a long-term relationship, but she still knew that sex had a way of changing a friendship.

Half of her soul said, "Finally!" The other half said, "I don't know if I'm ready for this."

What if she declined to have sex with him? What if he asked, sleep with me, and she said, no thank you, I'd rather just be friends? She knew Eric, knew he was honorable enough that he wouldn't push the issue if that was her decision. But would that not potentially change things between them even more? And wouldn't passing up the opportunity to be with Eric, in the biblical sense, be the most incredibly stupid decision she could ever make?

Or, maybe she was just overthinking this whole thing way too much. Maybe she should just boil it down to its basic components. He was a man. She was a woman. Neither of them was committed elsewhere. They were attracted to each other. Hooyah.

He wouldn't hurt her. He was her Eric, and she loved him.

Whoa. When did that happen? When did he evolve from her roommate Eric, her friend Eric, to just, her Eric? When had she fallen in love with him? Was it when they'd held hands on the helicopter flight? Admittedly, he had taken her hand at the beginning because she'd been scared. But on the way home, she had initiated the hand holding, and she hadn't been scared. Had it been when she'd seen the way his eyes glowed when he talked about his love for his work, or the day he'd rubbed her sore feet? Or, if she was being brutally honest with herself, had she fallen in love with him the day she'd run into his back, and he'd turned around, smiled and introduced himself? She wouldn't have admitted it at the time, but the way he'd put up with her craziness, had seen right through her fake bitchiness, had been life-changing.

What about all the times he'd touched her, and she's just considered it innocent and friendly? The empathetic arm pats, the friendly hugs, the supposedly fraternal cheek kissing – had he actually been flirting with her, hinting at a more than just roommates connection? What about when she'd cried on his shoulder? The second time, she thought she'd felt him petting her hair. But it had been windy that day, and at the time she'd thought he was just shifting her hair out of his face.

And then he'd kissed her. Despite how much she had fantasized about that, the reality of it had eclipsed all her imaginings by light years. Her heart kicked up a notch just remembering. She could close her eyes and continue to taste that kiss, sweeter than candy.

Could they still be friends if they become lovers? Was she brave enough to find out?

A horn beeped behind her and she realized she'd stopped in the middle of the street. She'd been so caught up in her musings, she didn't even remember driving home. She was lucky she hadn't run someone over. It was a good thing she was in front of her house and not down on Catalina Avenue.

<h1 style="text-align:center">37</h1>

When she walked in the door and set down her tool bag, the first thing she saw was Eric's knees. He was laying on his back on the couch with his legs bent up, but he wasn't napping. As soon as she closed the door he sat up and looked at her. He lifted his right hand, and she was just as mesmerized by it as she had been that day in the rain, and he beckoned her with one finger.

She didn't hesitate. Two quick steps took her to the couch to fling herself into his arms. The decision was made. The decision had always been made. The battle was lost, and all that was left to do was to surrender unconditionally. When he beckoned to her, she came to him, because that was where she belonged.

The force of her flinging had him flat on his back on the couch, with her on top of him, just like at the air show, but this time it was intentional, due to desire, not fear. She didn't grab onto him for protection this time.

She very much wanted to kiss him, that is, her being the kisser and him being the kissee, if there was such a thing, so he'd know that she wanted this, herself, on her own, and not just because he was her roommate or because he'd kissed her first in the rain the other day.

So, she kissed him. Right there, on her couch, with his sweet smiling face looking up at her, she kissed him, and *Freya*! Kissing him was positively addictive.

It was six-thirty in the evening, yet his cheek against hers was as smooth as a baby's butt. He'd obviously just shaved. Had he primped for her?

As usual, when she was at work, her hair was pulled back in a ponytail. Eric reached up and tugged the elastic band down the length of the ponytail until it was free. Dropping the elastic on the floor, he ran his hands through it, humming appreciatively against her mouth.

"I have so wanted to do this." He sectioned her hair between his fingers, smoothed it back, let it fall over their faces in a soft, dark veil before caressing it back again. She laid her face against his neck and enjoyed the feeling of him petting her hair.

She used a strawberry-scented shampoo he knew, from seeing the bottle in their shared bathroom, and from the faint residual scent of it he occasionally was able to detect. Smelling it now, in her hair as he pressed his face against it while smoothing his hands along its length, turned him on endlessly.

"Do you know how long I've wanted to kiss you?" she asked him.

"How long?"

"Since that day."

"You're going to have to be a little more specific."

"That day you bandaged my finger."

"Lord, you should have taken me, right then and there on that kitchen table," he said with fervor. That would have kept his compartment doors shut.

"The day you let me cry on your shoulder." He twitched a little in her arms.

"When you mistakenly thought I was going to jump off the pier."

"But wait, that was…"

"Yeah, it was," and she put her hands on his face and pulled him towards her for another kiss. It was a brief one, as he separated his mouth from hers, though not in rejection.

"Make love with me, Michelle," he implored. "I am so totally crazy about you. I've never wanted to be with anyone as much as I want to be with you. Since the first day I met you, I've wanted to be close to you. I haven't been able to stop thinking about you. About us. Together. I want to be with you, tonight. Now."

She still couldn't quite believe – it was impossible – that this man actually wanted to be with her, stupid pathetic little Michelle Diaz, when he could easily have any female in Avalon, or in California, with just a smile and those sparkly eyes. And yet he wanted her, bitchy little Michelle Diaz, the drunkard's daughter.

Her pulse racing, she melted from the inside out, and refused to consider the possibility that it was due to the convenience of having an unattached female living under the same roof.

"Don't think it's just because we share a house," he added, as if he'd just read her mind. "I hope you don't think I'm that shallow. I mean it when I say I've wanted to be with you from the start."

"Shallow?" she replied disbelievingly. "Remember how you always tell me that I'm not crazy?"

"Yes."

"Well, you are most definitely not shallow. I'll believe you if you believe me."

"I believe every word you say, sweetheart."

She'd seen the way female heads turned to stare whenever she and Eric were hanging out together – when they were meeting up with his friends who came over from San Diego. Girls would give him the eye when they sat on a bench on the pier eating ice cream cones on one of their non-dates. He had a genetic impossibility to walk by past an ice cream shop without stopping in to indulge in a couple of cones.

Even her friend Tracy had ogled him shamelessly, until she'd started dating Johnny Del Risco. Even women who had been accompanied by male companions, who had gold bands on their left hands, had glanced at him covertly.

She couldn't blame them. He was definitely a man worth looking at.

And yet, he'd never returned the appreciative glances sent in his directions. Polite man that he was, he never embarrassed his roommate by returning the flirtations in her presence. He did have a habit of smiling at pretty much anyone he saw, but she'd never seen him do it in any other manner than just his normal Eric Hanson friendliness.

"Are you serious?" she asked.

"Oh, babe, I am so very serious. I never wanted anything more in my entire life."

Laying on top of him, she could tell he was serious. A serious hard-on tented his shorts. She could feel it, just like the day in the rain, even through their clothes.

She was serious too, and her serious desire for him emboldened her to press her weight downwards against him, against his seriousness.

"This feels familiar," she commented, as he closed his eyes and hissed a little.

"Hey, when you jumped my bones at the air show, I did not-"

"Yeah, you were too busy laughing at me."

"I'm not laughing now." He wasn't laughing, but he was smiling. The most sinfully sweet smile she'd ever seen or could imagine.

She could live and die in that smile.

"The other day, in the rain, though," she reminded him.

He smiled beatifically, eyes closing briefly in remembrance, and she pressed against him again. This was certainly the sexiest thing that had ever happened here on her living room sofa.

"Oh, lord, you do that again and this whole adventure is going to be over a lot sooner than I'd like."

"Do you want me to move?" she asked, pulling back a little.

"No! Yes." He pushed her hair back and kissed her again. "Make love with me," he said again, whispering against her mouth. "Anywhere, as long as it's in my bed."

That should have made no sense whatsoever, but somehow, it made perfect sense.

Freya. That had been her go-to exclamation lately, ever since Eric had mentioned her.

The Norse goddess of love. And war. But mostly love.

Excitement raced through her, and she looked him in the eyes and said the sexiest, most erotic four words ever uttered in the history of the libido.

"Do you have protection?"

"Oh lord, yes."

In a nanosecond they were on their feet, as he grabbed her hand and tugged her to his bedroom, because that was where the requested protection resided. They bumped into the chair and the wall in their haste, and once in the bedroom they were drawn to the bed by forces both sexual and primeval. But rather than getting immediately prone, Eric knelt in the center of the mattress, on the smooth blue comforter, and drew Michelle to kneel facing him, so close that the tips of her breasts brushed his chest. He ran his hands down her hair, threaded his fingers through the long dark length of it, and kissed her slowly, tantalizingly, nibbling on her lips and stroking her tongue with his.

The feelings bubbling through her at this moment were sensations more erotic than she'd ever known. She had never wanted anything, anyone, more in her entire life that she wanted this man in front of her. She put her hands along the side of his face, smoothed them over his head above his ears, pressed them through the soft, short hair.

They undressed each other slowly, despite their haste in getting into the bedroom, fingers followed by lips as they felt and tasted each bit of skin. She knew, because she'd been sharing a medicine cabinet with him for months, that he didn't use cologne or any scented products, and she pressed her nose, and her mouth, to his shoulder, breathing in his natural sweet scent of soap and sunshine, and just, Eric. She'd always felt that removing one's clothes in anticipation of sex was awkward and ungraceful, but with Eric, it was a sensual revealing of skin and curves and new areas to kiss.

Despite the fact that they both knew perfectly well that they were here for sex, still he gave her that small, sweet glance that asked permission, as he smoothed her shirt up from her waist, over her breasts, her face and her raised arms, to drop it away behind her as her hair fell through the neck. She didn't know where it ended up, and she didn't care, as long as it was off.

In turn, she grasped the bottom of Eric's tee shirt, tugging it up over his waist, as smoothly as he'd just done with her. Skimming the fabric up his torso, she caught a brief glimpse of a tuft of brown hair in each armpit as he also raised his arms to facilitate the shirt's removal. For a moment she held the white fabric in her hands, as she recalled holding his shirt that first day, then squeezed the soft cotton briefly in her hand before tossing it back over her shoulder, as his smile turned sexy and hot.

Again, she cared little for where the shirt ended up, as long as it was off him.

She'd seen him bare-chested before, of course, but had not gazed at it with the possessiveness of this moment. Now, it was different. This time, she would do more than ogle. Rather than guilty glances, she felt emboldened to run her hands across his shoulders and arms, to press her mouth into the hollow of his throat, exploring with her hands and her mouth as he murmured appreciatively, "Ooh, yeah, I like that."

She had admired his muscles before, but even more so now as she allowed her hands to feel them, the shoulders, arms, and chest taut beneath the smooth skin under her fingers and lips. With her palms running over his back, she felt his muscles move with him. She closed her eyes and clung to him, feeling the surge of sensation.

At the same time, his hands were sliding up her back, under her hair, searching for a clasp he wasn't finding.

His lack of success in unhooking her bra was only a momentary setback. He slid the straps down her shoulders as she forced herself to take her lips off his skin long enough say, "This one unhooks in the front."

"Of course. I knew that." He transferred his efforts there, smiling at her. That sweet sexy smile made her toes curl. The slide clasp on the front of her bra was a bit stubborn and he stopped smiling for a moment to look down at it with consternation. "What structural engineer designed this thing?" he asked, as he finally defeated the piece of plastic. As soon as the bra cleared her shoulders to join their shirts in oblivion, he cupped her breasts, and the feel of them in his hands made her shudder as he leaned forward to kiss her.

His mouth on her breast was a gift. "Oh, lord, these are lovely," he breathed, and she gasped with delight when his lips touched her. It wasn't even a kiss at first, but more a caress, like butterfly wings against her skin. His gentleness almost drove her crazy. Crazier.

Every sensation was heightened, every perception revealed in to be retained in memory. The feel of her hair against her back. The smoothness of the bed's comforter under her knees. His hands, moving to her back, his fingers warm and possessive against her flesh. The soft feel of his lips on her skin, her fingers at the back of his neck, made her oblivious to anything but the sensations of the moment.

That beautiful sexy mouth that had made her fantasize about his kissing skills since the day he'd moved into her house, and those sexy warm lips on her made her forget her name, didn't just kiss her.

He talked. He complimented, he appreciated. Every spot his lips touched, everywhere his tongue lingered, between sighs and moans, he proved himself to be a man of many talents, who could kiss and talk at the same time.

She had never known before that her hair was silk, her skin satin, that the underside of her breast was luscious, and that her nipple, puckered under the moistness of his mouth, could make a dead man get hard. She suspected that last part was a quote from a song, but didn't care as long as the words came from Eric's lips, and she involuntarily arched her back and clutched at his head with yearning.

"Your breasts are like warm, soft, round globes of delight," he murmured as that masterful, clever tongue traced a ring of fire around her resurrection-inspiring nipple. "I've laid awake at night fantasizing about kissing you right ... here." The hot lips moved, breathing warm, deliciously against her skin. How could the simple touch of lips on flesh arouse her more than she could ever have imagined?

"I had no idea you were so poetic," she told him, breathing out with a gasp of pleasure.

"You might be too if you listened to enough country music." When he shifted so that his tongue captured her right nipple – because it was only fair that both girls should get equal adoration, her breath hissed between her teeth and she pulled his head even more tightly against her, certain he could feel her heart beating like a rabbit on a double dose of speed.

"You feel so good. You smell so good." His tongue caressed her skin. "You taste so good."

Freya, that tongue of his was so talented, it deserved its own category at the Academy Awards.

She felt his hands skim down her waist to the top of her shorts. The soft sexy lips left her breast just long enough to glance at her eyes as he murmured, "I so want you naked," a pronouncement that turned her joints to jelly as he tugged them down, over her hips.

It wasn't so much that she fell to her back to facilitate his desire for her nakedness. It was more that she flowed, as she raised her butt and the shorts also disappeared, off, leaving her only in her pink panties. But he still had his own shorts on, and she wanted him just as naked as he'd said he wanted her, and she leaned up enough to grasp at this waist too, and his hands joined hers as the pants came off somehow, without even unzipping the fly, disappearing over his cute feet and wiggly toes. He wore boxers and they were blue, but they weren't on him for more than another second, and that was not a banana in his pocket. He was definitely glad to see her.

Together they skimmed her panties away. "Pink," he breathed. "I knew they'd be pink," as he hooked a finger into the elastic to urge the panties downward.

"You've been thinking about my underwear?" she asked as they dropped to the floor.

"Constantly. Endlessly. Obsessively. And about getting you out of your underwear." And finally, all those pesky impediments of clothing were gone.

Naked. She was naked. *They* were naked. She and Eric, her roommate, goofy, smart, sweet, sexy Eric, whom she'd thought of as the world's most annoying person the day she'd met him on Catalina Avenue. How wrong she'd been. She was, at this moment, the luckiest girl on the face of the earth. In a flash, she realized that she had been wondering, since the moment she'd met him, what he would taste like, feel like.

He slid his hands over her hips. "Lord, you're so soft," he said, in a breathy voice. He explored her body with his hands and mouth as if he was a starving man at a banquet.

Her hands were sliding over him as well. "Lord," she mimicked. "You're so hard."

She was right. He was a damn steel rod, all for her.

She would absolutely, positively die if she couldn't feel his body on hers now, this second, and yes please, thank you Freya, they were prone, kissing, touching, his knee between hers, nudging, his hands smoothing her hair back, cupping her face, his lips brushing her temple, running a hot sexy line around her ear, possessing her mouth.

"Tell me what you want, my Michelle," he murmured, his lips warm on her skin.

He'd called her *My Michelle*. She had never heard anything sweeter in her entire life.

As for what she wanted? She wanted his body, his soul, his babies. She wanted this moment, the two of them, here, naked and entwined while he called her "my Michelle" to last until the end of time.

She whispered in his ear. There was really no need to whisper. It wasn't as if there was someone in the next room to hear them. She could have shouted. But somehow, this seemed like a situation that called for a whisper, soft and sensual against the curve of his ear. She smoothed his hair, pressed her lips to his ear, and whispered low. "I want you, Eric. All of you."

His response to her whisper was a shudder that she felt under her lips and her hands, as he drew back just enough for them to look into each other's faces. She was used to seeing him smile, because he did it so much, but this smile that spread across his face now was infinitely sexier than any other he'd ever shown her before, his eyes giving off a huge amount of sparkle.

"I'm all yours, babe."

With a flowing impulse, they were entwined, ankles mingled, almost connected.

This moment, this man, was the reason for her life up to this moment. He was the reason she hadn't been terribly upset that she'd never seen her prom date again after that night. He'd gone to the mainland for college and never returned to Avalon. This man with her now, about to become her lover, was the reason she has resisted Justin Douchebag, the reason she had declined a second date with Christopher Wong. Even before she ever knew someone like him existed, Eric had been her man, to the point where she came perilously close to blurting out, *I've always loved you.*

Being under him, on his bed, looking up at that sweet sexy smile and sparkly eyes intent with desire, made her suddenly wish that she had multiple hands and arms. A pair to encircle his neck, another to slide down his arms, another to reach down between their bodies to guide him-

Their eyes popped, and they spoke in unison. "Protection!"

He rolled off her and yanked open the drawer of the nightstand. As he reached in, a brief look of panic crossed his face as his hand swept around inside, just for a moment, then with a breathed, "Aha!" he pulled out a shiny blue box. It was still sealed, she noticed, and he ripped it apart in his haste to pull out a foil pack, the other eleven condom packets spilling onto the floor with the remains of the torn-apart box. Opening the foil pack with his teeth, he spit the foil away and covered himself in record time. Guinness would have been impressed.

"I'm not a virgin, you know." As soon as the words left her lips, she realized how stupid they sounded. He knew that already. She had told him about her first time within an hour of meeting him. But Eric didn't miss a beat.

"Neither am I," he murmured, and then yes, *yes*, thank Freya, with one strong, incredible thrust, he was inside her and the sensation of it, smooth and powerful, shook her to the core. She couldn't remember ever feeling so alive. He held her hands in his on either side of her face and pressed his face against her neck.

"Oh, god, Michelle, I can't believe we're finally here together. I can't tell you how much I've wanted this and hoped you would want me too. I never hated anything so much in my life as much as that wall between your room and mine. I've been wishing for it to disappear. I've wanted to kiss you and touch you and taste you-"

"Eric?" she murmured against his neck.

"Michelle!" His voice was breathy.

"Has anyone ever told you that you talk too much?"

"More than you can imagine."

"They were wrong."

She had always before held back a part of herself, never truly let go with the complete abandon of passion. She'd been afraid before, to give herself emotionally without reserve. Giving everything of oneself made a person vulnerable, open to hurt, disappointment, grief.

But no person she had ever met had treated her as Eric had, had been what or who Eric was. She looked into those eyes, lost herself in that smile, and she trusted. Trusted him to keep her safe, in body, in soul, in her heart.

When she wrapped her legs around his hips, as she tried to pull the entire world, the entire universe, which at this moment consisted only of Eric and herself, into the center of her, he stopped talking and moaned. She loved hearing that moan from him, not only for its sensuality, but also because it showed that even cool, competent, always in control Eric, was able to let loose. Doc was finally off duty.

His moving in her was at this moment, her sole reason for existing. She couldn't think anymore, could barely breathe. She could only feel. He was the river and she was the sea, flowing one into the other. The pleasure was almost terrifying in its intensity.

All that existed was right now, Eric's eyes, his smile, sweet yet intense with desire, the sensation of his hands on her and the feeling of her ankles against the back of his legs, his firm calf muscles bunching with his movement.

It was like a dream, but better. She almost begged him, for more, for everything, for that nameless, all-important *Something* that she craved above everything else in the universe. But she knew there was no need to beg. He gave it willingly.

"Open your eyes," he requested, and she did so immediately, getting lost in his sparkle. At that moment she'd be willing to do just about anything he asked, up to and including laying her heart at his feet.

They climaxed simultaneously. She'd always thought he was cute, handsome, sexy, but the look on his face when he came was more than that. It was beautiful. He shuddered, and moaned. She screamed, and clung, and wrapped herself around him, and the force of it pushed their bodies six inches across the bed.

****

"Oh. My. God."

Her voice was muffled under his shoulder.

"Yeah," he breathed, panting a little. "You said it." His breath stirred against the top of her head.

"Sweetie?"

She'd called him sweetie. It was the best thing he'd ever heard in his life.

"Mmmh," he murmured, nuzzling her ear.

"Sweetie, could you move your arm? You're on my hair."

"Jeez, I'm sorry. Am I squishing you? I'm such a clod." He immediately rolled to the side and leaned away to deal with condom disposal awkwardness.

"You are many things, Eric Hanson," she said as he turned back to her. "But you are not a clod."

Feeling reassured, he cuddled close again, but making sure he wasn't on her hair, and resumed his nuzzling.

"So that's why you screamed? I was pulling your hair?"

Damn. He'd hoped her scream had been due to the throes of passionate lovemaking, not from the pain of having her hair pulled.

"No, you weren't pulling my hair at that moment."

The scream had surprised even her. What had also surprised her had been the intensity and depth, and the heat of sensation. To describe it as merely an orgasm seem woefully inadequate. At that moment, she wouldn't have noticed if Eric had pulled her hair out by the roots. It was only afterward that she'd noticed her hair stuck under him.

Freya, she was happy and satisfied.

Eric leaned on one elbow next to her and played with her hair, gently and taking care not to tug, pressing a strand against his lips as he showed her a smile replete with satisfaction. "Poets should write poems about your hair," he said. "A mere paramedic can't possibly do it justice."

She made a sound of satisfaction and cuddled closer against him.

"Do you know how long I've wanted this?" he asked.

"How long"

"Since the first minute I ever saw you."

She put a disbelieving hand on his shoulder. "You can't mean that. The first minute you saw me, I was telling you to fuck off and generally treating you like shit. I'm surprised you even wanted to talk to me after that."

He closed his eyes for a moment with a blissful expression on his face and murmured, "Foreplay."

Her left arm was under his neck and starting to go numb but she didn't care, and she put her other hand on his chest. Under the soft fair hairs, she could feel his heart pounding. He didn't have a lot of chest hair, but what he did have was very soft, and she enjoyed the feeling of the skin going to goosebumps under her fingers. He looked at her hand, laughed a bit and said, "My knees are weak too." His breathing was ragged, and she knew if she were able to take his pulse, it would be way higher than his usual seventy beats per minute. Perhaps closer to that of a rabbit on speed.

"Feel my heart pounding," she invited, and he placed his hand on her left breast, spreading out his fingers.

"Can't tell, too much interference." He moved his hand down to her waist and placed his lips where his palm had rested. "Ooh, yeah, I feel it now. 120 beats per minute."

Sitting back up, he smiled at her. Actually, he looked at her as if she was some kind of angel or goddess. "Can I ask you something?"

"Sure." She expected him to ask about her previous experience, though she didn't dare ask him his number.

"Would you go out with me?"

"You mean, like a date?'

"Not like a date. An actual date."

She giggled, and he smiled. "Is my asking you out on a date that funny?"

"No, it's not funny. I would love to go out on a date with you. I was just thinking that we did this backward."

His eyebrows quirked up. "I don't know about you, but I was paying attention. We did it face to face. Although, I'm totally open to alternative suggestions."

"I wasn't referring to that. Which, by the way, was wonderful."

"Just wonderful?"

"Amazing."

"That's a little better." He wiggled his eyebrows at her.

"You're just fishing for praise, aren't you?"

"You know me. I'm totally shameless."

She traced a lazy finger across his chest. "OK, how about, fantastically awesome, mind-blowing, best experience of my life?"

He grinned. "Now you're talking! Same goes for me, by the way. So, what's this backward stuff?"

"Well, most people go out on dates, then have sex, then live together. We did it in the opposite order, backward."

"You're right. And here I thought I was so squared away." He brushed a strand of hair away from her face.

"Your hair is a little messy," he observed.

"I wonder whose fault that is?"

He totally took the blame. "Mine. And I had fun doing it. I'll brush it for you later. A lot later. So, because I am such a shameless glutton for praise, let me be certain. Was it good for you?"

She looked up at the ceiling as if considering various responses, then looked back at his face.

"No."

From the look on his face, it was obvious that she'd finally managed to do what she had failed to accomplish the day they'd met when he'd walked her home. She'd shocked him.

"Good is an ice cream cone. Good is mascara that doesn't clump." At his quizzical expression, she assured him, "Yes, that is a thing. Good is birds singing. This was miles, eons, light years away from being merely good. Good doesn't even begin to describe it. It wasn't even in the same universe as good. It was like, the best experience ever."

She sat up to emphasize her words.

"*Ever.*"

"So it really was fantastically awesome and mind-blowing for you?"

"Even better. It was better than my wildest fantasies."

His face lit up and his eyes went wide/ "You have wild fantasies? Do tell!"

"Yeah," she replied. "Lately I've been fantasizing about getting it on with my roommate."

"I like the sound of that." His eyes gleamed. "Details, sweetheart, I want details."

She batted her eyelashes at him, a silly, playful gesture she'd never utilized before, but with Eric, it seemed the most natural thing in the world to do.

"Well, I fantasized about kissing him." He obliged her by kissing her again. "And I fantasized about us being naked together."

He looked down at the two of them, cuddled on his bed, naked. "Well, that part is fulfilled. I hope it lived up to your expectations."

"It way exceeded them," she assured him.

"You took the words right out of my mouth."

A moment later she was on her back again, as he took her hands in his and stretched her arms above her head so that their bodies made tingly, delicious contact everywhere from fingertips to toes.

"Your neck is beautiful," he told her, as he kissed it. "And so is your cheek, and your ears. Your eyebrows turn me on." Each of those features received its own feathery kiss.

The man certainly enjoyed his post-coital cuddling, and so did she. She'd never realized how much fun it was to cuddle with your lover.

"Sleep with me."

Her eyebrows twitched up. "I don't know about you, but I was paying attention. We already did that."

"Yes, and it was glorious. I meant literally. Stay here with me all night. Don't go back to your room."

"Are you kidding?" she asked. "Do you think I'd get up and leave this?"

He sat up, tugging down the bedspread they had been lying on and nudging her under the sheet with him.

"I'll try not to hog the covers," he said. "It's been a while since I've shared a bed."

The man had told her, from day one, ask me anything you like, my life is an open book.

"How long?"

"Remember that day you crashed into my back on the sidewalk?"

Of course. How could she forget?

"Since before that."

She was flabbergasted. That had been over a year ago. And yet, for a guy who claimed to have been celibate for that long, he'd sure been prepared for today with an extra fun-sized box of protection.

"What was her name?"

"Whose name?" he asked warily, hoping against hope that Michelle had a sudden, out of the blue desire to be told the name of his sister, his psychiatrist, or the math teacher he'd had a crush on in the eighth grade.

No such luck.

"The last person you shared a bed with."

"Aw jeez Michelle, do you really want to know? Name, date, cup size?"

Yes, she wanted to know. She wanted to know everything about him, everything he'd ever done and experienced. Every girl he'd ever been with, every high and low of his career.

At the same time, she didn't want to know about his past, obviously very active intimate life. She wanted to fantasize that it had always been only him and her. A completely unrealistic fantasy of course, but one that she couldn't help having.

Curiosity won out over fantasy today.

"I'll tell you about mine if you tell me about yours."

He sighed, but knew he had no choice but to tell her.

"Linda." He hesitated, looking thoughtful. "Lisa. No, LeeAnn."

"Does she have a last name?"

"Most people do."

"Do you remember it?"

"I would have if she'd ever told me."

"Date?"

"The day of the last funeral I went to," he said, and she sat up suddenly with dread in her heart, remembering the day he'd come home from attending a funeral, less than a month ago.

"A funeral?"

He obviously could tell what she was thinking of.

"Not that funeral. A different one, before I met you."

How sad that he'd had to attend so many funerals. She was also curious to know more about his post-funeral encounter, considering that he wouldn't even let her get near him the day he'd returned from the mainland after attending a more recent service.

"Cup size?"

"Seriously?"

"Hey, you brought it up."

He held up both of his hands, curved into breast-like shapes. "D."

"I'm jealous. I'm only a C."

"I can tell. You have absolutely no cause to be jealous."

She turned away for a moment. Suddenly she no longer wanted to know about Linda Lisa LeeAnn. However, there was more on her mind, and she turned back to him.

"When did you buy the condoms?"

"The day after the rain, when I had to go to L.A. with a patient. We airlifted him to UCLA Medical Center, and after I was done, they let me crash in the doctor's lounge until morning. I was going to get an Uber down to San Pedro to get on the boat there, but one of the nurses getting off duty said she was heading down there to visit her daughter, and she gave me a ride to the Catalina Express terminal. I asked her if she had time, could we make a quick stop at Macy's on the way, because I wanted to buy something special before I went home. She looked at me and said, something special for a special young lady? When I told her yes, for an extremely special young lady, she said she'd be glad to stop there."

"But what did you buy at Macy's?" She was pretty sure that an upscale department store would not be the place to purchase condoms.

"I got this," he patted the second pillow on his bed. "Just in case. I was … hopeful."

"Wow, you got a pillow for me at Macy's? Target would have been OK, you know."

"Nah, you deserve Macy's." He drew her back close to him with an arm around her shoulders, and she gladly cuddled back against his chest.

"When I came out to the car with this in my shopping bag, Sylvia took one look at it and drove me straight across the street to Rite Aid, put her car in park, and said, 'I think you have another purchase to make before you head home with that special pillow, young man.' I kind of stared at her for a minute saying, um, because I just couldn't believe that this lady who reminded me of my mother was actually telling me to go buy condoms. I didn't have the heart to tell her that I could get them at Leo's Drugstore right here in town. So I went in and bought them there, and also bought her a box of candy as a thank you for the ride. That's when she asked for our address so she could send us an invitation to her grandson's bar mitzvah."

"You are such a charmer," she told him, with a thumb caressed over his cheekbone. She gave the expensive Macy's pillow an experimental pat. "It seems like a great pillow, but I don't think I'll use it much."

His face fell.

"I'd rather use this for my pillow." She slipped down a little and put her head on his shoulder. Automatically he put his arms around her, and his voice came from the top of her head.

"What about you?" he asked. "How long has it been?"

"Well, there was this day, I was walking down the street minding my own business, and this wall just sprung up in front of me. Since before that."

The man who at first glance she had thought to be a wall murmured against her hair. "I thought maybe – well – you know I'm not blind. I've seen your birth control pills in the medicine cabinet."

"I thought you were a medical professional."

"Most of the time." He took a strand of her hair in his hand and played with it.

"They're also to regulate my period and reduce menstrual cramps."

"So, you hadn't used them for the birth control aspect in over a year?"

"I told you I hadn't dated in that long. In fact, I told you a little lie."

He looked just a bit concerned.

"The real reason I hadn't gone out with anyone was because I only wanted you. I think, even before you moved to Avalon, after we'd met and you were," she waved her hand a bit, indicating the whole wide world, "OCONUS."

He smiled at her remembering the term.

"Everyone else was, well, not you."

"No even Christopher Wong?"

"Not even him."

His arm tightened around her and she lay there for a moment, her face against his warm shoulder, running her fingers across his chest and digesting what he'd told her about his last encounter, marveling that he could even bring himself to tell her, his current lover, about it when most people most likely wouldn't be able to discuss it. After a moment she realized he was sitting up, dislodging her from her extreme spot of comfort to look down at her face, his eyebrows curved up in a question.

"Well?" he asked.

"Well, what?"

"I distinctly seem to recall someone saying, I'll tell you about mine if you tell me about yours. I told you about mine. I'm not proud of it, in fact, I'm downright embarrassed by it, but I told you. And a promise is a promise, girl. So, spill."

"Aw jeez, Eric, do you really want to know? Name, date, um, shoe size?"

He chuckled a bit at her parroting his turn of phrase, and managed to both shake his head no, and nod it yes, at the same time.

"His name was,"

"Wait," Eric interrupted. "It wasn't Justin Douchebag, was it?"

"No way. I wouldn't have gotten that close to him if he'd been the last living, breathing man on the planet."

"What about Shooting Range Guy?"

"Who?"

He mimicked a gun pointing at the middle of his forehead, saying, "I missed my first shot."

"I never slept with him either."

"OK, cool. Pardon the interruption. Continue."

"David."

"Does he have a last name?"

"Most people do."

"Do you remember it?"

"Yes, I do. It was Vargas."

At least she'd taken the time to get the guy's full name. He hadn't always been so conscientious with his previous partners.

"Date?"

"Shortly before I finished technical school. After breaking up with Shooting Range Guy. David seemed like a nice guy and he didn't drink, at least not around me. But after I spent the night with him, or rather, part of the night, I found out that he'd only pursued me to make his girlfriend, who I didn't know existed at the time, jealous."

"Did it work?"

"Yeah, kind of too well. The girlfriend found out and dumped him like a hot potato. So he called me again and I said, too bad so sad, and blocked his number. I'll admit, part of the reason I slept with him was to show Shooting Range Guy that it was possible to be charming naturally, without finding your appeal in a bottle or three. But at least I wasn't in another relationship at the time, and if I'd known that David had a girlfriend, I wouldn't have had anything to do with him."

Another person who had disappointed her and let her down.

"OK, last question. Shoe size?"

She smiled. "Just average. Same goes for skill level. Unlike you, who is way above average, in every respect."

He grinned broadly. "Thank you, ma'am."

"I'm sorry about Christopher Wong," she said impulsively. As long as they were having awkward conversations about previous relationships, or non-relationships, she might as well banish the last of them.

Eric made a "Hmmph" sound, crossed his arms over his chest, and looked away from her.

"Are you pouting?"

"Trying to."

How could the man possibly get more adorable? Despite her best efforts, her lips twitched, and in a moment she was lost to a full grin.

"Why, exactly, are you pouting like a kindergartner?"

"It's what I do when I'm insanely jealous."

"You were jealous that I went out with him?"

"Too right I was. It killed me to see you walk out the door with him."

"Then it worked."

"Worked? Wait, are you saying that you went out with him just for that reason, to make me jealous?"

She nodded guiltily. "Yes. But when you just let me go without saying anything, I thought maybe you didn't mind. I was hoping you'd tell me not to go."

"I minded like crazy. But – what if I had said something? If I'd actually said, don't go out with him, stay with me?"

"I would have sent him away in a heartbeat. But you were too good-mannered to say something like that."

Despite the pout, he cut her a little side-eye and the corner of his mouth twitched. Encouraged, she poked him in the ribs. He twitched but kept his arms crossed over his chest. She reached for his hands and pried his arms out of their crossed position, laying her head against his chest, and giving his rib another poke at the same time. The mouth twitch turned into a laugh and he tried to grab her hand to push it away from his ribs.

She banished all thoughts and jealousy over Christopher Wong by tickling him until he gasped for mercy.

Then he narrowed his eyes a bit. "Wait, a minute. Back up here a little. You said the last time you, um, shared a bed was while you were at tech school. Didn't you complete that like, two years ago?

"Yes," she admitted

"So it's been two years since you…"

"Yeah. Is that so weird?"

"More like, astonishing."

"I told you, everyone else was just that, everyone else. Not you."

He shook his head sympathetically. "Oh my lord, you poor deprived little thing, you. No wonder you fell into bed with a broken-down retired sailor." He winked.

"Broken down? I don't think so."

"I'm honored to be the man you chose to end that drought."

How could using the word "honored" be so utterly sexy?

The last thing she saw, just before she closed her eyes, was a pair of sweet, sexy, sparkly hazel eyes smiling at her. She picked up his hand and held it close to her cheek.

"Your eyes are like Fourth of July sparklers, reflecting off a pool of honey."

"Hey," he replied, "You can be poetic too. We'll make a cowgirl out of you yet."

She let go of his hand just long enough to touch his lips with one finger. "When you first moved in here, do you know what the first thing I thought was?"

"That I was playing my music too loud?"

"OK, the second thing I thought was, I wonder if he's a good kisser."

"Am I?"

"The world's best."

38

She was glad she woke up first, because she realized that the sweetest thing she had ever seen was Eric sleeping.

Of course, she had seen him asleep before. But that had been on the couch, fully clothed. It was a whole different situation this morning, in his bed, with him curled up naked beside her. Sometime during the night, they'd crawled under the covers and cuddled.

Freya, she could get used to this. The first hint of sunrise peeked in between the window curtains, diffusing a soft glow of subdued light over them.

It wasn't surprising that he smiled in his sleep. She hoped that she had been the one to inspire that sleepy smile on his face, but realistically, it was most likely his natural expression. There was the tiniest little blond streak in his light brown hair. So maybe his adherence to sun protection wasn't quite as rigid as he let on. The tiny laugh lines next to his eyes were adorable.

He lay on his side, facing her, his bottom arm tucked under the pillow beneath his head. She couldn't decide which she'd rather do, watch him sleep, or wake him up to see his sparkly eyes.

It was a situation requiring a basis for comparison. She put a hand on his cheek, and rubbed a thumb over the faint stubble there. His eyes opened immediately. He didn't blink or yawn or seem to need to adjust his consciousness from slumber to wakefulness. He was just awake.

"Hey there, gorgeous."

The eyes. Definitely the eyes. Although the sweet sleeping face came in a real close second. "It wasn't a dream. You really are here." He reached up and held a strand of her hair. "I've fantasized about this, but the reality is so much better."

From anyone else, that might have sounded corny. But not when Eric said it.

"Hey there, handsome," she replied. "Where have you been all my life?" She could be corny too.

"Right here, waiting for you."

They just sat there smiling at each other for a moment, sharing air, then Eric said, "I like sleeping with you. You're cuddly."

"So are you," she replied immediately.

"I am, aren't I?" He proved it by cuddling her, then asked, "You want breakfast? Food," he clarified. "I'm cooking."

Wow. Mind-blowing sex, a hot guy sleeping next to her, and breakfast in bed? It didn't get any better than this.

He made a quick stop in the bathroom on his way to cook their breakfast, and she smiled at the sound of him closing the door behind him. Under the circumstances, seeing that they had spent the night together, she thought it would be OK if he let her hear him pee. But no, Eric was still too polite for that. His mama had raised a gentleman. She stretched out her feet and enjoyed the sensation of laying in his bed while he cooked her breakfast. The sheets were crisp, and very tight. He still made his bed like a sailor. You could probably bounce a quarter off it.

Both the bedsheets, and the coverlet that had been shoved to the foot of the bed, were blue, like the ocean. Michelle hadn't been inside this room since she'd prepared it for her new roommate, even before she knew that roommate would be Eric. The place was very neat. It didn't surprise her. He kept everything neat and tidy in the rest of the house also.

No dirty laundry was laying on the floor, other than the clothes they'd discarded last night. There was a small laundry hamper next to the door, and its lid was closed, any contents being contained inside without so much as an odd sock peeping out, and nothing piled on top.

Michelle wasn't exactly a slob, and her room wasn't a total mess. But there might be a few items of clothing and other assorted possessions kicked under the bed as a more convenient method of straightening up her room, and she'd have to confess she didn't always make her bed every day, and when she did, it was never as neat and tight as Eric's sheets. A fair amount of miscellany existed around her room, piled on the dresser and nightstand, and yes, admit it, the back of her closet was a testimony to indifferent housekeeping. She smiled to herself at the memory of Eric teasing her about helping him clean his room. Maybe she should have asked him to help her clean her room instead.

There was no miscellaneous clutter piled on his dresser or nightstand, only assorted photographs in simple, neat frames. The poster of Catalina Island still hung where she'd put it before he'd moved in, and on the other wall, he'd put another poster. It was a ship, specifically an aircraft carrier, with dozens of airplanes parked in precise rows on the deck, and hundreds of crew members lined up in another precise row, along the edges of the deck. The number 68 was painted on the side of a tower-like structure on one side of the deck. Eric's cap had the number 68 on it also.

So that must be the Nimitz. She wondered if Eric was one of those sailors along the edge of the deck in that photo, but she was not going to get out of his bed just now to scrutinize it more closely.

There was another frame hung on the wall, across from the two posters. It was the sketch she'd given him the day they'd hiked up the mountain to find the buffalo – the view of Avalon she'd drawn from the vantage point of her flat rock where she'd spent so much time in her youth. She thought he'd only asked for the sketch to be polite, but he'd obviously liked it enough to purchase a frame and hang it on his wall. If that wasn't the sweetest thing ever.

Lovers. They were lovers now. The concept both thrilled her and scared her. No one else she had ever known had made her feel like this. Not only sexually, but also safe, both physically and emotionally.

All those teasing little touches, the fake flirting, the supposedly fraternal cheek kisses – had they actually been leading up to this? The empathetic arm pats, the way he'd held her hair on more than one occasion – had he actually been flirting with her for real? Had she been so secure in their friends and roommates status that she'd stupidly not noticed? Or had this, their falling into bed together, becoming lovers, been the natural conclusion of it all?

He was both familiar – her friend, and roommate, her silly, joking, teasing Eric, whose off-key singing had filled her house, and her life, for months – and yet at the same time, her new lover, exotic, fascinating, a little mysterious, a different person in her life than he'd been yesterday.

She remembered the awesome foot rub he'd given her, which as she looked back, seemed to show somewhat less than fraternal affection. Not to mention the day he'd manhandled Justin Douchebag for insulting her, like her own personal knight in shining armor. All the times he'd called her sweetheart – she'd thought it was just something he said to every female he was acquainted with. She'd heard him use the endearment to Susan, to Natalie, to the girl at the ice cream shop who scooped their cones. But did he mean it more seriously when he said it to her?

The way he'd held her when she'd cried on his shoulder – was he just being a friend? Or showing romantic affection? The second time, she'd thought she felt him petting her hair. But it had been windy that day and at the time she thought he was just shifting it away from his face.

And most importantly, would the sex, as awesome and erotic and mind-blowing as it was, diminish their best friends relationship? Or would it enhance it? Why did she feel like this was what her life had always been leading to, to be with him?

Sex with Eric was fun. It was hot and passionate and satisfying, but it was also fun. They had laughed, they had giggled, they had talked and joked. The few other guys she'd been with had taken it all so darn seriously, with only one goal in mind, and once they'd achieved that, the fun was over. Until now she'd been afraid that was how it was always supposed to be.

He'd said some pretty amazing things to her last night. Things like declaring himself to be totally crazy about her. But did that sentiment hold the same sincerity when expressed during sexual foreplay as it might in the cool light of the morning after?

What were they, really? Roommates with benefits? Lovers, with all the uncertainty that went with a name like that? A Committed Couple with capital C's? Or just a silly boy and girl having screaming hot monkey sex without anything resembling a commitment?

Was this supposed to be a casual affair, roommates with benefits, or the inspiration of hope for happily ever after? It was fascinating how quickly sex could transition from an occasional bit of fun, to a full-blown addiction, once one found the right man.

Yes, Michelle, admit it. You are addicted to this man.

She didn't know how all that was going to play out, but one thing she did know. This was the best thing that had ever happened to her, and she was going to make the best of it.

She just wondered if Eric felt the same.

In just a few minutes, the delectable scents of bacon and coffee started wafting through the house, along with a quick yelp of "Ow!" from the kitchen.

"Are you OK?" she called out. "Do you need help?"

"No, I'm fine," he called back. "You stay there, I've got this."

She lay back on the crisp sheets, then heard him yelp again.

"Ow! Shit! Ow!"

"Are you sure you don't need help?"

"I'm sure!" he called back. "Don't worry, it's almost ready."

Taking his word for it, Michelle resisted the urge to go check out his issues in the kitchen and leaned over the side of the bed to picked up the shredded blue condom box and the other eleven foil packets that had fallen on the floor, and replaced them in the nightstand drawer that had remained open. As she was closing the drawer she noticed a metal chain inside, next to a small, leather-bound book, and she picked them both up. Yes, she was being nosy but under the circumstances, didn't she have the right? He'd told her his life was an open book long ago. If he had things he wanted to keep private, he could have locked them up in his gun case.

The metal chain held two metal tags-his Navy dog tags. She read the stamped wording, Hanson, Eric P. A number, it must be his social security number. A-POS, his blood type? And at the bottom, the word

Lutheran. That was odd. She recalled him telling her the first day they met that he wasn't much for religion.

The book had no wording on its cover, and when she opened it, saw it was filled with incompressible writing in a delicate, vine-like text, like baby worms playing tag. It was justified at the right, rather than on the left like English. Her guess was that the book might be in Arabic.

There were three frames on his nightstand-two photographs, and a small plaque depicting a ship and the words, "Home is where the Navy sends me." One of the two photos showed Eric and four other sailors standing on the deck of an aircraft carrier with huge grins and thumbs up. However their uniforms were different from what Eric had been wearing when he returned from reserve duty. These guys wore a pattern of shades of ocean blue.

The second photo was also a group of people-seven, including a younger Eric in a dark uniform that looked like the guy on a box of Cracker Jack, two older men and two older women, and next to him an elderly gray-haired couple, the man in a wheelchair with Eric's hand on his shoulder.

When she heard him in the hall outside the door, she instinctively pulled the sheet up over her breasts. Which was an utterly silly thing to do, considering he'd already seen, touched and tasted pretty much every-thing she had. It was simply a reflex, in the light of the newness of their intimacy. He could take the sheet off her later, if he was so inclined.

As he walked in the room with a plate in one hand, piled with toast and bacon, and two coffee mugs held by the handles in the other, she said, "I know things about you."

He grinned as he handed her the plate, set the mugs down on the nightstand, and sat down next to her on the edge of the bed.

"Under the circumstances, I should think so. You now know the loca-tion of all three of my freckles."

"Yes, and they're very adorable." At first, she hadn't noticed any freck-les, but then he'd turned around and bent down to pick up his skivvies and step into them. Aha, there they were, on that cute butt. Even cuter, when it was naked, three little freckles in a row, like Orion's belt.

"And also, that you read Arabic, and you're a Lutheran."

"Nope, and nope." His grin said, "Fooled ya!"

"You've been looking in my things, haven't you?"

She nodded guiltily as she bit into a piece of bacon. He held up a piece of toast in front of her face and she bit that too, then he ate the rest. He didn't seem concerned about her looking in his things.

Sitting there together, companionably eating bacon and toast, Eric looked down at himself and said, "Uh, oh. I've broken a rule."

"You mean there's a rule against rocking a girl's world? Please say it isn't so!"

"There better not be a rule like that. But I've broken my promise not to walk around the house in my underwear."

She waved a hand at him as she swallowed the last of the slice of bacon.

"I grant you a dispensation. You may now walk around in your skivvies, as long as you take them off when I ask."

"And when will that be?" he asked hopefully, eyeing the sheet.

"As soon as I finish my breakfast."

"FYI," he said, "not a good idea to cook bacon in your skivvies." She followed his glance to see several red marks on the fair skin of his belly. "It spits," he said ruefully. Now she understood his yelping and swearing.

"You were wounded in order to feed me. What a sweetie."

"Sweetie is my middle name." This time she didn't dispute it.

He set the plate on the nightstand, next to the photos she'd also examined, handed her a cup of coffee, and opened the drawer. His eyes widened a bit when he saw the pile of condom packets she had dropped in after picking them up off the floor. "Thanks for picking up after me."

"Not a problem, Doc."

He picked up the dog tags and looked at them. "I only had them put Lutheran on these for my family, in case, you know... Anyway, it would have looked dorky to put Jedi, though some guys tried to."

He was a Star Wars fan, quoted Clint Eastwood movies and sang country music out loud. The man was looking at dorky in the rear-view mirror. But he was absolutely the world's sexiest, most adorable dork.

Dorky was the new sexy. He put the chain over her head and the two tags clinked as they settled between her breasts.

"Oh, that is so hot," he breathed.

She looked down at the two metal tags resting between her breasts and couldn't help thinking that wearing them somehow made her his woman. More than his roommate with benefits, more than his lover. His Woman.

"Did you actually wear these things?" she asked.

"Not since boot camp. No one does. If you're somewhere hot, like in a ship's engine room, or somewhere like Iraq, the metal gets too hot to have near your skin. It was literally a hundred and twenty degrees there, in the shade. You let metal touch your skin at that temperature, and you're asking for a second-degree burn. If you're somewhere magnetic, like near a ship's engine, you can imagine how dangerous it could be to have them on. And the medical staff especially never wears them." He put his hand around the chain. "I'd rather get a black eye from a disoriented patient, than get choked. When I was on the green side, we'd lace one into a boot."

He picked up the small book, rubbing a finger over the cover with affection. "This was a gift, from the parents of the first baby I delivered."

"What is it?"

"It's the Koran, the holy book of Islam, but I can't read any of it. Except for this. I had a translator explain it to me." He pointed to some words written by hand on the first page, following them with his finger, starting from the right side instead of the left like it was in English.

He read the memorized words slowly. "*Barakatih ealayk.*"

"What does that mean?"

"It's 'blessings upon you'."

"It was thoughtful of them to give you a gift, but I would have sent flowers or a basket of muffins."

"I suppose so, but there aren't too many flowers or muffins in Iraq."

"I looked at your pictures too," she admitted.

"Well, that's what they're there for."

He put the book back into the drawer and picked up the plaque, rubbing a thumb over it in a gesture that she was realizing he used when the item held sentimental value for him. "My mom gave this to me when I left for my first deployment. Some of the guys teased me about carrying this around wherever I was stationed, but after my mom died, they let up."

He set the plaque down and picked up the photo of him and his buddies. "This is from crossing the line."

"You don't look like you're doing anything that crosses a line."

"Not crossing A line. Crossing THE line. The equator."

"Oh." The furthest line she'd ever crossed was the I-15 freeway. "You guys are wearing different uniforms from what you were wearing when you came back from reserve duty."

He touched the image of him and his shipmates. "These uniforms are called blueberries, or aquaflage. They've phased them out since then and replaced them with the green camouflage."

"I like the blue ones better," she said. "They just seem more Navy-like. No offense, but the green one you were wearing almost looks like you're in the Army."

Eric chuckled. "The blueberries are great for camouflaging someone if they fall overboard. In which case, you'd rather be seen than camouflaged. They were also uncomfortable, didn't breathe, and the fabric was prone to melting and potentially worsening a burn injury. They may look more naval to a civilian, but the green ones are actually an improvement. The Navy is an evolving institution, constantly striving to improve itself." He set down the flight deck photo and picked up the other one.

"That one is my family and me, the day I graduated from boot camp."

"Are those your grandparents?"

"No, that's my parents." He pointed at the two men standing on his right. She'd thought perhaps one of them was his dad. "My brothers, Oliver and Philip." Then he indicated the two women on his left. "My sisters, Diane and Brenda."

"May I?" she asked, reaching for his family photo. He smiled and gave it to her, and she looked more closely at them.

"You look like your dad." Despite the fact that the man in the wheelchair was elderly and gray-haired, she could still discern the origin of Eric's twinkly smile and sparkly eyes.

"Yeah, he used to say he was glad one of his kids took after him.

My brothers both look more like their mother, my dad's first wife. And my sisters were Dad's stepdaughters. Their father was our mom's first husband. My parents were both widowed when they met. We're a real blended family."

She handed the photo back to him and he ran a thumb along the image of his father before setting it back on the nightstand. "That was the last time I saw my dad. He died a month later. I think now, he knew it would happen soon, and that would most likely be the last time we saw each other. I think that's why he made such an effort to come to my boot camp graduation. It wasn't easy to travel from Florida to Illinois with a wheelchair, especially with having to change planes in Atlanta. I was lucky that my parents and all my siblings were able to come. We were really only supposed to have four guests each, but a couple of buddies whose families couldn't make it gave me their extra tickets. I still remember the last thing my dad said to me. When they were getting ready to leave, I knelt down next to his chair so we could be face to face, and I hugged him and thanked him for coming. We're a pretty affectionate family but it was extra special when he hugged me back, and he actually kissed my cheek and he said, 'I'm really proud of you, son.' And I said, 'I love you, Dad.' They left then, and a month later, I got the call that he'd had another stroke."

She pressed her face into the warm curve of his shoulder and ran a finger along his collarbone.

"I envy you. The last thing my dad said to me before he died was, don't wait up." Then she sat up and looked at his face, at his sweet smile tinged with just a bit of sadness while recalling his father's death.

"I'm sorry," she said. "I'm sorry you lost your dad like that, and I'm sorry I said that about mine."

"You don't need to be sorry, if it's the truth."

"It was the truth, but I'm sorry I brought it up here, now." She swept her hand, indicating his bed and the pleasure they'd experienced there. "I'm going to stop doing this. I've got to stop doing this."

"OK, I'll bite. What are you going to stop doing? I hope you're not going to give up ice cream. If you did, I'd feel obligated to give it up too and I would hate that. If you're concerned about the calories, we can burn them off with some more hiking. I wouldn't mind seeing those buffalo a little more up close. Or, there are a couple of other things I could think of to burn off the extra calories."

He pulled her close and kissed her neck, making it clear what he thought those other calorie-burning activities might be.

"I'm trying to be serious, Eric."

He switched to his serious smile. It was an oxymoron, but yes, he did have a serious smile.

"Being serious is highly overrated. Although I am seriously into ice cream."

She gave him a look that stopped his teasing.

"I'm sorry, sweetheart. I'll be serious. What do you want to stop doing?"

"I want to stop my whining about my former shitty life. Pardon my language. My cosmic existence. The past is past, and I've been such a downer all these years, whining and moaning, oh woe is me. I've whined about it to you so much, you're probably sick of hearing about it."

"You're not whining, and I'd never be tired of listening to you," he said, but she held up a "stop it" finger in front of his face.

"You always argue with me when I'm trying to be serious."

"No I don't."

"You just did."

"I just can't win here, can I?"

"It's not a competition. I just need you to listen to me for a minute without cracking a joke or trying to distract me."

"OK, I can do serious. But I don't know how long I can go without trying to distract you."

He actually did assemble a serious expression on his face, not a joking serious. A serious serious.

"I'm going to change," she said.

"There's nothing wrong with you the way you are now."

She stuck a finger in his face again, almost tapping his nose. He snapped at it as if trying to bite it.

"You're arguing again!"

He rolled his eyes at her. "Can't a guy express his honest opinion?"

"Not right now. Maybe later, if you'll be serious and listen to me."

"Sorry, Ma'am." He made a zipping motion across his mouth.

"Remember when you told me that I could compartmentalize my bad memories?"

Eric nodded but kept his lips pressed tight together, so tight they were starting to turn white.

"Well, I'm going to do just that. I'm going to quit with this woe is me, my parents didn't love each other, didn't want me, didn't care about me or themselves and didn't let themselves live." She saw his eyes light up with the urge to argue that point, and she struck preemptively with a shushing finger on his lips. She'd meant only to forestall the denial of her negativity with that finger, but couldn't help but run it along his lips, which made him sigh dreamily and not argue the point.

"Maybe that's true and maybe it's not. Like you said, we can't know any of it for sure. But it doesn't matter anymore. I intend to put the bad stuff in its compartments and keep it locked up tight and enjoy my life."

Let me know how that works out for you, sweetheart. Even the strongest compartment doors manage to open themselves up every so often.

He didn't say that out loud, because Michelle would probably smack him. Keeping his big mouth shut was really hard.

"OK, I'm done. You can talk now."

His breath rushed out as if he'd been holding it for an hour.

"Thank you! I was about to pass out there."

"Do you believe me? Are you taking me seriously? Or are you going to make some joke or argument?

He grinned for a moment, but somehow managed to reign in his goofiness.

"I'm totally taking you seriously. And I think you're the most amazing and extraordinary person I've ever met."

"This is the best thing that's ever happened to me and I'm not going to ruin it with my whining," she promised.

He put his hand under her chin and tilted her face towards him.

"Sweetheart, having you here like this, with me? Nothing could ruin it. You can whine if you want to. But I'd rather have you kiss me."

That was a request that she was more than happy to accommodate, with her arms around his neck and her breasts pressed against his bare chest as the blue sheet slipped down to her waist.

Freya, how had she ever lived before, without being able to feel that sensation? His mouth tasted of bacon, butter from the toast, and – mint.

She looked at him, narrowing her eyes a little. "You brushed your teeth!"

"Well, yeah. Is that a bad thing?" Obviously, relieving himself hadn't been the only thing he'd done in the bathroom on his way to make breakfast. She was suddenly embarrassingly aware of the fact that she hadn't brushed her teeth in almost twenty-four hours. She'd walked in the door yesterday afternoon at six-thirty, and by six-forty she'd been here in bed with Eric, and she hadn't left it since. She'd kissed him with, *eeww,* morning breath. Gross. She backed away and put her hand over her mouth.

"What's this?" he asked. "Are you tired of kissing me already?"

"No, I'll never get tired of kissing you," she mumbled from behind her hand.

She could kiss him every day for the rest of her life and never get tired of it. I'll kiss you in bed, I'll kiss you in the kitchen, I'll kiss you here, there and everywhere. Like Dr. Seuss for adults.

"But my mouth, my breath, um," She edged towards the side of the bed. "I need to go brush my teeth too."

He prevented her by running his hands through her hair. *Freya,* she could be convinced to commit treason when he touched her like that. He pried her hand away from her mouth and insisted on kissing her again. The bacon and toast and coffee sat forgotten on the nightstand next to his photos.

"Your mouth is like sugar. Like honey. Like a golden delicious apple."

"An apple? Really?"

"Yes, sweet and delicious. You taste better than bacon. Better than ice cream, and you know how much I like ice cream."

His sexy compliments were turning her into jelly inside, but she still squirmed away. "You're sweet," she assured him. "You're the sweetest, sexiest person I've ever met in my life. But not only do I need to brush my teeth, I need to, um," she nodded behind her. "You know, use the head, like you say."

He relinquished his hold and as she reluctantly dashed to the bathroom across the hall, he insisted, "Hurry back. If you think I have nice things to say about your mouth, just wait until I get started on how beautiful your breasts are."

With a prospect like that to come back to, she took care of business in the bathroom really quickly, though she did brush her teeth real thoroughly.

39

He was laying on his back with his arms behind his head, satisfaction oozing from his very pores when she scampered back into the room, and turned to her with his sexiest smile as she slid back under the sheet with him.

"I want to do it again," she said, and Eric's smile nearly split his face.

He started to get up from his prone position, breathing out a hearty, "OK!"

She put a hand on his chest. "No, stay like that."

He glowed. The man actually glowed. "Is this one of those alternative suggestions we talked about earlier?"

"You could say that." She pulled open the nightstand drawer, pulled out a fresh condom package, and handed it to him.

"Are you up for this?" she asked, and he didn't fail to miss the double entendre. With a quick glance downwards, he gasped, "Yes, Ma'am!"

Again, he started to move over but she pressed a hand against his chest to stop him.

"Lay still," she insisted, pushing him down into a prone position.

"Far be it from me to disobey a direct order, ma'am, but I'm afraid that's not possible."

She looked down, where *things* were rapidly progressing from laying still to awesomely *not* laying still.

She swung a leg over and straddled his lap, and he sprang to attention in a way that even the snappiest military sale couldn't come close to. Yes, ma'am! He had never been so completely, utterly turned on in his entire life.

"How fast can you put that on?" she asked, with a glance at the foil packet she'd given him.

He could, and did, put it on very fast. With lightning speed, actually.

"Oh, yeah, right, alternative suggestions! I like-"

His sentence went unfinished as she grasped him for steadiness, her knees straddling his hips, then slowly, agonizingly slowly, she slid down on him until he was fully encased, surrounded, possessed.

All he could utter for a moment was a small moan, with throat stretched tight and eyes closed.

But when she moved, starting to raise up a little, he grasped her hips with his hands and this time held her still.

"Wait," he said, and she adored that look of absolute bliss on his face. "Just stay like that for a minute. Don't move. I want to just feel you there. Oh, lord!"

When he took his hands from her hips, and moved them up to her breasts, she realized Eric wasn't the only person who could moan with pleasure. She moved on him then, feeling the hot friction, the fullness of him in her, and they both moaned.

Leaning forward, she put her hands against the wall above his head for better stability.

"You know what I'm calling this?" she asked.

"Heaven," was his quick, panting reply.

"No, that should happen in a few minutes."

"Oh, you bet it will."

She leaned forward to kiss him.

"I'm calling it, Saving a Horse."

"Oh my ever-loving God."

It was funny how a man got religion at a moment like this.

******

"Damn," he said later. "Damn."

"Is that a good damn, or a bad damn?" she asked.

"Good. Definitely good. Wonderful, in fact. No, wonderful is woefully inadequate. Stupendous, amazing, soul-shattering. That was the whole thesaurus under the heading awesome."

They spent the rest of the morning napping, talking, and not napping, and by early afternoon were hungry again. For food as well as each other. This time, Michelle insisted on providing the nourishment and told Eric to wait for her in bed.

She didn't have his confidence to walk around the house in just her panties, even if she could find them, so she swiped his bathrobe from its hook on the back of the door. It was an ugly green color, but it smelled like Eric, and she wrapped the sash around her waist as she glanced back at him, sitting there in bed watching her and smiling as she took an appreciative sniff at the terry cloth.

"You wait here," she insisted. "I'll fix us something to eat this time."

"I could help," he suggested, putting one foot out from under the covers, but she held up a hand.

"Nope. My turn to provide nourishment. I'll be back in a minute."

"I can't wait," he said

In the kitchen, she got out bread, mayonnaise and lunch meat and was making sandwiches when she felt Eric's hands on her hips, warm even through the fabric. Dang, he walked quietly. He pushed her hair aside with one hand and kissed the back of her neck.

"You were supposed to say in bed," she admonished, as she spread mayonnaise on the bread.

"I know. I missed you. You've been gone a whole two minutes." He turned her around to face him, barely giving her a chance to put down the knife. A spot of mayonnaise was on her finger and on impulse she dabbed it on the end of his nose.

He went cross-eyed looking at it. "Hey, take that off."

She obligingly removed the mayonnaise spot from his nose. With her tongue.

When she kissed him this time, she was certain her mouth was fresh, and the kiss went quickly from tender, to heated, to pure sexy desire. His hands went to the sash of his robe around her waist, undid the knot, slipped inside the green terry cloth to encircle her waist beneath it. She leaned close to him, clinging, feeling the muscular smoothness of his back, his shoulders, his gluteus maximus. Just as she was beginning to wonder if the kitchen table would bear the weight of both of them, Eric suddenly tensed and stared at the clock on the microwave behind her.

"Crap, I have to be at work in half an hour!" he yelped.

"Do you want me to get dressed real quick and drive you over to the fire station in the golf cart so you're not late?" she asked.

"No. I want to remember you like this, naked underneath my robe." He ran his hands briefly over her hips and waist, cupping her breast briefly.

"Oh, Lord!" he breathed, then with obvious regret in his eyes, folded the robe back across her body and retied the sash. He kissed her briefly and said, "I have to say it. Thank you for the best night of my life, sweetheart."

She tried to put her arms around his neck, to kiss him back, but Eric, being the completely honorable person that he was, wouldn't let her, and sprinted back to the bathroom.

He really could SSS in ten minutes, Michelle observed, and all too soon was out the door with a brief goodbye kiss and a muttered, "Damn, I never got to brush your hair," carrying the sandwich she'd made in a plastic baggie, and singing one of his country songs as he dashed towards work.

40

He shouldn't wake her. It was 7:30 a.m. on Sunday morning, but the thick fog blanketing the island this morning defied one's belief that the sun was actually up. His walk home from work was eerie and surreal, like walking through a cloud.

He shouldn't wake her. Even if she was asleep in his bed, and he'd walked into the house after a fifteen-hour shift.

He'd barely made his three-p.m. call time yesterday, stashed the sandwich Michelle had made him in the fire station refrigerator, and offered an enthusiastic high five to each and every person he'd gotten within five feet of. Five minutes later, they were called to aid a hiker who had fallen up on Stagecoach Road and injured his ankle. As he hopped into the passenger seat of the ambulance, Tony had grinned knowingly from the driver's seat and said, "I'll bet dollars to donuts that *someone* got laid last night!"

There'd been no way Eric could have denied it even if he'd wanted to. His answering grin was blindingly happy. "Oh man," he'd replied. "I am the luckiest son of a bitch on the planet."

So now this morning he stood in the doorway of his bedroom, leaning against the door frame watching her sleep in his bed, and it was the sweetest thing he'd ever seen. The blanket covered her demurely to the waist, and she wore a white shirt, way too big for her. She lay with her back to him, her long dark hair smooth and shiny against that pillow he'd bought at Macy's.

Best hundred bucks he'd ever spent.

As if she'd sensed his presence, she turned over and opened her eyes, smiling at him. Lord, he wanted to capture this moment forever – Michelle, in his bed, her beautiful dark hair across the pillow, that sweet smile across her face. She picked up one hand and beckoned him with her finger, and in a nanosecond, he was at her side, sitting next to her on the edge of the bed, leaning down to smooth her hair away from her face and kiss her.

His hand touched the cotton over her back. "Is this my shirt?"

"Yes," she admitted, with her arms around his neck and her breath warm against his ear. "But it's not the one you were wearing yesterday. I hope you don't mind." He could see the metal chain of his dog tags was still around her neck, under the shirt. Lord, that was sexy, to think of that part of him laying against her breast, close to her heart.

"Where did you get it?" Had he left his clothes in the washer or dryer?

Michelle nodded towards his dresser. "You were gone at work forever. I just wanted to feel you close to me."

So, she'd taken it from his dresser when he'd been at work. He didn't mind a bit. His room was her room. And seeing her wearing his tee shirt was almost as much of a turn-on as seeing his dog tags around her neck.

"It smells like you." She pulled up the neck of the shirt over her mouth and nose, inhaling.

"What do I smell like? Nothing bad, I hope."

She breathed in. "Soap. Sunshine. Maleness. Warmth. A hint of Navy petty officer."

"A hint of petty officer? I didn't think that had a smell."

She smiled. "It's a unique Eric Hanson scent."

"Are you wearing anything underneath it?"

She picked up the blanket and looked underneath. "Don't be mad. A pair of your boxers. The blue ones."

"Well if you're going to be rummaging through my dresser, I'm going to have to find a new place to hide my dirty magazines."

A look of shock filled her face.

"I'm kidding, sweetheart! I don't have any dirty magazines."

"Because all that is online now, right?" Her shocked expression switched to teasing.

He looked completely, utterly, one hundred percent innocent. "I have absolutely no idea about that. You can wear my skivvies any time. Let me see them on you."

"I can't stand up. They'll fall off."

"In that case, please please stand up."

"Sorry but no. I'm staying right here in this bed. I hope you don't mind I slept here while you were at work?"

"Are you kidding? I'm thrilled."

She smiled. "But there's one problem."

"What's that?"

"You still have your clothes on."

He stood up and grabbed at his boots, almost falling over in his haste to try and get them off, and why did the Avalon Fire Department make him wear these stupid-ass boots that Would. Not. Untie. Finally, he was able to loosen them enough to yank them off and cast them aside, but now his belt was stuck together with superglue and his fly was welded together like a ship's hull. It took a superhuman effort to get them undone.

He hated that belt. He punished it by kicking it away from him, still looped into his pants.

Somehow, he managed to get his shirt off without ripping out all the buttons, tossing it towards the chair but not bothering to see if it landed there. Michelle sat there watching and waiting, a sexy smile on her face that made his hands sweat as he struggled to get his clothes off. There were just too many damn pieces.

He was just about to deep-six his skivvies when Michelle held her hand up in a "stop" gesture.

"Wait a minute," she requested.

Wait a minute? Was she kidding? She got him all hot and bothered and now she wanted him to put on the brakes? He couldn't keep a look of dismay from crossing his face.

"You haven't changed your mind, have you, sweetheart?"

She shook her head. "No. I just want to look at you for a minute."

"Again?" he asked with teasing in his eyes and put his hands on his hips, allowing her to ogle shamelessly. "I haven't changed any since the day I moved in."

"You're right." She peered over the edge of the bed and looked at his feet. "Your toes are just as cute as they've always been."

"My cute toes want to have a conversation with your cute toes," he told her.

Her eyes moved up his body, all the way to the top of his head. "And you're still gorgeous." He was too gorgeous for his own good. Or for her own good.

When he rolled his eyes she insisted, "You're beautiful."

He was. She'd thought so when she first saw him, standing shirtless in her kitchen, and she still thought so. He was unbelievably gleaming, standing at attention, ma'am! Gorgeous, with all that smooth, light skin, fair but not pasty. The smooth freshness outlined and emphasized the definition of his muscles, deltoid and bicep, pectineus and sartorius. Pectoral and abdominal, not bulgy but smooth, subtle and oh so sexy. But it was the eyes and smile, of course, that were his most attractive features, especially now, as they glowed with desire.

"You are too," he responded, sitting next to her on the bed. "My Michelle, you are like a goddess." How could saying something so corny come out sounding so erotic? "Your hair is like a river of chocolate."

"You mean sticky and wet?"

"No, silky and warm and delicious." Warm anticipation flowed through her as he ran a hand over the hair he had just complimented.

"Even when I have bed head?" she asked. So maybe she was fishing for compliments, as he had been yesterday, but she couldn't get enough of hearing them from him.

"Yes, even when it's tousled and messy from you sleeping in my bed on your new pillow. Do you know that your eyes are the color of the ocean? Every moment since I left here yesterday, I've been thinking of ways to make you smile."

"Your being here is what makes me smile," she said, and she was suddenly, desperately needing the feel of his heartbeat against her skin.

She couldn't yank the shirt off herself fast enough, but when her hands touched the chain hanging around her beck, he put his hand over hers.

"No," he breathed. "Leave those on."

"Eric." It was only the sound of his name, sighing from her lips, but it was the most sensuous sound ever uttered.

He grabbed a condom from the drawer as she yanked away the covers and pulled him down into bed with her.

******

For their date, Eric took her to dinner at the Bluewater Grille. Unlike other times when they had eaten together, rather than take their chances with seating, he had called ahead and reserved them a table on the patio, looking over the bay. He even held her chair when she sat down, which may have been a totally old-fashioned gesture, but she loved it. Apparently, chivalry was not dead after all.

After dinner, they strolled down Crescent Avenue, and to anyone observing them, it was obvious that Eric and Michelle were On a Date, and no longer just roommates hanging out and grabbing a bite to eat.

The first clue was that they were walking down the street holding hands. This time, it wasn't an 'it's crowded, I don't want to lose you' hand-holding. It wasn't 'reassuring you that you'll survive your first flying experience' hand-holding. It was definite, full-on 'we're together' hand-holding, for everyone in town to see.

The second clue was how they were dressed. Rather than the usual island uniform of tee shirts, shorts and flip flops, Eric wore crisp jeans and a shirt with actual buttons that wasn't part of any uniform, and Michelle wore a flowy pink sundress and lots of mascara.

Being the small town that Avalon was, it wasn't surprising to run into someone they knew. Tracy came around the corner from Clarissa Avenue, stopped, looked them both up and down, and smiled a huge, knowing grin.

"Hey, you two," Tracy was practically purring "What are you guys up to?"

Michelle and Eric glanced at each other, then back at Tracy, who had a serious "I thought so!" grin on her face.

"Good evening, ma'am," Eric said in his best, most polite Navy Chief Petty Officer voice. "Nice to see you again. We're just looking for a good place to watch the sun set."

Michelle smiled at her friend with an expression that said, "Yeah, what he said."

Tracy pointed south past the boat dock, where the road curved around the bend. "Lover's Cove is just around the corner."

"That sounds perfect, ma'am. Thank you."

Michelle stifled a giggle at the way Eric was drawling out his slight southern accent a little dramatically for Tracy's benefit.

"Enjoy the rest of your evening," he said dismissively as he led Michelle past where Tracy stood, and towards the curve in the road leading to Lover's Cove. Michelle gave her friend a little finger wave as they walked away.

They could positively feel Tracy staring holes in their backs as they strolled down the street towards Lover's Cove. Before they reached the curve, Eric let go of Michelle's hand, put his arm around her waist and drew her close.

She hadn't been a fan of PDA's in the past, but she sure liked it now.

"I have a suggestion for our next date," he murmured in her ear. "Let's go to the mainland, find a nice hotel, in Long Beach maybe, with a big bed and room service, and put the Do Not Disturb sign on the door."

"That sounds heavenly. You don't have any friends in Long Beach, do you?"

"Yes, but I won't tell anyone that I'll be there. And I'll only answer my phone if it's work."

"That sounds like the perfect date to me." The perfect date, she thought, with the perfect guy.

"Is she still watching us?" Eric asked a few steps later.

Michelle snuck a brief glance behind her. "Like a hawk."

"Well then, let's give her something to look at," Eric said with a gleam in his eye. He put his hands on her hips, drew her close, and kissed her, right there on the sidewalk on Crescent Avenue, in front of Tracy and everyone else.

A couple of people whistled. Another called out, "Get a room!"

"Are we the scandal of Avalon now?" he asked, smiling into her eyes.

She nodded. "I think so. You know, the last time we stood on this spot, you were taking my pulse."

"Maybe I need to take it again," he replied, and picked up her hand and pressed his lips to the inside of her wrist. "Like a rabbit on speed," he murmured. "Are you having a panic attack?"

"No. I'm having a lust attack."

******

Of course, the first thing the next morning, Tracy was at the dock by the Casino.

"You sly little vixen you! Just roommates my eye! Don't you try and tell me you two aren't doing the wild thing."

"Shhh, someone will hear you." But Tracy didn't care about being overheard, she wanted details.

"You have to tell me what he's like, and does he have a brother? Spill, girlfriend!"

"He has two brothers but they're both married." Michelle refrained from adding, *and they're grandfathers.*

Tracy's face fell, but she didn't give up her quest for details. "And?"

"Well, he's a great guy. He's sweet and funny and strong and smart and..."

"Yeah yeah yeah, that's great, but what I'm asking is, what is he like in bed? Is he a screamer? A moaner? Does he invoke a deity? Details, girl-friend, I want details!"

"Jeez, Tracy. I'm not telling you that." There was no way on God's green earth she was going to tell Tracy that he was indeed a moaner, that she was the screamer, and they had both invoked a deity. But the unbidden smile of satisfaction that lit up her face as she remembered it told her friend all she needed to know. But Tracy wasn't done. "Does he call you 'Ma'am'?"

"All the time." In fact, she felt like she'd heard the term about as much as the Queen of England. However, far more than being called Ma'am, Michelle really preferred the breathy way he said her name in bed, though Tracy was never going to know that.

"And how long has this been going on?"

Michelle pretended ignorance. "What?"

"You know! You and the hot paramedic. Doing the horizontal tango."

"Um, since Friday."

"You have to be kidding me. I thought you two had been living together for months."

"We were."

"I can't believe you waited so long to do the deed with him."

Sometimes Michelle couldn't quite believe it either.

Tracy looked wistful, and a bit jealous. "That man has such a fine ass."

Tracy was right. He did have a fine ass. Michelle had seen it. She'd had her hands on it. It was fine.

41

The day she took his hand and led him into her bedroom, he was touched, and not just because it got them on a bed three seconds faster than taking the three additional steps into his room. Since the day they'd become lovers, they'd always slept, and not slept, in his bed. She only used her own bed when he was away on the night shift, and on the days that pink box came out of the medicine cabinet. He'd perceived that she didn't trust people easily, and taking a man into your bedroom, even a man you were already sleeping with, revealed a big amount of emotional trust.

He didn't need to be a rocket scientist to figure out what had happened to her to make her so distrustful. Life had happened to her. Her mother's premature death, her father's alcoholism, were primary contributing factors to her shuttered eyes and compressed lips. He suspected her previous romantic relationships had been less than inspirational as well. That he found really difficult to believe, how a girl as beautiful and charming as her had apparently not had a satisfying romantic relationship. Obviously the men she'd met up with hadn't bothered to look past the pretend bitchy exterior to find the charm beneath.

He was perfectly aware that she'd had other lovers before him-guys she'd dated while attending tech school, and, from what she'd told him about her high school experiences, a totally undeserving prom date. But he'd be willing to bet none of them had ever been invited into her pretty pink princess sanctuary.

As they lay on the flowered bedspread, he said, "Could you do something for me?"

Her eyes gleamed. "What did you have in mind?"

He nodded towards her dresser. "Deep-six the teddy bear. He's staring at me. He's going to give me performance anxiety." She laughed, because that was the last thing he needed to worry about, but obligingly banished the teddy bear to the closet.

"Sweetie, you would give other men performance anxiety," she assured him.

"Did an old boyfriend win that for you at the county fair?"

She blinked at him. "No, I won it myself."

"Of course you did. Sharp shooting?"

"Yeah, but just those water pistols aimed at a painting of a clown."

He started to get up and she looked upset. "Where are you going?"

He jerked his head towards his room. "Condoms."

She ran her hand down his arm, caressing his tattoo briefly, stroking his wrist, then twined her fingers firmly in his. "You know, I'm on the pill." Sometimes, over the past year, she'd wondered why she'd bothered to keep refilling that prescription. It hadn't been as if she'd need the protection lately. But she kept it up for the reason she'd started taking it in the first place, to regulate her period and reduce menstrual cramps.

She looked up at him, hope and expectation and the big question in her eyes. She didn't have to say it; he knew what she was asking. *Are we exclusive?*

He tumbled back down on the bed, right on top of those pink and yellow and blue flowers, held her hair in his hands and pressed his face against her neck.

"Oh, Jesus." She had no idea just how exclusive they were.

******

"Are you licking me?"

She moved her mouth off his skin just long enough to admit, "Yes."

"OK, I love it. But why? I feel like an ice cream cone. Not that I'm complaining, mind you."

"You taste good. Way better than ice cream." Just as Tracy has surmised, he was lickable. But Tracy would never know just how much.

"I love the feel of your lips on me," Eric said appreciatively.

"Really?" She had to ask. "Where"

"Anywhere."

"Like, here?" She kissed the side of his neck.

"Oh, yes!" She pressed her lips to his shoulder.

"There too," he assured her.

She scooched down and caressed his right nipple with her tongue. Interesting. A man's nipple could pucker under a loving tongue just like hers did. The sound he made when she did that was a cross between a sigh and a moan.

Then she took her mouth off his skin again and looked up at him.

"Can I ask you a question?"

"Yes. Yes! I'm sure that whatever you want to ask me, the answer will be yes."

"Why do men have nipples?" she asked, just before she licked it again.

He didn't answer the question, just tilted his head back and made a slight moaning sound. "Oh, lord! I like that!"

She sat up and looked at him. He loved the way her eyes it up, the way she smiled at him as if making love with him was the most fun she'd ever had in her entire life. But he was disappointed at the cessation of her licking.

"Well?" she asked, teasing him with her eyes.

"Well, what?" he countered, a bit breathlessly.

"Why do men have nipples?" she repeated.

"Shit, I don't know," he moaned, trying to get her back into licking mode with a hand cupped at the back of her head. "You're the smarty pants who got all A's."

"They never covered that in my high school biology class. You're the medical professional who's into anatomy."

"We can Google it later," he promised. "Just, please, do that again."

She murmured hums of appreciation along the lines of his pectoral muscles, breathed along his ear, felt bold enough to slide her hands down over his cute, firm butt, an action that had him moaning and shuddering, as the soft skin of her breasts pressed against the hardness of his chest.

Later, much later, they lay replete and drowsy on the tangled flowered bedspread, basking in the afterglow.

"I'm dead," she murmured against his clavicle.

Eric shoved the weight of her hair away from his face. "No you're not."

"Yes, I am." Despite being dead – killed with the exhaustion of love-making – her tongue was able to lick him a little more.

Eric lifted a fatigued hand and pressed a finger against the very not-dead pulse in her neck.

"I feel a pulse. You're alive. You're just arguing for the sake of arguing."

He turned over to face her and pulled her against him.

She said, "OK, so maybe I'm not completely dead."

"Uh, huh." Eric kissed the sweet spot where her neck met her shoulder.

She murmured something indistinct, and Eric picked up her hand, kissed the palm, then sucked on her fingers.

"Are you listening to me?"

"Of course. I always listen to you. You said, I would like Eric to kiss me – here."

"Did they teach you mind reading in the Navy?"

"I told you, I have spidey sense." She didn't argue with that one.

He kissed her some more, then said, "I'm an idiot."

"You know that really isn't something a girl wants to hear her lover say."

"I mean," he clarified, "I'm an idiot for not suggesting this sooner. I really feel sorry for him."

"For who?" she asked.

"Christopher Wong. Because he's at home in – where does he live again?"

"You know perfectly well where he lives."

"Yeah. He's at home in Redondo Beach and not here with you like I am."

"There was never any chance of that happening," she assured him.

"Ha! So you really did go out with him just to make me jealous."

"Were you?"

"Insanely."

"Tell me about Florida," she requested, running a smooth finger over the rope design inked onto his arm.

Lord, how could the simple feeling of one finger against his skin be such an awesomely erotic sensation? It was such a turn-on that his body sustained a brief tremble of desire, despite the fact that it was way too soon to expect arousal again.

"Does that tickle you?" she asked, feeling his shiver.

"Not there," he replied. "But touch me behind the knees, and I won't guarantee I'll be responsible for my reaction."

Michelle chuckled and laid her head on his shoulder as he talked, basking in the pleasure of simple pillow talk.

"Well, Florida has two seasons. Hurricane, and monsoon. During hurricane season, you check the weather channel like every fifteen minutes to track them. Unlike earthquakes here in California, which strike without advance warning"

She shuddered a little. As a California girl, hurricanes sounded way more terrifying than earthquakes.

"We don't get as many on the west coast of Florida as they do on the east side, facing the Atlantic. But I do recall evacuating up to Georgia a couple of times when a hurricane came knocking, but fortunately, we never had any serious damage to our house. During monsoon season, it rains almost every day. It'll be sunny and bright and then all of a sudden the storm clouds roll in and it starts pouring like crazy. It's practically biblical. It comes down so sudden and so hard, you just can't believe it. The earth can't absorb it fast enough. The streets start to run like rivers, and you start wishing you'd thought to build an ark. Then all of a sudden it just stops, out comes the sun and dries up all the rain. And the itsy bitsy spider climbs up the spout again. An hour later, we're back to earning our reputation as the Sunshine State."

She giggled, a little huffing sound against his collarbone. "And there are alligators," he announced solemnly.

Michelle sat up hearing that. "Alligators? Just running loose?"

He nodded. "Once we had one walking down our street. I was about ten. Maybe eleven. I thought it was cool. I wanted to go out and play with it."

"You didn't do that, did you?"

"No. My mother had other plans. She locked all the doors, told me to stay put, and called animal control to come wrangle it."

"Your mom was a very sensible person." She returned to her place against his shoulder and he tightened an arm to keep her there. "But in general, it was a wonderful place to live. I don't want to make it seem like it was all bad weather and alligators. Of course, being in the Pensacola area was a bonus. When it wasn't storming, or even sometimes when it was, we could always count on planes from the air station roaring overhead."

"And I know you love the smell of jet fuel in the morning."

He grinned. "Yeah. It smells like freedom."

42

Eric was, for the most part, a very quiet sleeper. He didn't snore or snuffle or toss and turn. He fell asleep quickly, woke up alert, and was still and quiet in between. Except for one night, when he twitched in his sleep, forcefully enough to wake Michelle up, though he didn't wake up himself. She heard him mutter, in a desperate voice, "Breathe, damn it, breathe!" and his arm, which had been across her waist, tightened, his hand clenching into a fist.

This was awful. This was scary. She was, admittedly, unfamiliar with the bed-sharing parameter, but she was still certain that having one's usually contented lover twitch and moan in his sleep was outside the norm.

She reached over and rubbed the taut muscle of his arm, petting him like a baby, then moved her hand to his shoulder and shook gently.

"Eric, wake up. You're having a bad dream," she whispered. It was so dark, and she was so close to him, that she couldn't see his eyes, but she could tell from the set of his body that he'd awoken. He breathed out the word, "God," then his arms tightened around her. He said three more words, the first almost a sob, the second two almost a command. "Please. Kiss me."

She turned and groped for his face in the dark, found his mouth, holding him tight. She didn't just kiss him, she wrapped herself around him, so he'd know that she was there, that she was alive, that she wasn't going anywhere. That she cared about his despair, even though she didn't understand it. The kiss he returned to her was hard, and not sexy. It was almost brutish. It was an affirmation of life, and after releasing her mouth, he sighed against her hair, then laid back, shifting apart from her a little.

"I'm so sorry I woke you up like that. I wanted to wake you up with kisses, not with … that." Even in the dark, she could feel his embarrassment at having this nightmare in her company. A slight shudder flowed through him. "I would totally understand if you wanted to go back to your room so you can get some sleep without me thrashing around on you. Or I could go to the couch."

"Uh, uh." She moved her foot and hooked it over his ankle. Anchoring him so he couldn't get away. His normally warm skin was chilly. "I'm not going anywhere and neither are you."

That sounded kind of bossy, she realized. But he had told her that he liked that, so she curved a hand around the back of his neck and nudged his head to her shoulder.

He complied with a murmured, "Yes, ma'am," as he snuggled against her obediently.

"I always wanted to do that," she murmured back. "I always wanted to have you put your head on my shoulder and tell me what was bothering you."

For once he wasn't talkative, just cuddled against her in the surreal dark. But she knew he hadn't fallen asleep. After a moment she said, "That was a hint, sailor."

He twitched again, just a tiny movement of protest.

"Tell me about your dream," she insisted. "Have you had it before? Is it a memory of something real?"

It was a moment before he answered, with a simple, "Yes," and she took that as an affirmative to both her questions.

She waited expectantly, and after another hesitation, he asked, "Do you really want to hear about it? It's not pretty."

"Yes, I really want to hear about it. I figured it wasn't pretty if it made you have a nightmare."

She could sense him looking up, seeing not the ceiling above them, but things thousands of miles away and years in the past, but which were nonetheless right here in the room with them at the moment.

His arm tightened around her and he nuzzled her neck briefly before he spoke.

"I wasn't in the truck that ran over the IED, in fact, I never was. I thought maybe my presence was some kind of charm against it. Stupid, huh? Would it have turned out differently if I'd been in that truck?

"There were four Marines, blown up by that IED. Three were in surgery. It was too late to do anything for the fourth guy. I wasn't usually in the surgery bay. The corpsmen's jobs were to transport the patients from the truck or helicopter they arrived in, start the IV's, relay whatever info we had on their wounds to the doctors, insert a breathing tube if necessary, then step back and get out of the way. But we were short-staffed that day, that whole week, so that's how I ended up assisting the surgeons on one of the patients. I didn't know his name and I didn't care if the guy had a family back home, what his rate or rank was, or what his life would be like if he survived. Didn't care what kind of music or food or sports team he might like. I didn't even notice what race he was. All I wanted was for him to breathe. Just to breathe. It's not that hard, billions of people do it every day, all day. Just breathe. Just be alive. Is that so much to ask? You know how the cardiac monitors make a beeping sound. You've probably heard it in TV shows. Beep, beep, beep. It means the patient is alive. He's breathing. They really aren't very loud. But when that beep beep stops and the guy flatlines and that beep beep becomes a single fucking whining sound, it's the loudest thing you'll ever hear. Louder than a gun or a bomb or a hurricane. I've heard all of those and none of them are as loud as that stupid whine that means the poor bastard isn't breathing anymore. The surgeon was up to his wrists in the guy's guts and he's gone through three pairs of gloves just working on him because they get so damn bloody, and the guy's guts are still warm and then it gets absofuckinglutely silent, except for that damn he's-dead-Jim whining heart monitor. You just want to grab that stupid thing and smash it into a wall to make it stop whining, but you can't because you need it to use on the next poor bastard who's going to come in bloody and shredded and missing parts that you and I take for granted, and it all runs in a loop over and over. It wasn't the first time I'd seen a guy die and it wasn't the last either."

He paused for a moment, then sighed against her skin. "I'm not bragging when I say that I'm good at what I do, and the surgeon I was assisting was the best. Maybe the guy was too far gone when we got him. But still, God, I hate that flat-line sound. You don't ever get used to it. For some reason, my brain picked that particular day to stick with me. Maybe because the next day, I delivered a baby for the first time. It was amazing to bring a new life into the world, but it still didn't make up for the three that were lost."

He drew in a deep breath.

"Just another day in fucking paradise."

She was accustomed to hearing him swear, and he always asked pardon for his language. But somehow this curse held a whole lot more emotional meaning than the casual four-letter words he usually flung around.

She petted his hair as if he were a child, and his arm tightened around her.

"Oh, Eric," she murmured. "I'm so sorry." She could feel moisture where his face touched her neck, and the feeling of his tears on her skin broke her heart into multitudes of sharp, tiny pieces. "The Marines who died that day – were they friends of yours? Buddies?"

"I never met them before that day. But they were all buddies. Comrades. Brothers."

He was still for a moment, but she knew he was still awake.

"Have you ever had to cry quiet, so people around you can't tell?" he asked after a moment.

Yes, that was something she'd gotten good at in her adolescence, keeping her tears secret so her dad wouldn't see how his neglect had hurt her. One thing she had learned being Gregory Diaz's daughter was to pretend that big girls didn't cry. Somehow that seemed kind of petty now.

She had heard the cliché, realizing something like a lightbulb going off over your head, and she felt that same feeling at this moment. Eric's twinkly sparkle, his outgoing friendliness, the corny movie quotes and his love of singing. They weren't just his personality. They were also his armor.

You could cry, or you could sing. Either way, the dead would still be dead.

That was empathy. The trouble was, empathy could be painful.

This was so unfair. He didn't deserve this. Sweet, adorable, caring Eric didn't deserve to wake up in despair over a death that had not been his fault, that he had worked so hard to try to prevent.

She lay awake long after he'd fallen back asleep, holding him and wondering how many times he'd had this kind of dream before they'd been together, when he'd slept here alone, and how long it had lasted. She held his head against her shoulder, and her heart broke for him, just cracked into pieces.

In the morning, he was his usual smiley, way too perky before caffeine self, as he bounced into the kitchen, humming off-key, buttoning his shirt and sniffing for coffee. Michelle was almost sure she had finally mastered the correct cinnamon to coffee grounds ratio, and was putting hers into a travel mug, about to walk out the door. She was running late, but before she stepped out the door, she hesitated.

"Eric?"

"Yo."

"You're a hero."

He looked at her then, and she'd never before seen such a serious expression on his face. "No," he said with harshness. "I am not a hero. The heroes are the guys who came home missing a leg. Or an arm. Or in a body bag. If I never have to attend another funeral for the rest of my life, it will be too soon. You don't know how much it cuts you up to see a Marine on one knee, giving a folded flag to someone's mother. Or widow, or widower."

She didn't have his gift for glib conversation, of knowing the right thing to say to people to make them feel better, so all she could do was set down her cup, step in front of him and put her arms around his neck. It must have been the right thing to do because his arm curved around her waist and held her against him, tightly, clinging almost desperately, while his other hand held her head against his shoulder.

"You're wrong," she said against his shirt. "You are a hero too. I bet there's a lot of mothers and spouses who didn't get those folded flags because you were there to help save their lives." He didn't respond, just held her even tighter. He couldn't see that she was holding her mouth tightly closed, keeping in the words she wanted to say.

I love you. She'd never uttered those three words to anyone, and she didn't say them now. She wanted to, but she couldn't.

They stood there for a minute, just sharing air, until he stepped back and smiled down at her. Twinkly Eric was back.

"I'm sorry I woke you up."

She put a hand on either side of his face.

"You have nothing to be sorry for. Remember you said I could cry on you any time I felt the need? Well, you can twitch with me any time you feel the need. Or cry, if you need to."

Sweetheart, you're not ready to hear about my issues.

When he'd said that to her, she'd thought he was just trying to make her feel better. But no, he'd meant it.

"You have PTSD, don't you?" she said.

He looked rueful. "You figured it out, didn't you? That's what the shrinks call it."

"I'm sorry you have to experience that," she said. "But I'm glad you told me about it."

"I don't think I was actually doing you any favors there."

"You're the one who told me that we should talk about our issues and not keep them bottled inside," she reminded him. "How long have you been having these nightmares?"

"Years," he replied. "But I've never told anyone other than my shrink the details, until now."

"What about your ex-wife? Or Gabriel?"

"My ex wasn't interested. Gabriel knows the basics, but I haven't even told him all the gory details. You're the lucky one who got to hear it all."

"I'm glad you felt you could tell me," she assured him. "I wish I could make them stop tormenting you."

"Thank you, sweetheart," he said solemnly.

"For what?"

"Last night. For being there. For staying, and being – comfort. It means a lot to me."

"So that's why you see a shrink?"

He nodded. "But having you there to kiss me, and to order me to stay put with you despite the twitching and moaning – that helps just as much as talking to a shrink. I mean, that helps too, but being with you is an extra added bonus."

He kissed her and then added, "Now shoo, you. I don't want your boss calling me to complain you're late for work."

She picked up her stuff, her throat felt tight, but she managed to give him just a quick goodbye kiss before she walked out the door.

You may leave the war, but it never leaves you. And yet despite the dream, despite the twitching, despite the need for secure mental compartments, he'd do it all again in a heartbeat.

43

Eric arrived home at nine-thirty, even though his shift had been over at six. It wasn't surprising. Emergency calls and the required reports that went with them frequently left shift schedules as more of a suggestion than a reality. But what was surprising was that he walked in and sat silently on the couch, rather than changing out of his uniform and hanging it up as soon as he got home, as he usually did. The man was anal about keeping his uniforms neat.

Michelle sat down next to him. Something in his face made her refrain from asking how his day had been. He smiled briefly and took her hand in his and held it, kind of tightly, but said nothing.

Uh-oh. No conversation, no teasing, no joking, no sparkle.

"Eric, did you lose a patient today?"

"Yeah," he said.

After a minute she asked, "Do you want to talk about it?"

The look he showed her exuded gratitude. He squeezed her hand.

"His name was George. I'd seen him walking around town with his wife a couple of times. They were retired here, lived up in Hamilton Cove. We chatted once or twice."

Michelle would be willing to bet that Eric had walked up to them and shook hands, saying, "Hi, how you doing?"

"He was eighty-three. It was his second heart attack. He'd had a long, full, happy life. But still... He was already unconscious when we got to their condo, and he was gone by the time we got to the hospital. But I kept doing chest compressions, I couldn't make myself stop, even when the doctor called it. He practically had to push me off the gurney rail."

Eric stared in front of him with that "not quite here" look that she hated to see on his usually smiling face. "I stayed with his wife after the doctor came out and told her George didn't make it. No one should have to be alone at a time like that. They have a grandson going to UCLA, and he was able to get on the next boat out here. Nice kid, he's studying architecture." He looked at her then with a sad smile, and of course, being Eric, thought of her feelings too. "I'm sorry to lay this on you. But I'm glad you're here."

That sad little smile broke her heart. All the commitment, all the passion he had to make people feel better, to heal, to live – today had been punched in the gut and thrown to the ground. Michelle knew that Eric had seen death in much more traumatic circumstances in the service, people who weren't eighty-three-year olds who'd lived a long, happy life. She also knew, it didn't matter.

"I'm glad I'm here too. I'm really sorry about George. You did everything you could, Eric." She didn't bother asking him if he wanted anything to eat. Instead, she put her arm around his neck, kissed his cheek and said, "Come to bed."

"I don't want pity sex."

"OK. How about, I lust for your body sex then, instead?"

"Oh, yeah, I want that. But there's something I need to do first. Wait here, I'm going to change."

That was a bit confusing, but she waited on the couch as he dashed into his room and came out a minute later, having traded his paramedic uniform for his civilian uniform of tee shirt and shorts. Slipping his feet into his flip-flops, he said, "Let's go for a walk."

A walk? Was he kidding? Apparently not, since he held out his hand and opened the door. He led her quickly down the hill towards town, but still insisted on walking on the side closest to the street. When they got to Crescent Avenue, his destination, and his reason for wanting to walk, became obvious.

Even though it was dark by now, the Green Pleasure Pier was full of tourists. Eric and Michelle stopped at the first empty space along the rail that they encountered, between the boat hoist and the fish and chips shack, and looked out over the dark ocean, listening to the faint slap of waves and seeing the glint of reflections from the lamps on the pier.

It was there, as always, never changing, never disappointing, always there, always listening. Even when you didn't speak, it still listened. It was the Ocean. They ignored the bustle of people around them, looked out at the water, and got calm.

"When anxious, uneasy and bad thoughts come," This time she started it, the words that had somehow become their mantra, their path to calm.

"I go to the sea, and the sea drowns them out with its great wide sounds," he replied.

"Cleanses me with its noise."

"And imposes a rhythm upon everything in me that is bewildered and confused." It was not at all surprising that he had memorized the quote. But what did surprise her was when he started to sing, still in the same low soft voice, and of course, still off-key.

Only one line floated out, something sad, and then he looked at her with an apologetic half-smile, before turning his gaze back to the water, and spoke in an even softer voice.

"You can sing, or you can cry. Either way, the dead will still be dead."

She looked at his profile as he gazed out. Across the bay they could see the last Catalina Express boat of the evening pulling away from the dock, heading towards the mainland. He put his arm around her shoulder and she leaned against him, smelling the fresh cotton of his shirt and the warmth of his skin underneath. When he looked towards her, she had to say what she felt.

"Eric, I," she didn't get to finish it because someone bumped into her back, startling her. She looked down to see a boy, about ten, saying, "Sorry!" as his mom came up and secured his arm.

"Stevie, watch where you're going!" she scolded. She looked at Michelle apologetically. "I hope he didn't hurt you."

"No, no it's fine," Michelle assured them. The mom and boy apologized again and went on their way, and Eric smiled at her with some of his sparkle returning to his eyes.

"Do you still lust for my body?" he asked.

"Always." She didn't finish what she'd started to say a moment ago. Maybe it was for the best that she'd been interrupted. She wasn't sure how Eric might respond if she told him that she loved him.

It wasn't like she wanted to get married or anything. Her only observation of the state of matrimony had been her parent's marriage, a state of unwilling obligation and resentment, and a depressing lack of regret when death parted them.

But wait. She'd spent significant time at Tracy's house in her youth, and her parents were happily married. They did have their occasional differences, but in general, had for the most part exhibited love and affection. Michelle had been invited to their twenty-fifth anniversary party. Her father had declined to attend, but Michelle had gone, and Tracy's mom and dad had obviously been happy, loving and committed.

Then there was her other friend Ashley from tech school, whose wedding Michelle had attended the weekend that Eric had moved in. Ashley and her new husband had glowed with happiness at their wedding, and Michelle had, frankly, been jealous, watching them kiss at the altar until the priest had to clear his throat loudly. Unlike Michelle's parents, Ashley and her groom were marrying for love and desire, not obligation.

So what did that mean, in the grand scheme of things? That some marriages worked and some didn't. Eric's marriage had failed, and Michelle found that to be astounding. How could any sane woman let a guy like him go, even if he did have to leave on deployment? She could only guess that somehow he had gotten himself hitched to the most idiotic woman imaginable.

She'd heard him mention his parents and siblings with affection. He seemed particularly close to his sister Brenda, another relationship Michelle, as an only child, was jealous of.

So maybe marriage wasn't only a prison of sadness. Maybe some of them were happy and worth the effort.

"Let's go home," Eric said. He took her hand and they headed back down the pier towards Crescent Avenue.

His phone rang, and she knew he would answer it. He always did, in case it was an emergency. He pulled it out of his pocket and glanced at the display, saying, "It's Tony," before swiping it open.

Anxiety swirled in her heart at the possibility that Eric's partner might be calling him away to another heart attack or accident or premature childbirth. But despite that concern, Eric still managed to hold his phone with one hand, hold Michelle's hand with the other, and still look out for traffic as they crossed the street.

"Hey there, dude. Yeah, I'm OK. Yeah, it sucks." He listened for a moment, then said, "Sure, great, yeah, let's get together and shoot the breeze." Another pause. "You can have a beer, I'll have coffee. Yes, that really is a thing." He glanced at Michelle and rolled his eyes. "Not today, dude, I'm with my girl."

Happiness sparkled inside her to hear Eric refer to her as "his girl".

"No, not at this exact moment, you perv!" Another eye roll. "Sure, tomorrow. Afternoon. I'm sleeping in." He looked at Michelle and winked. It buoyed her spirits to see him coming back to his normal happy self. "Later, dude," he finished, then pocketed his phone as they hurried back home.

44

Michelle loved the fact that, now that she and Eric were lovers, she could just touch him wherever and whenever she wanted, and he'd smile like a five-year-old being offered ice cream. She traced the outside of his ears with her finger, and he closed his eyes and looked dreamy. She messed up his hair, and he opened his eyes and smiled broadly. Somehow, despite her messing it, his hair obediently just fell back into place. It brought back a memory.

"It was me," she admitted.

"Like I said, I pay attention. I know it's you."

"The day you came home from reserve duty and fell asleep on the couch, and said you had a dream that someone brushed your hair. That was me."

"Yeah, I know."

She ran her finger down his nose and he gave her that silly grin she adored. Then she went back and felt the nose again, rubbing the cartilage back and forth a little.

"You like my deformed nose?" he asked.

"It's not deformed," she assured him. She ran her finger over the bump again. "It's cute."

"Oh, if that isn't the last thing a guy ever wants to hear from a girl in bed. Cute." His fake look of outrage was hysterical.

"You make me laugh."

"I take it back – THAT is the last thing a guy wants to hear."

"I mean it, Eric. Nobody has ever made me laugh before. In bed or out."

He recognized that for what it was, an admission from the deeper part of her that she didn't share lightly.

"Well we're just going to have to make up for lost time, aren't we? Are you ticklish?"

"No." But the speed with which she scooted away from him was suspicious.

"I don't believe you. Come here." He grabbed her waist and twitched his fingers over her ribs. "You little fibber, take this, you are such a liar."

She was already at the edge of the bed and she collapsed against him, twisting and gasping, trying to avoid the tickling.

"No, no, stop it, don't do that! Stop it!"

"Don't stop that."

******

Later, he sat up and wriggled his shoulders a little as if they hurt.

"What's the matter with you?" she asked innocently.

"My back hurts. You scratched me." He twitched again. "I don't think I'm ever going to be the same." He grinned and made eyes at her.

"Lay down," she requested. Obediently he slid down to a prone position.

"No, on your stomach."

Flipping the covers aside, he turned over, throwing the pillow on the floor as he propped his head up on one elbow and looked over his shoulder at her. "Are you going to spank me?" His voice was hopeful.

"Have you been bad?"

"I could be very bad."

She traced her fingers over the faint red marks on his back. Eric shivered at her touch. "You are such a baby, I didn't even break the skin."

"There's always hope for next time."

She ran a hand down his spine, starting at the base of his skull, pausing at each vertebra. "Which one is T2?" she asked.

"Keep going," he instructed. "One more."

She stopped at the spot he'd instructed. "That one is T2."

Bending down, she kissed the spot briefly. "I'm sorry I hurt it with my forehead like a rock."

"I'm not sorry. It was the best collision I ever experienced."

"I have a bone to pick with you," she said seriously.

His reaction surprised her. He quickly turned over, pulled her into his arms, pressed his face against her neck, and murmured, "I'm sorry. Was I too fast? I couldn't help it. You're so gorgeous and sexy, I couldn't wait."

Although she seriously enjoyed the physical affection, his timing had not been the bone she wished to pick.

"No, you weren't too fast. You weren't too slow. You were just right.

"That day you went to the funeral. I know you were grieving the loss of your friend, but still – I only wanted to comfort you. It really meant a lot to me to have your friendship when I was in that situation, when you emailed me after my dad died, and said you would have come to the funeral if you'd been able to. If I'd known about your friend, I would have come with you to that funeral. But you treated me like I had something contagious"

"I didn't mean to be rude," he said. "I thought about asking you to come, but I didn't want to make you miss work, or bum you out over it." He looked away for a moment. "I knew I wouldn't be able to trust myself. I was afraid you might touch me, and I wouldn't have been responsible for my actions.

"I would have loved to have your sympathy. But if you'd hugged me at that moment, I don't think I'd have been able to restrain myself from dragging you back into the house and into bed."

He had refused to take advantage of her at that time, despite his attraction to her. It had cost him a lot to rebuff her.

The thought kind of thrilled her. "I don't think I would have objected."

"It wouldn't have been right. I don't think I would have even talked to you, told you how much I wanted you and wanted to be with you. And I sure as hell didn't have protection on me that day, but I wouldn't have waited or cared at that moment. That would be so wrong, to treat you like that. To treat this like that. It wouldn't have been lovemaking. It would have been just sex. And I would have felt like a dog after."

He'd done that in the past, and he hadn't liked himself afterward.

Just because one doesn't drink, doesn't prohibit one from picking up a girl in a bar. In fact, not drinking had actually given him an advantage over guys who not only couldn't drive, but who couldn't even find their own asses with their two hands.

He remembered waking up next to Linda. Lisa. No, LeeAnn, and feeling like scum for charming his way into her bed for his ulterior motive, which had been to temporarily forget the funeral he'd attended that day, to wipe out the sound of Taps and Amazing Grace and the family's tears with hot but meaningless sex, to shield his eyes from the sight of the kneeling Marine, the folded flag, the brave widow and even braver little boy trying not to cry and failing when hearing the words, "On behalf of a grateful nation."

His sitting up and pulling on his clothes had woken up Linda Lisa LeeAnn and she'd entreated him to stay. But he couldn't have. He would have felt even worse, and he already felt like scum.

No, he wasn't just scum. He was excrement. He was not going to give her false hope that this was the start of a relationship.

What only added to his guilt and self-recrimination over this one-night stand pickup, was that he'd left his dress uniform in a crumpled heap on the floor next to the bed. He'd never disrespected his uniform like that before, not even in the throes of lust. Now when he got back to base, his roommates would see him walk in wearing his wrinkled dress whites rather than his working uniform, and would know immediately what he'd been up to. They'd been at the same funeral. For the first and only time, he wished he'd paid more to live in his own place off base. But until today, he'd enjoyed the companionship of his shipmates and the proximity to naval operations. He usually didn't mind the morning after, walk of shame ribbing he'd get, and even bragged about his conquests. But he wasn't going to be bragging about this one.

As he opened the door to leave, she'd asked, "What's your name, sailor?"

He'd replied with the name that applied to the person he was at the moment.

"It's Dirtwad."

That had been six weeks before his last sea cruise. Six weeks before he and three buddies decided to spend their last day ashore on a day trip to Catalina Island. Six weeks before he'd stood on the sidewalk outside the Marlin Club and had an angry, panicky girl run into his back. Six weeks before he'd met his Michelle.

His Michelle. Gabriel had asked him if Eric had a pet name for Michelle, and he'd declined to answer the question. But he realized now that he most definitely did have one.

His.

"Can I comfort you now?" she asked.

"Please," was the heartfelt reply.

"But, Eric?"

"Ma'am?"

"It won't be just sex. It will be lovemaking."

"I'm counting on it."

45

∽

The woman was blonde and beautiful and tall, wearing a blue dress. Heads turned as she walked by, including Eric's. In fact, he stared at her in a manner Michelle had never seen before, and a devastating the jolt of jealousy coursed through her at the sight of it.

Keep it casual, Michelle. The easiest way to drive him away is to get all clingy and possessive. Though she, of course, could not help getting clingy and possessive, any more than she could help breathing. After all, Eric did call her "My Michelle" in bed.

All the more reason to resent his staring openly at another woman. But when she looked at his face, she realized he wasn't staring at her with a look of lust, like all the other men in the vicinity. Rather, he was looking at her as if he'd just seen a ghost. His naturally fair skin went even paler about the lips.

"Oh my god," she heard him say, low and disbelieving.

"Do you know her?" Michelle asked, trying to resist the urge to grab him and yank his attention away from the gorgeous blonde in the blue dress as she emerged from the Island Threadz dress shop and ambled down Crescent Avenue. The words in her head escaped her mouth. "Should I be jealous?"

Eric cut her a look. "Not in the least."

Despite that disclaimer, Michelle was jealous. She couldn't help it. Her Eric was staring at another woman, even if it was with a weird expression on his face. The woman was gorgeous and blond and sultry and all the things Michelle wasn't, and Eric apparently knew her.

His voice was low. "That's my ex-wife. That's Karen."

"That's the bitch who sent you divorce papers while you were at sea?" She tried to keep her voice low but it was very difficult. "What is she doing here? She'd better be here to apologize to you, though it's kind of late for it."

Eric's gaze turned from staring at his ex, to staring at Michelle with amusement.

"I seriously doubt she came here to see me. I haven't talked to her since before the divorce, and that was seven years ago. I'm sure she has no idea I live here now. She probably still lives in San Diego, so I'm sure it's just a coincidence that she's here. Probably just visiting like all the other tourists."

Michelle stared at the beautiful blonde woman who had been previously been married to, had slept with, lived with, her Eric and had foolishly thrown him away.

She wanted to run over there and pull the woman's hair out of her head as punishment for cruelly serving Eric with divorce papers while he was deployed.

She wanted to go over and thank the woman for setting Eric free, because if the marriage had been successful, he wouldn't be here with Michelle now.

"I suppose we should go over and say hello," Eric said.

"Why?" Michelle asked, still torn between the warring desires in her to either pull hair, or offer thanks.

"To be polite," Eric replied, and he walked towards the blonde. Michelle followed, unwilling to leave him alone with her.

"We have to be polite?" she asked. "After the way she treated you? Your mama really did raise a gentleman. What did he think of her short-term daughter-in-law?"

Eric stopped for a moment and looked at her somberly.

"My mother never met her. She had already passed away. She died of pancreatic cancer seven years after my dad died, at age sixty-seven. You don't have to come over if it will make you uncomfortable."

She shook her head. "Oh, no. I think I need to give her a piece of my mind."

He took that final step that brought him next to his too-beautiful ex-wife.

"Hello, Karen."

At the sound of Eric's voice, the blonde turned and looked at him a bit disbelievingly.

"Well, what a surprise," she said coolly. "I certainly never expected to see you here. Shouldn't you be off floating on the ocean out there?"

She waved a well-manicured hand towards the water. The look on her face was positively disdainful.

"It's nice to see you too," Eric said with heavy sarcasm in his voice, a tone which surprised Michelle completely. She'd never heard him talk like that before. Apparently seeing his ex-wife brought out the worst in him. But his voice softened a bit as he told her, "I've retired from the Navy. I live here on Catalina Island now."

"Well isn't that just sweet," the other woman said, with a complete and utter lack of sincerity.

Michelle put a proprietary hand on Eric's arm, a movement that the Ex noticed with amusement curving her lips.

"This is Michelle Diaz," Eric introduced. "Michelle, this is Karen Butler."

He had introduced her to his ex-wife as just Michelle. No qualifier as to their relationship. Not, this is my girlfriend, my lover, my woman. Not even as his roommate. Just plain Michelle. The omission cut out a little piece of her heart.

From the look on Karen's face, Michelle could literally read her thoughts. *You quit the Navy to be with* her? *My, you really traded down.*

Michelle at least said, "Hello."

Eric, obviously, was trying to keep things civil. He leaned towards Michelle a bit, apparently to put himself in a position to intervene should she try to start pulling Karen's hair out.

"How have you been, Karen?" he asked politely, as if it actually mattered. "Are you visiting the island?"

She nodded, still with the unfriendly look on her face. "My fiancé is renting a golf cart. He'll be here to pick me up in a minute."

"Your fiancé?" he asked with surprise in his voice.

There was a flash and glitter from Karen's left hand, as she pushed a lock of hair behind her ear, and Michelle stared at the diamond ring there. Was she still wearing Eric's wedding ring? No, it couldn't be. He'd said she'd been married and divorced again since they had broken up. The ring looked like an engagement ring, with no accompanying wedding band. Michelle was certain, given the precipitous nature of their marriage, that Eric hadn't given Karen an engagement ring. Karen waved it a bit, showing off the highly heated and pressurized bit of ancient carbon in its gold setting.

"Yes. I'm engaged. To someone who isn't going to leave me and run off to some stupid ship first chance he gets. We're getting married next year."

"Congratulations." Eric actually smiled at his ex as if he were happy for her. Sometimes the guy was just too damn nice. "I hope you're happy."

"I'm sure we will be," Karen said, with a scathing look at Eric that radiated the unspoken words, *as I never was with you.*

"Do you still live in San Diego?" he asked, and Michelle had to fight back the urge to scream, *why are you carrying on a polite conversation with this person after the way she treated you?*

"In the area," Karen replied. "We bought a place in Del Mar Heights. Roy wanted to live in La Jolla but I said, no way. That neighborhood is way too close to your base and all those nasty noisy airplanes." She gave Eric a dirty look as if it were somehow his fault that the Navy's jets weren't quiet.

Eric gave Michelle a wry glance, and she was quite certain that wherever he and Karen had lived during their brief marriage had been within sight and sound of naval aviation.

He confirmed it by telling her, "We lived in the East Village." Karen wrinkled her nose and made a face when he mentioned the area. "You could smell the jet fuel and read the call signs on the planes from there."

"That place was horrible," Karen said. Michelle thought it sounded like a fun place to be.

This was quite possibly the weirdest conversation Michelle had ever witnessed, standing with her lover calmly talking to his ex-wife about the merits and disadvantages of various neighborhoods. He wasn't even getting upset over the rude, untrue, narrowminded things the woman was saying. But then that was Eric. He took things in a level-headed stride, probably due in part to his medical training which required him to remain cool, calm and collected in all situations.

"I'm sorry you were unhappy there," he said to his ex.

"No you weren't," Karen declared. "If you were, you wouldn't have been in such a hurry to sail away from me."

"Sail away from you?" Michelle interjected. "Is that what you really think?"

Karen opened her mouth as if to argue the point but didn't get the chance.

Boom. The sound that interrupted their weird conversation was almost gentle, but the sound waves that followed it blew over their faces like a quick breeze, halting all conversation around them as the three of them, and everyone else in the vicinity, stared out towards the water, in the direction the explosive sound had come from. A bright bit of flame seemed to pop out of the water on the horizon.

"What was that?" Michelle gasped.

"The oil rig," Eric replied. "My god, I think it exploded. That can't be good. There are people working on that rig. They could be injured, or," he shuddered. "Dead."

Michelle stared at the flame on the water. It looked small, but it was eleven miles away, halfway between the island and the mainland. Eric took a step away, towards the beach, scanning as if he could assess potential injuries from his spot on the sidewalk on Crescent Avenue.

As if on cue, the voice pager he always carried clipped to his waistband started to chatter. He grabbed it and held it to his ear, holding up a shushing hand towards Michelle and Karen as he listened.

"I have to go," he said brusquely, as he jammed the pager into his pocket.

"Of course you do," Karen said with a sigh. "You've obviously been on dry land longer than you feel comfortable."

"We're launching a rescue boat to go out there for the crew on the rig. And another is coming from Los Angeles." He was looking at Michelle now, paying little heed to Karen's bitter words. "I'm heading to the rescue dock to get the dive gear."

Michelle was sorry now that they'd walked into town rather than bringing the golf cart. He could have gotten to the rescue dock, which was on the far side of the Casino, quicker using it.

"Sorry to dash off on you. I'm not sure when I'll get back." He put a brief arm around Michelle's waist, kissed her really quickly, and said, "Take care, Karen," to his ex, before dashing away up Crescent Avenue in the direction of the casino.

"What, no kiss for me?" Karen inquired with a whole lot of snark in her voice as they watched him go. He didn't so much as give her a backward glance.

Karen turned as if to walk away, obviously finding Michelle to be beneath her notice. For a moment, Michelle found herself tongue-tied under the cool dismissal of Eric's ex. She'd fully intended to give the woman a piece of her mind about how she'd treated Eric, but under that chilly, unfriendly demeanor that obviously found Michelle to be unworthy, she faltered. But just for a moment, then she gave the other woman what she hoped was an intimidating look.

"How could you do such an absolutely cruel thing to Eric like that?"

Let's go right from, Hello, to full-on evisceration in zero point three seconds. Do not pass go, do not collect two hundred dollars, do not waste time with chit-chat.

"Excuse me? What are you talking about?" Karen turned back with an icy, astonished expression.

"He told me about how you served him with divorce papers while he was deployed at sea. How cruel can a person get?"

Karen's chilly glare shifted momentarily in the direction Eric had gone, up Crescent Avenue towards the casino. "What has he been telling you? He is such a little gossip."

"He's only told me the truth. That he married you because you thought you were pregnant, and that you sent him divorce papers while he was deployed at sea, rather than in person." She gave Eric's ex her best Raging Bitch glare. "Go ahead, deny it."

Too late, Michelle realized how much the words she had chosen echoed the way Eric had talked to Justin during their unpleasant scene on the dock. *Go ahead, make my day.* And she had called him a dork for it. Was she being a dork, berating his ex-wife over their long-ago divorce?

Perhaps, but still, Karen should be grateful that they were on the sidewalk rather than the pier. Michelle might have been tempted to imitate Eric further and push his ex into the water.

Karen, however, refused to be ashamed. "I don't have to justify myself to you. To either of you. He walked away from me without a backward glance. Just like today. Just like he always does."

Michelle channeled her inner Raging Bitch, although in this circumstance, it was directed solely towards Karen Butler rather than the world in general, and rather than lashing out for herself, she was angry on Eric's behalf.

"You had your chance to be with him," she said. "And you threw him away. I should actually be grateful for that."

"Yeah, you and every other girl he's screwed since then, and I'm sure it's been a lot. I heard stories about his social life, both before we got married and after we got divorced."

Michelle wondered if Eric's ex would believe her if she told her he'd claimed to have not slept with anyone for a year before he and Michelle had gotten together.

"He never cheated on you, even though you trapped him into marriage with your fake pregnancy claim."

"Fake? Is that what he told you? I took a test. It's not my fault it turned out to be wrong. When I told him about it, he practically dragged me to the county clerk's office before I even had a chance to verify it. How was I supposed to know it was a false alarm? And you know what? He didn't really want a wife. He just wanted a kid. He only wanted to get married because he thought he'd get a kid out of the deal. Once we found out there wasn't going to be a kid, he was off on his ship like a shot."

What an incredibly obtuse person Karen Butler was. It was almost unbelievable that a smart man like Eric could have gotten close enough to her for them to suspect pregnancy.

He had told her how, she recalled. It was a bar pickup, a moment of lust, not a meeting of the minds.

"You really think he left you because he chose to?" she asked incredulously. "Don't you understand how the military works? He was deployed. It was what he signed up for when he enlisted. He would have been on that ship even if he'd never met you, if he was married or single."

Karen shrugged. "Whatever."

Hey, Michelle, you're the one with a reputation as a bitch in this town. Surely you can out-do her. But maybe after hearing some of the things Karen had said, you should pass the Raging Bitch crown over to her.

"Maybe three times will be the marriage charm for you."

Karen stared at her in disbelief.

"What?"

"You dumped Eric. Did you dump husband number two also when he left to do his job? Did he last longer than Eric did?"

"Actually, it did last longer – almost two years. Husband number two cheated on me. At least Eric was too polite to do that."

Of course. Eric was the King of Polite. He would never cheat on a spouse, no matter how obtuse she was.

"That must have sucked," Michelle said with little sincerity. "Maybe husband number two found someone who actually cared about him."

"How dare you? You don't know anything about me."

"True. But I do know Eric. He's the nicest person in the world. He'd never hurt anyone."

"Oh, he's nice all right. Nice when it suits him. Nice when it gets him what he wants. He's a real charmer when he wants to get laid. But put a ship in front of him and that niceness turns real quick into, so long, see you in six months. Then he takes off and leaves you in a dinky little apartment with jets practically landing on the roof."

Michelle looked harshly at Karen. How deep had the connection between her and Eric been? Had he told Karen things, shared emotional experiences, that he hadn't with anyone else, including his sister, as he had with her?

"I know about his PTSD too," she said.

"His what?" Karen actually looked confused.

"PTSD. You know – post-traumatic stress disorder. Didn't you know about that? It's what causes the nightmares he has sometimes."

"You mean that twitching? He still does that? God, it was annoying."

Karen was even more obtuse than Michelle had suspected. Or maybe she was just uncaring.

"Look, honey, I'm sure you're enjoying your little fling with him, but don't get too comfortable with it. It won't last, I guarantee you."

"It's not a little fling. It's more than that. I-"

She stopped herself. She hadn't yet told Eric that she loved him. She certainly wasn't going to tell his ex-wife first.

"Oh, I'm sure he's trying to make you think that. How long have you two been together?"

How long had they been together? Well, it depended on when one considered their togetherness to have begun. Since they'd first slept together? A few weeks. Since he'd moved to the island, into her house? A couple of months. Since the day they'd met on the sidewalk in front of the Marlin Club? Over a year. She seriously doubted that Eric's ex would take the nearly twelve months between meeting and becoming roommates as togetherness. Not when you considered that Karen had drawn up dissolution of marriage documents practically as soon as he'd left port.

"A while," she muttered vaguely.

"Sailing off on his stupid ship was more important to him than being with me. I'm sure whatever he's running off to now is more important to him than you are. Don't get your hopes up about him, honey. He's not good husband material. He doesn't do long-term. For someone who doesn't drink, he spent an awful lot of time socializing in a bar."

"Of course, he was making sure his friends got home OK. Didn't you meet him in a bar?"

"Yes. Where did you meet him?"

"On the sidewalk outside a bar," Michelle admitted.

"Oh, so he picked you up even before you got into the place. That's fast."

"Fast? Not as fast as sleeping with someone only a few hours after you met."

"Hey, it was fun." A smile of remembrance softened Karen's mouth, and the jealousy Michelle felt at the sight made her fingers itch to slap that smile into the middle of next week. "One thing I do have to say about him is, he was good in bed. I have to give him that."

Thinking of another woman appreciating Eric's bedrooms skills made Michelle see red.

"Do you not understand at all what he does? What he did? He was in the military, and he was deployed. It wasn't like he went off on a vacation. He was putting his life on the line to defend our freedom, and you sent him divorce papers while he was doing it. He saves people's lives. He's on his way to try and save people's lives right now, and you think he's using it as an excuse to get away from me? You have got it all wrong, sister."

"Go ahead and think that if it makes you feel better," Karen replied. "But don't say I didn't warn you. He likes to have his fun and when he's tired of you, he'll find some reason to skedaddle away, to something else more interesting. To someone else more interesting. You should have seen him when he went off to sail the ocean blue on that stupid ship of his. He was smiling. I never saw him that happy when he was with me. And he was making a big deal about some test he'd passed."

"The chief's exam." Eric had told her how intense and difficult that had been, and how proud he'd been to pass it with an excellent score.

"He actually studied for it like it was some high school final. That was something else he found more interesting than me."

"That's kind of hypocritical, coming from someone about to embark on marriage number three. Maybe the problem was more that you're not good wife material."

"Oh, and you think you are good wife material?"

Actually, Michelle realized, suddenly, she would be excellent wife material. She actually loved Eric and would never use him the way Karen had. If she'd been married to him while he was in the service, she would have put on her bravest, proudest face when he left for duty, would have been there on that dock to see him off and been back there when he got home.

A rental golf cart pulled up next to them and the man driving it waved in their direction.

"That's my fiancé," Karen said, making a little hand gesture that set the rock to sparkling.

The fiancé had a smarmy smile that set Michelle's teeth on edge as he looked towards the two of them. Even from six feet away, she could feel him trying to look down her cleavage. Apparently, after giving up the best (that was, Eric), Karen now had to settle for somewhat less. Michelle wondered what husband number two had been like.

"Congratulations," she said with a complete lack of sincerity. "Good luck with that. Are you going to take his name, or keep your own to save on paperwork when it doesn't work out?"

"I think you're going to be the one needing luck," Karen replied, ignoring Michelle's crack about her name as she got into the cart's passenger seat.

"Who's your friend?" the fiancé asked, giving Michelle the eye.

"Nobody," Karen told him crossly. "Let's go. I'm hungry. I hope they have some decent seafood in this town."

Michelle could have recommended several places that served excellent seafood in town, but she didn't. As the golf cart pulled away, she wondered how long Karen Butler not Mrs. Hanson was going to last in marriage number three.

She also wondered how long Michelle Diaz and Eric Hanson were going to last.

46

∿

After Karen Butler and her smarmy fiancé pulled away in their rental golf cart in search of seafood, Michelle hurried down Crescent Avenue and up the Green Pleasure Pier, restraining herself from pushing aside the tourists who were looking out towards the flame on the horizon and speculating as to its meaning. Did these people not understand that the man she loved was even now racing towards a catastrophe that everyone else would be fleeing away from? She finally secured a spot along the rail when a couple turned away to walk back down the pier, discussing their reservation for the zipline tour up at Descanso Canyon.

More than watching the fiery evidence of the explosion to the east, she stared and squinted towards the Casino just north of town, visible across the bay. The county rescue boat was moored just on the far side of the casino building, on the side away from the dive park and Casino entrance that most people visited. After a few minutes she did see a boat appear from behind the Casino's white façade, racing in the direction of the fire. It was too far away to identify any occupants, but she could still envision Eric and perhaps Tony or their colleagues, shimmying into their wetsuits, zipping up them up the back and pulling on dive hoods as the boat raced towards danger. Despite being located in a tropical climate, the water temperature off the California coast was barely over sixty degrees at best, thanks to the coastal Alaskan waters pushed down towards Southern California by the Pacific current. They would pull on their buoyancy compensators and oxygen tanks, check their regulators, and prepare to roll off their boat into the chilly waters, in search of victims. Flippers would go on last, just before they splashed into the water.

It always looked so cool, so intriguing, to see divers roll backward off a boat, falling blind into the water. But this would be no pleasure dive. If the bit of flame visible from Avalon's shore was any indication, Eric would be rolling into waters covered with burning oil, most likely being fed by more oil spurting from the damaged derrick. And below that flaming petroleum and flying debris lurked curious great white sharks, swishing beneath the surface, just waiting and hoping for some tasty human victims, as well as their rescuers, to flail about in their hood.

Please be safe. She didn't pray, because like Eric, she had no religious beliefs, but she still silently asked the universe for his safety and tried to take comfort in the fact that she knew Eric was trained and certified for this type of rescue.

Maybe she could try to contact Gabriel or Susan to inquire if Gabriel would be involved in their rescue, but realized that a charter helicopter wouldn't be called in. Any aerial evacuations would be performed by the Coast Guard. And besides, she was suddenly reluctant to talk to Eric's friends, afraid they might confirm what his ex-wife had asserted, that Eric didn't do long-term, that he would be easily distracted towards a new love affair when he tired of his current relationship.

Her phone in her pocket chirped with a text message and even though she knew it was way too soon to hear from Eric, she quickly grabbed it out to read the message. It was from Tracy, saying she had a date that night and what should she wear?

When Michelle responded asking if Tracy was aware of the oil rig explosion, the reply was simply no, she wasn't, and more discussion about wardrobe choices for tonight's date.

What difference does it make if you wear black or red, Michelle wanted to scream, which in text message protocol, would mean typing her response in all capital letters. Although, if Tracy's hair was still red, Michelle would, if she was as frivolous as her friend, recommend against the clash of pairing red hair with red clothing. But she couldn't be certain about Tracy's hair color this week, since she hadn't seen the girl in person for several days, due to Tracy's current infatuation with the manager of the Portofino Hotel and the fact that Tracy had been spending most of her free time casually strolling past that hotel in hopes of accidentally on purpose bumping into Johnny Del Risco.

The oil rig explosion had occurred at a little after six p.m., and by that time the next day, when Michelle arrived home from work, there was still no word from Eric. Again, she was tempted to try to contact his friends, to see if they had heard from him, but again, she decided against it. What if Eric had been in touch with them, and not with her? She didn't want to have to endure the sympathetic silence from them that might ensue if that was the case. So she didn't contact Gabriel or Susan, and she didn't text Eric to ask how things were going. He was, after all, busy responding to a life-threatening situation.

His absence gave her plenty of time to obsess over what Karen had said about him, to vacillate from taking the woman at her word, to dismissing her claims as simply the bitterness of an Ex after a less than amicable breakup. Eric hadn't sounded bitter when he'd told her about his failed marriage, in fact, he'd managed to seem actually sympathetic towards Karen's reason for cruelly dumping him the way she had, but then Eric was a unique and special person. Would he be sympathetic towards her, Michelle, if and when he told his next girlfriend or lover or significant other about them? Would he say, I had this roommate and we slept together but she wasn't The One?

Or was she over-analyzing something that had ended years ago and maybe wasn't nearly the big deal she was making out of it? It was really a question that only Eric could answer, but like the information she had gotten from her father's former drinking buddy, she was quietly terrified of hearing the answers.

But when she arrived home the second evening, his work boots were lined up neatly next to the door and he was asleep in bed, his door open, an obvious invitation to join him.

She didn't join him. There were several reasons.

One, she had no idea how long he'd been home. She didn't know if he'd been asleep for five minutes or five hours, or when he had to return to work. Let the man rest when he could.

The other, more disturbing reason, was that the conversation with his ex-wife had unnerved her, more than she cared to admit.

He doesn't do long-term. He'll find some excuse to leave you.

Though one side of her wanted to believe that Karen said those things out of spite, lashing out at her incorrect perception that Eric had somehow left her voluntarily, rather than as his duty, along with thousands of other military personnel.

But, still, could there be a ring of truth to his ex's claims? Was he incapable of sustaining a long-term relationship, regardless of his situation when he'd been in the Navy? Lots of sailors, and other military personnel, had relationships and families and somehow made it work even when deployments kept them apart. But Eric, despite his social nature, had never entered into any other long-term relationship that she knew of, other than his very short marriage. Could the few weeks that the two of them been lovers count as "long-term?" Or possibly the beginning of long-term? Or was he going to find a way to walk away from her, from them, sometime soon?

They had never discussed the nature or timeline of their love affair, never verbally exchanged the words I Love You. Was it because of the newness and excitement of the affair? Or was it because he was too polite to say, this is fun but it's not forever?

She could ask him, of course. She could come right out and say, where is this going? What do you feel for me, deep down in your heart? Is the desire more than sexual? He had said he could ask him anything, and she didn't doubt he would answer her honestly.

But maybe she didn't want to hear the honest answers. She'd asked her father's drinking buddy for answers, and the honest replies she'd gotten had cut her heart and wounded her soul. She wasn't sure if she could handle the continued turning over of stones, if doing so revealed more brutal honesty in the form of the kind of feeling that Karen Butler seemed to think Eric harbored.

She wasn't hungry, but she sat at the kitchen table picking at a salad anyway. Having doubts about the strength and length of your love affair would be a great way to lose weight. Call it the Heartbreak Diet.

Eric ambled in wearing just cargo shorts, and smiled when he saw her.

"Hiya, gorgeous," he said with his usual sexy grin. "I'm sorry I didn't text you while I was gone. My phone battery died and I just plugged it in now when I woke up."

"How did it go out there?" she asked.

"Not as bad as it could have," he replied with relief in his voice. "No fatalities, thank goodness. Several seriously injured, but none life-threatening. They were all airlifted to UCLA Medical Center. The worker's chemical release monitors had gone off, so they were already evacuating when the thing blew up. The oil rig is a total loss though. I imagine lawsuits will be flying."

She nodded, looking at the salad she'd been picking at with no interest.

"How long have you been home?" She picked up her salad bowl and took it over to the sink

"About an hour." So he hadn't been asleep long when she got home. He'd barely gotten a nap. Good thing she hadn't disturbed him. "I have to go back in at six a.m. Tony got a little bit of smoke inhalation. They kept him overnight at UCLA, so we're going to be short-handed for a day or two. We have," he squinted at the clock on the microwave. "Ten hours."

She scraped her uneaten salad into the trash, then turned on the water to rinse out her dish, and heard him step up behind her. One warm hand rested on her waist and the other brushed her hair aside as he nuzzled her neck. "Ten hours," he repeated in a suggestive murmur. "Let's make the best of them."

She stepped aside, out of his embrace, even though the feel of his hands and lips made her knees wobble.

"Not tonight," she mumbled.

It didn't take him any time at all to pick up on her avoidance.

"Sweetheart, is everything OK? Are you mad at me or something?"

His look of concern, of contrition for anything he might have done to upset her, was so sincere she almost crumbled.

"No, I'm just tired." If that wasn't the most pathetic excuse ever. He'd just spent the past thirty-six hours rescuing injured people out of shark-infested waters, and *she* claimed to be tired? *What an idiot you are, Michelle.*

"Then come lay down and take a nap," he suggested, trying to put his arms around her again, to lead her to his room, his bed, for a nap.

Freya, she couldn't think straight when he touched her.

"You need your sleep if you have to be back at work at six. I'd just disturb you."

"Yes, please, disturb me. I'd love to have you disturb me. And after we disturb each other, we can do that nap thing. We've got a whole ten hours."

She evaded him again and looked at the center of his chest, because she suddenly didn't want to look at his eyes. Those sparkly eyes would seduce her in a moment and as much as she wanted to, craved to be seduced by him, the conversation she'd had with his ex-wife still rang in her head.

Suddenly her excuse to be tired became a reality. She was so emotionally exhausted, she felt like she could just sink down on the floor at any moment.

"I think I'm going to sleep in my room tonight." She could see him twitch at her tone, which silently added the words, *without you*.

"Why?' he asked. "Sweetheart, tell me what's wrong. You don't seem like yourself. Are you sick? Is it something I did? Do I stink? I showered as soon as I got home, so I shouldn't smell like fish or petroleum anymore."

He was too good at math for her to use the girl's excuse of it being that time of the month, so she didn't bother, because it would have been a lie. And he certainly did not stink. She knew, if she let herself get close enough to him, that he'd exude only his usual sensuous scent of warmth and sweet, clean male skin.

But she was still too chicken-shit cowardly to tell him the real reason she was putting him off.

"No, it's not you. I just need,"

What did she need from him? Space? Affection? Understanding? Sex? Love? This moment? The rest of their lives?

All of the above. And that was just the problem. And, maybe, the problem was him and his alleged inability to do long-term. And the problem was her, too scared to find out for sure.

God, she was so confused.

"I need to think about stuff," she finally said, and left her salad bowl unwashed in the sink as she went to supposedly sleep, alone and undisturbed, in her own room, closing the door on his bewilderment, feeling like a complete idiot. She could be sleeping in the arms of the man she loved, enjoying their togetherness while it lasted. But instead she lay awake, lonely and cold, and yearned for him, on the other side of the wall, knowing for certain that he'd have left his door open just in case she decided to come in and disturb him.

He stared at her door for several minutes after it shut, thinking, *what the hell?* And feeling a bit peeved. It was a guy thing. Guys hated rejection. While he was far, far from the misogynistic ass Michelle had once mistakenly accused him of being, still, he was a guy. He had no choice in the matter. He hated rejection.

Michelle thought she'd probably lay awake all night, but somehow, she did finally fall asleep, and didn't wake up until after he'd left for work at six a.m.

The next day he sent her a couple of text messages, between calls and other tasks, brief and friendly, just saying hello. Late in the afternoon he sent one that said, "I miss you," followed by, "Let's talk."

She wanted to talk to him, but she was afraid to.

I don't deserve you, she thought.

She also thought, *I want you so bad I can taste it*. Not just sexually, though she craved that with a passion. She also wanted the closeness, the laughter, the simple happiness they'd had since becoming lovers, even if they had never discussed the future.

She suddenly realized what that feeling in her soul was.

It was an ache.

She ached for him. She'd always thought of that as a silly, unrealistic term used in silly, unrealistic stories. But she was so wrong. She literally ached for him, for his touch, his smile, his embrace, for the feeling of his warm skin against hers.

A dozen times she had awoken last night and almost got up and went next door to his room, into his open bedroom door and into his bed, the bed they'd shared often enough that she'd started thinking of it as their bed. And a dozen times she picked her foot up off the floor, tucked it back under her bedsheet, and stayed in her room, feeling too insecure to go tell him, "My little talk with your ex-wife scared me into a complete insecurity about our relationship."

He'd probably laugh his head off at that.

What did he know about insecurity? He was the most self-confident person she'd ever met.

And yet. The way he'd talked about his father, he must have fallen apart when his dad had died. He'd told her he'd had to pull over and cry when he'd left the Navy base for the last time. He'd begged her to kiss him when his nightmare had consumed him.

He used jokes and music and nerdy movies to deal with his insecurities, while she'd used insults and bitchiness to deal with hers.

She slapped herself upside the head. Not literally, just figuratively.

Enjoy this time with him. Savor it. Treasure it. Even if it doesn't last forever. Even if he breaks your heart.

Michelle had always strived to be as much not like her father as she could be. And in her refusal to drink, or to get involved with people who drank, she had accomplished that goal. But, she realized, there was another way in which he could live her life in a manner the opposite of how he had. She could care, about something, someone. She could be happy. She had the right to be happy. It was promised in the Declaration of Independence.

Her parents certainly had never been happy. Why, she didn't know. But she was going to be happy. She was happy. And the reason she was happy was a certain hazel-eyed paramedic who couldn't carry a tune in a bucket, despite how much time he spent trying to.

When he put his phone in the speaker dock, turned up the volume, and started singing, she put her hands over her ears. He just laughed, grabbed her hands away from her face, and made her dance around the kitchen with him. His dancing at least was a lot better than his singing, and the dancing led to kissing, and kissing led to other dancing, the kind he was an expert at.

She could tell him anything. Well, almost anything. There was one thing she couldn't say to him, despite how easy he was to talk to. Maybe it was because she'd never said the words before. Maybe she was afraid of rejection. Maybe she had commitment issues. Or maybe he did. Whatever the reason, she found herself unable to utter out loud the simple words that revealed her innermost soul.

She couldn't say to him, "I'm in love with you."

There were times when Michelle had no idea exactly why she did the things she did, and tonight was one of those times. Had she lost her ever-loving mind?

Yes, she had. She was crazy. Crazy about him.

Eric was the best thing that had ever happened to her, and she was going to make the best of it. She'd realized that the morning after they'd first slept together.

He'd once suggested she compartmentalize her bad memories, to allow herself happiness in the present. She should take his advice. She could compartmentalize his ex-wife and her unhappy suggestions into the unpleasantness compartment, and pursue happiness with Eric.

She'd always run off and hid in her room in the past when anything upset her. She didn't want to do that anymore. She wanted to be with Eric, and maybe one of these days she'd get brave enough to tell him right out loud that she was in love with him, and hope that he might feel the same. All he'd had to do was kiss her, really kiss her, and she belonged to him, body and soul, with all her doubts and fears and her stupid bitch of a psyche be damned.

She sat in the pitch-black darkness on her sofa, not even tempted to sleep despite it being oh-dark-hundred, as Eric would say, and she waited.

When the key jiggled in the lock and the door opened, she saw a glow of light in front of him. He'd turned on his phone to use as a flashlight. Of course, being the polite man he was, he would make sure he didn't bump into anything in the dark that might make noise and disturb his sleeping roommate when he came home late. Even under the weird circumstances of the past few days, he was still a gentleman.

When she stood up and stepped towards the glow, he yelped softly with startlement.

"Michelle? Is everything alright?"

She didn't answer, just stood in front of him.

"Is something wrong? Why are you sitting here in the dark in the middle of the night? Are you sick? Do you need something?"

His voice was wary, and a bit breathy. Not surprising, consider how she'd startled him by appearing in the dark like a ghost, and with the low tone that somehow surfaced when talking in the dark of night, even when there was nobody sleeping to be disturbed.

She put her hands on his chest and grasped the collar of his uniform shirt.

"Yes, I do need something." She kept her voice low and breathy too.

Even though his phone screen had gone dark, she could still tell he was staring down at her, wide-eyed.

"Michelle," he repeated. "Oh-"

She cut him off with a kiss, pressing her tongue into his surprised mouth, pressing herself against his surprised body which immediately responded to her, releasing her hold on his shirt to encircle his neck. He didn't hesitate to kiss her back - hot, wet, and mobile. His arms quickly went around her waist. She could feel the square of his phone, still in his hand, pressing against her back.

She ended the kiss so abruptly he gasped, and took his hand, pulling him across the room towards the hall. As they passed her door, he said, "Wait, Michelle, does this mean-"

She said, "Shh!" as she reached for the doorknob of his room, but of course, being Eric, he would not shush.

"Sweetheart, what's up? Well, I know what's up." He emphasized the word 'up'. "I thought for a while maybe you didn't want to be with me anymore. Does this mean-"

She flung his door open, with a bit of force. It made a thump as it hit the wall, and in the same movement, she pressed her hand over his mouth, just like he'd done to her once, with another ordered, "Shh! Don't talk. Don't say anything. Not a word. Just feel."

He licked the inside of her hand. She removed it from his mouth and started unbuttoning his uniform shirt. When she got the second button undone, he put his hands over hers to facilitate the unbuttoning, but she twitched them away.

"Don't. I'll do it."

"Sweetheart, I have questions."

"I said hush. That's an order. Be still." She put her hand over his mouth again, using the other on the shirt buttons, but when she got the last one open, he disobeyed her order to be still and pulled the shirt back, dropping it on the chair and pulling off his tee shirt in the same fluid motion. She had to remove her hand from his mouth then, but pressed a quieting finger to his lips briefly, and this time he obeyed, because he liked it when she was bossy, not speaking but only emitting a hissed intake of breath as she pulled open the sash of the robe she'd been wearing, let it drop away to reveal she was naked beneath it, and reached for his belt. At least this time it didn't seem to be superglued in place. No sooner had the pants and his skivvies dropped to the floor than the two of them were tumbled to the bed, pulling each other down, desperate and fast, needing no light nor words to feel, to arouse, to caress the places they each knew the other liked to have caressed.

Her lips against his throat could feel the strain of his accepting her order to be speechless, and his lips on her breast, her nipple, made her arch her back, and utter a low sound, not a word but a primeval sigh of desire.

"Oh, Jesus!" He moaned disobediently, and then they didn't talk anymore.

They made love without further words, their only vocal sounds being the gasps and moans of pleasure and climax. The absolute and utter dark made it even more surreal, with no visualization of each other's bodies or faces, perceiving with only lips and fingers and skin, exclusively tactile. As if the surrounding dark and silence was a cocoon, an infinitely small space, they wrapped arms and legs about each other as if there was no space for outward movement, restricted only to the portion of the universe allotted to the shape of their bodies.

Even Eric's climactic moan was muted, his lips against her cheek, the gratification even more intense for its speechlessness.

Afterward, she still wouldn't let him talk, again pressing fingers against his lips, murmuring, "shh, shh," when he tried to inquire as to what, exactly, had just happened. A kiss was also effective in keeping him speechless, and he finally seemed to realize there would be no post-coital conversation tonight as she rested her head on his shoulder and her hand against his chest.

He didn't understand why she was acting like this, but then men had been not understanding their women ever since the first cavewoman had told the first caveman that she had a headache. But from the look on Michelle's face that he'd glimpsed by the light of his phone when he walked in the door, it seemed more like a heartache than a headache.

He pulled the covers up, tucking them around her shoulder as she cuddled him, and neither of them spoke in the brief minutes before sleep.

******

Eric was determined to have a conversation with Michelle in the morning when he woke up, whether she wanted to talk or not, determined to clarify what this was all about, why the silent passion of the night before after her request to sleep apart the previous night. No matter if she tried to hush him again, he was going to talk.

But he'd slept harder and longer than he realized. He'd slept little the night before, missing Michelle's presence and wondering what he'd done to push her away. Why didn't she yell at him and let him know exactly what had bothered her, like she usually did? Why, when she did come back to his bed, had she refused to let him talk to her? The silent passion had been undeniably erotic, but he still wanted to talk to her. However, having her back with him, making love even though it was silent and dark, had finally released him to sleep soundly afterward.

When he came awake and turned over, he found himself alone in his bed, the only indication she had been there being the slight indentation in her pillow. The robe she'd been wearing was gone, Michelle was gone, and her bedroom door was firmly closed. She'd already left for work without kissing him goodbye.

Apparently, silence was still the order of the day.

******

When Michelle left work that afternoon, she should have been happy. All her repairs had gone smoothly. The boat owners were all happy, and none of them had hit on her today or even looked at her with anything other than respect. Her boss had stopped by and complimented her on her work and told her he was glad he could trust her to get the job done with little supervision.

The weather was beautiful, she was having a good hair day, and she'd gotten laid last night. So why did she still feel grouchy when she picked up her tool bag and walked towards her golf cart?

Because she was an idiot, that was why.

Eric was waiting for her, leaning against her golf cart, the pink beads right next to his head as he leaned against the frame, his arms and legs crossed, and – what had she done to deserve it – his gorgeous killer smile lighting his face. He pushed his sunglasses up onto the top of his head when she got close and gifted her with a gaze from his sparkly eyes.

How could she ever resist those eyes and that smile?

He stepped towards her and took her tool bag, placing it on the back seat of the golf cart, then turned back to her.

"Talk to me."

"Kiss me first."

"Yes, ma'am," he said obediently, caressing her cheek briefly before sliding his hand around to the back of her neck and pulling her close.

He didn't just kiss her. He possessed her, inhaled her, made her forget they were standing out in public. If he'd started undressing her right there, she probably wouldn't have resisted.

But fortunately for her reputation, he refrained and released her, then held out one hand.

"Keys," he demanded firmly.

"You want to drive?" she asked stupidly.

Duh. Of course, why else would he demand the keys?

"Yes. It will make it easier for you to talk if you don't have to watch the road."

She handed him the keys and got into the passenger seat, putting a brief finger on her lips, which were still tingling. He started up the cart, but rather than making the U-turn onto Casino Way, he drove around to the other side of the casino, where the rescue boat was kept. For a moment she was afraid he was going to be heading out on another rescue. But he had chosen this spot for its relative privacy, on the far side of the building from the dive park and the casino entrance and the road leading into town in one direction, and towards the Descanso Beach Club and Hamilton Cove in the other.

"Talk to me," he said again, and he might as well have been a five-star admiral and she might as well have been the lowliest, newest sailor in the Navy, because she obeyed his request immediately.

"Last night I wanted you not to talk," she started.

"You mean when you ordered me not to talk?"

"Yeah, that. Did it freak you out?"

"What? You mean, not talking to me except to tell me to keep quiet? You mean, doing it in the pitch dark so I couldn't see you, couldn't see your face or your body? Nah it didn't freak me out at all." The look he gave her was almost a glare. "Of course it freaked me out! What the hell was up with that? I mean, why the order to not talk? After avoiding me the night before? I mean, yeah it was hot and sexy and I loved it, but it was kind of disturbing at the same time."

I needed it to be quiet because I knew if I let you talk, I'd talk too and what I would have said was that I love you and I was afraid you wouldn't return the sentiment.

That was what she said only in her mind.

"You said it – I have control issues," she actually said verbally. "I wanted to be in control. But more than that, it was Karen. Talking to her kind of freaked me out and I wasn't sure how to proceed. I wanted you, but I didn't want to have to talk about her just yet."

"You don't ever have to talk about her if you don't want to. Lord knows I'd rather not talk about her. Wait, did she say something to you after I left? Was that the reason you wouldn't sleep with me the other night?"

"She said a lot of things to me. I'm sure she was wrong about most of it, like saying you were running off on her when you got deployed, and that you were running off on me the other day when the oil rig blew up."

"Yes she was definitely wrong about that."

But was she wrong about the other things she'd said? Like, Eric doesn't do long-term. She wanted to ask him but was afraid to hear the answer.

"It kind of bothered me," she admitted vaguely.

"Look sweetheart, don't let her get to you. I don't think she means to be a bad person."

Yeah, it wasn't intentional. It just came completely naturally.

"She said a lot of unpleasant things about you."

"Well, she didn't like me very much."

"And yet she married you."

"I kind of bullied her into it. I think her problem is that she's just not a big-picture type of person. She just isn't capable of seeing beyond the end of her own nose, and it tends to give her a kind of skewed outlook on things. Do you know what she does for a living?" he asked.

"No, we didn't get to the point of exchanging personal histories."

"She's a jeweler. She spends her days peering through a magnifying glass at small objects, searching for imperfections, and I think it affects how she looks at life – the small picture, only how it affects her person-ally."

Whereas Michelle had recently, suddenly become very much of a big-picture type of person, imagining all sorts of improbable futures.

"Look, Michelle, neither the marriage, nor the divorce, was exclusively her fault or exclusively my fault. We both failed, but it's over now we're past it and. Ancient history. The only reason I ever even think about it is because my sister Brenda keeps bringing it up, just to remind me how stupid I was."

"No offense to your sister, but that's kind of insensitive."

"Oh, she means it in a good way. Just to make sure ancient history doesn't repeat itself. I'm sorry you had to talk to her. I promise, if we ever run into her again – and I hope we don't – I will turn and walk the other way."

"I was very civil to her," she said. "You would have been proud of me."

"Sweetheart, I am always proud of you."

"I really don't want to talk about her anymore."

"Good, because I don't want to talk about her either. Hopefully knowing that I live here now will encourage her to not to want to spend any future vacations on the island." He leaned towards her and cupped her chin in his hand. "Sweetheart, Karen is ancient history. Whatever she says or thinks, it doesn't matter to us. Don't let her intimidate you, OK?"

She nodded and leaned forward to give him a quick kiss. "OK. Now, let's go home. I'm starving."

"For a steak? Or for me?"

"Both. Though not necessarily in that order."

He laughed as he started up the golf cart and turned it towards Casino Way. "And you'll talk to me? Let me talk to you?"

"As long as the talking includes things like, ooh baby, just like that."

"You bet it will. And not just when you're eating the steak I may eventually cook tonight."

47

The Casino movie theatre did run a Star Wars marathon, and of course, Eric dragged Michelle to see it. "Just the original trilogy," he promised, as if that made a difference. "I can't believe you've never seen Star Wars."

"Yeah, I know, my education has been sadly lacking."

Eric was familiar with the Casino building, but only from the outside. The Los Angeles County Baywatch rescue boat was docked on the casino's east side, around the building from the public area of the dive park. Though the building was as tall as a twelve-story edifice, the interior had only two levels, with the movie theater on the ground floor and the ballroom above it.

After purchasing their tickets at the ornate steel and leaded glass ticket booth, Eric gazed up at the art deco style underworld water scene above the door, created from the famous Catalina Pottery tile.

"She's cute," he teased, looking towards the slender nude mermaid surrounded by swirling purple kelp and energetic fish and seahorses in the tile panel over the door.

"Humph," Michelle muttered dismissively. She saw that artistic mermaid almost every day. "Redhead."

The lobby inside curved in circle around the inside wall, as befitted a round building, and the buttery yellow chairs and blue sofas set against the warm, luxurious wood-paneled walls were intended to evoke seashells and the ocean, with gold stars on a rounded ceiling painted the color of sunset, all of it exuding the glamor of the nineteen twenties.

If Eric's eyes were wide with appreciation in the lobby, they grew saucer-sized when they entered the theatre itself.

The art deco theme was continued in the bright murals covering the theater's walls. Perhaps this venue didn't seat as many patrons as a twenty-screen multiplex on the mainland, but the chairs they sat in here were upholstered in red velvet. Above the single screen, Venus rose on a half shell, her hands and hair strategically placed to cover breasts and genitals. It wasn't an exact replica of the Birth of Venus painting in Florence, but it evoked the same artistry. Colorful, ornate art-deco murals covered the walls, depicting stylized mythical scenes including god-like hunters, lush scenery in artistically unnatural colors, unicorns, leaping stags and other exotic creatures around huge colorful beds of fantastical flowers. Birds darted amongst clouds swirling to meet tall, rounded, wave-like mountains. Above the doors were a pair of three-foot-tall Chinese theatre masks depicting tragedy and comedy.

"Are you sure this is a movie theater?" Eric asked. "It looks more like an art gallery."

"It's a theater," she assured him. "The only one in town." She pointed up at the ceiling, decorated with more stars, painted in real gold. "There's a ballroom on the upper level. It was used as Avalon's first high school, back in the olden days."

"This is positively the most beautiful movie theater I've ever been in." Michelle felt a bit of home-town pride in Eric's admiration.

Before the movie started, Eric propped his legs on the seat back in front of him and tossed up pieces of popcorn to catch them in his mouth. Without looking, he tossed a piece in Michelle's direction. It missed her mouth by inches, and fell down the front of her tank top.

He craned his neck, trying to look down her cleavage as if to try and retrieve it, but she smacked his hand away with a smile.

"You're so bad," she whispered at him reprovingly, and he nodded in agreement with a wide grin, his eyes going hot as she reached in and retrieved the piece of popcorn herself.

He picked up a second piece out of his bag, and looked at her questioningly, offering it in her direction. She held out her hand but he shook his head and gestured towards her mouth, so she opened her mouth and let him put it directly on her tongue.

"I'm a big girl. I can eat my own popcorn," she told him.

"I know. But it's way more fun this way."

The second time he did it, she bit his finger.

She would have gone to this movie marathon just to watch Eric's obvious enthusiasm for it, but actually found herself enjoying it for its own sake. She had been afraid that watching three movies in a row might be long and boring, but it turned out to be just the opposite. Part of it was the vicarious enjoyment she gleaned from observing Eric's evident pleasure. However, as they watched, she found herself getting into it for its own sake as well. Eric held her hand during most of the movies, which only increased her enjoyment.

When they blew up the Death Star, Eric yelled out, "Hooyah!" with a complete and utter lack of self-consciousness. When Darth Vader revealed himself to be Luke's father, Michelle clapped her hand over her mouth in surprise, then looked at Eric who, she discovered, had turned to her with a gleaming smile that said, "Didn't see that one coming, did you?"

It was midnight when the movies finished and they drove down Casino Way. The night was clear and moonless. Michelle let Eric drive the golf cart again, but he drove right past their house and turned up Avalon Canyon Road.

"You don't have to go in to work tonight, do you?" she asked as they passed the fire station. She didn't mind at all dropping him off at work, but didn't he need to stop at home to change into his uniform?

"No, I'm off tonight and tomorrow," he replied. "But it's such a clear night, I thought we could look at the stars."

He parked the cart in front of the Sand Trap, which was shuttered and dark, and they walked across the street to the golf course. Out of habit, he put a shushing finger on his lips as he glanced across the green towards the fire station.

"Come on," he whispered. "Lay down."

He actually laid down on his back on the grass at the edge of the golf course, which Michelle was fairly certain was not allowed, but it was so dark it was unlikely they would be noticed. The street lights were spaced far apart on this street, and they chose a dark spot between two round slices of light. Michelle just wondered what the schedule was for the sprinklers to go off.

She knelt on the grass next to him, and he took her hand and nudged her down so that they lay flat on their backs, holding hands as they gazed straight up at the sky.

"Look at those stars," Eric breathed appreciatively. "Imagine, each and every one of them is like our sun, with potentially planets revolving around them, possibly supporting life. And we're only seeing a tiny fraction of them."

"Like little green men?" she teased. "Do you believe in E.T.?"

"Little green men, big green men, seven-foot tall Wookies, who knows? It seems like it would be an awful waste of space to think that we were the only living creatures in the universe.

"Let's see if we can pick out any constellations. There's Orion's belt – see those three stars in a row?"

He pointed, and she murmured, "I see it. They look like your freckles."

"When is your birthday?" Eric asked her. "Maybe we can find the constellation for your zodiac sign."

"I'm a Virgo. My birthday is September 11."

He went still beside her. "September 11? That's – sad."

She turned her head towards him. "Why do you say that?"

He squeezed her hand a little. "Well, to have your birthday on the same day as the attacks. It kind of takes away from what should be a happy day, since it was such a day of tragedy."

"The attacks?" She thought for a second. "Oh, you mean the World Trade Center attack."

"And the Pentagon and Flight 93. So many people died that day, I'd think it would be hard to celebrate your birthday on the same day."

"Well, since I was only seven that year, I didn't realize what had really happened until years later when I was older and we read about it in history class."

A lump of ice started to form in Eric's stomach, crystallizing as Michelle's words took on meaning and substance.

"I suppose," he replied, feeling his throat clench as he tried to keep his words causal. "Well, there doesn't appear to be any constellations visible tonight. Let's head home. I'm really tired."

As they clambered to their feet and walked back towards the golf cart, Michelle couldn't help teasing Eric. "Did the excitement of seeing Star Wars again wear you out?"

"Yeah, I guess," he replied briefly as he turned the cart back towards their casino.

Later, she cuddled against him as she usually did in bed, her pillow pressed against his as they lay with her back against his chest, curved together like two spoons in a drawer. He'd yawned and drooped enough that she suspected nothing of his thoughts when they didn't make love before sleeping. It was after all close to one a.m. and she had to work in the morning.

He pulled the covers up, covering her shoulder, tucking the sheet under her chin, and she murmured drowsily just before her breathing smoothed and quieted, and he knew she was asleep. But Eric didn't sleep, at least not right away. Not after realizing the significance of what she'd mentioned as they lay on the grass looking at stars, words that had seemed like idle conversation to her but which had been a catalyst of despair to him.

Where had she been on September 11? On *the* September 11? In the damn second grade and too young to be scared of the tragedy that had happened and the possibility of what might happen next. Him, he'd been at sea on his first WestPac deployment, and old enough to be scared enough to practically toss his cookies over the side. While she'd been playing with Legos, he'd been treating wounded sailors and Marines in Operation Enduring Freedom. He'd already been in high school when she'd been born. She'd been in preschool while he was raising his right hand, swearing to defend his country against all enemies, foreign and domestic. When she'd been twelve and experiencing trauma during a fire on the island, he'd been twenty-seven and experiencing the trauma of a war zone in a field hospital in Iraq.

She stirred a little in her sleep, whether due to a dream, or just restless sleep, he couldn't be sure. He put his arms around her and nudged her against his shoulder, and she willingly cuddles against him, murmuring something indistinct against his neck. He petted her hair, wishing like hell that this could be forever.

Why couldn't it be forever? Because it just couldn't, that was why. It was fate or kismet or karma, or whatever weird thing one might call it. But whatever title you hung on it, it was still definite.

This just couldn't be forever. He could lay here and do the math all night, but it wasn't going to change.

Why can't this be forever? an inner, almost childish voice in his head asked. Why can't we, and by we I mean this lovely young woman and myself, be a forever couple?

You know why, dirtwad, the inner voice mocked him. A classy woman like her isn't going to want a man who's had as many one-night stands as you have. A guy who got married and divorced in less than a year, because the woman apparently couldn't stand to be around him any longer. Michelle was sweet, fresh, adorable, and he was a reformed man-slut. She might be happy with him now, but give her time. She'd get over it.

He feigned sleep when she got up to get ready for work in the morning, even when she tiptoed back in the room and kissed his cheek just before she left.

It still didn't matter how he did the math, it always came out the same.

They were so completely and utterly different, not really the twins separated at birth that he had joked about. He was a little bit country, she was a little bit rock & roll. She liked to read, he preferred movies. When he went out back and lifted weights, she did yoga. She liked sushi while he preferred a nice juicy steak, well done.

He'd been around the block, actually around the world, a time or two or six; while she'd barely been out of the state of California. But the biggest thing, the gut-punch doom to the possibility of a future together, was their age difference. The inescapable fact was that he was thirty-seven years old, and she was only twenty-two. A fifteen-year gap. That verged on almost old enough to be your father territory. He was such a perv for being in love with her. What would his family, especially Brenda, think of him, sleeping with a woman fifteen years his junior? Brenda had never hesitated to give him her honest opinion of his actions and life choices. The way she'd figuratively raked him over the coals over his marriage had illustrated that.

He'd always been aware, in the back of his mind, that he was so much older than Michelle. It had been obvious the first day they'd met, when she didn't know that Paul McCartney had been in the Beatles. But he'd attempted to disregard the age gap, for two reasons, and they both started with the letter L.

Lust. And Love.

He wasn't sure when the one had evolved into the other, or if they'd both possessed his psyche simultaneously.

Did it matter, that he was crazy, stupid in love with her? Was it any justification that she was the only woman he'd ever been with whose embrace had any chance of keeping his compartment doors closed and banishing the dreams?

He should consider himself lucky. He knew guys who had it a lot worse than him. The shrink he had seen after his last deployment had said Eric was one of the most well-adjusted vets she'd ever talked to.

He was lucky. He knew guys who had to spend the Fourth of July in a closed room wearing noise-canceling headphones, unable to enjoy the Independence Day fireworks. For them, the words "bombs bursting in air" were much more real than just a line from the Star-Spangled Banner.

He knew guys who were forced to avoid ever being within earshot of a construction site, because the sound of nails being hammered was too similar to the sounds of gunshots.

He'd known guys who had committed suicide.

When Eric had gotten the call about his buddy whose funeral he'd attended recently, he had for one panicked minute been afraid the guy had offed himself. He hoped he'd be forgiven for feeling relieved when he'd heard it was a car accident, completely the other driver's fault.

Compared to some guys he'd known, a little night-time twitching wasn't so bad. But it still shook him up.

He also realized that it wasn't only service members who suffered the effects of traumatic experiences. While Michelle didn't twitch in her sleep and wake up demanding proof of life, still he could tell she was sometimes still affected by memories of her idiot of a dad and his indifference during his life.

Maybe she hadn't seen guys bleed out in front of her eyes. Maybe she hadn't gone out in full battle rattle to pick up the pieces of guys blown up by IEDs. But still, she'd been affected by what she'd experienced. He was glad to hear Michelle talk about her lonely, loveless childhood, not because he enjoyed it or pitied her, hearing about it, but because he felt that letting it out, expressing it to someone who cared, was a whole lot healthier than keeping it all bottled up inside until you burst from the pressure.

And he did care, way more than he ought to. He not only cared, he loved her.

The concept half fascinated him, and half scared the hell out of him.

He'd only had the one night-time dream incident since he and Michelle had been together, and that was a distinct improvement over the norm. He dared to hope that it would be the last time, that her love would banish it forever, but now that he'd stupidly driven her away, all bets were off.

He'd hoped that once he retired from the service, that the dream of memory would stop. His shrink had warned him not to place too much hope in that possibility, and she'd been right.

It had even happened once while he was staying with Gabriel and Susan before moving to Aalon, sleeping on their couch. That time, he wasn't awakened by a tender nudge, followed by kisses and embraces from the woman he loved.

That time, he woke up when he fell off of Gabriel's living room sofa and landed on the floor with a thunk, his leg bashing painfully against the coffee table with an even louder thunk.

A moment later, the light went on and Gabriel loomed above him, as Eric was pulling himself back onto the sofa. Gabriel's brow was furrowed with concern, his dark eyes round and black.

"Dude, you OK?" he asked.

Eric breathed deep, pressing a hand against his chest.

"Yeah, I'm good. What are you doing up at this hour? It must be one a.m."

"Would you believe me if I told you I just happened to need a midnight snack right about now?"

"No, I don't think I'd believe that. You never get up for midnight snacks."

"Ok, then would you believe me if I told you that my wife put an elbow in my ribs and said, go check on Eric. I think he's crying in his sleep."

"Yeah, that I'd believe. But I wasn't crying."

"Whatever. Susan said you sounded pretty bad. You know she's got that Vulcan hearing thing."

It had happened several times during his short-lived marriage, in the even shorter time that they'd actually cohabitated. Karen hadn't held him or kissed him or called him a hero, nor had she ever bothered to ask him what his nightmare was about. She'd just kicked his ass to the couch when his twitching disturbed her sleep.

They'd never even been in love or anything close to it. They'd only gotten married because, six weeks after their one-night fling, she'd called him to say she thought she might be pregnant. It wasn't the first time he'd had to ask a woman's last name after the fact, but it was the first time the P-word had been uttered. As a result, he'd gone all honorable and bought wedding rings the same day. He'd been insane to do it. But he'd been blindsided by the thought of having a family. They'd been married at the courthouse the following day, and he'd managed to find them an apartment, small and less than elegant, and way too close to the sounds of military aviation for Karen's liking. Deployment was fast approaching, and he'd wanted his kid to have the protection of his benefits if anything should happen to him.

Then, it had all turned out to be a false alarm. She'd recently started taking medication for a thyroid issue, a medication that contained hormones, and like any medication containing hormones, it had interfered with her female rhythms. He of all people, working in the medical field, should have known better, should have insisted on a second pregnancy test and waited for confirmation before rushing into marriage. His brothers and sisters had given him a lot of grief about it, and Gabriel had called him a few choice names. His mother had already passed away by then so at least he'd been spared her disappointment.

He should have known the whole thing was doomed when they'd found out she wasn't pregnant after all. At his suggestion that they try for a baby anyway, seeing that they were already married, her refusal had been harsh and instantaneous.

They hadn't even had sex again from that point, not even with protection, and he had spent the remainder of his nights until leaving for deployment sleeping on the couch. When the day to leave arrived, she did drive him to the dock, but only dropped him off at the curb, rather than parking and accompanying him to the ship's gangplank as most of the other families were doing. She remained in the car as he retrieved his sea bag from the trunk and he'd had to lean into her window to kiss her goodbye, a farewell whose response could only be described as chilly.

He walked alone to the ship, making his way among crewmates who were with their spouses, children, or parents, saying their goodbyes with smiles, tears, kisses and hugs, some family members carrying posters or wearing custom-printed shirts proclaiming their pride in their sailor. A lump formed in his throat, quickly swallowed down, at the site of one of his crewmates kissing his wife, then leaning down to bestow a tender goodbye kiss on her bulging tummy as well. Judging from the size of that bump, when they returned six months from now, that wife would be there greeting her husband with a baby in her arms.

The ones whose goodbyes were faintly heartbreaking were those spouses who refused to show emotion no matter what they might feel inside. The ones who stiffened their spines, straightened their shoulders, and said their goodbyes dry-eyed. It was only when turning away that their lips trembled and their eyes filled with tears. Others wept copiously, paying little heed to anyone who might notice, clinging to their departing sailor as if the two bodies were fused together with welding solder.

He saluted a female lieutenant urging two toddlers – twins from the look of them – into her husband's arms with kisses and hair petting and a teary smile. Eric wished he could stop and embrace those two kids also – a boy and a girl, wasn't that just perfect – and tell them that it was their futures that he and their mom and the five thousand other sailors here were leaving to protect. He wanted to tell them that they weren't boarding that ship because they wanted to get away from them, because they found the company of their shipmates more interesting than them, but because of their commitment and honor and duty to the service and their country.

But of course he couldn't do that, barge in on another family's precious last few minutes together, and that of an officer as well. He could only murmur a respectful, "Ma'am" as the lieutenant returned his salute, and keep walking, trying not to feel bitter at the fact that his own spouse had just dropped him off with barely a goodbye and was probably at Starbucks right now picking up a latte with one of those cute little designs swirled into the foam, and not giving him a thought.

He couldn't blame Karen, really. It would be easy to blame her completely for the marriage's failure, considering the way she'd served him with divorce papers via email while he was deployed. But he had to shoulder just as much of the responsibility. They both knew perfectly well they weren't in love. One night of lust after a bar pickup rarely translated into true love. They were totally wrong for each other. And he'd been unable to hide the fact that he was in it only for the prospect of parenthood, and once they realized that wasn't happening, it had been pretty much over from that moment.

The divorce rate was abnormally high in the military under the best of circumstances, and his marriage had been the exact opposite of the best of circumstances. While he had truly not been terribly upset when Karen had ended it, other than a slightly peeved resentment at the sneaky way she'd waited until he was deployed to serve him, he was still certain he wasn't good husband material.

But now he looked at his Michelle, and wished like hell that he was good husband material.

Michelle was young, and lonely, and vulnerable to some older, more experienced man swooping in and taking advantage. And what had he done? Swooped in and taken advantage.

What had happened to respect? What had happened to the gentleman his mama had raised?

If he was being brutally honest with himself, and he usually was, he'd been pretty much of a hound until he'd met Michelle. Though he did pride himself on never having cheated during his entire six months of wedded non-bliss.

He knew of at least two other guys, in addition to Christopher Wong, who would ask Michelle out in a heartbeat, if Eric hadn't been in the picture.

One was Eric's friend and former shipmate, Danny Gonzalez, and the other was Gary McNeil, the bartender at the Marlin Club.

He'd noticed that manner in which Gary had hovered protectively the first day Eric had brought Michelle into the Marlin Club, the warning look Gary had flashed when Eric had sat down at his bar with her. It was more than just his acquaintance with her due to her having to come there to drag her drunk father home, though it was obvious Michelle was unaware of Gary's interest.

Eric also realized that Michelle probably wouldn't have accepted invitations from either of those men, even though they were both closer to her in age than Eric was. Danny due to his excessive drinking, and Gary due to his profession as a bartender, serving those drinks.

As for other men, he had to wonder if it was, as she had said, really due to the limited local dating pool and her supposed unpleasant reputation, or, as she had also claimed, due to her desire to only be with him, even though he was totally the wrong man for her.

They had finally had the opportunity to go diving last week, and after surfacing, they sat on the dive park steps, pulled off their flippers, then walked over to where they'd left Eric's dive bag. When Michelle peeled down her wetsuit, revealing the cute pink swimsuit she wore beneath the black neoprene, Eric noticed two guys, also divers peeling down, ogling her from a few feet away. Her back was to them and she didn't notice how their eyes lit up with interest, and one of them started to walk towards her, probably planning to say something like, "Hey, babe, see any interesting fish down there today? I have a cool fish tank at my place, you want to come see it?"

Eric had headed off the potential pick-up attempt by picking up Michelle's towel and placing it over her shoulders, and behind her back gave those other guys a "back off dudes, she's taken" glare.

The dudes backed off.

Now, he reflected, perhaps he should have stepped aside, not interfered as they approached her, let them talk to her, and let Michelle make the decision whether or not to respond.

Those two guys had both been at least ten years younger than Eric.

While in high school, she'd worked whatever odd jobs she could scrounge up, repairing lawnmowers and things like that.

Eric had worked part-time when he'd been in high school too. He'd bagged groceries at the supermarket, served as a lifeguard at the community pool, and been a caddie at the golf course. He'd like the caddying work the best. The tips were great, and his brothers had really appreciated the free passes he'd gotten for them. He had used what he'd earned to buy scuba gear and skydiving lessons. His eighteenth birthday had been spent on his first jump.

Because it was his first jump, he'd had to do it in tandem with the instructor. Even though they were strapped together, he still felt that fraction of a second of absolute regret as he faced the open door of the airplane, that momentary, though unvoiced, thought of, "Shit, I changed my mind." There was another moment of mind-numbing terror, just for a second, as they stepped out and he found himself free-falling away from that perfectly good, safe airplane. But the terror and regret were only fleeting, quickly displaced by a complete and utter thrill, and a desperate hope that there would be no malfunction in the Go-Pro camera mounted to his helmet.

When the parachute deployed, it jerked him upwards for a moment, but he'd been told to expect that. His entire family, and Gabriel, had come out to the landing field to see him land, with the exception of his mother, who'd refused to watch. Despite the difficulty in getting the wheelchair over the bumpy, uneven ground, his dad had insisted on being there "to see his crazy kid fall out of the sky", and Oliver and Philip had simply picked up the chair between them two and carried it to the landing spot. Brenda had held up a sign saying, "Welcome to Earth, G.D.", while Diane had taken video.

He'd been eternally grateful that the landing was smooth and that he and the instructor both stayed on their feet. He would have been embarrassed to stumble down into an undignified heap in front of his family. He also kind of wished that Brenda hadn't put the nickname "G.D." on her sign. He'd long since outgrown the Gross and Disgusting impression she'd had when he'd been born, hadn't he? Even worse, he'd had to explain the reference to the instructor, who'd asked, "Who's G.D.? I thought your name was Eric Hanson?"

And while he'd used his earnings for fun and thrills, Michelle had used hers to pay her father's bar tab, to fix and maintain her house, to buy serious tools like pipe wrenches. The thought of it made him feel a bit frivolous and immature.

Never before had he analyzed his reasons for sleeping with a woman. He'd meet someone, sparks would fly, and they ended up naked, sometimes all on the same day. The only time it had come to more than that had been with Karen, and hadn't that been an utter fiasco.

But with Michelle, it had been totally, completely different. She entranced him a way he'd never known before nor dared to expect to deserve. He didn't deserve her. But her eyes were the color of the ocean on a calm sunny day, and he had been helpless to resist her.

Their relationship was all kinds of wrong, for all kinds of reasons, the main two being their fifteen-year age difference, and his totally deserved man-slut reputation.

But the truth was that he burned for her. It wasn't just lust. It was longing. Not only sexually, but emotionally. He should never have seduced her, but his need for her was way more intense than any addict's need for a fix.

He shouldn't have even responded to her roommate ad, knowing that the seeds of attraction were already there, that they had started germinating the moment he'd turned around on the sidewalk after feeling a rock-hard forehead connect with his T2 vertebrae.

He should never have seduced her, but then, guys did crazy shit when they were in love.

In love. It was a basic human experience, felt by millions of people all over the world, including him. He was totally, desperately in love with her. He wasn't quite sure when it had happened. The sensation had inserted itself into his soul via osmosis, almost without him realizing it. But had been unable to tell her.

It was unlike him, the bigmouth, to be unable to express himself.

Well, actually, he could express himself. It was more that he didn't dare. It would simply be unacceptable for him to tell her the honest truth, that he loved her desperately, that he'd never felt for another person what he felt for her, that he'd want to marry her if he wasn't so positive that he was bad husband material. Someone with a moral past like his did not deserve a sweet, wonderful, adorable person like Michelle Diaz.

48

It was his day off. There were a lot of things he could have done while Michelle was at work. He could lift weights. He could call Tony and see if he wanted to play golf. He could go swimming or diving or watch the game or take a nap.

He did none of those things.

He spent the day pacing and fretting and debating with himself, mentally bouncing back and forth from being selfish to being honorable to doing what was morally right. He was surprised he hadn't worn a groove in the living room floor by the time Michelle arrived home from work.

She saw him there standing in the middle of the living room and the happy smile that filled her face was almost painful to see. A tiny frown of concern replaced the smile when he caught her hands and wouldn't let her kiss him, saying, "Let's sit down, we need to talk."

Obligingly she sat down next to him on the couch and smiled at him, but he couldn't make himself smile back or even look her in the eyes. He hated what he was going to say, but he had to say it.

She spoke first, mentioning last night's dinner. "Sweetie, if this is about the sushi, I told you, if you don't like it, you don't have to eat it."

"No, it's not about the sushi." Though he still had to admit, the sushi had been pretty unpleasant. He'd been surprised; he thought he'd eat just about anything. But apparently, he was enough of an old-fashioned southern boy to want all of his meat cooked well-done, even the fish.

He almost started out by calling her Sweetheart, as he usually did, but reminded himself, *you have no right to call her that.*

"Michelle," he said. "You know that I'm thirty-seven years old, right?"

An expression of slight bewilderment crossed her face. Of course, she knew that. She had a copy of his driver's license saved on her computer. She knew his height, his weight, his date of birth. His birthday had been a week before he'd moved to Avalon.

"Of course I know that, Sweetie. So?"

He wished she hadn't called him Sweetie. It just made things harder.

"Well, you're twenty-two." She nodded. She knew that too, of course.

"Don't you think you would be better off dating someone closer to your own age?"

"No, of course not. I don't care about what our ages are." A slightly suspicious look of hurt crossed her face.

"It's just not right. You should be with a guy your own age, someone you have more in common with. I really think that would be the best thing for you, what would make you happy."

"No, what makes me happy is being with you."

This was killing him. *It's what best for her*, he reminded himself.

"In the long run, you'd be better off with a younger guy. I mean, look. We're fifteen years apart, Michelle, and-"

She tried to put her arms around his neck, to protest what he was saying, but he wouldn't let her. He could see the small look of concern in her eyes. She was starting to get upset.

She was going to get a lot more upset before the evening was through.

"Are you saying that I'm too young for you?"

No, she wasn't too young for him. She was perfect for him, but this wasn't about what he wanted. It was about what was best for her.

"I really think we shouldn't date, shouldn't sleep together anymore. You should find a guy closer to your own age to-" Lord, the thought of her sleeping with another man was like a knife to his gut. "Be with," he finished lamely.

Her eyes narrowed at him and her head jerked as if she'd been slapped, the blue eyes going huge and teary. That passion of anger that usually turned him on, now devastated his soul.

"So you got what you wanted, and now you're done with me?" she demanded.

"No, it's not like that."

"I thought you were my best friend. I thought you cared about me. I thought you-"

He was certain that the words she bit off were going to be, "I thought you loved me." He wanted to shriek out, "I do love you, and you are my best friend," but he had to keep his fucking big mouth shut about that.

She jumped to her feet, away from him, her fists bunched and her body taut with distress. He stood also, and involuntarily reached a hand towards her.

"Michelle, I-"

She shrank away from him. "Don't touch me." She literally paced back and forth a bit, much as he had been doing most of the day.

"Oh my god, the books."

He glanced at the coffee table where several of her books lay, then back at her in confusion.

"What about the books?"

"The books!" she practically shouted the word. "You bought me all those books. I knew I shouldn't have let you. You were paying for it. You bought me those books because you thought it would get you something."

"Absolutely not," he insisted. "I never thought any such thing when I bought those books."

Yeah, right. Men had been making excuses like that forever.

"You could have saved yourself the money. The sad part is, I would have slept with you anyway, even if you hadn't bought them."

"I did not buy you those books to get you into bed," he protested again.

"Yeah, because you've never had to lie in order to get laid, right? That's what you really meant to say the day we met, isn't it?"

He couldn't deny that. It was true, in his hound-dog past, that he'd never had to lie or pretend in order to attract a girl, to entice a woman into bed. But he had never, for a single moment, thought of what he and Michelle had shared as merely getting laid. Getting laid was fleeting, shallow, meaningless. The kind of thing he used to indulge in, before he'd met her. With her it had been miraculous, soul-warming, the best thing that had ever happened to him.

Something he was never going to experience again.

"So let me get this straight. You move in here, help me with all my emotional shit just to get me to have sex with you, make me feel like it's wonderful, and now you decide I'm not sophisticated enough for you? I'm some kind of stupid little country bumpkin and now that you've screwed me, I'm just a little bitch who's too young for you. Is that it?"

She had it all wrong. No that wasn't how he felt, not how he'd ever felt. His reasoning for doing what he was doing was not getting through to her. He was screwing it up because he hated having to do this. Maybe he just needed to fall on his sword, for the good of both of them, to keep this whole scenario from spiraling out of control.

For the first time in his life, and certainly for the first time to Michelle, he told an outright, boldfaced lie.

"Yes. You're too young for me." The knife in his gut twisted and wounded as the words left his mouth.

"You jerk! You made me fall in love with you and now you're dumping me? You jerky jerk!"

She was obviously too upset to think if any more creative bad things to call him. But even if she could, he'd deserve them. He couldn't help but take a step towards her, and she stepped back as if he was Jack the Ripper.

"Go jump in the Persian Gulf!"

The wounded look of hurt in her eyes killed him inside. It was how she'd looked back when they'd first met, that weird, exciting afternoon starting on the sidewalk outside the Marlin Club. He'd hoped that wounded look had been gone forever, but he'd managed to put it back on her face, idiot that he was. A dragon jabbed its jagged claws into Eric's gut and twisted.

She dashed into her room and slammed the door so hard, the whole house shook. Eric stared at the closed door for a moment, feeling his insides ripping open, then went into his own room and slammed his door too. Not because he was mad at her. But because he was mad at himself.

In his career, he'd treated everything from a bee sting to a severed limb. But he'd never torn out a human heart before.

******

Michelle flung herself on the bed and let loose with all the tears she'd refused to let Eric see. She cried until she was dry, then she found more tears and cried some more. It was doubly tragic to sob in despair without being able to do it on Eric's shoulder, in his arms.

He was abandoning her, passing her off to some theoretical other person. Of course. Everyone in her life abandoned her. Her mother had abandoned her. Her father had abandoned her. And now Eric, who she loved desperately, was abandoning her too. He probably thought she was an unsophisticated country bumpkin, and he'd prefer a blonde with D cups.

And she was reacting exactly the way she used to, the way she'd sworn she'd never act again – running away and crying.

She had dared to hope that Eric would be different, that she could trust him not to hurt or disappoint her. Perhaps she had hoped in vain. But she had been so certain that their affair would evolve into something more, into a real loving relationship, even deeper than their current best friends having incredibly hot sex relationship. She'd dared to dream about forever.

What had happened to her best friend? What had happened to 'my girl,' to 'My Michelle'? What had happened to 'the best night of my life'? She had trusted him, as she had never, ever trusted another person in her life. She loved him and he was kicking her to the curb, metaphorically speaking, because of something as unimportant as a date on a calendar. Did what they had shared, both physically and emotionally, mean nothing?

She was well aware that Eric had had quite a few former lovers, and she had at first been intimidated by the possibility that she might compare unfavorably to them. But the way he looked her, the way he told her things like "best night of my life," had given her hope that she did compare favorably. It appeared now that she'd been wrong to hope that.

She loved him, but she had never told him so, not in words. Would this situation have turned out differently if she had? In her misguided youth, she had thought true love was a myth. Maybe Eric thought so too.

She loved his face, his body, his muscles, the three freckles on his cute butt. But mostly she loved his soul – the man who had been an armed warrior, who saved lives as a first responder, and yet who was sentimentally human enough to cry at a movie with a sad ending, which had been a true story. She loved how he rescued kittens from trees, bought gifts for his friend's children for no other reason than that he loved them, and secretly ran his hands along her hair when he had washed it. She loved his loyalty, his corny sense of humor, the big mouth that got him into trouble.

He thought she was too young for him. Why should she doubt him? He had always been forthright and truthful with her, from day one, with a complete lack of artifice. There was no reason to think he wasn't being sincere in his claim to be acting in her best interests with his insane suggestion that she seek out a man closer to her age. Just because his idea was ridiculously incorrect didn't mean he wasn't sincere about wanting to do what was right for her.

Someday, she would find this funny. Someday in the dim and distant future, she would call Tracy, or send a text to Susan, and say, "Remember that time when Eric dumped me?"

And they'd say, "Yeah, I remember that." And they would all laugh and laugh and laugh.

Yeah, right. Now she was lying to herself.

Michelle truly envied what Gabriel and Susan had – an easy, loving relationship and a beautiful family. The manner in which Gabriel had looked at his wife while caressing the belly containing their new son had warmed her heart. She could only wish to experience something like that. Those two were obviously so much in love and had made a happy life despite the obstacles. Despite it being the twenty-first century, there were still challenges in being a mixed-race couple.

She should have expected this. Eric's ex-wife had warned her. *He'll find some excuse to leave you.* He'd found his excuse, a reason that was lame and stupid, but a reason, nonetheless.

Karen Butler had been right. She had after all been married to Eric. It stood to reason that she knew him better than anybody. Michelle had been a fool to think that it would somehow be different now, that Eric would change and do long-term with her.

Maybe it was a good thing she hadn't told him her true feelings, hadn't let him know how much she loved him. It would only have confirmed sooner what he had just told her tonight.

His own words mocked her. Would it be better to know the truth even if it's unpleasant? In this case, no. Knowing the truth was breaking her heart and killing her soul.

Or maybe she was wrong to put so much stock in what Eri's ex-wife claimed. Why would she believe the bitter words of a selfish, self-absorbed woman who didn't really know Eric and apparently didn't care to? Karen had lived with him, but she didn't really know him and obviously was too selfish to try to understand him on any more than a physical level. The woman hadn't even understood that Eric's nightmares were caused by PTSD, and that was why he'd been seeing a shrink. She'd only noticed that he'd disturbed her sleep, and had been uninterested in the reason for it.

Somewhere in the tears that soaked her pillow, she realized she was wrong about Eric, about what he'd said to her tonight. Eventually she had to stop crying, or she'd choke to death, and she lay on her wet pillow fuming at him for his misguided notions of honor and what he thought was "right" for her. She'd been wrong. He wasn't abandoning her. He was trying to make things right for her, the big goof. Damn his stupid noble intent.

The fact that he wouldn't look her in the eye should have set off a warning bell. It was not like him to hide his expressive eyes. Hearing those words had hurt her to the quick. But despite the stabbing pain in her heart, she'd still managed to glimpse the emotion in his eyes despite his avoidance, and it had told her that his brutal pronouncement had been the only untruthful, insincere thing he'd ever said to her.

She knew Eric, knew how he operated. He fixed things. He stepped up, assessed the situation, and he fixed it. He thought he'd fixed this situation, but he hadn't, no matter how well-intentioned he'd been. This was one situation she was going to have to fix herself, even if he was thirty-seven and she was only twenty-two.

She sat up, looking for something to wipe her eyes on. Of course, there was nothing to hand that she could use, not even one of Eric's shirts. She had to wipe her face on the edge of her bedsheet. For about a second, she considered calling Tracy to ask her advice on this situation. But Tracy would probably suggest that Michelle color her hair blue, to match her mood.

Instead, she gathered up her keys, purse and phone and opened her door a crack, not wanting to see Eric just yet. His door remained closed. She was tempted to drag her old pink hoody out from the back of her closet as she headed out the front door. But no, she didn't need that anymore.

When the going gets tough, the tough go shopping.

******

Eric heard her leave and for a second was tempted to run after her and take it all back. But he remained sitting on the edge of his bed in misery, regretting what he'd said, feeling lower than whale poop that he'd hurt her. Lord, he hated to see her cry. Especially when he was the one who inspired it. He leaned his elbows on his knees and let his hands dangle between them.

It was what was best for her. If he kept repeating it enough, maybe one day he might actually believe it. Maybe he'd start to accept it. Maybe it would make sense. Maybe it would make him happy.

Fat chance. He felt grief, as if someone had died. Yes, something had died, and he'd killed it.

Eric had, fortunately, never been wounded in the line of duty. A nose broken due to youthful over-exuberance, a bruised eye inflicted in confusion, were inconsequential. But now, this moment, he felt a hundred wounds knife through him. And he'd caused those wounds himself, with his own stupidity, inflicted them viciously, and yet completely unnecessarily, with words he'd regretted almost the moment they'd left his lips.

It was an annoyance when his phone chirped and lit up with a text message. The last thing in the world he felt like right now was being sociable, but it might be a work emergency so he picked it up and swiped it open. It was just Gabriel, not an emergency, but by then he'd already revealed his wallpaper photo.

It was the picture he'd taken of Michelle standing in front of the Stealth Bomber. After attending the air show, he had set up that photo on his phone, replacing the one he'd used previously – the picture of her he'd taken sitting on that rock on the mountain. She was holding her cap to her bosom in the new photo and smiling as if she'd just won the lottery. After he took the picture he'd walked over and put her cap back on her head - because it was his weekend off and he didn't want to have to treat anyone for sunstroke - and couldn't resist threading her ponytail through the back opening. She'd turned around and let him do that and he'd almost kissed the soft, sweet spot at the back of her neck, but she stepped away just at that moment and said, "Ooh, let's go look at that one," and skipped across the way to inspect a Harrier, unaware of how close he'd come.

He set the phone down and lay back, putting an arm over his eyes. *Well Hanson, you really FUBAR'd this one.*

******

Eric waited at the boat dock feeling anything but sociable. Gabriel and a couple of friends were coming over and while the last thing he wanted to do today was hang out, he knew if he blew them off, his phone would light up like the Battle of Baghdad. Gabriel knew something was seriously amiss when Eric barely managed a fist bump of greeting. Of course, they hustled him right into the Marlin Club. Gary saw him walk in and immediately opened the fridge, took out a cold can of Coke and set it on the bar in front of where Eric sat, while the guys snagged a pool table. He made no move to join them and after a minute there were head shakes and raised shoulders that said, *what's up with him?*

Gabriel came over and sat down next to him, on the same stools Eric and Michelle had sat on the day they'd met.

"What is up with you, man? I ain't seen you this low in like, ever. And where's your girl?"

"I don't want to talk about it."

Gabriel staggered back and put his hand over his heart. "You? You don't want to talk? Who are you and what have you done with the real Eric Hanson?" Eric just shrugged and played with the condensation on the outside of the Coke can. He finally spoke, but it wasn't much.

"I screwed up."

"What did you do?" Gabriel glowered. "Wait, you didn't cheat on that pretty lady, did you?"

"God no!"

"Good, because if you did, I'd have to pound you." Further details were not forthcoming. "Can you fix it?"

"No, this was a goatfuck level screw-up."

Gabriel hadn't served in the military, but he had spent enough time with Eric and his Navy buddies to understand that a goatfuck level screw-up was damn near unfixable.

"Can you grovel?"

"Wouldn't matter. She hates me." Because he was a jerky jerk who should jump into the Persian Gulf. Had she chosen the Persian Gulf as the body of water to insist he jump into because of what he'd told her about his divorce? Maybe she thought he should sit there at the bottom, next to his former wedding ring, and think about the mistakes he'd made.

"I don't believe that," Gabriel insisted. "That pretty lady is crazy about you. And don't give me that we're just roommates BS. I know that ship sailed a long time ago."

"Ship has sailed, been torpedoed, and sunk."

"Dude, I'm not buying it. That girl is in love with you. In love with a capital L. I could see it in her eyes when you guys came to visit."

"Yeah, well I managed to kill it." The sadness of it crushed him. "You know what I said to her? Lord, I'm such an idiot. I told her she was too young for me. It was a ginormous lie, but I said it anyway. And now she hates me."

Gabriel's face filled with a mixture of shock and sympathy.

"You can't be saying you don't love her anymore."

Eric refrained from mentioning that he hadn't actually ever told Gabriel that he loved Michelle. Not that he wanted to keep it a secret, but because he knew that happily married Gabriel would immediately suggest the M word, and Eric had already realized that he, unlike Gabriel, was bad husband material. But that didn't restrain his big mouth now.

"I'll always love her. I'm pretty sure she was in love with me too, but – not anymore."

"Dude," Gabriel said. "Every day since you brought her with you to the air show, Susan's been waiting for the call that you guys were engaged. Or married."

Eric made a snorting noise. "Yeah, right. You know my track record. I'm the last person a special woman like her would want to be stuck with."

"If you're referring to She Who Shall Not Be Mentioned, I don't think the pretty lady will have a problem with that particular mistake in your past."

"You can say her name, you know," Eric replied tartly. "She's not Beetlejuice. She won't appear in a puff of smoke if her name is uttered."

"Maybe, maybe not. I'm not taking the chance."

"We ran into her a little while ago," Eric said. "She was visiting the island with, get this, her fiancé. You remember the oil rig explosion last week?"

Gabriel nodded. "It was all over the news. There's already millions of dollars worth of lawsuits flying around. Everyone is blaming everyone else for it." He hesitated and looked around warily, apparently uncertain if he should believe Eric's claim that it was safe to say his ex-wife's name out loud. "Are you saying that - Karen - is getting married again? What is this, number four?"

Eric shook his head and held up three fingers.

"You know you dodged a serious bullet there," Gabriel went on. Eric shrugged in indifference. "You know, dude, if you ever need a place to crash my couch is always available."

"Thanks." Gabriel had never heard a more pathetic thank you.

Suddenly Eric's usually big mouth just shut down. He didn't want to tell his friend how much he loved Michelle, how much he regretted pushing her away, how he'd dared to hope that she might love him too despite his unsavory sexual past. How he'd screwed up the possibility of their intimacy going deeper than just the biological urges of their libidos. He just wanted to crawl into a hole and not crawl out until he'd figured out a way to fix things.

"You want to shoot some pool?" Gabriel asked. "It might take your mind off ... things."

"No, I think I'm going to just take a walk." The guys would just have to find their way back to the boat dock on their own, no matter what condition they were in.

"Well call me anytime if you want to-" but Eric was already out the door. "Talk."

He hadn't even opened the can of Coke.

His walk took him around the corner to El Galleon, which despite its Spanish name, seemed to specialize in German beers. He'd gotten to know Gary back at the Marlin Club since he'd lived in Avalon, and had told him about his allergy, so he knew the guy wouldn't serve him anything stronger than Coke.

At El Galleon, he chose a seat at the far end of the bar, as far as possible from the people with lives. As he looked at the confusing wall of bottles on display behind the bar, it occurred to him that this was the first time in his life he'd ever been in a bar all by himself. Until today he'd always been with his buddies, to hang out, shoot pool, see them safely home.

Above the bar were mannequins of a 1920's era jazz band, and clocks indicating the supposed time in places like New Orleans, Munich and

Cape Cod. But the clocks indicated wildly different hours and minutes and it was highly unlikely any of them were even close to accurate.

Despite being only about two feet tall and depicted only from the waist up, the jazz band mannequins above the bar were detailed and life-like. The keyboard player's tie even fluttered wildly, and the saxophone, trumpet and other instruments looked like the real things, placed into those painted plaster hands. An exuberant singer in a shimmery blue dress channeled Billie Holiday.

The bartender here, who looked barely old enough to drink himself, was standing there looking at him expectantly. After some hesitation, Eric indicated a bottle at random, and the bartender set a glass in front of him and poured out something tawny colored. Eric waggled his fingers and the guy poured him a double. He looked at the glass for a long time, his hands on either side of it, but he couldn't make himself touch it. After a lifetime of avoiding booze for the sake of his health, he found now that he couldn't stand the smell of it.

"You're supposed to drink it, dude," the bartender said with some amusement. Eric gave him a dirty look.

"No shit, Sherlock." The bartender shrugged and moved away to serve another customer.

The whisky swirled in the glass, a little snake-like, and he stared at the brown liquid for a long time, wishing it could somehow teleport him back to the day before he'd become the world's biggest idiot. If it could, he'd risk the nausea, the hives and the anaphylactic shock. But even so, it wouldn't change the idiotic things he'd done and said. Quickly, before he changed his mind and did another really stupid thing, he pulled money from his pocket and put it on the bar next to the glass. The too-young bartender walked over and Eric told him, "Enjoy," as he got up and walked away. The bartender picked up the untouched glass, lifted it in the direction of Eric's back, and said, "Cheers, dude," as he downed the eight-dollar shot of Glenfiddich that Eric had paid twenty bucks for.

He seriously doubted that even looking at the ocean was going to make him feel better today, but he might as well try it.

He didn't for one moment regret the path his life had taken. Not even the transfers, the deployments, the nomadic, almost gypsy-like lifestyle he'd had in the Navy.

Actually, he did have one regret – that he'd never had a family of his own. He of course had a lot of family in general. He needed a spreadsheet to keep track of the nieces, nephews, great nieces and nephews, cousins, spouses, and a few ex-spouses. But he more than occasionally wondered what it would have been like if his ex-wife really had been pregnant, if the kid had actually existed. He had no idea how parenthood would have worked out, other than that he would have loved it, but one thing he knew for sure – he'd still be divorced. Moral of the story, don't marry someone you don't know. Don't marry someone after only a four-hour acquaintance, during which time very little conversation had been had, including the lack of exchanging surnames.

But he certainly knew Michelle, and not just because he'd seen her naked. There had been a time in his life when that would have been sufficient. But not so with Michelle. He knew her on the inside too. He knew what made her laugh, what made her frown. He knew just where to touch her, where to kiss her, that made her arch her back and grab his face to pull him down for a kiss. He knew that look she got when she found herself reminiscing about her lonely childhood, and the look she tried not to show that revealed her craving for affection. He knew that look of fierceness that took no BS, and her look of whimsy and laughter when he joked, acted silly or sang. He knew how her tears felt on him when she grieved, and how her lips felt on him when she was aroused. He'd seen her at her worst – blotchy and blubbery – and at her best – soaring in ecstasy.

He knew her, and because he knew her, he loved her.

He may have thought he'd been in love once or twice, though ironically never with the woman he'd married, but it had never lasted and when it ended without regret, he'd realized it hadn't ever really been love. Until now. His plan with Michelle had been to stay with her until it ended. And it would end. It always did, with him. He'd just never realized it would hurt so much.

You don't know what you've got until it's gone.

Wasn't that right.

He'd had Michelle, physically, emotionally, sensually. According to what she'd said, he'd made her fall in love with him.

Only fair. She'd made him fall in love with her as well. And it hadn't even been when they'd slept together. He'd succumbed to her ocean-blue eyes practically at first sight. He sometimes wished he'd met her sooner. But it was a good thing he hadn't. If he'd met her much sooner, and had made love with her, even so much as kissed her, he'd have broken the laws of both man and morality.

He'd stayed with Gabriel and Susan for three weeks before moving to Avalon, living on their living room sofa, and he had spent most of that time with their kids. He'd spent hours helping Tyler build his Lego Death Star, and hours helping Natalie scour the internet for fighter jet posters and models, and had paid for what they'd found with his credit card, so that her allowance could go into her flight school savings fund. More than once, Gabriel had complained, "These are my kids. Get your own."

He would have loved to get his own kids. He yearned for them. But it had to be with the right woman. His experience with Karen had taught him that. Well, he'd finally found the right woman. He couldn't help conjuring up an image of a smart, dark-haired, blue-eyed kid who didn't take BS from anyone, least of all him.

He'd always walked away from relationships. Usually not by choice, mostly due to a transfer or deployment. But whether by choice or by commitment, he'd still walked away. Walked away from his family, girlfriends, lovers, his marriage. Now he had no one ordering him to walk away, he had no need to walk away, and he certainly didn't want to walk away. He wanted nothing more than to be with this woman he'd fallen in love with. And yet like a stupid idiot, he'd tried to push her away for a stupid reason that didn't really matter. He'd only wanted to spare her hurt, and yet, he'd hurt them both instead. His picture should be in the dictionary next to cruel, fucking idiot, pardon his language.

The moment his feet hit the sidewalk, his phone rang and he yanked it out of his pocket with considerable irritation. If it was Gabriel calling to try and cheer him up, he just might have to go back to the Marlin Club and ram it up his ass. It wasn't his friend, but he recognized the number.

He quickly slid the little green phone icon to accept the call and put it to his ear.

"Sir?"

49

Eric was really, really surprised when Michelle texted him at work the next day and asked what time he'd be home. After sitting at the edge of the Green Pleasure Pier for hours the previous evening, he had found no calm nor answers this time. Obi-Wan Kenobi didn't appear in spirit form to advise him. Not even every sad country song he'd ever heard contained the right words. Instead, Gabriel had sent him ten texts demanding to know what was going on, until Eric had finally sent a terse reply text simply saying, *I need space*.

He rubbed salt in his self-inflicted wounds by looking at his phone photos of her. Damn, but he wished he could step into one of those images, take her in his arms and only let her go long enough to slap himself upside the head, and tell himself – what?

How about the absolute honest truth?

Too late for that now. He'd had his chance, and he'd blown it big time. Too late now to tell her, I need you, I love you, don't leave me, don't push me out of your life.

The words she had thrown at him kept thrumming through his head, like rain, like gunfire. *You made me fall in love with you.*

When he finally returned home, he and Michelle had managed to avoid each other. Sleeping alone, he had the dream again, and without Michelle to wake him up, it went on and on in a horrible loop before he was able to twitch himself out of it, waking up sweaty and despairing.

Puzzled at her text, he decided that brevity would be best and merely replied, "6:00 p.m.". Within a minute came her even briefer reply, merely "OK"

When he arrived at the house, it was quiet and dark. He understood now. She'd wanted to know when he'd be home so she could be elsewhere. Maybe she'd gone to the mainland, and was even now at a shooting range, aiming at a target with his name printed across the forehead.

He'd be willing to bet money she wouldn't miss any of her shots in that case. He almost went into his bedroom to check and make sure his gun case was still there on the closet shelf.

He went into the kitchen for a bottle of water, unbuttoning his uniform shirt and draping it over the chair, before taking a bottle from the fridge and sitting down in his tee shirt to drink it, wondering what was going to happened now, wondering if his life was going to continue on as it had before, filled with meaningless one-night stands and fleeting, casual relationships while he looked for The One.

No, it wouldn't. He'd found The One, and no matter what he did or what happened to him from this point on, he'd never need to look further.

He didn't want those meaningless encounters anymore. A sweet, spicy, unique woman with control issues and pseudo-bitchiness had slid her hand around his heart and taken possession. And he'd never even told her how she owned his soul. The one time his big mouth had remained shut.

He thought he was alone in the house, but he sensed movement out on the patio, so he stepped outside to investigate.

She was standing with her back to the door, on the exact same spot they'd first kissed that morning in the rain, and turned around when she heard him.

The clingy red dress she was wearing could only be described as *slinky*, with thin spaghetti straps and a low V neckline. She'd gotten a – what did the girls call it? – a mani-pedi, and the polish on her fingernails and toenails matched the bright crimson of her dress. It looked fabulous combined with the blingy gold sandals on her feet. He'd always adored her legs, and the short silky skirt enhanced them even more. He had to restrain himself from reaching out to touch her smooth, shiny dark hair, which he'd also always adored. Hell, he'd always adored every part of her, inside and out.

He simply couldn't restrain himself from letting out a low, appreciative whistle. "Wow, you look gorgeous. Got a hot date?"

Damn his big mouth! He really needed to work on that.

She smiled slightly. "I hope so."

Eric thought he'd already ripped out his heart, torn it to shreds, and stomped on the pieces, but he found there was still some left to hurt, at the thought that she was already dating someone else. If her date was coming here to pick her up, he didn't want to see it. He turned to leave, calling out a choked, "Have a nice time," over his shoulder, hoping he could change out of his work uniform and be out the door before the date arrived.

What if she'd made up with Justin from the boat dock? What if she'd reconnected with her high school prom date, or the guy in Los Angeles who had cheated on his girlfriend with her? Oh, lord, was Christopher Wong from Redondo Beach on a boat to Avalon right now? Would any of them be invited into her pretty pink princess sanctuary? If so, would he have to lay there in his room, the room he'd thought of as *their* room, and listen to them?

Kill him now.

"Eric, wait," she called out. He stopped but didn't turn around. "I want to ask you something."

He knew what she was going to ask. *How soon can you move out?* Gabriel's couch was looking more and more like a reality. It was going to be a hell of a commute to Avalon.

Actually, that wouldn't work out at all. His contract with the Avalon Fire Department required him to live here in Avalon. Well, at least he was sure he wouldn't fall in love with his next roommate. He forced himself to turn around and look at her.

"Come here," she requested with a smile, holding out her hands to him.

This was surely the weirdest breakup he'd ever experienced or heard of, as he found himself stepping back to stand in front of her. It was even weirder than getting divorced by email.

She took both his hands in hers. Standing close to her now, he could smell a delicate perfume. He didn't know what it was, but it smelled expensive. It was light, flowery, seductive. Just enough fragrance to make him want to discover exactly where she had applied it.

She gripped his hands tightly, squeezing hard. So hard that his phalanges complained, but he was mesmerized by the feel of her hands and the small smile on her face.

In a nanosecond, he saw his life flash before his eyes. Michelle laughing at his off-key singing, fussing over him when he returned from reserve duty exhausted and with a black eye, tracing the lines of his tattoo as they lay in bed.

"Eric Paul Hanson." Uh-oh, his full name. He was really in trouble now.

"Will you marry me?"

If she'd hit him over the head with a baseball bat, he couldn't have been more shocked.

"You're proposing to me?" He couldn't help the way his voice squeaked a little with his exclamation.

"Yes. And I believe the appropriate response in this situation should be, yes ma'am."

His first impulse was to throw himself to his knees, say yes, and beg her to go make babies. But there were other considerations in play now, things she didn't know about yet.

Before he could speak, she went on, "I have a Plan B, you know."

He could only stare at her, his usual gregariousness stunned into silence. Plan B?

"When you moved in here, your old captain wrote you a letter of recommendation. He included his email address. I still have it. I'll write to him and have him order you to love me."

He finally found his voice. "Michelle, you cannot do that. That is the most frivolous thing I ever heard of. You can't bother an important naval commander with something like that. Besides, nobody needs to give me orders for me to love you."

From the brilliant smile she showed him, he quickly realized that her plan to contact his former captain had been a bluff.

"I love you too," she said. "Now that we've established that, we can move on to Plan C."

Plan C? She had a Plan C?

She'd said, "I love you too." He forgot to breathe for a moment and almost missed what she said next.

"Plan C is your parents."

His parents? What did his long-deceased parents have to do with this? Although, he could just imagine the conservation that might transpire between his mother and Michelle, were his mother still alive.

"Hey, Mrs. Hanson. This is Michelle. You may have heard about me. I'm the love of Eric's life. Well, here's the thing. He was mean to me, but I know he didn't mean it. I just need you to have a little conversation with your son about what is really the best thing for both of us. If you could do that, I'd really appreciate it. Thanks. Love ya!"

"Did I tell you that I got all A's in high school?" she continued.

Wait, now she was talking about her high school transcript? Was this Plan D already? What had happened to Plan C?

He was starting to feel a little dizzy. This girl had as many plans as the Secretary of the Navy.

"Yes, I remember you telling me about your good grades. But what does that have to do with this? With us?"

"It means I'm good at math, you big goof!"

He had it so bad, he even loved it when she called him a big goof. "OK, so you're good at math. And?"

"So, you told me that when you were born, your mother was forty-two and your father was sixty."

"You're not only good at math, you have a good memory too."

"So that means your father and mother had an eighteen-year age gap. That's three more years than us."

"Well, yeah, but,"

She interrupted him. "Did your father ever try to kick your mother to the curb because he thought he was too old for her?"

"Not that I know of."

"Did they love each other?"

"They were devoted." In fact, as a teenager, he'd found his parent's public displays of affection to be downright embarrassing. Even after his father's first stroke had put him into a wheelchair, Eric had still caught his father patting his mother's rear when she walked by. Embarrassed as only seventeen-year-old could be at that sight, he'd hissed, "Dad!"

His father had grinned at him. All their relatives said that Eric had inherited his father's grin. "If you're lucky, son, someday you'll find someone as special as her." Dad had looked towards Eric's mother with affection.

I found her, Dad. It took a while, but I found her.

"Were they happy together?"

"Until the day my dad died."

"Then what is your problem?"

"My problem is, I love you too much to keep you from being with someone your own age."

"And my problem is that I love you too much to care about anyone else, no matter what age they are."

"Fifteen years is still a pretty big age gap to most people."

"Tell that to a paleontologist."

He blinked and stared at her. "A paleontologist?" he repeated with amused eyes.

"It's someone who studies dinosaurs."

"I know what it is. I just never expected to hear it used in a conversation about everlasting love."

"Love doesn't always stop to do the math. Love hates math. In fact, love totally sucks at math. And that's the problem."

Now he was confused. More confused.

"What? Being in love with me is a problem?" He'd been right after all – he was bad husband material.

Michelle shook her head. "No. Being in love with you is the easiest thing I've ever experienced in my life. The problem is that I didn't tell you sooner. It would have saved us both a lot of heartache. But I'm not nearly as brave as you seem to think I am."

"Why didn't you?"

"I was scared you might not feel the same."

"Sweetheart, I think I've been in love with you since before I even met you. But I was certain of it when you held my hand in Gabriel's helicopter on the way back from San Diego."

"I knew I was in love with you when you woke me up the night of the earthquake."

"Why didn't you tell me?" Her question, so like his, was a challenge.

"I never thought you'd actually want to marry me," he said ruefully. "But Michelle, it's not only our ages. You know I've got a pretty unsavory past-"

"Pfft." She released one of his hands just long enough to wave her hand in an *I don't care* gesture, and just like that, every other girl he'd ever slept with in his unsavory past, just disappeared.

"I know, and it's not the important thing. I care more about the future. Our future. Do you really think I'm too young for you?"

"No. That was a lie. I'm sorry. Not only was it a lie, it was a whopper. I hated saying it. Not only because I hated the lying, but because it hurt you, and I apologize for that. You're not too young. You're perfect. But at the time, I honestly felt I was doing what was best for you."

"You were wrong."

"I know that now." He hesitated. "There's something else."

"Something? Or someone?"

She had to be kidding. There hadn't been so much as a hint of someone else in his life, or in his heart, since the day he'd met her.

He tugged her towards the love seat nearby. "Come sit down. We need to talk."

She resisted his attempt to have her sit.

"No. The last time you said, sit down, let's talk, it didn't end well."

"OK, fair enough." She was right. It had ended with tears, name-calling and slammed doors. It had almost ended with him allowing himself to risk a serious allergic reaction, thinking it might somehow change things.

He remained standing with her, their hands still clasped.

"The Navy wants me back."

He was surprised at her lack of reaction. But it was obvious she'd misunderstood.

"You have to go back for more reserve duty? I thought it was only two weeks a year?"

He shook his head. "No. Permanently."

That got her. "Can they do that?" The word 'do' came out a little screechy. "Can they draft you like that? I thought you were retired!"

She was still holding his hands, and her grip got even tighter, as if to prevent him from changing into his Navy uniform and sailing away. His hands were starting to cramp with the pressure. She stared at him in shock, her eyes starting to get suspiciously moist.

"Well, technically, yes they can. As a reservist, I could get called back to active duty any time they deem it necessary. But in this case, it's not for active duty. They want me as a civilian contractor. They're offering me a job teaching at advanced corpsman training school. It's at Fort Sam Houston. In San Antonio, Texas. That's actually an Army base, but they've consolidated all of the military's medical training there now."

She relaxed then, released his hands, and actually smiled. "Texas, huh? I've never been to Texas."

"I have. It's hot. Not sexy hot, just plain hot. Not as hot as Iraq, but still hot enough to be uncomfortable."

"Are you going to take it?"

"I don't know. I signed a one-year contract with the Avalon Fire Department and I can't do anything until then. Plus, I'm not sure if I'm ready to give up hands-on patient care. So, I don't know." His indecisiveness since getting the call about this new career opportunity surprised him.

"Well, if you decide that's what you want to do, I can call Randy Zimmerman and put the house up for sale. The real estate market is so tight here in Avalon, all I have to do is whisper and I'll have five offers."

"You'd sell our little casino? Why?"

"The proceeds will make a great down payment on a place in San Antonio, Texas."

"But this is your home."

"No. It's just a house. It's just wood and glass and stucco." She stepped close and put her hand on his chest, over his heart. "This is my home."

He was unable to refrain from putting his hand over hers against his chest, so that she couldn't take it away.

"So, you don't have a date then? You're dressed up all pretty. I mean, you're always pretty, but this is special." He gave a brief wave at her to indicate the dress, the nail polish, the perfume, and praying that Christopher Wong from Redondo Beach wasn't about to show up.

"This is for you, you big goof. It isn't every day a girl proposes, is it? I thought if I couldn't get you with love, I'd have to resort to stunning you into submission. My next option was going to be handcuffs."

Eric gulped and his normally excellent blood pressure went up just a little at the images that slid across his brain when Michelle uttered the word handcuffs.

"Sweetheart, you have both, my love and the stunning. We can talk about the handcuffs later."

She smiled. "The only date I'm anticipating is the one I'm hoping to set with you. How does Thursday sound? We could go over to Long Beach and-"

"You don't want to marry me."

"Oh yes, I do. I wouldn't have asked you if I didn't."

"You could do so much better."

"Oh no, I couldn't."

"Why would you want to marry me?" He glanced down at those gold sandals and red toenails for a moment before looking back at her. "I don't think I'm good husband material. Do you really want to be stuck with a guy who might twitch in his sleep with nightmares at any time? My shrink said that might not ever stop, although it hasn't happened again since the night you were there to kiss me."

He should have felt utterly humiliated at having that nightmare while with Michelle, the way he'd felt when it happened while he was married to Karen. The way he'd been embarrassed when it had happened while with women he'd dated or when he'd visited Gabriel and Susan and slept on their couch.

But with Michelle, he hadn't felt humiliated. He'd felt relieved. Like he didn't have to go through it alone anymore.

"Oh, I don't know," she replied with just a touch of her spicy snottiness showing through. "As an only child, I've always wanted a sister, and you have two I thought I could borrow. Three if you count Susan."

She held up a hand and started counting on her fingers.

"One, I want to marry you because I love you, of course. I thought we already established that. Two, because I need you more than I need air. Three, because you saved my life. And I don't mean, just when you kept me from stepping out in front of a taxi."

"And a golf cart."

"Yeah, that too. But more importantly, you saved my emotional life. I'd still be a Raging Bitch running around like a crazy person if it weren't for you. Four, because I can't imagine a fate more horrible than not spending the rest of my life with you. As for the nightmares, I don't see that as an impediment. As long as I get to be the one there to kiss you when you need it. But I mainly want to marry you because I love you. I don't care if we live here in Avalon, or in Texas, or in Florida."

"Florida?"

"I would like to meet your family. In fact, maybe we should call your sister Brenda and ask for her opinion. Ask her if she wants you to be happy."

"Of course she wants me to be happy. She loves me. She's my sister."

"Well, I love you too. Not exactly like your sister, of course, you know, due to that whole sex thing. But I still want you to be happy, and I want me to be happy. I want us to be happy together."

She glanced away from him for just a moment, and he could tell from her expression that she was wondering if his family would approve of her, of them. He'd wondered the same thing, and it had been stupid to wonder. His family, especially Brenda, would adore Michelle not only for herself, but because Eric adored her.

"Sweetheart, they will love you." The real Eric, the guy with the big mouth that got him into trouble, or into heaven, took over. "They will adore you. I love you. Yes, I said it. I've never said those words before other than to family. I'm in love with you, my Michelle. Always have been." He tasted the words on his lips, and they tasted good. 'I should have said them sooner. Much sooner. But I was stupid and maybe scared."

"You were scared?" She smiled, almost a giggle. "I never thought you'd ever be scared of anything. You're the bravest person I've ever known. I'm the one who was scared. I tried to say it a hundred times but I always chickened out. I know you think I'm strong and brave, but not about that."

"Twins separated at birth."

"Huh?"

"We both chickened out, I guess. But Michelle, sweetheart, my Venus, you don't have to sell your house, even if we do move away from Avalon."

"But-" she started to protest, and he smiled into her eyes.

"I can buy us a house. I have plenty of money. I have almost a million dollars in the bank."

"You do?" she asked disbelievingly. She hadn't thought that working as a paramedic was that lucrative a career.

He nodded, amused at her surprise. "My father was a CPA. He had his own accounting firm. He called it By the Numbers. He said that a regular name like Hanson Accounting Services was too ordinary and he wanted to dispel the stereotype of accounting as dull. It worked because it was very successful. When he died, my mother sold the business and the proceeds were divided between my two brothers and me. Since I was only eighteen at the time, my portion was put into a trust until I turned thirty, but I never touched any of it. Though I almost had to in order to pay off my credit card after a certain visit to the book store recently. Now, don't look guilty, sweetheart. I'd drop every penny of it for that if it made you happy."

She stepped closer, leaning into him, and he breathed in that perfume she'd bought to entice him. Although the scent and feel of her hair, her skin, were infinitely more enticing to him than any perfume.

"I told you, being with you is what makes me happy," she said.

"Same goes for me," he asserted.

"I don't care about your money," she assured him, her eyes wide and honest. "I'll sign a prenup. You can keep it or spend it or give it away. It doesn't matter. But-"

"But what?" he asked.

"Are you sure you can handle being married to someone like me, a bitch with control issues who can't handle talking to a shrink about them?"

"Hey, you proposed to me and now you're trying to talk me out of it?"

"No, but I want you to realize what you're getting into, so you don't think I've deceived you about me."

"Yes, I can handle that. As long as you use some of those control issues to control me, I'm down with it. Look, Michelle, I meant it when I said I love you too. Remember that first night we spent together? Lord, that was so sweet, to wake up and see you there. You remember what I said just before I left for work the next day?"

"Yes, I remember. It was, crap I have to be at work in half an hour."

"After that. I said, thank you for the best night of my life. I meant that with all my heart. And not just because of the sex, although it was the best, don't get me wrong. It was being with you, close to you – with you. If I'd died at that moment, I would have died happy."

He extricated the hand he'd been using to hold her hand against his chest, and at her quick look of panic, assured her, "I'm not going any-where." Instead, he laid that hand against her cheek, touching her cheek-bone with his thumb.

"I don't want a courthouse wedding this time," his big mouth said. "I want the real thing. In a church with flowers and guests, and Gabriel standing next to me while you walk up the aisle in a white dress. If you want someone to escort you, I'm sure my brothers will fight each other for the opportunity. I want the whole old-fashioned, sentimental, here-comes-the-bride, tears of joy shebang."

Her face lit up with a glow that was almost painful to see. "That sounds like the most wonderful thing ever. There's just one problem with making plans like that. We're not engaged yet."

He'd been stupid before, but he wasn't going to be stupid again. He took her hands in his in the same manner she had done.

"Michelle Ramona Diaz." Her eyes, those eyes that were his ocean, gleamed. "Are you going to quit arguing with me and ask me again?"

"Will you quit arguing with me and say yes?"

"Try me."

She didn't hesitate. "Will you marry me?"

Joy filled him like sunshine.

"Yes, Ma'am!"

50

AVALON, SIX MONTHS LATER

Michelle was thrilled to finally meet Eric's sister Brenda, and equally thrilled that Gabriel and his entire family had come over to Avalon at the same time. But with their wedding taking place on the mainland in two days, it seemed a bit unnecessary for them to come out to the island, just to return the next day. Brenda could have been sightseeing in San Diego with her husband Alex and Eric's other siblings who had all flown in from Florida for their wedding. But she and the Jones family had all come over to visit, with Brenda staying at Michelle and Eric's house overnight and the Jones family staying at the Portofino.

When they all met up on the sidewalk in front of the hotel, Gabriel laughed at her notion.

"We all came out here to make sure neither of you tried to chicken out at the last minute," he said.

"No chance of that," Eric declared.

"I can't believe my baby brother is finally getting married for real," Brenda said, as the group started down the street to get dinner.

"Believe it," Eric replied, picking up Michelle's hand and giving it a quick kiss, right next to her engagement ring.

She had told him not to buy it. It was an unnecessary expense and a sexist tradition. But she'd wasted her breath. He'd bought it anyway, and she loved it.

Johnny Del Risco, the manager of the Portofino Hotel, walked out its door at that moment. Not surprising, he did work there.

"There's our maid of honor." Eric grinned at Tracy, who had followed Johnny out the hotel's front door. Again, not surprising. She had set up a gift shop in the hotel lobby and managed it with much more diligence she did the other shops her father owned. Which was probably due to the fact that she had been dating the hotel manager for months now, ever since Eric had introduced them.

Avalon is a small town, so it was probably mere coincidence that Tracy and Johnny were walking in the same direction as Michelle, Eric, Brenda and the Jones family, but it did still gave the impression of an entourage. Eric took charge of pushing baby Cameron's stroller while the little guy snoozed inside.

Susan gave Michelle's arm a little squeeze as the group walked down Crescent Avenue.

"It was so sweet of you guys to set your wedding date for after Cameron's arrival." She looked at her husband and Eric, walking just ahead of them, Eric refusing to relinquish control of the stroller to Gabriel when his friend tried to take it over. However, Eric heard Susan's words and turned his head briefly towards them.

"Well we just wanted to make sure you didn't steal the attention away from me by going into labor during the ceremony," he joked.

"Yeah, right," Susan retorted. "You actually think anybody is going to be looking at you at all, once Michelle shows up in her wedding dress?"

"It's gorgeous, isn't it?" Tracy offered from behind them.

Eric stopped pushing the baby stroller and turned to look at the women, smiling at the mention of Michelle's wedding dress.

"Tell me how gorgeous," he requested with begging eyes.

"Nope," came four replies in unison. Brenda shook a finger at her brother.

"We are going totally old-fashioned here. No details, no hints, no peeks until Saturday."

The soon-to-be bridegroom turned towards his soon-to-be bride, and though he kept one hand on the handle of the stroller he was guiding, still managed to get his other arm around Michelle's waist and pulled her in for a kiss, as he murmured, "I can't wait."

As always, his kiss overwhelmed her, promised passion, and she completely forgot about all the people around them, until, through the haze, she heard Natalie's voice.

"Uncle Eric! Not again!"

And Tyler added, "Not more mushy stuff! Gross!"

Eric released her mouth and looked at the two kids. He ruffled Tyler's hair and said, "Kissing my beautiful fiancée is not gross, young man. Just remember that if you're going to be our ring bearer."

"I'm sorry, Uncle Eric," Tyler said quickly. "You're not going to fire me, are you?"

"Nope dude, you're good," Eric assured the boy. "Just you wait a few years. You won't think kissing girls is mushy or gross, I assure you."

Tyler looked doubtful but didn't argue the point.

"For goodness sake, G.D.," Brenda put in. "Save it for the wedding night."

Eric released Michelle from his romantic grasp, but held her eyes with a blissful gaze. "Can't wait for that either," he told her.

"You know," Brenda continued. "Between Tyler in his tux, and Michelle in her wedding dress, I'm sure nobody is going to be looking at Eric at all."

Eric pouted. "Not even in my dress whites?"

"Maybe one or two people might notice you," Tracy said from the back of the group, but even as she said it, she squeezed Johnny's arm and smiled into his eyes. Then she turned and stepped past Brenda towards Michelle, saying, "What do you think?" as she ran a hand over her hair, which was a different color again.

"That's beautiful," Michelle replied. It was actually the best color she'd seen on her friend, and she'd seen many different hues over the years.

Tracy glanced back towards her boyfriend, who apparently liked the new color too. It was a glossy sable brown, though not as dark as Michelle's hair, the color of caramel silk, subtle and shiny.

"It's mine," Tracy said.

"Yours?" Michelle asked. Her eyes widened. "Do you mean?"

"Yep. This is my natural color. I had the dye stripped off and had it deep conditioned. Johnny asked me to do it. He said he liked the real me the best." Tracy leaned a bit closer and lowered her voice with a small catch of emotion. "I might just have to marry that guy."

"It's gorgeous, Tracy," Michelle assured her. "You're gorgeous. Thank you for agreeing to be my maid of honor."

"I wouldn't miss it for the world," Tracy replied. "Maybe one day you can do the same for me."

At that point, Eric reached over and took Michelle's hand again, at the same time relinquishing custody of the stroller to Gabriel.

"Come on," he said. "I have something to show you."

"I thought we were going to eat at Maggie's?" she protested, as they approached the steps next to Steve's Steakhouse which gave access to Maggie's Blue Rose Mexican Restaurant on the second floor.

The whole group followed Eric without argument as he led them all right past their planned dinner spot, though she did see Susan look at her kids and put a finger to her lips in a "be quiet" gesture.

What was that about?

Even Tracy and Johnny were still following them down the sidewalk. What was up with that? Of course, Avalon was a small town and surely wherever those two were going might simply be in the same direction.

"What do you want to show me?" she asked, as they turned from Crescent Avenue onto Catalina Avenue.

Something was happening on the sidewalk outside the Marlin Club, because there were a bunch of people standing around there. For a moment she thought perhaps there was some kind of medical emergency going on, because she could see Eric's boss and his work partner Tony among the group. But they were wearing civilian clothes, and didn't appear to be doing much of anything other than just standing on the sidewalk chatting with Randy Zimmerman, the realtor who had helped her place the roommate ad which had brought Eric to her house. When she'd told Randy that she and Eric were getting married, Randy had grinned and declared he was thrilled to have been their matchmaker and planned to add that service to his business. Even her boss and a couple of her coworkers were there.

Eric turned in that direction, but he didn't hurry over to assist his coworkers, so apparently there wasn't an emergency happening. Gabriel followed him and Michelle thought she saw a small, secretive glance pass between the two men.

Even Gary emerged from the door of the bar to stop and chat with the people gathered there. Maybe he was on a break, or had come out in curiosity to see why a bunch of random people were standing around in front of his bar.

It seemed like everyone she knew in Avalon was standing there as if waiting for something to happen. Was that – really? Her once long-ago date Justin even stood at the edge of the group. She almost didn't recognize him. The peroxide streaks in his hair were gone and it was cut short- almost as short as Eric's.

She glanced from Justin to Eric, hoping there wasn't going to be any unpleasantness when Eric noticed him there.

But, surprise, surprise, Eric saw Justin, walked over to him with a smile, and shook his hand. Michelle followed quickly, in case the situation went south and she needed to intervene.

"Did that recruiter call you?" Eric asked, and Justin nodded.

Recruiter? *Recruiter*?

Justin actually smiled at Michelle before looking back at Eric.

"Yeah, we talked. I'm going to Long Beach next week to take the ASVAB."

"Wait a minute!" She stared at Justin. "Are you saying you're enlisting in the Navy?"

"We're just talking," Eric assured her. "Nothing's been signed yet. Taking the ASVAB doesn't commit you to anything."

Whoa. Justin, considering the military, and with Eric's help? Pigs had just flown, Hell had frozen over, and the Dodgers were going to use a designated hitter.

"Can I talk to you for a minute?" Justin asked, with a glance towards Eric that clearly requested, *privately*?

Despite his changed appearance and attitude, she had no interest in a private conversation with the guy. She looped an arm through Eric's, and Justin winced a little as he noticed.

"Anything you have to say, you can say in front of him," she said firmly. "We're engaged, you know. We're getting married on Saturday."

After a moment's hesitation, Justin spoke.

"Look, Michelle, I just wanted to apologize to you. I was a jerk to you when we were in high school, and after that too, and I'm sorry for the rude, mean things I've said to you over the years. I wish I could take them back. I wish you every happiness in your marriage." He gave a little nod to Eric.

Despite her absolute astonishment at hearing Justin's words of apology, she managed to say, "Thank you, Justin."

If that wasn't the weirdest, most unexpected speech she'd ever heard. Of all the unbelievable things she could have imagined, having Justin apologize to her was one of the most unimaginable.

But she had little time to wonder over her former tormenter's change of attitude. Before her brain could explode at the thought of Justin in the military, Eric tugged her away with a brief nod of dismissal in Justin's direction.

"I don't believe it," she said, glancing back at her former date. "Is that the real Justin, or did you clone him into someone else? It's like he's had a whole new personality implanted."

"I think he's just matured," Eric replied. "He's not really a bad guy, just a little misguided."

"When did you start talking to him about the Navy?"

"A couple of weeks ago. I ran into him at the Chi-Chi Club."

She raised a brow at her fiancé. "And what, precisely, were you doing at the Chi-Chi Club?" she asked, just teasing, because she knew he would only have gone there in an official capacity.

"Mostly I was pressing a gauze pad against a laceration on a guy who'd had a beer bottle broken over his head, assessing him for a skull fracture, and assuring him he wasn't about to bleed to death. Head wounds bleed like swamps, so the patient tends to freak out even more. He was also trying to apologize for making a pass at another man's girl, which is how he ended up getting a bottle smashed on his head, but I had to tell him that I was just the paramedic. I didn't have time at the moment to be a relationship counselor, or the go-between for him and his buddy."

"Was Justin the victim or the bottle wielder?"

"Neither. He was an observer who just happened to be there. Though he did hold the door open for us when we left. The next day he came to the fire station and asked to talk to me. He said he was tired of being a jerk and having everybody hate him. So I told him,"

"Let me guess," Michelle interrupted. "If you're nice to people, they're usually nice back."

Eric's special grin warmed his lips. "Yep. That's my motto. So we got to talking, he asked how I came to live here, how you and I met, and, end of story, he gave me his phone number to pass along to my recruiter friend."

"He's not going to train to be a corpsman, is he?" She couldn't imagine anything less likely than Justin calming people down and treating patients.

"Nah," Eric replied. "I think he's more gunner's mate material."

She hugged her fiancé briefly. "You could talk a leopard out of his spots."

"As long as I can talk you into staying married to me forever."

"That's a given," she assured him.

"I have a surprise for you," he said, anticipation glowing in his eyes.

"Another one?" He had already surprised her with two tickets to Paris for their honeymoon. He had wanted to present them on their wedding day, but had been forced to tell her about it sooner so that she could get her passport.

"Yes, another one," Eric affirmed. She was still trying to figure out what all these people were doing just standing around on the sidewalk.

Eric gave a nod towards, of all people, Randy Zimmerman, and the other man made a shooing motion, so that the group of people moved aside. Susan picked baby Cameron up out of his stroller, and Gabriel pushed the stroller off to the side, so there was room for Tracy and Johnny to stand next to them. It was looking suspiciously as if this were no coincidental meetup amongst a random group of people. It looked like they had all come to this spot at this time on purpose.

Eric took Michelle's hand, and indicated – the sidewalk bench. At least, she thought he was indicating the bench that she'd sat on in her childhood, traumatized by the island fire and her father's indifference. But at the moment it was, weirdly, covered up with a white cloth. At Eric's nod, with a ceremonious gesture, Randy removed the covering to reveal – the green bench.

"Look," Eric suggested, as if there were some special reason why she should.

Was this some kind of aversion therapy, to expose her to the things that upset her in the hope that it would dilute the trauma? It was uncharacteristically insensitive of Eric to be urging her close to a bench she hated, and in front of all these people who happened to standing there watching. It seemed like everyone they knew in Avalon was here.

Except that – it wasn't the bench. When she looked at it she could tell, it was different. It was still green, but a brighter, fresher shade. It still had a back, a seat, cement sides – but they weren't the same. The planks comprising the seat and back were wider, heavier pieces, the wood smooth, and with less space between them than on the original bench. It looked sturdier, more solid, and it wasn't even positioned in the exact same spot. This bench had a slightly different footprint. She could see that the bottom of the cement side supports, where they sat on the sidewalk, didn't line up exactly where they used to. The footprint of the bench was an inch or two different.

She looked at Eric, whose thousand-watt smile was spread from ear to ear. All the people standing around watching were smiling at them too.

"It's not the same bench, is it?"

He nodded. "It took a lot of negotiation with the city of Avalon, but I was able to get the other bench replaced. Randy helped – he's in the Chamber of Commerce. I bought this bench to put here in its place."

She raised her eyebrows at him in disbelief. "You bought it? A whole new bench? That must have cost a fortune."

He shrugged, with as little care for the expense as he'd had for those books he'd bought her, or the one carat diamond ring on her left hand.

"I wanted to have it painted pink, but they said it had to be green like the old one."

"I can't believe you did this." Her mind was boggling. "What happened to the other bench?"

"We had the original bench relocated." He waved a hand to indicate a general, unspecific someplace else.

"So let me get this straight. You bought a bench – I have no idea how much that costs and I'm not sure I want to know – and you had the bench that was here taken away and this new bench put in its place? Why?"

He took her hands in his, reminiscent of the way they'd held each other's hands the day she'd proposed to him, and smiled into her eyes.

Freya, she loved this man.

"Sweetheart, I know the bench here was a part of a really traumatic experience for you, and that it's affected you ever since. I thought if that bench went away, and a totally new one was put in its place, that the trauma and despair might go away, or at least be diminished."

She felt a lump form in her throat. "You did this for me?"

"Sweetheart, I would do anything to make you happy. I'd spend every penny I have if it made you feel better."

By now, she was so choked up she couldn't speak.

"Come and try it out," Eric urged. "Tell me what you think."

She had once sworn she would never sit on that bench again. But this was not the bench she had sat upon as a traumatized twelve-year-old. It was fresh, new, a completely different object, both physically and symbolically.

She let Eric take her hand, allowed him to seat her on the new bench. It was just a bench, with a back, a seat, side supports attaching it to the sidewalk. Just a place to sit down and rest. It wasn't a source of trauma or fear or despair. She felt those childhood burdens drop away from her, as if she were dropping rocks that she had carried around for way too long, leaving her feeling light and happy.

But there was more. "Look at the plaque," Eric said.

In her amazement over the bench itself, she'd failed to notice the shiny brass plate affixed at the center of the new bench's back support. She put a finger on it, tracing the raised lettering.

"In Loving Memory of Rachel Emerson Diaz"

By now her eyes were swimming with tears. "You had it dedicated to my mother? How did you know her maiden name?"

"I called your cousin in Temecula and asked her. She said she'd be glad to talk to you about your mom someday if you want."

"This is the second nicest thing you've ever done for me," she told him.

"Only the second?"

"The first was when you said yes, ma'am at the appropriate time."

He smiled, that wide happy smile she loved. "That was nice of me, wasn't it?"

Through the veil of happy tears that blurred her vision, she heard applause from the group of people gathered to share the unveiling of the new public bench, as well as a few discreet sniffs as a few secret, sentimental tears were wiped away, and not all of them from the women in attendance. In fact, she saw Susan quietly passing a tissue over to Gabriel.

At the edge of the group, Gary McNeil, the bartender from the Marlin Club, who'd had Michelle's number programmed into his phone for years but who had foolishly only used it to call her to come get her dad, looked at Eric and muttered, "Lucky bastard."

Next to him, Justin Moore, who had once had a date with Michelle and had blown it, muttered back, "You got that right."

The two men looked at the new bench and its lovebird occupants. "I need a drink," Justin said.

"Me too," Gary replied. "Come on. First one is on me." The two men turned away and went into the bar to nurse their broken hearts.

Back at the bench, Michelle, with her head on Eric's shoulder as she wiped happy tears on his shirt, asked him, "Did you arrange for everyone to be here to see this?"

"Yes," he admitted as their friends and family gathered around them.

Since the moment she and Eric had announced their engagement, not one single person had said anything about their fifteen-year age difference. Not so much as a peep. "I wanted everyone to see the unveiling of the new bench."

His arm was across her shoulder and his fingers caressed a strand of her hair as Michelle traced her fingers over the lettering on the brass plaque.

"I have a surprise for you too," she said.

"Really?" His smile was warm and dreamy. "Is it ice cream?"

She laid a soft hand on his cheek. "No, it's not ice cream."

"I'm pregnant."

THE END

Dear Readers,

I would like to address one aspect of this story that some people might perceive to be a glaring error in research, but which is in reality a bit of creative license on my part. For the purposes of my story, I have insinuated that the USS Nimitz, the queen of the American Navy, is currently based in San Diego. Anyone with access to Google will quickly realize that the Nimitz is in reality based at Naval Base Kitsap in Washington State. It has in the past had its home port in San Diego, but transferred to Naval Base Everett in 2012 and from Everett to Kitsap in 2015. However, for the purposes of my story I have kept this amazing ship ported in San Diego. My apologies to the Nimitz, its crew and the Navy for my fictional alternative.

Some people have asked me about what is real and what is fictional in Avalon as depicted in my story. I would like to confirm that all of the locations – the bars, restaurants, hotels, Casino, Green Pleasure Pier, etc. really do exist in the places I've mentioned them. You can visit them on an excursion to Catalina Island and if you have the opportunity, I highly recommend you do so. The Casino building really does house an ornate art-deco theatre, and the fire department rescue boat really is docked on its far side. The Avalon Fire Station and other municipal buildings do sit upon the site of the former Chicago Cubs practice field, and it's true that William Wrigley would call under-performing players onto the carpet at his home there.

The fire which played such a traumatizing role for my heroine blazed on Catalina Island in 2007, burning ten percent of its area, necessitating significant evacuations assisted by the Marines and Coast Guard, and threatening the town of Avalon before being dampened by a convenient marine layer (which is California-speak for fog). I can recall seeing the glow and smoke even from the beach in Los Angeles, and thinking back then, long before this story was conceived, how terrifying such a fire had to be for the residents of Avalon.

However, all of the people in this book, all of the Avalon residents with whom I have populated it, are completely creations of my own fictional imagination. No comparison to any real Avalonians is intended. While the oil rig explosion is also my creation, there are oil rigs located in the Pacific Ocean between Catalina Island and the mainland. I can assure you from personal experience that oil-producing facilities are potentially hazardous work-places.

Also, I don't know if the Casino movie theater has ever run a Star Wars marathon, but they should. And as far as I know, the green bench in front of the Marlin Club has not actually been replaced in recent memory.

"When anxious, uneasy and bad thoughts come...", quoted from Letters by Rainier Maria Rilke, 1890-1912, is in the Public Domain

I would like to thank the following people without whose assistance this story would never have been written:

First and foremost, my husband Rick, whose love and encouragement made it all possible

My awesome daughter Jennifer, my personal graphic artist, for cover design and website development

My awesome daughter Jessica for her invaluable research assistance, especially in the realm of country music

My son-in-law Jason, for firearm instruction

My brother Richard, for medical and paramedic information, and for critiquing the medical text

My late father, Allan R. Carlson Jr., for telling me his Navy stories. I just wish I had listened to more of them

Michelle Warner at the Catalina Island Chamber of Commerce, for information on living in the unique town of Avalon

Cheri Webb at the Catalina Island Museum, for helpful information and for guiding me to excellent research material

Mike Krug, Avalon Fire Chief, for information about paramedic and rescue operations on Catalina Island, and for informing me that the staff there are allowed to have visible tattoos, when many other public employees are required to cover them up.

Peter Villanueva, United States Navy, for information regarding the USS Nimitz and Navy life in general. Thank you for your service.

Any mistakes I may have made, or liberties taken, are entirely my own.

Glossary of Navy Terms

"A" school – Technical training school for specific Navy jobs, after completing boot camp

A-stan – Afghanistan

ASVAB – a military entrance test taken by potential recruits

Aye – Yes, I have heard and understand your command

Battle rattle – full combat gear, close to 50 pounds, including a flak vest, Kevlar helmet, gas mask, ammunition, weapons, and other basic military equipment.

Blue Angels - the Navy's flight demonstration squadron

Blue side – serving on a Navy ship

Blueberry - blue digital camouflage Navy uniforms, also called aquaflage

Boot camp – Basic military training for the Navy

Bow – Front of a ship

Brig - naval military prison or jail on a ship or navy base, derived from an obsolete abbreviation for a brigantine, a type of ship.

BUD/S – Basic Underwater Demolition/SEAL – Part of the training undertaken by candidates training to become Navy SEALs.

"C" school – Advanced technical training school for specific Navy jobs

C.O. – Commanding Officer

Chief Petty Officer - (CPO), the seventh enlisted rate (E-7) in the Navy, just above petty officer first class and below senior chief petty officer

Chief's Mess – Living and dining quarters aboard ship reserved exclusively for Chief Petty Officers, off-limits to all other sailors, including officers, unless given specific invitation.

COD – Carrier Onboard Delivery

Corpsman - an enlisted medical specialist of the Navy, similar to a civilian paramedic

Cover – hat

Crossing the Line – Crossing the Equator

CVN-68 – The hull number of the USS Nimitz. The initials CVN indicate that it is a nuclear-powered aircraft carrier

Davy Jones's Locker – a term for the bottom of the sea

Deep six – to throw something away or dispose of it. Derived from a nautical term in which an item thrown into the water at a depth of six fathoms (36 feet) would be impossible to retrieve

Doc – Nickname for a corpsman, a mark of respect

Don't Ask Don't Tell - The official policy, instituted in 1994, requiring gay military service members to remain "in the closet" or risk dishonorable discharge and/or brig time. DADT was repealed in 2011.

Dress Whites – Formal naval uniform worn on special occasions

Embrace the Suck – the situation is bad, deal with it

Fantail – The deck just below the flight deck of an aircraft carrier, at the stern of the ship

Force Recon – United States Marine Corps special operations forces

Friendly fire – being shot by your own side, not from the enemy (hopefully accidentally)

FUBAR – Acronym, "Fucked Up Beyond All Recognition"

General Quarters - an announcement made aboard ship that all hands report to battle stations immediately

Goat locker - Navy slang for the Chief's Mess, in reference to ship's livestock that used to be kept in the Chief's quarters for safekeeping.

Goatfuck – really really bad

Great Lakes – Naval Station Great Lakes, the home of the Navy's only boot camp, located near North Chicago, Illinois

Green side – serving with a Marine unit

Head – Bathroom

Hooyah - a word used in the Navy to build morale and signify verbal acknowledgment, or as a cheer. The Marine equivalent is "Oorah"; the Army and Air Force equivalent is "Hooah".

IDC – Independent Duty Corpsman, specialized hospital corpsmen who serve on land or at sea in support of the Navy and Marines in military treatment facilities around the world.

IED - Improvised Explosive Device

Island – the command center on an aircraft carrier for flight-deck operations, and the ship as a whole. It is about 150 feet tall, but only 20 feet wide at the base, so it won't take up too much space on the flight deck

Jarhead – What Navy personnel call the Marines, semi-insulting

Knee Knocker - The bottom portion of a watertight ship's door. Being several inches off the deck, they tend to trip up those who fail to pay attention

Leave – time off from duty

Landstuhl – Landstuhl Regional Medical Center (LRMC) in Germany serves as the primary medical center for casualties of U.S. military operations in Europe, southwest Asia and the middle east.

M16 – Rifle used by the United States military

Master Chief - the ninth enlisted rate (E-9) in the Navy, just above senior chief petty officer

MRE – Meals Ready to Eat – military rations. Sometimes called Meals Rejected by Everyone

NAS – Naval Air Station

Nimitz – see USS Nimitz

Norfolk - Naval Station Norfolk, Navy base in Norfolk, Virginia.

OCONUS – Acronym, Outside the Continental United States

Operation Inherent Resolve – the ongoing military intervention against the Islamic State of Iraq and Syria, starting in June 2014

Petty Officer - a noncommissioned officer ranked above seaman and below chief petty officer.

PO3 – Petty Officer Third Class

Port – the left side of the ship, facing forward

Primary Flight Control, aka Pri-Fly - The section of the island from which the air officers direct all aircraft activity on the flight deck and within a 5-mile (8-km) radius.

Rack - Bed

RDC – Recruit Division Commander – a Petty Officer or Chief Petty Officer in charge of training Navy recruits

Reserve Duty – Temporary military service, one weekend every month and two weeks every year

Sea bag - a large cylindrical bag made of cloth with the closure at the top, used by the military

SEAL - "Sea, Air, and Land" Teams, the Navy's special operations force

Senior Chief - the eighth enlisted rate (E-8) in the Navy, just above chief petty officer and below master chief petty officer

Shore Patrol – the Navy equivalent of military police.

Six, Got your six – Got your back, watching out for you. Refers to aviation positioning in which six o'clock is directly behind you

Skivvies - underwear

Squared away - perfectly arranged or organized

Squid – What the Marines call Navy personnel, semi-insulting

Starboard – the right side of the ship, when facing forward

Stern – the back of the ship

TAD – Temporary Additional Duty

Terminal leave - transitional leave service members accrue before they transition out of the military

UCMJ – Uniform Code of Military justice – the judicial code which pertains to members of the United States military

USS Nimitz – a nuclear-powered US Navy aircraft, the lead ship of her class, and the oldest and largest American carrier in active service.

V.A. – Veteran's Administration

Vulture's Row – Located on the same level as the Pri-Fly, a narrow balcony platform with a great view of the entire flight deck.

WestPac – Naval sea deployment in the western Pacific Ocean

It started with an article about a 60's pop band.

Although the article was never published, and in fact was read only by a seventh grade English teacher, it was nevertheless the beginning of Peggy Hoffman's love of putting words onto paper.

Peggy was born in Chicago, Illinois and lived in four states before settling in her current home of Kuna, Idaho. She decided to become a writer at age twelve, after crafting the above-mentioned article, despite the challenges that Real Life tends to present. A love of history, both medieval and military, research and travel have been the inspirations for her stories. When not writing, she has married her high school sweetheart, raised two children and is currently living in Idaho. Two more novels are currently in progress.

And just in case you're curious, the subject of the unpublished seventh-grade article was Paul Revere and the Raiders.